PENGUIN MODERN CLASSICS

When the Time Is Right

BUDDHADEVA BOSE (1908–74) is widely considered to be the successor to Rabindranath Tagore for the versatility and breadth of his literary work. A multifaceted writer and one of the leading lights of modern Bengali literature, Bose combines lyricism with a style of writing uniquely his own to create an unmatched legacy.

ARUNAVA SINHA translates classic, modern and contemporary Bengali fiction and non-fiction from Bangladesh and India into English. He also translates fiction from English into Bengali. Over ninety-five of his translations have been published so far in India, the UK and the USA. He teaches creative writing at Ashoka University, where he is also the co-director of the Ashoka Centre for Translation, and is the books editor at Scroll.in.

BUDDHADEVA BOSE

When the Time Is Right

Translated from the Bengali
by Arunava Sinha

PENGUIN BOOKS

An imprint of Penguin Random House

PENGUIN BOOKS

Penguin Books is an imprint of the Penguin Random House group of companies
whose addresses can be found at global.penguinrandomhouse.com

Published by Penguin Random House India Pvt. Ltd
4th Floor, Capital Tower 1, MG Road,
Gurugram 122 002, Haryana, India

Penguin
Random House
India

First published in Bengali as *Tithidore* by New Age Publishers Pvt. Ltd, Calcutta 1949
First published by Penguin Books India 2011
This edition published in 2025

ISBN 9780143416388

Typeset in Bembo by Guru Typograph Technology, New Delhi
Printed at Gopsons Papers Pvt. Ltd., Noida

www.penguin.co.in

BOOK ONE

First Sari, First Rain

1

Rajen-babu was a man of delicate taste. But he was not a dandy. He had no objection to rolling his dhoti up to his knees and plunging into the filthy vegetable-and-fish market with a shopping bag in each hand; but he needed a little fragrance on his pillow at night. He would go to work in the same clothes six days in succession, but wouldn't drink water in anything other than a crystal tumbler. If the maid stayed away, he would get out of bed before sunrise to light the stove, then sit bare-bodied on a rickety plank on the veranda, humming a morning raga.

These small fancies of his greatly amused his wife Shishirkana—named for a dewdrop—when she finally came to stay with him, having been married at fifteen and spending another year in her parents' home. She had even indulged him a little, hiding vials of fragrant wood under his pillow, and, on some nights, even tying at the end of her sari a few bokul flowers she'd collected with the help of her maid. Fragrance was good; but there was nothing wrong with making the source of the fragrance even better.

When Shishirkana became pregnant a few months later, and Rajen-babu said, 'This is wonderful! A lovely little baby girl—perfect!' she retorted, not very pleased at this new fancy of her husband's, 'Baby girl? Why a baby girl?'

'A boy is nothing but shorts and bat-and-ball. But think of a girl! Frocks of different colours, ribbons, long curly hair—and then, when she grows up a little, just imagine!'

3

But Shishirkana did not appear elated at the prospect of increasing the population of her tribe. The future mother echoed what she had heard from her own many times over: 'Frocks, ribbons—wonderful! Excellent education for your daughter!'

'Whatever you may say, a daughter will light up our lives.'

A few months later, their lives were indeed lit up; and three days later, Rajen-babu demonstrated another example of his delicate taste: he named his daghter Shweta.

'Please, no,' said Shishirkana's widowed aunt from the door to the labour room, 'don't call her Sita—Sita had such a sad life.'

'Not Sita—Shweta,' said Rajen-babu gravely, enunciating the name clearly to show the difference with the tragic heroine of the Ramayana.

'We can't pronounce all those foreign names, but yes, your daughter will certainly be as lovely as a white girl.'

'But it's not foreign . . .'

Rajen-babu was cut short by a different voice coming from the labour room. 'Why do you pay attention to him, Pishima? You know what he's like! I've named her Manju.' Shishirkana made sure to declaim the last few words extra loudly, so that they would accurately find their intended target.

They did, but the target was unmoved. Within a month or so, a battle broke out over the name. Shishirkana would coo to her daughter, holding her to her breast, 'Manju—Manjul—Manjulee . . .' while Rajen-babu would harmonize, 'Manju—Jhumjhum—Lozeng-eu!' Then coming nearer to his daughter, he would stroke her cheek, saying, 'Shweta.'

The daughter would blink rapidly, as though this was the name she preferred—which was quite possible, given that her fair complexion lived up to her name.

Those who say that the first child is a thorn in the father's side must never have seen Rajen-babu. He rocked her to sleep on his knee, fed her her milk in a bottle, walked up and down with her in his arms all evening and changed her sheets at night. Not once during the first six months was the new mother's night-time sleep disturbed—nothing could be more surprising in a Bengali family.

But there was a price to be paid for this pleasure.

'Where's Shweta's frock?'

'Can you pass Shweta's powder?'

'See how soundly Shweta's sleeping today.'

Having to hear things like this all the time, even Shishirkana referred to her as Shweta sometimes. At first, she would jokingly say 'your Shweta'—for instance: 'Everyone's admiring your beautiful Shweta' or 'Have you seen how your Shweta smiles?' And eventually, just Shweta. Not Sita, not Situ—it was Shweta, pure and simple. Manju was exiled, having lost the war; like a great warrior, Rajen-babu accepted his victory with humility.

When another daughter was born one and a half years later, Rajen-babu immediately named her Mahashweta. The third daughter didn't even wait that long—just fourteen months afterwards, Saraswati came to Shishirkana's arms.

'No more! Don't go showering your love on them any more with your names,' Shishirkana exclaimed.

'But they do have to be named, do they not.'

'Rot!' Shishirkana rhymed unknowingly.

She had been convinced that her second child would be a boy. Still, she had tolerated Mahashweta for the sake of future expectations. But again! Three girls in a row. Her annoyance, her unhappiness could no longer be hidden.

'What lovely hair Saraswati has,' said Rajen-babu.

'All right! Enough, go now . . .' Out of the corner of her eye, Shishirkana glanced at the newborn's head full of curly hair.

'Three lovely girls—don't you love this?'

'I see. You want more daughters. It's because of you that I keep having girls. Don't even talk of girls any more.'

But so what if he didn't, when it came to fulfilling this one fancy of Rajen-babu's, the Almighty proved extraordinarily efficient. After lying low for seven years, Shishirkana was galvanized into activity again. And after seventeen years of married life, Rajen-babu was the father of five daughters. A son also popped in between them, however. Highlighting the difference between him and his sisters, Rajen-babu named him Bijon, the solitary one.

'What!' Shishirkana's eyebrows shot into her hair. 'The world has been turned upside down with the glory of the daughters' names, but the son is merely Bijon!'

'Simple names are best for men. You don't know what he will grow up to be—saddling him with a mouthful of a name now...'

'And what kingdoms are your daughters going to be princesses of?'

'Well, considering they're *my* daughters, they *are* Raj-kanyas—princesses.'

'Then why shouldn't the son be a prince too?'

'That doesn't mean he can be named Vikramaditya now, can he?'

With just the one son to speak for so many years of pain, Shishirkana couldn't tolerate her husband's indifference about him. Flaring up, she said, 'Here you are losing your head over your daughters! I guarantee they're going to heap disgrace upon you one day.'

It was true that Rajen-babu was a little too taken up with his daughters. And as luck would have it, you couldn't turn your eyes away from whichever of the five girls you looked at. While Shishirkana was an old-fashioned beauty—fair of complexion, with almond eyes—and Rajen-babu was handsome too, no one could have predicted that each of the girls would turn out to be so beautiful. It could so easily not have happened that way. And it was not just beauty, either.

Of course, Rajen-babu wasn't fortunate enough to have all five of his daughters living at home at the same time; Shweta was married before Swati was born. Shishirkana—who had married relatively late by the customs of the time—clearly remembered not being happy until she got married; it was as if marriage had saved her. So, no sooner had her eldest daughter turned fifteen than she became restless for her wedding. Shweta's beauty earned her the son of a minor landowner from Mymensingh as a groom. Shishirkana approved of the groom from his photograph; the groom's father approved of the bride after viewing her in person. The wedding took place.

Swati was seven months in her mother's womb at the time. Shishirkana did feel a little embarrassed in the presence of her new son-in-law. But what option did she have?

Bijon had been born two years earlier. He wanted a brother, being reluctant to grow up alone in the company of sisters—such was Shishirkana's logic. It didn't work. Yet another daughter! When the thirteen-year-old Mahashweta, the twelve-year-old Saraswati and the five-year-old Saswati crowded around the door to the labour room, if she didn't slap all of them soundly, it was only because she lacked the strength even to get up.

Rajen-babu said, 'This is nice—one daughter gets married and leaves, and another one arrives.'

Shutting her eyes, Shishirkana prayed, 'Let this be the last one, O Lord.'

The lord heard her prayer. However, by mistake—since he made such mistakes quite frequently—he granted a little more than was asked for. Within a few months of Swati's birth, it became clear that not only would Shishirkana not bring any more lives into existence, but her own life was also waning.

A month went by, a year went by, her health simply did not mend. Fed up with the doctor, Rajen-babu took two months' leave. At great expense, he took his huge family off for a change to Mihijaam. Shishirkana recovered greatly, even being well for some time after their return to Calcutta. But again her health deteriorated, she had to take to her bed once more.

She finally settled down to this state of existence. Sometimes the doctor had to be called and the treatment worked, but as soon as the doctor said, you will definitely recover now, there was a new complication. Sometimes she would be quite well even without treatment; at other times she would have to stay in bed a fortnight. Rajen-babu made it a point to whisk everyone off for a holiday once a year—the seaside, the mountains, places with dry climate, medicated natural springs—but all to no avail. One fine day Shishirkana suddenly lost her appetite, and with it her spirit. And so it was back to bed.

Chaos ensued in the household; they kept running out of things. From her bed, Shishirkana helplessly watched the servants pilfering, the daughters' extravagance, the son's ragamuffin-like appearance. Her family! She had nurtured them day by day, fulfilled their needs little by little, made up for every lack with her physical effort, her body. After all, what did women have but their bodies? Men could achieve so much with their strength, their courage, their money; whatever women could achieve was only with their bodies. It hadn't been very long, after all, since her husband had started earning as much as he did now; they used to be poor, really, but had she ever allowed the slightest discomfort to creep in, had they ever had to wear dirty clothes or eat a poor meal, had her husband ever had to be informed that they had run out of money.

Raising her weak voice, she called, 'Mahashweta! Saraswati! Mahashweta!' What mouthfuls these names are. I haven't been allowed to shorten them even after all these years.

Mahashweta came in. 'What is it, Ma?'

'Can't you see how filthy Biju looks? Why don't you clean him up in the bathroom?'

'Saraswati's in the bathroom, Ma.'

'Then take him to the tap in the yard downstairs. Can you check the wardrobe for his clothes?'

Mahashweta took out velvet knickerbockers.

'How clever! In this heat! He's outgrown it, too. Take out the white shorts and vest.'

But the vest was not to be found anywhere. Mahashweta went red in the face, perspiration gathered on her brow—in trying to get one garment out she dropped three on the floor. Exercising all her patience, Shishirkana said, 'That poplin shirt—oh, can't you put everything away carefully! And fix your sari, it's all over the place.'

Mahashweta went out quickly with her brother's clothes. Returning in a few moments, she said, 'Biju won't come, Ma.'

'What do you mean won't come! Make him!'

'You think I can?'

'Of course not, you're such a big girl, why should a small boy listen to you!'

'He beats me up.'

'What kind of big sister are you if you don't get beaten up?' Shishirkana smiled. 'That too, a big sister old enough to be his mother!'

Mahashweta clicked her tongue in annoyance, tossing her head.

'Why do you react that way to anything I say?'

'Don't I have to study? Don't I have exams?'

Shishirkana was taken aback by her tone. That you could talk to your mother in that tone had been beyond her wildest imagination when she was a child. 'All right, go and study,' she said, after a pause.

Mahashewta disappeared at once, seeming extremely relieved.

That same evening Shishirkana told her husband, 'You'd better start looking for princes for your princesses now.'

'All in good time. You must recover first.'

'I know just how much I'll recover. Make arrangements for both together—that way, you'll save both money and me.'

'What's the hurry? They're still so young, they should go to college. Times have changed . . .'

'Times have changed,' Shishirkana spoke softly but clearly, 'because people can't find grooms easily these days, so no one says anything. That doesn't mean girls are taking longer to become women.'

'Is marriage the only cure for that illness?' Rajen-babu smiled.

'Yes—it's not a joke. Your girls aren't in the same boat as the rest, their looks alone will see them through.'

Maintaining the jocular note, Rajen-babu said, 'In that case the princes will come on their own, seeking their hands.'

'One or two seem to be here already. What's all the noise in the other room?'

'They're having a wonderful time in there.'

'Who are?'

'Who do you suppose. Mahashweta, Saraswati . . .'

'I can hear someone else too.'

'Oh, that's Arun.'

'Arun?' Shishirkana frowned.

'Have you forgotten Arun already? Shweta's brother-in-law, the one who's studying to be a doctor . . .'

'Is Arun here? What for?'

'He comes quite often.'

'Quite often? But he never visits me.'

'He doesn't disturb you, that's all, he knows you're not well.'

'Does he meet you?'

'Oh, I don't need him to meet me specially. They're children, after all, they spend their evenings together . . . I don't disturb them.'

From the mass of plumped-up pillows, Shishirkana's exhausted almond eyes came to a halt on her husband's face.

'And you didn't tell me all these days.'

'But is this anything to . . .?'

'What kind of a person are you!' Shishirkana sat up straight. 'What *will* happen to you after I die?'

'What nonsense . . .'

'Ask Arun to see me, will you?'

'Are you mad? Don't forget he's one of Shweta's in-laws . . .'

'So what,' Shishirkana thought about it for a while. 'He's not Shweta's husband's brother, only a cousin. And what if he were, anyway . . .'

'Come on, Shishu, there's a good girl, don't work yourself up into a state unnecessarily. You've seen him, haven't you, very nice boy, wonderful boy . . .'

Storming into the room, the five-year-old Swati flung herself into her father's arms—'Baba, listen!'—and instantly burst into tears.

'What is it, what's the matter?'

'Nothing, Baba,' said Biju, standing behind her like a warrior, arms akimbo. 'Chhordi only wanted a look at her chocolate . . .'

'No, Baba,' Swati said, flooding her father's clothes with her tears, 'she took mine . . .'

'Liar! So jealous!' yelled Saswati from the door, dressed in a colourful frock and shaking her curls. 'She's a crybaby. It's not like he gave them to you.'

'As if he gave them to *you*!' retorted Swati through her sobs.

'He gave them to Shejdi!' It wasn't clear which side Biju was a soldier for.

Shishirkana was startled. 'Tell Shejdi I'm looking for her, Biju,' she said.

'Give me my chocolate!' Swati issued a nasal appeal.

'Here! I don't want any! Spoilt brat!' Saswati's long fair arm flashed, and a few bars of chocolate—wrapped in glittering magenta, green and silver foil—fell in a scattered arc on the floor by Shishirkana's feet. A sudden contortion twisted Biju's tiny figure—in an instant, he swooped down on all of them and leapt across the room. Saswati shrieked and gave chase. Swati kept whimpering.

'Quiet, Swati!' Shishirkana roared despite her frail health.

Swati became inaudible at once, but her heaving doubled. 'Stop crying this instant!'

Rajen-babu went out to the veranda quickly with his daughter in his arms. Walking up and down as he ran his fingers through her thick curls, he crooned, 'Swati, my lovely Swati, don't cry, my pretty girl, my sweetest girl, don't cry any more . . . Let me see, what lovely eyes, what a lovely smile!'

And she *was* truly lovely. Her hair was even more beautiful than Saraswati's. Swati—the youngest of the youngsters in the family, the most beautiful of the five beauties, the sweetest of the five names. He could have chosen this name for any of her sisters—for Saraswati, or for Saswati—but thank goodness he hadn't. It wouldn't have suited anyone else. Unknowingly, he had reserved the best name for the last.

Swati calmed down, became quiet, her head resting heavily on his shoulder. Poor thing, she had fallen asleep. All that running around, stomping around all day—how can children ever have normal lives with their mother so ill! How much can I do by myself? I have to be in office all day. Besides, can a father do all of this, do everything? The girl was a little too spoilt—too demanding, too obstinate—but that wasn't surprising, considering she hadn't really got a chance to have her mother by her side. Moving her hair away from her face, Rajen-babu kissed her on her soft, wet, cool lips, then put her down carefully on his own bed.

Shishirkana was in bed, shielding her eyes from the light with her arm. Without a glance at her daughter she said, 'She's fallen asleep, hasn't she? She never has her dinner . . .'

'Never mind,' said Rajen-babu quickly, 'I'll wake her when it's time to eat.'

'What a way to spend your time after a long day at work. God!'

'Don't say that, Shishu! I quite enjoy all this.'

Taking her arm away from her eyes to look at Swati,

Shishirkana said, 'You're so much in love with your daughters—and all for what? When you already have three growing girls, do you imagine that your beautiful Swati will do any better than them?'

'What rubbish! How can my daughters be ordinary . . . What is it, Saraswati?'

'You called, Ma?' Saraswati said, standing in the middle of the room.

'Long ago.'

Not realizing the significance of this, Saraswati smiled sweetly.

'Who brought all that chocolate?'

'Arun-da.'

'For you?'

'He got some for Mahashweta the other day, so he got some for me today. We share whatever he brings. What a lovely box! Want to see, Ma?'

Saraswati ran out and ran back in with a large colourful box wrapped in transparent paper. Putting it on the bed within her mother's reach she said, 'Here, Ma . . .'

'I can see,' said Shishirkana sternly. 'Why has he brought you all this?'

'What do you mean, why?'

'Does he bring gifts like this often?'

'What if he does?' Saraswati stretched the 'what' out a little self-indulgently.

A shadow of apprehension clouded her bright, lovely, guileless face, instantly dispelled by the blind faith of happiness. Looking at her, Shishirkana couldn't summon up an answer at once, and Rajen-babu took the opportunity to say, 'Nothing, run along now.'

Saraswati glanced at her mother.

Exhaling, Shishirkana said, 'Yes, run along. Send Arun to me.'

As soon as she left, Rajen-babu said urgently, 'Do you really need to meet Arun now? You're not well . . .'

'That box of chocolates must cost at least ten rupees, mustn't it?'

'Are you mad! Can't possibly be that much! . . . And what if it does . . . He likes doing these things . . .'

'All this isn't good.'

'You and your . . . Don't go and say anything to him now . . .'

'Don't worry, I'll say exactly what needs to be said.'

Shishirkana discerned from her bed that Mahashweta and Saraswati had left after escorting Arun to the door of her room. Slipping his shoes off outside, Arun entered a little diffidently. He was thin, tousled, a trifle bewildered. Stepping forward, he offered the ritual *pronaam* to Shishirkana stiffly, touching her feet with his hands, probably wondering whether he should do the same to the head of the family. Rajen-babu delivered him from his dilemma. 'Sit down, sit down. All well? Everything all right at home?'

Ignoring the chair, Arun sat down on the bed, near Shishirkana's feet. Smiling shyly, he said, using the oft-used term to address a friend's mother, 'How are you, Mashima?'

'I'm actually your *maoima*,' said Shishirkana, explaining the technically accurate form of address to describe their relationship.

'Maoima! What on earth is that? No, it's horrible, I can't address you that way!' Arun's plea sounded positively plaintive.

Shishirkana couldn't help laughing.

'What are you suffering from?' Arun asked like an expert.

'Nothing, the doctors are all frauds.'

'I'm sure you haven't given the doctors a chance?' the would-be doctor protested instantly.

'If you'd been the doctor I'm sure you'd have cured me. But by the time you get to be one either the illness will be gone, or I will.'

With a quick glance at Shishirkana, Arun consoled her in the manner of a medical expert, 'I don't see anything particularly wrong with you.'

'I got better the moment I saw you,' said Shishirkana. 'You're a very good doctor.'

Arun left after a few more exchanges. Shishirkana didn't say any of the things she had been planning to. She couldn't. Bad! But why bad? He seemed a nice enough young man. But then, does everyone who spells danger necessarily have to be a bad sort?

Except on the days she felt utterly exhausted, Shishirkana began to send for Arun now and then. The young man seemed a little distracted and scatterbrained, but his conversation was lively, and sometimes he said funny things without being aware of it. Shishirkana noticed that her daughters never came into the room during those visits—even Saswati stayed out of the way, clearly emulating her sisters. Sometimes she deliberately kept Arun in her room up to an hour, imposing greatly on her own health. But the young man was never restless—there was no indication that his heart actually lay elsewhere. Deep in the recesses of her mind, in the dark, unseen part, Shishirkana even felt a little sorry for him; in the hope of getting close to the daughter, he was being forced to make countless pilgrimages to the depressing bedside of the mother.

There *was* another companion on his visits, however. As soon as there were indications that Arun had arrived in her mother's room, Swati came running. She would either flop down on the floor, flat on her back, reading a torn copy of a children's book, or else turn over on her tummy to draw pictures with great concentration on a blank sheet in one of her sisters' abandoned notebooks, using a broken pencil which she kept licking. Glancing at her, Arun said, 'Are we drawing?' That would do it. She would tuck the drawing under her chest, dying of embarrassment. 'Show me, show me, please!' It only took a little coaxing for Swati to raise her face and say, 'No, it's terrible!'

But she would stand behind Arun with the drawing in her hand. Looking at the notebook, Arun said, 'Which one is your drawing?'

'This one.'

'Oh my God, is that yours! I thought one of your sisters had drawn that. You actually drew this? This tree, this river, this sun—all of them? How beautiful!'

'No, it's not! Not at all!' The curly hair on Swati's head started dancing, her tiny, supple frame rippling through several poses. Looking intently at Arun, she said, 'You really think it's good?'

'What do you mean good? Do you suppose there's another five-year-old girl in Calcutta who can draw as well!'

'What about other cities?'

'I don't know,' answered Arun with unwavering solemnity. 'Maybe in England.'

England was remote enough for Swati to smilingly accept the possibility of a peer in that country. Her next question was: 'Arun-da, what does a tamarind tree look like?'

'Tamarind tree?'

'I want to draw a tamarind tree next to this banana tree, but I simply cannot remember what a tamarind tree looks like. Ma, have I ever seen a tamarind tree?'

'Stop your chattering for a bit, will you!'

Swati had long stopped expecting a gentler answer than this from her mother. Without looking the least bit miserable, she said again, 'Arun-da, tell me please, what does a tamarind tree look like?'

'Right now, I can't remember, either,' Arun smiled. 'I'll tell you tomorrow.'

The next day Arun brought a jet-black painting box and an enormous drawing book. When she got them, Swati flashed a dazzling smile. 'Mejdi! Shejdi! Chhordi!' she shrieked, disappearing like the same flash.

Shishirkana didn't let go of this opportunity. 'This is wrong of you!' she said, a little sharply.

'Wrong? What did I do wrong?' came Arun's agitated question.

'Waste of money.'

'It's not a waste. Children always break their toys—that doesn't make them a waste of money.'

'Look, Arun, let me tell you something. You're like one of the family—you can come and go as you like. But I don't like the fact that you spend so much money on gifts.'

Looking at Arun's downcast face, Shishirkana realized this was completely unexpected, like a bolt from the blue. It was cruel, but she couldn't stop herself from continuing, 'If you do have so much money, there's no lack of poor, deprived people in the world. What's the point of indulging the waywardness of a bunch of immature girls. You seem quite intelligent for your age. I'm sure you know what I mean.'

Arun couldn't raise his face for a long time. When he did stand up, Shishirkana was pained by his expression.

A little later, Mahashweta came to ask, 'Where's Arun-da, Ma?'

'He left just this minute.'

'Left! Now who's going to explain this sum to me?'

Two days, four days, seven days went by. Arun didn't visit any more. In the evening Shishirkana got out of bed slowly to enter the girls' room. Swati was the first to see her. 'Ma! Ma's here! What fun!' she cried as she ran to hug her mother. Unable to withstand the force of her daughter's physical affection, Shishirkana flopped on to the first of the three beds placed side by side. Swati jumped into the bed next to her. Putting her arm round her mother's neck, rubbing her own face against her mother's, she kept saying, 'You're all right, then, Ma? Ma, will you take me out today, Ma? Please, Ma, let's go!'

Saswati came and sat on the bed too, straightening an errant strand of hair on her mother's forehead. 'How long it's been since you've been in this room, Ma!' she said.

The elder daughters came near, too. The room faced west, allowing a long shaft of sunlight to stream in. There was even a breeze. For a moment Shishirkana imagined she really had recovered.

'Shall we go out, Ma?' pleaded Swati, slightly nasally.

I've not been able to do anything with this little one, thought Shishirkana. She still craves for her mother.

'No?' The nasal component doubled.

'But I don't have the strength to walk, Swati.'

'Then let's take a taxi. Or a rickshaw.'

'Not today . . . Another time . . .'

'Whenever I ask, it's not today, not today!' Swati let go of her mother to roll on the bed. 'It's no fun . . . At least if Arun-da were here it might have been!'

Saswati laughed.

'She's right. Arun hasn't been here for a while. Why?' Shishirkana looked at Mahashweta.

Neither blushing, nor lowering her eyes, Mahashweta went on plaiting her hair. 'No idea,' she said indifferently.

'He isn't angry, is he?' Shishirkana turned her eyes towards Saraswati.

'Maybe he is,' Saraswati smiled. 'Swati tugged at his hair so hard the other day, oh my God!'

'I did not! Of course I didn't tug at his hair.'

'What do you mean, you didn't?' Saswati added fuel to the fire. 'You practically pulled it all out.'

'If I did, I'm glad! He didn't give any of you the painting box, did he? He gave it to me.' Tumbling out of the bed, Swati took her painting box from beneath Saswati's desk and went out proudly.

'She has a lovely walk,' Shishirkana said, almost to herself.

'Do you know, Ma,' said Saswati, 'she can dance. She often

performs for us, and even dances before the mirror by herself. Don't you want to see her dance sometime, Ma?' Saswati squeezed her mother's hand with both of her own.

'No need for her to dance.' Pouring cold water on Saswati's enthusiasm, Shishirkana rose slowly.

The three sisters got dressed and went out. She could hear them warbling until they reached the bottom of the stairs. Laughing, they left, and had fun together in the evening as usual—they did not seem to have been affected in the least. What *were* girls like these days? Stupid? Or heartless? Or experts at deception?

Arun's prolonged absence continued to prick Shishirkana.

He did arrive a couple of days later. Going directly to meet Shishirkana, he said shyly, 'College holidays have begun; I'm going home tomorrow.'

Looking at him, Shishirkana said, 'Why haven't you been coming?'

'I had a lot of things to do before the holidays began,' Arun answered without any stiffness.

'And how are you?'

'Very well, Mashima. Ah, Swati. What have you been up to?'

Swati had been running full tilt, she stopped suddenly and proceeded to contort herself.

'Come here, don't be shy. Just a few days I've been away and you're shy already? At this rate you won't even know who I am when I'm back after the holidays.'

When Swati came nearer Arun put his arm around her, overcome, she instantly slumped against him. Running his other hand through her hair, Arun whispered in her ear, 'How many pictures have you drawn?'

In the same secret, intimate tone, Swati replied very softly, 'Lots'.

'Aren't you going to show me?'

Swati nodded.

'Bring the drawing book.'

Swati ran.

'Swati simply doesn't want to let go of you,' Shishirkana smiled. 'The poor thing doesn't get much attention from her sisters.'

'What do you mean, Mashima? Who dares not give her attention?'

'She tears your hair out if you don't, doesn't she? . . . Swati, go into the other room, there's a good girl. Show Arun-da your drawings. Not too loudly, I've got a horrible headache . . . And Arun, have dinner with us, all right?'

That same night, Shishirkana told Rajen-babu, 'You couldn't do it, could you? And I've finalized a groom for her without leaving my room.'

Pouring out the medicine she took before going to bed every night, Rajen-babu said, 'I'm no match for you.'

'Arun's a suitable boy, there's no doubt about that. It's only because we know them that I was hesitating. Do you suppose I would have taken so long otherwise? But I was wondering . . .'

'Here's your medicine.'

Shishirkana transferred the medicine from the glass directly to her throat with years of practised ease. 'I was wondering which of them he actually likes—Mahashweta or Saswati.'

'Probably both.' Rajen-babu passed a glass of water to his wife. 'Can't make up his mind.'

Making a strange face, Shishirkana said, 'What a father you are—of daughters, too.'

'You'd better decide on his behalf.'

'What do you mean, decide. The younger one cannot get married before the older one, can she? You'd better look for another groom. And write to Arun's father tomorrow.'

'Why are you in such a hurry, Shishu. Mahashweta's matriculation exams are just a few months away. Considering the effort she's put in, shouldn't she get a chance to take the exam!'

'But so many girls take their exams even after they're married.'

'But that's not possible all the time, is it?'

'And what if she can't. Marriage is the most important thing for girls.'

Rajen-babu came closer to Shishirkana. After a little silence, he said, 'But they're both such babies still. Let them stay a while longer—eventually they *will* have to go.'

Shishirkana looked at him.

'What do you think?'

'I know what you mean, but—no, don't say no! Don't you see, I could die . . .'

Rajen-babu put his arms around his companion of twenty years. 'Die indeed! You think dying is that simple?' But he did write to Arun's father the very next day.

The reply came promptly. Arun's father wrote that since one marital arrangement between his family and Rajen-babu's had already proved a happy one, he hoped that a second arrangement would, too. But his son's wish was that the third daughter . . .

'There!' exclaimed Shishirkana.

'Amazing!' said Rajen-babu. 'So Arun could be so . . .' He didn't say what exactly.

The brides knew nothing, continuing to read their geography, geometry and magazine stories serenely. On his part, Rajen-babu sent his spies out in all directions in search of another groom.

Shishirkana chose Hemanga Bardhan of Rangoon. He was a rich man, the owner of a successful iron business venture. Having built his fortune with his own hands, he hadn't had the leisure to get married all this while. Now he was in Calcutta with the intention of going back with his wife. He was a little on the older side, but that was only to be expected.

Bardhan came himself, along with two friends, to survey the potential bride. Mahashweta had been informed just a day in advance; she screamed and cried a great deal—am I an exotic creature to be paraded before people, am I a doll to be displayed in a shop—but eventually, the dutiful girl that she was, she did make an appearance at the appointed hour, dressed in a sky-blue silk sari from Murshidabad, her long hair left loose, her feet reddened. Saraswati was kept hidden away, lest she overshadow her sister, and Bardhan, like Arun, said yes.

Clean-shaven, thin-lipped, with close-cropped hair, Bardhan sat with his head bowed most of the time, not talking much. But there was a certain niceness in his expression. And the next day, he sent word that the wedding must take place in early Aghran—just after the middle of November.

'I told you, didn't I!' Rajen-babu hadn't seen a smile like this on his wife's face in years. 'We'll never have to worry about your beautiful daughters! Get going now, two weddings together is a lot of work, isn't it!'

Two weddings together. Two of them would leave at the same time. Rajen-babu suddenly felt an emptiness in his heart.

In the evening Saswati told Swati, 'Guess what, the person who had come yesterday is marrying Mejdi, and Arun-da is marrying Shejdi.'

About to twirl the skipping rope she held in her hand, Swati froze. 'Of course not.'

'What do you mean of course not.'

'Of course Arun-da is not marrying Shejdi!'

'Of course he is!' Saswati was furious. 'All right, let's take a bet!'

After a couple of turns with the skipping rope, Swati moved the hair out of her eyes, curled her lips in a sneer, and said, 'I'm going to marry Arun-da. What do *you* know about it!'

Laughing and clapping, Saswati called out loudly, 'Shame! Shame! Swati will marry Arun-da! I'll tell! I'll tell everyone.'

Dropping the skipping rope, Swati stood erect, her arms straight by her side. With shining eyes, she said, 'I shall. Of course I shall.'

'Shame! Shame! Swati, really! Mejdi, Shejdi, have you heard?'

'What's so funny?' asked the five-year-old Swati, standing

as rigid as a willow. Her two elder sisters burst out in laughter at the sight.

'What are you laughing at?'

'Not laugh indeed! You idiot!'

Swati's eyes flashed, her breath quickened, her body arched like a cat's. She raised her right hand like an unsheathed sword, and delivered a resounding slap on Saswati's cheek, a full head higher and five years older than her.

Saswati didn't submit, offering a suitable counter-attack. A ferocious battle broke out between the sisters.

Emerging from the bathroom and walking along the veranda, Rajen-babu heard the commotion. Rushing into the room, he saw utter pandemonium. Saswati stood dishevelled against the wall, Swati kept bouncing up and down in a bid to slap and punch her, while the two elder sisters alternated between collapsing with laughter and trying to stop them.

'What's the matter?'

The two elder girls covered their faces, laughing, when they saw their father.

'What *is* it?'

'Listen, Baba,' Saswati began, 'Swati was saying . . .'

'What if I did!' roared Swati. Her contorted face was red-hot with perspiration, rage and tears, and blackened with grime. 'I'm glad I did. Of course I'll marry Arun-da! Yes, I will! What business is it of yours?'

Rajen-babu turned his gaze from one daugher to another. No longer laughing, Mahashweta said, 'Saswati laughed, so . . .'

Solemnly Rajen-babu said, 'That's true, there's nothing to laugh at. Saswati, go wash your face.'

'She's been punching and kicking me, Baba, aren't you going to say anything?'

'As if you haven't too. Come on, now, no more quarrelling. Don't you know Ma's not well?' Advancing, he called, 'Swati.'

'Baba!' Swati was overcome by a fresh bout of tears.

As soon as Rajen-babu held out his arms, saying, 'Listen to me,' Swati immediately flung herself away to sprawl face down on the floor—exactly like the swooning heroine of a play, thought Rajen-babu.

Rajen-babu bent to put his hand on her head. 'I will. Of course I will. What business is it of anyone's?' Swati hissed through her tears.

Picking her up from the floor, Rajen-babu made her lie down on Mahashweta's bed. She buried her head in the pillow, sobbing as though she would melt and disappear like a piece of ice.

'Swati! My sweetest Swati!'

'Baba!'

Swati clung to her father's hand, and Rajen-babu sat quietly by her side. How eccentric the girl had turned out to be—absolutely refusing to understand, or maybe she understood too much? So competitive with sisters so much older than her, not willing to settle for a smaller share of anything just because she was younger. She had taught herself to read and write simply out of jealousy for Saswati, treated her sisters' friends as equals, preferred her own company to playing with girls her age. There would be sheer murder if she didn't get whatever she wanted instantly. Who in the world would fulfil all her whims? How would such obstinacy be accommodated? Come to think of it, she did have many faults. Faults? In such a little girl! Rajen-babu looked at her head full of hair. Who else had such grace? Who else had such a beautiful gaze? She was the one who slept nights with her arm around him, who called out 'Baba' in her sleep. How could she have faults? So sensitive, such pride, she needed to be showered with love. She was the one who most needed a mother. O Lord, even if it means spending the rest of her life in bed, let her mother stay alive, keep her alive always . . .

Rajen-babu frequently feared she wouldn't last much longer, but somehow Shishirkana survived, though she had suffered a great deal the last few months.

Swati was just past ten when it happened. Eleven was still some way off, though she looked thirteen. In height she had almost caught up with Saswati, and her physical development was noticeable too—offendingly noticeable, even. Ever since she had sobbed her heart out, saying she wanted to marry Arun-da, Shishirkana had never stopped worrying for her youngest. The girl simply refused to put on a sari. Her mother was adamant too, and would force her best saris on her, but within half an hour Swati would be seen in a shameless frock again.

Requests, rage, the lure of new saris—nothing worked. Shishirkana was forced to sit up despite her frail health and use the sewing machine to stitch undergarments to veil Swati's budding womanhood. She pursued Rajen-babu to buy even longer frocks, but Swati outgrew any frock in no time at all, and finding frocks that fit her became increasingly impossible. Would they eventually have to buy the gowns that foreigners wore? Till the very last month of her life, Shishirkana used up much of her limited lifespan in teaching Swati how to conduct herself when awake, when asleep, when walking, when talking. Perhaps the end came a little suddenly for that very reason.

The three married daughters, along with their three husbands and, between them, the five children who had come—not all had been brought by their parents—left one by one after the funeral. Rajen-babu sat in silence on the veranda. So a new life would start now. When he had got married, Shishu had joined him in the flat in Beleghata that he had rented at eighteen rupees a month. The life that they had begun then had ended long ago, but a living symbol of it had remained all these years. Now that too was obliterated. From Beleghata to the two-roomed first-floor flat in Shankharipara, then the south-facing flat on Hazra Road—how smoky it would get in winter! And then, just the other day, at seventy rupees a month, an entire two-storeyed house on Jatin Das Road.

Shweta had come for the birth of her son. There used to be an unobstructed view all the way to the Dhakuria Lakes. The wind in Choitro—mid-April to mid-May—was like a storm, but it was the stinging of the mosquitoes that made the baby cry at night.

'Baba.'

'Swati—have all of you eaten?'

'We have.'

'Biju?'

'He's asleep. Chhordi too.'

'You're the only one awake? Not going to bed?'

'You should too, Baba.'

Rajen-babu rose. Emerging from the darkness of the veranda into the light, he said with a hint of a smile, 'Sari, Swati?'

'Yes, Baba. Only saris from now on.'

2

But it took much more time for Swati to get accustomed to the sari. She simply couldn't go to school in one, embarrassed at the thought of being seen by her friends. How much time did that leave to get used to it? One holiday, she solemnly emerged from the bathroom in a sari. After lunch, when she sprawled on the floor with a book, rubbing her toe on the ground as she read, the sari rose to her knee, and Saswati chided her, 'Cover your leg, Swati.'

Pulling the sari lower with two toes of the other foot, Swati plunged deeper into her book.

'Stop sprawling on the floor like that! You aren't a little girl any more.'

Just like Ma, thought Swati. But she said, 'What's wrong with sprawling?'

'What do you think is wrong! The floor's dirty, isn't it?'

'But it's quite clean . . .'

'Get up. Go sit on the chair. Or use the bed if you like.'

Saswati had started college a few months ago. She already behaved like a full-fledged young woman. Swati really wanted to be like her, but she simply couldn't stand some of Saswati's habits, such as wearing her sandals all the time even when at home, or religiously tying up her hair before bed, and so on.

Depositing the big toe of one foot on the raised ankle of the other, she said, 'No. I like this.'

'Terrible habit . . .!' Without another word, Saswati sat down at her extremely neat desk. Opening her textbook on inductive logic, pencil in hand, she felt herself a much more evolved creature than Swati. After a while, with a small yawn she shut her textbook, picking up a contemporary Bengali novel borrowed from her friend strictly for two days. With the open book on her lap, she rested her head against her desk, lowered her eyes, and then had no idea where the rest of the afternoon went.

Biju came and called, 'Chhordi.'

'Mmm?'

'Chhordi! Listen!'

'Uff!' It was not so much a sound of annoyance as an exhalation of pity for the heroine. Was this any time to abandon a book?

'Please listen to me . . .'

'What is it!'

Taking a couple of steps forward, Biju said, 'Shubhro-babu is here, Chhordi.' His tone suggested a momentous announcement.

'Shubhro-babu? Who on earth is he?'

'Oh my God!' Biju, dressed in shorts, the hair just beginning to sprout above his upper lip, raised his eyebrows in consternation. Then, lowering his voice—even though not even a shout would have reached the ears of the stranger who had arrived—he said, 'Shubhro-babu! He sang at Triangular Park during Saraswati Puja. Don't you remember?'

'So what?'

Stamping the floor fretfully, Biju exclaimed, 'Which world *do* you live in, Chhordi? Shubhro-babu—he sings at so many events these days—lives just down the road . . .'

'Oh, Shubu!' Swati suddenly spoke from the other corner of the room. 'Just the other day he used to go to school with a pile of books, wearing those round glasses! Now he's become a singer! Shubhro-*babu*!'

Glaring at Swati, Biju said, 'And you were there to see him, of course! Do you know how much older he is than you?'

Saswati mediated quickly. 'All right—but why is he here?'

'I made him come; he was passing by,' Biju announced proudly. 'Can you imagine, Chhordi, Shubhro-babu has agreed to give me singing lessons.'

'You don't need singing lessons, Dada,' Swati quipped. 'You're singing all seven notes quite naturally these days.'

'Swati!'

As Biju tried to shout, three or four different notes battled each other in his throat. Without attempting to protest any more, he turned his back on ignorant feminine audacity in a manner that suggested he was the only living representative of the glory of the older brother and of the gravity of the male of the species. And he wasn't far from the truth, either.

The information he animatedly provided in hushed tones was not new, however: 'Shubhro-babu is waiting downstairs, Chhordi.'

'What am I supposed to do?'

'Aren't you going to meet him?'

'Of course not!'

Biju's face fell. His worthy college-going elder sister—how much she would have contributed to raising him in Shubhro-babu's esteem.

'You're the one who got him here, you should keep him company.'

Of course! But would Shubhro-babu be happy with only

Biju for company? What was the point of visiting someone at home if you didn't get a chance to meet the others who lived there?

'All right—send some tea, please?'

Biju presented his request that evening: 'Baba, I want to take singing lessons.'

'Singing lessons?' Rajen-babu paused. He used to be addicted to music too when he was young. Swallowing the insults of gatekeepers at the mansions of the Mullicks, the Borals, the Debs, he had listened to the music of famous classical singers, both male and female. If they simply wouldn't let him in, he would wait on the pavement, praying that the music would drift out. But the world of music wasn't a pleasant one—you had to dig through so much dirt before getting to the gold that the very desire for the gold often died. Besides, that old music was no longer to be heard.

'It's very difficult, Biju,' he said. 'You have to give it everything you've got.'

'Not at all! Two hours of practice are all you need for modern music,' Biju quoted the opinion of the teacher he had selected.

'What's modern music?'

'Don't you know modern music, Baba?' Saswati came forward in aid of her brother. 'Don't you listen to the radio? Current hits.'

'I see. But do you have to *learn* how to cry?'

At this, Biju fled, Saswati stopped smiling, but Swati collapsed with laughter.

Biju solicited Saswati's help. 'Chhordi, tell Baba, there's a good girl. I've given Shubhro-babu my word—if it doesn't happen now, I'll lose face.'

'What do you mean you've given him your word, you little fellow?' Saswati laughed.

Biju was insulted, but he brushed it aside to plead further, 'Come on, Didi. You can get him to agree if you want to.'

Saswati didn't find this last statement unpleasant. In an authoritative voice she said, 'All right, start your lessons. Baba agrees to everything eventually.'

That was exactly what happened. Shubhro-babu began his twice-a-week lessons. Biju kept playing the harmonium and asking the rajanigandha in his fourteen-year-old's baritone why it was taking so long to bloom. No reply was possible, since this was how the rajanigandha normally behaved, which was why the question had to be repeated often, far too often. Even when Shubhro-babu wasn't there, Biju could be heard practising his music downstairs.

'Biju is determined to be a singer, it seems,' Rajen-babu commented one day.

Saswati defended her brother quickly, 'Don't say anything to him, Baba.'

'Who's the teacher?'

'Some Shubhro-babu . . .'

'But what will Biju do with singing lessons? The two of you could have taken them instead.'

'Not me,' said Swati quickly. 'God! How horrible Dada looks!'

'What about you, Saswati?' Their father looked at Saswati.

'How can she take lessons from that Shubu,' came Swati's immediate response. 'When did he learn to sing well enough to teach others?'

'How rude!' Saswati left with slow footsteps.

Biju drove everyone mad with his plan to have Shubhro-da sing at their house one evening. 'If I request him, I'm sure he'll find the time . . .'

'Quiet, you smart alec!' Saswati smiled. 'As if your Shubhro-da lacks for time. His only occupation is to request to be allowed to sing in people's homes.'

'You know it all!' Biju said, red-faced with rage. 'Do you know how many invitations he turns down?'

'Then what's the point of inviting him.'

'No, no,' Biju said with twice as much enthusiasm. 'If I ask him he will certainly sing. As many songs as you like.'

Saswati felt the teacher's enthusiasm was no less than the student's. And if he did want so badly to sing, would it be right to disappoint him?

Rajen-babu agreed happily. There hadn't been any excitement at home in ages—things were far too peaceful, sleepy, quiet. How few people there were at home; the three who still lived here had grown up so much that quarrels didn't bubble up between them either. Children all, how could they survive without celebrations and excitement? Fine.

A soirée was no good without an audience. Saswati invited a few people herself. Shubhro-babu arrived with much pomp and ceremony, accompanied by his own harmonium, his own tabla set, his own tabla player, and three or so friends. Friends, meaning proven and avowed acolytes. The small room downstairs looked quite full. Playing a melody on the harmonium, Shubhro glanced at the audience. Having used Saswati's talcum power liberally on his hands, the tabla player prepared himself, his sleeves rolled up. And the silver wrapping around bundles of paan glittered in the breeze under the fan, as though very happy.

Rajen-babu was present too—and not just to keep his children happy, either. But as soon as the first song was over he quietly went upstairs. They called this music! What *were* things coming to!

He thought he had come away quietly, but it hadn't escaped the singer's attention. However, Shubhro wasn't heartbroken at the absence of the helpless-looking middle-aged gentleman; after a few passes on the harmonium for a couple of minutes, he suddenly broke into his second song of the evening.

An elongated face, backbrushed hair, even a small, thin moustache. Swati couldn't quite reconcile him with the adolescent she had seen going to school with an armful of books. Where *did* people leave their childhood behind? Did the child suddenly disappear in thin air, a grown-up taking their place? Where will the 'I' that I am today be a few years from now? Will I grow to be like Chhordi, and later like Ma—but I quite like the way I am now, why do I have to let go? That school-going Shubu wasn't a bad sort; what did he have to gain by suddenly growing a moustache and becoming Shubhro-babu who sang to the accompaniment of a harmonium?

Swati simply couldn't bring herself to like Shubhro. After singing half a line, he looked around for praise—his three friends nodded violently—only after which he sang the rest of the line. Looking at the tabla player with round eyes, he stroked the reeds of the harmonium with three fingers to convey the rhythm; occasionally letting go of the bellows, he raised his left hand to launch into an extravagant gesture that suggested he was going to topple over on the person next to him. Did one have to do all this to sing? Tiny bubbles of laughter rose in Swati's throat, but she didn't see similar signs on anyone else's face. Everyone listened in rapt attention, and seemed to be enjoying the music. Swati tried to coil herself up too, to listen to Shubhro's music with her ears instead of looking at him with her eyes.

Shubhro stopped after singing three songs in a row. Wiping his face with his handkerchief, he said, 'Now one of you . . .'

'Who could possibly sing after you,' exclaimed the elder brother of one of Saswati's college friends, himself a student too and currently his sister's escort.

Accepting the analysis gracefully, Shubhro said, 'So what. Somebody must sing . . .'

A ripple ran through the room. Behind their glasses, Shubhro's eyes wandered here and there before settling on Swati's face. 'Why don't you sing a song.'

'No,' Swati shook her head.

'Why not? Do sing!' Shubhro said encouragingly.

'I don't know how to.'

'But you look like you do,' Shubhro duelled with the sparkling young girl.

'Looks can be very deceptive,' said Swati, suddenly raising her eyes.

One or two people laughed. So did Shubhro. Maintaining the note of laughter, he smoothened his appearance before turning his eyes towards Saswati. 'How about you?'

'No, no!' Saswati looked as though someone had asked her to swallow nails, or broken glass, or powdered pebbles.

'Ask her, ask Chhordi,' Biju shouted from the corner. 'I'm sure she'll sing.'

A glance was shot off towards Biju like a bolt of lightning; some of those present thought it the epitome of womanhood.

'Will it be very difficult for you to sing a song?' Shubhro pleaded.

'Do sing, Saswati,' contributed her college friend from the back of the room.

'Just one!' urged one of Shubhro's three friends.

'I've wanted so long to listen to you sing,' Shubhro gathered courage.

Saswati had to sing. In a hesitant voice, she sang a song of Tagore's, with one error in melody and two in the lyrics. The chorus of appreciation that followed as soon as she had ended sent beads of perspiration, like tiny ants, down Saswati's spine.

Shubhro resumed his position, singing one, another, and then, at everyone's request, a third before ending the soirée. Then it was time for snacks, tea and conversation. Everyone enjoyed the evening.

As soon as the guests had left, Biju rolled in joy on the sheets laid out on the floor. 'How grand it was, Chhordi. Oh, wonderful!'

Swati was sitting on a sofa pushed back against the wall. Staring at a slice of black sky through the window and refusing to look at him, she said, 'Let's hear you spell "wonderful".'

'Shut up, Swati. I'm not talking to you.'

'His singing wasn't bad,' Saswati consoled her brother.

'Not bad! Hmmph—what do you mean! And how he praised your singing. Do you know what he told me out on the road? He said, if your Chhordi were to concentrate a little on her singing . . .'

'Oh, shut up,' Swati spoke again. 'You're rotten, and your friends are rotten too!'

'What!' Biju leapt up to grab a clump of Swati's hair.

'Of course! You look exactly like a lout with all that paan you've had,' said Swati, freeing her hair with a jerk of her head and slowly leaving the room.

An angry Biju stopped talking to Swati, and, to underline the point, kept brushing against her as he stomped past, nose in the air. And he continued practising his music morning and night, in stiff competition with the radio. This too was revenge on Swati.

But Swati herself offered the best revenge. One day, as she emerged from her bath, Biju heard her humming the same song about the blue sea that Shubhro had sung at the very end that evening. Forgetting his vow, he said, 'Swati! Well, then?'

Swati smiled with her eyes, and continued humming.

'Lovely! How nice it sounds when you sing it!' Biju forgot all his enmity with Swati in a moment. Putting his arm round her, he said, 'Why don't we sing together a bit, with the music?'

'What rubbish!'

'Please, there's a good girl! Really, Swati, a little more seriously and you . . .' he said, using English for 'serious'.

'Please, Dada, no more English!'

Instead of losing his temper, Biju melted even more. 'Really, Swati! Really! All right—not me, why don't *you* sing? I'll just listen.'

But Swati sat down to her books instead. Biju loitered for a while, then, unable to hold back any longer, ran off to his harmonium, floundering in the currents of the blue sea all morning.

'I do hope Biju manages to get an education.' Rajen-babu didn't seem able to tolerate the whining of the harmonium as he left for work.

'He's very intelligent, Baba,' Saswati said quickly.

'That's reassuring. Why don't you help him with his studies?'

Saswati's enthusiasm about her talented brother waned visibly. 'He refuses to sit down to his books,' she had to acknowledge.

'Is Saraswati the patron goddess of the harmonium too?' asked Rajen-babu, popping another paan into his mouth before leaving.

Amazing! In a month or so, everyone saw—heard, actually— that there was no harmony in the harmonium any more. Such a major development was not easy to believe, and before conviction could take root, another plea for help suddenly rose waveringly from the room downstairs—much more tearful, much more terrifying, through teeth clenched tighter than when playing the harmonium. It jolted Rajen-babu who had just submitted his work-weary body to the cool mat on the floor of the veranda.

'What on earth is that?' he asked, and then answered his own question. 'It's a violin! Is Biju learning the violin?'

'I don't know. No idea,' said Saswati.

'Come on, Chhordi,' said Swati, 'didn't you see Sukomal-babu turn up with a violin the other day?'

'I don't know. You're the one who notices these things!' said Saswati, touching the bun on her head.

'Shubhro's friend Sukomal. You remember the one who said after you sang—'

'All right, shut up! No need to refer to older people by their names.'

Later that night, at dinner, Rajen-babu said, 'Why the violin now, Biju?'

Biju replied with a gracious smile, 'I have no future as a singer, Baba.'

'If it can't be singing, does it have to be the violin?'

'I can master the violin.' Biju was confident.

Looking at his plate, Rajen-babu said, 'If you studied a bit instead perhaps . . .'

Nodding in enthusiasm, Biju said, 'I'll do that too—don't worry a bit, Baba.'

There was a pause. 'Where did you get the violin?' asked Rajen-babu.

Biju's face brightened. 'Sukomal-da got it for me. Costs forty rupees. We don't have to pay at once—will you give five rupees a month, Baba?' Biju looked at his father, whose head was bowed. Here was an opportunity to own a fortune like a violin at just five rupees a month—and still Baba wasn't pleased! What *was* . . .

The violin strings rusted before the violin was fully paid for. However, the musical atmosphere persisted; Sukomal visited at times, so did Shubhro, as well as Saswati's friend with her brother, and some of the neighbours. Saswati had many friends— she was at the right age for an entourage of friends—many of them stayed nearby too. Every evening, while Saswati's court was in session upstairs, Biju had gathered his musical elders in the room downstairs; waves of laughter cascaded downwards from the first floor, snatches of song took wing upwards from the ground floor. The first floor grew wistful, the breath quickened on the ground floor, and Bijon the bold leapt across the divide. Then—it wasn't clear precisely how, it must have been through Biju's efforts—the ladder of freedom was put in place, the flag of equality was hoisted, and as for affinity, there had never been any lack of it. Some evenings, when Rajen-babu returned with tired steps, as soon as he entered he was greeted by happily chattering young voices.

Swati wasn't unhappy about the whole thing; she finally realized for herself that she loved music. When he sang at a soirée, Shubhro seemed rather silly, but when he simply hummed—

why, he was quite nice. While bathing, or when she was by herself in her room, at least when there was no chance of her brother hearing her, she hummed too—just the tune, without the words. To her, the song was just that—humming, nothing—not the harmonium, not the tabla, not lights, not people—harmonized with it. Just humming—like a leaf rustling in the wind, or like lying on your back to watch the moon gazing at your face. If only the moon's silent gaze could be *heard*! Did anyone sing such songs? No, no one knew, but still, whenever anyone sang, *this* was the kind of song they thought up; whenever anyone listened, *this* was the kind of song they tried to hear.

'If one could sing silently,' Swati couldn't help saying what was on her mind, 'it would be so nice. Wouldn't it, Chhordi?'

'What on earth is that!' replied the young woman who was almost eighteen.

'Tell me, Chhordi, on a train, haven't you ever felt someone singing all over the sky?'

'Oh, that!' Saswati smiled. 'You can make the sound of a train say anything, sing anything—everyone knows that.'

'No, that's not what I meant . . .'

Never mind, she wouldn't say any more. No matter how much the wheels of the train clanked, they simply could not drown that song, the song of the sky, she had heard it clearly, mile after mile, crossing stations in one flash after another. But as soon as the train entered a large station, a wave of human sounds would take over, you couldn't hear it any more. Everyone rode in trains—hadn't anyone else heard it?

In the evening, Swati went downstairs, looking for Saswati. She found Shubhro whispering to Saswati, who quickly said, 'Oh, Swati. Where were you?'

'Where do you suppose?'

'Wait here. I'll be back soon.' Saswati weaved her way out of the room.

There was half a glass of water on the table, drinking it up, Shubhro rose.

'Leaving already?' Swati was surprised.

'Yes, I have to.'

Shubhro left. No one else visited; Saswati didn't say much either, the evening passed quite gloomily.

'Swati, come here,' Saswati called her a couple of days later, 'go and give this book to Shubhro-babu, will you.'

'Where is he?'

'He's waiting downstairs. Tell him I'm not feeling well.'

Taking the book, Swati said, 'Didn't he give it to you yesterday? When did you manage to finish it?'

'I've read it before.'

'Keep it a little longer, Chhordi, I want to read it too.'

'No, give it back.'

'Shan't! Why don't *you* go—you're not really ill, after all!'

'There's a good girl. I'll get it for you again later, all right? Go, give it now, please.' Pressing on her temple with two fingers, Saswati added, 'Oh, such a bad headache.'

Shubhro opened the book as soon as Swati gave it to him. A blue envelope among the black and white pages flashed before her eyes. Shutting the book immediately, Shubhro asked with a smile, 'Where's Chhordi?'

'She's probably got a headache.'

'All right, then . . .' Shubhro rose. Suddenly he paused and said, looking at Swati, 'Why don't you take singing lessons? You have such a lovely voice.'

'Lovelier than Chhordi's?' Someone else seemed to have put the words in Swati's mouth.

'Yes, lovelier than hers,' Shubhro answered at once. 'Why don't you come to me? I'll teach you properly,' he said, pinching Swati's cheek with three fingers.

Going back upstairs, Swati went straight into the bathroom. She splashed her face with water and rubbed her cheeks with soap till they turned red, as if trying to peel the skin off, if possible. Then, taking off her pink organdie frock, she put on a blouse and a sari—a simple white cotton sari with a black border. Drawing it around herself, she was suddenly reminded of her mother—she had never thought of her this way in the past two years, had never questioned why her mother wasn't there, given her perpetual illness she had always assumed she wouldn't be there some day. But today she thought, that's not true, people don't always have to die when they fall ill, Ma could just as easily not have been ill. Never, never again will I dress in anything but a sari . . .

The more she said this to herself, the more her eyes filled with tears as she looked at herself alone in the mirror.

∾

Swati could no longer be seen in the evening sessions downstairs. 'What is it?' asked Saswati after a few days, 'what's the matter with you?'

'Why should anything be the matter?'

'You spend so much time by yourself.'

'Not at all!'

'Guess what, Swati,' Saswati tried to cheer her sister up, 'Shubhro-babu and the rest of them are starting a music school in the neighbourhood. There'll be dance classes too—want to join the dance classes?'

'No.'

'Why not? You used to dance so much as a child, remember? You'd be very good at it if you took lessons. You have such a lovely figure . . .'

'Be quiet, Chhordi,' Swati snarled.

Saswati was quite cheerful that day. Placing her hand on her sister's back, she said, 'What's the matter with you? Why are you in a bad mood all the time?'

Swati wound the end of her sari round her fingers without answering.

'All right now, get ready—don't be late,' Saswati bustled.

'For what?'

'Don't you know? The magic show at the club!'

'I'm not going.'

'What do you mean? Everyone's going.'

'I'm not.'

'Come along, it'll be a very good show, come now,' Saswati tugged at her hand.

'I shan't go.'

'Drop it then.' Saswati shook off Swati's hand and went off to get dressed. There was no time—her friends would be arriving any moment.

There were scattered clouds in the sky that day, gusts of wind. Pacing up and down on the terrace, Swati watched a broad, ash-coloured road like Chowringhee in the sky, and—like red fire engines racing along that road—long strands of sunlight. She had nothing else to do: she had read every book in the house at least ten times, there were no borrowed books to read either, and there was no more humming—not even by mistake—these days. Gradually, the light went out in the sky, the clouds gathered more closely, Swati saw her father approaching slowly along the dim road under the gas lamps that had just been lit.

Rajen-babu arrived upstairs just as she was rushing downstairs.

'You're very late today, Baba!'

'This job, this job,' Rajen-babu sighed as he walked towards her.

Walking alongside, Swati said, 'As if no one else has a job. They all came back ages ago!'

'Is that so,' Rajen-babu stopped near the clothes-rack beside the bathroom door.

Snuggling up to her father and running her finger round

the button on his coat, Swati said, 'Why do you wear these coats, Baba? Why not a suit or something.'

'Spare me!' Rajen-babu took off his coat and shirt.

'And your trousers! All of them short!'

'And a good thing too. I like them that way.' Rajen-babu freed his feet from the ten-hour jail sentence of his shoes.

'No, Baba,' said Swati, woebegone. 'It looks terrible.'

'Naturally good-looking people don't have to dress up, do they?' winked Rajen-babu, entering the bathroom. He emerged barefoot after a wash, dressed in a dhoti and vest.

'I've laid the mat out in the veranda for you, Baba,' smiled Swati.

'Heavenly!'

Rajen-babu lay down promptly. The tea came, along with some snacks fried two or three hours earlier.

'Baba, why don't you eat properly?' Swati asked.

'What's that supposed to mean?'

'We eat so much: taalshash, guava, gur,' she rattled off the local names of delicacies. 'You're the one who buys them all, but how is it that you don't have any of it?'

Rajen-babu looked at his daughter in amusement. Was it just amusement?

'Want some litchis, Baba? Yes, Baba, you *have* to have some litchis.' Without waiting for consent, Swati ran off to get four large magenta litchis hidden in her pencil box. Placing them near her father, she said, 'Here you are.'

He had to take one.

'Aren't they nice?'

'Delicious.' Taking one of his daughter's hands in his, Rajen-babu put the other three in it.

Leaning back against the railing and drawing up her knees, Swati said, 'I'll put litchis aside for you every day, will you have them?'

'How is it that you're home this evening?' Rajen-babu asked.

'What do you mean? I'm at home every evening!'

'All alone today?'

Swati was a little hurt by the question. She didn't say anything.

'How are the music sessions going?'

Without answering the question, Swati asked, 'Why do you stay at home every evening after you get back, Baba?'

'Because I like it that way—and because it's a habit.'

'You could go out sometimes . . .'

'Go out where?'

Peeling a litchi with her teeth, Swati said softly, 'You could visit your friends, or go for a film on Saturday or Sunday . . .'

'All right, all right, that's enough! And why do *you* stay home in the evenings?'

Stretching herself from the waist upwards, Swati said, 'Just . . . like that.'

'Your sister can hardly stay at home these days, and your brother of course is the best friend of the entire world. Don't *your* friends visit you?'

'I have no friends,' said Swati, putting the entire peeled, bluish white, perfectly rounded litchi in her mouth.

Rajen-babu's evenings had been a trifle lonely of late, now they suddenly brimmed over. Swati had so many things to say! It was like a balmy breeze blowing over his worn-out body, carrying tiny raindrops. One day Swati said, 'Baba, there's this shiny new black car that goes down our road, have you seen it?'

'Really?'

'You know that large house at the head of the road with the huge compound—that's where it belongs. They have four cars. They're very rich, aren't they, Baba?'

'Must be.'

'But you can't ride in all four at the same time, can you? What do they do with four, then?'

'They're probably a large family,' Rajen-babu said after

some thought, 'and none of them stays home like you do, all of them go out a lot.'

'Buy a car, Baba.'

'Will you go out if I do?'

Swati smiled. 'Not a bad idea. If you have to, it's best to go out in a car. I don't like it at all that girls have to walk.'

Rajen-babu laughed at this.

'There's nothing to laugh at,' said Swati, 'that's the way it is! And if you get a car, you won't have to take a tram to office either.'

'But I like trams.'

'Horrible! How crowded they are! Yes, Baba, buy a car.'

'Let's see.'

'Tell me, Baba,' said Swati, drawing a finger slowly through the parting in Rajen-babu's hair, 'can't we move into a smaller house? We don't even use two of the rooms.'

'But we need them when your sisters come, don't we?'

'Who knows when they'll come—just for that . . . Why haven't any of them visited since then?'

'It's not easy, you know.'

'But when Ma was here they came so often . . .'

'When their mother's gone, daughters don't visit their father very frequently,' Rajen-babu smiled.

'They don't! What do you mean!'

'Do they?'

'What about me? Aren't I your daughter any more?' Swati lay down on her stomach, nestling against her father. With his eyes, Rajen-babu kissed the head covered with dense black curls for a long long time.

∼

An amazing development took place, an unprecedented proposal was made!

One Saturday, Rajen-babu asked as soon as he came home from office, 'Where are you, my princesses, would you like to go for a film today?'

Swati ran up to put her arms round her father. 'Really, Baba, really?'

Saswati was in a spot. On Saturdays she had classes at Gitayatan, the school that Shubhro and the rest had set up, on the other hand she was reluctant to disappoint her father too, since the fancy *had* caught him! 'Which one do you want to go for?' she asked coolly.

'Whichever you want.'

'*The Prisoner* is not bad, I heard . . .' Saswati observed sagely.

'Nonsense!' Biju's white dhoti swayed near the door. 'If you have to, the film to watch is *The Revenge*—oh, glorious!'

'Have you seen it?' Saswati seemed to challenge her brother to a duel.

'A-a-ages ago.'

'So you won't go again, will you?' said Saswati.

'Who wants to!' Biju's heroism flashed behind the door. 'I wouldn't have even if you'd asked me to—I have rehearsals, don't I!'

'Rehearsals! Theatre?' Instead of asking his son directly Rajen-babu looked at Saswati.

'The local boys are putting up something—and you can't possibly have anything in the neighbourhood without Biju being involved!' Saswati said quite proudly.

But eventually Biju managed to resist the rehearsal. They all went in a taxi, and the most expensive tickets were procured, with seats on the first floor. Saswati sat back against the cushion as if she were a veteran, her eyes scanning the audience till the film started, and from the moment it did Biju talked indefatigably next to her . . . 'Now she'll storm off to her parents in a rage . . . He's going to fall ill, that's why his eyes look like that!' Saswati even boxed him on the ear, quite hard, but Biju was unrelenting.

Even in the taxi, on the way back home, his chattering went on and on. 'You know, Chhordi, Shiben's songs were actually playback numbers. Someone else sang them, he only mouthed the lyrics.'

'All right, enough, be quiet now!'

But even as Saswati spoke, Rajen-babu interrupted with 'Really?' He had been quite surprised on watching—watching *and* listening to—the film. Aeons ago he'd watched the silent bioscope—they used to be called bioscopes those days. This was his first talking film, that too in Bengali. What goings-on, my God! How did they *do* it?

'Of course it's real!' His father's enthusiasm made Biju bubble over like boiling water. 'Shashanka Das sang all the songs—he lives in Manoharpukur, has a Studebaker, latest model!'

'You know a lot about these people, don't you?'

Biju interpreted the observation as a compliment, accepting it with a smile. 'Shashanka sings for so many films these days—and he does sing very well too, doesn't he, Chhordi? Shubhro-da's going to be singing playback very soon.'

After some thought, Rajen-babu said, 'But whatever you may say, mouthing the lyrics is no less difficult. And the hero's quite—'

'—handsome!' Biju took the words out of his mouth. 'That's Sujit—made his debut just the other day in *Dream Palace*, and already . . . Not surprising! You just have to look at him!'

'He's horrible!' Swati spoke at last. 'Stupid lips!'

'Did you know,' Biju threatened her, 'Sujit got the most votes in *Style & Star* for his appearance?'

'So what! That other man—that friend—he's *far* better looking.'

Making an effort to recollect the appearance of the hero's friend, Rajen-babu said, 'You liked him?'

'Yes, Baba, he's very handsome. A little like you.'

'Like me!' Rajen-babu laughed. 'If I'd been as handsome that would have been something!'

'You're not handsome? Whatever do you mean?' Swati's small, immaculate teeth gleamed as she laughed.

The discussions on the film went on for some time even after returning home. Using his Chhordi as the excuse and his father as the target, Biju unlocked his storehouse of astounding knowledge on the subject. Swati stayed more or less silent, as though she was looking at something else, thinking of something else. In the dark veranda, with the lights yet to be lit, Rajen-babu suddenly said, looking at her indistinct face, 'Swati, your birthday's coming soon.'

Swati turned swiftly to look at him.

'You're quite grown up now—we must celebrate your birthday properly this time.'

'Yes, Baba, yes,' Saswati clapped. 'That'll be lovely. What fun!'

'What a soirée we'll have!' Biju leapt up. 'Oh! I'll get Shashanka Das himself. There'll be so many people to see him.'

'Very good—a soirée—what else? Whom will you invite?'

'Shobha-di, Leela-mashi, Mithu-da . . .' Biju rattled off the names of relatives.

'Fine. And what about you? Your friends?'

'Oh, they will . . .' Biju paused suddenly before resuming, 'Chhordi, Harit-babu. Shall I invite Harit-babu?'

'You and your . . .'

'What a speech he gave at the club the other day! How intelligent, isn't he? If only you'd stayed a little longer, Chhordi, I could have introduced you to him.'

'You haven't given up yet!' Saswati laughed loudly.

Before going to bed that night, getting hold of her father by herself, Swati said, 'Listen, Baba . . .'

'What, Swati?'

'No birthday party or anything, please.'

'Why not?'

'I don't enjoy things like that.'

'What *do* you enjoy, Swati?'

What did she enjoy? Did she know for herself? On short-lived holiday afternoons, a sudden extraordinary joy took hold of her. Films, going out, dinner invitations, fun with friends—nothing else did this for her. And if that couldn't happen, however nice something was, *was* anything a joy? The sky sang in her ears, the world was nothing but a train, no station, perpetually running, the song never stopping, morning or night, we don't hear it, nobody can hear it, only I can, and if I can, why don't I hear it all the time?

'Tell me, Swati, what do you enjoy?'

'All right, do whatever you want to,' Swati smiled and went to bed.

On the morning of her birthday, after his morning tea, Rajen-babu said, 'Saswati, come with me, will you?'

Swati stepped forward quickly. 'No, not you today,' said her father, 'you must stay at home today,' addressing her with the more stilted *tumi* rather than the friendly *tui* he normally used.

Swati seemed rooted to the spot, then she went away slowly. What upset her most—even more than not being taken along— was that her father had addressed her that way. She couldn't remember his ever having done that before. Was it her fault it was her birthday?

The sounds of their return were heard on the staircase about an hour later; hearing them call her, she said in irritation, 'Wha-a-at?'

'Come quick,' Chhordi was bursting with excitement.

'I'm busy with arithmetic!' She started writing out the decimals swiftly. Arithmetic was very good, arithmetic was the best—nothing was as effective at distracting you when you were feeling miserable.

'Please!'

'I can't now!' Swati blasted her.

'Here you are!' Something dropped on her table, and Biju ran away. A large square box with the name of the shop printed on it. Oh! How she had been longing for a box like this, how heavy it was, and how nice, you could put so many things in there—she wanted to play with dolls again as soon as she saw it. Where had her brother got it? And why was he being so nice, giving it to her instead of keeping it for himself?

Putting her pencil aside, Swati opened the box. Oh, a sari! What lovely golden needlework on green! A blouse too! And in a small, slim box, under shiny paper—just like a geometric triangle—were folded yellow, pink and light blue handkerchiefs.

Swati ran outside. Flowers, sweets, new cups and saucers, shining spoons—what a sight!

'Well?' said her father. 'Doesn't it look like a birthday now?'

From a distance Biju said, 'Don't imagine you're the only one who got a present. Here's my new dhoti, and Chhordi's sari. What fun we'll have!'

Swati was quiet, blushing. When her mother was alive, their birthdays did get celebrated, new frocks; paayesh, the traditional birthday rice-pudding; even guests sometimes—but not like this! So many flowers! So many sweets, cool, soft and swollen, with green pistachios! All this for her? Because it was her birthday!

'What do you think of the sari?' asked Rajen-babu. 'Do you like it?'

'It's silk . . .'

'You don't like silk?'

Without raising her eyes, and twisting herself a little, Swati said, 'It's like the saris you dress dolls in . . .'

'But then who is it for but a doll?'

'Not at all!' Swati laughed. Looking at the things scattered all over, she said, 'Baba, you've got something for everyone, but nothing for yourself?'

'But it's all for myself,' said Rajen-babu.

∽

She had to dress in the green silk sari and the satin blouse. Saswati forced a new hairdo on her, the sandalwood marks on the forehead were not forgotten either. Rajen-babu was reminded of the glow on Shweta's, Mahashweta's, Saraswati's faces on their wedding nights—so beautiful, so joyful. How well this look matched Swati's still-immature face—a face he had seen in the grip of so much sadness for so long! After just a single glance, Rajen-babu turned his eyes away.

Swati, too, felt like a new person when she appeared in the large upstairs room in the evening. So many pairs of shoes on the floor, a roomful of people, everyone nice, everyone happy. Granted, Biju hadn't been able to get hold of Shashanka Das, but Shubhro and his cohorts kept everyone enthralled till nine at night. Swati felt all the songs were sending her the same message, 'You're so lovely, we love you. All the people here love you. Lovely, very lovely, this world is lovely, everything in this world is lovely; why else do people sing, dance, laugh, make merry; where else does such joy come from?'

'Your turn,' said Shubhro, pushing the harmonium towards Swati.

Instantly, the spell was broken. Crushing all the joy she had built up till then to a pulp, an impossible embarrassment took hold of Swati's throat—as though everyone were staring at her, looking at her strangely, she didn't seem to have put her sari on properly, something had gone wrong somewhere. How awful! She wished she could go away, but so many eyes were watching her!

'We *will* hear you sing tonight,' she heard Shubhro's

suave voice, like a cat wailing at night, continuing to use the more familiar *tumi* instead of the formal *aapni* when addressing her.

Completely spontaneously, she suddenly raised her face and said, with the entire room her audience, 'Don't you address me so familiarly!'

An indistinct murmur ran through the room. Behind his glasses, Shubhro's shining eyes went out instantly like a light switched off, wiping off whatever joy and poise there had been in his expression, leaving him looking like a different person altogether. Breaking through the uncertainty created by everyone wanting to say something but being unable to, someone very lively spoke up clearly: 'All of us would be very happy if you were to sing.'

Swati discovered the speaker leaning against the wall, his denim-clad knees drawn up, one arm half-covered by a half-sleeved shirt resting on a knee, the other one holding a pipe upside down. She didn't think she had seen him before. But how did that matter, a reply sprung to her lips: 'Would you be happy to hear *anyone* sing, or just me sing?'

'Let's say it's you.' The pipe-wielder looked amused.

Swati looked in amusement too at his dark, smooth face. 'I don't how to sing,' she said.

'You don't? But haven't the people here heard you sing before? I've also heard that you can sing,' the pipe-owner had a crooked smile at the corner of his lips.

'You may still have heard me sing, but it's impossible that you may have heard that I *can* sing,' said Swati, taking her eyes away from the dark man's face. Laughter coursed around the room, in voices deep and thin.

'How impertinent you are! Shame!' Saswati wasted no time as soon as she met her sister afterwards.

'Why?'

'Insulting Shubhro . . . babu like that!'

'Insult?'

'Of course! He's known you since you were young . . .'

'But I'm not young any more.'

After a momentary glance at Swati's sparkling sari, Saswati said, 'How can you switch from casual back to formal?'

'Why not? You can switch from formal to casual, can't you?'

'Impertinence,' Saswati blushed.

'Don't keep using that word, Chhordi!'

'Of course I will. Impertinent, uncivilized, arrogant! You think you can joke around with Harit-babu too, don't you?'

'So that dark man is your famous Harit-babu.'

'Don't imagine, Swati, that a twenty-five-rupee sari makes you grown up,' Saswati flared up. 'You'd better remember you haven't yet earned the right to rub shoulders with adults as an equal.'

Swati had never seen such blind rage on Saswati's face. Scared, she said, 'Chhordi.'

'You obviously think everyone in the world is Baba. That you can get away with anything. You cannot! You think you can win every battle with your childishness. You cannot! If you cannot behave decently, politely, no one will tolerate you—no one!'

'Chhordi, what did I do—what have I done—why are you talking to me like that?' Swati put her hands out, stepped forward, stopped, trembled, retreated; the end of her gold-embroidered sari tumbled to the floor.

'You're not such a child any more,' Saswati contradicted herself. 'If you still cannot rid yourself of your conceited ways, your arrogant behaviour . . .'

Swati almost started sobbing on hearing such stern rebukes. 'Don't scold me, don't scold me any more . . .' Somehow managing to keep her long sari on herself, she ran off to her father, wrapping her arms around him and crying, 'Baba!'

'What's the matter, Swati?'

Looking at her father's calm, pleasant, reassuring face, Swati swallowed her tears.

'. . . No, nothing.'

'What's happened?'

'Nothing.'

'Did Chhordi scold you?'

'No.'

"What is it, then?'

Swati was quiet, her face buried in her father's shoulder. Running his hand over her curly black hair Rajen-babu said, 'How fashionably Chhordi's done up your hair!'

'Baba,' Swati said, rubbing her face softly against his clothes, 'Baba, I'm going to live with you. I'll never leave you and go anywhere. Never.'

'Very nice. That's wonderful. Such joy! But why do you have to cry? Do grown-up fifteen-year-old girls cry!'

'Oh God!' Swati raised her eyes, brimming with tears, to laugh. 'What do you mean, Baba? I only turned thirteen today.'

3

I won't go anywhere, I'll live with you . . .

But go they had to. It was Saswati's turn.

Rajen-babu had moved into his own house a few months back. Long ago, when the opportunity had arisen, he had bought a small plot of land, quite cheap, in Tollygunge, near the bridge, a little to the west of Russa Road. Suddenly he decided that it needed a house. But not all that suddenly, either.

Despite regular visits from private tutors six months in advance, Rajen-babu's fears came true—Biju failed in his matriculation exams. For a few days he remained sunk in gloom, and then immersed himself in the preparations for staging *Sita*— this was no laughing matter, for he was playing Tungabhadra!

It was best, thought Rajen-babu, for someone like Biju not to have cash at his disposal. Not that he had any to speak of. While it was true that, having ascended the government ladder step by step, he was now on a seven-hundred-rupee level, all his life he had had to take many loans, pay back many loans. Ten years of treatment for his wife, the weddings of three daughters, and unrestrained spending for his children's happiness—how much could that leave? Still, despite all the blows it had had to withstand, the provident fund had survived, and the two insurance policies were about to mature too. Of the two methods most employed people in Bengal used to save money, Rajen-babu practically emptied out the first one to get his house built.

It wasn't a large house—single-storeyed, with four bedrooms or so. Nor was it modelled on a ship or a plane or the racecourse at Labong—just a simple house where people could live, eat, sleep. Saswati wasn't happy at all. On top of that the road was named Bidhu Ghosh Lane—she didn't like that either.

'Why did you have to build a house here, Baba?' she couldn't help saying one day.

'You don't like it here, do you?'

'This area is too . . .' Saswati was about to say *full of poor people*, but Harit had taught her to respect the poor—indeed, they were the ones who ran the world, they were all that counted! Pausing for a bit, she finally settled on '. . . too petit bourgeois'.

Rajen-babu was astounded at what his college-going daughter had just said. Petty . . . what? Pettycoat? Petty cash? Petty quarrels?

'Too . . . what?'

'Oh, nothing!' Saswati smilingly pardoned her father's ignorance. 'Don't you see how congested the place is, how dirty the children are!'

Swati was on the window seat, munching a green guava; swinging her legs, she responded at once to Saswati's remark.

'Congested! What do you mean, Chhordi? See how open it is this side—fields, trees, so much sky! Oh God! I feel claustrophobic at the thought of Jatin Das Road now.'

Saswati laughed at her reaction. 'Why didn't you put up another floor, Baba?' she said.

'You want me to do everything? Let Biju do the rest.'

'What would we do with another floor anyway? This is fine—just as much as we need. I don't like having too much of anything!' Holding on to a window-bar with one hand, Swati swung her leg, adding at once, 'I like the ground floor best— the outdoors are so close at hand on this floor. Just wait and see what a lovely garden I'll make! Is there anything as beautiful as a small, single-storeyed house?' declared Swati, taking on the mantle of judge and ruling in favour of herself, without giving her opponent a chance to speak, and bit into her guava with great satisfaction.

But the opponent didn't let go, resuming the argument in the privacy of the room. 'Tell me, Swati, why do you assume everyone must like exactly what you like?'

'What do you mean! Am I not allowed to say what I like?'

'You behave as though the world and everything in it is ruled by your wishes.'

'Not the world and everything in it—just one or two people . . .'

'Not even two,' Saswati interrupted, 'you can't have more than one person like that, and there'd be trouble if you did.'

'Meaning?'

'So innocent! As if you haven't digested all those novels already!'

Swati really hadn't understood at first—she did only after her sister smiled contemptuously. Turning graver in response to the smile, she said, 'But why do you have to quarrel over the house—you won't be here much longer, after all!'

'As if you will!'

'Of course I will!' The words forced themselves up from within, but seemed to lose their force as they rose, eventually not hitting their target at all. After a silence she was about to say something else: 'Listen, Chhordi . . .'

'Be quiet now,' said Saswati, taking a book from the desk and flopping on to her bed.

'Listen, please . . .' Swati pleaded.

'No!' Saswati opened her book.

'Please, just a minute!' Swati begged almost tearfully. 'Do you *have* to read Markas right now?'

'Marx, not Markas,' Saswati corrected her smugly. 'I'd better leaf through it. Harit-babu will be here in the evening, after all.'

Swati was surprised, forgetting what she had been dying to say. 'So what?' she asked. An entirely logical question.

'Harit-babu lent me the book, you see.'

'Do you have to return it today? Won't he let you keep it a few more days if you tell him?'

'These books are not really for reading,' Saswati smiled slyly. 'Just to leaf through—so that I can say something about it when he comes!'

Swati had never heard anything so peculiar in her fifteen-year-old life. Although you haven't read the book, you have to pretend that you have. Why? If you don't like it, don't read it—what's the problem! She looked at Saswati, her eyes full of questions, but her sister's face was hidden behind the book's yellow cover emblazoned with black letters.

Saswati rose in a few minutes, carefully placing the unreadable book on a row of books to be read for college, and went for a bath. Swati suddenly felt sad at her sister's anxiety. Standing by the desk, she picked the book up and began leafing through it. She was afraid, her heart thumping; who knew when a blue envelope would peep out from between the pages. It would take a long time to go through the entire volume. Turning it upside down, she shook it vigorously a few times. No, nothing in there. She put Marx back in its place. How harmlessly the book lay there, but . . . but . . . but . . . what?

Wrapping a towel round her head, Saswati said as she returned, 'Your turn.'

'Later.'

'This is a terrible habit of yours, Swati,' Saswati put the towel away and picked up her comb. 'Shouldn't you freshen up a little for the evening?'

'I'm always fresh,' Swati flopped down on the bed.

'What're you lying down for?'

'Why not?'

'Is this any time to . . .' Saswati's fair fingers ran up and down her black hair rapidly.

'Tell me, Chhordi,' Swati pinched the skin on her forehead, 'what news of Shubhro-babu?'

'How strange! How would I know?'

'He's never come to this new house, has he?'

'He didn't visit much in the other house either recently. Works so hard, he has no time. Pass that ribbon.'

'You stopped going to his singing classes too . . .'

'So much concern for him now—you couldn't stand him once upon a time!'

'The world doesn't run according to my wishes, you see.' Turning on her side, Swati placed a palm under her cheek. 'A person needn't be bad just because I can't stand him.'

Without replying, Saswati unscrewed the lid on a jar of cream. Swati's glance fell again on the book with the black-and-yellow cover.

'What's Marx, Chhordi?'

'Marx—Marx was a person.'

'He wrote the book?'

'It's about—about him.'

'About, meaning?'

'Meaning . . .' Saswati's powder-puff stopped on her face. 'Oh, simply . . .' Pausing, she brushed the puff across her cheeks, and concluded, 'If you want to know, ask Harit-babu.'

'Does he know all this?'

'Of course. He's such a scholar! Graduated from the London School of Economics!' Saswati proceeded to put on a sari whose colour was exactly like the inside of a blackberry.

'Does he teach you economics?'

'Of course not!'

'Why not? He could—he comes over quite often.'

'How funny! He hardly visits.' Saswati tucked the lower part of her sari in at her waist, and then wrapped the upper part around her back, saying, 'They have a lot of conferences— he comes by with news about them. I've asked you to go so many times, why don't you ever go?'

'What happens at the conferences?'

'So many things. Songs, speeches, arguments . . .'

'Rubbish!' Swati sneered.

'What do you mean, rubbish? Harit-babu speaks so well— you can learn so much just listening to him.' Adjusting her sari with a crimp here and a tug there, Saswati stood before the mirror once more.

Looking at her for a bit, Swati said, 'Didi, the powder in that square tin of yours is awful.'

'Awful?' Saswati laughed.

'Too strong.'

'It's face powder, you see.' Saswati dismissed what Swati had said, but also took a covert look at her own reflection. Had she overdone it? No, it was fine. Still, she picked up her powder-puff once more, saying, 'Who's this writer who made his fashionable heroine use Cuticura powder on her face? No sense!'

'Why?' Swati was amazed again.

'Do you think Cuticura should be used on the face?'

'It shouldn't?' The vehemence of her own protest made Swati sit up. 'I do. So have you, many times.'

Pretending she hadn't even heard, Saswati said, 'How people laughed about him the other evening. Eventually Harit-babu brought up the thing about the powder . . .'

'There's so much to learn from him.' Swati appeared overcome by the breadth of Harit-babu's knowledge.

Happy at seeing her sister soften, Saswati said, 'Try this— you'll see how good it is; nothing compares with it.'

'But whatever you may say, nothing smells as good as Cuticura,' said Swati as she got up.

Rajen-babu returned from office a short while before Harit came. Swati had just brought her father tea in a small pot. Pouring out his tea, Swati smiled, 'May I have some tea, Baba?'

'Why bother to ask for permission every day?'

'Then I'll have tea every day from now on—all right, Baba? I'm grown-up now, aren't I?' Putting her arms round her father briefly, Swati went near the teapot. 'Do you want some, Chhordi?'

Saswati was seated on a reclining chair near the window, all dressed up, the book with the black-and-yellow cover open before her. 'No,' she answered succinctly.

Drinking her tea with a spoon, Swati said, 'How good this tea is—lovely!'

'Swati, stop drinking your tea with a spoon,' the cultured Saswati hurled a comment at her.

'Why, what's wrong?'

'Nobody drinks their tea that way.'

'Don't they just! I've seen many people . . .'

'All idiots!'

'And those who don't drink their tea with their spoons are not?' Saying this, Swati put down her spoon and picked up her cup with two fingers, as adults do, saying the very next moment, 'No, I prefer the spoon!' She glanced at Saswati, but Saswati suddeny stirred and focused her eyes on her book in sudden seriousness. The crunch of shoes was heard outside, followed by three muted but clear, Westernized knocks on the door.

'Find out who it is,' said Rajen-babu; but without getting off her chair, Swati said, 'Please come in.'

Parting the curtains, Harit entered, dressed in a pair of floppy trousers and an open-necked shirt. Greeting Rajen-babu with a two-handed wave, he said, 'Ah—all well?'

'Tea, Swati!' Rajen-babu started bustling.

'No, no tea, I just . . .' Harit looked at Swati, bending forward. 'Am I intruding?' His behaviour suggested Swati was the most important person of the three.

Swati laughed. How he emphasized his words. *Tt*ea for tea, *inn*truding for intruding. 'Not at all,' Swati paused. 'Do sit down.'

Harit couldn't ignore her request, taking a few steps to the chair next to Swati's. 'Well? Done reading?'

'Not finished yet.' Saswati's eyes were downcast, her voice faint.

Crossing his legs and stuffing tobacco into his pipe, Harit said, 'It's a difficult subject—but then, there's no other subject that's relevant today. We of course are happily spending our days stuffing our faces and writing poetry about the moon, while a major battle . . .' he put his pipe in his mouth before concluding, '. . . is about to break out. So we should in advance . . .' As he was about to light a match, he lowered his pipe and turned to Rajen-babu, who was in a vest, saying—in English—'I am sorry.'

'Not at all . . . I'd better . . .' Rajen-babu made as if to get up.

'Please stay,' Harit raised his arm like a god granting a boon. 'Not that there's any offence . . . but since we have a custom in our country . . . I'll just take a short walk . . .' Oozing respect for his country's traditions in every step, Harit went out, pipe in hand.

A little later, after a final sip of his tea, Rajen-babu left slowly. Still sitting, Saswati put herself through various physical contortions, and kept sitting.

Swati went with her father. 'Come for a walk, Baba?'

'Let's.' Rajen-babu was ready immediately.

'Let's take a walk there in that field.'

'Fine.'

Swati was ready in two minutes. 'Baba? You're lying down? Don't you want to go . . .' With a quick glance, she said, 'Never mind, Baba, let's not go.'

'Why not? Let's—I was just resting for a moment.'

Swati sat down near his head. 'No, Baba, go on resting. Let me pluck out some of your grey hair.'

'Isn't it too late?'

'You've hardly got any grey hair—you don't have to be so proud of it.' Parting his hair with her hands, she added immediately, 'Oh, so many!' Out they came.

'That hurts,' Rajen-babu squirmed.

'Don't behave like a child! Quiet now!' Swati manoeuvred her father's head according to her requirements; running her hand through his hair, she said, 'Such lovely hair, Baba!'

'Has to be! I'm Swati's father, after all!' His voice sounded indistinct again.

What had her father looked like when his hair hadn't greyed at all? She seemed to have always seen her father this way—it appeared he couldn't possibly have been any other way, ever. But obviously that wasn't so! There were a couple of old photographs of his; he looked so different, it was funny, but it must have been fine when the photo was taken!

'Baba,' called Swati, 'Baba!'

She heard deep breathing in response. Asleep! Swati was surprised, somehow, seeing her father drop off in the middle of the evening. Not stirring, she sat quietly; the light fell and night entered the room. Suddenly sounds of laughter filtered in, a mixture of deep and high voices.

Later in the evening, as she sat down to her studies, Swati exclaimed, 'Chhordi, Harit-babu's book!'

'What about the book?'

'You might as well have returned it. Since you're not going to read it . . .'

'What business is it of yours?' Having told her off, Saswati began to wonder how she would be able to go to the University Institute on Sunday afternoon, as Harit had suggested.

The next day, too, she wondered about just that as, books in hand, she stood on the pavement opposite her college with two of her classmates. All the meetings she had been to so far had been at the house of a well-off man who lived on Rashbehari Avenue—going there was easy enough, but College Square! She hadn't revealed her problem to Harit—what would he think, after all—girls travelled all over the city by themselves all the time these days, but she . . .

'Get in,' a small grey car rolled to a stop in front of her. 'Get in,' Harit said again, beckoning.

'Oh, it's you!'

'Come in,' Harit opened the door.

Saswati looked like hesitation personified. Stammering, she said, 'No, I'll . . . the tram . . .'

'Who is he?' whispered the girl next to her in her ear.

Harit said a little more loudly, 'I see, you're with friends, that's why. I would have been happy to have given all of you a lift, but as you can see, there's no room for more . . . Therefore, if you permit . . .' He smiled at the other two.

'Go along,' one of them nudged her. 'Don't you have any consideration?'

'There's our tram,' said the other one, running off.

The tram left with them. Saswati kept standing with a sort of missed-my-train expression amidst the ten-thirty bustle in the morning. 'What else is there to ponder on now,' said Harit.

'Many thanks, Mr Nandy,' said Saswati gravely, 'But . . .'

'Oh! Don't be silly!' Speaking in English, Harit made such an impatient yet amused face that Saswati got into his car without further delay.

The car turned right on Hazra Road. 'Where are you going,' Saswati shouted, her hand on the door. 'Not this way!'

Without answering, Harit brought the car to a halt slowly at a petrol pump. Saswati breathed in relief, the words 'I see,' escaping her lips.

Taking his pipe out of his pocket, Harit knocked it against his car to get rid of the residual tobacco. Turning his head to look at Saswati, he said, 'Did you think I was running away with you?'

Saswati's virginal face was inflamed. Enjoying the sight, Harit said again, 'And even if I did have such an evil motive in mind, why should you be afraid? Can't you defend yourself?'

Saswati turned away to watch the pale gold stream of petrol bubbling its way down the glass tube. After a while the car started moving south along Russa Road in the bright sunshine. She noticed all the trams and buses were packed, many of them with girls from her college heading home—how uncomfortable it was!

'It appears I have committed a crime,' said Harit mincingly.

Saswati finally found something to talk about: 'Your car— very nice.'

'It belongs to a friend; I use it. Rather too small—are you cramped?'

'What to do even if I am?'

'You could at least remove the books from your arms.'

'Never mind.'

As they crossed Rashbehari Avenue, Harit said, 'I really have discomfited you. But then, I did not request you to get in for your pleasure.'

'For whose then?'

'Mine, obviously!'

Saswati lowered her eyes.

'I hope you're coming on Sunday?'

'Let's see.'

'Why the doubt?'

'It's so far away...'

'Far? What do you mean far! You have to come.'

Saswati swept the hair off her forehead with one hand. Glancing at her slightly lowered profile, a new thought suddenly flashed through Harit's mind. 'All right, don't worry, I'll pick you up on the way.'

'No, no...'

'Why such vehement protests?'

'So much unnecessary trouble...'

'Not more than taking a tram or a bus...'

'It's not that...'

'Well, then, that's settled. Please be ready by six, I have to get there a little early.'

'No, really, see...'

'Really, see!' Harit joked with her own words. Saswati laughed.

Getting off the car on the main road, Saswati walked the rest of the way home. How would it have mattered if he'd dropped her all the way? Really, how horrible my thoughts are! All rubbish! Makes no sense! I *shall* go with Harit in his car on Sunday—I shall, I shall!

But she couldn't. 'How can you go alone with him?' said Rajen-babu.

'Why not?'

'No particular reason—it's not done. Say no to him.'

No! The father who had never said no to anything was now saying no! Was she so subservient that she couldn't even go, of her own volition, where she could learn about different things! And all these years she had thought her father was not like other fathers!

Shaking her head, she said, 'I can't say no to him now.'

'Then I will.'

'No, please . . .' but by then Rajen-babu had disappeared. A little later, Saswati, dressed in an expensive silk sari from Dhaka, heard the small car depart.

Re-entering the room, Rajen-babu said, 'What, are you very upset?'

'What did you tell Harit-babu?'

'I said, Saswati won't go today.'

'You said that?' Saswati raised her hand in a plea.

'What should I have said then?'

'Couldn't you say I'm sick?'

'Why, *are* you sick?'

Saswati wanted to rip her clothes in rage. How would she meet him after this? And what kind of a person was her father, blandly saying she wouldn't go. He had insulted an important person. Would Harit bother to visit her again? Not only would he not, but now he must surely think her to be some pathetic, awkward kind of bumpkin! If only she could still go to the conference now, at least she could explain . . .

'If you do want so much to go,' Saswati heard her father articulate her heart's desire, 'take a bus with Biju.'

But Biju didn't want to go. He was about to step out to meet his friends, his collar cocked. 'Lecture? Impossible! Not me!'

'Why don't you make an exception for your Chhordi?' Rajen-babu requsted him.

'Not me!' Biju vanished in a jiffy.

'Then I might as well . . .' said Rajen-babu.

With her father? Never mind, at least she was going. Saswati rose to refurbish her make-up. 'Want to go, Swati?' said Rajen-babu.

'Where, Baba?' Swati ran in from the next room.

'I'm taking your Chhordi to a conference . . .'

'Why you?'

'Why not? A chance to go out.'

'No, you won't . . . What are you laughing at? Just the Sunday, just the one holiday a week—and you want to go all the way to College Square? Are you crazy?'

'There's nothing to do all Sunday . . .'

'Nothing, my foot! Why can't Dada take her?'

'He has no time.'

'And you have all the time in the world! You make me so angry!'

Saswati came into the room, complete with her bag. 'Chhordi, Baba isn't going,' Swati announced as soon as she saw her.

Saswati halted abruptly.

'Let me.' Rajen-babu observed Saswati's face clouding over, while lightning flashed in Swati's eyes. 'Let's go, all right?' he said helplessly. 'You come too.'

'What kind of person *are* you, Chhordi?' Swati confronted her sister. 'Now you're dragging Baba along . . .'

'But she didn't say anything . . .'

'Swati!' Saswati thundered, 'when did *you* become the head of the family?'

'You mustn't!' Swati raised her voice too. 'You mustn't go, Baba. I forbid it!'

'Don't want—I don't want to go! I won't stay here any more!' Saswati ran to the window, grasping the bars and sobbing.

❧

Her words didn't prove untrue—before a month had gone by, Harit proposed.

It was another Sunday. After his morning shopping, Rajen-babu was reading the newspaper in the drawing room, when Harit marched in. His attire—possibly because winter had

legally arrived—fitted him better . . . crisply ironed trousers,
clean tie. Rajen-babu welcomed him hesitantly. 'Have a seat,' he
said, gathering up the pages of his newspaper with a view
to leaving the room. But Harit stopped him: 'Don't leave, I
need to talk to you.'

Rajen-babu looked calmly at the young man.

'The thing is . . .' sitting upright in his chair, Harit tapped
the handle twice, 'I want to marry Saswati. You must have realized
this is Saswati's wish too, now all that's needed is your approval.'

Saswati's name didn't sound pleasant at all when Harit
said it. Why is it that I don't like this young man!! There's
nothing wrong with him—quite suitable, in fact! Well educated,
even been abroad, enthusiastic, intelligent. But still—his behaviour,
his demeanour, the way he spoke—all of it sort of . . .

His three other sons-in-law floated up in his mind's eye—the
large-hearted, jovial, eldest son-in-law Pramathesh; the slightly
short-tempered Hemanga, but very intelligent behind his thin-
lipped taciturnity; tousled-haired, bewildered Arun; and next to
them, this . . . this what? Who knows! Maybe today's best young
men were this way; I'm old-fashioned, the problem is with me.

Since the bride's side seemed silent, the suitor added, 'I
have some information for you. I work at the insurance office;
my current salary is three hundred, the prospects are good.
My father is a lawyer—writes law books, lives in Bhowanipore,
in a house built in my grandfather's lifetime, both his younger
brothers live there too—I've recently taken a separate flat
on Rashbehari Avenue.'

'Why?'

'For your daughter's happiness,' Harit answered without
hesitation. Leaning back in his chair, he said, 'So what do
you think?'

'I'll talk to your father.'

'Of course, all those formalities do have to be completed.
But since my father has no independent viewpoint on this,

I'm the one . . .' Harit looked at Rajen-babu, seeking an answer. Not getting one, he stood up. 'I have to go. I'll be back at the same time tomorrow.' Stopping in front of Rajen-babu on his way to the door, he lowered his voice and said, summoning a disinterested look in his eyes, 'Let me say something. We *shall* get married. I do hope there won't be any pointless objections . . .'

'We'll see.'

Rajen-babu remained in his chair after Harit left. What was the matter? What was wrong with Harit? Why couldn't he think of this as wonderful, why couldn't he feel happy, why couldn't he see in his face Pramathesh's pleasantness, Hemanga's sharpness, Arun's charm? Why was his heart revolting at the thought of placing him by their side? But my daughter has selected him, my daughter will be happy—who am I here? But am I no one? Aren't they mine? . . . No, did the fruit really belong to the tree? The seed belonged to the tree, the flower belonged to the tree, but the fruit belonged to the earth. The moment it ripened, it had to be given to the earth, or else the fruit would rot, the tree would die . . . What if it fell on abandoned land, on fallow land, on a desert? Who knew, could anyone tell? Whom could he ask? Whom could he discuss it with today? Even when confined to her bed, suffering intensely, barely surviving her illness, she had at least been there. Where did she go? Has she really gone then, will I never see her again, will I not even see her at her daughter's wedding, not even once?

'Baba!'

Swati, who had just bathed, entered wearing a white sari with a red border, her wet hair left loose. Looking at her, Rajen-babu couldn't say a word. There was nothing to say, no one would listen if he did; I have to let go, I too will have to let go, I too owe the world three, four, five daughters.

'You seem worried, Baba.'

'Let me ask you something . . .'

'What, Baba?'

'What do you think of your Chhordi's getting married to Harit?'

'Why shouldn't she?'

'Why shouldn't she? Do you like Harit?'

'Me?' Swati didn't say anything more.

'Will Saswati be quite happy, do you think?'

'Why shouldn't she be?' Swati turned round, perhaps a little shyly. The red border of her sari flashed before his eyes. This had happened before. Once before, remembered Rajen-babu suddenly, exactly this way, on just such a November morning; a similar moment, a sari with this same dazzling red border, the same cascade of wet hair, the thrill of watching an identical turn of the head. When? When? Was it in this lifetime, or another? Was it in this world, or another? Was that me? Was that really me? That other fifteen-year-old woman— don't you remember? Don't you remember me? Don't you remember me any more?

'Should I call Chhordi, Baba?' Swati leaned forward to rest her chin on her father's shoulder. Moving his head away, Rajen-babu drank her in with his eyes, as though he had never seen her before. This curly-haired head, the loveliest of all the faces he had seen in his life! This face too had changed. The face that had once held only joy, only heavenly bliss, why did it now hold anxiety, disquiet? Was it afraid of something he didn't know? Her eyes had never appeared as large, as slanted. Her face had never seemed so unusual, so unusual that it almost appeared unfamiliar . . . Although he had seen four daughters grow up already, Rajen-babu still could not believe this was his daughter too.

'Why don't you speak?' Swati asked again.

'All right,' said Rajen-babu, rising from his chair.

That very day he began to arrange the money for the wedding. The date was set for the middle of December, in no time at all, the excitement of the wedding spread over the neighbourhood.

∽

And what a wedding it was! Swarms of people; commotion and celebration; unending rounds of cooking and eating.

Although all his three daughters had visited sporadically over these past few years—once Shweta and Saraswati had even arrived at the same time and both had stayed through Durga Puja—Rajen-babu had not, despite his best efforts, succeeded in getting all three of them together at the same time. He was very hopeful that it would happen at Saswati's wedding, but it didn't. Hemanga was suffering from renal colic, he could neither travel nor be left behind. Mahashweta wept to her father in a long letter, sending a bank draft for five hundred rupees in the same envelope, along with a parcel containing examples of the work of Burmese goldsmiths.

For his daughters and sons-in-law, this was the first time in the new house. Rajen-babu allocated the largest room, open to the south and the east, which Saswati and Swati lived in—used to live in, to Shweta—not because she was the eldest, but because she had the largest brood of children. His own room went to Saraswati, and, handing over Biju's room to the two youngest daughters, he took the drawing room—which meant nothing else but spending the night in it.

'And me? Where will I sleep? Biju glowered.

'Why, there's so much space in the drawing room,' said Rajen-babu.

'On the floor?'

Rajen-babu had a cot brought in. Swati said, 'So you'll sleep on the floor, Baba, and Dada on the cot?'

'It's much more comfortable on the floor.'

'Where am I going to study?' demanded Biju. 'I have exams too.'

'Swati has exams as well,' Rajen-babu scratched his head, perplexed. 'For a few days, then . . .'

'As if you're studying all the time!' Swati sneered. 'Very convenient for you, since you have a lovely excuse now.'

Flying into a rage, Biju went off to a friend's house with two or three books and a pillow. 'He's right . . . why him, he could have . . . after all, his exams . . .' Shweta said tentatively.

'Just as well,' said Rajen-babu. 'If he actually studies a little out of sheer rage, it might prove useful.'

'Aren't you going to call him back?'

'He'll come on his own.'

Having spent the entire day elsewhere, Biju returned just before evening, calling out, 'Swati, give me my mosquito net!'

Shweta came up to him quickly. 'Funny boy! Where have you been all day? Come along—what do you want to eat?'

'I'm going away right now,' said Biju heavily.

'Go to your room now. I've tidied it for you.'

Biju was astonished when he did. The desk was neatly arranged, the bed covered with a new bedspread, and there was no sign of the two sisters. He flopped down on the bed immediately—he had been on his feet all day.

In the evening Shweta said, 'Baba, I've asked for the beds to be made in the drawing room. Saswati and Swati on one cot, you on the other . . .'

'Why?'

'Let Biju stay in his room.'

'And you, with all the children, it's so cold . . .'

'What cold—as if Calcutta winters are cold. We'll make a lovely large bed on the floor, lots of space for everyone.'

'Oh yes, that's best—they roll around so much!' Pramathesh said, laughing in a way that suggested rolling around was a lot of fun.

'Biju shouldn't be indulged like this,' said Saraswati.

'What do you mean, indulge?' said Shweta. 'When everyone else can be comfortable, why should he be the only one to suffer?'

'Suffer! Why can't he make a few sacrifices for his sisters? It's only a matter of a couple of days, after all.'

'He's a child, after all—how can he . . .?'

'As far as I can see, his childishness will never leave him. I told you, Baba, let him come and live with us in Delhi—he'd have grown up properly there.'

'Really? Then let me get my Dalim to come and live with you—the monkey simply won't study!'

Arun appeared in a warm, grey suit. 'Can you get me a handkerchief?'

'Check in the suitcase,' answered Saraswati without glancing at her husband.

'But I can't find it . . .'

'As if you can ever find anything. Geeti, get a handkerchief out for your father, will you?'

Geeti had also dressed up to go out with her father; shaking her head like a doll, she said, 'Can't.'

'Can't. There's nothing you people can do. What's the point of having children if I have to do everything myself!'

'Poor fellow—why don't you get him the handkerchief,' Rajen-babu said.

Pummelling her daughter as punishment, Saraswati stood up, having covered her head first. 'Let me have your sari,' said Shweta, 'I'll add a border.'

'This one?' Saraswati was surprised. 'These are meant to be worn without borders.'

'Really? The new fashion is to wear saris without borders? Oh God!' Shweta didn't seem to believe her own eyes.

'Don't you remember Mrs Dey, the judge's wife . . .?' The room echoed with Pramathesh's loud laughter.

In bed that night, Saswati told Swati, 'Bordi's changed, hasn't she!'

'Changed to what?'

'Sort of rustic.'

'No, not that. Something else,' said Swati after some thought.

'Like what?'

Nestling closer to her sister under the quilt, Swati whispered, 'Like Ma.'

'It's very warm!' Saswati kicked the quilt off.

'Do you remember Ma, Chhordi?'

'Of course I do.'

'But I feel I've practically forgotten. The day Bordi came . . . I was startled at first glance . . . Exactly like—'

'What rubbish! Ma didn't look like that at all! Check the photographs.'

'I don't know, maybe it's because I didn't get to see much of Bordi . . .'

'Her husband's stupid,' Saswati remarked after a while, 'that's why she's become that way too.'

'What rubbish, he's very nice.'

'It's Arun-da who's very nice. But how old he seems already. The two of you don't seem so thick any more.'

'I hardly get to see him.'

'You remember, Swati—' Saswati shifted to bring her face close to her sister's—'how you had cried because you wanted to marry him?'

'What rubbish!'

'You cried buckets! And how you kicked and punched me! Don't you remember?'

'Rubbish!'

'You really created a scene. Mejdi and Chhordi died laughing!' Recollecting the incident, Saswati laughed the same way her two elder sisters had laughed ten years ago. But was it exactly the same way?

After a pause, Swati said, almost to herself, 'It's Friday already, next Friday by now . . .'

'Go to sleep now.'

'Chhordi, tell me something.'

'What?' Saswati looked a little embarrassed.

'How does it feel?'

'How should it feel!' replied Saswati, and turned over abruptly.

On Saturday morning, following the wedding night, Harit felt contented—as though, having spent an afternoon watching a film, he had re-emerged into the glow of the early evening sun. The winter morning had blended into people, movement, laughter, conversation and activity. He awoke on the floor of an unfamiliar room in an unfamiliar house, traditional motifs drawn in white on the floor next to him, a yellow thread on his wrist, dressed in silk. As though the film were over, everyone had melted in the crowd on the road, leaving him alone on the staircase. No—he simply had to go out after a cup of tea. Stretching, Harit stood up.

After a wash, and exchanging his silk for an everyday dhoti, he returned to the room to find quite a crowd. Tea was laid out on an enormous silver tray on the floor. And not just tea—bread-and-butter, poached eggs, plump golden bananas, puffy *luchis*, fries, three kinds of sweets. Harit was about to faint.

'Well, Mr Nandy, did you manage to sleep at all?' asked Saraswati.

'Very soundly.' Harit sat down grimly on the floor, since there was no chair.

'Oh dear, you've taken off your wedding clothes!' Shweta was alarmed. 'What about today's rituals?'

'I'm going out,' said Harit even more grimly.

'Now? Where do you need to go now?' Shweta was horrified. 'So many things to be done . . .'

'Come on, now,' the corpulent Pramathesh positioned himself on the bed. 'Forget all those rituals of yours. Young men don't care for all that! Give him a cup of tea.'

'Swati, go call your Chhordi, will you? Perhaps the young man would like that?' Saraswati darted a glance at Harit.

'Don't embarrass the poor girl unnecessarily,' said Shweta, covering her head even more elaborately with her sari.

But no! Dressed in her wedding sari and jewellery, Saswati smilingly sat down beside her brother-in-law, leaning against the bed.

'Wrong choice. Why don't you go sit next to *him*—give us something to look at!' said, Pramathesh, looking around for support.

'Stop bothering us!' Shweta squatted on her haunches near the tray, handing Harit a plate laden with food.

'What's all this for?'

'For you to eat a little?'

'A little?'

'You had to fast yesterday . . .'

'No! Why should I fast?'

'All right, you didn't fast yesterday,' Shweta laughed. 'Doesn't mean you will fast today, does it?'

'Just some tea, please.'

Saraswati poured the tea. 'What about the rest of you?' said Harit.

'We had ours a long time ago,' Pramathesh gestured with his hand. 'We're used to our small-town ways, you see. Been awake a long time.'

'What about you?'

Saraswati was the object of the question.

'You should have told me earlier,' Saraswati smiled mischievously, 'I'd have waited for you.'

Dressed in a loose dhoti and *panjabi*, Arun entered and sat down on the floor, sweeping the hair off his forehead and saying, 'Some tea for me.'

Saraswati handed a cup to her brother-in-law first, then to her husband.

Looking at the bed, Harit said, 'You, Saswati?'

Pramathesh burst out laughing, Shweta concealed her smile behind the corner of her sari, and Saraswati asked without any stiffness, 'Want some tea, Saswati?'

Shweta raised her eyes towards Harit: 'You don't have to worry about her—eat up!'

Harit ate an egg, then sipped his tea.

'That won't do! You have to eat everything.' Shweta pushed the *luchis* towards him. Harit shuddered.

'Eat up!'

'No.'

'E-e-e-eat up!'

'No, really—I don't normally have breakfast . . .'

'Do you get married every day? You needn't eat like you do every day either. You think you're very clever? Eat up quick!' Rolling a *luchi* around a large lump of chips, she wedged it into Harit's hand. Harit ate it in distress.

'What will you have now?' Saraswati entered the fray.

'Nothing else.'

'Oh, so you'd prefer Bordi to feed you. All right, Bordi, put some more food in Nandy's hand. He doesn't know how to eat by himself.'

But when it came to the sweets, Harit almost lay down in vehement refusal. It was a veritable moral protest. The sisters-in-law didn't relent either, soliciting his patronage from either side.

'What kind of obstinacy is this!' said Saswati from the bed. 'Why can't you have some, they're asking you so nicely?'

'Oh my God! Already!' Shweta collapsed on the floor with laughter.

Saraswati announced, perhaps a little drily, 'All of us have failed—see if you have better luck, Saswati!'

Standing near the door, Rajen-babu said, 'It's terrible to force food on people. They should be allowed to eat as they choose.' He spoke softly, but everyone heard.

'So . . . so . . . if that's what he . . . Never mind!' Saraswati's face fell.

'Not everyone follows the same customs,' said Rajen-babu as he left.

Arun, who had put down his cigarette at the sight of his father-in-law, now picked it up quickly and said, 'If the wife sits a mile away, who can possibly enjoy their food?! Come closer, Saswati.'

Running his hands over the soles of his feet in a princely way, Pramathesh said, rolling a little from side to side, 'You're a clever man. Already got your wife near yourself, and on top of that . . .'

'Does that mean I cannot even sneak a look at someone else's wife! Please don't mind, Harit.'

Seated by the window, at a little distance from the rest, Swati raised her eyes when Arun spoke.

'Inspired by your sister-in-law's wedding, I see!' Saraswati fired an arrow at the smiling man with perpetually tousled hair.

'Simply won't eat,' said Shweta, wiping her face and getting up.

But she wasn't to be cowed down; at lunch she served her new brother-in-law a perfectly sculpted bowl-shaped mound of rice on an enormous silver plate, surrounded by different-sized brass bowls arrayed around the plate like the strands of a necklace—just like the moon and his twenty-seven wives.

As soon as Harit sat down, Shweta said, 'Not for eating, just to look at.'

'Extremely worthy of being looked at,' Harit had to admit. 'Tell me which the best items are.'

Pleased, Shweta said, 'Try everything.'

'Everything! Won't the leftovers go waste?'

'You don't have to worry about that.'

'What extravagance! So much food wasted!' Harit said to himself as he surveyed the rows of bowls.

'What's the point of a wedding otherwise!' Ignoring the *shukto*, Pramathesh began with the daal. 'Don't you know that story about C.R. Das—for his daughter's wedding, the treasurer had estimated the expenditure at one lakh rupees. One lakh will be pilfered, Mr Das had smiled, how much will it actually cost!' Pramathesh laughed loudly.

'That's why we are where we are today!' Harit broke off a corner of a fish cutlet to put it in his mouth. 'But that day is not far away—it's almost here! This time too Chamberlain has managed to keep it at bay, but war is inevitable—then we'll see how such extravagance can continue!'

'You seem quite excited at the prospect of people not being allowed to enjoy themselves any more?' said Arun the doctor, slurping up his *shukto*.

Rajen-babu was squeezing the juice of a lemon into his daal. Without raising his eyes, he said softly, 'But he's right, we *are* needlessly extravagant.'

'Since we *have* been extravagant, let's make the most of it!' announced Pramathesh, attacking the bitter-flavoured curried fish.

'Do you suppose we'll learn easily! People must die of starvation on the roads—only after that!' Harit selected the lobster, cooked with poppies and coconut.

'Those who help people face such a problem,' said Arun, mixing a whitish sauce of gourd into his rice, 'they just cannot be happy when people are.'

Leaning her head against her father's shoulder, Swati suddenly laughed with a sound like flowing water. Harit raised his eyes to give her a fleeting glance, then continued eating in silence.

'Aren't you eating, Swati?' Pramathesh changed the subject.

'I'll eat with my sisters.'

'But Swati and Biju could have eaten with the groom.'

'Biju ate and went out ages ago,' answered Shweta. 'And Swati . . .'

'No,' Arun exclaimed, 'eating together and all that—it isn't hygienic at all.'

'Is that you speaking?' Saraswati smiled. 'There was a time you couldn't eat unless it was with Swati.'

'But that was for a different reason—don't you remember, Swati?' Arun threw a glance at Swati.

'Nandy isn't enjoying your old-fashioned jokes,' Saraswati called a halt to the exchanges.

'Let's hear a few newfangled jokes, then!' The object of Shweta's comment reddened a bit, but didn't raise his eyes from his plate.

Swati came away. She had a misty memory of how much she used to like Arun as a child; she had never liked anyone as much again. Shubhro, Shubhro's friends, Harit—was any of them like the Arun of that time? But why wasn't he the same any more, what had happened to that Arun? Do the favourites of your childhood no longer remain your favourites as you grow up? How fortunate it was she had grown up—from now on she would be constant about whom and what she loved, it wouldn't change any more. Or would it? How horrible! Swati seemed to stop breathing for a moment. If that was the way it was, how could you have faith in your love?

Going to Saswati, she said, 'Tell me, Chhordi, if we like someone once, do we like them all our lives?'

'What a stupid question!'

Swati looked in silence at her sister's hair now with a line of powdered sindoor in the parting. Suddenly she said, 'You'll go away today, Chhordi?'

'Where's Biju?'

'No idea.'

'I haven't seen him in a long time.'

'But Dada's always out...'

'Can you check whether he's back?'

Coming back, Swati said, 'No, Chhordi, Dada isn't home.'

Till the moment she got into the taxi, Saswati kept asking about Biju, but it wasn't before dusk that Biju returned, sunburnt, his sandalled feet caked in dust. He didn't like the brooding silence he encountered. Peeping into different rooms, he asked Swati, 'Where's Chhordi?'

'Gone,' said Swati heavily.

The word seemed to deal him a body blow. Recovering, he said, 'When?'

'In the afternoon.'

'Why wasn't I told earlier?' Biju's voice rose.

'You have to be told specially?'

'Why didn't you tell me?'

'Don't shout, Dada.'

'She kept asking for you,' Shweta sighed. 'I know, why don't you pay them a visit now, she'll be delighted.'

'Couldn't care less.'

'Don't ask him to do anything, Bordi,' said Swati. 'Is he even part of this family, that he would feel bad?'

'Of course I'm not! Of course I'm not a member of this family!' Biju shouted at the top of his voice. 'If I'd been a member of this family would I not have known when Chhordi was leaving!'

'There you are,' Swati answered.

'I know!' Biju tried to vaporize Swati with his eyes. 'I know everything. This house is yours, you're the only one that matters here, everyone listens to you—there's no room for me here. You were so jealous of Chhordi all these years, and now she's gone as well. So why aren't you dancing for joy now?' His face red, his mouth foaming, the veins in his neck swollen,

Biju took what was in his heart and planted it in the ears of each of the saddened, exhausted people at home.

What the recent departure of a daughter and a sister had not been able to do was now accomplished by an unexpected onslaught from the heavens.

'But do you know why?' Biju's voice was heard again. 'Do you know why I'm not part of this family? Because of you! Listen carefully, Swati, it's all because of you that I never stay at home, that I roam around all over the place, that I had to give up my studies! Did you think I would also live in your kingdom! Not any more! I'm leaving now!' Smiting himself theatrically on his chest and jumping up, knocking over a kettle near his feet with a clang, Biju left like a bullet from a gun.

'So insolent,' Rajen-babu said softly in the next room.

Everyone else was transfixed for a few minutes. Then Pramathesh whispered, 'Go find out if he's really left.'

'Why do they leave things lying around!' Putting the kettle away, Shweta went to her father. 'You could talk to him sometimes, Baba. He's grown up now. . .'

'Wild!' Saraswati couldn't think of any other English word. 'Completely wild!'

'Ma isn't here,' Shweta said quickly. 'All boys become a little wild at this age. If only Baba would . . .'

'No,' Saraswati interrupted. 'It's not like that. He needs discipline, strict discipline. It's because Baba is such a gentleman that he's got this way.'

Rajen-babu didn't respond to any of his daughters. Suddenly the stomping of footsteps was heard again. Looking like he had been beaten up on the road, Biju came into the room, glaring at everyone and saying, 'You couldn't tell me? None of you could tell me? No one?' He flung himself down on Saswati's bed, burying his head in the pillow and, with a horrible, bloodcurdling groan, cried out, 'Chhordi! Chhordi-i-i-i!' bursting into loud, outrageous tears.

Leaning on a pillar in the veranda, Swati seemed to have melded into the grey winter darkness all this while; she was startled by her brother's extraordinary outpouring of grief. Biju didn't let up, and as she listened, Swati choked, her lips trembled, her face crumpled in countless creases, and warm, soul-wringing teardrops rolled down her cheek.

4

Tears. Was this what tears could be like? When they took her mother away, when her father returned without her, that first night at home without her mother—she had all but died weeping. And yet this was not how she had felt then. She had been swept away on a wave of tears, as though she were sinking into the deepest ocean, but every time her breath was about to stop someone had taken her hand to draw her head above the waves. But now, these tears seemed to break her heart as they welled up within, rising, rising, and then falling, making her eyes burn on the way. She tried to conceal them, but could not—they made her feel ashamed, but who cared about shame? The tears for her mother had held only pain—the more the pain, the more the relief. And the strongest message of these tears is that I have lost, there is something that I had meant to say but could not—those words have been wiped away by the tears.

Swati remained in the grip of her tears during the next few days. Whenever she thought of Saswati she cried; she flooded the room with tears when Shweta and Saraswati left; tears seemed to lie in wait to ambush her in the house, now emptier than ever before, in the same way that—as she had heard—police detectives stalked freedom fighters. At one point, simply unable to shake them off, she scolded herself like Alice in Wonderland: 'Shut up! I'm asking you to shut up! Aren't you ashamed to be such a big girl and still cry? Stop at once.' And indeed, how could she go on this way? Weren't her exams round the corner?

'Let's study together, Dada,' she told Biju.

Running his tongue over his lips, Biju said, 'I've finished.'

'See, Dada, I simply can't understand geometry...'

'All right, I'll explain it to you another time. Is there a clean dhoti somewhere?'

'The washerman's due... Don't mess around in there!' Swati put her book aside to carefully pull out a crisp dhoti from beneath the trunk.

'But this is Baba's,' Biju said, examining it.

'So what?'

'Too coarse, too short.'

'If Baba can wear it why can't you?'

'But I'm taller than him. And do you suppose it fits him either? Terrible habit—as if we'll save money if he wears short dhotis. If only he'd spend less!' Biju was very pleased to be able to echo what he had heard one of his sisters say at some point of time. Laughing uproariously, he then said, 'All right, since there isn't another one...'

'The geometry, Dada...'

'Wait. After lunch...'

Dhoti in hand, he went off for a bath. When he met his sister again at night, he asked, in quite a superior manner, 'I hope all's well with your studies...'

'So-so.' Swati didn't bring up the subject of geometry any more.

'How many essays have you memorized?'

'Memorize essays? Whatever do you mean?'

'Haven't you memorized a single English essay? Not even the one on the plane? That's the one they'll tell you to write this time—mark my words.'

'Good god!' Swati burst into peals of laughter. 'You don't memorize essays, you make them up.'

As if for the benefit of his sister, Biju proceeded to stay up nights studying English at the top of his voice. Rajen-babu was startled. 'Biju's studying—I'm surprised!'

'Why not wait and watch?' Swati reassured her father.

But it was all in vain—Biju failed again. Finding an opportunity at some point, Rajen-babu diffidently raised a question to his son: 'What now?'

'Not going to study any more, Baba,' Biju answered benevolently.

'In that case . . .?'

'Don't you worry, I've got it all planned.'

Rajen-babu looked at his son.

'I'm going to be an artiste, Baba.'

'Artist!' Rajen-babu was flummoxed. 'You mean a painter?'

'No, Baba,' Biju sweetly informed his father, 'even singers are called artistes these days. Actors, too.'

'Has Biju gone mad?' Rajen-babu asked Swati in private afterwards.

'Nothing new there,' Swati smiled, before adding quickly, 'But Dada's very intelligent, Baba; if only he'd concentrate.'

Rajen-babu didn't reply. Unless he could get Biju involved in some kind of gainful work immediately, wouldn't it be too late afterwards? He was only two years away from retirement; the regime under which he had joined had all but ended; if he requested the powers that be even now, it might be possible in his department . . . But without even a matriculation degree . . .

'And besides,' Swati comforted him, 'passing exams isn't everything. There are so many other options. He might do something worthwhile suddenly—who can tell?'

'He will remain without an education,' Rajen-babu sighed.

'Uneducated! What do you mean? Does he lag behind anyone in conversation or conduct! Never mind how he behaves with us—just watch him with others!'

'Even Saswati passed her BA exams after she got married . . .'

'Does passing exams make you educated?'

Although Swati argued, she was no less sorry for her brother. Wouldn't he even go to college ever in his life? She was going, and what a good college it was—completely different, completely new. So many new ideas, difficult ideas, things she couldn't even have imagined a few months ago—truly! It made her happy.

∾

One day during the English class in college, Iva Ganguly said, sitting next to her on the back bench: 'What's the point of all this English? England isn't going to rule us forever!'

'No?' Swati was amazed.

'Just wait and watch where this war goes . . .'

Really! War! So Harit was right! 'Will there really be a war?'

'What do you mean, really?' Iva laughed.

The professor paused in his reading of 'The Ancient Mariner', throwing them a fleeting glance before continuing. Suppressing her laughter, Iva said quietly, 'Don't you even read the papers?'

Instead of answering, Swati concentrated on the professor. He was very nice to listen to, but the way he was holding the book, you couldn't see his face. Looking at her book, Swati matched the sounds to the words.

'Such deep attention!' A pencil poked Swati in the back.

'Uff!'

The reading stopped suddenly; raising her eyes, Swati saw the book had moved from the professor's hands to the desk, and his quiet gaze was on her face. 'Is anything the matter?' he asked softly.

Iva looked away disinterestedly, while Swati's blushing face announced her wrongdoing. The plump Maya Sanyal sprang to her feet from the front benches, 'We can't concentrate on studies today, sir.'

'Why not?'

'Tell us something about this war.'

'But this isn't the place for that discussion,' said the professor, standing up to recite in a deep voice:

'Nor dim, nor red, like God's own head
The glorious sun uprist:
Then all averr'd I had killed the bird
That brought the fog and mist.
'Twas right, said they, such birds to slay,
That bring the fog and mist.'

Swati couldn't look any more, her eyes were glued to the pages of her book, she drank in every note, rhythm, emphasis; like the three-year-old that the poet had spoken of, she listened, enraptured.

'The fair breeze blew, the white foam flew,
The furrow followed free;
We were the first that ever burst
Into that—'

'Sir, what does "like God's own head" mean?'

The music broke off abruptly; Swati shuddered as one does at the sound of a metal bowl screeching across the floor; she fired an angry look at Maya Sanyal's back.

'Let me read a little more,' answered the professor in English, 'before we discuss this.'

'Didn't understand "nor dim, nor red" either, sir,' protested Alaka Nag.

'There's nothing to understand for now,' the professor looked above the students' heads at the wall. 'Listen with your ears first, think with your minds later.'

'But why did he call the sun "God's own head"?' Maya questioned unrelentingly.

'Very difficult poem, sir,' said someone else. 'We can't follow unless you explain it properly.'

Swati saw the blood rise in the professor's gentle, reserved face. His eyes grew sad, his lips curled a little, he explained deliberately, with what seemed to be an expression of amusement on his face. There was no need, Swati burned within, there was no need—it would have been lovely if he'd just continued reading.

'The way he read—it really reaches out to you,' Swati told Iva after class.

Not hearing her properly, or perhaps deliberately misinterpreting her statement, Iva replied, 'How can he even think of teaching! He's so young—graduated just the other day!'

'Really! How young he is! And so shy? Never even so much as looks at anyone,' added the plump girl.

'Isn't he Satyen Roy? The famous student? I've heard my brother speak of him.' A petite girl in glasses spoke for the first time.

'Good students don't necessarily make good teachers!' Iva quoted her uncle, who was the vice principal. 'He's teaching the girls' class because of Anadi-babu's illness. He actually takes tutorials for the boys, earns seventy-five rupees. He was in such a state at the sight of so many girls together!'

Iva was the oldest among the girls in the class. She was accomplished, and had her uncle's backing. Many of the listeners laughed; not that everyone found it funny, but not laughing would mean losing face.

'So unfair!' Swati's sharp voice drowned the laughter. 'First you didn't let him read—and now you're joking. How beautifully he was reading, and how lovely the poem is!'

Looking at Swati's face, which had colour in it, Iva said gravely, 'That's why they shouldn't let young male teachers take classes for girls,' following it up with a naughty smile. The girls started warbling again.

'So old men aren't dangerous?' Swati responded quickly and marched out. What nonsense! You had to squash them with replies like these. It was so sublime—how much she was enjoying it—and they had to spoil it all. Never mind the history class today, I'm going home. Or else Anupama and Chitra and Supriti will all come along, chattering all the way—so nice to be alone now.

'We were the first,' Swati stopped suddenly on the pavement as a car brushed past her. 'We were the first that ever burst into that silent sea . . .' Oh, how did they make them this way, who made them? Another step . . . 'Into that silent—'

Swati retreated hastily—a bus! So large and so loud! The din of buses, the clanging of trams, fifty different noises on the road. But Satyen Roy's deep, gentle voice rose above all of them:

'Nor dim, nor red, like God's own head
The glorious sun uprist . . .'

What did it mean—'Nor dim, nor red, like God's own head'? Did it matter? You could see it with your eyes: the sea—endless, silent, just the sea; a solitary ship, just the sea; black fog, shadowy light, just the sea; and over that sea rose an extraordinary sun—extraordinary, what could be more extraordinary than this . . .

There were a hundred sources of commotion—the tram making a fuss, the din of the bus, crowds, sunlight, tall buildings, people rushing off to work. For a moment Swati saw nothing, heard nothing—she saw the sea, just the sea, and on that lightless, chiaroscuro sea, the extraordinary sunrise; she heard those extraordinary words in a gentle, deep voice, so extraordinary that she had never heard them before: 'Nor dim nor red . . .'

'Dying to be run over in the middle of the road?' Anupama put her hand on Swati's shoulder.

'Oh, Anupama!' Swati was a little late greeting her classmate.

'I came right behind you. Really, Iva is very vulgar . . . Let's go.'

Back home, Swati read the long poem from start to finish. She enjoyed it, but not all that much. If only she could have heard Satyen-babu read the whole thing. His class wasn't till next Tuesday. But how much could you do in the classroom anyway, and these girls . . .

Next Tuesday the girls seemed even more restless, the Durga Puja holidays being just two days away. Satyen-babu didn't take the class, presumably anticipating as much. And after the vacation, Anadi-babu came back. Of imposing appearance and stentorian voice, it wasn't possible to tell whether he was reading poetry or making a speech; it needed intelligent guesswork to determine just when during his speech he started dictating notes with the words: 'Take down . . .' You could hear a pin drop during those forty minutes.

Had the door opened a crack for just a moment only to be closed? But I have seen what's inside, and it's extraordinary! Will it never open again? Will I never get a glimpse inside again? Will I never enter? . . .

Over and over again Swati turned the pages of the fat textbook with red covers. The melody that her ears had caught could no longer be heard. Just as a very gentle, subtle, intangible breeze suddenly creates a little bit of heaven on a sultry night before disappearing, so did her heart feel an occasional balmy touch—but then it went back to being silent and sultry once more, still and sultry.

She brought the subject up with the girls in her class. 'Hasn't the writer of "The Ancient Mariner" written anything else?'

'Nothing else in our text,' said that petite dark girl, who had won a scholarship in her matriculation exams.

'One's bad enough!' Maya Sanyal, who had wanted to know the meaning of the poem, shook her head. 'It's such a horrendous poem!'

'Old wives' tales!' said Supriti, who had written an article on the enlightenment in China in the college magazine. 'What if he killed a bird? The age of fairy tales is long past!'

When Saswati and her husband visited them next, Swati

asked in the course of the conversation, 'Harit-da, do you have any poetry books?'

'Poetry?' Harit smiled contemptuously. 'I don't read all that poetry stuff.'

'Why not?' Swati was a little surprised. The college girls may have been stupid, but Harit was a knowledgeable man.

'What can poetry do for you? Can poetry fill your stomach?'

'What do you mean!' Swati broke out in peals of laughter. 'Why should poetry fill your stomach? For that you need food.'

Harit pardoned his young sister-in-law's levity with a generous smile, but on the way back he told his wife, 'Swati's education is misguided.'

'Swati's quite brilliant,' answered Saswati. 'If only she'd been a boy and Biju a girl . . .'

'Can't women be brilliant?'

'Women can't do what men can, can they?'

'Oh!' Harit said in agony. 'How much more, how much longer do we have to hear all this! Aren't you ashamed as a woman to talk like that?'

'Can't—meaning aren't allowed to,' Saswati corrected herself immediately.

'Exactly!' Harit was pleased. 'It's nothing but a question of opportunity. In the Soviet Union women are even driving train engines!'

Travelling comfortably in the car—the one that belonged to Harit's friend—the chiffon-sari-clad Saswati imagined herself before the demonic furnace in the engine, and expressed her gratitude to God (God! But no one was listening, after all!) for not having been born a woman in the Soviet Union.

'It'll happen in our country too.' His hands on the steering wheel, Harit smiled and looked at her, and Saswati looked back at him, glowing with eagerness.

Meanwhile, Swati had to resort to the college library,

asking a little apprehensively, 'Do you have Coleridge's poetry?' Without bothering to check, the aged librarian said, 'No, we don't have Coleridge.'

'Not even one?'

'No . . . Utpala Sarkar . . . *Gora* . . .'

After Utpala Sarkar had left optimistically with a copy of *Gora*—tattered, dog-eared, smeared with numerous hand-prints and tattooed with various bizarre comments—Swati tried again: 'Do you have anything else? Any other poetry?'

The librarian raised his face to look at her with bespectacled lifeless eyes. Rummaging through books on the racks, his back turned to them, someone said, 'Why don't you give her Palgrave's *Golden Treasury*?'

'Palgrave is a textbook, we don't issue it to students.'

With a brief glance over his shoulder, Satyen Roy resumed browsing, then pulled out two books and approached the librarian's desk. Swati looked at him, then looked again. Satyen-babu noticed her suddenly. 'Why don't you help her out,' he told the librarian.

Entering the names of the two books in his register with great effort, the librarian said, 'No more books to be issued today.'

Swati returned in disappointment. She had barely reached the library door with slow footsteps when a book appeared to fly through the air and drop like a stone near her feet. Satyen Roy bent at once to pick it up with his left hand, somehow balancing a pile of books in his right at the same time. 'So many books!' the words escaped Swati's lips.

Smiling shyly, Satyen-babu divided the books into two piles, one for each hand.

Swati stopped too, touching the books quickly with her eyes before asking hesitantly, 'You . . . you don't take classes with us any more?'

The professor's fingers became animated on the two piles of books. 'Which year?' he asked softly.

'First year. You were teaching us "The Ancient Mariner"...
It was wonderful.'

'It's a wonderful poem . . . I'm not surprised you like it,'
said Satyen-babu; about to leave, he stopped, looked at Swati
and asked, 'Do you like poetry?'

'Poetry? I . . .' Swati didn't know what she should say,
what the right answer was.

'Have you read Rabindranath?'

Swati couldn't answer this either. 'Read Rabindranath,' said
Satyen-babu again, looking at the books he was holding.
'And . . . don't expect anything from this college library . . .'
Skilfully extracting a book from the pile in his left hand with
two fingers of his right, he said, 'Try this one.' Swati took the
book he held out between his fingers. Reading the name
inscribed inside, she was about to speak, but without giving
her the opportunity Satyen-babu left, his two piles of books
swaying a little.

It took Swati seven or eight days to go over all the pages
of *The Golden Treasury*. Whichever page she opened the book to
absorbed her. So much everywhere! Which should she read
first? If she happened to read a short eight-line poem, she felt
the urge to read it again and again, but the next poem called
out to her too, so did the one after that. 'Spring, the sweet spring
is the year's pleasant king . . . the spring time, the only pretty ring
time . . . mistress mine . . . full fathom five . . .' What *was* all
this? What? If printed words could sing, wouldn't they drive
people mad? How long would it take her to finish this book, how
many months, how many years? Even a single line would stay
with her the entire day—if it went on this way she wouldn't be
able to finish it in her lifetime! He hadn't said when it had to
be returned, but that didn't mean she could keep it for a long
time. Swati took it every day to college to return it, but where
was Satyen Roy? He taught the boys, and here the classes for
boys and classes for girls were held separately—how would she

meet him? And as for him, he had completely forgotten that he'd lent her a book, he could at least have asked for it back. But whom will he ask, he doesn't even know my name. It's not right to lend books this way, I would never have if I were him—how will he get it back now even if he needs it, I should return it, it's wrong not to return it . . . Swati became very worried about the whole thing, but Satyen Roy just wasn't to be found; the days passed, winter gave way to summer, exams came and went, the summer vacations began.

∽

During the vacation, her father said one day, 'Swati, you seem a little depressed these days.'

'Not at all,' Swati smiled brightly.

'You're alone all the time.'

Swati was silent.

'Don't you visit Saswati?'

'I do.'

'You could spend a few days with her.'

'No, Baba . . .'

'Why not? Saswati was saying the other day . . .'

'I don't like it anywhere except at home.'

'Then why don't you ask your friends to visit you at home?'

'What friends do I have?'

'Why, now that you're in college, I'd expected lots of girls in colourful saris to visit every evening. Laughter, music, conversation—lovely!'

'Chhordi's the expert there, isn't she, Baba? How lively it was back then, and how silent now. I'm sure you hate it.'

'Do you, Swati?'

'Not I.'

Looking at his daughter, Rajen-babu said, 'Your sisters are all so fond of people. How did you turn out so unsocial?'

Twisting her body like she used to as a child, Swati said, 'I *am* unsocial. Unsocial is best.'

'Aren't you friendly with anyone in college?'

Swati didn't reply.

After a pause Rajen-babu said, 'Any idea what your brother is up to?'

Adding a bit of wishful thinking to information, Swati said, 'Dada is an apprentice at some radio shop, I think.'

'Good,' Rajen-babu remarked disinterestedly.

'Don't you meet him at all these days?'

'Hardly.'

'He has this strange notion that you don't love him.'

'The stupidity of the ignorant is boundless.'

'There you are! If you say things like that do you suppose he doesn't understand?'

'Is it untrue?'

'Do you have to say something just because it's true?'

'It's not as though there's anything left to say . . .'

Rajen-babu clamped his lips together.

'You know, Baba,' Swati changed the subject quickly, 'I found an old book the other day—*Geetanjali*—with Ma's name on it. I've never seen it before.'

'It's so old,' said Rajen-babu after some thought. 'Is it really there still?'

The cover had long been torn off. As soon as he took it Rajen-babu's eye caught the name on the first page. He almost appeared not to recognize the handwriting, the name. The white paper had become yellow, the black ink brown—but still that old-fashioned slant in the writing, those smiling faces of the repeated letters, that name . . . the name. Even as he tried to wrench his eyes away he turned them again towards the name.

Observing the look in her father's eyes, Swati asked, 'Did Ma like this book?'

Placing the book face down, Rajen-babu said, 'Everyone had

a copy of *Geetanjali* those days—it was all the rage! Everyone sang those songs. I had a friend named Haren—he sang so many of those songs for us—and your mother . . .' Pausing suddenly, Rajen-babu forced the remaining words out somewhat stiffly: '. . . your mother used to have people over all the time.'

'Tell me, Baba, tell me,' Swati sat close to him.

'What else is there to tell?'

'Ma used to love music, didn't she?'

'Oh, you know, she'd be cooking in the kitchen and making requests from behind the door for specific songs from time to time.'

'Why behind the door?'

'Do you suppose women used to come out before other people those days?'

'How terrible!' Swati commented at once. 'Thank goodness I wasn't born back then! And then?'

'And then? Did you think this is a story?'

'Where did you live then, Baba?'

'In Shankharipara.'

'Where on earth is Shankharipara?'

'Somewhere in Calcutta.'

'Had I been born?'

'Of course not! Saraswati was the last one to be born there.'

Her parents' life, with two and then three children, songs on request, the orthodoxy—all of it seemed like a dream to Swati. So much happiness! Her heart seemed to ache: will I ever know such happiness? Ma wasn't allowed to come out, she had to sit in the kitchen and listen to the singing. But still there was so much happiness. I am free, I can do so much more, but . . . but . . . does that make for greater happiness? Is Chhordi happier than Ma was? Can Chhordi and Harit-da even be compared to Ma and Baba in Shankharipara? But why not? Chhordi's very happy, she goes to new places, meets new people, her face radiates happiness . . . but . . .

'Baba,' Swati said faintly, 'will you show me that house in Shankharipara?'

Without replying, Rajen-babu glanced again at that copy of *Geetanjali*—a relic from another time. And Swati, running her hand gently over the face-down book, said softly, 'Beautiful songs, aren't they, Baba?'

Rajen-babu agreed with his eyes.

'Baba,' Swati exuded embarrassment, 'will you give me ten rupees?'

'Is there something you need?' Rajen-babu's expression changed immediately.

'How about buying some more of Rabindranath's books?'

'How will only ten rupees do?'

'Oh Baba, do you suppose I'm going to buy the whole lot? They said at the shop that the whole set will cost a hundred and fifty or two hundred rupees.'

'That's not much. There must be a hundred and fifty or two hundred books too.'

'All right!' Swati's face lit up with joy. 'A few every month . . .'

'So practical already.' Rajen-babu held her head between his hands and shook it affectionately.

Manasi, Chitra, Kalpana, Kshanika, Balaka—spreading out the fresh new books on her bed, Swati lay down quietly in the afternoon. The sky was clouding over—smoke-coloured, shadow-coloured, night-coloured clouds, blackening the tips of the tall coconut trees, skipping from one musical note to another on gusts of wind. Slowly, the clouds in the sky spread all over Swati's heart. Why do I feel so sad? What do I have to be sad about? Nothing really. Well, then? Has poetry done this to me? Is Harit-da right, then—are Iva and Shobhona and Supriti and the rest not stupid after all? Is it true that whatever is not useful is no good at all?' 'Just read economics, all the fog in your mind will be cleared,' Harit-da had said. Fog . . . Clouds were foggy too, but were clouds bad? If there were no clouds, no rain . . .

' . . . Swati.'

Swati sat up happily on seeing her brother.

'Give me the wardrobe keys, will you?'

'It's unlocked. Need a sari?'

Without answering, Biju tried to select one, his back turned to her.

'How long will you go on playing women, Dada?'

'Not much longer,' Biju turned his head to smile. 'Men and women are doing their own drama these days—the drama of life.'

Ignoring him, Swati said, 'It was one thing when you were a child, but now a clean-shaven man hardly suits the role of a woman.'

'In any case everyone is clean-shaven these days,' Biju answered. 'And as for suiting the role of a woman, I acted in *Sweet Sixteen* at Dhakuria, people were speechless with wonder for three whole days after that.'

Swati laughed.

'If you had watched me you wouldn't have laughed. Don't you have a really nice sari? Chhordi had so many! This blue one . . .'

'Don't take that one, Dada! That used to be Ma's!' Swati shouted.

'Let me have a look.'

'No, you don't have to—put it away!' Leaping out of her bed, Swati came forward, hand outstretched. Looking at her for a moment, Biju said, 'All right, never mind, they're *your* mother, *your* father—no one of mine.'

Returning her mother's sari where it belonged, Swati said, 'That doesn't mean you have to take it into that chaos—no. You lost my lovely silk sari last time.'

'Lovely, my foot! Five rupees is all it cost!'

'But it was such a beautiful light green. And five rupees is not all that cheap either!'

'As if you lack for money. All you have to do is ask Baba . . .'

'And you?'

Biju didn't answer. Looking at the books scattered on the bed, he said, 'Did you buy these? Why didn't you tell me—I could have got them cheaper for you.'

'How can books be cheaper?'

'What do you know anyway?' Biju's eyes shone with the pride of knowledge. 'We're staging *Last-minute Escape*. We needed six copies, and Dhruba Datta got the price down from one rupee to fifty-six paise . . .'

'Who?'

'Haven't you even heard of him? And you claim to be in college—he's such a famous poet! We'd got him over to watch *Sweet Sixteen*. He told me after seeing me act . . .'

'Poet? Does he write poetry?'

'What do you mean does he write poetry?' Biju clucked. 'He's published so many books. That's why he can buy books cheap. Can you believe it—he's coming to watch *Last-minute Escape* too!'

'To watch a clean-shaven Indumati?'

'As if you and your friends can do better!' Pacing up and down, Biju said proudly, 'Do you think they had actresses in England in Shakespeare's time? They still don't in China. Didn't Jyotirindra Thakur himself play a female dancer on stage?'

Looking at her brother, Swati asked, 'Whom did you learn all this from?'

'Never mind who.' Biju sat down on the bed to try and recollect whether Dhruba Datta had told him any more on the subject. Giving up after a while, he said, 'Why don't you come to a show?'

'No . . .'

'Of course, why should you! Can you possibly bear to watch

me accomplish something! It was a huge mistake to ask you to do something you have never done in your life!' Biju stood up, his face red with rage.

'Why do you get angry so easily, Dada?'

'It's not anger! No matter how much others might praise me, nothing I do is good enough for you.'

Swati laughed. 'I don't like praising you, but I like it when others do.'

'You have no idea what others say,' Biju softened immediately. 'I'm also thinking,' suddenly melting, he revealed his secret to his sister, 'of not playing women any more. If I can play the hero a couple of times, I'll get a chance in films.'

'Films . . .?'

'Don't tell anyone yet,' Biju winked. 'I'll spring such a surprise!'

'Dada, that thing you were doing in the radio shop . . .'

'Never mind,' Biju stood up busily, quickly wrapping the three saris he had selected in paper. 'Will you come tomorrow, then?'

'Only if Baba goes too . . .'

'Why do we need him? It's close by—at the crossing of Southern Avenue and Lansdowne Road. Besides, Chhordi also . . .' Biju couldn't even stay long enough to finish what he was saying.

Alone again in her room, Swati began to feel a sadness on that cloudy afternoon. The neighbourhood was silent; a tram could be heard suddenly on the main road—exactly as though someone had sighed in the room. She wished she could go off somewhere, wished she could do something, wished she could watch something, listen to something, learn something . . . No, Swati said to herself, running her hand over her forehead. Nothing. Through the window she could see blue through the gaps among the clouds in the sky, the green tops of trees full of tender leaves, and, between the blue and the green, flying slowly, a quiet, confident, black crow . . . How happy that crow was—even the sight of it made you happy . . . But what kind of happiness was this that made you feel even sadder.

The next day, she went to watch her brother's *Last-minute Escape* with Saswati and Harit after considerable planning. How she had laughed on reading the play! If someone had told her earlier, 'Read Rabindranath . . .' where would she have been by now? Where did reading get you? Did reading make people happy? . . . Did poetry fill your stomach? . . . That was what Harit had learnt abroad. Reading poetry only makes you sadder, that's why no one reads poetry. . . Sadness?

Given a special seat in the front row, Swati looked back to survey the audience. It seemed every young loafer and fat housewife and crotchety old man in the world had gathered here. But people had no control over their appearance—but then did appearance mean nothing at all? Who couldn't tell from one look at her father what a good man he was! And you could tell immediately from Satyen Roy's face that he read poetry—that's why the girls were as bold as they were . . .

'There's Dhruba Datta.' As soon as she heard, Swati turned her head to see three or four of the organizers dripping humility from every footstep as they escorted the principal guest of the evening to a chair placed at a slight angle, beside the sheet laid out for the children. They had probably delayed the play for him—the curtain rose soon after his arrival, and the play began.

Swati's eyes kept shifting from the stage towards Dhruba Datta. A poet! He was a poet! She was seeing a real living poet for the first time. Less than half his face was visible, he was sort of slumped in his chair, his head bowed, his legs stretched into the distance. But there was no serenity about him. Even in that position he kept shifting continuously, smoking one cigarette after another . . . Was this a poet? Would he know how to present words that way? Could he make mute letters sing? Someone who looked like that? Close-cropped hair, thick neck, muscular arms—not like Satyen Roy at all! But why should he be. After all, was

Satyen Roy a poet? . . . And what if he was; do poets have to look similar? Could two people ever be identical? . . . Why did she think—really, how silly it was! She looked away, trying to concentrate on the play.

After the first act, Harit said, 'Shall we go now?'

'So soon?' Saswati protested. 'I'm enjoying it—and Biju is looking like a real woman.'

'Not too bad,' Harit said, clamping his teeth on his pipe. 'What else can you expect in a capitalist regime?'

'You mean it isn't good?' Saswati asked, crestfallen.

'They all speak with such exaggerated politeness!' Harit chuckled drily. 'People who haven't done an ounce of work in their lives . . .'

'How true,' said Swati, looking at the back of her sister's head. 'How exactly do working people speak?'

'At least they don't speak with exaggerated politeness,' Harit answered.

'They speak through clenched teeth,' was Swati's instant riposte.

Harit lapsed into a grim silence, and stood up decisively after the second act, saying, 'No, that's enough.'

Fidgeting, Saswati said, 'Want to go, Swati?'

She didn't get the answer she wanted. 'I'll go whenever you do,' said Swati, her eyes swivelling towards Dhruba Datta.

Saswati looked quickly at her husband, but saw no hope there. She was in a spot—who knew that even *Last-minute Escape* was a poisonous fruit of malignant capitalism! She had been quite enjoying it, and there wasn't a long way to go either.

Suddenly Harit said, 'Why don't the two of you stay? I'm off.'

Saswati stood up instantly, followed by Swati a little later.

'Why don't you stay if you want to,' Harit paused while walking ahead of them through a gap between the rows of chairs.

Saswati only heard him, without seeing his expression.

'Can we?' The joy in her voice was palpable. 'Will you come back for us later?'

'Why do you need me to take you home—can't you get home on your own? You needn't necessarily return tonight either, you can spend the night at your father's,' said Harit, looking at his wife.

Without another word, Saswati left slowly, her head bowed . . . Is he angry? So much anger over *this*? That too in Swati's presence! How angry he can get! Why didn't he say straightaway what he wanted, it's not as if I would have resisted.

As they reached the street, Harit began to walk at a masculine pace.

'A little slower, Harit-da,' said Swati.

'Too quick for you?'

'Not for me—for Chhordi. She's put on weight, you see.'

'I find it hard to keep pace with you,' said Harit, condescending to slow down his a little.

'You don't have a choice . . . since it's all thanks to you . . .' Swati looked at Saswati out of the corner of her eye, but Saswati didn't say anything. Harit was silent too. Walking furiously, they soon saw Tollygunge Bridge coming into view. At the head of the street Harit said, 'Let's take a tram here.'

'Of course not!' Swati dismissed the idea.

But Harit remained at the tram-stop, unbending. A wave seemed to ripple through Saswati, the wave subsided—words rose into her throat and fell back, the hollow in her throat trembled. Swallowing, touching her necklace, she pulled the end of her sari over her head and steadied herself.

'Come along home—you simply must!' Swati called out to Harit.

'Not tonight.' Harit looked away in expectation of a tram.

Under the electric street lights, the two sisters exchanged glances for a moment. Saswati was the first to lower her eyes, she bowed her sindoor-streaked head, turned her slightly

made-up face away. A tram with headlights was visible at the
bend in the road.

'All right, then . . .' Without looking around, Swati quickly
entered the lane that led to her house.

Rajen-babu was in bed, eyes closed, his arm on his forehead.
Hearing Swati, he sat up, asking, 'Where are they?'

'They went home, Baba.'

'They wouldn't come?'

Without any hesitation, Swati answered, 'Someone is
supposed to visit Harit-da at nine thirty. Very important, so . . .'

'They couldn't come for even a minute?'

'Never mind—they're so close by, maybe they'll be here
tomorrow.'

'Whom did you come with?'

'Me? So many people from the neighbourhood . . . Dada
was so—he did so well . . . Wait, I'll tell you everything . . .'
Swati ran off to change her clothes, releasing her thick black
curls. She proceeded to describe the play in detail, imitating
the different characters, their way of talking—so well that Rajen-
babu laughed several times.

Swati was awakened by what seemed to be a commotion.
A storm whistled outside, the wind buffeted everything inside,
the window kept banging. Suddenly afraid of being alone in the
dark, she quickly turned on her side, opening her eyes, and
called out, 'Chhordi!' Her sister's bed still lay in the other
corner. Unoccupied, it looked horrible—took up space too,
unnecessarily . . . How childish—I just can't sleep alone. For such
a long time I used to sleep in Baba's room . . . Then after Ma,
Chhordi and I have been together ever since. So what if Baba
made us use separate beds? I used to chatter on and on in
Chhordi's bed, then come back to my own after quarrelling with

her, and then call her again, 'Chhordi!' Swati seemed to hear that hoarse voice of hers, thick with sleep . . . Who'd have thought, alone in a room . . . But what was so unthinkable about it, everyone knew it would happen. Am I still a child that I should be scared when I wake up in the middle of the night! Get up, switch on the light, shut the window!

Even as these thoughts passed over her mind, a light assaulted her eyes. Swati shut her eyes at once, but continued to peer through them. Fastening the window near her and opening the windows at the other end of the room, her father came up to her bed. 'Baba,' she opened her eyes, laughing.

'Awake now?'

'Why did you get up?'

'At least it's cooled down a bit. Such a relief!'

'Is Dada back, Baba?'

'Not yet.'

'Best not to come back so late at night, don't you think?'

Without answering, Rajen-babu took a shawl from the clothes-stand and arranged it over his daughter, saying, 'Sleep now.'

'Will you stay with me a little, Baba? . . . Never mind, go to bed.'

Sitting down, Rajen-babu said, 'It's raining at last. Lovely rain, isn't it?'

'Very nice, Baba! I love it *so* much,' Swati's voice began to slur in warm, secure comfort. 'That bed is of no use, Baba . . .'

'Yes, I'm going to have it removed.' Rajen-babu looked at the unmade bed, just a mattress on it, and then took in with his eyes his youngest, most beautiful, his last, his only daughter. Sleep had settled into Swati's eyes—she could see crowds, people; the play would begin any moment, Dhruba Datta was smoking; but Saswati wasn't there, nor Harit; unfamiliar faces everywhere, an unfamiliar place too . . . Where was she? How had she got here? Oh, there was Baba!

'Baba!' she called once in a sleepy voice. 'Is this your hand,

Baba?' Stretching out to take his hand and draw it to herself, she fell asleep at once. Outside, it rained, it rained.

5

What grandeur the monsoon displayed that year. As though it would blow you away, sweep you away. Swati had lived through so many monsoons, after all, but she had never seen anything like this. She seemed to see the grass getting thicker before her very eyes, the trees growing, the joy of the earth, the happiness of the roots. A long cloudy, lonely afternoon; an evening melting with the ecstasy of colours; and the drizzling night, interspersed by cloud-torn, moist moonlight. it felt so good, because it felt good it felt lonely, but company wasn't welcome either—in this twilight she felt her breath being taken away; she'd be relieved when her college reopened.

That morning the city was all bathed and dressed up, as though it knew that Swati's college was reopening today. Books in hand, she left home on light feet; green earth, sparkling sunshine; she couldn't contain her happiness, had there been no one on the road she would have pirouetted. Ignoring the seats reserved for women on the tram, she sat right in front— such a lovely breeze, and how beautiful the road was till it crossed Southern Avenue; so many trees, so much grass, and the grey trams moving under the trees like ducks winding along on water—every minute they pass by, but no one sees them, does anyone see? How hard people try to go somewhere for pleasure—the cinema, the theatre, the stadium. Crowds thronged to fairs, wherever they might be, shops brimmed over with customers, people took trains to distant lands—but actually there were so many things to make you happy all around you, without a name, without a price, without a ticket, in such a big city and yet no one knew. As if you had to go somewhere for happiness, as if you had to do something—there was no lack of happiness even without any of this, did people have a choice but to be happy?

Anadi-babu's class was in the very first hour. He was looking rather nice today—new glasses?—no, they were the same—he was quite good-looking—how strange—but why was it strange, couldn't Anadi-babu be nice to look at? And was his teaching all that bad? Swati opened her textbook, but after the roll-call Anadi-babu added more gravity to his normally grave expression and announced, 'Roll No. 19 of your class, Maya Sanyal, has passed away during the vacation . . .'

What! Ten or twelve girls buzzed with suppressed exclamations—Maya Sanyal's friends—while the rest looked on in surprise.

'. . . As a mark of respect, there will be no classes today. You may go home.' Anadi-babu left immediately.

'How shocking!'

'What happened?'

'When did she die?'

'Do you know anything, Alaka? She lived near your house . . .'

'I met her just a month ago—then I went off to my uncle's . . .'

'We should hold a condolence meeting,' said Iva, speaking louder than the others.

'Of course!' Alaka supported her enthusiastically.

'When do you want to do it?' The question came from Supriti.

'Today! Right now!' Iva bubbled. 'We'll pass a resolution and send it to her home today.'

'But so many girls are leaving already . . .'

Iva jumped up on the professor's platform. Rapping on the desk with her knuckles, she spoke as though she were making a speech, 'Friends, please don't leave. We will hold a condolence meeting for Maya Sanyal. Please don't leave—please sit down—please sit down quietly.'

Some left nevertheless, some sat down as they were about to leave. 'We have enough people,' said Iva, checking the numbers.

'Who's the chairman?' protested someone.

'We don't need one,' Iva answered quickly. 'This is our own meeting—a students' meeting—and a chairman is an anachronism today.' Iva was rather pleased with herself at being able to apply the newly learned word correctly—surely none of the girls knew what it meant? 'Why don't one of you say a few words while I draft a resolution . . .' Iva continued, solemnly occupying the professor's chair. If they were so keen on a chairman, let them assume it was her.

After a bit of nudging and pushing, Alaka rose to say a few words, followed by Supriti, then by two other girls. They stammered as they spoke, made mistakes, giggled, the rest giggled too, it didn't seem like a condolence meeting at all. Then Iva rose to read out the resolution, everyone stood up to accept it, and at the end Iva delivered a rousing speech, using grand words and speaking at a furious pace. The girls were amazed and Swati kept feeling that Maya had died in order to create an opportunity for Iva to deliver this speech.

She looked now and then at the spot on the bench in front of hers where Maya used to sit. That plump girl who had wanted to know the meaning of the poem. She had died. Was it so easy to die? Could anyone die any time? Me too? Thank goodness—the words leapt into her mind—thank God I haven't died. What would have happened if I were no longer among the billions of people on the planet? Nothing—if I hadn't even been born, how would that have made a difference? Not in the least. Here was Maya Sanyal, converted from a 'yes' to a 'no' so suddenly—what difference had it made? Ma died, and yet all of us are alive and thriving; fine—yes, we're all fine—suddenly there was a hammer-blow on her heart, it broke from anguish because she no longer mourned for her mother, does this mean that the absence of an individual makes no difference at all? I can't survive a moment without the world, but the world will survive till eternity without me. These rains, this air, this sunlight—are they actually meant for me. Do they even need me? I have been born in this world by chance, I don't know how I have survived without dying—that's what lets me experience all of this, this sunlight, rain, air, all of it seems to be for me; they do need me, it's me they need—if they don't, how did I even come into existence. It could have been someone else instead of me, why me?

Out on the road Swati looked at the sky, at the light, at the trees with the rustling leaves—listen, don't any of you have anything to do with me? Young clouds were running around in play in the courtyard of the sky, long shadows raced along the shining surface of the main road, the wind shook the hair of the trees, laughing uncontrollably—don't you know who I am? No answer. You had to make up the answer, you had to make them say the words that the heart wanted to hear.

'What're you thinking of?' asked Anupama, walking alongside.

'Nothing at all.'

'Are you thinking of Maya?'

'Of Maya? No.' Why should I think of Maya? Is anyone thinking of Maya any more?

'You must be thinking of something,' said Supriti. 'It's another matter that you don't want to tell us.'

'You look funny!' Chitra turned to face Swati after they had crossed the road. 'What's the matter?'

'What could possibly be the matter?'

'Not in love, are you?'

Supriti and Anupama laughed, and Swati said, 'What are you laughing at? Is falling in love a laughing matter?'

'Then it's *true*!' The three of them drew out the word loudly into laughter.

'How can it not be true?' There was a suppressed smile in Swati's eyes.

'Will you tell us who?'

'Do you suppose I know that I can tell?'

'Very funny . . .!'

'There's the tram,' Supriti nudged Chitra. How annoying to have to interrupt a discussion they were savouring! Chitra wasn't happy, but the tram wouldn't wait, after all.

The seats reserved for women were all full. The four of them stood holding the aluminium poles. It wasn't as though this was a problem for them, but it was for the men, so from the long back row of seats first one, then two, then two more—reluctance turning their faces to thunder—men stood up to make room for the women. Holding on to one another as the tram rattled around, they made their way to the seats, then looked out of the window disinterestedly, as though none of this had anything to do with them.

It was embarrassing, really. Two men always stood up to offer one woman a seat. Maybe the woman was on her way to Dhakuria Lakes for an evening walk, while the men were returning home, exhausted after a hard day's work. But what was the alternative? Swati swept the hair off her forehead. It's true we're weaker, and besides—no matter how much we assert ourselves—we do find it difficult. We may shout from the rooftops about being equals, but our bodies have handicapped us—physical contact in a crowd—horrible! And yet, because of us others have to travel without a seat, that too . . .

'There—Satyen Roy!' Anupama whispered into her ear.

'Who?'

'Satyen Roy—the professor—remember Iva's fight with him?'

The moment she turned her head she saw him. He was standing, holding on to a leather strap with one hand, balancing two thick books in the other with considerable skill. He must have been sitting here. Only for us . . . If he could at least put the books down—it's easy enough for me, but how do I tell him? He's looking straight ahead. Swati saw that his hair had almost reached his shoulders—he needed a haircut now; one of his pockets was torn—did he even know that? Or did notes and coins keep slipping out? She also observed the slender ankle-bone swollen by the pressure of the foot. There was simply no hope of talking to him.

Swati spent the ten-odd minutes in the tram very uncomfortably. Couldn't she have mentioned that book of his that was still with her! So difficult being a woman! If she'd been a man, she could simply have got up and gone up to him to talk. When would she see him again?

Swati was usually the first to get off. Bidding goodbye to her friends with her eyes, she rose to discover Satyen-babu getting off at the same tram-stop! But so what—by the time she had reached the road he was already marching off to cross it, and before she could cross the tram-tracks he had already entered the lane next to theirs. As though he had got to know and was deliberately avoiding her. But why was he here? Did someone he knew live close by? Did he come by this way now and then? Watching the white *panjabi* disappear down the lane, Swati felt a ray of hope too.

Exactly two days later she saw Satyen Roy again, waiting at her tram-stop, a shawl draped over one shoulder, reading a newspaper-covered book held in one hand. Swati looked at him, took a step, then retreated; his eyes didn't budge from his book. The tram trundled up, about to get in, Satyen-babu let go of the handle on seeing a woman, Swati also stepped back after stretching her arm out, to show deference to her professor, the tram left in the meantime. 'Stop!' cried out Satyen-babu. But the ever-practical tram paid no heed.

'What fun,' the words escaped Swati's lips.

Satyen-babu looked at her for a moment. He conveyed clearly with his expression that it was his fault that they had missed the tram, but that he had not expected this comment from the lady.

'Don't . . . don't you recognize me?'

'You . . .' Using the formal *aapni*, the professor noticed the books in Swati's hands. Pausing abruptly—and avoiding both the formal *aapni* and the less formal *tumi*—he mumbled, 'From college?'

'You had lent me a book a long time ago . . .' Swati wasted no time broaching the subject.

'Really?'

He didn't even remember? Swati was a little hurt. He had forgotten the book, and with it the person he had lent it to as well? Faintly she said, 'At the college library one day . . .'

'Is it a library book?' Satyen-babu's question was a little anxious.

'No, yours. *Golden Treasury* . . .'

'Oh yes.' A smile spread across Satyen-babu's face. 'Have you read it?'

'I haven't been able to return it all this time, though I did try . . .'

'Why, didn't you like it?'

Not understanding, Swati raised her eyes towards him.

'How could you finish it so quickly?' Satyen-babu said again.

'It's been seven or eight months . . .'

'You finished it in just seven or eight months!'

A little embarrassed, a little perturbed, Swati raised her eyes again.

'I never borrow poetry books . . .' Satyen-babu answered the question in Swati's eyes, 'and I don't lend them either. You must keep the book.'

'No, I—why you—how odd . . .'

'It's not strange at all,' Satyen-babu smiled a little. 'With other books, when you've read them you're done with them—but you're never done with poetry, are you, how can you do without having the book for yourself?'

Swati was amazed. Overcoming her diffidence, she said, 'But does that mean you'll give away any book to anyone?'

'No, it doesn't. But you have to, to those who really love them.'

'Then you won't have any books left of your own.'

'There's no fear of that. There are very few people like that, you see.'

Am I one of those very few people? Swati asked herself. How do you know? You don't even know me. As she wondered whether she could say this—even *how* to say it—another tram came. Swati was embarrassed to go to the front of the tram like she did every day, she sat down quickly in the seats meant for women. Unable to forget even for a moment that Satyen-babu was seated at the back, she couldn't enjoy this tram journey the way she usually did.

The tram-stop was directly opposite the college. Satyen-babu stepped aside for Swati as they were getting off the tram, then they entered the college together. Girls converged from all sides—some alone, some in small groups—as soon as they passed through the gate Swati seemed to lose herself in the crowd—but oh! The conversation remained incomplete! . . . What conversation? She couldn't think of what she'd have said; but still she felt there was so much to say.

They met again another day.

After the rain, sunlight glistened just before evening. Swati was on her way back after a walk in the open field to the west. It couldn't really be called a field any more, though; houses were coming up, a road was being built, bullock-carts had flattened the grass, there were large bald patches in the green. But still she felt sad the moment she left the field to turn into the lane—although in a short while they would all become lanes.

Nestling against the field was a west-facing two-storeyed house, face-to-face with the sunset. Standing in its narrow ground-floor veranda, his hands on the railing, Satyen Roy saw a girl with black hair in a violet sari, emerging in a blaze of yellow light. When she came nearer he recognized her. As she crossed the house Swati raised her eyes and stopped suddenly. What a surprise! Him? 'You!'

The word escaped her throat so quickly that it sounded awkward even to herself, she lowered her eyes, reddening slightly.

'How are you?' the professor asked after her politely. 'All well?'

'You here?' Swati asked very softly.

'This is where I live.'

Of course. Why else would he take the tram from that particular tram-stop? How silly I am—I should have thought of this earlier. I wouldn't have been so inappropriately surprised. Trying to gather herself, she said, 'Didn't someone else live here?'

'They still do.'

'Relatives?'

'No, why should they be relatives?' Satyen-babu smiled. 'They live on the first floor; I've rented the ground floor. It's a nice place.'

'Do you like it here?'

'The view doesn't look like Calcutta at all.' Satyen Roy looked in turn at the many-hued clouds in the distant sky and at the yellow-ribbon-in-dark-hair light. As though he couldn't decide which to look at.

'It was much more beautiful earlier,' Swati said. 'They've cut down so many trees now.'

'No less beautiful now,' said Satyen-babu, looking at the light shining in the black hair.

Swati was silent for a few moments, then she suddenly remembered when, at Jatin Das Road, new neighbours had moved into the house next door, her mother had sent them dinner, pitchers of water, milk for the babies, her father going back and forth four or five times, climbing up and down the stairs. 'Do you,' she quickly inquired, 'have everything you need? If there's anything . . .'

'I'll tell you if I do.' Satyen-babu walked down the steps from the veranda. 'Do you live close by?'

'That single-storeyed building at the end of the lane,' Swati pointed. 'If you happen to . . .' She didn't finish.

'I can't ask you to come in, there's no one else here, you see . . .'

'When will they come?'

'There isn't anyone else. I live by myself.'

'Absolutely by yourself?'

A smile appeared on the corner of Satyen Roy's lips. Absolutely alone—'alone' was heaven! How horrible that crowd in the Bhowanipore mess had been, like getting off one tram only to get into another . . . He had found this house by sheer luck, because the neighbourhood wasn't sophisticated and the house old, at a rent of only eighteen rupees. He looked again at the pink cloud turning brown in the distant sky, and the piled hair on the bowed head looked even darker in the grey shadows. 'What's your name?' he asked suddenly.

'Swati Mitra.'

'Swati Mitra? Swati?'

'Swati.'

'Lovely name.'

Lovely!

When Satyen-babu didn't say anything for another minute or so, Swati raised her eyes with a half-spoken 'Well . . .' and took her leave, nodding goodbye to the professor.

Back home, she said, 'Baba, one of our professors has come to live here.'

'Where?'

'That house by the field . . .'

'Ah, Rebati-babu's house.'

'How do you know everyone here, Baba?'

Rajen-babu smiled. 'When you meet them you get to know them. I'm glad Rebati-babu's got a professor as a tenant.'

'Why are you glad?'

'Naturally. Professors are usually quiet, nice people.'

'Really?'

'Do you suppose they can be so learned without being nice?'

'Whatever you may say, all the learned people of the world have a long way to go before they can be as nice as you.'

'Enough—everyone thinks of their own father as wonderful!'

'Rubbish!' Swati shook her head. 'Not that easy!'

Rajen-babu returned to what they had been discussing. 'Did you meet the professor?'

'Yes, Baba. He lives by himself . . .'

'Why?'

'How would I know? Don't people live by themselves?'

'There you are. Do you suppose he'd have been able to rent the house had he not been a professor?'

'Why not?' Swati was surprised.

'Didn't you know—nobody in Calcutta wants a single man as a tenant. He must have a wife—or at least a mother or a sister or something.'

'Why?'

Rajen-babu answered after some thought, 'A house doesn't become a home without a woman in it.'

Swati's heart suddenly skipped a beat. She was distracted.

'You must find out from time to time if he's all right.'

'How can I find out . . . If you'd . . .'

'All right, I'll go with you.'

'You have to know everyone in the neighbourhood, don't you, Baba?' Swati smiled.

The next Sunday, after his morning shopping, Rajen-babu took off his shirt as usual, popped a paan into his mouth, and then rose immediately to put his shirt on again.

'Going out again!' Swati half-asked, half-protested.

'Just checking on Anukul's house . . .'

'Stop it!' Swati raised her voice. 'You don't have to check every day. It's just fine—it hasn't grown wings and flown away, or been stolen for that matter.'

'Don't you understand—he doesn't live here—if there's a problem . . .'

'What if there's a problem, why do *you* have to worry?' Swati shook her head. He made her so angry, honestly!

Some distant relative, who worked in Delhi, was having a house built on that plot of land, and whenever he could, her father went and supervised the construction, standing in the sun endlessly. The relative had visited them once at the Jatin Das Road house—what elaborate meals they had had, her father really could go to extremes! But despite that, when the relative hadn't been able to find a dhoti of his one day—the servant had put it away with her father's clothes by mistake—he had created such a fuss that her mother had been close to a heart attack.

'I'll be back soon . . .' Rajen-babu hesitantly sought his daughter's permission.

'No, you mustn't go anywhere.'

'You come too . . .'

'Couldn't be bothered!'

'We could drop in at your professor's house too on the way back.'

'Do you really want to?' Swati said after some thought.

'We should, shouldn't we? Find out if he's all right?'

Swati suddenly said, 'No, Baba, I won't go.'

'Why not?'

'No.' Scrunching up her face, Swati shook her head.

'Oh, come along now, it'll be nice—such a lovely morning.'

Swati left the room, coming back in two minutes, dressed to go out, and said, 'Change your dhoti, Baba.'

'Oh dear!'

'Honestly, Baba, your clothes!' Swati handed him a freshly ironed set. Looking at him, she added, 'You could get a shave too.'

'Enough!' Transferring himself from the soft intimacy of clothes worn for two successive days to the crisp civility of fresh garments, Rajen-babu stepped into the road with his daughter.

∼

It had rained early that morning, and there was a faint cool, sweetish scent of grass mingled with a whiff of overnight bokul flowers. Crossing the professor's house, they stepped into the field; Swati looked just the one time at the ground-floor room, then began to explain to her father as they walked that he would have to give up this bad habit of taking every responsibility upon himself. Listening to his daughter with his ears, Rajen-babu reflected that Anukul's contractor must be cheating him; he would have to talk to him—he was sure the contractor didn't come to the site very often, a young assistant of his in a dhoti and a sola hat was about to leave on a bicycle when Rajen-babu stopped him to tell him a few things, and Swati stood at a distance, looking at the half-completed house. How ugly a house looked while it was under construction! You just couldn't imagine that one day people would live in it, laugh, love, chat over tea, quarrel as they chatted. Right now it just appeared as though those eight or ten scattered piles of bricks were festering like boils on the body of the field. Swati's eyes wandered into the distance, towards the old house across the field; standing amidst the lime and the cement and the dust, the whole neighbourhood seemed quiet, shaded. The road seemed only half as long on the way back.

Looking at the closed door of the ground floor of Rebati-babu's house, Rajen-babu said, 'Is the professor even home?' Swati's body suddenly grew heavy with reluctance. Tugging at her father's shirt, she said, 'Never mind, let's go.'

'Come along,' Rajen-babu said confidently. Climbing on to the veranda, he knocked on the door.

A servant opened the door.

'Is Satyen-babu home?'

'Please sit down,' the man said, wiping his spice-stained hand on a rag.

Four chairs were arranged around a cane table in the middle of the room. 'Sit down,' Rajen-babu told his daughter and settled down quite comfortably.

'Please wait a minute,' said the man, making a respectful gesture with his shoulders and disappearing behind blue curtains.

Swati seemed a little relieved at not meeting Satyen-babu the moment they had arrived. She saw two bookshelves against one of the walls, one large, one small, but both simple and unadorned—English books in the large one, Bengali books in the small—the books were in different positions—standing, lying, slanting, upside down—maybe he hadn't had the time to arrange them yet, or did those who read usually keep their books this way? A small desk lay between the windows, a jet-black pen tucked into a blue pad—a letter! To whom? Oh my God, did he lack for people to write to? He lived here by himself, he had to write to people at home. But the violet-tinged blue colour of the pad seemed to . . . Suddenly rage flared in Swati's brain, she felt they had been waiting far too long, why were they waiting, what need did they have to wait, why did they even have to come?

'Baba . . .' But she couldn't say anything more—Satyen-babu entered the room. In a flash Swati saw he had just had a bath—his hair was perfectly combed, he was dressed in a thin, floppy *panjabi*, and when he came closer a subtle fragrance distracted Swati for a moment. Why, he could be quite elegant!

Satyen-babu seemed taken aback when he entered, then he advanced quickly to say, 'Oh, it's you, and . . . I was having a bath, so . . . Waiting so long, how . . .?'

Standing up, Swati said, 'My father.'

'I see.' A smile appeared on Satyen Roy's lips as soon as he looked at Rajen-babu.

Rajen-babu smiled too. 'My daughter dragged me here.'

'Of course, of course . . . That is to say, I should have gone myself . . . You took the trouble . . . Why don't you sit, do you plan to keep standing? Such a strong sun today . . . and he hasn't turned the fan on either, how odd . . .'

Satyen-babu ran to the corner and switched on the

table-fan, checking whether both the guests could feel the breeze of the fan—but what breeze? He unplugged the fan and plugged it in again, fiddled with the switch for quite some time, but the fan didn't run. Raising his face, wiping his forehead with the back of his hand, he smiled faintly. 'These hired fans . . .'

'Never mind,' Rajen-babu said, 'no need for a fan, there's a breeze in any case! Please sit down.'

'It came only yesterday . . .' Looking sadly at the fan for the last time Satyen-babu took a seat.

'Is it from Ghosh & Co.?' asked Rajen-babu.

'How did you know?' the professor was surprised.

'There's just the one shop for electrical goods here, after all. Which is why they're so . . .' without finishing Rajen-babu said, 'Is there anything you need?'

'Need? No, what could I possibly need?'

'Has Rebati-babu kept the other room for himself?'

'Yes, he has some things in there, I don't need it either— even two rooms seem too much for me.'

'What about a kitchen?' asked Rajen-babu next.

'There probably isn't one,' said Satyen Roy after some thought. '"Probably" meaning,' he smiled and added quickly, 'there isn't one in fact. And there's not that much of cooking to be done, so . . .'

'Can your servant cook?'

'He does cook, but I cannot say whether he *can* cook.'

Rajen-babu burst out laughing at this. Turning his eyes towards his student, Satyen Roy said, 'Why so quiet?'

Swati dragged her eyes away from the bookshelves.

'Want to look at the books? Go ahead.' Satyen-babu got up and went up to the shelves. 'Come here.'

How lovely books were. So many colours, so many different kinds of binding, and names—so many names—and so much happening between two covers! She touched a few books lightly with two fingers.

'Do you want a few? Would you like to take some books? . . . Which ones do you want?'

Swati put her fingers slowly on a light grey book lying on its side, not for any other reason but because of the amazingly beautiful colours of the cover.

'Chekhov,' said Satyen Roy happily.

Che . . .?

Understanding the unarticulated question, the professor enunciated again, 'Chekhov.' The *kh* sounded guttural and the *v* very soft. 'Anton Chekhov. Russian. But the translation is so very good . . . and the stories . . .' Stopping suddenly, he asked, 'What English storybooks have you read?'

Swati shook her head.

'None?'

Swati shook her head again. In her cloud-hued eyes Satyen Roy saw the contest between embarrassment and curiosity, the hide-and-seek between politeness and enthusiasm. 'None! So many good books, and such fine translations of practically every good book in the world! Amongst all the disadvantages of British rule, this is the only advantage we've had.' As he spoke, he put the light grey book—along with three others he selected himself—into her hands.

Swati seemed to bend over with the weight of the books, of embarrassment and gratitude. 'So many all at once . . .' she said softly.

'It's not all that many—one wants to read several things at the same time. Start with short stories; once you're used to them you can read longer novels.'

The final statement was a teacher speaking. Swati tried to speak, tried to say something, anything, but she could not.

Once outside, Rajen-babu said, 'Profitable visit for you, Swati.'

Swati was looking at the title pages of the books, one by one. 'I know!' she said, raising her eyes.

'Very nice man!'

'How can you make that out so quickly?'

'How gentle he looks. I don't think I've seen anyone so gentle.'

'You overdo everything!' Swati's laugh tinkled like water being poured into a glass.

'. . . And how childish he was about the fan!'

'Honestly!' Swati laughed again as she recollected the incident. 'Scholars like them need someone to look after them! I'm sure the servant steals money!'

'I suppose you'd like to do his shopping every day?' Rajen-babu smiled mischievously.

A little later Swati said, 'Why do you say these things, Baba?'

'Say what?'

'You went and said I'd dragged you there. I was so angry with you!'

'But he's *your* professor . . .'

'Yes, he is, but then you seemed much more interested!'

'But I like meeting nice people too!' said Rajen-babu as they reached the steps to their own home.

'You're so nice yourself, you think everyone else is, too!' Swati bounded up the steps to enter the house before her father.

Going to her room, Swati put the books on her desk, sat down on the chair and picked one up. But she stopped as she was about to open it—a blue envelope flashed before her eyes . . . The black pen tucked into the blue pad . . . The moment she opened the book a poisonous insect would leap out, sting her. What stupid thoughts these were, was there any comparison between Shubhro and Satyen-babu? Shubhro was just a bad . . . but why bad? If Shubhro was bad so was Saswati! And what was so terrible about all this—but the stories she heard the girls in her class exchange with each other—no, no, horrible, it was all horrible, all of it bad, everyone in the world was bad—but was that Satyen-babu's fault? Swati sat stiffly for some time, then slowly, very slowly, with great concentration, she turned over all the pages of all four books. 'Come in, come in,' the pages rustled. 'Listen, listen,' the black letters in English hummed. A wave of happiness, as intense as the depression she had felt a short while ago, washed over her breast—would she ever have got her hands on these books had she not met Satyen Roy?

That evening, as she read out Saraswati's letter to her father, the maid appeared to say someone had come. 'Who is it?' asked Swati in annoyance.

'How would she know who it is—let me find out,' said Rajen-babu, getting up.

'Must be someone we owe money to—don't go.'

'How difficult life is for creditors—they not only have to sell things on credit, but also have to face people's rage when they try to collect their money!' Rajen-babu laughed as he left the room.

Returning very soon, he said, 'It's your professor.'

Swati stood up instantly.

'He's left.'

'Left!'

'I told him so many times to stay a while, but he refused—probably has tuition classes to take or something.'

Sitting down again, Swati said lifelessly, 'Why did he come?'

Rajen-babu smiled without a word.

'Why?'

'Nothing much, just . . .' Rajen-babu said a little guiltily, 'I'd sent that table-fan of ours to him, you see . . .'

'Sent?'

'We have no use for it any more—and the poor man would suffer in the heat all day—wasn't it a good idea?'

'Haven't I told you, Baba, not to do these things without asking me first?'

'But what's wrong?'

'He doesn't even know us very well . . . And now suddenly something like this . . . What must he have thought!'

'Why should he be offended? He said such nice things just now. Really, it's such a pleasure to hear him talk.'

'You get these pleasures far too easily, 'Baba,' said Swati gravely.

'Read Saraswati's letter once more now,' Rajen-babu tried to appease his daughter.

Swati read it, but only to get it over with. He'd left! Couldn't wait a minute! When would he come again . . .

But they didn't meet again soon, and Swati seemed relieved. For some days now it had been raining every evening, she simply couldn't go out any more; she stayed in her room, reading and raising her eyes occasionally to look outside. The sky was blue, the clouds black, the grey spread everywhere, the rain was torrential, torrential. The light was low, it dropped even more, died, impossible to read now, impossible to see, the book open in her lap, she sat musing, dim, alone, silent.

BOOK TWO

The Path of Pensive Colours

1

What did Swati think of? Sitting by the rain-evening window, in a light blue sari, her hair loose, the rainwater splashing on her face, her lips, what *did* the seventeen-year-old Swati think of? What? . . . What *could* she think of, all thoughts had already been claimed by others, even thoughts she had never thought possible to think of—tentative, unclear at first; then, when they opened up—but where would this road take her, into a terrifying darkness, into some hidden, smiling hell lurking below everything?! Could there be stories such as these in this world! Since childhood, she had read not a few stories—hundreds of stories in monthly magazines, all of Saratchandra's, all of Rabindranath's—but nothing like these! Merely reading them was enough to be on the verge of madness, didn't people go mad writing them? Of course they did—what about Maupassant—it was right there in the book—he really had gone mad and slit his own throat. And those who had not killed themselves—they went mad, too; but most people could probably hide it; only a few couldn't, not at all . . . Hide? And the things that blazed on these black-and-white pages—that the paper didn't burn was surprising. Extraordinary—so intense, so brazen, so cruel—and so . . . so true! Did they know everything, how did they know everything in your heart, no one ever says these things out loud—how can they, people don't even know that such things exist in their hearts, they cannot possibly know, either . . . until they read all these books. Here I am, they've even written of so many of the things in my heart—not some of them, they've written about all of them, whoever they've written about, it's nobody but me—sometimes it's almost embarrassing to read it, but if all of these characters are me, then how can it be embarrassing to be with any of them, and it wasn't just embarrassment, but also the opposite of embarrassment, and that opposite was just as extraordinary—and no matter how strange it all sounded, life *was* like this, it was exactly like this. So much so that I wouldn't have known these things about myself had I not heard it from them; who I am, what I'm like, how bad and how good I am—all of it has been written down all those years ago by these madmen from distant lands! Incredible!

It was impossible for the seventeen-year-old Swati's thoughts, dense as clouds, to gauge just how incredible it all was; all thoughts were obliterated in the pale, damp evening spread out against the sky.

On such an evening, as Swati was hunched over Tolstoy's ethics, Rajen-babu came back from office and called her, 'Swati.'

Swati didn't hear him.

Coming closer, Rajen-babu said, 'Must you read in the evening too?'

Startled, Swati smiled when she saw her father, standing up as she inserted her finger in the book to mark the place.

'Whenever I see you these days you're reading. Is it good to be such a bookworm?'

'Isn't it?'

'All these books . . .' Rajen-babu glanced at Swati's desk, 'Do you understand them?'

'Why shouldn't I?' Swati answered, a trifle embarrassed.

'It isn't good to be reading all the time,' Rajen-babu said again.

'What else is there to do, tell me?'

'Why,' Rajen-babu's face brightened as though he had just made a new discovery, 'you could do some housework.'

'You're right,' said Swati, holding up the index finger of her right hand, then she too made a new discovery suddenly: 'You're sopping wet, Baba.'

'Not all that much . . .'

'Don't you care, Baba? Do you have to get wet every day!' Her hair danced on her back as she ran off to fetch dry clothes. Saying, 'I'll get your tea in a minute,' she ran off again. But the book remained in her hand even while they drank their tea.

All four were finished, one by one. They had to be returned, she wanted more books too, but . . . she didn't feel like going . . . Would it be right to send them through someone, however? Satyen-babu delivered her from this dilemma himself. Suddenly at three o'clock one afternoon he knocked on the door of Rajen-babu's house.

Opening the door, Swati seemed blinded for a moment. The sun was very strong after the rain. Satyen-babu stood on the steps, his face flaming red, and, of course, a pile of books in his hand.

'It's you!' the words escaped Swati's lips.

'I brought a couple of books for you . . .'

'Please come in!'

Entering, Satyen-babu handed Swati the books without sitting down. Glancing at them, Swati said softly, '*Shanai, Nabajatak*. New books?' She had meant they looked like newly purchased books, but Satyen-babu replied, 'New books by Rabindranath. We're so fortunate that we're still getting new books from him. But what I hear about his health . . .'

'He's ill?'

'He hasn't quite recovered from that last time!'

Swati did not know when and from what illness Rabindranath had suffered, so she said, after a brief silence, 'Do sit down.'

Putting his books by his side, Satyen-babu sat down on

the sofa in a manner so composed that it suggested he would spend the rest of his life on it. 'Have you read those other books?' he asked.

Swati smiled indistinctly, shaking her head.

'Not yet?'

'Do you . . .' said Swati quickly.

'I don't particularly need them right now, but you have to read more. This is the time, after all.'

Bowing her head, Swati started twisting the end of her sari round her wrist.

'Did you like them?'

Swati raised her eyes without saying anything.

Could there even be an answer to this question?

Looking at her, Satyen-babu said, 'All right, I'll give you more books,' and stood up immediately.

'You're going?'

'Yes . . .'

'So soon?'

'I have to go home and then go out again soon afterwards.'

'How strong the sun is,' said Swati, looking out of the window.

'When you go out it's not as strong as it seems in here. All right then . . .!'

Swati remained in the drawing room after Satyen-babu had left. She hadn't offered him any tea, not even a glass of water—he must have been very tired when he came in from the sun. Oh well—if you left abruptly like that, how could anyone remember! Still, the mistake kept pricking Swati for a long time. To distract herself, she opened *Nabajatak*, running her eye over it and flipping pages at random, then, forgetting everything else, she began to read the poems, one after the other, peace descended on her; after the incredible madness of the stories she had been reading all these days, this seemed to be an even more extraordinary tranquillity, emerging from the storm, the darkness and the intolerable lightning, she seemed to enter a land where all was bright, all was good, all was beautiful. The comfort she felt in her heart made her eyes droop; she went to her room and lay down on the bed, and instantly sweet slumber took her in its lap like a mother.

Swati went herself to return the books two days later. As soon as she knocked lightly with one finger Satyen Roy opened the door. 'Come in,' he said, standing face-to-face with her.

Swati paused as soon as she entered. There was someone slumped on a chair, his feet up on the cane table, a hand with a cigarette between two fingers dangling from the chair, the eyes half-closed. Oh! I know him, I've seen him before! Who . . . Where?

'Come in!' Satyen Roy welcomed her again.

Stepping into the room, Swati saw two half-finished cups of tea on the table, cigarette butts on the floor. They were having a chat by themselves, why did I . . . Would I ever have turned up at this hour if I'd known! Only now did the other gentleman seem to realize there was someone else in the room; casting a quick glance at her through sleepy, reluctant eyes, he suddenly opened them wider—jolted, Swati sat down on the nearest chair, and immediately she remembered that this was the famous Dhruba Datta, whom she had heard of from her brother, who had cut such a disappointing figure when she went to watch her brother's play.

'This is Swati Mitra—a student from our college. And this is Dhruba Datta, the poet,' said Satyen Roy, looking pointedly at the enormous feet raised close to his student's nose.

Dhruba Datta lowered his feet, but continued to slump in his chair. Nodding indistinctly in response to Swati's gentle greeting, he drained the rest of his teacup.

'Would you like a cup of tea?' Satyen-babu tried to compensate for Dhruba Datta's indifference by paying extra attention to his student.

'No . . . I . . . In a minute . . . Just these books . . .'

'Stay a while. Listen to a poem of Dhruba-babu's.' Picking up a slim magazine from the table, Satyen Roy looked at the poet, saying, 'Why don't you read it?'

'Oh no, I can't,' the poet answered in a deep voice.

'Please do—this girl, she loves poetry too.'

'Really?' Dhruba Datta opened his eyes wide again to look at Swati. She saw that there wasn't a trace of joy on his face— beneath his smooth dark complexion he seemed to be plagued by a constant restlessness. She hadn't been able to see him properly the night of the play. Today she could, and it disappointed her. This was a poet? Perhaps!

'Please read the poem,' Satyen Roy requested him again, but, raising his cigarette to his lips, Dhruba Datta waved away the request.

'Then let me read.' With a look at the poet and at the student, without any further ado, Satyen Roy Roy read out the poem from the magazine, clearly, with precise diction. After finishing, he said brightly, 'It really is very good!'

Dhruba Datta curled his lips slightly, but it was obvious that he was pleased.

The professor turned to his student. 'What did you think of it?'

'It's very nice!' Swati had loved the way it was read, but she hadn't quite grasped whether the poem was good or bad, which was why she didn't manage to bring much conviction to her judgement. Suddenly Dhruba Datta smiled, wrinkling his nose in a funny way, and said, 'The moment I hear that expression "nice" about my poem, my feet start itching. I'm off.' Straightening his tall frame in a few energetic moves, he stood up, and without any ceremony of leave-taking, wound his way out of the door. Suddenly peace descended on the room, just like a radio that had been switched off after playing for a long time.

Swati was taken aback. Was Dhruba Datta angry? Did I say

'very nice' rather stupidly? But really, am I important enough, does my opinion even matter! But how is it my fault, it was Satyen-babu who . . .

'The first time you see him,' said Satyen Roy, finally putting down the slim magazine in his hand, 'Dhruba-babu seems peculiar, but . . . he's a real poet!'

Swati did not feel enthused enough to talk any more.

'He left rather abruptly,' Satyen Roy seemed to say to himself. 'I only met him for the first time today.'

'The first time today!' Swati looked at him in surprise. 'When I saw the two of you together in this room,' she couldn't hide what was on her mind any more, 'I imagined he was an old friend of yours!'

Sidestepping the issue, Satyen Roy said, 'Did you think then that I was praising him only because he's my friend? Of course, I would have had to praise him even if he'd been my friend—even my enemy, for that matter.'

After a short silence Swati said, 'Do you know everyone who writes well?'

'Not exactly everyone,' Satyen Roy seemed a little embarrassed by Swati's question. 'But his . . . his book—I had written a critical essay after reading it . . .'

'And he couldn't stay away after he was praised?'

Glancing at his student's guileless, smiling face, the professor felt like smiling too. But retaining his solemnity, he said, 'He doesn't like the very fact that people like it when they're praised. The artist's temperament.'

'But people who read books are actually nicer than those who write them,' Swati chuckled as she spoke.

'It's true that the writer's book is often better than the writer,' Satyen Roy responded after some thought. 'But Dhruba Datta's appearance is so remarkable!'

'Really?' Trying to match the description with reality, Swati said, 'But he's . . . old!'

'At your age many people seem old, not at mine,' laughed Satyen Roy.

'As if you're very old yourself,' the words jumped to Swati's lips. But would it be right to say this to your professor? So she said, 'But he's so much older than you!'

'That doesn't make him old!' A little later he added, 'You don't like poets being old, do you?'

'Nobody does,' Swati agreed.

'What about Rabindranath?'

'I've never seen him.'

'Never seen Rabindranath! How can you live in Calcutta and not have seen Rabindranath!'

Her head bowed, Swati accepted her transgression.

With a sudden laugh, Satyen Roy said, 'I mustn't assume it's your fault. Not everyone gets the opportunity—and girls have so many problems besides. Why don't you ask your mother to let you visit Santiniketan.'

'My mother's dead,' said Swati.

Looking at her a while, Satyen-babu said, 'Dead. Well, you have your father—and such a wonderful father too!'

After some thought, Swati summoned up enough courage for a domestic question: 'Don't your parents live here?'

'Neither my mother nor my father is alive,' Satyen-babu smiled faintly.

Swati was surprised. But why was it so surprising, so many people in this world were in similar circumstances. But his father wasn't alive either! Would her own father also not be alive one day?

For a moment, Swati felt she couldn't breathe. She stirred, was herself again. 'Brothers or sisters?'

Satyen-babu shook his head.

'Not even one? How odd!'

'It's odd, is it?'

Swati didn't say anything. Suddenly she felt sad. How nice

it would have been if there were a mother here in this house. She positioned the memory of her own sick mother in this room, saw her smile, heard her talk, and, sitting quietly in the room now filled with shadows, she felt that the mother she was thinking of was nobody but herself.

Satyen-babu rose to switch on the lights. 'Tell me which books you want to take.' Without waiting for an answer he picked out a few English books himself, then, turning towards her, asked, 'Would you like to read Dhruba Datta's poetry?'

Swati's brow furrowed, unknown to herself. There he went again! What little she had tasted from Satyen Roy's reading had not whetted her appetite for Dhruba Datta's poetry; so she did not respond.

'You may not like it straightaway,' Satyen-babu read her mind in her expression, 'but if you give up, you'll be the loser. Try reading him.'

Swati rose with the books in her hand. 'I'm going now.'

'I enjoyed the afternoon,' said Satyen-babu as he walked with Swati. She was expecting him to come up to the street, but he stopped at the door, going back inside after a minute. I enjoyed the afternoon, the words played over and over again in Swati's mind. Why? Because of Dhruba Datta, perhaps?

Swati entered the house through the back door, running into her brother immediately. Bijon was having a cup of tea at the dining table, along with an enormous omelette.

'Dada! Home at this hour?'

'Why, isn't it allowed?'

Putting the pile of books down on the table, Swati sat down opposite her brother, sweeping the hair out of her eyes, she said, 'That's something we could be asking you.'

Cutting a piece of his omelette with his spoon, Bijon put it in his mouth, biting into a slice of bread held in his left hand. His cheeks bulging a little as he chewed, he smiled and said, 'And what's the news here at home?'

'Will you tell me honestly what you're doing these days?' Swati frowned at her brother.

'Nothing but the truth?' Bijon moistened his throat with a sip of tea. 'How's your professor?'

'What professor!' Swati seemed to have temporarily forgotten that Satyen Roy was her professor!

'You know—the one Baba sent my table-fan to.'

'But you have a ceiling fan in your room now.'

'Still, the fan had been brought for me. I should have been asked before giving it to someone else.'

A sharp response had sprung to Swati's lips, but it would only lead to a quarrel—and how did a quarrel matter to her brother—he just had to walk out to shake it off; she was the one who would feel low for a couple of days. So after a short silence Swati changed the subject. 'I met your Dhruba Datta a short while ago.'

'Dhruba Datta, the writer? Don't even mention him to me.'

'What!' Swati raised her eyebrows. 'Wasn't it just the other day you were obsessed with Dhruba Datta!'

'I *had* become obsessed when I was under his spell!' Bijon laughed uproariously. 'He had promised me passes to the theatre—asked me to visit him at home—but whenever I did he was not at home! If you're never going to be home, why bother to have one! So rude!'

Recalling Dhruba Datta's feet on the table, Swati was tempted to agree with that last remark of her brother's, but lest that meant indulging him too much, she said with a smile, 'But you're a little cleverer than Dhruba Datta, Dada—you never invite anyone home.'

Without a reply, Bijon finished his bread and omelette, his head bowed. He wolfed down his food like ravenous people eating in station refreshment-rooms between a change of trains—swiftly, only half-chewing, without a glance left or right. Pushing away his empty plate, he drew the cup of tea towards himself, wiping his mouth with a handkerchief before finally replying to Swati. 'Imagine comparing Dhruba Datta with me! I'm a twice-matric-failed vagabond, while he's a famous man, a married man, with four or five children; his words should carry some weight, shouldn't they—rubbish, all rubbish!'

'But Satyen Roy says he writes wonderful poetry.'

'Let him write as much poetry as he likes, it doesn't matter to me.'

'Why did you have to go asking him for passes?'

'But he was the one who wanted to . . . Never mind, you can concentrate on your professors and writers, Swati; count me out. They might be vaults of learning, each of them—but do they ever get to see any of the money! What use is that kind of learning, tell me, in this day and age?'

Sitting up straight, Swati placed her elbows on the table. Lacing her fingers together, she said, 'When's your next play?'

'Didn't you know?' Running his tongue over his lips, Biju smiled slyly. 'I've given up all that.'

Without being the least bit perturbed by such a momentous announcement, Swati rested her chin on her interlaced fingers, saying, 'So what now? Films?'

'I can get into films any time I want to, but . . .'

'Why the "but", then?'

Glancing at his sister through lowered eyes, Biju said, 'Laugh as much as you want to now, you won't laugh much longer.'

'But what's the matter, why have you decided not to join films?' Swati said, wiping the smile off her face.

'No, I'm going into business.'

'Into what?'

'Business.' Biju pronounced the word with solemn reverence.

'Bijon's business!' Swati couldn't control herself any more, flinging her arms and breaking into peals of laugher.

Bijon laughed too, which was completely unexpected. 'It's all fixed. The company will be named B. John. Isn't it a good idea?'

'What else have you thought up?'

'You'll see! Listen, Swati,' Bijon suddenly said furtively, leaning towards her, 'can you ask Baba to give me two or three thousand rupees? I can get going immediately.'

'Shouldn't you be the one asking him?'

'Of course I should! But it doesn't always turn out that way, does it. What fathers should be like is not—'

'Dada!' Swati's voice declared war.

'Forget it,' Bijon got up boldly from his chair. 'I don't have time for your lectures. You don't have to ask him—I'll do it on my own.' Looking back from the door, he added, 'Unfortunately, your father doesn't consider his son a member of the human race at all. But even if you people don't give me the money, I'll get hold of it somehow. I *must* have the money!' Shouting out the last few words, Bijon stormed out, the calendar on the wall flapping at the impact.

One by one, the calendar shed the leaves for July, August, September, the leaf for October, full of dates marked in red, came into view. Holidays! But was there any reason to be specially happy about that? Joy had already filled Swati's days and nights, her dreams when she slept, every waking moment, she had discovered a new world, the world of literature, lands, scenes, people, such waves of laughter, such tremulous tears, such sweet, ruthless, terrible, beautiful descriptions—embarrassing, horrifying, dreadful—but, eventually, joy, just joy. Was there so much to life? How fortunate that she had met Satyen Roy—how else would she have got all of this, known so much joy?

Could so much happiness be kept all for oneself? How could you do without someone else? One day, as Saswati was leafing through the books on her desk, Swati took the opportunity to ask, 'Have you read Gogol, Chhordi?'

'Gogol!' Saswati laughed at the funny name. 'Whose goal is this Gogol!' Opening the book, she said, 'Who's this Satyen Roy? So many books of his here!'

'Don't you know him? He's a professor at our college.'

'Satyen Roy?' Saswati knitted her brows. 'No idea—he wasn't there during my time, must be new! So he has lots of books?'

'Lots. And what wonderful books! Chhordi—if you'd just read this one, this story about an overcoat . . . Oh!'

Leafing through the pages, Saswati shut the book as soon as she saw the polysyllabic names.

'Want to read it, Chhordi?' Swati pleaded. 'So wonderful . . .'

Saswati shook her head. 'Doesn't he have any Bengali books?'

'As many as you want! All books of poetry. . .'

'Who on earth reads poetry? No storybooks? Novels? Your Harit-da doesn't read Bengali books, and as for the English books he reads—'

'But you could easily buy some Bengali books.'

'What—waste money on books!' Saswati left the room, her expensive sari glittering.

Then Swati tried Harit. She had just finished an Oscar Wilde novel. The words were arrayed like priceless gems and jewels, colours that dazzled the eye, as though each of them could be lifted off the pages of the book and held in one's hands. She had been in something like a drunken haze—very softly, as though saying something very intimate, she asked, 'Harit-da, have you read *The Picture of Dorian Gray*?'

'Wilde!' Harit burst into laughter. 'Emperor of escapists! Relic of Romanticism! You're reading Wilde! Meanwhile the hour is nigh!'

Surprised and hurt, Swati looked at him. Wasn't it proper to like all this, then? But how could there be rules about what to like? No idea!

Having no other option, Swati began to chase her brother. Bijon spent the afternoon at home sometimes, taking a long nap after lunch and going out just before his father came home from office. 'Want to read a storybook, Dada?'

'What book?'

'Very, ve-e-e-ery good book, here!' Swati handed *Dorian Gray* to her brother. She felt so selfish at times—let her brother read it too.

Glancing at the book, Bijon said, 'Not now—I'll read it later.' Lighting a cigarette, he lay down on his bed, pulling out a book with lurid colours from beneath his pillow, the cover displaying a white woman in a cleavage-revealing dress threatening a black-masked rogue with a gun.

'Why do you read this rubbish, Dada?'

'Rubbish! Hmmph!' Bijon blew smoke-rings. 'You have no idea, I'm learning how to speak English. So fluent. A damn at the drop of a hat.' He continued a little later, 'You have to speak English well if you want to be in business, you see.'

Swati saw, she went away slowly, bearing the burden of her enjoyment all by herself.

Just like the small boy at Holi who, unable to get hold of anyone else, empties his tin of colour on his mother's back, Swati also got hold of her father one day.

'You know, Baba, all those books Satyen-babu gives me to read—I can't tell you how wonderful they are.'

'Naturally! A man is known by his taste.'

'You keep accusing me of reading all the time, but if you started one you wouldn't be able to put it down either.'

'Then I'd better not start. I have office, after all.'

'All right, I'll tell you the stories,' Swati smiled. 'Shall I, Baba?'

'Of course,' Rajen-babu was instantly willing.

'Now?'

'Now? It's best after dinner. Swati, since Satyen gives you so many books, shouldn't you give him something too?'

'But what can I give him?'

'You could invite him for lunch or dinner, you could even send him something nice that's been made at home . . .'

'I can't do all that.'

'That's not good enough. Now that you're a grown-up, you have to do these things.'

Swati only raised her head, shaking it in response.

'All right, I'll invite him during Durga Puja. Shweta will be here too by then.' Rajen-babu's face was tinged with happiness.

'Is Bordi really coming?'

'So she's written.' Rajen-babu's face glowed with joy.

But as soon as the holidays began Satyen-babu went off somewhere out of town, and after spending the actual days of Durga Puja at her husband's home, Shweta arrived two days later with husband, five children, one servant and lots of luggage in tow. As soon as she arrived, she unpacked the hold-all herself, pulling out a bundle of new clothes for everyone as gifts, as well as all kinds of homemade sweets and savouries packed into biscuit tins. Laying out a plateful before Swati, she said, 'Go on, eat up.'

'Oh my God! So much!'

'What do you mean so much? My children can put away four such plates—you can't believe how I had to hide them in that hold-all, if those monsters had got wind of them, do you suppose there would have been any left, they'd have finished them all during the journey!' Laying out two more plates, she said, 'Biju, come along. Baba?'

'What's all this, Shweta?' Rajen-babu smiled. 'You've barely got in!'

'They haven't gone bad, have they?' Shweta's voice betrayed anxiety, only after holding one up to her nose and sniffing several times was she relieved. 'No, they're all right . . . What?' She chased her own children away now. 'Why are all of you here? All right, here's one for each of you—no more, run along now! Not eating, Swati?'

'With my tea.'

'All right, you can have them again with your tea, but for now . . .' Picking out a fish-shaped sweet Shweta wedged it into Swati's mouth.

'Oh, Bordi!'

'Isn't it nice?'

Swati chuckled as she felt cardamom-flavoured coconut taking over her tongue.

'This one—Biju, you—oh, there you are.' Spotting her husband, Shweta covered her head with her sari. 'Do you want one too?'

'As if he has a choice with you in command,' Rajen-babu smiled.

'Don't I know!' Bringing up a smile to the folds of fat on his face, Pramathesh said, 'My blood pressure is climbing, but your daughter . . .'

Looking at a point midway between her husband and her father, Shweta said, 'As if anyone can force you if you don't really want to.'

'Everyone's had some—what about you?' asked Rajen-babu.

'Spare me!' Shweta shuddered. 'I'm sick of all this. Will you get some *deem*-shondesh for me. And some *shonpapri*. And *doi*.'

'All right,' Rajen-babu got up.

'But your tea, Baba . . .'

'No tea now.' Without further delay, Rajen-babu took the tram to the well-stocked Jogu-babu's Market. Saswati and Harit arrived a little later, a fresh wave of joy erupted.

While tea was being made, Shweta reappeared after a wash, the sindoor bright on her hairline, keys tied to the end of her newly worn sari. Despite being the mother of five children, she looked as young as ever—she hadn't put on any weight, her slightly dull-complexioned face seemed pure grace. Swati was enraptured.

At tea, Shweta was like the bird dancing about on a spring morning. Here she was putting her arms around Saswati, there she was stroking Biju's immaculately parted hair, and elsewhere she was exchanging old-fashioned evergreen banter with Harit. Handing everyone their cup of tea, she suddenly stopped before Swati, saying, 'Swati! How lovely you look!'

'And you!' Swati replied with a shy smile, 'you're getting lovelier by the day.'

'Listen to her talk.' Shweta's hand travelled around the enormous bun on Swati's head. 'You don't *see* such hair on girls these days.'

Stroking her own small, compact bun, Saswati said, 'Long hair is no longer in fashion, Bordi.'

'Really? Then I have nothing to worry about. I didn't have a bad head of hair once upon a time—and look at it now! Barely a fox-tail.'

Everyone laughed together in response.

'How long does a woman's hair last anyway!' Bijon suddenly said gravely. 'Only until marriage. As soon as she's had a child or two—that's it!' He had heard Dhruba Datta say this a long time ago—now he was thrilled to be able to repeat it so appropriately before so many people at home.

When Dhruba Datta had said it, most of the listeners had laughed, but Bijon's audience didn't respond the same way, only Pramathesh said, 'Right! Right you are, Biju! Absolutely correct!'

'It's terrible when children talk like old men,' Saswati said, shifting a little.

'How much longer can you go on calling him a child! Hasn't he grown up now?' Shweta smiled at her brother. 'More tea, Biju?'

'No, no more,' said Biju in a deep, mature voice. 'I'll be back, Bordi.' Without looking at anyone else he scraped his chair back to get up quickly. He couldn't bear to remain amongst these so-called elders of the family any more, he was dying for a cigarette.

'A little more for you, Harit?'

'Yes, please,' Harit pushed his cup towards Shweta.

'Now sit down, Bordi. Have your tea,' said Swati.

'Yes, I will.' Filling Harit's cup a second time, Shweta sat down in the chair abandoned by Biju, between Saswati and Harit. 'Give me some tea, Saswati. Extra sugar.'

'How many spoons?' Dipping the spoon into the sugar bowl with perfection and poise, Saswati raised her eyes.

'Three.' Smiling, Shweta added, 'I won't say no to four either . . . What's this?' Shweta suddenly clamped two fingers around the wrist of Saswati's right hand, which still held the spoon. 'Where's your *shankha*?' she asked, referring to the thin white bangle traditionally worn by married women.

Without answering, Saswati poured the tea out, her face lowered, and sat down again.

'Did you break your wedding *shankha*? You must get another!'

Bringing up a cutting smile to the corner of his lips, Harit said, 'What's the point of displaying all those symbols of slavery?'

'Slavery? Oh my God . . .' Shweta poked Saswati with her elbow. 'Well? Do you call it slavery?'

But Saswati neither smiled, nor raised her head. She did feel a prick of sadness over this *shankha*. Harit had been waging a holy war against the *shankha* right from the beginning.

Having run out of adjectives like 'uncivilized', 'barbaric' and 'medieval', Harit had finally said, 'I feel embarrassed going out with that *shankha*-and-sindoor figure!'

'Very well! Don't then!' Saswati had retorted angrily,

'What? You want to stay homebound like the perfect wife?'

'I'll do whatever I please—how does it matter to you!'

'Of course it does—because you are my wife. And in this day and age I don't want just a wife, I want a companion.'

'You don't lack for companions, do you!'

There was some history behind the last remark. They'd been to a party a few days ago, they were raising money for some poor country—Saswati didn't quite remember whether it was China or Spain or Czechoslovakia—there, Harit had chatted a little too long with a lipstick-wearing Punjabi woman in a salwar. Saswati was unsmiling on the way back home that night, but Harit was so engrossed in describing the plight of China or

Spain or Czechoslovakia that he hadn't gauged anything from his wife's expression, but the moment Saswati said what she did, Harit thought of the Punjabi woman. She was the sister of a man he respected immensely. Looking at her, he said, 'You're quite illiterate.'

In the midst of such an argument six months after their wedding, Harit grabbed Saswati's wrist and snapped her *shankha*. Saswati wept buckets that night—for the first time in her married life—but she didn't even think of getting another, and gradually she came round to the idea that it had been for the best, none of Harit's friends' wives wore them, she used to feel a little out of place anyway.

Getting no response from Saswati, Shweta turned to Harit. 'But if it's a matter of slavery, that's your fault, why take it out on the *shankha*?'

Harit seemed to feel a moment's discomfort, then he said, 'If the symbols are eradicated the slavery will be too.'

'Why, can't there be slavery without symbols?'

'Your sister-in-law's right there, Harit. Take us—we *are* their slaves—but we don't have any symbols or anything.' As Pramathesh spoke, there seemed to be a small landslide of laugher in the folds of fat on his face. 'Halfwit!' Harit thought to himself, looking at him.'

But since thoughts cannot be heard, Pramathesh had another stab at humour. 'Why don't you start a protest movement instead, Harit—for men to have a symbol of slavery too after marriage?'

'Many men do have them. Diamond rings, silk kurtas, gold buttons, and a shiny new umbrella.' Harit snorted in laughter, a dry, joyless laugh. 'Some carry them temporarily, some all their lives.'

Except for the umbrella, the description clearly fit Pramathesh, but he didn't even realize it, nodding in appreciation, he said, 'How right you are, how right, how right!'

'Well said, Harit!' Laughing, Shweta clapped him on the back. Harit couldn't make out what all the hilarity was for.

'You've hit the nail on the head! He refuses to give up the wedding ring and those buttons of his. See for yourself,' Shweta turned to her husband, 'how smart Harit looks in his half-sleeve zippered sports shirt—don't worry, Saswati, you can use that zipper to drag him behind you!' Shweta fell on Saswati, rolling with laughter.

Maintaining a supercilious smile, Harit stood up, holding the folded newspaper like a royal sceptre. 'I'll be back.'

'Oh, what's your hurry, don't go now, there's so much more I want to talk to you about,' said Shweta.

'Later. Lunch isn't going to be before one or two o'clock, will it? Let me finish my work meanwhile.'

'Work—even during Durga Puja!' Pramathesh was wonderstruck.

'It's the office that has holidays, not me.' Clamping his teeth on his pipe, the champion of work left with long strides.

Looking goggle-eyed at the door, Pramathesh said, 'Smart lad, our Harit!'

'And as for you,' Shweta said with a tap on Saswati's head, 'men have all these whims, why do you have to get worked up! Come with me, I'll buy you *shankhas* from the temple at Kalighat.'

Swati noticed Saswati's mood change completely as soon as Harit left. She became comfortable, her face looked relaxed. It wasn't just today—Swati suddenly felt this was how Saswati was nowadays—as long as Harit was present, her ways, her words, her smiles, all seemed tentative, stifled; and whenever Harit deposited her here to go away for some time, she was a different person. It's wrong to think this way—maybe I'm making a mistake; but the more she looked at Saswati, the more she listened to her talk, to her chatter with Shweta, the more surprised Swati was that this hadn't occurred to her earlier. Really, what *had* happened to Saswati? She had put on weight, she looked even more glamorous in her sari and jewellery, but . . . but where was the grace in her face . . . Why didn't her eyes dance any more; she was like a fresh flower that had wilted under the sun. Was this how it happened? *Could* such a thing happen? Glancing at Shweta's face, rippling with joy next to Saswati's, Swati felt a pang of sorrow.

Rajen-babu returned, having bought out the entire market, and Shweta promptly tied the end of her sari around her waist to enter the kitchen. Over and over again Rajen-babu told her not to, but who was listening? 'How fresh this fish is—I can't possibly let anyone else cook it! The fish-head too—and cabbage! Oh my goodness, cabbage in October! And how large the crabs are. Really, this was Calcutta for you. Was there any joy in cooking if not this way!'

'This girl, really!' Rajen-babu mumbled.

'But,' Pramathesh exclaimed, 'it's best to let each one do what they love.'

'The truth is,' Swati smiled, 'nobody but Bordi's cooking is to your taste.'

'Not true. If the sisters-in-law cooked that'd be even more to my taste, but they . . .' Pramathesh finished in an explosion of laughter.

Swati went off to stand at the door to the kitchen. Two stoves blazed, the pans crackled, the pots bubbled. The smells made Swati sneeze immediately.

'Swati! What is it?'

'Nothing.'

'Want a snack? Should I fry you a piece of fish? Or some *alusheddho*?'

'Oh my God, all those sweets just now—how can I eat again so soon afterwards?'

'All my children love *alusheddho*. Whatever I make, they can't do without it.' Dipping her ladle into the pot in which the daal was bubbling, Shweta brought out three potatoes, poking each with a finger to examine their readiness, then twisted her wrists to dispatch two of them back into the boiling water, sending the third unerringly into the hollow of a bowl. Plunging her left hand into cold water, she peeled the boiled potato immediately, and then deposited the round, golden, fragrant potato on a saucer, the vapour still rising from it, adding salt and pepper before presenting it to Swati: 'Here you are.'

The whole thing took less than a minute. Swati was reminded of a Japanese tennis player—Arun-da had taken her as a child to South Club to watch.

'Sit down now and eat,' Shweta pushed a low stool towards her, immediately asking the maid whether she had finished slicing the cabbage.

Swati ate the potato in small bites, reflecting that there was no tastier food in the world. But the smaller the potato got, the more the heat of the kitchen reduced the pleasure of eating it. As she marinated the crab, Shweta said, 'Run along now.'

Swati rose when she had finished her potato. Watching for a while, she said, 'Bordi, how do you manage to spend so much time at the stove at a stretch?'

Wiping her face with the end of her sari, Shweta smiled at her sister. 'You will, too.'

She would? Even she? Swati spent the rest of the morning wandering around distractedly.

It was two o'clock by the time lunch was over, and then afternoon sped swiftly into evening. Had the days become so short suddenly?

Immediately after tea, Harit said, 'We'll be off now.'

'Oh no, not right away?' Shweta protested at once. 'After dinner . . .'

'One meal was enough for two. More than enough. Get ready, Saswati.'

'What's the hurry?'

'A friend of mine is coming at seven thirty.' Harit, glanced at his watch.

'You have friends over every day,' Shweta said gently. 'For a change—'

'I can't. We have an appointment.'

'Then they have to go, that's true . . .' Pramathesh nodded.

'Let Saswati stay then,' Shweta made a last attempt.

'Yes, good idea,' Pramathesh was instantly enthusiastic. 'Let Saswati stay—she'll go back at night after dinner, all right? Biju will drop her—and if he doesn't, I will—no need to worry.'

'The friend's coming with his wife, which is why Saswati needs to be there,' Harit's lips curled as he spoke. 'But if she doesn't want to go, let her stay. She can stay the night, in fact.'

Stretching, Saswati said faintly, 'No, Bordi, let me go.'

Observing their expressions in turn, Shweta said, 'All right, that's better. It's true—if you have guests at home, how can the housewife be missing. Come again. Come every day, all right? Let me do your hair.' She put her hand on Saswati's head.

She got late getting her hair done and changing into her sari. Harit had to take a taxi to get home by seven thirty, and because of this needless expense he was even more put out. Saswati sat near the door, her face turned away—after they had travelled in silence for a while Harit suddenly said, 'So you're crying.'

Saswati neither responded, nor turned towards him.

'If you're so attached to your family, you shouldn't have got married!'

Harit didn't get a response this time either.

'Fool!' Harit pronounced this powerful English monosyllable just once to recover the taxi fare, as it were.

2

Saswati wasn't crying; she was only thinking of the darkening evening after the golden day. She would now have to glow in

the drawing room, smile while suppressing yawns,; and be on
tenterhooks lest she laugh at the wrong places. Their guest was
unbeatable in the country when it came to economics—at least,
so Harit felt. He was always singing his friend's praises. And
indeed, how well informed they all were, how knowledgeable,
how well read, and how much each of them could talk!
Saswati couldn't make head or tail of any of it, even their jokes
and their humour didn't make anyone but themselves laugh.
Another problem was that there were non-Bengalis too in
the group, whenever any of them was present the conversation
was always in English, and although Saswati had passed her
BA examinations with honours, she still found it difficult
to converse in English, she started gasping for breath after a
couple of set phrases. If the men came with their wives it was
better—although it was forbidden by law for the women to
talk among themselves in a group, at least you could breathe from
time to time. But very often she was the only woman among
men in trousers—if she came away her husband would lose
face, and if she stayed she would lose her life. She couldn't
converse in English; she simply hadn't managed to memorize
the list of places where Fascist monsters had done—and were
still doing—terrible things; it was her fault, she felt embarrassed,
she tried her utmost; but how could anyone enjoy slaving all
the time like preparing for an exam? Harit couldn't survive
without these sessions with his friends; either someone called on
them, or they called on someone, every evening was spent this
way; in these past two years, come rain, come illness, Saswati
couldn't remember a single evening that the two of them had spent
together by themselves. At first she would be upset, she would
be angry, she would be heartbroken . . . But having passed
through that phase long ago the longing itself had died by
now . . . Now all she wished for was that someone should
visit, someone else, a woman, a woman to whom another woman
could bare her heart. Swati had only progressed up to novels,

it would be nice if she got married—but who knew what she would be like after marriage.

Today she had got a new life with her eldest sister. Climbing up the clean, lifeless, melancholy stairs to the tiny second-floor flat, she sighed twice.

'Shall we go over?' asked Harit the next morning.

Saswati looked away in detachment.

'Come on!' said Harit, pronouncing the word as 'khome'. 'I can expect something from you too, can't I. After all, you *are* my wife. Come on now.'

'You needn't come, I can go by myself.'

'Your sister didn't ask me to go, of course, but . . . might as well.'

Saswati was surprised to see Harit choose a dhoti and kurta.

She went over some time or the other during the day, and Harit arrived to take her home some time before ten at night.

The days and nights at home were transformed. Swati felt her joyous childhood had come back—even her brother was spending a lot more time at home. He had frequent secret confabulations with his brother-in-law, after each such exchange he went out, returning with a bunch of tickets for a play or a film; the entire family packed itself into two taxis with much excitement, heading to the theatre in Shyambazar—good God, they had filled an entire row by themselves. And films? Not only did a single Bengali or Hindi film remain unwatched—they even went to Metro for an English film in Harit's honour, after which the then-most-wondrous Lighthouse wasn't ignored either. When Bijon lightly mentioned the name of yet another play, Harit said quickly when he heard, 'Bijon, are you planning to bankrupt your brother-in-law?'

'Not at . . .' Pramathesh conveyed his point of view with nothing but those words and a matching expression.

'The amount you've spent just on entertainment these past few days,' Harit calculated, 'is what many people spend over an entire month. Many, meaning that fortunate four or five per cent of the population that earns that much.'

'Er . . . er . . .' Stammering, Pramathesh suddenly discovered a rationale, 'Even the people in the film and theatre business have to earn a living, don't they?'

'Of course they do!' Harit smiled derisively. 'Only because the rich man wastes money copiously for his pleasure does the poor man get two square meals a day.'

'Why is it a waste if it's for pleasure?' Pramathesh sounded like an obedient student asking a question of his teacher. 'Isn't money meant for pleasure?'

'Pleasure's fine, but reining in expenses is even better.' Harit said this with great confidence, flashing a look at his wife, but Saswati was looking at the album of family photographs with Bijon, her head bowed, she didn't hear, or, at least, it wasn't clear whether she had heard. Harit was enraged—for Saswati didn't seem to be absorbing any of the lessons he had been imparting, either on politics or on domestic economy—why, just the other day she had made the absurd suggestion of taking everyone to the cinema or something—not that she'd managed to finish, for Harit had cut her off halfway with a 'Are you mad!'

But Saswati hadn't spared him the question: 'Mad! Why?'

'Do I have that kind of money?'

'How much can it cost?' his wife had argued. 'Jamai-babu takes us so often,' she added, referring to Shweta's husband.

'Then I'll say you shouldn't have gone—you know your finances.'

'Why, are we all that badly off!'

'We will be if we follow your wishes.'

Saswati was hurt, but what choice did she have, if only she would follow the rules strictly there would be none of this heartburn. Harit saved a quarter of his salary scrupulously—if they needed money near the end of the month he preferred borrowing ten rupees to dipping into his bank account; to ensure they didn't waste any money, he didn't even bring his chequebook home. Pramathesh's extravagance almost sent him into convulsions.

'Reining in expenses . . . Hmm . . .' Pramathesh seemed to like the idea. 'I wish I could, but somehow it never happens. You see . . . the children . . . such a big household . . .'

'Bad days are coming, very bad days!' Harit's expression instilled fear in everyone.

'Why?' Pramathesh asked in anxiety.

Why! He was asking why! Heavens, were there still such people! And it was because there were that the country was in such a plight! 'War,' answered Harit briefly.

'But the war is thousands of miles away—what does it have to do with us?'

'I don't need to answer that, the bombs will,' said Harit through clenched teeth.

'What!' Pramathesh said in consternation. 'Bombs! Is Hitler going to bomb us from so far away! It's possible, Hitu is capable of anything—what a walloping he's giving our lords, eh!' Every one of Pramathesh's paan-stained, discoloured teeth became visible.

Fascist! A Fascist through and through! Harit jumped out of his skin as well as his chair. But Pramathesh didn't realize anything, still laughing, he said, 'But yes, you're right, Harit. Times aren't good.'

'How does it matter to you!' Harit's face reddened with the hue of revenge. 'Landowners!'

'What landowners!' Pramathesh sighed. 'I'll be happy to get rid of it. But the thing is—it isn't easy to change your habits, and as long as it's there, might as well spend it—there's no doubt about the pleasures it brings.'

❧

No, there certainly wasn't any doubt. It wasn't just the cinema and the theatre, Pramathesh had started a regular competition with his father-in-law over the daily provisions too. Rajen-babu had brought cabbage, so Pramathesh got a basketful of cauliflower all the way from the wholesale market— tiny and very expensive. Rajen-babu got chicken, so the very next day Pramathesh had to get the best mutton from Hogg Market, along with fresh green peas and tomatoes the size and colour of bright red apples. So Rajen-babu bought the special *amriti* of Dhaka. That was it—Pramathesh whizzed off to an exclusive shop near Sealdah to order two kilos of another special sweet, the *pranohara*. But on the day of Kali Puja, he hit the jackpot, returning at noon, panting and perspiring, with a trussed-up turtle, which a servant placed in front of the kitchen door, upside down.

Swati was transfixed! Running up to it, but not getting too close, she said, 'Oh my God, what's this?'

'It's a turtle,' said Pramathesh, wiping his neck. 'Never seen one before?'

'But why a turtle? Whatever for?'

'Whatever for?' Pramathesh chuckled. 'To eat.'

'To eat!' Swati was astounded.

'You've never had turtle? But how would you—you can get everything in Calcutta, but not this. Sometimes you get tortoise, such a fuss over that. For heaven's sake, tortoise meat is medicine for gout, it's not fit for human consumption. This is the real thing—the real turtle! Whatever you may say about chicken or mutton, there's no meat like this one.' Concluding his eulogy, the corpulent Pramathesh started panting like an engine.

'Where did you get this?' asked Rajen-babu.

A victorious smile appeared on Pramathesh's face. 'You just need to make the effort. One of the tillers on my land has a shop in Baithakkhana, his wife's from Nobinagar in Comilla district. I sent him—'

'What! You sent someone to Comilla for this!'

'Not bad at all. He got to visit his in-laws, and we can have the best turtle from Comilla without leaving Calcutta—not bad at all!'

'Really, Pramathesh,' Rajen-babu laughed, covering his mouth with his hand.

Blinking at his father-in-law, Pramathesh said, 'I haven't had any in a long time, and you love it too . . .'

'Very well done,' Shweta spoke at last, her survey of the turtle completed. 'Lots of fat, too. Anukul, you can slaughter it, can't you?'

Rubbing his hands, Anukul, Pramathesh's special servant, said, 'Of course I can, Ma, don't you worry.'

'O-o-o-oh!' Swati said, 'are we going to kill it and then eat it! How awful!'

'I suppose you eat your regular fish and meat without killing anything,' Pramathesh laughed.

'But still,' Shweta intervened quickly, 'it's not nice to see it happening before your eyes. And the way you have to kill these . . .' Shweta ran her hand affectionately over the helpless turtle's black-and-white stomach, then told Anukul, 'Outside, all right?'

Anukul was ready to start immediately if he got the word, but since Harit's office had reopened, they had to wait till Sunday. Pramathesh supervised the turtle-slaughter personally, and Shweta cooked it with quite some ceremony. But the special guest folded his hands at the table.

'Eat up!'

'No.'

'Come on, now, eat up!' Pramathesh mediated. 'It isn't tortoise—it's turtle. Real turtle. Just try it.'

'Here you are!' Using the back of her hand to ensure that it was still warm, Shweta pushed the bowl close to Harit's plate, practically touching it.

'Wonderful! So much fat! Eggs too! And the cooking's very good!' Pramathesh gushed.

'You could just try it,' requested Rajen-babu.

Looking at the meat in the shining brass bowl, reddened with oil and spices, Harit again pronounced a determined, definitive 'No'.

'A little—just try a little! If you don't like it don't have any more. Just a little!'

There was a regular tug of war for two or three minutes. Shweta almost prostrated herself over his plate—she'd feed him herself if she could.

'Simply refused!'

Having failed, Shweta was almost in tears.

'Such willpower, Harit! Everyone's requesting you . . .' Pramathesh was quite hurt at this unexpected insult to his turtle.

'Can all kinds of meat really be eaten!' Holding his plate in his left hand, Harit helped himself to a little tomato chutney.

'That's quite true,' Pramathesh nodded his assent immediately. 'I've heard they eat frogs in England. Is that true?'

'That's a different kind of edible frog,' answered the veteran.

'This seems quite edible to me too,' said Pramathesh, putting a little meat, a little egg and a lot of fat into his mouth at the same time. Transferring the load from one side of his mouth to the other, he said, 'You know, Harit, there's hardly any kind of meat I haven't tried, but I am yet to taste frog meat, that's a bit of a regret. Is it good? Have you tried it?'

Without answering the question, Harit said, 'It's not very good for you to eat too much meat or fish.'

'No meat? No fish? What does that leave?'

'But since your blood pressure is high, what's the alternative?'

'All those are doctors' games. If you follow their advice you'll have to starve to death. It's better to gorge yourself to death.' Pramathesh helped himself to the rest of the meat, scraping the bowl to ensure nothing was left behind. 'Done already, Harit? Really, it's embarrassing for us to have a meal with you. Tried the meat, Saswati? Did you like it, Swati?'

'It's delicious,' Swati responded enthusiastically. When Harit categorically refused to try the meat, she was feeling quite bad for Shweta, for Pramathesh too—in fact, more for him. Such a nice man—though he did look exactly like the god Kartik with his moustache and the central parting in his dense, curly hair; and though he usually had his *panjabi* off and his dhoti raised to his knees, and chomped far too loudly when eating—but still nice. You felt a tenderness for him, like he was one of your own.

After lunch Swati sat down next to him, accepted a paan from his container, listened to his account of how he had gone hunting in the Garo Hills ten years ago, until he started snoring. Then she went into the drawing room, where her eldest sister lay on a sheet on the ground with her youngest child, while her father dozed in the easy chair.

As soon as she entered Shweta said, 'A letter for you, Swati.' Taking out a dark blue envelope from beneath her pillow, she gave it to Swati. Swati saw her own name sparkling on the envelope, written in a beautiful hand. Did she know this handwriting? Who had written to her? Opening the envelope, she first took a look at the name at the bottom of the letter: Satyen Roy. Her face reddened a little and, realizing as much, she unfolded the letter before her face to read it. She couldn't, she just glanced at it superficially, then said, 'Satyen-babu has written, Baba.'

'What does he say?' said Rajen-babu drowsily.

'Here you are . . .' Swati stretched out her hand with the letter, but Rajen-babu said, 'What? He's all right, isn't he?'

'Yes, he's asked after you too . . .'

'Who's Satyen-babu?' asked Shweta.

'A professor of mine.'

'A professor! Professors write to you! And long letters, too! They must think very highly of you?' Her elbow on the pillow, her head on her hand, breastfeeding her baby, Shweta looked with affection and pride at her sister.

'Bordi, really!' Swati wandered around the room a little before escaping. She sat on the steps of the veranda inside. It was quiet; the evening session hadn't yet begun in the kitchen; a cool four o'clock November wind was blowing. Sweeping the hair out of her eyes, she lowered her gaze to the notepaper.

Swati,

I've been travelling a lot. On the last day of Durga Puja I took the boat on the Ganga at Benares—it was like seeing the Taj Mahal by full moon, or Diwali in Delhi; half a day at Fatehpur Sikri, two in Jaipur in between; Lucknow, Allahabad, Patna on the way back—all done, and now in Santiniketan. I read about Rabindranath in the newspaper—came here directly, couldn't stay away. He's seriously ill; there's no hope of meeting him. The golden boat is floating along the river of light towards darkness—but perhaps that is the larger ocean of light.

Although the poet is a prisoner to his pain, Santiniketan in autumn is just as lovely as ever. It seems a little cruel, doesn't it? But this is what is right; this is what the poet has sung about all his life. Not just Rabindranath—all poets, every poet in the world. The world is beautiful, life is wonderful—what else do we have to talk of, after all.

Do you know how I feel here after having seen so many lands, so many sights? As though, after a sumptuous feast, I am in bed in my own little home. Santiniketan feels like home every time I come—I've been to school here, taught, too, for three months—do you suppose there was anything missing from the welcome just because the holidays are here and no one is to be seen? No! The sky is blue, the tall flowers growing in the grass are white, the sun shines all day, the moon peeps down in the evening, and after the moon thousands of stars arrive; the more the night advances, the more their light spreads, like a very fine dust. There's no need to spend nights at railway stations and days on tongas to see such extraordinary sights; all you need is to wait in silence. If you can develop that ability to wait in silence, you'll be fine—but how many of us can do it, we cannot be silent ourselves until everything else is silent too, that's why we *have* to come every now and then to a place such as this, open everywhere, silent everywhere—what a silence that is. So devoid of sound that you think you'll be able to hear a butterfly pass. Does that mean everything is silent, though? Oh no. Making their stage beneath a tree, a group of child archers jumped on it with shrieks, the branches cried out, the north wind ran away after shaking the trees by their shaggy mops, a letter arrived from winter.

Now look how I've been immersed in my own feelings of joy: my day was not darkened at all by the fact that the one who taught me these joys is now on his sickbed. Man is very selfish—what do you say?—sometimes I feel drowsy as I sit here, I try to remind myself that this is not all there is— there's Calcutta, work, the war, the exam scripts to be marked. I have sudden bouts of unhappiness too: I'm not taking more than my due from the world, am I? Is it only for me that the day drops like a ripe fruit from the golden tree of the sun? I'm not a poet, I cannot return the compliments. But why talk of that? Does this pleasure I get hold no value? Is my love for all this not true simply because I cannot express it?

How are you, what are you doing? I'm sure you're very well. I'm sure you've spent the holidays very happily. I want to hear all the stories when I'm back. You could write a letter before that if you like. I'm going to be here a few days more—not longer, the holidays are nearly over.

Tell your father I asked after him.

Satyen Roy

Swati looked at the letter after she had finished it. Two sides of a large sheet of paper: the words packed densely together towards the end, as soon as the sheet was filled, the letter was finished, too—as if he couldn't have written another page! Turning the sheet over, she started reading it again slowly, she had an indescribable feeling. She hadn't thought of Satyen Roy even once all these days; the books he had given her before leaving lay untouched—the joy of Shweta's arrival had made her forget everything else. But then he wasn't exactly suffering either; first the huge tour in the north, and now he was in Santiniketan to watch the moon and the stars. With no one there, nothing to do, he had written a letter to pass his time. Swati was angry, she was envious of Satyen Roy; he could wander wherever he liked, at will—how free he was, how happy he was! And at the end of all the details about himself, a dry 'how are you'. Of course I'm well—I'm very well, I'm very happy; different people in this world are happy in different ways. Different, yes, but—and this was that Swati hated the most—she seemed to read in Satyen Roy's letter that the things she was engrossed in— the lunches and dinners, the cinemas and theatre, the fun and laughter, all of which was good—but only in an adolescent way. Why adolescent? And was she still one?

Leaving the blue notepaper on her lap, Swati began to ponder: am I still an adolescent? She saw two crows perched on a branch of the tree by the road—how beautiful! Black amidst the green, interspersed with the yellow of the sunlight—matching colours, all! Here too the sky was blue, the grass green, the sunlight golden—then why bother to go anywhere else? Anywhere else! Anywhere else didn't mean another land, it meant another . . . what. She had no idea, but all she felt was that even the greatest pleasure you could get out of meals and dressing up and going out and having fun could not match the joy to be had in this anywhere else, this particular joy seemed to be endless. She wasn't grown up—what did she know about it—but didn't she know anything at all? When she heard a song, when she read a breathtaking book, when she suddenly saw gold between the green, and black amidst the green?

'What are you doing, Swati?'

It was Saswati. She had just woken up from her nap, her face swollen, her clothes crumpled, a fragrance rising from the hair left loose. Sitting down next to her, Saswati said, 'Is that a letter? For whom?'

'For me,' answered Saswati.

'Who's written it?'

'I told you about Satyen Roy, remember?' said Swati, putting the letter back in its envelope.

'That professor of yours? He's written? Let's see!' Saswati snatched the envelope from Swati's lap. 'Swati, do me a favour, go get that tamarind pickle from Bordi's room, will you? . . . Why aren't you going?'

Swati rose to contribute to her sister's post-nap munching. Dabbing the pickle thickly on the fingers of her right hand and licking it off, accompanied by appropriate sounds, Saswati pressed the letter down on her knee with her left hand. Swati stared at her sister's hand with anxious eyes, any moment now the letter would have a pickle-stain on it.

Returning the letter, Saswati said, 'Why has he written all these things about his feelings to you?'

'Then whom will he write to?' answered Swati solemnly.

'Why's that?' Saswati smiled. 'He doesn't have anyone else to write to?'

'Maybe he has, but will anyone else enjoy reading about his feelings?'

'Oh my God! This pickle's delicious, isn't it? Hats off to Bordi! Don't you want any?'

'No, Chhordi—my fingers get too sticky.'

'Silly!' Saswati seemed to have accepted Swati's silliness smilingly; without any help, she put away all the pickle in a few minutes.

After sunset, in the dim darkness, Shweta murmured with her father, while Swati sat silently, leaning against the wall. Saswati had left, Pramathesh had taken Ata–Tata–Chhoton out for eight-for-a-rupee photographs. After all the fun and excitement a sort of cold drowsiness had descended on the house, as though there was nothing for anyone to do. And it really was so—so much food had been cooked for lunch that the stoves would have to be lit only to make some rice; Shweta's baby, whose crying usually ensured that this time of the day was a noisy one, had unexpectedly fallen asleep on her own; seizing the opportunity, the maid was making the beds early in every room, as though she were advancing night with her own hands. Evenings made you sad—Swati always felt—they made you melancholy. In that grey period, when the light died, but darkness didn't blossom, when the shadows fell, a couple seemed to be parting forever—whenever she was alone Swati felt like crying; luckily, electric lights existed, the tears of the shadow spreading across the sky were swept out of the room by Aladdin's magic lantern.

But the lights in the veranda had not been lit; the light in the room cast a beam or two near her father's feet through the gaps in the curtain, and Swati could see, from where she sat, a spot in the sky with a large, green, solitary, pulsating star; was this the evening star—out of all the people in the world, the unblinking eye in the sky was gazing at her. The star appeared the way things do when your eyes fill with tears, so transparent that it seemed to be made of tears, looking so much as though it wasn't attached to the sky, that it had detached itself, that it would melt into drops any moment, just like your tears overflowed from your eyes on to your face . . . Suddenly, she did not understand how, she did not know what happened, very simply, without the slightest pain, two drops of water rolled out of Swati's eyes, how strangely silent everything was, and a misty fog had appeared, such a strange, cold, drab, listless evening, just like in winter—but then winter *was* on its way, and why should you feel sad because winter was coming, why should you cry! Swati felt like laughing now—luckily it was dark, no one had seen—and how fascinating that star looked through her tears! Wiping her eyes on the end of her sari, Swati listened to the conversation.

Baba was saying: 'So you *have* to leave on Friday?'

'Yes, Baba, his courts have reopened, and we've been here quite some time.'

Shweta would go away? On Friday? But how could she not? She'd have to go. Have to? Yes, have to, of course . . . I wonder how it feels. How does it feel to go away for the first time? And after that? And later? How strange this life was for women—they were born only to go away, and that was their way of getting everything in life. Bordi must be feeling very bad about going—Baba must be feeling worse. But still Bordi didn't say, 'All right, let's stay a little longer.'

'How much longer before you retire?' asked Bordi.

'Not much longer at all. Just a year to go.'

'How long you've been working, my God! . . . Baba, didn't we live in a house in some kind of a lane once upon a time?'

'You remember Shankharipara? You were so small then.'

'I have faint memories of you going to office, and me crying because I wanted to go with you. I fell down the stairs one day, didn't I?'

'You remember quite a lot!'

After a silence Shweta said, 'You've worked so hard all your life, Baba. Now, after retirement, you mustn't work a single day any more.'

'Really?'

'What do you mean really? We won't let you. First of all you will come and stay with me for a few months.'

'All . . . right.'

'Don't just say it, you have to do it. Meanwhile, you have to try to get Biju into something.'

'Let's see.'

'Just because studies didn't work for him, it doesn't mean nothing else will,' Shweta encouraged her father.

'I hope something does.' He didn't sound too enthusiastic.

'One more thing, Baba,' Shweta glanced at her sister and smiled covertly. 'We shouldn't delay things further for Swati.'

'For what?' Rajen-babu was flabbergasted.

'It's time she got married.'

He didn't reply, a shadow fell across his face, Swati saw it even in the darkness.

'Well, Swati?' Shweta turned towards her. 'Isn't that so?'

Swati stood up, biting her lips. 'Don't go away,' Shweta joked. 'No need to leave like that with flowing hair and distant eyes. Those days are long gone when . . .' But Swati did not wait to listen, she went into the room.

Looking at the trembling curtain, Shweta said, 'This daughter of yours is so beautiful . . .'

'All my daughters are beautiful,' Rajen-babu smiled indistinctly.

'What do you mean, do you think any of us can stand up to her?' Shweta brimmed over with happiness, then said gravely, 'But really, don't delay any more. It must be done before your retirement. And then, nothing more to worry about— you'll be completely free.

'That's quite true,' said Rajen-babu faintly.

Looking at her father, Shweta felt a wrench. Still, and because of this, she said, 'Besides, their marriage won't be like ours. And,' Shweta tried to cheer up her father, 'if she stays on in Calcutta, that's perfect!'

But Rajen-babu remained quiet, and Shweta didn't seem to have anything more to say either. Suddenly a kind of silence descended, as though it were late at night, as though a train had come to a stop at a tiny station in the middle of a field in the darkness, and in that darkness someone was going off somewhere, leaving her home behind.

∾

Back in her room, Swati sat down at her desk. Before her eyes lay Satyen-babu's letter. Picking it up, she read it once more. Should she reply? What did she have to say in reply? 'You could write if you like.' Which meant he wasn't all that interested. But whether he is or not, I know how to be polite. All right, might as well write then. Now's the best time—the house is quiet, and I'm sure there'll be no time tomorrow.

Swati armed herself with paper and pen. But how would she address him? When had she ever written to someone who was neither a relative, nor a girl her own age? What would she write? 'Sricharoneshu'—the classic way of addressing older people? But was he an old man to be addressed that way? But couldn't you use it with someone even if they weren't all that old? He's a learned man, after all. And he's my professor—older than me too—and . . . Never mind, what's the point of debating so much—might as well use it:

> Your letter was wonderful. How much you travelled, how many things you saw, and then how beautiful Santiniketan is. But the letter was wonderful not because of all that, it was wonderful in itself.
>
> You wrote of winter, didn't you—here, too, there's a wintry feeling this evening. Perhaps it's been there for quite a few days, but I didn't feel it earlier. Winter is nice, but when it arrives, you feel a little sad. Don't you?
>
> Are there rules about when people feel sad and why? Things are fine, all is well—suddenly Mr Sadness arrives! And that's it! As though he will never budge any more in his life! Of course, he's not a bad person. I mean, it's not as though feeling sad is necessarily bad—it feels quite nice, in fact, sometimes.
>
> It's nice, but you can't talk about the niceness of feeling sad with others; you can only talk about the niceness of feeling happy. It's not that either, you don't even have to talk about the niceness of feeling happy—it spreads on its own; and it's the niceness of feeling sad that you have to talk about—that people want to talk about, but cannot. And

is it because they cannot that they compose songs or write poetry? How sad Rabindranath must have felt, how often he must have felt that way, to have composed all those songs. Isn't that so? Will you ask him if you meet him?

How am I? I am well. What am I doing? Nothing at all. I mean, what I'm doing can hardly be given a name. And as for what's known as doing something, do you suppose I'm capable of that?

Swati

As soon as she put it in the post the next day, Swati started hoping for a reply. Would he write again? It was almost time for him to come back. But if that *was* so, why did I have to write either? She hadn't written because she needed to say something—there was no news to give either—why, then? For what?

As she nursed her cup of tea the next morning, Swati thought: my letter has reached by now. As soon as the thought occurred to her, she imagined Satyen-babu opening the envelope to read her letter, embarrassing herself so much that she lowered her eyes at once, looking at her teacup for a long time lest her eldest sister ask what the matter was. And the next day she wondered whether the reply to her letter would arrive that very day.

The reply didn't arrive—Satyen Roy himself arrived.

It was eleven in the morning. Done with the cooking, Shweta was chasing two of her children for their baths—they were jumping up and down before the mirror, shrieking at the top of their voices—apparently they were singing and dancing! Swati helped her sister collar them, they ran away, Swati gave chase. Entering the drawing room at a run, she saw Satyen Roy standing near the door, smiling.

Swati stopped abruptly, so did the children at the sight of a stranger, Satyen Roy said, 'All well?'

There was a buzzing in Swati's head, she didn't seem to be

able to hear clearly, the burning sensation in her face descended to her neck. She would have run away if she could, but her feet refused to move. Satyen-babu had never seen his student so dishevelled and bewildered—her face cherry red, beads of sweat on her lips, small strands of hair plastered to her forehead. Looking at her a while, he spoke again, 'How are you? Well, I hope?'

Swati made up her mind, wound the end of her sari round herself, stood up erect and raised her face. With an effort, she said, 'When did you get back?'

'Last night.'

Swati didn't feel like talking after that. Having slept all night, lazed all morning, dressed up after that, at last he had found the time.

'Tata . . . Chhoton . . .' Shweta appeared, calling her children by their names. 'Here you are—the two of you just drive me up the wall . . .' She stopped suddenly, taken aback.

'This is my eldest sister,' Swati had to speak finally, 'and this . . . this is Satyen-babu, a professor at our college.'

The professor greeted her with bowed head—he bowed it a little too deeply. A wave of irritation swept over Swati.

'What's this, Swati,' Shweta smiled faintly, covering her head with her sari. 'You haven't even asked him to take a seat.'

'No, no, I'm not going to—I was going out, thought I'd—besides, it's lunchtime for you,' Satyen-babu said, looking at Shweta.

Oh, he was going out! So, on the way to the tram-stop he thought he'd . . .! Back in Calcutta after one and a half months, the first thing he must do is to roam around town and meet his friends, mustn't he? Why would he be happy unless he had met that feet-up-on-the-table Dhruba Datta—there was no one else worth having a conversation with!

'The things you do!' Shweta said, entering. 'Just like that he left—couldn't you stop him!'

'What do you mean just like that?' Swati's voice was acerbic.

'But he was visiting after the Pujas . . . Some sweets or something . . .'

'Hmmph!' Swati jerked her head. 'As if he could be bothered to have your sweets! He's happily off to meet his friends after lunch!'

Shweta couldn't help but laugh at what Swati was saying, at her tone. A little later she said, 'Your professor is almost a child!'

'What did you think?'

'He was the one who wrote to you?'

'Yes.' Swati fidgeted a little before going off for her bath. The restlessness did not lessen afterwards; the day passed like the smoke from a stove before it actually starts burning. As if I'm even worth being considered a person, as if my letter means anything, as if he feels the need to talk about what was in it! When he wrote, his feelings were overflowing. Chhordi was right—why did he have to write me a letter brimming with feelings—but it wasn't really for me, it could have been sent to absolutely anyone—no harm publishing it in a magazine either, it didn't even need a letter! I'm stupid too—I actually replied—I shouldn't have posted it. Or had he not received it? Let that be so, oh God, let that be so. But how will I know whether he got it or not?

In the evening Shweta said, 'Baba, I'm arranging dinner tomorrow.'

'You've arranged every meal this past month,' Rajen-babu's face turned tragic as he tried to smile. 'You haven't let up on your cooking even for a day.'

'If she hasn't yet for a day, then why let it happen even for a day.' Pramathesh guffawed. 'And tomorrow's the last day, after all.'

'Actually, I should be the one throwing a farewell party for all of you.' Rajen-babu looked timidly at his son-in-law.

'Of course not—since your daughter wants to . . .' Pramathesh immediately started preparing the menu verbally—if he could he'd go shopping straightaway.

'Really, Pramathesh's energy!' Rajen-babu smiled. 'If your professor had returned while Shweta was still here, you could have invited him too...'

'But he came today!' Shweta exclaimed.

'No, Baba, no!' Swati raised both hands in protest.

'Why not? I'd been thinking for a long time—such a nice boy...' Rajen-babu looked at Shweta as he finished. 'Besides, he lives by himself.'

'Alone? Why?' asked Shweta.

'I don't know why, but I don't see anyone else there,' Rajen-babu answered.

'Not married!' Shweta was stunned. 'A graduate with a job, and not married!'

Rajen-babu laughed loudly at this. Widening his eyes, Pramathesh said, 'Your daughter... What can I say... The moment she hears someone isn't married she can't restrain herself—she's become quite a famous matchmaker already.'

'Naturally!' Rajen-babu smiled covertly. 'When you're happy yourself you want others to be...'

'The things Baba says!' Shweta looked away.

'Come along, Swati,' Rajen-babu took the initiative the next morning. 'Let's go invite your professor.'

'I'm not going!'

'Come along, now...'

'Why, can't you go by yourself?'

'You come too.'

'No! I don't even know why you want to invite him!'

After a brief silence, Rajen-babu said, 'What's the matter with you, Swati?'

His daughter bowed her head at once. But she didn't answer.

'Why are you so annoyed?'

Swati didn't reply this time either.

'Never mind, I'll go by myself.' Rajen-babu dressed and went out slowly, and saw Swati by his side the moment he reached the road.

'Same sari . . .?'

'So what?' Swati smiled. 'It's quite a nice sari.'

'You order me around so much, but look at you.'

'What do you mean?'

'Don't you even comb your hair in the morning?'

'It's fine.' With her hand Swati brushed the hair off her forehead.

Satyen-babu was half-sitting, half-lying in his easy chair with the newspaper. His pose signalled so much of comfort, so much of a reclining indolence that the moment she saw it, Swati's head began to buzz with irritation. And as soon as he saw them, Satyen-babu rose, and remained standing in a deferential, almost servile, pose, instead of reducing her irritation, this only aggravated it.

'We came to tell you something . . .' Rajen-babu skipped the preamble. 'Our house this evening—er . . . You must stay for dinner, of course . . .'

Her father, honestly. If only he could say things properly!

'Of course . . . of course . . . of course . . .' After three 'of courses', the professor suddenly discovered other words. 'But . . . what's the occasion?'

'Nothing. Just, you know.'

'Nothing?' Satyen-babu looked at them with the hope of getting some information.

However, Rajen-babu disappointed him: 'No occasion at all.'

'No . . . er . . .' Suddenly Satyen-babu turned to Swati, speaking in a completely different tone. 'Oh yes! Your letter . . .'

Her heart jumped.

'. . . came last night. They had forwarded it. Fortunately.'

Fortunately? If only . . .

'Your daughter writes very well,' the professor turned to the father.

Very well. Was this an exam paper? Swati wanted to tear that accursed letter to shreds before his very eyes. Can you ask for a letter back?'

The outcome was that the fun of that evening was soured for Swati. She lay on her bed, wandered around the house, sat with Saswati for a bit, getting up in a moment to chat with Ata and Tata, she couldn't concentrate on anything. When Satyen Roy came, Rajen-babu welcomed him ceremoniously, then, looking for Swati, he said when he found her, 'Satyen's here, Swati . . .'

'So what can I do?'

'What do you . . .?' Rajen-babu couldn't find any more words.

'Is he all alone?' Pramathesh became anxious. 'In that case . . . All right, I'd better go and talk to him . . .'

'A *panjabi*, Jamaibabu,' Swati shouted softly.

'This will do fine . . .' Pramathesh's round belly wobbled under his vest as he laughed.

'No, never.' Trying to keep her voice down, Swati sounded tearful.

'Where will I now get a . . .'

'Never mind then.' Without looking at anyone else, Swati stomped off to the drawing room.

Calm, composed, immaculate, Satyen Roy was sitting on a chair by the window. Smiling at her, he said, 'Well, Swati, are you still feeling sad?'

Silently, Swati bowed her head.

'I could not present your question to Rabindranath, but he may have written the answer into his songs—see if you can find it,' said Satyen Roy, extending a brown paper package towards her.

'What's this?'

'*Gitabitan*,' he answered. 'His songs are not just meant to be heard, but also to be read with care.'

Still standing, Swati unwrapped the package to extract two volumes of *Gitabitan*. Inscribed inside were the words: 'To Swati—Satyen Roy'.

'Why did you get me these?' The question sounded as though she was demanding justification.

'Why do you suppose. For you to read.' Satyen Roy continued after a pause, 'You could think of it as a birthday gift too.'

'Birthday!' Swati laughed in surprise.

'It isn't? But it could have been, couldn't it?'

'How strange! Is *that* what you thought?'

'So what if it isn't your birthday—it's nice to get new books at any time. Especially books such as these.'

Then Pramathesh entered, in no less than a silk *panjabi* with gold buttons, and immediately Harit came in too from the street, in a bright red tie with a light blue shirt. Swati introduced them to one another; Pramathesh offered a gratified smile in response to Satyen Roy's greeting, and Harit raised a hand to his forehead, like a sword pulled out of its scabbard. 'How much longer before dinner?' he asked, sitting down.

Jiggling his knee, Pramathesh said, 'But you only just got here, already—'

'What does one do, so many responsibilities!' A superior smile appeared on Harit's lips. 'Bengalis spend so much time feasting and hosting, when do they have the time for work!' Harit looked at Satyen Roy, though it wasn't clear whether it was in the hope of support or to educate the harmless-looking teacher.

'I've heard it's worse with the Chinese.'

'That's why China is in the state that it's in. Japan is tearing it apart. But finally they have become wiser after the hiding they got—now they've even learnt to go to war themselves.'

'Does wisdom always lead to war?' asked the unintelligent Pramathesh.

Harit settled down in his chair. No, it was just no use talking to fools—wasted your time, spoilt your mood. But this was Saswati's family—couldn't avoid them either—such a problem!

'When the Chinese used to cook for six hours and eat for two,' Satyen said softly, 'they did write very good poetry.'

'Poetry!' Harit reared backwards like a stallion. 'Putting your feet up and tasting Chinese poetry may not be a bad experience, but was it able to save China and its billions of people?'

'It does appear it could not save everyone,' Satyen Roy agreed. 'I heard from Nandalal Bose in Santiniketan this time that young Chinese men in leather coats place their old landscape paintings on the floor and stomp on them till they crumble to pieces.'

'They're right. What use are all those paintings. Here . . .' Harit reached out to grab one of the volumes of *Gitabitan* from the table—Swati felt a cat had just pounced on a mouse— 'what use is Rabindranath either?'

'What do you mean?' Swati couldn't help saying. 'What's wrong with Rabindranath?'

'What's wrong,' Harit had a ready answer, 'is that no one can become a warrior because of his poetry. Finally he has realized his own mistake—this is what he wrote recently . . .' He chanted the words like running prose in a monotone, eliminating all punctuation: '*Shantir baani shonaibe byartho porihaash, bidaayer aagey daak diye jaai daanober shathey jaara shongraamer tawrey prostoot hotechhey ghawrey ghawrey.*' The cry for peace shall mock in futility, ere I leave I call upon those in every home who prepare for battle with the monster.

Overcoming the kind of shudder brought about by biting on a stone inside a fruit, Satyen said, 'I think it's *shantir lolito baani* and *bidaay nebaar aagey taai . . .*' The sweet call of peace and hence ere I leave.

'It's one and the same. The fact is that all that business of peace will achieve nothing now—we need war now—war!' said Harit, boldly knocking his pipe on the handle of the chair.

Pramathesh's mouth had been falling open wider and wider as Harit spoke, sighing, he said, 'But war is inevitable!'

'This is nothing! Japan the predator is lying in wait . . .'
Harit would have said more, but Pramathesh suddenly remarked
independently, 'Russia too . . . Apparently Finland has also
been massacred—is that true?'

'You have to do these things in self-defence,' Harit became
very serious. 'What would you do if your home were to be
attacked by robbers?'

Pramathesh simply couldn't understand just when Finland had
tried to commit robbery in Russia. But he had no idea—he
wasn't very well informed, didn't understand much either. And
why did people have to go to war anyway, why not live together
happily. He couldn't help speaking his mind, 'Whatever you may
say, war's a terrible thing. Humans killing humans, bah!'

To Harit the 'bah' sounded like 'baa'. Nothing but sheep,
the whole lot of them. The professor seemed to be part of
the flock too—let's see. He resumed the argument with Satyen:
'What do you think? If art isn't going to be a weapon now,
what good is it?'

'For what?' Satyen Roy asked with trepidation.

'For what! For breaking chains, obviously.'

'What chains?'

'Chains of hunger, of misery, of slavery!' Harit smiled
contemptuously at having to explain in such detail.

'Hunger, misery, slavery—what do you mean?'

'Mean?' Harit hadn't expected this question, but taking the
catch like a champion, he lobbed the ball back immediately.
'Can one explain the meaning in words? If someone were to truss
you up and abandon you to darkness, forcing you to starve day
after day, maybe you'd understand then?' Harit tried to smile
pleasantly—that would have lent more edge to his banter—but
he didn't quite succeed, his smile emerging as a snort and a snarl.

Intimidated by this angry noise, Satyen stammered, 'Oh,
you're talking of food and clothing. I thought you were
talking of art.'

'Yes, food and clothing!' Harit roared now. 'That is exactly what people want—food and clothing, work, rest, shelter, a wife. And those who don't get any of that are becoming extremely insolent these days, they're making too much noise all around the world—the sages are about to have their meditation rudely disturbed.' Concluding, Harit looked around with glittering eyes, as though he wanted to say, 'So?'

But the professor offered no response. He didn't have one, obviously! Harit took a quick look at Pramathesh's and Swati's faces—both looked dispirited. His barbs had obviously worked. When the call for dinner came a little later, he was the first one to stand, saying quite suavely, 'Come, Satyen-babu.' Having succeeded in nudging them from the darkness towards light, even if only a little, he was quite pleased with himself, besides, the conversation had whetted his appetite.

Harit and Saswati left immediately after dinner; Satyen stayed for a while. When leaving, he bid goodbye repeatedly to Shweta. 'You're leaving tomorrow? So soon!'

'We are, yes.'

'But you're going as soon as I came back.'

'At least we met—that was nice.'

After a silence, Satyen said very gently, 'Is there no way you can stay a little longer?'

'We'll be back,' Shweta smiled.

'You will, won't you?' Satyen seemed unable to tear his eyes away from Shweta.

'Such a nice boy,' Shweta said to her father after Satyen left.

'Anyone who's had even a single one of your meals, Shweta,' Rajen-babu smiled, 'can never forget you.'

'Doesn't he have any family?'

Swati didn't quite like that; she said derisively, 'Oh, please—a grown-up male—what does he need anyone for.'

'But didn't you say he has no parents or brothers of sisters?'

'That doesn't mean no one, does it?'

'Poor thing,' Shweta didn't register this last remark of Swati's. 'At least he got a taste of a home here with us. Being a man—so many battles to be fought all day—but you need a home at the end of the day, after all.'

Suddenly putting her arms around Shweta, Swati said, 'Don't go, Bordi.'

Shweta put her hand on her sister's head.

'No, don't go—really . . .' she choked, trembling with her face hidden in her sister's shoulder.

'What! Are you crying? Silly girl!' Shweta gave her sister's head a shake, looking at her tearful eyes, she said, 'How silly! What are you crying for . . . Come along, come to bed now.' As she rose, she put her arm around Swati's waist to pull her to her feet, continuing, 'It's so easy for you to start crying—have you ever thought how it makes me feel? Stop now, or I'm going to start crying too.' She made such a comical face that Swati laughed through her moist eyes.

She went to bed alongside her sister that night, talking in whispers till she fell asleep—as though she had never slept in such comfort for ages—she awoke late the next morning, Shweta was already busy with the packing. Swati went to work too, gathering the children's clothes and shoes scattered all over the house, kneeling on the floor to fold the saris. Shweta was taking back a lot more than she had brought—so many new clothes had been bought—Pramathesh had been clever enough to buy the children's winter clothes too—but fitting them all in was proving to be a problem now. The big suitcase was so stuffed the lock simply couldn't be put on it; the sisters pressed down on either side to shut the lid, but as soon as they tried to put the lock in place, it snapped open and they laughed in unison, eventually Swati sat on the suitcase, and the sisters tried again, but the lid was very disobedient, and the more its recalcitrance, the more fun Shweta and Swati seemed to have. Meanwhile Rajen-babu arrived with a large cardboard box, putting it down carefully near Shweta and settling down lightly on the bed, at a distance.

Sitting on the floor, one knee drawn up, her chin resting on it, Shweta slowly pulled out alta, sindoor, powder, cologne, hair oil, hairpins, ribbons, soap, cream, and a box of *deem*-shondesh. Gazing at them without a word, she ran her fingers lovingly over each of them before putting it all back in the same box, retying it with the same string, and then raised her eyes towards her father. Rajen-babu disappeared into the other room.

The day became topsy-turvy after that. Rajen-babu went to office, came back from office—no one knew where the time in between went, no one could tell, the train of the day raced from its starting point to its destination. Saswati came, there was some laughter and conversation, there seemed to be extra laughter that day—and between it all Shweta was reminded of a hundred things to be done, Anukul ran to the shops repeatedly, the gasping suitcase was reopened two or three times, Biju came up with his sleeves rolled when it was time to pack the hold-all, Pramathesh abandoned all hope of a nap and maintained a steady diet of paan and jarda. Suddenly the packing was complete, two cases full of food stood by a pitcher of water slotted into a wooden platform, the children, smartly dressed, walked around in their new shoes, their heels clicking. Rajen-babu came up to Shweta, 'Is this any time to make paan? Get up, it's time.'

'Swati, paan for Baba . . .'

'What am I going to do with so much,' Rajen-babu said. 'Take some more for Pramathesh, on the way . . .'

'I've taken enough for him.'

Shweta rose, went for a bath and, putting on a maroon handloom sari—it wouldn't look dirty during the journey—

helped Saswati with her sindoor, did her own, then sat down on the veranda steps.

Saswati said, 'What are these sandals you've got on, Bordi, didn't Baba get you a new pair the other day?'

'As if I'm going to spoil those lovely red sandals on a train journey. What's wrong with these—they're quite nice.'

'Shweta,' Rajen-babu twinkled with laughter, 'do you still like to go to bed with new shoes?'

'Even if I wanted to, do you suppose that daughter of mine would let me! She destroys all my shoes!'

Pramathesh cleared his throat, 'Biju, now . . . a taxi . . . No, two—Saswati will come to the station too, you'll take her back home, won't you?'

'Of course!' Biju left swiftly.

'Isn't Harit coming?' asked Shweta.

'He was supposed to . . .' Saswati said faintly.

'He doesn't get enough time—he has so many things to do, and how well he talks, excellent!' Pramathesh nodded in appreciation. 'Not like us, lazy and fat.'

'Baba, Satyen didn't come at all today . . .'

'He doesn't come very often—once in a while . . .'

'Really? Doesn't he stay close by? But he's so shy . . . It would be so nice if he visited us. Tell him, Swati. All right?'

'Aren't you coming, Swati?' asked Saswati.

Swati had been sitting quietly, her cheeks cupped in her hands, she asked, startled, 'Where?'

'Aren't you coming to the station with us?'

Swati shook her head.

'Why not, come, do.'

'N-n-no . . .'

Biju arrived, announcing in a baritone, 'The taxis are here.' Suddenly everyone fell silent, and exactly at that moment, as it were, evening descended on earth. Swati felt just like she had that day when she received Satyen Roy's letter, and saw the glittering, glistening evening star, it was that same heartbreaking evening, grey, permeated with shadows, misty with fog, the same unbearable heaviness of parting filling the earth and the sky. Silently two servants loaded the luggage, silently Rajen-babu made a survey to ensure everything had been loaded, he did a round of the rooms—nothing important had been left behind, had it?—the shadows spread, deepened, and like a shadow Swati saw Shweta say goodbye to her father, so did Pramathesh, panting at the effort, leaning on his cane, then Shweta came up and put her hand on Swati's back, touched her cheek to Swati's; everyone walked slowly to the side of the road, about to get into the taxi, Pramathesh turned towards her suddenly, saying, 'Swati, we're going now . . . We haven't enjoyed ourselves so much in a long time, don't know when we'll be back next, we're going now, all right?' He smiled, the smile was far too silly.

A little later, in that empty, stilled, dead house, Rajen-babu came up to Swati and and sat near her. 'Why are you crying, Swati?'

On her stomach, her pillow clenched between her teeth, Swati heaved.

'Don't cry any more. There's a good girl, my lovely Swati, no more tears now.'

But Swati's tears just did not stop. How would they? Who was it who had left? Bordi? No, no, I, I—Swati screamed at the top of her voice in her head—this is me; the one who leaves every evening making the skies weep is me; the one who gets off the train at the tiny station by the empty field in the shadowy darkness is me too! I shan't go, Baba; I shan't go, Baba! But who was listening, and why could she not say it with conviction? And because she couldn't, more tears flowed.

'Swati . . . Swati . . . my Swati . . .'

Swati didn't open her eyes, didn't raise her face. Her father gazed at his daughter's round fair arms wrapped around the pillow, at her back as it shook, the black hair billowing over it . . . So she has sorrows even I cannot understand, so she has tears even I cannot staunch. He sat by her side in silence, not calling to her any more, not moving, not touching her; he recalled a hundred different things, so much came to mind. Not a sound was to be heard anywhere, gusts of tears from Swati's breast swirled up inside the silent, heartbroken house, and through the window, from time to time, coiled-up streams of cold air brought forth the first shivers of winter on the body.

3

Winter arrived, filling the world with melancholy. Such forlorn, colour-shredded evenings, and tiny short-lived afternoons—thin, narrow, apprehensive, existing for a flash before vanishing into the darkness. Just the other day the late afternoon had held so many colours—violet and brown and green, yellow and green and golden; some days the evening seemed to be an ocean of pink, fragments of cloud, golden trees, and the golden grass, golden trees on the surface of the ocean—now, everything had vanished. Twilight's vermilion gown became mousy brown, the sky resembled a widow's brow.

Jingling, tingling, winter came, and Swati saw it come, all by herself. It came a little closer every day, the closer it came, the better it became, the more it could be loved; the melancholy dropped away slowly under the cold wind, like one leaf falling at a time from the tree; the cold water brought peace, and after the morning bath the soft blue day was like a rare gift that the earth held in its hand. Swati found it astonishing—astonishing because winter, too, was beautiful, the sky was never as calm, the days never as soft—was everything that happened wonderful, then, and was all that existed, beautiful? Did people know just how beautiful? But their faces didn't suggest they did. What kind of faces did you see out on the road, on the tram? Haughty faces, naughty faces, gloomy faces, the young men flippant, some sharp, some stupid, but none of the faces had it written on them that . . . what? Swati's mind halted for a minute, a finger pressed down just once on the logic textbook on the lighted desk of the evening, and then she saw before her eyes Satyen Roy's face—the grace in it. The first time she had seen him, she hadn't thought of the man as beautiful, it would not have been possible either to think that way—if at all she had thought about it—but yes, definitely beautiful. Whatever was beautiful appeared beautiful to his eyes—and that's why his glance . . .

Someone's hand pressed down on her shoulder, Swati turned with startled, wide eyes. Smiling, Saswati said, 'My goodness! What *were* you thinking of, lost to the world?'

Swati stood up. 'When did you come?'

'Just now, and will go just now, too!'

Flashing a look at her, all dressed up, Swati asked, 'Are you invited somewhere?'

'To meet the royal family of Pirozepore.' After a pause. 'Lots of people, we won't be leaving for some time, so I thought of a quick visit. It's close by.' She shifted, displaying the lustre of her sari under the electric lights. Since Swati didn't say anything, she added, 'That big pink house on Southern Avenue!'

Swati felt bad about disappointing her; she pretended to know where the royal residence of Pirozepore was on Southern Avenue. 'Hasn't Harit-da come with you?' she asked.

'No—he's deep in conversation with them! The king's son is a friend of . . . Harit's.' With only a little effort, Saswati pronounced her husband's name quite easily. 'They met in England. After five years there, followed by a tour of America, China and Japan, Makaranda Mukherjee got back just the other day. You won't believe . . .' Pleasure was reflected in every fold on her face, 'so incredibly rich, and yet so courteous!'

Thinking about this a little, Swati said, 'Are rich men never courteous?'

Without paying any attention, or maybe without registering what Swati had said, Saswati passed on important news, 'Japan will definitely join the war!'

'Really?'

'We don't have any hope if they do.' Lowering her voice, almost whispering in Swati's voice, Saswati said, 'The Japanese are ve-e-e-ry evil!'

'Really?' said Swati again.

'We're usually kept in the dark, do you know what's going on in China . . .' Saswati regurgitated all that she'd just heard from the prince of Pirozepore while it was still hot, and Swati heard Harit speak—even the pronunciation was similar. She gazed at Saswati—she was quite plump now, very fair, pink, everyone would call her pretty, but beautiful?

'What?' Saswati suddenly became self-conscious as she was describing the Japanese beast. 'What are you looking at? The necklace?' Pleased, but in an embarrassed manner, she lowered her eyes towards her throat, two clear creases appearing in her neck. 'But you've seen this before—my father-in-law gave it to me at my wedding . . .' Saswati touched the red noose studded with thick discs. 'Beautiful, isn't it?'

'What does "beautiful" mean, Chhordi?' Swati asked faintly.

'Oh no!' Saswati burst out in laughter like men do. 'You're becoming too much of a thinker by the day. Of course, some girls do get that way at your age—but they are cured too . . .' laughter sparkled in her eyes, purely feminine laughter this time, 'when the time is right.'

Saswati left after chatting with her father for a few minutes. Rajen-babu walked with her till the gates of the royal residence, so did Swati. On the way back, she said, 'Baba, shall we sit by the Lakes for a bit?'

'Fine.'

It was the fortnight leading up to the new moon, and cold to boot, there weren't many people by the lake, although not as few as there might have been. Not a single bench was empty. After wandering around a bit, Swati said, 'Come, Baba, let's sit on the grass.' She hadn't stepped out of the house at all for the past few days, now that she had, she was enjoying being under the open sky.

Slipping his foot out of his shoes to test the grass, Rajen-babu said, 'No, Swati . . .'

Someone stood up from a bench by the water suddenly and said, 'Why don't you sit here.'

'Oh it's you . . .!' Swati exclaimed, perhaps a little loudly.

'Sit down, Swati.' Satyen Roy spoke as though this were his drawing room and Swati, a guest.

Swati sat on one end of the bench, settling himself next to her Rajen-babu said, 'All of us can fit in.'

'Of course,' said Satyen Roy, occupying the other end.

Resting her elbow on her knee and her chin on her hand, Swati asked, looking straight ahead, 'You and the Lakes?'

'Am I not allowed here?'

'But everyone else comes to the Lakes.'

'And so?'

'You'd said you don't like coming here because everyone else does.'

'When did I say that?'

Swati wasn't sure whether Satyen Roy had indeed said such a thing, or whether she had assumed at that very moment that he had. And in that silence he said, 'But just as well I did—or else I wouldn't have met you,' and leaned back, erect, on the bench.

Rubbish! If he really wanted to meet her it was so easy—he stayed only a couple of minutes away. Many thoughts bubbled up within Swati but she couldn't very well reveal them, could she. You spend your whole life hiding the truth. Without moving her hand from her chin, her elbow stiffening on her knee, her back aching, Swati gazed at the water twinkling under the starlight, at some places the electric lights seemed to be skimming the black water, but the water refused to flow, and so everything seemed half-dead. So much water, an island packed with trees in the middle, a small bridge in the distance; and yet it all seemed artificial, contrived, not natural—but then artificial things were bound to appear artificial. Was everything artificial just like this, and everything natural, beautiful? But poetry was artificial too, yet it didn't *seem* artificial, did it?

Sitting up straight and looking at the professor over her father's back, Swati said, 'Have you ever seen a lake?'

'I'm seeing one now.'

'No, a real lake?'

'I've seen that too.'

'What's it like?'

'What's it like?' Satyen Roy raised his face, it appeared he would provide a detailed description, that he was composing it in his mind, but although she was all ears for a couple of minutes, Swati didn't hear him say anything. She was just beginning to feel disconcerted—just as a boy feels when he has said something with utter solemnity at a gathering of older people only to feel foolish a little later—when, as though after a great deal of thought, Satyen Roy said softly, 'Everything on earth is beautiful.'

Swati leaned back again, as though she hadn't even heard, turning her head she tried to think of the island in the distance as an enormous mountain and the dense darkness of the clumps of trees as an impenetrable jungle, the headlights of a car lit up her face suddenly, she covered her eyes, but it hadn't been necessary, the light had moved away immediately.

In the silence Rajen-babu sneezed loudly. Wiping his lips with the back of his hand, he said, 'Shall we go now? It's quite chilly.'

'Yes, Baba, let's go.' Swati rose, standing with her back to the water, and Satyen Roy's eyes gradually moved from the water and air behind her to her face.

Seeming to shiver a little in the chilly wind, Swati suddenly asked, 'Tell me, what does "beautiful" mean?'

After a short silence, the professor answered, with a hint of laughter in his voice, very softly, 'Never mind all that now, you have exams coming up.' Then he rose too, facing Rajen-babu. 'I wonder why they allow cars on the roads by the lake!'

Swati didn't say another word on the way back; suddenly she felt exhausted; exhausted, empty, unsure.

All right then, might as well prepare for the Intermediate exams. The college closed in January, after which there was little else to do but study. But how much was there to study, anyway? She spent the rest of the time reading other books of all kinds, trying to decide during lunch which of her unfinished books to resume reading with her back to the sun, there would never be any lack of books so long as Satyen Roy was there. As she read, the sun shifted from her back to her face, she rotated her cane chair to keep pace with this movement, then, when the sunlight no longer flooded the room but the warmth remained, the printed letters began to jostle with one another before her eyes, she nodded off intermittently, but reopened her eyes wide at once to leave the world of imagination behind and look outside—the narrow road in front of the house was empty, not a sound was to be heard, only the golden sunlight of the winter afternoon and the sapling planted by the corporation played with each other.

At just such an hour one afternoon, Biju turned up to ask, 'What're you doing, Swati?'

Pleased to see her brother, Swati smiled, 'What do you suppose.'

'You seem to read novels all day. What about studies?'

'Those too.'

'Nobody but you knows just what you read.'

'How can anyone else know—and why do they even need to know.'

'Oh-ho, it's one thing to just read, another to study for exams,' Bijon spoke from his experience of double failure.

'You must know if you're doing it right. And you have an advantage.'

'What advantage?'

'You can request Satyen-babu to—'

'Oh no!' Swati interrupted him. 'I couldn't possibly ask him to . . .'

'Why? As a professor, his job is to help people pass exams, isn't it? Why, he could even tell you what questions will be asked.'

'What! Does anyone give away exam questions?'

'Don't they!' Bijon laughed contemptuously. 'All the time! Both times during the matric exams I had got to know the topic of the essay—'

'Did it help?'

'Of course, you must *know* the questions to give them away. Satyen Roy is a junior professor—how would he know.'

'I like the colour of your shirt,' Swati changed the subject.

'You do?' Bijon looked down at his shirt, then said dismissively, 'Got a few new shirts made. The first requirement for bagging business deals is to dress flashily.'

Glancing at his light grey trousers and black-and-white two-toned shoes, Swati wanted to know, 'Does flashy dressing automatically bring in business?'

'You'll see,' Bijon let out a mouthful of smoke. Wandering round the room, he suddenly stopped before his sister. 'Will you ask Satyen Roy if he can draft a couple of letters for me? You know my English isn't all that—'

'Job applications?'

'Of course not, why should I apply for jobs? These are business letters. Have to write to the government, you see, so it needs a little . . . Will you ask Satyen Roy?'

'I can't ask him.'

This was the answer Bijon had been expecting, and he had decided beforehand not to be angry. 'Never mind,' he said at once, 'I'll manage. He may be very learned, but what does he know of commercial correspondence, after all? How do you spell commission, Swati?'

Swati laughed, covering her face with the end of her sari.

'What're you laughing at?' Putting his hands in his pockets, Bijon thrust his chest out. 'Very troublesome word. All that memorization of commission and omission, but what's the use? One M, two S-es, right? Or is it one S, two Ms?'

But then, people with work to do were not to be put off by issues of spelling. In just a few days, an impressive letter box was visible beside the front door, written on it, in white capital letters, was the name B. JOHN & CO.

Rajen-babu was flabbergasted at the sight. Had someone rented his house without his knowledge? He asked Swati, 'What's going on?'

'What?'

'Whose letter box is that?'

'Whose do you suppose. Ours, of course. Dada's put it up.'

'But it has some company's name on it.'

'Oh my God! You didn't understand? B. John—meaning Bijon.'

'Oh! Hahaha!' Rajen-babu burst out laughing. He hadn't laughed so loudly or so long in many years.

'But it's not a bad plan at all,' Swati defended her brother.

'Yes, very clever! And a company too!' Rajen-babu threw his head back and laughed.

Swati said, 'Dada is *definitely* doing something—what a lovely letterhead he's had printed, in black and green—and bills and so many other things . . .'

'Well organized, I see.'

Swati's eyes shared a laugh with her father, but she said, 'There's nothing to laugh at—do you know, letters have started arriving for B. John & Co., in a khaki envelope, one of them even had OHMS printed on it, do you know?'

'Good.'

After some thought, Swati continued, 'Dada must be doing something useful now—he's earning a lot too.'

'Did he tell you?'

'He doesn't have to—you can make out. So many new clothes, and I can't tell you how many razor blades he's buying, Baba.'

'What did you say? Buying blades!'

'So-o-o-o many! Enough to fill a biscuit tin!'

The laughter was now replaced by creases on the forehead. Had the boy finally gone mad! Or was Swati mistaken? 'Have you seen the blades?' Rajen-babu asked.

'He keeps them hidden beneath his clothes in the suitcase—he was counting them the other day when I went into his room. "What on earth are you going to do with so many blades?" I asked. "I'm collecting blades. Soon they won't be available any more." He started laughing . . . Is that true, Baba, are blades really not going to be at all available? Will everyone have to grow a beard? God, how awful!'

The creases on the forehead deepened, the face paled. After a minute's silence, he said to himself, 'Where's the money coming from?'

'Didn't I tell you,' Swati tried to allay his fear, 'he's earning a lot of money. He asked me, "Guess how much these blades are worth." I mentioned the highest figure I could think of—twenty-five? He burst out laughing. "I already have two hundred rupees worth of blades, I'm going to buy more." Can anyone buy two hundred rupees worth of blades unless they have a lot of money! But just as well—when they're out of stock, we can give blades to everyone we know. . .' As she spoke, the bluish tinge on Satyen Roy's clean-shaven cheeks swam up before her eyes—'You're not listening to me, Baba' she said, nudging him.

'Oh yes! I *was* very worried!' Rajen-babu smiled at his daughter.

But, secretly, he began looking for an opportunity to talk to Biju. When the father was home, the son usually was not, which meant it took a long time for the opportunity to present itself. And because it took time, Rajen-babu's anxiety did mount, but somewhere deep within he was also relieved—the moment he asked a question, Biju was certain to get into a confrontation and shout, and if Swati happened to say something, that would be it—he would get nasty with her. And yet how can I not ask, I must find out whose money he's using for all this reckless behaviour.

Next Sunday, they ran into each other in the afternoon. As Bijon came into Swati's room, saying, 'What do you think of my new suit . . .' he found not her but his father on the chair, writing up expenses, glasses perched on his nose. He stopped in his tracks.

For a moment, Rajen-babu thought, not now. But immediately he gathered his willpower—lowering his pencil, clearing his throat, reddening a little—and said, 'Biju, I wanted to ask . . .'

'Me?' Biju walked up to him confidently, not letting him realize how much effort had gone into this casual response.

Rajen-babu looked through his lifeless, old man's eyes at the fashionable young man in a shining navy blue suit. Then he mumbled, 'The thing is . . . er . . . What are you doing these days . . . ?'

'Oh, please!' Bijon made a stifled sound of impatience, he would have to hear an entire litany now! It was better to make a clean breast of everything—as much as was possible, at any rate. Summoning a smile to his lips, he said clearly, 'I've got a break in my business, Baba—B. John & Co. will do well. Mark my words.'

'Who else is in your company?'

'No one else—just me. Many people want to become partners, of course, they make a lot of tall claims, but they can't fool me! I can do it by myself—I *will* do it by myself.'

'What can you do? What will you do?'

Bijon chuckled. 'Have you forgotten, Baba, that there's a war on?'

Rajen-babu was somewhat surprised. Had Biju really learnt to talk like this? It was possible—it's been such a long time since I talked with him—and he was hardly a child any more. 'B-b-but,' he stammered, 'the war is even more worrying. These are bad times.'

'Let's see which way it turns out.' Answering the question that sprang up momentarily in his father's eyes, he said, 'Don't worry about all this unnecessarily, Baba. Everything is all right.'

'Where did you get the money?'

'I got some, that's how . . .'

'Where?'

'Someone gave it to me.'

'Who?'

Blinking twice, Biju answered, 'I can't tell you the name.'

Rajen-babu felt his face and ears go red. After a pause, he said, 'How much?'

Bijon didn't answer.

Rajen-babu started taking deep breaths, even coughing in between. Then he said, very softly, 'Forget about all this. Return the money. Get a job.'

'I'm not going to, Baba. And there's no question of returning the money. He hasn't lent it to me—he's given it to me, once and for all.'

Rajen-babu began to pant. Swati came in, planting herself on the bed and saying, 'I've got some vests for you, Baba. All of yours are torn.'

Running two experienced fingers over his sister's purchases, Biju said in a low voice, 'Third rate.'

'I thought so too,' Swati answered quickly. 'This Manohar

Stores is no good, but there's nothing else in the neighbourhood. You go to so many places, can't you get some?'

'I will.' Bijon left without another glance at his father, perhaps a little hastily.

'Dada looks nice in the suit, doesn't he?' said Swati.

Rajen-babu was silent.

'Are the vests really third rate?' Swati said to herself. 'Let me return them then.'

'What?' The protest, Swati felt, was rather too vehement for her father. 'They're very nice! Wonderful! I've never had such nice vests in my life!'

'No, Baba,' Swati shook her head, 'you say too many things to please people! Very annoying! Of course,' she added after some thought, 'you're not wrong either. If you'd bought them yourself you wouldn't have bothered to get anything but the cheapest ones!'

'He works so hard for the family, of course,' glowered Rajen-babu, 'that he is entitled to dismiss others' efforts as third class.'

'Oh God! Is *that* why you're angry with Dada!' Swati's teeth sparkled in the gap between her lips.

'Make a fortune from the war!' Rajen-babu's body quivered. 'Of all the . . .'

Then there were other reasons for his anger? Looking at her father's creased brow, Swati asked, 'What's the matter, Baba?'

'Your brother wants to make a fortune from the war!' Rajen-babu could no longer contain the steam building up within him. 'Don't you see him all suit and style?'

'What of it? It's good to be rich.'

'But who makes a fortune from war? Cheats!' He rose from his chair as he spoke. Swati was astonished at his agitation. 'I saw what happened during the last war, didn't I! All the thieves and scoundrels looted the government treasury.'

'Harit-da says each and every rich man is either a robber

or a thief,' Swati informed her father. 'If not him, then definitely one of his ancestors.' As she spoke she was reminded of what she had heard Saswati say about Makaranda Mukherjee, Harit-da's friend. People said a lot of things, but did that mean they really . . .

'The boy's going to be a thief—a thief!' Rajen-babu choked.

Swati simply could not think of her brother in the navy blue suit and backbrushed hair as a thief. A thief! That was dirty, horrible—policemen frogmarched them on the road with ropes around their waists; small boys clapped and hooted all the way behind them. Was there any other kind of thief? Really, Baba made a mountain out of every molehill! No provocation whatsoever, and suddenly he calls Dada a thief. Thief my foot!

'Where did he get the money?' Rajen-babu muttered to himself.

'What money, Baba?'

'Give me one of those vests, Swati.' Swati was pleased at this, but seeing her father slip on his *panjabi* too, she asked, 'Going out, Baba?'

'Yes, I'll be back in a while.' Without another word, Rajen-babu went out.

∾

He went to Bhowanipore, from Bhowanipore to Ballygunge. Over the next three or four days he covered the other parts of the city—Behala, Moulali, Maniktala—all of them far-flung areas, no mean task! He didn't leave out anyone who could be considered a relative or a friend. Has Biju borrowed any money from you? Have any of you given Biju any money? No. Of course not! Why should Biju take money from us? Why . . . What is it?

Trying to list people he might have omitted, Rajen-babu jumped. Good God! What about Biju's sisters! He should have thought about his own daughters first—but no, he had scoured the entire world instead! Who else would give him money if not his sisters? But which of them? He ruled Saswati out straightaway—Harit was somewhat tight-fisted, and Saswati didn't have the gumption to give the money in secret. Which of the other three? Mahashweta was in Rangoon, Saraswati in Delhi—could something like this have been accomplished at a distance, simply through letters, without my getting to know anything about it? . . . No, this had to be Shweta's doing! Biju must have softened her up when she was here—and she was soft anyway, how much effort did it take to make her melt? Of course! Must be Shweta. Rajen-babu breathed a sigh of relief—thank goodness he hadn't taken the money from or tried to cheat someone outside the immediate family! He would be able to confirm his suspicions with a letter to Shweta, and as soon as he did, he'd return the money.

Rajen-babu wrote to all three daughters. Saraswati was the first to reply. 'Baba, I'm amazed by your letter. Do you think I would ever give Biju money to waste under the pretext of going into business without telling you first? I've been telling you for such a long time now, control him, or he'll get you into all kinds of trouble afterwards. Now see what's happened! Even after this if you don't . . .' This was followed by copious advice and regrets. Mahashweta hadn't been home in years, so she had greater trust in her brother, and obviously she had great faith in enterprise. In a succinct letter she informed her father that she had not given any money, nor had the question arisen, but why all this anxiety, going into business was a good thing—why assume at once that Biju wouldn't succeed—maybe he would. Shweta's letter was the last to arrive, though she lived the closest. 'Sorry for the delay in replying, Baba, these children don't give me a moment to call my own. I haven't given Biju any money—in any case I don't have any of my own. If anyone had to give him money it would have been your son-in-law—when I asked, he said, are you mad! He also said Biju had told him quite a few times that he wanted to go into business, since he *is* inclined that way right now, why not wait and watch? Tell your father, he said, not to work himself into a state over this. I think that's for the best, Baba. You needn't worry so much—we're all here, aren't we?'

Mahashweta's assurances, Saraswati's advice, Shweta's consolation—none of them had any effect, and precisely because it had abated a little, the anxiety now darkened his mind twice as much as before. Where did he get it then? It wasn't a small sum either—all those fancy clothes, and two hundred rupees worth of blades! Who was this wise man who had trusted Biju with all this money? No need to return it either! Let him do whatever he wants to with the money—blow it, burn it, lose it—as long as I can return the money to whoever it was. He hasn't bankrupted some widow somewhere, has he? Is there anyone like that among relatives or people we know? No. The more he worried, the more he lost himself in his worries. It remained like a thorn in his side, puncturing the minutes of leisurely luxury over his paan, shattering the peaceful slumber of his nights.

'Biju,' he said, getting another opportunity, 'just tell me whose money it is and how much. I'm not going to scold you.'

'Why are you worrying so much about this?' asked Biju smilingly.

Why, indeed? Shweta had said the same thing, Mahashweta too. Really, what business *is* it of mine? Rajen-babu was angry with himself when he heard himself say, 'Tell me who it is, I'm going to return the money.'

'I told you it doesn't have to be returned.'

'So what? I'm going to return it anyway.'

'If it has to be returned I'll be the one to do it,' Biju said grimly.

'Please tell me,' his father almost entreated him. 'If I were to die, this task will remain unfinished . . .'

'What nonsense . . .!' Biju said, stifling his words. Then, raising his head to meet his father's eyes, he said, 'I give you my word I'll return his money—many times over. Happy now?'

Indeed! He's giving me his word! Quite the right person for promises. Rajen-babu was agonized by his son's behaviour. He lowered his eyes, as though *he* was the culprit.

He had to abandon all hope of finding out whom his son had performed his first-ever act of sleight of hand on. What option did he have anyway . . . Mocking all his efforts, his letters, his entreaties, the letter box of B. John & Co. continued to stand proudly by the door, not entirely unutilized either—letters were indeed dropped into it from time to time.

∾

By the time Swati's Intermediate exams had ended, Biju had begun to get visitors, some of them even arriving in cars. They called him Mr Mitra, each of them carried cigarette tins, they held closed-door confabulations in low voices. They looked through Rajen-babu, and when they ran into Swati, they displayed extraordinary civility, stepping out of her way with puffed-up chests. These people stalked the lions and tigers of Clive Street, snagging leftovers in the form of other game, and sometimes hunted small beasts on their own. Rajen-babu knew who they were at a glance.

One day he couldn't hold back any longer, telling Swati, 'Let Biju do what he wants to, but why does he allow these scoundrels into the house? Tell him not to.'

'As if he'll listen.'

'If he wants to be in business, let him get an office in the city.' A frown appeared above Rajen-babu's eyes. 'Who has ever heard of having your office at home?'

Swati didn't say anything more then, but as soon as her father returned from office in the evening, she ran up to him, putting her arms around him and saying, 'Ba-a-a-ba!'

'What, Swati? What is it?'

'I have a big surprise for you.'

'Are your results out?' asked her father, recovering his breath.

'So soon! Of course not!'

'There's nothing else I can think of.' Rajen-babu flung himself on the bed without changing out of his clothes.

'Here . . .' Swati ran to her desk, opened her *History of India*, said, 'Where'd it go?' then pulled out the book *Bhanushingher Pawdaboli* from beneath it, and the thin, bluish-green, hundred-rupee note emerged from it immediately Extending it towards her father, she said, 'Here.'

'What is it?'

'Take it. Have a look!'

Rajen-babu looked briefly at his daughter's face, overflowing with happiness, then turned his attention to what she was holding. 'Money? Where did you get that?'

'This is from Dada for you,' Swati forced the note into her father's hand. 'Well? You thought Dada was a good-for-nothing. And now?'

Rajen-babu sat up, the note in his hand. 'Why is it for me?' he asked softly.

'What do you mean? Who else would it be for if not you? He's embarrassed to give it to you himself, so he told me, give this to Baba, all right? He really does love you a lot, Baba.'

'So money is proof of love?'

'Baba, you . . . Really!' Swati couldn't find words to express herself.

After a few moments of silence, Rajen-babu said, 'I don't want to have anything to do with his money. Return it to him—here.'

But Swati didn't stretch her hand out; surprised, she said, 'You won't take it? You're returning it?'

'Tell him to return it to whoever he took the money from.'

Getting off the bed as he spoke, Rajen-babu put the currency note on the desk, placing a book on it.

'Who's he taken money from now?' It sounded like a protest, not a question.

'If I knew that . . .' Pausing suddenly, he said, 'Tell him this. He should return it to the person he borrowed it from.'

Swati had been brimming with hope all day. How pleased Baba would be that Dada wasn't really a good-for-nothing, that he was really concentrating on work now. She had expected him to say, "So Biju really has become a man!" And now, returning the money, her father had poured black ink on that colourful canvas of her imagination. How would Dada feel? He had given the money with so much eagerness.

'Why do you behave this way with Dada all the time, Baba?' Swati couldn't help saying.

'Which way?'

'Like now—when you didn't take the money—if I gave you some money and you didn't take it, do you think I'd ever speak to you again!'

'So you think it'll make a big difference if Biju says "I'll never speak with Baba again!"'

'No, Baba, no!' She herself didn't understand which 'no' she wanted to convert into a 'yes', but a protest rose from within her nevertheless.

'Besides,' said Rajen-babu in a placating tone, 'I don't need money—as long as I live, I can fend for myself.'

'Do you take money only when you need it?'

'Enough now, Miss Know-it-all!' Her father dismissed her argument.

What could she do, Swati had to return the hundred-rupee note to her brother. She broke the news with trepidation, beating around the bush to soften the impact, but how strange! Biju didn't seem heartbroken at all, not even upset, with a smile he put the note back in his leather pocketbook, saying, 'Just as well! . . . Do *you* need some money, Swati?'

'Me? What'll I do with money?' Swati laughed.

'Good! The longer you can do without money, the better it is,' said Bijon, humming happily as he left.

Swati said to herself, 'What kind of a person is he? Honestly, you can't blame Baba. It's Dada who's a bad sort—always been that way, still hasn't changed. His behaviour, the things he says . . . Really!' The more she pondered over this, the angrier she got, but the next day her anger melted, her heart flooded with remorse when Bijon deposited nine or ten bars of chocolate on her desk.

'Nestlé!' Swati screamed in delight. 'Oooh—you don't even get to see these red wrappers these days. Where did you get them, Dada?'

'I have my sources!' Bijon smiled knowingly. 'If there's anything else you need, you just have to tell me.'

Without another word, Swati unwrapped one of the bars, broke off a small bit and put it in her mouth, gradually, she finished an entire bar, all the while feeling a long-forgotten pleasure spreading inside her mouth. Suddenly she said, 'Have some, Dada!'

'No, I don't like all this stuff.'

'I don't all that much either,' Swati said quickly. 'Really, how fond I was of chocolate when I was young. You don't want any, Dada?'

'Have one more.'

'Oh God! I'm so full after just one!' said Swati, unwrapping another bar with two fingers.

Bijon started bringing his sister a gift or two quite regularly—perfume from Paris in an egg-shaped blue box, foreign soap wrapped in rustling tissue in a golden case. Swati had been under the impression you didn't get these any more, and here her brother was asking, how many do you need! Amazing! He's never brought presents for me before—for anyone, in fact.

Baba hadn't taken that money, Biju may not have said anything in as many words, but it must have hurt! Why else would he give me all these. Swati's heart melted at the thought. Then, when news of her results came, on the pretext of a gift Biju gave her a parrot-green sari, and said, handing her two ten-rupee notes, 'Now that you've passed your exams, it's time to spend some money of your own.'

Reddening a little, Swati said, 'So what if I've passed, everyone does.'

'Not everyone—take me,' Bijon smiled affably. 'Do you like the sari?'

'Ve-e-ery nice colour.'

'I don't know anything about saris—Majumdar chose it for me.'

'Who on earth is that?'

'He comes to see me sometimes—tallish . . .'

Swati was silent.

'Majumdar said the colour would suit you very well.'

'What! When has he seen me?'

'Why shouldn't he have seen you, do you live behind a purd—purg—whatever the word is . . . You're not one of those, are you?'

Swati didn't think much of this. She identified Majumdar mentally—she had never seen such highly polished shoes before. 'Why do you let these types into the house? Don't you know Baba doesn't like it either?' The words jumped to Swati's lips, but she stopped herself even as she was about to utter them. Never mind—he'd just got her these gifts, if she straightaway . . . Not now—but she wouldn't spare him if the subject came up again.

Swati spent the twenty rupees on two Scissors dhotis for her father. With the money left over, unable to think of anything else, she bought the new volume of Rabindranath from the local shop. In the evening, she placed the dhotis and the books before her father.

'Here, Baba!' Before he could say anything she explained everything. 'You must wear these dhotis.'

'They're so wide, I'm going to trip over them, Swati.'

'I knew you were going to say that! But what can you do, since your son has given them to you, you must wear them.'

'Is the book for Satyen?'

This question was beyond Swati's imagination. 'Why?' she asked, almost as though she had been slapped.

'Wouldn't that be the right thing to do?'

'What's the use,' Swati said, winding around her fingers the strands of hair on her forehead. 'As if he hasn't read this book already.'

'That shouldn't matter to you; you must do your bit. He has given so many books to you. Now that you've passed your exam, you—'

'But . . .' Swati stopped, apparently without finishing what she had wanted to say.

'How is Satyen?' Rajen-babu asked. 'I haven't met him in a long time.'

'As if I do.'

'Doesn't he come ever?'

'Ha-a-ardly!' Swati said in a laughing tone. 'He came twice after the exams—no, thrice.'

'Ask him to dinner one of these days.'

'That's all you know of, Baba. Dinner. Lunch. He doesn't have time for all that—doesn't like it either!'

'Didn't look that way the night Shweta was here . . . You'd better learn these things now—having people over for meals . . . looking after them . . .'

'I don't know how to do all that!'

'You will, you will.' Tenderly, Rajen-babu's eyes touched Swati.

Bordi had said the same thing. I will? I will too? Like Bordi, like Ma? . . . My memories of Ma seem to be fading more and more—is it the same with Baba? Baba never speaks about Ma, but doesn't that silence actually speak volumes? But then, does Baba really never speak of Ma, or is everything he says actually about Ma in some way? 'Ask him to dinner . . .' Had Ma been here he wouldn't even have had to say it. Images from her childhood came to mind. So many relatives from all sides of the family, so many of Baba's friends with their wives, so much of cooking, feasting, laughter, conversations, joy—Shweta had brought back that same atmosphere of her childhood. She left—and her father's solitude returned—after her mother's death they had even fewer guests than before—now it appeared he had no family, no friends, no one; in the morning he went to the market, spent all day at the office, then in the evening he either went out again on errands or sat quietly, the lights switched off—there was nothing more in his life. But why, I'm here . . . I? The sharp question mark lodged in her heart, she gasped for breath for a moment. Till just the other day Saswati had been here too. And now? How many times had she visited since Shweta had left?

Swati walked away from her father. Suddenly she was struck by a thought: her father fulfilled every wish of hers, but she didn't do anything to fulfil any of his. Baba wanted to inquire after Satyen Roy from time to time—if Ma had been here all this would have happened automatically—but no matter what might have happened had Ma been here, was it at all possible now? . . . But then I don't invite him over either—even when he comes I don't ask him to stay longer . . . Why should I, but who else will . . . Baba knows him only because of me; he doesn't mean anything to Baba. Indeed . . . the way he . . . the way . . . the way he's so polite with me, in comparison, I . . . But is it normal to be so measured in one's ways?

Swati reflected for a while in silence. She had the impulse to go over immediately and give him the book. The moment the thought occurred to her, a wave of happiness lapped at her heart. Was the joy of taking as much as the joy of giving? But it was late . . . No, hardly late—evening had barely fallen . . . She may not find him at home, or maybe she would find him with his friends—but what if he was home, what if, let's assume, he was alone at home . . .?

Again the question pricked her. There had never been so many questions in Swati's mind, never so many pinpricks in her thoughts. Her life used to be unrestricted—who had taken away her freedom; her life was a straight line—who had led her to this winding path. April's silken evening slowly became velvet night, and Swati's heart grew proportionately heavy.

∾

Barely a day or two after this, Satyen Roy came. As soon as Swati entered the room, he said, 'How are you, Swati?' Every time they had met in recent times, this was always the first thing he said, how are you, Swati? And Swati would answer correctly, 'Very well', but today she couldn't help asking, 'Why do you ask the same question every day?'

'Every day? Do I meet you every day?'

'That's up to you,' answered Swati.

'Besides,' Satyen Roy paused for a second to go beyond her answer, 'I do want to know how you are.'

'Can that ever be answered in a few words?'

'Use several.'

'You won't have so much time.'

'*So* many things to say?'

Swati didn't answer.

'Tell me!'

After a bit, Swati said, 'Aren't you going anywhere in the holidays?'

'I am.'

'You are!' Swati was embarrassed as soon as she spoke,

because even to her own ears it was obvious she had been hoping for the opposite as the answer.

'Shouldn't I?'

Satyen Roy's tone seemed to hold a hint of banter, as though he were asking Swati for advice about whether he should go or not, and if Swati said no, he wouldn't budge. Swati bowed her head mentally, her voice choked, but at the same time, being only eighteen pushed her to the frontiers of boldness, she said, as though returning banter with banter, 'Must you go just because holidays are here?'

'Do I have any reason not to go?' Satyen Roy also returned the question with a question, but surely the question was not for Swati, but seemingly for himself, as though he was trying to discover his fate in the wedge of sunshine visible through the parting in the curtain. His eyes moved away immediately, met Swati's, laughing away a breathless moment he said very innocently, 'You could take a holiday too somewhere.'

'Where would I go?' Swati breathed a sigh of relief too.

'Why not to your Bordi?' Satyen Roy answered promptly. 'Bordi had asked you to visit her.'

'Didn't she ask you?'

'As if she has to ask me!' Swati smiled.

'In that case . . .'

'Baba has no holidays, so . . .'

'Can't he get leave from his office?'

'No idea!'

'Your Bordi could visit again too.'

'It isn't easy for her either. Not everyone is as independent as you.'

'Independent? What does that mean?'

'Independent means independent.'

'Is being independent a good thing?' Satyen Roy said, savouring his own independence mentally.

'How would I know!'

Satyen Roy glanced again at the sliver of sunlight filtering in through the opening in the curtain, and rose immediately.

This sudden departure looked disjointed, much too abrupt. 'Leaving?'; 'Leaving already?'; 'Won't you stay a little longer?'— which of these was best, what was the best way to say it, or would it be best to say nothing at all—Swati was rescued from these dilemmas by Rajen-babu's return from his office on heavy feet. A smile appeared on his tired face on seeing Satyen. 'Ah, how long have you been here?'

'He came just now, and he's leaving just now too,' said Swati.

'Why? Stay a bit longer. I'll be back in a minute.'

'So you're staying a bit longer?' Swati said after her father had disappeared inside the house. She didn't like his agreeing so readily; a little later she continued, 'You don't seem to be in much of a hurry today.'

'Hurry for what?'

'Why don't you tell me?'

'Am I always in a hurry?'

'I can't say about always.'

'But?'

'I can tell you about what I see . . . Anyway, at least you kept Baba's request . . .'

'I like keeping requests.'

'Everyone's?'

'Some people's.'

'Whose?'

'Definitely your father's.'

After a little silence, Swati spoke. 'So requests have to be spelt out for you.'

'Not always.'

'But unless they're spelt out it doesn't seem to work.'

'That's for the best.'

'That's normal.'

'Don't you like normal?'

'Do you?'

'It's quite nice to be normal.'

Swati thought a little more. 'I think . . .'

Waiting, Satyen Roy asked, 'What is it that you think?'

Looking the other way, Swati said, 'Shall I get the tea, Baba?'

At the sight of Rajen-babu in a dhoti and vest, Satyen's expression appeared to relax, he seemed to settle down in his chair more comfortably. 'How are you? Well, I hope?' said Rajen-babu.

Satyen replied with a gentle smile.

'No . . . no problems, I hope?'

'Problems? But why?'

'We haven't been able to inquire . . . er . . . You're well, I hope?'

'I am.'

This conversation between two individuals far apart in age didn't progress further. They sat looking in different directions until the tea came, and Rajen-babu made his escape as soon as he had finished his cup. It was almost evening, but night was a long way off, the most pleasurable time of the summer months permeated across the city.

'Tell me, Swati, what is it that you think?' said Satyen Roy.

Arranging the cups, saucers and teapot on the tray, Swati stood up. In the fading light of the room, against the backdrop of blue curtains, she appeared uncommonly fair to Satyen's eyes, very tall, and older than she actually was.

'What, tell me.'

'What?'

'What is it that you think, tell me.'

'What would I think.'

'You stopped just as you were about to speak . . .'

'Really?'

Swati saw Satyen Roy run his hand over his face, take his handkerchief out of his pocket, but put it back without using it. Then he rose slowly, took two steps towards her and said softly, 'Goodbye, Swati.'

Swati immediately walked with him to the door, watched him walk down the three steps, cross the small yard slowly, turn around to put the latch on the low gate in place, then begin walking swiftly, disappearing around the corner. And the shade of the evening turned into bliss in Swati's heart, the breeze of summer changed to joy as it wafted into her heart.

The letter came from Sylhet a few days later. A short letter: 'I'm staying with a friend . . . It's a lovely town, but this is just the appetizer—the feast will begin when I leave for Shillong . . .' Her reply sprang to mind even as she read, but how would she send it, there was no address anywhere on the letter or the envelope. Rage flared up, but she subdued it instantly—whom was she enraged at? If you couldn't convey your anger what use was it getting angry? When another letter came three days later, as soon as she saw the envelope Swati said: no, I won't write . . . But, looking grim, even keeping the letter unopened for two or three minutes, she couldn't convince herself that Satyen Roy would keep writing even if he didn't get a reply. So, slitting open the envelope, she gazed at the broad sheet of paper filled with the curly black script before actually reading the letter—the sight of the inky scrawl gave her so much pleasure that she couldn't even read everything the first time round. All she gathered was that he had reached Shillong, and that the scenery on the road from Sylhet to Shillong was breathtaking. Putting the letter down, Swati put on her sari the formal way, took a walk outside for no obvious reason, ran into her college friend Chitra on the road, she didn't seem as silly any more, quite nice, in fact! Back home she read the letter again, then once more in the early evening, and all the time that she didn't read it she thought about the letter—but whenever she caught herself at it she chided herself, trying to fasten on to a different strain of thought—Bordi, Harit-da, joining the BA classes soon—but the mind lagged behind, returning to the same point, she seemed to find this game amusing, she accepted the demands of her heart, just as we eventually quite enjoy the naughty boy's demands although we're annoyed at first . . . She stayed up late into the night to write her reply, another letter, one more reply; every buzzing day in that long, blinding summer was replete with getting letters and writing letters and thinking letters.

She had fallen asleep that afternoon, when she awoke it was four o'clock; but still afternoon, the entire afternoon, the long day, reigned like a king, even if you used it all up it didn't end. Alone at home, she wandered around for a while from one room to another, you could almost touch the heat in the drawing room, its doors and windows shut—Swati went to the wall to switch on the fan, opened the front door, searing gusts of wind made the curtains fly instantly, searing her face— she savoured it, savoured the blinding glare of the sunshine, the powdery dust, the whirling gravel; her soles curled at the red-hot touch of the baked steps, still she pressed down on them deliberately, forcibly—from her feet to her spine, from the spine to the brain, numbing pinpricks of heat—she enjoyed those too. After looking at the road for a while, she stirred, turned back towards the house, as soon as she did her eyes fastened on the letter box of B. John & Co., she spotted a letter through the glass window, a sunlight-coloured white envelope displaying Swati's name reposed inside peacefully.

Bijon had developed a new habit: locking the letter box, locking the suitcase, even locking his room when he went out. What to do? Nothing—she would have to wait patiently till her brother deigned to return home, whether it was in the evening or in the dead of night or the next morning. She looked at the envelope for a long time, from this side and from that—but what use was it roasting needlessly under the sun—was the letter a bird that could fly to her, and even if it were, how would it have escaped that cage? Back in the room she opened all the windows, sat down quietly, listened to the sound of the roads being watered in the distance, then closer, and after that—she didn't know exactly how much later—saw her brother enter the room, returning home much earlier than on all other days, she wasn't the least bit surprised—in fact she felt as though she had dragged him home with the infinitely long rope of her need.

'What's the matter? Why're you looking like that?'

'Give me the key to the letter box,' said Swati.

Bijon didn't give her the key, he unlocked the box himself and brought her the letter. Before handing it to her he glanced at it, asking, 'Who's it from?' As though justifying his question, he added, 'It's quite heavy.'

'From Satyen Roy,' said Swati, taking the letter.

'That infant professor of yours! Has he lost his job?'

'What do you mean?'

'Why isn't he in Calcutta?'

'It's the summer vacation, isn't it? He's gone to Shillong on holiday,' Swati had to explain.

'Vacation!' Bijon curled his lips. 'We can't even think of one. These college teachers have easy lives—losers on salary but winners on holidays, although frankly speaking I just can't tell how they manage to pass their time with so many holidays.'

'How would you?' Swati consoled her brother before going into her room.

A little later Bijon entered too. 'Read your letter?' He began a conversation with his sister, a smile on his lips.

Putting the letter back in the envelope, Swati said, 'Even our letters are put into your box—leave the key with me.'

'Why not tell the peon.'

'I will, but I'd better keep the key too.' Swati raised her eyes towards her brother. Bijon took the key-ring out of his pocket, held it up before his eyes, turning it round and round, then used two fingers to take one small key out of the ring and, saying, 'Keep the duplicate, then,' handed it to Swati as though he were parting with an extremely valuable possession just to keep his sister happy. Looking around, he seemed to choose the cushioned cane chair after considerable thought and sat in it; leaning back, lighting a cigarette, he said luxuriously, 'I'm thinking of inviting Majumdar to tea.'

Swati didn't reply.

Keeping his eye on the ash at the end of his cigarette, Bijon continued, 'If I can make this business work it'll be because of Majumdar. I should invite him home once in a while.'

'That's fine—take him to a restaurant.'

'A restaurant. We're sick and tired of restaurants.' Bijon paused, seemed to ponder a bit. 'Besides, he'd be pleased if I invited him home.'

'Who'd be pleased?'

'Aren't you listening?'

'All right . . . ask Baba, if he approves . . .'

'Ho! Why do I have to ask Baba about this?'

'You should.'

'Why should I? Can't I invite a friend for a meal if I want to?'

'A friend!' Swati laughed.

'What are you laughing at?'

'That forty-year-old creature is your friend!'

'Forty?' It was Bijon's turn to laugh. 'What do you mean forty—thirty-one or thirty-two at most. A fine man—he's made lots of money too.'

'Is that why he's fine?'

'Whatever you may say,' Bijon confessed, 'to make money you have to be clever and passionate about your work. Majumdar didn't have anything to begin with, he's made it on his own—a totally self-made man. He isn't married, has nothing to do with his family, nothing but work and work and more work all day.' Biju glowed with pride for his friend.

'Wonderful! So he's your ideal man now?'

'Is the ideal a bad one?'

'You'll know better than I.'

'I cannot understand why Majumdar does so much for me,' Bijon seemed to be talking to himself. 'So many people queue up for an audience with him every day, but I didn't even have to ask, a single glance—'

'—enabled him to tell gold from dross!' Swati finished on her brother's behalf.

'Must be!' Stretching, Biju rose with a detached look in his eyes. Frowning at his sister, he said, 'Why do you always look so shabby?' using the word 'shabby' in English.

'Too much English these days, Dada!'

'This is nothing—the English they use in business circles—blast your bile! My left foot!' he exclaimed, using the last two phrases in English. 'Have you ever heard such things? Just reading piles of books at home will not . . . But why do you look so unkempt all the time? Don't you have any decent saris?'

'What do you mean!' Swati spread out the end of her sari in both her hands. 'As if this sari is a bad one! What a beautiful sari it is—a little dirty, it's true—but it's more comfortable this way.'

'It's lousy! You get such beautiful Bombay prints these days . . .' About to say something more, Biju stopped suddenly. Jingling the keys and coins in the pocket of his trousers, he said, 'I'm inviting Majumdar to tea on Saturday, then, have some food ready.'

'I shan't do anything of the sort.'

'Why not?'

'What do you mean why not. I shan't, I tell you.'

Bijon looked at his sister through narrowed eyes, as though he couldn't decide what to say next. Looking at his glittering eyes, her father's words leapt into Swati's mind, suddenly she blurted out, 'Why must you have your business partners over at home?'

'Oh, is that it!' Suppressed all this while, the anger finally flared.

'Don't you know Baba doesn't like all this? All these types . . .'

'These *types*!' Bijon leapt to confront Swati, shaking a fist under her nose, saying, 'How dare you! What insolence! But then, like father like daughter . . .!'

'If only it had been like father like son,' Swati spoke up in the middle of Bijon's outburst.

'Of course, if all men were sheep you people would be so happy, wouldn't you?'

'You can shout for all you're worth, but you have to stop all these sessions of yours here at home!'

'Have to stop? On whose orders?'

'On the orders of the owner of the house.'

'Is the house yours?'

'It's not yours either.'

'Of course it's mine!'

'Indeed!'

'Look, Swati! I'm not going to argue with you any more, but listen carefully—this is my house, I'll do as I please here, if he doesn't like it why doesn't Rajen Mitra tell me directly, why does he complain to you?'

'Because you're bull-headed, and because no decent man can talk to you.'

'I see a lady can!'

'Because she has to! If I don't look after Baba's interests, you'll probably throw him out.'

'Shut up!' Bijon really did bellow like a bull now. 'Another word and I'm going to throw you out—like this—by the scruff of your neck!' Curving his fingers like the coils of a snake he brought them near Swati's throat. 'Like this! I'll throw you out on the streets—Rajen Mitra will stare open-mouthed! When it comes to my friends he will not allow it, but he can rush off fifty times to invite your mewling, effeminate, sly Satyen Roy!'

Swati's face turned ashen, and then red hot like a coal furnace. Her voice stuck in her throat as she tried to talk, she looked at her brother with wide eyes, his face was like a bad-tempered cat's, and when Bijon spoke again a little later, even his voice sounded hoarse and angry, like a cat's.

'Baba's a fool . . . but . . . I . . . will take care of your rudeness!' Bijon's wiry finger wagged under Swati's nose before moving away. Swati retreated a little too, a little more, but didn't take her eyes off her brother's face, grinding his teeth, Bijon said, 'I'll take care of you. Not just you . . . Also . . . that scrawny professor! Writing letters! Rascal! Let him return—I'll thrash him till he's forced to leave the neighbourhood!'

Swati had retreated all the way to her desk, her back against it now, heaving as she breathed partly through her parted lips and partly through flared nostrils, the corners of her eyes inflamed, a vein throbbing beneath them, even after Bijon had finished she didn't say anything, but as soon as Bijon opened his mouth to continue talking, she flung a thick book at his face with her long, fair arm. There was a loud thud, and when the book fell open on the floor, Swati said, 'Get out!'

Bijon circled his face with his right hand, swept his hair back to the left, after a quick glance at the book he kicked it out of the room, and then left, his head high and chest held out. Before leaving he said, 'That's what will happen to you too one day.'

4

What will happen to me? Will I meet the same fate as that book? But that book has conquered the world. Flying out of the room, crossing the veranda, Keats's poetry had stopped at the second step of the staircase—face down, the wings of its covers spread wide, like a bird hunted down; in the slanting beams of the late afternoon sunlight the poet's name shone—golden letters, golden signature. Swati picked it up, cradled it and wiped it clean with the end of her sari, opening the covers to glance at Satyen Roy's name written inside, she smoothened the dog-eared pages with her fingers, concluding that never, in no circumstances, should you be so angry that the name of the writer does not stall your arm in mid-air as you are about to fling a book at someone . . . Dada was a philistine. Thank goodness Baba wasn't home—he wouldn't get to know either.

Lest her father come home immediately and ask her, 'What is it, Swati, what's happened?' the moment he saw her, and lest she too revealed everything on an impulse, Swati quickly went into the bathroom with her towel, trying to wash off through a bath all the acrimony, the rage, the heartburn, she blamed herself repeatedly, mentally taking her brother's side. The arguments were structured so perfectly, their logic so flawless, that she began to believe them within a few minutes. She realized the family was unfair to her brother—the unfairness of neglect, having to stomach everyone's indifference since childhood had upset his balance, now he was determined to score over them with his money—poor fellow! Swati saw neither the wiry finger like a snake's, nor the vein-bursting feline rage that could tear someone apart with its claws, but a palm upturned before her—the acknowledgement he didn't get from anyone else at home, probably not even outside home, was what he sought, with his palm upturned, from the only person at home who was younger than he was. Just as he went out of his way to quarrel with her, he also went out of his way to chat with her, on one pretext or another he seemed to want to tell her the same thing—acknowledge me, if not as your elder brother, as a man, as an adult, as a gentleman, as a male.

Swati felt remorse. It was true that she was often contemptuous of him, she said terrible things about him at the drop of a hat, never took him seriously. If she could have protected him—if, say, she could have been like Shweta, cool, soft, gentle—maybe Biju would have turned out like everyone else—in the sense that he would have been happy, her father would have been happy too, this conflict at home would not have existed. The responsibility for her brother to be happy—to be good, that is—had been hers, maybe it still was hers, perhaps there was still time. With this thought, seeing herself playing such an important role suddenly, Swati was astonished, a little thrilled, even before emerging from the bathroom, droplets of water still glistening on her, she vowed to herself that this time, for the first time, she would accept defeat to her brother. She made the vow but still, after her bath, having put on a freshly ironed light blue sari, and savouring the fragrance of the talcum powder, the stench of the altercation did not leave her, the bitter taste of the argument persisted on her tongue . . . But this unhappiness must not be indulged—her brother would have to be reformed even at a cost to herself—dabbing talcum powder on her face, Swati prepared for her starring role.

As they sat on a mat in the veranda with their evening tea, Swati broached the subject with her father.

'All right,' said her father.

'I know nothing makes you happier than having someone over for a meal,' smiled Swati, 'but I was thinking, all these business partners . . .' she looked at her father without finishing.

'Never mind . . . Since Biju wants to . . .'

Her father said this so spontaneously that Swati wondered whether she had overdone her battle with her brother by taking his side. Lowering her eyes, she said, 'I told Dada, Baba.'

'Told him what?'

'Just that . . . you don't like those types visiting our home . . .'

'As if Mr Bijon Mitra cares for my likes and dislikes.'

'No, Baba,' Swati said gravely. 'Dada looked quite doubtful after I had told him. "Never mind, then," he said. So I said, "All right, let me ask Baba . . ."'

'What's going on?' Rajen-babu smiled. 'Suddenly he's a dutiful son! What does he want?'

Again, Swati was puzzled by his tone. Had she got it wrong, was she barking up the wrong tree? Just as she had overdone it when berating her brother, was her present effort to be nice childish too? But there was no going back now, she would have to be nice to him, whether or not it was good for him.

The next day, not having run into him till nine in the morning, Swati had no choice but to go towards his room. As soon as she came near the door she heard a tapping inside, looking in, she saw her brother trying to use a typewriter, the extraordinary effort involved in this had made his eyes bulge, distorted the shape of his lips and given birth to three deep, clear creases on his forehead. Swati felt like laughing, but no—she wouldn't end up laughing, would she—summoning a light shadow of sadness to her expression, she called, 'Dada.'

Bijon raised his eyes as far as the red-and-black ribbon on his typewriter, then quickly lowered them to the keys.

Swati called again, even more gently, 'Dada, listen to me.'

Without raising his eyes, Bijon answered gruffly, 'What?'

Swati came into the room, watching the helpless writhing of the amateurish fingers, and then spoke in a voice like a bird's, 'What a lovely portable typewriter!'

Bijon moved his hands away to look at his new acquisition with a trace of pride.

'Did you buy it?'

'Yes.'

'But why do you type yourself—such a waste of time!'

Bijon's eyes flashed over his sister briefly. 'I'll get used to it soon enough,' he said, searching for the letter S amidst the shining rows of black and white with a frown on his face.

'I'm sure you will,' Swati said softly, 'but people have clerks for all this, don't they?'

Bijon couldn't help being pleased at this—that is to say, he couldn't help showing his pleasure, for he was already pleased, had been for some time; there was nothing else in the whole world this morning that could please him as much as Swati's contrite, forlorn expression. Leaning back in his chair, he said casually, 'So will I.'

After a silence Swati said, 'I could type your letters too for you from time to time . . . In fact, I really feel like doing it right now, Dada.'

'Will you?' Bijon tried very hard not to show that his heart was melting, but in vain.

Advancing a step, retreating a step, Swati said, 'No, never mind . . . I'll make mistakes.'

'I make mistakes too!' Bijon couldn't hold back any more, he laughed. 'See, my eyeballs are popping out looking for the S.'

Without joining him in his laughter, Swati said, 'You'll get used to it soon enough.'

This was the first time Bijon heard an echo of his own statement from Swati without banter or suspicion, without an attempt to dismiss or ignore it. Shoving his chair back, he stood up and finally looked directly, fully, at his sister, saying, 'Try right now.'

'Not now. If you leave it with me in the afternoon, I'll practise a little . . .' Stopping suddenly, putting her finger on the rounded edge of the typewriter, she said, 'When did you buy it, Dada? Why didn't you tell anyone?'

'Nothing to write home about,' he said, running his tongue round his mouth. 'I didn't buy it. It belongs to someone else.'

'But it's new!'

'Of course it's new! The person who bought it gave it to me to use.'

'He gave it to you? Very generous, I must say.' The old note of sarcasm seemed to creep into Swati's voice, but so subtly that Bijon didn't quite perceive it—or did he?—which was why he suddenly wiped the smile off his face, looked very serious and said, drawing himself up to his full height, 'Yes, he's a very nice man.'

Appearing not even to notice the change in her brother, Swati said casually, 'Doesn't he need it?'

'Him? He has so many machines in his office!'

Swati concluded that she might as well get her brother to mention Majumdar by name. So she smiled, saying, 'You're very lucky when it comes to friends, Dada.'

'One needs to be lucky somewhere!' Bijon said this as though he had perceived a hint of an attack by the enemy and was ready with his weapons, and had decided at once that offence is the best defence. Loudly, sternly, he said, 'I shall always say that you have to be very lucky to have a friend like Majumdar.'

Swati exhaled mentally, waited a little longer, the more her brother spoke, the less she would. That was just what happened, a little later Bijon said, 'And this is the Majumdar you people insult.'

'Oh my God!' Now Swati had a marvellous opportunity to speak. 'Who on earth insulted him, when did all this happen!'

'Wasn't all that an insult!' Bijon hissed.

'I have an idea,' said Swati gently. 'Why don't you invite your friend to tea.'

'No. Forget it.'

'Why not? I've told Baba—he has no objection. And if he doesn't, why should I?'

'You mean,' said Bijon, placing a cigarette between his lips and concluding, with her help, as it were, 'you still have objections?'

'It doesn't matter to you if I do, does it?'

About to answer right back, Bijon stopped suddenly. Lighting his cigarette, and transferring it from his lips to his fingers, he said, 'But why the objections?'

'Why should I object to you inviting your friend to your house? I told you, didn't I—do as you please.'

'All right, I will,' said Bijon, putting his cigarette in the ashtray and sitting down at his typewriter again, his teeth clenched. Swati waited another minute or so, all of which Bijon spent hunting for the E after the S.

But that evening he came himself to inform Swati, 'I told Majumdar. Saturday isn't convenient, so it's Friday instead.'

'Fine.'

'You . . . Will you be civil at least?'

'Do you imagine I know how to?'

'If you don't, you have to learn—since there's no one else here but you.' Swati liked this, which was why she didn't respond.

'Friday is the day after tomorrow—don't forget, all right?' Bijon left with a wave.

On Friday, Swati not only did not fail in her role as the courteous hostess, she passed with flying colours. She poured the tea, made it clear that her happiness would know no bounds if the guests agreed to have some more of the food, she had some herself, but no one could make out, it wasn't as though she talked a lot, but whenever the conversation flagged, she gently breathed new life into it—whether in her conversation, or her expression, or the way she conducted herself, it was never evident that she was so young and so inexperienced—but then, why consider her inexperienced, she had read so much—wasn't that experience too?

Bijon had never imagined his Friday would have sparkled quite so much. You could never trust Swati—to be on the safe side, he had also invited Saswati and Harit. He had thought—possibly hoped—that Harit would not be able to make it, but a long-overdue payment and a long-pending increment had made Harit particularly cheerful that day, besides, there wasn't any exciting meeting or conference in town, so he opted to attend his brother-in-law's first-ever party. And it wasn't a bad party, either—three men and two women made the place look quite full; and although the conversation here was much paler than with his friends, there was at least an opportunity to draft a new person to the cause.

Harit fired his first shot at the same old target. 'What have you done, Swati! Who's going to eat all this?'

'We will,' said Swati.

'But this isn't appropriate—prawn cutlets with tea!'

'Oh, they don't go together, you mean?' Swati was embarrassed. 'I rather like them that way, actually.'

Prabir Majumdar laughed at this.

'The amount of time and effort we waste over food in our country . . .' Harit specifically speared Majumdar with his glance, 'And as for the amount of food we waste, the less said the better!'

'That's true!' said Majumdar eagerly, 'and it's all homemade! I wonder when you found the time!' He looked at Swati.

Swati was embarrassed again. She hadn't made any of it herself, however—her father had done the shopping for provisions, everything had been prepared through the afternoon by Hari, the servant they had had since her mother's time, he was the one who had laid it all out on different plates—all she had done was dress up and hand people their plates, and yet she was the one being praised! But could you possibly respond to polite clichés with 'No, really, I didn't make any of this!' But she couldn't determine what else to say, so she reddened a little and bowed her head, and she looked exactly as she would have had she accepted the praise as her due.

With an oblique smile, Saswati asked, 'Which one did you make, Swati, let me try that.'

'If you asked me, Mrs Nandy,' Majumdar got it wrong this time too, 'I'd recommend the cutlet. If you must have prawn cutlets in Calcutta, the only place to go to is Chang-Aan, but these cutlets beat theirs hollow!'

Swati raised her eyes at this, and immediately exchanged glances with Saswati. Chuckling, she said, 'It wasn't me.'

'You know what I mean!' Majumdar busied himself establishing the quality of the cutlets in practical terms.

'Mr Majumdar is an expert on the best food in Calcutta,' said Biju.

'Really?' Harit's raised eyebrows held a dash of sarcasm.

'He can distinguish between Puntiraam's shondesh and Jalajog's blindfolded. And besides . . .'

'Oh, Mr Mitra!' Raising his left hand, Majumdar interrupted the advertisement of his skills, and then said, looking at everyone, 'The thing is . . . eating regularly at home is not what fate has in store for me . . . I have to wander all over town, so there's no choice but to . . .' Without completing, Majumdar laughed, displaying his prominent, shining teeth.

'His factory is in Dum Dum, office on Canning Street,' Bijon seized the opportunity to expand on his friend's credentials, 'and his work extends from Barrackpore to Diamond Harbour.'

'That means . . . you're a capitalist!' Harit wrinkled his flute-like nose.

'Not yet, but I'm trying to be.'

From experience Saswati knew that Harit's war bugle had sounded, so she tried to change the subject quickly. 'What do you make in your factory?'

'Useless things,' Majumdar smiled affably. 'Jute, copra . . .'

Saswati was genuinely disappointed. It would have been nice if it had been a factory for saris or something—she could have paid a visit. Looking at her sister out of the corner of her eye, Swati said, 'Not useless at all. Copra is needed for so many things—doormats . . .'

'Doormats.' Bijon burst out laughing.

'That's right! You're right!' Majumdar glanced at Swati solemnly. 'We work so hard all day precisely so that all of you can wipe your feet.' Then, without changing his tone, he turned to Harit. 'What do you think? Is the war going to intensify or fizzle out?'

'Wage slave-driver!' Harit muttered to himself in English. Then, to overwhelm the man, he counter-questioned with a sly look, 'What do *you* think?'

'I don't know—the way they're all dropping by the wayside . . . Paris has fallen too, now all that's left is for Hitler to have England for breakfast, and it'll be all over.'

Harit was enraged at his jovial stupidity; patiently, he said, 'Is that all it'll take?'

'Who's left to fight after that?'

'Russia, of course!' Harit roared like a lion.

'Russia?'

Majumdar may have said more, but Harit couldn't wait any longer, he delivered the death blow: 'Russia is the world's only hope.'

Majumdar clearly choked at this, stopping midway as he was about to raise his cup to his lips, and looking at his large, ruddy, thick-lipped face Harit realized that this wood-for-brain would-be capitalist of Bengal was hearing for the first time what every intelligent person in the world today believed. 'Russia is the world's only hope,' he relished the repetition.

'Thank goodness I learnt this from you, or else like everyone else I too would have assumed that Stalin was happily fiddling while half the world was burning,' said Majumdar, sipping his tea.

'Let it burn,' Harit said, red-faced. 'If Russia survives, the world will survive.'

'I see. The world means nothing but Russia, and therefore Russia is the world's only hope?'

The red on Harit's face turned to grey. He was tempted to teach this lump of flesh a lesson or two and leave, but instantly he remembered the advice of the leaders of the party: you need patience, you must never lose your temper; you have to teach, you have to explain, you have to convert people—even subtle deception is allowed when necessary—he'd seen some of them too, arguing for hours together with the haute bourgeoisie, the petite bourgeoisie and the lumpen proletariat, just in case drafting some of them to the cause would benefit the party—and so Harit averted his face and distractedly ate up the very prawn cutlet whose arrival with the tea he had shuddered at. Majumdar was taken aback by his reaction; Saswati's head was bowed, only Bijon looked on with shining eyes, his chest thrust out—a friend who could match a man as erudite and articulate as Harit word for word was no ordinary mortal.

In that silence Swati's voice bubbled up, 'I love Russia. The people drink tea and argue all day, the stationmasters sleep all the time, and the women stay awake nights to—'

'Where do you get all this?' Harit snorted through his nose.

'Turgenev.'

'Turgenev!' Harit snipped Swati's hesitant answer ruthlessly. 'He lived the life of a dandy abroad—what did he know of Russia? What has he done for his downtrodden country? That's why no one in Russia reads Turgenev any more!'

'They don't?' How sad, they don't read such books, such wonderful books! Swati felt very sad for the people of Russia; she said, 'Then Russia's people are still miserable!'

Harit had been simmering for such a long time, waiting to talk, that he didn't even listen to Swati, but hearing the word 'miserable' he roared, 'No—Russia's people don't live in misery any more. The stationmasters there don't sleep all day any more, the women don't sigh all night, now there's . . .' For five straight minutes Harit described heaven-on-earth Russia, seeing the plump, fleshy Majumdar gradually wilt, with his neck drooping to one side, Harit realized his diatribe was working, and as soon as he had finished Saswati exclaimed, 'Really, what an amazing country!'

'Amazing!' Majumdar echoed.

To tell the truth, Harit hadn't finished, he had only paused for breath. But he was so pleased by the defeated and reverent expressions on everyone's faces that he said, 'Some more tea, please, Swati.'

The meal ended, the dishes were removed; Majumdar held out his cigarette tin to Harit to propose a truce. 'Please . . .'

'Thank you, my pipe . . .' Harit began, but then noticed that it was a State Express tin. Smiling generously, he said, 'All right, I'll take one.'

Majumdar held the tin out to Bijon next.

With a smile, Bijon looked guiltily at Harit, at Saswati too. 'Please give him your permission,' Majumdar winked. 'Why unnecessarily . . .'

'Of course!' Having ensured victory for Russia in just five minutes, Harit was now even more cheerful than earlier, smiling benevolently, he said, 'Bijon, why do you even . . .'

For the first time Bijon lit a cigarette honourably at home, in the presence of adults, openly, and that made him feel so proud that he couldn't smoke it properly. What liberties he takes, Saswati thought to herself. So impertinent! But she didn't say anything, lest Harit get into a bad mood.

Lighting a match and offering it to Harit, Majumdar said, 'Please don't mind, Mr Nandy, for my arguing with you like a fool.'

Harit guffawed, then coughed as he tried to light his cigarette. Waving his hand before his face to dispel the smoke, he said, 'Not at all . . .'

'We have so much to learn from people like you! But where's the time!'

'Why don't you come to one of our meetings some time.'

'Meetings!' Majumdar looked apologetic. 'I'm terrified of meetings.'

'Nothing like that—just some friends . . .'

'What will a fool like me do at a gathering of wise men?'

Accepting this without demur, Harit said, 'You could come for the music.'

'Music? What kind of music?'

'Working-class music.'

'Warring-class music?'

'You're quite right, working-class songs will indeed become warring-class songs soon! Farmers' songs—oh, if only I could describe them!'

'What are they like?' Majumdar wanted to know.

'You'll know the moment you hear them—one of us has picked up the songs after touring different districts—he has a wonderful voice . . .'

'Oh!' Majumdar half-shut his eyes to bring back some pleasurable memory. 'But I'm yet to hear a voice like Shashanka Das's!'

'You know which Shashanka Das, don't you, Chhordi?' Bijon stirred in his chair.

'The one whose car number you knew by heart—that one, right?' Saswati joked with her brother, but became mentally animated. How wonderful his songs were in that film, *The Revenge*—that was the only time Baba had taken us to the cinema—it had never been repeated the same way. And soon after that, I met Harit for the first time on Swati's birthday!

Saswati's mind had started floating away, when she registered the conversation again, she heard Majumdar say, 'It's our misfortune, it's this country's misfortune, that Shashanka Das has to sing in films to earn a living!'

'But he doesn't seem to be singing in films these days.' Saswati spoke in a way that suggested she did not agree with Majumdar about the misfortune.

'He's in Bombay now—if there's no option but films, you might as well be where the money is. But I'm trying to get him back to Calcutta.'

'You know him!' Saswati was thrilled.

'Know him? Shashanka is an old friend.'

The words 'old friend' made Swati want to laugh—in fact,

she did laugh, and to justify the laugh she said quickly, 'Chhordi is very fond of films.'

'So am I,' Majumdar said immediately. 'It's not that films are bad, it's just that we're not capable of accepting what Shashanka can offer.'

'But if the best people aren't involved,' Bijon remarked sagely, 'how will films improve?'

'That's true too.'

'Which Bombay films has he sung for?'

The discussion was all about films after this. Majumdar did most of the talking, Bijon didn't give up without a remark from time to time, and with a gentle smile on his face Harit set a record with almost ten minutes of patience, then brought up Russian films, flying Eisenstein's flag a couple of times, but the conversation rolled back to the plains of Indian films. It turned out Majumdar knew a number of actors. Saswati was charmed—she desperately wanted to ask whether he knew any of the actresses too, but she baulked at actually asking—that . . . that wouldn't be right. The thing was, Saswati couldn't see half as many films as she really wished she could; Harit never took her to more than two every month, and that too English films only, unless she could join her sisters-in-law at Harit's parents' home she hardly ever got to watch Bengali films, so she tried to satiate her suppressed desires as much as possible by listening to Majumdar talk.

After a few more minutes of silence on his part, Harit couldn't take it any more, glancing at his watch, he said, 'I have to go.'

'So do I!' Majumdar stopped talking and stood up with an air of finality.

'I . . . I'll stay a bit,' Saswati said a trifle morosely.

'Yes, of course . . . I'm not going home now in any case . . .'

'Which way are you going? If it's towards the city, I could drop . . .'

'All right.'

'Then we're meeting at nine in the morning tomorrow, Mr Mitra?'

'Certainly.'

'Many thanks, Mrs Nandy, many thanks, Miss Mitra,' Majumdar bid goodbye to each of them. 'I hope to meet you again.'

'Certainly,' said Bijon again.

'Oh yes . . .' Majumdar seemed to remember suddenly, 'Paul Muni's new film is coming to Metro, would you like to go the Saturday after next? I mean,' he elaborated the very next moment, 'I'll be delighted if you accept my invitation.'

'Well . . . we could,' Harit was the first to respond. He had been thinking of going for this film—this was a godsend—a quick calculation of how much money meeting this man would save him played through his mind.

'You'll come, won't you?' Majumdar stopped in front of Swati.

'Let's see . . .'

'Why not?' Majumdar inclined his head towards her.

Swati had stood up as the guests were leaving, she took a good look at him now that he was close by. Parted in the middle, his hair cascaded in waves on either side; the small eyes were set far apart; he had an enormous face and thick red lips, his glittering silk *panjabi* reached almost down to the knees, the crinkled and embroidered end of the dhoti sweeping across his moss-green sandals. Swati suddenly felt as though she had been knocked backwards—her heart seemed to tremble with a terrible dislike; all her politeness, civility, attempts to please her brother—all of them were swept away, her senses filling with that horrible, bitter stench.

'I've seen you many times,' she heard Majumdar say, 'but never met you. Since you were kind enough to grant a meeting today, can't you be kinder still?'

Saswati laughed to herself at this, and thought, every woman has her day, but how soon it's over! Had God not created women as complete fools, they wouldn't forget themselves because of anything men said, nor would they forget anything men said; they would have listened quietly to everything, then calculated the tax . . . Standing next to Swati, she said, 'Doesn't Swati want to go? That's what she's like! But why won't you go, all of us are going, how can you not go?'

After Majumdar departed in his car, Harit by his side, the first thing she said when she came back was to Swati: 'Well? Saw the state that Majumdar is in?'

'Of course I did,' Swati smiled in reply. 'Beware, Chhordi.'

'What do I have to be . . .'

'What do you mean! It's you who has to beware.'

'Naughty!' Saswati pushed Swati away, reddening a little too.

Swati reddened, became angry with herself because she did, and reddened more because of the colour of that anger— luckily it was shadowy, hazy, dark. She had been a little startled on seeing Majumdar standing before her, holding a glass with a straw in it, for she really was thirsty but hadn't said so, because only children and women unused to watching films felt thirsty at the cinema. Did he consider her a member of one of those two groups of people—how else would he have known?

'Please,' Majumdar extended his hand towards her, his head bowed.

'The others . . .?' Turning to look at Saswati, she saw she had moved up a chair to chat with Bijon.

'Everyone's got one—please take yours.'

Now Swati noticed the turban behind Majumdar, holding a tray. God! How could she have assumed it was only for her, that he had made out she was thirsty . . . God! But revealing this embarrassment would be an even bigger embarrassment; so she summoned up the courage to tear her eyes away from the advertisement for the world-famous watch; a little loudly, conscious of not using the more common English words, she asked in Bengali whether it was a cold drink.

'You don't care for them?'

'The best drink is water.' Although it sounded contrived, Swati said what she really felt, and noticing the smile on Majumdar's face, she added, 'And the best cinema hall is Metro, as it's the only one with arrangements for water.'

'Not any more. The rate at which the paper glasses were being pilfered . . .'

'But why pilfer them?' Saswati had heard. 'You didn't have to buy them . . .'

'Precisely why!' Harit grabbed at the discussion. 'If anything is available free, that's it! Because they don't charge for the butter in London restaurants, Bengalis don't leave any behind on their tables!' Harit threw his head back and laughed.

'But since there is no water, for now . . .'

Finally comfortable, Swati accepted the chilled glass, while Majumdar approached Saswati. 'No, not me!' Saswati shrank back.

'Something else in that case . . .'

'No, nothing for me . . .' Saswati didn't enjoy the air conditioning. It was already so cold that even considering anything else that was cold made her feel wintry.

'Why not, go ahead!' Harit craned his neck around Bijon's back to look at his wife.

A plea appeared in Saswati's eyes—an ardent plea—but Harit probably didn't notice it in the dark, and what if he did? 'Now that it's been bought, it'll be wasted if you refuse it.' Would she be able to escape the ultimate logic?

'For you, Mr Nandy?' Majumdar stretched his arm out to Harit.

Normally Harit was derisive in masculine fashion whenever the subject of cold drinks came up, but today he felt a wave of kindness for this male-money-sucking female-heart-pleasing object—for you had to return civility with civility—accepting the glass he took a sip through the straw, then told Saswati emphatically, 'It's rather good.'

Saswati was surprised at this. When out with her husband, she had sometimes wanted something cool to drink, only to hear Harit say immediately, 'Are these even meant for decent people? All rubbish!' This constant litany had genuinely led Saswati to believe cold drinks were lower class—she was even a little embarrassed at not yet having brought herself to dislike them vehemently—and now here was Harit recommending them! Maybe these were extraordinarily good—they were a rupee each—refusing would indeed be wrong! 'All right,' Saswati held out her hand.

'You don't have to if you don't want to,' Majumdar said with a smile.

'Why waste it,' Harit looked sideways. 'You'll have to pay for it, after all.'

'Does one have to have it because it has to be paid for?' Majumdar seemed to want to know from Harit.

'Show-off. Flaunting his money,' Harit said to himself. Audibly, he declared, 'I'm not in favour of squandering money.'

Seeing her husband's grim face, Saswati didn't hesitate any more; she took the glass, slowly absorbing the chill that made her shiver. Luckily for her, the interval ended immediately, and when all eyes were riveted to the screen as the actual film began, she placed the almost-full glass beneath her chair. She quite forgot to move back to the seat next to Swati's, so Majumdar had to sit between the sisters.

And from that vantage point, he couldn't help watching more than the film. Turning alternately to the right and to the left, without being noticed by either of them, he compared

their beauty, taking into account the fine distinctions. Unlike
old-fashioned people, he didn't discount the contribution of
make-up; a modern man, he knew that the world's eye would
always be fixed on well-groomed people; therefore it was real,
it was everything. Still, his astute eye penetrated the make-up to
look within too; that the elder sister was looking very fair
had much to do with talcum powder and the darkness in the
hall; observing the portion between the elbow and the sleeve of
the blouse, which was left uncovered, allowed him to discover the
truth quickly enough. Her face was round, the nose too straight,
the mouth too small; about to deliver the verdict in favour of the
younger sister, Majumdar's judgement paused—being youthful
was to the younger one's advantage—that was still the case,
she was still at that age when a difference of even three or four
years made the skin glow a little more, but after her wedding—
after spending a few years in uninterrupted repose and unending
comfort in her husband's home—would that egg-shaped face
and the slightly slanted eyes win the prize as easily? What
if she tended to put on weight like her sister? What if her
chin acquired folds? Majumdar tried to identify in Saswati the
Swati of the future; he made a careful inventory of the flaws that
today's freshness concealed; but when he looked once more after
all his bookkeeping, he instantly identified that quality on her
face, which we have termed—unable to find another word—
grace; all his calculations failed, he knew for certain in his mind
that this grace would never be lost even after the assault of years.

Majumdar almost made up his mind . . . He was now at
that stage of life where he needed a wife. It was not a physical,
emotional or domestic need. Only helpless people, or the poor,
used their wives to meet those needs. That most men were
willing to spend their entire lives with just one woman, their
wife, was simply because wives were the cheapest, and the least
troublesome. But he was neither in search of the cheapest nor
afraid of trouble. Then why? It was just that a wife at this

point would suit him well, look apt, and it was undeniable that there were one or two benefits that in today's civilized world you could only expect to get from your wife. Just as the painting had to match the wall, and the frame the painting, so too did you need a wife to match your money; or else there was something missing, things didn't quite fall into place. Money was invested in business, was moved around between banks, was pinned to a piece of land; how much money could a busy man like him blow up anyway, with a wife the money could be put to good use, the bright showcase could be decorated just the way one wanted to and displayed to everyone. It wasn't as though he had made a great deal of money—not at all!—but there was nothing standing in the way either; whether he made any more or not, the first fifteen years of hard work had already ensured that he had made reasonable arrangements to secure his future, at least he was no longer in danger of being poor . . . Being able to make this claim—even to himself—with conviction gave him goosepimples; he looked behind him—as though he really thought that the moment he turned he would still see the grotesque and horrifying shadow of poverty—but instead he saw indistinct rows of people who had the best food and drink and clothes and homes among the millions in Calcutta, who were, therefore, the happiest. Oh, he had had a close shave. How scared he had been, in what fear he had spent his days—until just the other day. Poverty had bared its teeth at him twice a day through the river of watery curry coursing through mountains of rice, cheap coats that shrank to the point of choking him, the rotting stench like that of seaweed rising from the noxious, damp bathroom. He suddenly remembered Sidhu Mistry Lane from his childhood; seven families sharing just one . . . From dawn there was a long queue of those who had to go to work— the women were done before sunrise . . . How his father had thrashed him one day for soiling his pants . . . A lavish feast was being shown on the screen now, Calcutta's happiest people sat all around him—he ran his eyes over them as though to satisfy himself that he had indeed escaped that prison of ugliness permanently.

Sometimes he was astonished when he thought about how he had done it. Was it meant to be this way? He, the eldest of four sons of a godown clerk at John Morrison & Co.! Bloating on his meals of rice and daal, he would somehow scrape through the matriculation exam, then get into any job, at any salary, once he had gone out in the world, what more could one expect from life, putting on an open-breasted coat over one's dhoti, proudly taking the nine o'clock tram! That's what should have happened, he shouldn't have been able to even think of anything else . . . But he had divine inspiration, a heavenly fire in his breast; he had felt intensely discontented; he had hated this existence, the existence that was his by the fault of his birth, on the first Sunday of the month, when a kilo of potatoes and one and a half kilos of mutton would be cooked, when his brothers would sing and dance all morning, when they would lick every available portion of their plates, he used to gag, choking on his food. Money, I need money—he had recited to himself even then—money before everything, money above everything, money somehow or the other, since you could get anything if you had the money, and nothing if you didn't. He had kept that vow, people would say it was incredible; but he knew that what was really incredible was the fact that this vow had actually taken root within him. Could he ever have nurtured such high hopes had fate not been especially kind to him?

And now—now he needed a wife. He had worried enough—worked enough—for money; he would have to worry, would have to work, for this too—if not as much, at least in the same way. For just as you needed money to live, to marry you needed your wife to be beautiful. When he went somewhere with his wife, they must be the cynosure of all eyes. Of course, this one wasn't particularly glamorous, she didn't make you stagger when you saw her, but all that was a matter of dressing suitably and make-up, the aspect of beauty that could never be purchased, the face—for a moment Majumdar almost melted—the face was indeed lovely. If the make-up was right, if the unkempt hair were done up properly, if the expression of I-catch-everyone's-eye-but-no-one-catches-mine could be mastered, she too would be like those vain women whom Majumdar saw in restaurants, at the racecourse, whom he admired in his mind, with all his heart, but whom he had been forced to omit from the list of women he wanted to marry simply because he had never caught their eye. Left with no option, he had cast his eye lower down, at middle-class Bengali families, and for such a middle-class family this one was of course high class—so high that if she could become adept at social behaviour and conversation, she would be able to take him to the summit; these very arms would propel him into the chariot of fortune, even into the exclusivity of Lady Ganguly's drawing room or Rani Rukmini's lake party. . . And Bijon would prove useful too, his own brothers were beggars by nature, unable to resist the lure of small change—he had employed them as clerks, they would remain clerks all their lives; he had appointed his father his cashier—why pay a salary to someone else for something his father could do perfectly well? But besides all this he had been searching for someone else too, someone who would know what he had in mind from the barest of hints, someone who wasn't happy earning a pittance. Bijon, whatever else he might be, had his nose in the air—he didn't gasp at the thought of money, he could reel off large sums easily . . . Shifting in his seat he pulled out a cigarette, asking softly, 'Will the smoke disturb you?'

Swati was intent on the film, she didn't hear.

Majumdar raised his voice a little to convey his request a second time.

'No, not at all . . .' After a brief glance at him, Swati returned to the screen at once, her elbow on the armrest on the far side, resting her face on the back of her palm.

Finally Swati was enjoying herself. She had come unwillingly, spent the time up to the interval uncomfortably. She had made up her mind already, but suddenly Saswati came that morning, the first thing she said was, 'You'd better be ready, we'll pick you up.'

'What do you mean?'

'Don't pretend!' Saswati dismissed Swati's gravity.

'But I've already told Dada I'm not going.'

'Oh, my little adamant sister!'

'Did Dada tell you to talk to me?'

'He told us that Prabir Majumdar has invited us to a Chinese restaurant after the film.'

Saswati sounded quite excited. But Swati repeated, 'I'm not going.'

'How stupid! He's made all the arrangements; we have agreed, not going now will be extremely rude.'

'You may have agreed. I haven't.'

'So you aren't going?' Saswati became inwardly angry.

'No.'

'Why not?'

Swati didn't answer.

'Has anything happened?'

'No. What could have happened?'

'Has Biju quarrelled with you?'

'Of course not!'

'You look upset.'

'Really?'

'Why don't you tell me what it is?'

'Nothing!' Swati smiled slightly.

Unable to hold back her rage any longer, Saswati flared up, 'All of us can go and you can't? What an important person you've become!'

'I must have, or else why are you pleading with me to go?' Swati replied loftily.

'I'm asking you because I'll feel bad about going without you—no, not even that—because you'll enjoy yourself!' Saswati stomped out.

Swati hoped Saswati would be too angry to bring it up again, but what happened was just the opposite. She could be heard talking to their father, and soon she returned with him in tow. 'Tell her, Baba, tell her!' Saswati's eyes glittered.

Rajen-babu recalled these sisters' quarrels, screams, fights when they were children—it was their luck that it still wasn't over, and my luck that I'm still witness to it. Smiling, he said, 'Well? What's the matter?'

Before Swati could open her mouth Saswati raised her voice, 'You've made her so unsocial, Baba—but she *will* have to mingle with people one day, won't she?'

'Have *I* made her that way?'

'Who else! You never let her go out . . .'

'Why should Baba not let me go out!' Swati exclaimed. 'I don't feel like going anywhere.'

'There! She thinks her own wishes are all that matter.'

'All right, all right,' Rajen-babu mediated. 'Let Chhordi's wish be all that matters today. But am I not invited?' He was pleased that Saswati had at last been allowed to spend money on her own.

'Baba . . .' Swati stopped as she was about to say something, and Saswati buried it by saying quickly, 'Didn't I tell you? That friend of Biju's has invited us.'

'Biju's friend?'

'Majumdar—the one he had invited the other day.'

'I see.'

'Although he's Biju's friend,' Saswati smiled, 'he's quite nice . . . We're going, can't Swati come too, Baba?' It sounded as though Swati didn't want to go lest her father object, and Saswati was here on her behalf to get him to agree.

'No, Baba, I shan't go,' Swati said immediately.

Even in these words Rajen-babu heard her wish to go. She should indeed be going out more, going to different places; girls her age had so much fun these days. 'Why not, you must go,' he said with extra insistence. 'You'll enjoy yourself.'

∾

Swati had to join the group almost as though she had no choice, she felt helpless when she sat in Majumdar's car. A suspicion lurked within her—although it was not evident, Majumdar was paying more attention to her, today's arrangements were all for her; at once she also chided herself—can anyone think this way unless they're very vain? Swati tried to relax—to join in the fun that the others were having, to join her brother and sister in their laughter and jokes—but her ears seemed more eager to listen to what Majumdar was telling Harit as he drove, her eyes repeatedly stopped at Majumdar's freshly shorn neck above the light blue collar, a little later she was cross with herself for thinking of him quite so much; even in the cinema hall her discomfiture didn't go, and she had almost been caught out during that cold-drink episode—she had almost lifted the lid off her vanity, her silliness! Majumdar must have concluded that she felt he was thinking of her alone— she wanted to slap herself.

But within two or three minutes of the start of the film, she forgot all of this. Perhaps because the film was above average, or because she watched films once in a blue moon, or maybe the controlled beauty of made-up stories appealed greatly to her because of the novels she read, the swift, bright, living images drew her in almost immediately. She had obviously enjoyed what she had watched; she had enjoyed, too, the place where she had watched it—she had never sat in the balcony seats of Metro before—at last she had realized how comfortable the chair was, how soft behind her back, how much room there was for her legs, she observed the carpeted corridor, the gilded ceiling, the paintings on the wall—but people watched films in the dark, what was all this for? But because of all of this, Swati had to admit, the film was even more enjoyable; she was entranced by the enticing conspiracy of the setting to make her forget everything else for the time being. She sank into physical comfort, into mental repose—for films offered no time to think—as she was caught in the sensation of what was a new luxury for her, Majumdar in the next seat receded a thousand miles—being able to forget him filled the cup of Swati's joy. And the warmth of that joy did not drop the instant the film ended, like other weary veterans of film-watching, she did not feel an emptiness as soon as she stepped outside; climbing down the glamorous stairs amidst the glamorous people, step by step, she even liked the idea that instead of going home immediately they would now go somewhere else that was new to her.

At Chang-Aan Swati seemed a different person. She spoke freely, laughed; in fact, her shining eyes and the colour in her face seemed to betray a touch of exhilaration. She was seeing Calcutta's Chinatown for the first time; narrow, winding, dimly lit lanes—you couldn't tell the turns in the lanes apart from the doors leading into houses, flat-faced, slanted-eyed Chinese people crowded together cheek by jowl; men, women, even children, eating rice with chopsticks, playing cards with great concentration, mothers stood on the road with their children in their arms—the road was only a step away from their homes, you didn't even need a flight of steps—so the entire lane, actually, the entirety of each of the lanes, appeared to be their home, the car seemed outsized, out of place. After about ten turns, Swati was surprised that Majumdar didn't lose his way even once—the two-storeyed house with a gate that he stopped in front of was the finest building in the neighbourhood, and so resembled a regular house that Swati didn't even realize at first that this was Chang-Aan. There were no glittering lights outside, no signboard; and it was very quiet inside too, just two old British men at a table with glasses before them, but they didn't even have the time to glance at the newcomers, they belonged to the ruling classes, after all! She thought it would be nice to sit at that corner table between the windows, but no—Cabin No. 4 had been reserved for them; this wasn't bad at all; it had a window too, the black darkness hung like a velvet curtain, but in just a few moments she spotted the sky beyond the darkness through the twinkling eyes of three stars. And as soon as she had had a spoonful of soup, a sharp hunger seemed to awaken within her—a hunger not just for food, but for conversation, laughter, a hunger for friendship, a different hunger—for the world of living people outside books. She was the one to begin the conversation, saying: 'What did you think of the film, Chhordi?'

'I liked it . . .' Saswati's words were not matched by her tone. All films seemed the same to her, more or less; at the time they all seemed good, afterwards she remembered nothing.

'The film was very good . . . It could have been . . . if the ending . . .'

'Hollywood logic.' Harit smiled toothily at Majumdar, for he was the only one among those present who was somewhat worthy of conversation. 'The hero even got rich at the end. Ha!'

'Don't tell me anything about the film!' Majumdar's laughter, though silent, seemed loud. 'I didn't watch the film at all. If you're going to the cinema to watch a film, then why bother to go?'

Harit laughed in a different tone in response to this masculine humour, and, unable to understand, Swati was surprised. 'Why didn't you watch the film?'

'I didn't watch half of it at all,' Majumdar told the truth.

'But why?' Swati didn't let up on her questioning.

'I was thinking,' said Majumdar gravely.

'Now that you've confessed, confess your thoughts too,'

Harit did a favour to Majumdar by adding a note of camaraderie to his voice.

'I was thinking of my good fortune at being able to spend this evening with all of you.' As he finished, Majumdar was about to take his eyes away after a brief glance at Swati, but Swati's eyes held him back.

'I think the biggest problem with films,' said Swati, 'is that you can't express what people are thinking.'

Swati's eyes had made Majumdar quaver in hope, but what she said deflated him completely. Still he tried to follow the thread back to the wish it had originated in. 'Do you wish you knew what people are thinking?'

'Rubbish!' Harit gave his opinion immediately. 'Nothing but a carbuncle of bourgeois culture! I can't even get myself to read fiction, other than detective stories!'

'Yes!' Bijon finally proved that he was listening to the conversation. 'Some of those detective novels—oh!' He immediately lowered his eyes to the plate of sweet-and-sour pork, which is why the flicker of contempt in Harit's eyes touched him without hitting its mark. Majumdar's expression supported Harit's viewpoint, and, addressing Swati, he kept the exchange alive with 'What kind of books do you like?'

'Books that tell the truth are the books I like.'

'How can made-up stories tell the truth?' Saswati laughed.

'They can,' Biju informed her. 'Haven't you seen *True Story* magazine?'

'Not exactly—what I was saying was . . .' Swati began, a little embarrassed at first, but eventually she spoke quite freely, 'people's thoughts are in their heads, and they don't say what they think, but you can get to know what's on their mind only when you read, and that's what makes reading stories so worthwhile!'

This created something of a sensation. 'Don't people say what they think?' said Majumdar, laughing more than was warranted. Harit paused as he was about to spear a piece of meat with his fork; pointing his fork at Swati after a quick glance at her, he said, 'Swati, you're intelligent, you have learnt to express yourself, but you're becoming morbid. You should now . . .' He was about to add 'you should now get married' because at that moment she appeared quite attractive, and his own wife appeared far too dull next to her; but he did not want to expose his soft spot to a relatively unknown person; he applied the brakes in time.

Swati sensed the warmth in Harit's voice and eyes, enjoying it in silence.

'Aren't you going to find out what it is that you should do, Swati?'

'What should I do? To gain Harit-da's approval I should be like you.'

Majumdar and Harit laughed in unison at this. Biju laughed too, even Saswati did, though her laugh was forced, out of tune.

'For instance,' Swati didn't notice Saswati, she was looking directly at Majumdar now, 'Harit-da stopped without finishing what he was going to say. Does anyone actually say what's on their mind?'

Like Saswati's last time, this time it was Majumdar's and Harit's laughter that was forced—brief too—both seemed a little stiff. Looking from one face to another, Swati felt herself to be bolder, freer; she continued, 'The hero talks as though he hates the rich, but in his heart he feels just the opposite.'

'Right!' Majumdar almost shouted in eagerness. First the pleasure of a different kind of conversation, and then a conversation after his heart! Lest he betray too much excitement, he tried to look solemn, saying, 'It's because they envy the rich that people throw such barbs at them.'

'There is, after all, this one advantage to being rich—you can be happy under the impression that everyone envies you.'

Majumdar's expression hardened, and Harit burst out laughing. 'Well, it's better to envy the rich than to flatter them. I'd say that's a wonderful quality.'

'Envy is the sincerest form of flattery.'

Leaning back, Majumdar burst into laughter and Harit's eyes, meeting his, almost became ferocious; but the same eyes softened when they fell on Swati; after a brief glance he forgave this impertinence.

Swati realized she was the queen of the conversation. Whatever she said either hit home or made people laugh; Neither the well-groomed, oversized Majumdar, nor the learned, contemptuous Harit dismissed what she said, on the contrary, they wanted to hear more; Bijon and Saswati had been wiped out, she alone was talking to two adult men, as an equal—merely an equal? Swati's opinion of herself changed, for she had never before talked to Harit—or in his presence—on such equal terms; the level at which she had placed herself now rose much, much higher at one jump, more things to say came to her mind, to her lips— she never knew that she knew enough to say all this, all that had lain scattered, knotted up, at the bottom of her mind after reading all those books from all over the world now seemed to line itself up in rows, emerging unaided and so aptly that not only was Swati herself amazed, but she also realized that so were the others. The more she grasped she had a winning hand today, the more she spoke, and the more she spoke, the more she won. The hour that they took over their meal seemed to last only five minutes to her and to two others among those present.

Since Harit was sitting at the head of the table, the bill was brought to him. Looking at it, he said, 'You've spent a lot of money today, Mr Majumdar.' He said it from his heart—he himself wasn't fond of spending money, he didn't like it when others did either, even if he had played a part in the consumption.

Majumdar took out a sheaf of fresh currency notes with his left hand, counting out a few with his right, saying even before the waiter had left, 'One ends up spending fifty every day anyway.'

Harit tried to look at him light-heartedly, though the look was tinged with bewilderment. Even the royal scion Makaranda

looked for cheap options when throwing a party. But then his
father was still alive, he had to make do with a monthly allowance,
and this man's money was his own, there was no one to justify
his spending to. But did that mean he had to waste fifty rupees
every day? On what! Could anyone possibly spend that much?
They could easily—if they were immoral. Harit regained his
self-esteem with the thought that the man was either a liar or
a degenerate; spearing Majumdar with a crooked look, he said
softly, 'There's no joy in life like having an abundant, profuse,
unending supply of money, is there?'

Not realizing Harit was speaking his mind, Majumdar
was embarrassed.

'Of course there isn't!' Bijon suddenly spoke up. 'Everyone
should try to achieve it.'

'But since everyone cannot, no one should!' announced Harit.

Looking at Swati, who had stood up, Majumdar found an
answer, 'Maybe you can enact a law when it comes to money—
but women's beauty, men's intelligence—what will you do
about all these?'

'So it's only beauty for women and only intelligence for
men?' Swati raised her eyes, arched her eyebrows.

Majumdar was captivated. How well a diamond necklace
would suit her! The admiration in his eyes flowed into Swati's
throat, into her vocal cords too, she forgot to speak; and Saswati
answered on her behalf, which meant saying what was on
Majumdar's mind, though in a different tone: 'There are very few
women like you whose beauty is matched by their intelligence!'

A long-suppressed sigh was released along with this statement.
Majumdar noticed, and blamed himself immediately; when
two women were present, if you failed to notice one of them
because the other one was as intelligent as she was beautiful,
there was no forgiveness for boorishness, being able to keep your
head in any situation was known as intelligence. His estimation
of his own intelligence went down considerably—if Mr Nandy

did not pay attention to Mrs Nandy that could be passed off as politeness, but my behaviour should be different—keep the target in your sight, get your technique right—and bull's eye! How could I forget that she had taken my side on her own, and when it comes to the crunch she may prove to be my strongest ally, a greater ally than even Bijon, because it was natural that the widowed, aged father would pay more attention to the advice of the married daughter, but if I make mistakes like this, how will I get anywhere.

Majumdar tried to make amends at once. Standing by the exit door, almost guarding it, he said, 'I have something to apologize to you for, Mrs Nandy.'

'Whatever for, exactly?'

'You must be anxious to get home now...'

'Why?'

'When people have homes they are anxious to return...' Majumdar cocked an eye towards Harit, then sighed as though envious of the couple's happiness, then finished, '...but if you'd allow me a little more time, just a little, we could have some coffee on our way back—the Chinese may have good food, but for coffee it's Kaufman. The one good thing that Hitler has done for us by driving out the Jews is that we have finally learnt what good coffee is.' Majumdar's entire speech was addressed to Saswati, his voice acknowledged her as the queen; realizing that his words were having the desired effect, he immediately turned his eyes towards Harit, 'Pardon me, Mr Nandy. I may have been wrong about Hitler, but not about coffee, as I hope to be able to prove.'

Harit couldn't help being urbane and civilized for the moment. 'Your hospitality...'

'...must be reciprocated? Of course—I am willing to turn up whenever you give the order.'

That was not what Harit had meant to say, he had been about to mouth some polite cliché, but after this he had to accept

Majumdar's statement, saying, 'That would be a pleasure—but you're such a busy man—how will we ever track you down?'

'Track me down? That's easy, I have to go to Bijon every now and then. I simply have to—no better place, right, Bijon?' Majumdar put his arm round Bijon's shoulder in a comradely way. Bijon laughed insincerely, unsure whether the shift from the formal respectability of 'Mr Mitra' to this familiar intimacy augured well for him,.

'Then let's not delay any more, because,' having presented his proposal and had it passed, Majumdar stood upright, holding a panel of the swing doors, 'Frau Kaufman hates staying up even more than she loves customers.'

It didn't end with the coffee; after a couple of rounds of the Lakes, and dropping everyone at their respective doors, it wasn't until eleven o'clock that Majumdar was alone again. And the moment he was, he shed the bubbling, enthusiastic demeanour, the creases by his nose deepened, the lower lip covered the upper one, the chin slumped, the skin at his throat went slack, an exhausted man emerged, very exhausted, almost old. He went directly to Gitali's house—yes, the film-actress Gitali. She had almost fallen asleep, waiting up for him; 'So late?' she said, rubbing her eyes. There was neither eagerness in her voice, nor curiosity, as though all she wanted to say was: if you're going to be so late, you might as well not bother.

Majumdar didn't reply; he slumped on the couch he had himself picked out and purchased, his shoes still on.

'Do you want dinner?'

'No.'

'Lakshmi!' she called, looking at the curtained door—and in that summons her voice regained life—'Lakshmi, my dinner.'

The dinner came. Gitali didn't waste a moment devouring it.

As he had nothing else to do, Majumdar watched her eat. The cheeks swelled and ebbed, the throat bobbed, the insides of her mouth became visible at times, the tongue kept licking the lips. Not once did she speak, not once did she raise her eyes. Tearing with her hands, chewing with her teeth, swallowing with her throat, the body had become an instrument of consumption. 'She was waiting so long for me, she's famished—poor thing!' This thought could have occurred to Majumdar, but didn't, because he himself was satiated, and because he had been visiting her for six months, all he saw was ugliness, unbearable ugliness—not just in her, but in all womanhood; suddenly he felt that even greater than the exhaustion of working hard all day was the exhaustion of visiting a woman afterwards; and he was being forced to accept that exhaustion for life—for an entire lifetime—not for any other reason, but just to brag, to make people marvel at him! How agonizing it was to be affluent!

5

At the muted sound of the car door being opened the lights flashed on in the drawing room as well as inside the house; and as soon as Rajen-babu opened the door, the bright red tail-lights of the car disappeared around the corner of the lane.

Biju went inside, while Swati sat down in the drawing room, turning the fan on before she did. The room was warm—and wasn't it very small too?

Rajen-babu looked at his daughter, saying, 'I know you didn't want to go, but aren't you glad you did?'

Swati didn't speak. The late night breeze from driving around the Lakes was still playing on her skin.

'Saswati didn't come?' Rajen-babu said.

'No, I suppose not. She left.'

'Just as well. She'd have got very late if she'd come—it's past eleven anyway . . .'

'That late?'

After a silence, Rajen-babu said, 'Go to bed now,' and yawned himself.

That's true, what else was there to do now but to go to bed? Nothing at all, nothing at all. Every night everyone had to go to bed at a particular hour, had to sleep, Swati stood up with a shake of her head, a little angry at this arrangement of the Almighty's, and saw her father—not as though for the first time after returning home, but as though after a long time; as though he had not caught her eye this way in a long time. Sparse hair—a mixture of white, grey and black—small creases around the eyes and long ones beside the nose, slack skin at the neck, a wobbling paunch looking even larger on his bare torso, the edge of the dhoti tucked into the waist—with a hint of the mark around the waist where the dhoti usually begun. Swati saw an old man—aged, fatigued, companionless, currently sleepy. She was startled, surprised, as though she couldn't believe her eyes, for never before had Swati perceived her father as an old man.

What did it feel like to be old? How did it feel to be alive despite being old? All those other old or nearly old men whom she saw on the street whenever she went out—did Swati, or anyone else her age, consider them among the human race? No—she thought about it on the way to her room—she didn't consider them human beings, she wondered why they existed— what difference would it make if they didn't—she felt the world was hers, only for her and her generation—those who were her age, or close to her age, all felt the same way. However deep their divergences in perspectives and ideas, on this one subject they all had the same viewpoint, the same thought, everyone aged between fifteen or sixteen and twenty-five or twenty-six was so united that they never even talked about it, meeting one another's eyes was enough—in the thick, voluminous book of all their laughter, their fun and games, their conversations, their quarrels, their tears, this was written on the first page in bold, underlined letters. Crossing twenty-five alone took people out of focus—Harit himself seemed to be from a different species, and as for that enormous Majumdar, he must be . . . Yet, to tell the truth, had she had her head turned today by Harit's twenty-seven, or even by Majumdar's thirty-two?

Switching on the light in her room, she sat down in her chair without changing out of her sari, trying to work out at what age people became old, or till what age they did not. Forty? Whom did she know who was forty? Right! Her eldest brother-in-law! How old was he? Must be forty or thereabouts—but old? Like her father? . . . Suddenly she felt a pang at having considered her father old, even if only in her mind. All those old—or nearly old—people in this world who were nobody, who existed only to crowd the trams—was her father one of them too? Her father!

Aged, fatigued, companionless, sleepy, unable to sleep. Her father rose very early—whether in summer or in winter, always before sunrise—and was fast asleep by ten o'clock. He hadn't been able to fall asleep tonight because of her. The timepiece on the desk—her father had given it to her after she had passed her matric exams—showed the time as ten past eleven: she had returned after a gap of nearly six hours. When had she ever stayed out for such a long time? She couldn't remember a recent occasion. Even college hours didn't last as long, and besides, she went to college in the morning, when everyone went to work—but at night? They had all been to the theatre in Shyambazar with her brother-in-law—all, except her father—why? But there was no question of his going to the theatre, and so Shweta had often stayed back too with the same eagerness with which the rest of them had gone—she would 'be able to talk to Baba in private'.

And she? She hadn't really wanted to go today, it was her father who had told her to go, and Saswati had insisted so strongly . . . But was it really because of her father that she hadn't wanted to go? No—Swati paused before answering her question to herself—she hadn't wanted to go because of Prabir Chandra Majumdar. Why was he the reason for her not wanting to go? She didn't like the man—didn't like? Had these six hours been very painful?

Swati saw herself on the velvet cushion of Metro Cinema, on the dazzling carpeted stairway, in the intimate cabin at Chang-Aan, during the breezy drive around the Lakes. And what of her father, all this time? Alone at home, on a mat in the unlit veranda, a paan or two, silent in the silent house—he wasn't in the habit of reading either—what must he have been thinking about? Pass the time somehow till nine o'clock, so that he could have his solitary dinner—two more paans, and then sleep as soon as he went to bed, but not even that tonight; alone in the dark he had stayed up for her; perhaps becoming anxious as the hours had gone by, but there was no one to share his anxiety with; he wouldn't say anything to her either, there was no one to say anything to her; truth to tell, what *did* her father have to tell her, and what did *she* have to tell him! Her eldest sister was fifteen years older than her; when she sat with her father she couldn't tell him enough about her life, but the restlessness of her own thoughts, how much of that could she tell him? Right now, for instance, after the film, the dinner at the Chinese restaurant, the coffee at Kaufman's, the rounds of the Lakes—after all of these did she want to go to bed and fall asleep as soon as she had returned home? Wouldn't she rather talk for some time, chat for some time, laugh, fall asleep while still talking, talking sleepily till she dropped off? But her father was dying to sleep, her brother was in bed too by now; she alone would get no sleep, no fulfilment.

Why?

Swati looked around her room. Neat and clean, everything in its place. The cane chair, the wicker stool, the saris neatly arranged on the low clothes-rack, the books on the small bookshelf,; the bed made already with the mosquito net in place, a covered glass of water on the desk, everything arranged perfectly, just the way she liked it. She looked around even more closely: freshly washed curtains on the window, books that had been scattered on the desk now neatly lined up in a row, her mother's fading photograph on the wall now a little less faded. Nothing new, it was the same every day; she spent her days as she liked, left things lying around, and the maid cleared up after her twice a day, under her father's instructions. She was fine, she lived in great comfort, none of her sisters had ever had a room to themselves, her friends at college probably didn't, if you came to think of it, how many people in the country had a room to themselves, she had got hers entirely by chance, only because she happened to be her father's youngest daughter. But whatever the reason, she was comfortable, away from prying eyes, independent, left to her own devices; why then did sleep elude her, why did happiness elude her, something was missing, but what?

What?

Swati stretched out for the glass of water, and as soon as she picked it up she noticed a . . . a letter. Putting the glass down without a sip of the water, she picked up the stiff white envelope, but didn't open it immediately. She looked at the name on the envelope, her name, wavy letters in black ink, when had it come, how long had it been waiting for her; had she gone to bed immediately she may not even have noticed it today. This was wrong! But wrong of whom? Where had Satyen Roy been all this while? Starting this evening, until a moment ago, she hadn't thought of Satyen Roy even once, just as she hadn't thought of her father till the moment she got home. And just as her father had seemed different the moment she stepped in, so too this letter . . .

Swati's breath deepened; sweeping her hair out of the way, she slowly opened the envelope, slowly unfolded the crisp folded piece of paper inside. A wave swept over her, a wave that spoke to her with black letters, a breeze blew over her, a mountain breeze, a cold breeze, of calm, of turmoil. She remembered, in that very instant she seemed to remember, all the other letters; all the letters she had received, all the letters she had written, starting with that first letter from Santiniketan; all of them returned, flying like a flock of birds, some white, some light blue, but the whites and the blues all flying in the same direction, into the distance, after which the blue couldn't be told apart from the white.

Finishing the letter, Swati picked up the glass of water, draining it slowly. The water flowed down like a stream within her, a waterfall cascading down the side of a mountain—cool, even from a distance. The more it cascaded the more the turmoil grew—two lines of white and blue waterfalls tumbled towards the faraway, distant sea, after which the blue couldn't be told apart from the white.

With one hand on the letter, Swati reclined her head, shutting her eyes.

'Swati.'

She was so startled at the call that she almost fell off her chair. As she regained her balance and stood up, her first thought was to put the letter beneath a book. But no—why should she hide it, from whom? With a smile, she said, 'Not asleep yet, Baba?'

'Nor are you.'

'Not sleepy.'

'Not sleepy, so sleeping in your chair?'

'I wasn't sleeping,' Swati said, 'I was thinking.'

'Oh my sleepless thinker!' Rajen-babu laughed loudly at his daughter's grave pronouncement and even graver expression. 'Go to bed this minute, not a minute later.'

'Yes, Baba, I will.'

Sensing hesitation on his daughter's face, he said, 'Need something? Shall I call the maid?'

'No, Baba, go to bed . . . I'm . . . In a minute . . .' Swati waved the letter lying on the desk between two fingers, then slowly put it back in the envelope, so that it caught her father's eye.

With a fleeting glance, Rajen-babu said, 'What has Satyen written?'

'How did you know who the letter's from?'

'Who else do we know with such lovely handwriting?'

'He writes very well, too,' said Swati. 'How beautifully he's written of the Tamu range—shall I read it to you, Baba?'

'Naughty girl! Any excuse to stay awake! Not another word—bed!'

Rajen-babu returned to his room, went to bed in the darkness. And, a little later, the curtained door between the two rooms mingled with the darkness too, and, even later, a humming in a soft, very soft, voice wafted into his ears; first a diffident, wavering, tentative humming; rising a little now, but still a humming; then dropping again, a gentle, liquid, humming; oh—this *behaag*, it can make you mad—Swati had gone and stopped her singing lessons, if only she hadn't—she hadn't even taken the lessons properly, just that little bit at Jatin Das Road; she didn't sing even by mistake these days—music had returned to her tonight after so many years, after so many years Rajen-babu rediscovered music in his heart. He listened with eager ears, he listened with a fulfilled heart—one or two words wafted in as well, possibly a song of Rabindranath's—that's why it was so beautiful—the words were drowned immediately, just the humming continued—let it not stop, it didn't stop, that night, in the silent darkness, in his sleep-laden bed Rajen-babu was gradually submerged in a sadness he had never experienced, in a happiness that only imagination could bring; all the fatigue of his life was washed away, all the world was wrapped in peace, and still, even after Rajen-babu fell asleep, the humming continued—soft, softer, in a fading liquid voice, a little haltingly—the humming words of a humming mind—distress, apprehension, prayer, questions.

∾

Ever since Saswati had used her as an emissary to pass a book to Shubhro, and Shubhro had smiled oddly on seeing the flash of a blue envelope as soon as he opened the book, Swati used to be terrorized whenever she saw a blue letter—that is to say, she used to feel a terror at the very thought that someone might write to her that way some day. But in Satyen Roy's room she saw a pen tucked into the dark blue pad on his desk, and it was on that notepad that the first letter came from Santiniketan. Her fear was dispelled, she even liked—liked very much—that dark blue, almost indigo colour. A few days later she too bought herself dark blue notepaper and envelopes, such an unusual colour was not available in the neighbourhood shop, nor the slightly coarse fabric-like notepaper, she bought the best she could get, and then wondered whom she could write to on this new blue pad.

But Swati had no one to write letters to. Sometimes she had to write on her father's behalf to Shweta in Mymensingh, to Mahashweta in Rangoon, to Saraswati in Delhi—how is Tata after her measles, which class is Iru in now, send a photo of Dipu's, I'm well, Baba's well, how are all of you—letters with fragments of news, the same every time, dry bone—were they even letters?

Even so, she attached some flesh and blood to them, she informed Shweta, 'Some mornings I long for *alusheddho*—but not any old *alusheddho* . . .' An entire page filled up this way . . . To Mahashweta, she asked, 'Why haven't you written about your holiday in Memio? What a lovely name it is—Memio, tell me, have you ever taken the steamer to Vamo, I was reading in a book the other day . . .' In her mind she travelled to Vamo. Vamo, Memio, Mandalay—the M sound was so sweet; all of Burma was one large bumblebee—and to Saraswati she wrote the other day, 'We suddenly found a book in the trunk with your name on it, can you guess what book? How would you remember—Satyendra Datta's *Song of Dusk*. Shejdi, I didn't know you read poetry back then, the book's mine now, all right? Your handwriting is just the same, the last few pages are missing, the paper's yellowed—the book's even better that way...' And so it went, with a profusion of dashes.

But when the replies to all these letters came, after long delays, Swati immediately realized her mistake. Mahashweta was so sick most of the time that her letters seldom progressed beyond a few lines; every letter from Saraswati bore the stamp of haste, wrong words, dropped words, repeated words—she didn't even have the time to read what she had written; and as for Shweta, she had long stopped writing letters herself, what else were grown-up daughters for. Three sisters living in different cities, and still no one to write letters to, but such a strong longing to write—was this regret any less intense than the other things that people referred to as regrets?

∾

She had once tried to exchange letters with Anupama from her college, when Anupama was on holiday with her uncle in Barisal. Turning tradition upside down, Swati had been the one to write first. The reply had arrived promptly too, inspired by this she had been rather verbose in her next letter, but Anupama's second letter never did arrive. When Swati asked after college reopened, 'Why didn't you reply to my letter?' Anupama smiled guiltlessly. 'What to write, and where was the time?' What did she mean? No time? What was time meant for in that case? Nothing to write? Then what was the constant turmoil in the heart for?

'Will you write to me, Chhordi?' She had made the proposal with trepidation, out of the corner of her eye, in a muted voice, to Saswati.

'Letters?' The question mark was sharper in Saswati's response.

'I'll write and you'll reply.'

'What on earth!' Saswati laughed.

Without answering, Saswati looked into her eyes and laughed even more.

'Don't you like writing letters?'

'I used to at your age, but . . .' Without finishing, Saswati left the room, her pearl earrings glittering.

After this, one afternoon, Swati wrote herself a long letter, and then, becoming a second person herself, spun an even longer reply the next day; after that, of course, she tore up both letters, because she didn't enjoy this game any more, and felt worse when she remembered Gorky's story about Teresa.

As a result, the pad with the blue notepaper hadn't become particularly slimmer over these past six months. Or, it had lost as much weight in the sixth month as it had in the first five, after Satyen Roy went to Shillong. Swati hadn't expected a letter—or perhaps she had—don't people have expectations? Though she hadn't really imagined . . . But the letter suggested it was obvious—as though he used to live here before he went to Shillong, and there was no one but Swati to write to about his holiday in the hills. Finally, Swati's dream of getting letters, of writing letters, materialized: as she let loose the major part of the long, lazy holidays—of the long May, of the long days of summer—in a flock of blue-and-white writing, a bright June arrived at her doorstep.

But why had writing letters suddenly become so difficult? Why was someone for whom words spilled out easily—from mind to pen and from pen to paper—now silent, pen in hand? She had filled four pages with a single tale, but when she read the whole thing after finishing it—oh dear, how terrible, childish, what on earth had she written!—she tore it up immediately, flinging the pieces to the floor, she started again, but simply couldn't get going in the next ten minutes. The problem was not that there was nothing to say; the problem was that there was so much to say that it was a problem to decide what to say and what to leave out. All the things she wanted to write about seemed trivial. And yet she had written letters about just such things just the other day, why had she? Why?

A simple, extremely simple, but strange, extremely strange question grew in the twinkling of an eye in Swati's mind, like the magician's tree which grows instantaneously from a tiny seed to a full-blown plant, complete with leaves and branches: why did Satyen Roy write to her, and why, for that matter, did she reply immediately on receiving his letter, how well did they really know each other, and in what way, there was no question of exchanging letters really, but this simple fact had not occurred to her all these days—why hadn't it?

The Sunday after that evening at the cinema went by in vain for Swati, she didn't succeed in replying to the letter.

The next afternoon, when she had almost finished her letter—feeling lighter at having been able to shed a weight, as it were—the maid appeared to inform her that a gentleman had arrived.

Her heart leapt into her mouth. Was it Satyen Roy? Had he returned suddenly? But the letter . . . Never mind the letter then. Rising, wiping her face with the end of her sari, she asked, 'Have you asked him to take a seat?'

'He has.'

'Have you turned on the fan?'

'Oh—I forgot!'

Swati was angry. Even after all this time she hadn't learnt that as soon as anyone came, the fan . . .

Her anger rose as soon as she entered the drawing room. How silly the maid was, really! Couldn't she have just said Biju wasn't home.

The end of his dhoti sweeping the floor, Majumdar stood up, setting off a sparkle of glitter on the edge of this dhoti as he greeted her, his eyes twinkled, his lips smiled, resuming his seat, he said, 'Bijon's probably not at home?'

'No. He never is at this hour.'

'I thought as much,' said Majumdar, leaning back even more comfortably in his chair.

'Is there any specific business you had with him? Should I give him a message?'

'No, there's no message. In any case I'm sure I'll meet him sometime during the day.'

After a brief silence Swati said, 'Didn't you have to go to office today?'

'Office? My office is wherever I am. Those who have jobs have it far better—ten to five at work, peace after that—but the way things are changing by the day, the way I'm getting involved in fifty different things—as though no one but me can solve all these problems—there's no escaping even if I want to—how long will this go on, where will it end . . .' Pausing suddenly and smiling, he said, 'But why am I telling you all this?'

Swati didn't reply, as though she agreed with him on this point.

Eventually, Majumdar answered his own question himself. 'But then so what if I tell you, you may not enjoy listening, but I like telling you.'

Thinking of her almost-finished, yet-to-be-finished letter, Swati couldn't say anything this time either.

'Are you annoyed at my intrusion at this unrespectable hour?' asked Majumdar.

'No, no . . . Not at all . . . Why should I . . .?'

'You seem distracted?'

'Me?'

'What were you busy with?'

'Oh, just . . .'

'Napping?'

'Why should I be napping?' So he thinks I nap afternoons.

'I understand your situation,' Majumdar said seriously. 'You're dying to leave, but politeness decrees otherwise—isn't that so?'

Swati was embarrassed. This was her shortcoming, as well as her problem—that she couldn't conceal what was on her mind, but still, to say it like this, really! She raised her eyes, lowered them, smiled faintly, tried to say something, and Majumdar himself rescued her from this disconcerting dilemma with an affable smile and a touch of pleasant humour: 'But you needn't worry... I'm leaving in a moment... I'm on my feet all day... I quite like sitting here awhile.'

Swati's heart softened a little. She remembered a similar afternoon, when Satyen Roy had come for a few minutes to give her Rabindranath's *Nabajatak*. Really, how difficult life was for men... What difficulty, they were so independent, they could do whatever they liked, whenever they liked, here he was holidaying in the hills of Shillong—would she able to catch the post today? She dragged her mind back from the letter, saying easily, 'Oh, please stay as long as you like.'

'Like!' Although he didn't stay home in the afternoon even on holidays, the very thought made him claustrophobic, he modulated his response for the occasion and the audience: 'Tell me, who wouldn't like to spend the afternoon just chatting under the fan with the windows shut.' But Swati now heard exactly the opposite of the independence that she had associated men with a short while ago. 'But can one really do what one would like to do. Why else would such a thing as work exist in this world?'

'But you're not unwilling to work!' Swati was relieved at being able to say something at least.

Majumdar was clearly pleased at this, for this was high praise in his lexicon. He now said—but with a little more softness—what he normally bragged about to people who worked for him, who asked him for help: 'But that unwillingness is so strong in others that I end up having to work four times as hard, unnecessarily. The unemployed beat their breasts all the time, but I only see lots of work to be done, and not enough people to do it.'

She tried to display her support with her expression, without saying anything, for she had to be polite.

Encouraged, Majumdar continued, 'I have to run right away to the factory twelve miles away—one has to supervise things personally all the time, every little thing gets held up otherwise—although I've got several people in my kennel, earning salaries just to do this.'

The words didn't appeal to Swati, a thought about her brother nipped at her. Almost abruptly, she said, 'There was something I wanted to ask you. Do you know exactly what business Dada has gone into?'

'Don't you know?'

'He doesn't tell us anything.'

The gravity of the office boss descended on Majumdar's face immediately, he said softly, with several pauses, 'Bijon's doing quite well . . . He will do well . . . He's a man of many parts.'

'Parts?' Swati's eyes held a question.

'Competent,' answered the master of competence succinctly.

Imagine! The man who thought no one was willing to work was actually saying this about her brother—who had been renowned since childhood as the ultimate example of uselessness! Swati didn't seem sure whether to believe this or not. So what she said next also emerged as a question, 'That's good, isn't it?'

'I think so, it should be,' Majumdar answered sagely, as serious as the proverbial boss. Then he relaxed his manner, 'Are all of you very worried about him?'

Trying to gauge from his expression what and how much her brother had told him, Swati said, 'Would it be wrong to be?'

'Certainly not—especially as he's not even been able to pass his matric exam. But then I . . .' Majumdar smiled, displaying his large teeth, '. . . haven't progressed beyond the matric exam either.'

Swati tried to imagine how she would feel if her brother turned out to be another Majumdar.

'Passing or failing an exam in school is different from passing or failing the exam of life.' Majumdar shared his experience with Swati, and, with it, a reassurance: 'Tell your father there's nothing to worry about. I'll keep giving him subcontracts regularly, and that's how he will establish himself one day—now if only the war lasts a few years more.'

So Majumdar was a contractor? And her brother was in the same business? Swati was saddened. Softly, she said, 'But how can Dada help build houses?'

A smile spread through the folds in Majumdar's fat cheeks, but he also enjoyed the girl's naiveté. Almost affectionately he said, 'These aren't contracts to build houses, but to supply material for the war.' Looking at Swati he realized she hadn't understood, but without trying to explain further he said, 'I must have met Bijon when the stars were aligned perfectly.'

'Why?' Swati asked artlessly.

'That's how I happened to meet . . .' he had wanted to say 'you', but he changed it just in time, '. . . all of you . . . Your sister is a wonderful person. Harit-babu too. When will they be here next?'

'Why do you . . .'

'If I know in advance I can make an attempt to be present—provided none of you has any objection, of course.'

Swati tried to smile in a way that would suggest there was no question of any objection.

Suddenly glancing at this watch, Majumdar leapt to his feet, taking his leave as he left, he got into his car without a single backward glance . . . But it wasn't really sudden, he had been stealing glances at his watch, and he'd left just as he had planned. He had achieved what he had come for; the objective with which he had scooped out a few of his valuable Monday hours to drive upstream against the casually meandering current, from Canning Street to Tollygunge, had been met, met quite effectively, he was rather pleased with himself. He had come for his chosen one, not so much to get her to himself—what was to be gained from that, he would soon have to stomach an excessive amount of her company in any case—as to catch her unawares at home, unsuspecting, as unprepared as possible. But reality had surpassed his expectations, for he hadn't remotely imagined he would really see her this way, without make-up, without embellishments, just the way she had been at home. He had once performed the preliminaries of getting acquainted with a danseuse, the angel was the brightest spot at the party, but the same woman was unrecognizable one morning in her own home, she seemed a different person; it wasn't just that her complexion was much darker—even her features seemed to be different. Then again, he had also seen aristocratic women who looked almost identical at home and outside it; what they really looked like—if there was indeed such a thing as *real looks*—was something that probably nobody but God—if there was indeed such a thing as God—knew. Majumdar, of course, had already known that Bijon's sister belonged to neither of these two categories, but he had not known, not imagined, that in this day and age a woman could appear before a man without even running a comb through her hair, without even a trace of powder on her face, that she could appear just as she was, in a creased, less-than-clean sari. He had been looking at her closely as they spoke: little strands of curly hair flying into her brow under the breeze of the fan, the face purple, like when you're perspiring—wasn't there a fan in her room?—ink stains on her fingers—had she been writing? Didn't she have a fountain pen?—the sari rather apologetic, and the blouse, despite being concealed under the sari, had been caught out by his probing eye—a cheap blouse, poplin, that too it didn't fit her properly, she had probably made it herself. Ordinary, absolutely ordinary; you could find a couple of hundreds of thousands of such right now in Calcutta . . . But was that really so? The little strands of hair blowing into her brow, the face, the eyes, the smile—that faint smile of reluctance—and bare, fair, slim feet that matched the floor so well, even this low-quality floor, what if it had been a white-and-grey marble floor? Far too homebound by today's standards, childish at times, she didn't follow what was happening in the world, didn't understand anything about the world beyond her home; but rather nice, all told.

Majumdar suspected that this mid-afternoon hour in that faintly lit room had passed pleasantly, he had enjoyed his time there just as he was now enjoying, from his fire-baked afternoon-car, the sight of the curved pond with green water at the Park Street crossing. Majumdar didn't enjoy the fact that he had enjoyed his time there—it didn't match his opinion of himself, he seemed to lose some of his self-esteem. Still, as he drove along Mayo Road towards Dalhousie Square as soon as the amber light turned to green, the fair, slim pair of feet on the floor swam up before his eye, at that precise moment that pair of feet entered a pair of sandals, emerged on the street, walked swiftly, traversed the lane, stopped at the postbox on the corner. Shy words hid themselves in the darkness, a tiny, shy, light blue bird flew into the sky.

When the letter reached him, Satyen Roy was busy trying to do adequate justice to the afternoon tea at Hillview Hotel . . . Trying? Was the fame of hill-hood exaggerated, then, or was Satyen Roy not keeping well? No, in summer of that year, a month before the monsoon, Shillong could have won a global prize for healthy climes; and Satyen Roy, at the peak of his youth, with the freedom to lead a tranquil, even unambitious life, had managed to seize the qualities of Shillong in a way that possibly no one among the fifteen-hundred-and-odd summer residents had managed to do. He had never felt as good in his life, so good that the afternoon tea at Hillview Hotel was extracting almost its entire price from him. And why shouldn't it; since it was called tea, there was tea, of course; and he had managed to secure the facility of a teapot instead of readymade tea—though not free of cost—and though the teapot lost some of its heat by the time it arrived in his room from the kitchen, and though this was a land of tea—or perhaps because of it—the tea leaves were not the best either—but still it was tea, and not just tea; it was accompanied by *luchi*, fries and some fruit; true, the *luchi* was like leather, the fries like a rag, and the fruit included only diced banana and cucumber, or at most sliced sour wild apple. Be that as it may, Satyen Roy didn't have too many complaints about all this; his was not a complaining nature, and there was an antidote in the active nature of his liver; he was grateful enough just for that teapot, even more grateful at having got a room to himself; a room, in the sense that . . . But then what did one need more for, most of the day was spent outdoors—you had to use a flight of wooden stairs, if you shut the only window you were in trouble and if you kept it open you froze, because the room was detached from the main hotel building there was no electricity, but none of this appeared to be much of a problem to its current occupant, they were in fact convenience, wasn't any problem a convenience when the option was to spend the night in the same room as three or four clumsy companions? Satyen Roy was sipping his none-too-hot tea with considerable satisfaction, imagining that he was sipping High Mountain tea instead at Queen's Hotel (which he had spotted while on a walk)—and really, would staying in Queen's Hotel actually have provided more pleasure? I'm by myself, comfortable with no dearth of splendid thoughts to amuse myself with, what more could one ask for?

Nothing more; but it was proved just a little later that there *was* something else that could make him even happier. A local tribal man, working as a servant, handed him a letter and promptly withdrew; conveying clearly even in that fleeting moment that the tip to be left for him when the guest was departing should be commensurate with the number of times he had had to climb up that flight of wooden stairs to deliver these small but special pieces of paper.

Whether it's fresh warm bread, or a yet-to-be-opened newspaper, or a book with uncut pages, none of them is as good as a letter with a cup of tea. Morning or evening, whatever the kind of tea and whoever the sender of the letter—even a bill from a bookshop is welcome—so long as it's not a postcard. And if it happened to be a letter from someone whom you . . . liked; the kind of letter that . . . Even thinking about it was wonderful . . . Putting his cup down, Satyen Roy picked up the letter, turned it around in his hand, held it up to the light, as though he wanted to get a glimpse of what lay inside this way; then, slitting open the envelope and reading the letter breathlessly he picked up his cup again, the letter still in his hand, and took a rather long sip, instantly twisting his mouth— horrible! Quite cold! Quickly swallowing the cold tea he banished tea-thoughts from his mind for the moment; then he read the letter again, slowly, with pauses; he trained his eyes briefly on the name at the end of the letter, Swati, Swati Mitra. The name resonated within him, the way it had when he had heard it during that gold-and-red sunlight. A beautiful name. Two short words, of equal weight, gentle, rhythmic; light, all told, but solemn too; it looked nice when written, sounded nice when spoken . . . That's true, have I been thinking so much about this name? I don't seem to have left out any of the ways in which one can think of this subject! But . . . Suddenly he felt a jolt— he was surprised that despite so much thought he had not yet arrived at the real conclusion, that the name was unformed, temporary, untrue in a sense. The balanced, spare Mitra would be replaced and occupied by someone else one day; not one day, but soon—it was clear that that day was not too far away.

Satyen Roy couldn't quite approve of this change of name. Putting the letter back in its envelope, and the envelope in his pocket, he rose, almost energetically, pushed the cup, saucer and plate under the bed, pulled his suitcase out from the same place, unlocked it to take a clean handkerchief out, locked it again and pushed it back in place, rose to take the black shawl from the back of the chair to wrap it around himself, paused abruptly to peep into his wallet. All of these tasks reflected his penchant for neatness, the uniformity of the slow pace of his existence; but as he climbed down the wooden staircase he himself felt as though he was in too much of a hurry, as people are when they're annoyed, or as though he was about to meet someone—though, actually, there was no one.

He didn't walk very far; he sat down beneath the pines at the first place that appeared to be tolerably secluded. It was beautiful—any spot here was beautiful—but for the first time, possibly for the first time in his life, nature's playfulness didn't seem all that palatable. Nature had other forms of playfulness besides mountain scenes—these conquered his heart right now. He didn't muse on the philosophy of life that day; he mused on life itself—his own life—which, in his own estimate, was rather an unworthy subject, for people who thought far too much about themselves were those whose minds and hearts ouldn't go any further. In other words, those who were silly, stupid—or unhappy.

Satyen didn't want to consider the possibility of belonging to either of the first two categories, so he concentrated on the third.

But he had never thought of himself till now as unhappy. Just the opposite, in fact: the first twenty-five years of his life had blessed him with the conclusion that fortune was a little biased in his favour. When his mother had died—this chapter of his life had a great deal in common with his student's—he was old enough for it not to be too difficult to survive without her, but young enough for the blow not to be too harsh. His father didn't remarry, nor did he do anything worth mentioning the rest of his life. Leading a migratory life across different locations with his son, at low cost and low salaries, he sent his son to school in Santiniketan, and when the son went to Calcutta for higher studies after winning a scholarship in his matric exams, he settled down next to the Dhaleshwari river in the village he came from; he set up a library in the village with considerable effort; and then proceeded to pass his time reading two newspapers every day and providing willing or unwilling listeners with analytical solutions to various national, social and international problems, not a bad life, all told. The most willing, the most receptive listener was of course his son; and gradually he no longer remained a mere listener, he discovered one or two things of his own to say too; accordingly, his father began to await his visits home during the holidays quite eagerly. The father was very keen that his son became a pundit of history, but the son preferred English literature, but still he honoured his father's wishes by using part of his hundred-rupee prize from his honours course to buy him a few chosen volumes on Mughal history—since his interest lay largely in that area. Nor was this the first time he was sending something home; he had started offering private tuition even while he was in his Intermediate course, and his scholarship was always there in any case; it didn't take him long, therefore, to reach a period in life when he could take care of his own expenses entirely and still send small sums of money home to his father. He had learnt frugal living from his father; none of the habits that people often acquired as students in Calcutta, ensuring future unhappiness quite disproportionate to present happiness, had been able to attract him, he didn't even smoke; and as a result, despite being much poorer than many of his classmates and others of his age, his encounters with penury were nominal compared to theirs. The only useless expenditure was on books—it wasn't useless, however, but extremely useful—but even if a particular book was unaffordable it didn't matter, it was bound to be available in the college library, or somewhere else—and people did have to borrow the majority of books they read. No, he had not suffered from not having money, to tell the truth, he couldn't recollect a single day when he had had to face any intolerable inconvenience for lack of money.

Then, somewhat unexpectedly, his father died a few months before his MA exams. Still, he had managed to reach in time, that is to, say, shortly before the final hours. Initially, he had felt a deep loss, and a sense of unfairness too—his father hadn't been all that old—why, he had just crossed forty the other day. And, come to think of it, there were just the two of us . . . But fathers were released from the seemingly permanent business of being alive first—meaning, that was appropriate, and the appropriate was good. My father would have felt a lot, lot worse than I do right now had I been the one to have died while he had lived. If, say, a messenger of death were to tell me, 'Come with me this moment, or I'll take your father away,' then what would I have said? Would I have said, 'I'll come with you, spare my father'? No, that would have been silly—far too horribly cruel. Of course, he could have lived another ten, twenty or thirty years—but what sense would that have made, what did he have in his life anyway.

Satyen had never seen much brightness in his father's life, for although he had long forgotten any sense of emptiness he might have felt for his mother, he had always felt unhappy for his father because of her absence. He had realized that a motherless young man had little to be unhappy about, the unhappiness was all reserved for the middle-aged widower.

With these thoughts Satyen had staved off his tears, even wrung out some bitter consolation from them. And over the next few days, many more thoughts sprouted in his mind, just like the stubble on his face; the looming exams gave him courage; where was the time to be upset, it would all be pointless if the MA exams didn't go off well. For he had arrived at two, and only two, unambiguous conclusions about himself: first, that there was nothing he was prepared to do for a living except teach; and second, that there was nowhere he was ready to live except Calcutta. His years as a student had taught him that the competition in Calcutta was intense, that the people who had power had no conscience, and that the authorities were natural nepotists; those who could moor their boats at college jetties despite possessing only insignificant degrees had to have the power of strategic genealogy. But because his identity ended with his name, and started there too, even the slightest flaw in his qualifications would not be permissible. With more thought, he saw that the pattern of his life that had existed when his father was alive continued to be the pattern even now, and that the trajectory that his life would have taken had his father been alive had not been altered either; in going away, his father had not brought about any remarkable change in his life. In a motherless home, in the company of a detached father, he had always been self-sufficient; and in other senses too he had succeeded in becoming self-sufficient by the time he was seventeen; his life had essentially been distributed between various hostels and his father's house—and this house was also another kind of hostel—his life continued the way it had been, would continue, could continue, the same way, there was no displacement at all; the only difference was that he would no longer have to come to this village thrice a year. And this appeared to be a matter of convenience to him, a matter of huge convenience, for Satyen was neither a lover of the rural life nor a patriot. All this while he had only been self-sufficient, now at last he was independent too. Now he could travel, go anywhere he could afford to during the holidays, there were no more impediments, no more worries. These last thoughts made him sigh; but after completing the rituals, putting the books on Mughal history into his hold-all, along with the six or seven other books that his father possessed, placing his father's shawl—received as a wedding gift and now full of holes—at the bottom of his suitcase and completing his packing, when he sat down on a cot as bare as his shaven head, the sighs did not return.

A distant uncle arrived. 'So you're leaving today?'

'I'm leaving today.'

'Really . . . how unfortunate . . . that Naren would . . . so . . .' He lowered his voice, though such caution was quite unnecessary here. 'Has he left you anything?'

'He's left me,' answered Satyen.

'I can see that,' the uncle wouldn't accept defeat, 'but what has he left for you?'

'The entire world,' Satyen was about to say, but he restrained himself lest it sounded facetious; but he couldn't think of another response; trying to run his hand through his hair, as was his habit, and taken aback by the bristly feel of his shaven head, he said, 'But I don't need anything.'

'Listen to the boy talk! It's not a question of needing anything, and besides, what do you know of your needs yet. But what about this house, all this land . . .' Observing the contempt in Satyen's curled lips, he said, conveying even more contempt, 'It's not paltry, you can make about three hundred a year, or don't you need that either?'

'I really cannot imagine,' Satyen said after some thought, 'all this proving useful to me in any way.'

'Then I have a suggestion,' the uncle became serious. 'Sell it—I can buy it from you, if you like.'

'What do you mean buy . . .' Satyen laughed, perhaps a little animatedly. 'Please take it if it's of any use to you.'

The uncle misunderstood, noting that it wasn't as though the boy had no business sense at all. He wasn't unhappy, saying quite gently, 'You understand, don't you—my daughter's come back home a widow—so many children . . . I was thinking, at least a roof over her head . . .'

'Certainly—if it's convenient for her here . . .'

'The inconvenience will be yours . . . you will visit now and then, won't you?'

'I won't come here any more,' Satyen said with a disarming smile.

'But why shouldn't you, you must—we're all going to be here—and you're the pride of our village. Though you mustn't imagine we haven't had other scholars here . . .' The titles and professions of the living and dead Roychowdhurys of Tamalpur were reeled off with great gusto by the Tamalpur Roychowdhury with the least accomplishments: Satyen was told that among his clan were, or had been, two principals (one of them a PhD from Göttingen), a deputy postmaster-general, an executive engineer, an editor of the *Lahore Daily News*, a horticulturist at the governor's country home, and a bunch of deputy magistrates; none of it appeared new, he seemed to have heard all this several times before, but still he managed to maintain an expression of interest. 'Tamalpur expects a lot from you too,' concluded the uncle.

'Tamalpur will probably survive without me,' Satyen said to himself, 'and I will probably be better off too in the process.'

As he sat in the late afternoon shadows in Shillong's thin air, Satyen relived this day from four years ago as a living experience—the warm sunshine on his shoulders as he tramped off to the jetty, and the damp smoky smell as he walked up the ramp of the steamer. He had enjoyed the whole experience, perhaps indecently more than someone whose father had died just a few days ago should have. He did feel genuinely independent as soon as he left Tamalpur; he did feel genuinely happy at the thought of not having to return. He had never liked the place, in fact, he hadn't liked the fact that his father had liked the place. From his childhood, he had felt impaled on the sentiment that everyone there—even his father—had, which he had mentally dubbed 'Tamalpurity' or 'Roychowdhuryness'. He had registered his protest by divorcing the 'Chowdhury' component of his surname as soon as he entered college, by mingling as little as possible when he visited his home; and he had taken revenge by answering vaguely whenever anyone asked him about his home. Home! What did home mean? That he was from such-and-such village, that it was his 'home' but wasn't within a thousand miles of his heart; that he hated it there, found it hostile, that besides his father he didn't feel a kinship with anyone else. With so many lovely places in the world, why did that claustrophobic Tamalpur have to be his 'home'! How unacceptable! . . . He listened closely to the rumbling of the steamer, heared the promise of the distant shore; raising his eyes to the watery expanse, he saw hope on the horizon.

He might have felt somewhat unhappy immediately after his father's death, but since that was not what happened either, Satyen assumed he would never be acquainted with an unhappy existence. And his life lent ammunition to this assumption too; things happened in the precise sequence that he had planned; his MA exams led to the repetition of history he had hoped for, getting a job required no particular effort; he proceeded to fulfil his wanderlust, dispensing forever with the compulsion of having to read prescribed books, he earned independence in his literature; the only pang he had felt was in leaving his hostel for an ordinary mess, but there too he had been saved by the two ground-floor rooms in Tollygunge. It had to be accepted that fate had smiled on him; till now, he had got whatever he had asked for, whatever he had really asked for; and he had not really sought the things he hadn't got.

He had gone for a recommendation to the person whose writ ran large in the English department of the university. Hearing the name of the college in question, he had wrinkled his nose slightly, saying, 'Why them? Try at BES, they'll accept you.'

'For now . . .'

'Yes, of course; but you'd better hurry—there'll be a vacancy soon at Krishnanagar too. Should I give you a personal letter for the DPI?'

Satyen bowed with gratitude. Gulping, wiping his face with his handkerchief, he managed to get the words out: 'I . . . I'd like to stay in Calcutta.'

'You could go for a bit now, how long can it be before you pull the right strings and get into Presidency. Or else . . .' the gentleman of advanced years, glanced at the young man's embarrassed, red face, 'you could take a research fellowship with me, the pay won't be any lower than at that college of yours, probably higher . . .' He paused, spotting the sparkle of keenness on the listener's face, and said more seriously, 'You can work on the second half of the eighteenth century, even in England they haven't done much work on that period . . . Get some of it ready and submit it for the PRS, by then you'll have got your lecturership . . . then a PhD in London with the Ghosh Fellowship and then . . .' The prime spirit of universal education unfurled the map of his own past before the job-seeking young apprentice's future, 'and that's it!' To emphasize that there couldn't possibly be any cause for concern after that, he leaned back against his leather-covered English chair; offering a sympathetic, kind wink, he continued, 'You needn't worry, I'll guide you all the way . . . I have some notes on Crabbe . . .' He didn't finish, conveying the value of the notes, and the importance of the master's generosity to the pupil.

He discovered the seeker to be just as silent, humbled, overwhelmed, as when one's wildest expectations are more than met, and this third glance of his—although Satyen did not see it—virtually betrayed paternal love. Almost forgetting his own exalted status, he asked like a friend, 'What do you think of Crabbe?'

Crabbe! Of all the poets in the English language, George Crabbe! Satyen wanted to ask, 'Who's Crabbe?' He wanted to say it calmly, in a deep voice, looking the professor in the eye, he wanted very much to say it, he felt a terror rising within him, that if he were to stay a little longer, he wouldn't be able to help saying it, so he rose suddenly, smiled like a fool, rubbing his hands together like a helpless fellow, and the professor was delighted at the fact that his entire body dripped with every possible sign of gratitude.

Indeed, circumstances had obliged him generously. His biggest advantage was being completely alone in a family sense. Since arriving in Calcutta, he had realized that the cost of his education would prove a little too much for his father to bear, and had therefore begun giving private lessons at salaries of eleven or twelve rupees at the first opportunity, the human appendages to a father—such as a mother, brothers, sisters and other relatives—had not cast the shadow of support upon him; just the opposite, in fact; to him any family relationship meant handcuffs, a burden, the end of comfort, because it was inevitable that if someone were close to him, they would start depending on him. Suppose he had had younger brothers and sisters, in that case . . .? Then that was what he would have had to do, do the rounds of the BES at Krishnanagar, at Rajshahi, at Chittagong; or else pursue his 'research' on George Crabbe to scrounge for the benediction of the university . . . He would have been forced to do all this, maybe a great deal more, things even more lethal than Crabbe or Krishnanagar! Where would his independent life have been then, where his literary freedom. Ashit Ghosh, who had been ranked second, after him, in the BA exams, had opted for the ICS instead of MA, he was an assistant magistrate somewhere now; Pranatosh Bagchi, who had been ranked second in the MA exams, did not consider a posting in Krishnanagar beneath his dignity, he had now been transferred to Dhaka; and Dhiraj Gupta, who had escaped the ignominy of a first class degree by the skin of his teeth, had gone off to Delhi as a ringleader of radio propaganda.

He still ran into some of his fellow students from college;

all of them would say, 'Come on now, do you want to rot all your life in that pathetic college of yours?' Satyen only replied, 'It suits me fine.' He wasn't pretending, wasn't fobbing off their accusations; what he told them was exactly what he believed. Didn't they understand how comfortable he was, how happy he was; he was in Calcutta, the workload wasn't demanding, the vacations were long, he didn't have anyone else's burden to bear, in fact, he had no burden to speak of, for he himself got by on very little. He earned a hundred and twenty from the college, he gave private lessons to one—just the one—student; what he earned in sum was more than enough for him, to buy books, to travel, everything included; if he earned more he would have been hard put to find things to spend it on. And there was no question of increasing his earnings either, unless he was ready to sell his leisure, to put his independence on the market; and if he didn't have what really mattered to him, what was most valuable for him, then nothing else was of any use either . . . Why, there was another professor from Calcutta in the same Hillview Hotel, advanced in years, unselfish, for he was slaughtering every golden morning of Shillong with jabs of his red pencil on BA answer-scripts! . . . Satyen was fortunate he had not yet been made an examiner for matric exams; he kept applying regularly—as far as his college was concerned, it wasn't proper not to—and every time he did, he prayed, 'Don't let it happen!' And because he had done nothing about it so far except to sign the application form, his application continued to be systematically rejected every time. What others couldn't do without was just what he wanted to do without . . . No, he didn't see a single person around him with whom he would want to exchange places even for a moment.

From one aspect perhaps this was a bit selfish, from another it certainly displayed an incredible absence of self-serving interest—a lack of a worldly sense, in other words—Satyen could identify both these qualities in his own attitude. And yet, why call it that? If he did not feel anything missing because of the absence of brothers, sisters or other family, who had either never been present or had existed only nominally, if he felt unburdened instead—was that selfishness? Did he have to acquire six or seven brothers and sisters so that he could be the humblest among the poor? And lack of sense—about what? In case he got into trouble? What kind of trouble? He could fall seriously ill, he could lose his job suddenly, several other things could happen, they did happen to others! But despite thinking about it as deeply as he could Satyen could not imagine a situation in which he would be in trouble, or, as far ahead as he could see, no trouble seemed like trouble. Feel afraid? Never! The murmuring pine-breeze whispered in his ear: feel afraid? Never. The blue eye of the sky between the leaves said the same thing. He simply couldn't equate his solitude with helplessness. He was happy, quite happy, very happy—he simply couldn't think of things any other way—because he was alone. This was—he realized just this moment—what was most valuable in his life, the real thing, and this was what he clung to, calling it leisure or comfort or independence. He had met many, many people during these nine years in Calcutta—many of them had liked him, he too had enjoyed the company of many of them, some had even drifted quite close to him, becoming his friends—well, almost—none of them had actually become a friend, not one, he had stopped them just in time, or perhaps they had stopped themselves, but that was as much as he had wanted, if it had developed further, he would have lost something, he would have had to give up a part of himself.

. . . Satyen touched the letter in his pocket. A letter from her? Whom? His student? What kind of exchange was this between teacher and student? A friend? Friendship between a twenty-five-year-old man and an eighteen-year-old girl? Had he not witnessed the outcome of such friendships in a thousand novels and stories? He hadn't been able to make friends with any of the well-read, cultured, articulate men he had met—not even the one or two genuine pundits or virtuosos in their fields. He hadn't been able to—meaning, hadn't wanted to—and eventually it was this naive, delicate, tentative, reticent wisp of a girl with downcast eyes who had become his friend! Just because she was a girl?

His home might be devoid of women—or perhaps he had nothing like a home—but it wasn't as though he didn't know any women at all. There had been girls in his college, and the mothers, sisters, sisters-in-law of select male college-mates too, and, towards the end of his sojourn as a student, the wives of some of the professors; why, thanks to his degree he had even managed to escort a flesh-and-blood woman through the BA exams despite his own dangerous age. But he had never courted danger, never even spotted the inkling of such a possibility within himself. He could have become intimate with certain young women if he had wanted to, could have made progress if he'd tried—and not very hard, either—why hadn't he? Was he immune to the sweet, oh-so-physical conspiracy of youth? Was that even possible! Had he never been attracted, lured, willing? He had, on one occasion. But the attraction of solitude had proved even stronger. So he hadn't been defeated.

Then what made Swati Mitra different? How did she happen to be different from the rest?

He clearly remembered the morning of that class on Coleridge at college, when he had set eyes on her for the first time. He had enjoyed—it was impossible not to have—the sudden sensation he had had, of evidence of throbbing life amidst the hostile, blank faces intent on passing their examinations. Then . . . yes, in the college library . . . He had made the astounding discovery that at least one among the students in whom he had tried to instil a taste for literature, at the cost of intense agony to his soul every single day, had acquired an appetite for poetry. It was even more astounding because she was a girl—since Satyen had observed that the handful of students who did read

poetry were all men, the girls preferring conversation. That day
she had appeared to be someone worth keeping in mind—those
who were interested in him did not interest him much, but he
was certainly more interested in someone who was interested in
the same things as he was.

But so what? This wasn't the first time he had come across
someone who loved books, they were a constant presence among
the people he spent his time with. What, then, Satyen asked
himself, has drawn you so close to Swati Mitra that you are being
forced to think so much about it today? Is it her beauty?
Her age? Her diffident, gentle, warm, awestruck femininity? Or
is it her enthusiasm, eagerness, loyalty, her wonderful, uncultivated
mind, where you are happily running the plough of the world's
great writers? You've never been given the responsibility for
nurturing anyone's mind—and that too, a mind worth nurturing,
ready to be developed. Is that how you have concluded that
you have never seen another like her, another person like her,
another woman like her? Satyen shut his eyes, smoothening his
brow with two fingers.

As luck would have it, she became his neighbour too.
There were more encounters, he came to like her even more,
he liked her father at their very first meeting, and although
he had kept himself unscathed to the extent that he had not
permitted frequent encounters, but their home still seemed to have
become a part of his life. Home! He discovered the meaning
of the word the day Shweta had invited him to dinner; and that
same day he learnt of the joys of family life. It wasn't just
that Shweta charmed him, it wasn't just that he felt an
unarticulated, undefined, embarrassed kind of affection for Rajen-
babu; everything combined to create a grace that touched
him, everything seemed to be in tune, moving to the same
rhythm, everything a carefully nurtured part of a complete
fulfilment, even Harit did not strike a discordant note till the very
end; and, most important, he never felt like an outsider in this

family gathering. He had been invited home from time to time by other people in Calcutta; he had not encountered coldness anywhere, had been treated with courtesy everywhere; but such a sense of comfort, such a special sense of comfort, had not been available anywhere else! The very next morning the desire to visit them again reared its head, which was precisely why he did not go.

It had been wise of him, but he had already made the mistake, the big mistake, earlier. Why had he written that letter from Santiniketan? What was the desire, the thought, the speculation or fancy, that led him to write that first letter? . . . And this time too! This writing of letters—what was it but an indulgence? He loved literature, but couldn't write himself—so he contented himself with a pale substitute by writing long letters to people now and then. But that time in Santiniketan, couldn't he have thought of anyone other than that slightly familiar, slender student of his? Did he have to pour his emotions out in halting words to this tentative girl? And this time—it seemed to be a foregone conclusion that he would write, as though there was no question of not writing.

He had made a mistake.

Had he made a mistake?

Once again he ran through his mind the essence of the letter in his pocket. No longer was it apprehensive, no longer tentative, but stronger, bolder, more confident—the hesitation was forgotten, the barriers were being pushed aside—was this woman going to reach where no one had reached before, was she going to cross the frontier? Satyen leapt up suddenly, saying almost loudly, no, no more. He wouldn't reply to this letter, he wouldn't write to her ever again. With these letters, was he going to bring on the unthinkable, the unbelievable, the impossible outcome that could not have transpired merely through encounters? Satyen felt a terror within him, the wind felt chilly, he lengthened his steps.

That night he read the letter again by the light of the lantern. He couldn't sleep for a long time, but woke up at the crack of dawn. Going out even before his morning cup of tea, he took a walk for several miles, and, returning to the hotel, sat down to write a reply to the letter immediately after his cup of tea . . . What a beautiful day!

6

It was a beautiful day in Shillong, but one of the worst of the horribly hot days of summer in Calcutta.

There was no blue in the sky—a slight, almost imperceptible, smoky hue stretched across it, unexpectedly casting cloud-like shadows here and there; but it wasn't clouds—just the opposite—for it dispelled the very hope of rain, and switched off the breeze to make the world gasp for breath. When you looked outside, the sun didn't seem strong—quite feeble, in fact; instead of the crisp, immaculate, fresh first heat of summer— which you can practically pick up in your hand and put away in a box—this was a slippery, twisted, obdurate, cunning heat: a bath couldn't wash it away, the breeze from an electric fan couldn't wish it away. There was only one way to fool it; with work—work that clung to the entire mind. But did Swati have such work? . . . She had bathed earlier in the morning, she was reading Rabindranath's *Chheleybyala*—the kind of book that sank its teeth into you—and yet her mind kept wandering, the fan didn't seem to be all that powerful today, she wondered how much time could be passed just reading.

Bijon called her by name. Swati glanced at him briefly, her eyes expressing no eagerness.

'Swati—Majumdar's here.' Bijon busily parted with the big news.

Swati's face hardened a little, just a little. Without looking at her brother, she said, 'Doesn't he get a chance to visit people any time other than the afternoon?'

'What do you mean afternoon? It's only ten o'clock.'

Ten? So many hours to go in the day? What a long day!

Bijon took advantage of this silence on his sister's part, adding quickly, 'He's come for a *specific* reason.'

But Swati seemed not to hear, or perhaps she heard only the last word. Raising her eyes from the book, but without looking at Bijon this time either, she said softly, 'What am I supposed to do if he has?' As soon as she said that, she remembered saying the same thing earlier when Satyen Roy had come. How differently we can say the same thing.

'What are you supposed to do?' Bijon answered briskly. 'Precisely what you're supposed to do when friends come home.'

'I certainly would have, if it were my friend who came.'

Bijon stopped. Swati realized that the expression with which he had begun his retort had changed. 'All right, you could condescend to meet a friend of mine instead,' he said with a smile.

'I'm busy now.' Swati lowered her eyes to *Chheleybyala*. She tried to provoke Bijon into anger, but could not. Bijon suddenly reverted to his natural, primal artlessness, asking, 'How busy? You're only reading.'

'That's why,' Swati had to say.

Gravely, but also with a smile on the far corner of his lips, Bijon said, 'That's true. Majumdar doesn't know you're such an important, busy person, you see. And how would he—you spent an entire hour with him the other afternoon.'

Swati lowered her book to her lap, sat up straight, and finally looked Bijon in the eye. 'I made a mistake,' she said.

'Amazing!' came the instant reply. 'So you can make mistakes too.'

Swati didn't reply.

Bijon waited. 'You could at least find out whatever it is that he thinks is important.'

'Does it have anything to do with me?'

'With you too.'

'Then you can find out for me . . .' Swati began speaking as though it were a question, but concluded it with the finality of a decision: '. . . and I can find out from you.'

'You can, but don't you even want to put in an appearance?' Bijon swept his tongue around the inside of his mouth, and then played his ace with a chuckle, 'Majumdar isn't here alone, he's even brought his niece.'

'His niece?'

'Yes, his niece.' Bijon now had the pose of the victor.

'He has a niece too?'

'Can't he?' Bijon smiled. 'Then will you . . .' Bijon didn't finish. Having performed the job of the messenger, he left.

Then was there no choice but to go? Swati didn't waste time. Unwelcome tasks should be done quickly; the sooner you started, the sooner you finished. She had expected to discharge her feminine responsibilities towards another woman and quickly get back.

But she was wrong, Urmila Ghosh didn't want to leave quickly.

As soon as Swati entered, without even waiting for the introductions to be made, Urmila said, 'We've been waiting a long time—come, sit here by me . . .' She indicated the spot next to her on the cane sofa.

Swati was about to sit at a distance, but she couldn't disobey this command. Turning her head to look at Swati through her clear hexagonal glasses, the newcomer said, 'I've heard so much about you that I couldn't wait to meet you.'

'Where did you hear about me?' If it were someone else— even a few days ago—Swati would have said this with a smile, in a pleased, bantering tone; but now she pronounced the question in the same tone that people used to ask at the station, 'When is the next train to Naihati?'

'Why, from Mama, from my uncle, of course!' she answered. 'And from your brother too . . .' Swati's admirer flashed two streamlined smiles at the two of them.

Addressing the first of the two, Swati said, 'Don't you have anything better to discuss these days?'

'Better than what?' Majumdar smiled. And leaving the significance of this question to the opacity of Swati's imagination, he smiled even more broadly, saying, 'Milu says whatever she likes . . . My sister's daughter, Urmila.'

Swati injected a courteous greeting into a nod of her head, but without noticing, the object of her greeting answered her uncle: 'Do I say whatever I like? No; I try to say what the person I'm talking to will like . . . Don't you think that's good?'

Urmila looked at her new acquaintance for confirmation, but Swati said with a smile, 'In this case, you've miscalculated.'

'Why? Don't you like hearing that others have been talking about you?'

'Not at all,' Swati said seriously.

'What! Don't you like being famous?'

'Famous!' Swati seemed to be hearing the word for the first time, repeating it lightly.

But Urmila wanted a clear answer. 'You don't like it?'

'I can't quite understand what it would be like to be what I'm not, what I'll never be.'

Urmila laughed loudly, turning this into a joke. Leaning back comfortably in her chair, she stretched out her green-shoe-clad feet on the floor, dangled an arm from the armrest and, swinging her bag, which was the same colour as her shoes, said, 'If you assume you won't be famous, then how will you be famous? It's nothing much; anyone whom people talk about is famous. Famous if they praise them, famous even if they don't. But they must talk about them—they mustn't be able to help talking about them. And it only needs a little effort.'

'A little effort?'

'Are you joking with me? But I am determined to be famous—I *shall* be. I've begun my efforts—you'll see when I am.'

'But I will remain one of the crowd; so I won't see, but I will hear.'

'Do you object even to the sight of famous people?'

'Can you see them whenever you want to?'

'You just have to try.'

'I can never try to try.'

Urmila laughed loudly again, throwing her head back, the bag fell out of her hand. She shifted in her chair, crossing her legs, put her bag on her knees, injecting gravity into her expression, as though she were finally getting to the 'real' point after the jokes and the laughter, she said, 'If I told you that we're here today to get you to meet a famous person, wouldn't you be happy?'

'I'm happy just the way I am,' Swati responded.

Through her hexagonal glasses, Urmila's eyes settled almost sternly on Swati. Lest she have to hear the word 'famous' again, Swati quickly continued the conversation herself, 'Besides, I don't particularly like famous people.' She hadn't thought of him when speaking, but she was instantly reminded of Dhruba Datta.

'Which famous person have you met?'

'I haven't actually met anyone, but I think . . .'

'Why don't you verify whether you're right . . . Come to our place tomorrow evening to listen to Shashanka Das—Shashanka Das will sing!' Urmila announced with great ceremony. 'We're here to invite you!' Urmila assumed that to invite Swati was to secure her acceptance, she threw sharp glances at the two men, then smiled, as though pleased with herself, her smile spread over her face, she jiggled her knee.

The other two hadn't said a word all this time. Swati had glanced at them once or twice—they hadn't noticed—and had observed that they were both watching Urmila and exchanging glances with each other. Their eyes encouraged Urmila, congratulated her; as though, having consulted with each other, they had decided to leave the stage to her—the stage was the right word, she was being treated to an acting performance—the acting was good—quite good—but it didn't seem to end there, they wanted to give her a role too, to make her appear on stage! After his niece had finished Majumdar started on cue, telling Swati, 'Shashanka came to Calcutta all of a sudden, I got hold of him the moment I heard.'

Swati had by then trawled the dark, spider-webbed recesses of her memory to pull Shashanka Das out of them; so she managed to say, 'The playback singer?'

'Yes, it's as a playback singer that people know Shashanka Das today.'

Swati hadn't expected this response from Majumdar, this tone—she was a little startled—but the speaker continued the thread without noticing. 'He's going back the day after tomorrow—very busy—but I don't give up easily!' Majumdar laughed at his own last statement, displaying his large teeth, although Swati didn't think it all that funny.

'No one in Calcutta has any idea he's here,' Bijon contributed his share, 'or else there'd be no hope—he'd have been mobbed.'

'Just one or two people know,' Swati corrected Bijon's mistake, 'so he's getting off lightly.'

'It's not that . . .' It wasn't quite clear which of them Majumdar was protesting against. 'I would have got hold of him in any case no matter how many people there might have been. He's agreed to come tomorrow. I haven't told too many people—mine's not the kind of house where you can have many people over in any case—just a few other friends, besides you . . .' Majumdar rose as he spoke. 'And yes . . . if you could tell your father too . . . I don't have much time—I'd better go . . . Bijon, if you could take Milu home . . .' Throwing the last few words at them from the door, Majumdar left abruptly, suddenly, unexpectedly.

'No one needs to take me home,' Urmila had begun to

tell her uncle, but he didn't wait to hear what she had to say, left with no option she targeted Bijon through her glasses. 'But you can come with me if you like.'

Swati was a little surprised at Majumdar's sudden departure, leaving his niece behind and entrusting her brother with the responsibility of taking her home, because her entrenched notion of etiquette did not match such behaviour. As though trying to understand the situation, she said, 'One big advantage of having your own car is that no one needs to take you home.'

'Do you need someone to take you home just because you don't have a car?' Urmila protested immediately. 'What do you take me for?'

'Still . . . your uncle will surely send the car for you.'

'Why should he? What are trams and buses for?'

'Oh, do you live close by?' Swati looked for illumination in a different direction.

'Don't you know where we live?' Urmila seemed surprised, and Swati was taken aback at her astonishment, silently accepting her ignorance.

'We live in Beniapukur,' Urmila threw some light on the matter.

'Where's that?'

'Oh my God, don't you know where Beniapukur is?' Urmila went off into peals of laughter.

Swati was embarrassed. 'Is it a very famous place?'

'Oh no, nothing like that—the neighbourhood is . . . not nice; but we couldn't get a suitable place anywhere else. We needed several rooms, a garage, gas—and a flat wouldn't do either . . .' Urmila parted with a lot more information than necessary. 'It's difficult to get all of these in a rented house?'

Urmila added a question mark to this absolute truth, and looked as though she expected Swati to start arguing, so Swati had to agree, 'Difficult enough even in your own house.'

'You're right—for most people it is—but when my uncle

builds his own house . . .' Even Urmila seemed to feel that saying anything more on this subject was redundant, she returned to her earlier subject. 'But this one isn't bad either—large rooms, wide verandas—you'll like it.' Urmila swept her eyes around the four congested walls of their drawing room.

'What are the other things that I'll like—let me hear it from you.'

But Swati's blow landed on water. Urmila answered as smoothly as flowing water, 'I can't tell, but I'm certain you'll enjoy the singing.'

'But I haven't said I'm going.'

'You don't have to—of course you're coming!' Urmila said this with her lips, and with her eyes she said, 'How can anyone let slip a chance to listen to Shashanka Das?'

Swati didn't reply.

'Did you imagine you wouldn't be going?' Arching her eyebrows and laughing as she took Swati's hand, Urmila said, 'I like you a lot. Really!' Then, glancing sideways at the small gold watch on her other wrist, she turned her head and said, almost as sweetly, 'Are you coming with me, Bijon-da, I can't stay much longer.'

Bijon had been watching all this while, entranced—possibly by both of them. He jumped up immediately when she spoke. 'I'll get ready even quicker,' he said, departing swiftly for his bath and lunch.

Even that 'quicker' was far too long for Swati. For as soon as Bijon left, Urmila turned towards her, their knees almost touching, her eyes wide and brimming. She said, 'Let's have a heart-to-heart, you and me,' signalling intimacy with a switch from *aapni* to *tumi*.

Was the lady going to bare more of her heart even after this? Swati moved away a little, pretending not to have noticed the use of *tumi*—she said, a shade too formally, 'Some refreshments for you . . .'

Swati bit her tongue almost as soon as she said it—how could she not have realized beforehand that her use of the word would lead to her companion's spilling over into peals of babbling laughter! But what ensued was even worse than she could have visualized with the full stretch of her imagination: Urmila practically drowned in laughter; swallowing several gulps of laughter, she managed to raise bubbles of speech: 'Refreshments? No . . . I don't . . . want . . . refreshments or . . . anything.'

'Nothing?' said Swati irrepressibly.

'No . . . refreshments! Oh!' Escaping death by drowning, Urmila emitted feeble hiccups of laughter.

'Dada's probably gone for lunch . . . I'll just . . .' Swati glanced in that direction.

'Why, don't you have servants?' Urmila climbed up immediately to the functional jetty on dry land.

'Not because of that . . .' Swati stood up urgently.

'Never mind, sit down,' Urmila pleaded, taking her hand, stopping her. 'Your brother can do without so much attention. Let's talk.'

Swati sat down colourlessly. Her eyes stayed riveted on the inner door, as did the thirst in her eyes.

'You've just passed the IA exams, isn't that so?' Urmila began her heart-to-heart talk.

Swati indicated silently that the guess was not incorrect.

'What do you plan to do now?'

'Study.'

'But you'll be done with that too some time.'

'We'll see then.'

'You'll be done soon,' Urmila predicted knowingly.

'Can you ever be done with learning?' Swati answered almost like a sage.

'So you haven't thought much about your life?'

'You seem to have, it appears?' Swati had meant to say, 'You seem to have been thinking about my life,' but Urmila

brimmed over: 'Certainly! If I don't think about my own
life . . . But must you be so formal with me, I'm not all that
older than you . . . I took my BA exams this year . . . And now
the problems start—my mother doesn't live here, and my father
is dead—you can understand what the pressure is about, and
Mama thinks so too—he's quite old-fashioned still, but then
how *can* he be modern like us . . . He talks as though women
have no option other than marriage! I keep saying, no,
never . . . Do we still have to hear this clamour for marriage—
even in 1941! Of course it's different for girls like you, anyone
can tell you're the type to get married . . . Consider this,
you've been in Calcutta all your life, right? And yet you don't
even know the city, you can't even imagine getting around on
your own—so marriage is the correct option for you—but
not everyone is a good girl like you, and people have different
kinds of likes and dislikes too. If you were to ask me why I don't
agree to marriage, will I never marry—if Mama were to ask me
that—I'd say, no, it's not that, maybe I *shall* marry some day,
when I want to I will, and on the day I want to—but not a
day before that—now? I can't even think of it now; right now
I want to see life, taste it, most of all I want freedom—which
men have had a monopoly on all these days. Besides, I have a
plan in mind too—it's a plan for becoming famous, as I said
earlier . . . I'm going to enter politics . . . You can't acquire fame
today except through politics, you probably don't need anything
else either for fame. I've thought up a programme too—since I
have been born a woman, I must first raise my voice over women's
rights; women must get a share of their father's assets, Hindu
marriages must have arrangements for divorce—what intolerable
tortures are forced on women under the Hindu Marriage
Act—men can marry as many times as they like, but women,
never more than once—I've planned it all, only, I can't decide
yet which party to join—the Progressive Democrats, the Radical
Liberals or the Advance Guard. Certainly it's best to join the

strongest of them, but all of them say we're the strongest—and again, the wrong choice might even lead me to jail—that's the one problem in our country with getting into politics.'

Waving her arms, stamping her feet, shaking her knees, spreading them too, rolling her eyes, undulating her entire body, pouring drollery into every word, shouting articulately, Swati's new friend delivered this peculiar speech. She paused sometimes, as though the listener might also have something to say, as though, in fact, the listener *had* said something; Swati, of course, said nothing at all, she didn't want to, she couldn't, she wouldn't have been able to even if she had wanted; she didn't listen to all of it either, listened to almost none of it; only watched, but after a while didn't even watch, only the cannonballs of chaos rang in her ears.

Urmila's heartfelt observations may not have ended there, maybe she had only just started baring her heart. But there was no more time for deeper disclosure, for Bijon came back. To save time he had skipped his bath; so what if it was hot, it was nothing but folklore that a bath made you feel cooler, once you went out it was the same, and Calcutta's happiest place for him then was the road baked to over a hundred degrees. The moment he stepped into the room, he said, 'Shall we go?'

Urmila had occupied her chair so permanently that Swati was surprised to see her rise.

'All right, time to go today, lovely chatting with you . . .' Suddenly, as though she had just discovered the mistake in her choice of words, she appended, 'But you didn't talk at all, maybe you didn't like me much—don't you think? But I like you a lot . . .' Generously, effusively, lovingly, Swati's admirer placed her hand on her shoulder. Then, standing directly opposite Swati, she opened her bag and proceeded to repair the damage in her make-up. Glancing at herself in the mirror with a frown, she gifted herself a sweet smile, then turned around to tell Bijon, 'Let's go.'

'Let me get a taxi,' proposed Bijon.

'Taxi? What for?' Urmila dismissed Bijon's proposal with a wave of her hand. 'I go all over in trams and buses.'

'Not for you,' Bijon answered adroitly, 'but for myself.' He probably didn't realize himself how profound he had been!

But Urmila did. 'That's the problem with Bijon-da!' She bubbled with laughter as she spoke. 'He's the emperor of extravagance! You must discipline your brother—he's getting out of hand!'

'Why don't you just address him by his name,' Swati suddenly heard herself say. 'He's probably younger than you.'

'No, that wasn't nice; do I really look that old?'

But Swati could not meet the slightest expectation of courtesy in response to this, she couldn't summon the energy to say anything at all.

'But it's true,' the unperturbed Urmila said, 'that the days of so-and-so-da and so-and-so-di are gone—we're all equal now—we'll address one another by our names, what have we achieved otherwise!' She finished with a dazzling glance at Bijon, this wondrous golden age—and its even more wondrous evidence— brought forth a glow of golden happiness on Bijon's face.

Alone in her own room, in the still afternoon, Swati's sensation of having been overwhelmed was slowly dispelled; she regained her awareness, her thoughts—but she couldn't quite return to the comforts she was accustomed to. Was this how people felt when they came to their senses after the chloroform had worn off? Her room seemed unfamiliar, the books meaningless, the day empty like a fever. A short while earlier she had been reading *Chheleybyala*, she was back in the same chair, the *Chheleybyala* was close at hand too, but she wasn't even going through the ritual of opening the book; something momentous seemed to have happened in the interim, as though a wall had been blasted off her room, or as though her right arm had suddenly become immobile; something so terrible that it had pushed her life back a long way with one single shove, all the way back to the beginning, as it were, she would have to work everything out again from scratch. The first truth that floated to the surface from the frenzied whirlpool at the bottom of her consciousness was that her mother was dead. As soon as the thought occurred to her—she had never felt this way before— she felt helpless, afraid! As though she had been abandoned by everyone—even her father—in some strange, unfamiliar land, amidst a huge mob. That her father was in office at this hour also seemed to be part of this displacement that had left her in tears. And now she had nothing to do during the long, intervening, claustrophobic hours but to wait for him.

Swati breathed deeply, wiped her face on the end of her sari—she was perspiring profusely—but the perspiration seemed to be cold, the heat seemed to hold a chill within. In utter silence, with the deepest concentration, she tried to work out what she would say when her father came home . . . What would she say? What would she have said now had he been home? What thought was clear in her mind, what articulation was prepared? She didn't know herself what the matter was with her. She didn't know why she was afraid. And she was afraid to know that too.

Suddenly she felt quite weak—tired, exhausted, close to sleep.

The maid, whom they called Ram-er ma, after her son's name, arrived to ask, 'Don't you want lunch, Didimoni?'

Her appearance, the sound of her voice, seemed to provide support to Swati. Without budging an inch from her chair, she said, 'You're always in a hurry, Ram-er ma.'

'It's so late, doesn't your heart cry out for food?'

After a silence Swati asked, 'What's your name, Ram-er ma?'

'Name? My name?'

'Yes, what's your name?'

'My name . . .' she had to make an effort to retrieve the information, '. . . my name is Manorama.'

'Then why don't we call you Manorama?'

'The things you say, Didimoni,' she smiled, arching her body in a way that suggested this was very embarrassing.

'You weren't Ram-er ma from birth, were you? Only after Ram was born.'

Ram's mother could not absorb this logic; she stared blankly.

'What did Ram's father call you?' Swati continued.

Ram's father's son's mother hid her smile behind the end of her sari; the pose that her body took on for a moment made Swati realize she wasn't very old. Looking away, she said, 'I can't tell you that, Didimoni.'

'Please tell me!' Swati seemed to be revived by this natural, earthly humour.

'That's very shameful. You won't be able to bear it.'

'That's all right, tell me,' said Swati after some thought.

'You wouldn't like it if you heard it, Didimoni . . .'

Not expecting such free thinking, Swati listened a little more closely.

'You'd faint if you even heard the half of it . . . But it doesn't matter . . . As a husband he could call me any name he wanted, but when he brought my parents into it as well . . .' Swati had not expected Ram-er ma to complete her sentence, but the maid said something beyond her expectations, '. . . I didn't spare him either!'

Swati was squashed. She had interpreted 'shameful' differently. She wanted to know a little more about the person she had seen all these years, but whom she knew nothing about. 'How long has it been since your husband died?' she asked.

'When did he die?' she confirmed the question, and then answered appropriately, 'A long time ago. We had lots of mangoes that year . . . Not a drop of rain that summer . . . He got cholera early in the morning, death seemed to just drag him away.'

After a pause Swati asked her next question, 'Don't you miss him?'

The maid looked at her to gauge the meaning of the question. Then, surprising Swati for the third time, she said, 'No, Didimoni, I won't lie to you, he didn't torture me, gave me food and clothing—a tongue like the gutter—that was the one flaw he had—but then is there ever a man without flaws? And he didn't beat me up, brought money home every day, hadn't ever been ill, but when death summons you . . .'

Swati remained quiet.

Covering her head again with her sari—it had slipped off—the maid proposed, as usual, 'Come and eat now.'

'All right . . .' Swati rose at once; and she felt much more like herself during the long, intense mid-afternoon hours following her meal. If someone were to suddenly drop unconscious on the road, a crowd, a din, an ambulance, and then the doctor saying, 'Nothing serious, he'll be all right soon'—this was a little like that. Now Swati could recollect everything, think her way through the whole thing. She arranged select portions of Urmila's incessant chatter in order—although it had appeared she hadn't been listening. She remembered her brother's demeanour clearly; his exchange of glances with Majumdar, his glance at Urmila, his departure with her, and the way he had avoided Swati. Majumdar alone was bad enough, on top of that his niece, and then that stupid appendage in the form of her brother! Again, for a moment, Swati shuddered; she repeated to herself, 'Girls should never lose their mothers, and even if they do, they should never have such brothers.'

But her brother—suddenly a wave of pride surged within Swati, courage lending wind to her sails—what *could* her brother do, after all? Was he even a human being? Did he have the power to cause her pain? Her mistake was in seeking comfort; a mother's, a father's . . . But why? Couldn't she be done with this the way she quickly turned the pages of an annoying book? Of course she could, all by herself, too. She was her own source of comfort—who else could it possibly be? If she only stood firm, if she only looked people in the eye, if only she was determined, who could affect her?

Immediately, and simultaneously, Swati reached two decisions. First: she would in no circumstances tell her father anything about all this; second: she would go the next day to Shashanka Das's soirée. Not really for the soirée, though, but to tell Urmila a few things. Somewhere else, some other time would have been better, the occasion was not quite suitable; but would she get another opportunity, and since saying all this would be uncomfortable anywhere, any time, it made no difference. And if she could talk to Urmila properly she wouldn't have to tell her father—he needn't know anything about this—her brother was trouble enough for him, why cause more turmoil?

The shadows lengthened on the road, the sunlight changed its colour; and just when a pleasant breeze brought the news that yet another turbulent day before the monsoon had ended, Swati rose from her chair, opened the windows, pulled out all the books from her shelves to rearrange them. All this while, she had worked out in her mind every single word that she was going to tell Urmila the next day, muttering them to herself many times over, she knew them now like a lesson for the exams. Urmila would interrupt repeatedly, would wag her tongue incessantly, her sticky words would ooze out like the juice from a flattened mango; Swati would only move away a little, so that her hands did not get gummy, she would slash Urmila with her eyes, slash her with all that she would say, with every single one of her words.

It wasn't long. Here's what it was:

'Your uncle is mature, he's made money, all of you are now looking for a suitable companion for him. He's looking too, or perhaps he's the only one looking. He now thinks—and, accordingly, so do you—that this quest no longer needs to be continued. But no—your conclusion is baseless, completely baseless; and if you were to act on that baseless conclusion, that would not only be a waste of effort, but unpleasant too. Unpleasant for many people. I am here today to prevent you from pursuing this misguided mission. Please tell your uncle this, explain it to him. Please do not leave anything unclear. He will have to search elsewhere for his companion.

'Commenting on your family issues displays a complete lack of decency on my part, but it is because of you people that I could not remain uninvolved—yes, all of you; therefore I hope that you will not be reluctant to forgive this exception to my customary civility.

'There's something else I should let you know. My brother and I may live in the same house, but we occupy two entirely different worlds. My brother's friends can never be mine. So if your uncle, or you, again experience the compulsion to spend your leisure in a way that makes it essential to visit our house, please visit only with my brother in mind, only my brother, only him.

'You cannot have enjoyed listening to all this, I enjoyed saying it even less, but it would have been worse not to have said it, and so I did.'

Having composed this short essay, Swati's mind relieved itself of its burden. Now all she needed to feel contented was to actually say it.

BOOK THREE

Curtain, Quivering

1

It was raining outside. A silent, almost invisible rain. The car took occasional turns on the unfamiliar, shadowy, dimly lit roads, and long, diagonal lines of rain were caught in the prying curiosity of the headlight. But only for a moment. Then it became murky again, once again, nothing was visible.

It was silent inside too. The car had been on the road for nearly ten minutes, and in this period not even a single casual word had dropped into the velvet-thick darkness behind the rolled-up windows. This darkness offered an opulent, very opulent luxury that everyone seemed sunk in; no one even realized that nobody was talking.

After another turn, Rajen-babu said, 'Torrential rain.'

It was like tossing a shard of glass on a pillow; there was no resonance.

Rajen-babu spoke up again a little later, 'But isn't the heat . . .!'

Swati woke up at 'heat'. Indeed . . .! This wish-fulfilling rain, this long-hoped for June; and to think its first onslaught had been squandered in this stifling car. For the first time after setting out she seemed to realize where they were going, the turns they were taking, where they were coming from. Shifting a little, she rolled down the window, and instantly the downpour struck; a cascading song in her ears, the touch of a cool-wet hand, no, not a hand, no hand could be as soft. Swati leant out, and an entire rainworld came rushing at her; the black of a rainswept Calcutta night, glistening roads slippery with lights, the even blacker trees, the dance of shadows on the pavements, and this splash of cool water from the ground on the face, body, mind . . . Aaah!

'Aaah!' Saswati's cry rose within the car. 'What do you think you're doing—now my sari's all wet!'

Rolling up the window again, Swati said, 'It was lovely.'

'You and your . . .!' Without finishing, Saswati started smoothing her brick-coloured georgette sari over her knee.

'Rolling it down a little wouldn't be bad.' Rajen-babu tried to roll down the window on his side, but either couldn't locate the handle, or couldn't make it work.

'Should I do it for you, Baba?' Swati leant across, stretching out over Saswati's knee, Saswati screamed thinly, 'What do you think you're doing!'

'What's the matter?' Bijon, seated next to the driver, looked back.

'I think she stamped on my sari,' said Saswati, bending to examine the area after pinching it out with two fingers.

'This sari of yours has taken over. Impossible to do anything.' Swati gave up, resuming her seat.

'What is it?' Bijon wanted to know.

'Nothing,' answered Rajen-babu.

A little later, as if to say something, as if to gloss over the fact that she had overdone it about the sari, Saswati said, 'Where are we, Biju?'

'Amir Ali Avenue,' Saswati got her answer at once. Then, without turning his head, without looking at them, he recited the geography of Calcutta fluently, 'Still on Amir Ali Avenue, Bright Street to the left . . . Store Road there to the right . . . Old Ballygunge Road starts here.'

What Saswati said next bore no relationship with any of this. 'Tell me honestly, Swati, how did you enjoy the evening?'

'What do you mean honestly?'

'I mean . . . you don't enjoy most things . . .'

'It's not that—you're trying to say that actually I do enjoy things but claim not to. But no, I never do that. Besides, I do enjoy things—almost everything.'

'That's news to me,' Saswati tried a little light banter. 'Then can I assume you did enjoy the evening?'

'For now I'd enjoy it a lot if you didn't object to this window being rolled down just a little bit.'

This time Saswati acceded readily to her sister's wish, but she moved away to sit as close to her father as possible, and Swati, too, rolled down the window fully—no—only till her nose. Saswati's sari received a new lease of life, and so did Swati now that she could get a gust of cooling wind and a little rain in her heart.

'Shashanka Das is rather nice-looking!' Saswati said this as though she had been thinking about it for a long time.

'Didn't I tell you!' Bijon swivelled quickly. 'He was very handsome earlier—now that he's put on some weight he doesn't look as dashing.'

'Better than many actors,' Saswati's comment didn't seem to include Bijon. 'I wonder why he doesn't go into films.'

'Looks and singing aren't everything,' Bijon solved the problem with an amalgam of knowledge, experience, expertise and even a little contempt. 'You must be able to act, too!'

'But his singing is actually even better than in the films.' Saswati paused, then targeted her sister directly. 'Don't you think so, Swati?'

Swati had been sitting on the edge of her seat, almost rubbing her nose against the rolled-down window pane, without changing her position she answered, 'What do you mean but?'

'You're demanding a lot of explanations today, Swati!' Saswati laughed, just the way a person laughs when irritated. She waited a while for Swati to reply, then declared loudly, with extra emphasis, 'I thought his singing was excellent.'

But Swati didn't respond to this either.

'Gariahat–Rashbehari crossing!' Bijon announced in a bus-conductor's baritone. 'You'll be home any minute, Chhordi!'

Finally Saswati felt like looking outside. After the oppressively snobbish darkness of Old Ballygunge, she thrilled to the sight of the lights, the shops, the crowds caught here and there in the rain. She was relieved to be back on familiar ground, able to breathe easily; in silence she savoured the intimacy of this section of Rashbehari Avenue after turning right—which no one else here had a share in—and then, without trying to draw Swati into conversation any more, she turned to the person on the other side. 'Baba, did you like the singing?'

'It was good . . .' As though he hadn't been effusive enough, Rajen-babu repeated, 'it was good.'

Saswati hadn't expected anything more from her father, so she wasn't disappointed, instead, with mounting enthusiasm, she said, 'Really, how beautifully he sang! How lucky we are to be acquainted with Majumdar, or else we'd never have heard him.'

Bijon's back assumed a bragging pose, evident even in the darkness.

Rajen-babu wondered if the driver had heard, and what he might be thinking if he had. But Rajen-babu was not capable of lowering his voice to the extent that would be required to warn Saswati—possibly no male is—so he tried to change the subject by asking why Harit hadn't accompanied them.

'He isn't fond of this sort of music!' Saswati answered quickly, confidently. As though she was not at all miserable about this divergence in taste with her husband—quite pleased, on the contrary.

Rajen-babu drew attention mildly to how Saswati had used the informal *o*, rather than the formal *uni* when referring to her husband. 'Is that how wives refer to their husbands these days?'

'But so do husbands,' Saswati's statement was half a question.

'In our time even husbands used *uni*.'

'Anything will do,' Saswati tried to make light of the issue, but a little later, she herself continued, 'What do you know of today's women in any case—and what do I know, for that matter?'

She was thinking of Urmila, who had a very strange hairdo that evening, so overdressed, such a gaudy shade of lipstick, and, every minute that they had lingered after the singing was over, not once did her words, those dervishes, stop whirling! Her father would certainly not approve of such behaviour, which was why she had tried to discuss it with him, but her profound observation evoked no response from Rajen-babu, there wasn't any more time either, Saswati was home.

Putting his hand outside to check, Bijon said, 'It's stopped raining at last.'

Although Saswati was much more used to it now, she still hated having to climb the stairs to the second floor, wending her way past all those other flats; she took Bijon along.

Swati had been silent all this while, looking out of the window, she hadn't said anything even when Saswati got off, but since the car had been parked directly under a lamp post she pulled away from the window into the darkness inside, and was so happy to see her father when she turned in that direction that it seemed she hadn't even expected to see him. Moving even closer to her father, she said, 'I didn't think, Baba, that you'd really go there.'

'Am I not allowed to go anywhere?'

'Anywhere else . . .' Swati fell silent, her eyes on the back of the driver's neck.

'I had also . . . just like you . . . I'd thought the same,' Rajen-babu said.

Instantly Swati turned her face towards her father—and just as instantly lowered it again. Her father did understand then—but how much did he understand? Had he learnt of, understood, the turmoil in her mind over these past two days, past few days, without saying anything, hearing anything, only from her face? . . . Swati was discomfited, but also reassured:

the first things she had become familiar with in life, those old simple things, obviously ran far deeper than these completely new and uncontrollably fearsome complexities of life.

Finally getting the hang of it, Rajen-babu slowly rolled down the window on his side too. The rainy night sprinkled itself all over the small, closed space.

'Thank goodness it rained,' Rajen-babu sighed.

Swati raised her face. 'It's been such a long time since you went anywhere with us, Baba.'

'Saswati was so insistent . . .' Rajen-babu tried to justify his transgression.

'I was sure I didn't want to ask you to come,' Swati's answer seemed to be a justification too.

'But I came only for you.'

'For me? . . . Why?'

'I thought . . . it would be better.'

This had an even greater impact on Swati. For a moment, she saw a different face to the father she had always known; simple, as transparent as water, never embroiled in anything, always willing to do as she proposed—but did he then actually run much deeper, as deep as the water, as convoluted as the undercurrent, deceptive, alien? This time her discomfiture was higher, as though her father had been eavesdropping on her heart, as though he was much closer to her than she thought he was, closer in a very different way than she imagined, as though she had no freedom even in her mind, even in her thoughts.

Bijon returned and, though there was room at the back, took the seat next to the driver again, and Swati returned to the window from her position near her father . . . She really had not wanted her father to go. Because, first, in her opinion, he had not been invited properly; even if he had been—secondly—not going would have suited him; and thirdly—this was the main thing—so long as he was nearby she did feel a little bit like an adolescent. She had not wanted to be remotely adolescent this evening; she had wanted complete freedom, so that, by some ploy she could corner Urmila alone at some point for a few minutes . . . And then return home in peace. To actually say the things that she had prepared would need her to be older than she was—the way they paint pictures of people larger than life, or the way they appear gigantic on cinema screens. She mustn't be a homebound Bengali girl of eighteen, a bookworm, she would have to stretch herself, would have to be like a fictional heroine, such as Portia, for instance—but if Portia's father had been sitting by her side, would she have succeeded in ensuring that Antonio won?

Sitting by her father in the taxi, Swati pondered over the enormity of her task, and she was young, young by any standards, and even younger with her father by her side. She conducted a complete mental survey of the adversities; unfamiliar house, unfamiliar people, the disadvantage of being a guest—and was that all? The whole thing was horrible, Urmila was horrible—but even to keep this horrible thing at bay she had to touch it, by uttering the words she had prepared would she not be a little defiled herself? And to brazenly say unpleasant things to someone who had no relationship with her—that was no mean feat either. She'd never had to say such things before, why was she being forced to say them now . . . Why did one have to? Why couldn't people just keep their emotions to themselves, everyone could be happy that way; why did people try to make others unhappy, and end up unhappy themselves?

Unhappiness? The word pricked Swati suddenly, in one corner of her mind. It wasn't a nice word, it made you more vulnerable. She tentatively concluded that since there were so many different kinds of people in the world, each with their own motive, it would be difficult to live unless being unhappy was the last thing, the rarest thing, that could happen to you. To live—that is, to live on one's own terms—you had to imagine, had to accept, had to believe that no one can make you unhappy. On my own, I can be as melancholy as I want to be; but why should anyone else be able to dislodge me from where I stand? The melancholia that Swati was so familiar with since childhood, she had finally realized, was not unhappiness. Unhappiness came from without, and melancholia was born within—and we do love everything about ourselves, don't we? Besides, melancholia brought its own joy, it was nothing but another face of diffused joy; joy was a bright colour, like the sky at sunset, red here, gold there, yellow even further back, but with gaps in between, lots of emptiness; then, when all of that was wiped out and all over the sky there was only the colour of a shadow, a shade of grey, a non-colour, melancholia too spread across the heart the same way . . . And what of unhappiness? Which made your throat dry, didn't let you speak, made you afraid? No, not at any cost.

With a small wave of her hand, Swati seemed to fling all familiar, unfamiliar and unborn unhappiness out of the moving taxi on to the road. She lifted the load off her mind—this is nothing, I'm not going anywhere special, but only to correct anyone in case they say things to me under mistaken assumptions. She went over her carefully composed speech once more in her mind; like the writer reading the final proof of the book, she thought over every word one last time, removed one here, added one there, checked the punctuation ruthlessly, was forced to admit that it was as good as anything she was capable of, she couldn't do better—not at this point of time, anyway—and got off the taxi feeling unburdened, confident, prepared, and, just as the writer is until the book is out in print, a little, just a little, anxious.

They'd been late getting out, having overshot the hour they had planned to leave. Rajen-babu had poured cold water on Saswati's reminders urging him to hurry, and Biju's fidgeting by announcing that being late was the norm when it came to music. But he was old-fashioned—what did he know of modern times, and he knew nothing at all about one of its unique representatives, Shashanka Das. Those who had 'inside' information from the world of musicians—even Biju had not yet been able to penetrate that deep—all knew that, no matter what the rest were like, when Shashanka Das had promised to sing somewhere, he would arrive by the clock, and, without waiting for latecomers, even avoiding conversation, would start immediately if he could. He was famous—infamous—as a person of few words. Fans didn't like his tight-lipped nature; they said his stock would have been higher had he been more social, yet others said it was a professional ploy, that it was his distant, egoistic image that added the zeros to the right hand side of his income.

And so, by the time Swati and the others arrived, Shashanka had already started strumming on the tanpura. The uncle and the niece could only offer an abbreviated welcome, they had to sit down quickly among the crowd—yes, it was definitely a crowd, and the room was enormous, though Majumdar had claimed otherwise—or perhaps that was why he had said so. But Swati did not have the time to carefully note the discrepancies between Majumdar's account and reality; an unfamiliar setting, new faces everywhere, cheap Western prints in gilded frames on the wall, a jungle of shoes by the door, Majumdar with a smile dripping all over his face, Urmila's cleavage-revealing dress—all harsh reality was drowned under the murmuring of the tanpura.

'You're late . . . we were wondering . . . anyway, you're just in time . . . he's just started . . .' she seemed not to hear any of the things that Urmila said, sitting by her side, and after that, 'Today's songs are all new, his own tunes . . . his own compositions . . .' Even this ray of light was obliterated by the resounding fog of the tanpura. After that, though, for quite some time—how long?—there was nothing anywhere except the music.

Majumdar glanced towards Swati now and then from where he sat, even trying to catch her eye, but Swati's eyes were shut, her body still—not entirely still either, swaying a little from the waist upwards, like a fresh bamboo reed—and her slightly parted lips seemed to have no awareness of the spoken word. She sat cross-legged, her hands gathered in her lap, her full, upraised face open to any willing eyes. Majumdar noted an unusual loveliness on that face—unusual, and new, he hadn't seen it before—like a painting, like a sculpted goddess, the face of a goddess seen hazily through the smoke rising from incense sticks, some distant, detached, loveliness, of no use to anyone, and on it—Majumdar sensed, although he could not link a word to his sensation—was painted a virginity that could never be defiled. Majumdar didn't quite appreciate it, he was perplexed, feeling as though he had suddenly been outsmarted while effecting some commercial sleight of hand.

Swati felt the way you do in Puri, when, wandering through the lanes and bylanes of the dingy town for hours together, the sea all but forgotten, you take an unfamiliar turn in an unfamiliar neighbourhood to find the sea suddenly appearing in view—that is to say, if she had retained the ability to think, she would have realized that she was in a similar situation. She had come to argue in the garb of Portia, armed with a plot to win the case with logic; but where was this she had ended up immediately on arrival? In the world of her early childhood— that free, simple, uncaring infancy—her heart was soaked in those memories, the house on Jatin Das Road, her mother, her sisters' weddings, and Shubhro . . . she even remembered Shubhro. But there was no emotion to any of it, not sadness, not rage, not happiness, only silence; the silence of all that existed no more, and, because they existed no more, would never end. Then, when a more profound, more intricate melody rose in the air, the magical world of memory vanished, instead of the smooth edges of the painted canvas came the horizon, space, the sky, all those impossibly high skies, where all parallel lines met, and where every wish was the fulfilment of that one wish.

This was where Swati's mind hovered. If asked, she wouldn't be able to tell what kind of song it was, what it was titled, what *raagini* it belonged to. The light suddenly seemed too harsh when she looked, and everyone seemed to be talking too loudly. Shashanka Das steadfastly rebuffed entreaties for more songs; and the moment he rose so did everyone else—the soirée broke up—there were twittering conversations, there were hunts for shoes, there was jostling at the door—Swati looked for Saswati, and immediately spotted her father next to her.

'We should also . . .' said her father.

'No, you mustn't go yet,' Urmila interrupted Rajen-babu, standing directly behind Swati. Advancing to Swati's side, she continued, 'Please wait a little—let the others leave—this is your first time here, you must stay a bit—Mrs Ghosh is going, I'd better talk to her, otherwise . . . when there are so many people how can you possibly talk to everyone!'

Despite this onerous responsibility, Urmila tried as much as possible to remain near Swati—to make her feel at home, to shield her, taking them upstairs after the crowd had departed. Small tables with chairs around them were laid out in the enormous veranda, like a restaurant, plates of food, tea, coffee, ice cream, have whatever you like—a few select friends, and maybe the family, and, of course, the focus of this gathering— Urmila took Swati by the hand to introduce her to everyone, starting with Shashanka Das—Majumdar took care of the others—presenting her to everyone as her friend, and as an extraordinary young woman. But Swati could provide no evidence to corroborate Urmila's description—unless not speaking was a sign of being extraordinary—and because she didn't say anything, she didn't understand anything either; she had no thought other than wondering when they could get out of there, when she would be able to listen once again in rapt attention to the songs that were still playing in her ears. She did hear Urmila say once: 'You're neither eating nor talking. What's the matter?'

Swati smiled slightly, offering an excuse at once, 'I have a headache.'

Majumdar overheard her. 'A headache? A bad one?' He rose, bustling, from his chair.

'No, not all that bad . . .' she had to smile again.

'Would you like an aspirin?'

'Come to my room, take an aspirin and rest awhile,' said Urmila.

Urmila had offered her a wonderful opportunity, but Swati didn't respond, only asking for permission to go home.

Fortunately her father was with them, and on top of that a few drops of rain began to fall from the overcast sky, so they could leave quickly. And as soon as they emerged from the lane into the main road, the rain intensified, in tune with Swati's heart. Even more than that, in the enclosed car, the silent rain so melded into her heart that until her father mentioned it, she didn't even seem to have realized that the rain was outside the car, not in it. But it wasn't just the rain; absorbing the rain into her body through the window opened a crack at the top, she understood more, much more; she remembered this was Majumdar's car, remembered—at long last—her objective, preparation, vow, and the failure of the vow.

Repeated rewriting, repeated proofreading, all of it was done; the book didn't come out. But—unlike most writers—Swati felt, so what? She had got what she had wanted for today; she had grown up, grown up more than she had believed possible; she was free—free enough to speak her mind, even free enough not to speak her mind. To say something was a kind of compulsion, wouldn't protesting against something imply it was worth protesting against? . . . But what protest? They were nice, Majumdar, Urmila, they were quite nice; from the peak she had climbed by virtue of growing up nothing could prevent her from saying they were nice; now, from this vantage point, they were nothing, absolutely nothing, they made no difference. Her train had blown its whistle, and they had been left behind on the platform—already so small—and sitting in that train which made the entire sky rise to a song, her arduously constructed, carefully arranged words became as irrelevant as those droplets of stations where the train doesn't stop, but which still have to make arrangements for the train to pass . . . At night, before falling asleep, she recollected Majumdar, recollected Urmila, a few times, through her closed eyes she saw the hope in their faces, their desire, their eagerness; she felt a stab of pity for both of them.

Before going to sleep that night, someone else was thinking of Majumdar too, but her thoughts were far removed from pity. Saswati had had a lovely time, she had wanted to stay longer, but the way Swati went on and on about leaving, and her father was at Swati's beck and call.

Even more enjoyable than the singing was probably the time spent upstairs afterwards; wonderful setting, excellent tea, shondesh that melted in your mouth, and over and above that, above everything else, the honour of being seated at the same table as Shashanka Das. Majumdar had reserved this honour for Saswati alone; he was at that table too, steering the conversation in a way that Saswati could join in. She hadn't said much, of course, she'd been busier listening, Shashanka's beautiful baritone, his beautiful, solemn expression, his occasional remarks, and the exuberance of Majumdar's powerful laugh. She had never liked Majumdar as much as she did that evening; and, all told, she could not remember having so wish-fulfilling, so wonderful an experience anywhere recently. She had been to no small number of parties with Harit, so many events arranged by their organization, at different restaurants, at mansions, at Prince Makaranda's invitation; glamorous affairs, she had felt a great deal of eagerness when going, but it had never been the case that, half an hour later, she had not wanted to come away, and even after that she had had to wait with an aching back for a long time—so very long!—because Harit would never   be done. These days she was beginning to develop a little courage—sometimes she wouldn't go, Harit didn't insist strongly either,   unless someone important was coming, in which case his wife had to be present—but the divergences in their respective worlds of pleasure—although Harit referred to them not as pleasures but as duty—had created a problem, which was that even if she had avenues for pleasure elsewhere she could no longer talk about it, as she would have liked to once back home until she had digested it—since there was no one else at home—and at these moments Swati, her father, Biju—her entire life before her wedding—their conversations on the mat laid out on the floor upon their return from wherever they'd been— Swati's colourful descriptions, Biju's excitement, her father's soft laughter—the unbearable memories of all of these were never stronger than at these moments. They had hardly spoken in the car on the way back today—although there had been plenty to talk about and listen—she wished she'd gone back home with them, spent some time there, chatted a bit—but it was past nine, and did any husband like coming back home to find his wife missing? . . . But now, lying in the darkness, Saswati repented for this too, for Harit returned almost an hour later, and every minute of that lonely hour in the flat sank its fangs into her.

At dinner Harit said, 'Do you think Hitler will attack Russia?'

How would I know? Saswati did try to be enthusiastic about these things nowadays, but right then she could think of nothing to say, she was ashamed not to be aware of Hitler's hidden motive.

'I had a bet with someone today; he claims the war will be over in three months—apparently there's nothing left to it. They're all living in a fool's paradise.'

'The longer you can live in it the better it is,' said Saswati.

Harit lifted his eyes to look at his wife, a knife seemed to bare itself momentarily on his curled lips, but suddenly a note halfway between incredulity and plea entered his voice. 'Do you really feel it will make no difference to you if the world burns or roasts?'

Saswati's response was odd. 'Tell me, couldn't we live there?'

'Where . . .'

'At your—at our Bhowanipore home?'

Harit snorted with laughter. 'Why this sudden fondness for my parents?'

'Because if there's a crisis, it's better for everyone to be together, isn't it? And . . . it saves on expenses too.'

But Harit paid no heed to the second piece of logic either. 'Not even I can survive in that house, never mind you.' With a wave of his hand he dismissed this absurd proposal.

'But I quite like going there . . .' Saswati said.

'. . . To visit,' Harit completed the sentence on his wife's behalf. 'But to live! You'd have gone mad in no time—driven *me* mad, that is. Don't I know! Is there even one woman today who doesn't consider her mother-in-law poisonous! And that's fitting, too—now the mothers-in-law are being paid back in their own coin!' He elucidated by translating the English idiom, and as he did, he noticed his wife's wooden posture. 'You're not eating!'

'I ate already over there, and . . .' Saswati finally got her chance and seized it, 'what wonderful music we heard.'

'Eating at untimely hours is an incurable disease of the Bengali! If you're going to invite people for a meal do it properly—either tea or dinner—people know what's coming, they can go prepared.'

Still Saswati chanted, 'Ve-e-e-ry nice songs.' Pausing, she added, 'If only you'd come along . . .'

'Film songs? You already have records for those, and they play them so incessantly on the radio that you inevitably have to listen to them everywhere when you go out, and on top of that if . . .' Harit concluded with a demonstration of the unique skill that he had picked up in England, a shrug of the shoulders.

'It's not that . . .' Saswati was about to try once more, but Harit rose after his meal, planting himself before the radio to absorb all the news about the enemy. However, suddenly it seemed there was nothing but music in war-ravaged Europe; annoyed, he switched off the lights and went to bed.

Saswati glanced at the man fast asleep next to her. Harit slept in pyjamas—he even wore them quite often—tailored long-cloth pyjamas, Saswati was surprised yet again—as she had been many times in the past—that he didn't have them made looser. She had tried to argue about this and, inevitably, lost . . . Her mind went back to the evening she had spent; everything at Majumdar's house was out of proportion, excessive—and excessive was the norm. What luxury the man lived in—he let his fancy go in any direction it wanted to, was happy to spend money on any pretext . . . and his fancies were nice too, like his friends . . . and indeed, anyone who could claim Shashanka Das as a friend had to be an important person himself.

Walking down the stairs with them, Majumdar had paused halfway down the staircase to say, 'I hope the evening was not unpleasant, Mrs Nandy.'

'It was wonderful,' Saswati couldn't find anything more to say in reply.

'That will be proved only if you come again.'

'Another soirée?'

'How will I get hold of Shashanka again, but if there's someone else whose songs you like . . . and . . .' Slowly walking alongside Saswati down the stairs, he suddenly jumped a step lower, then turned around to face her directly, 'Will I ever be so fortunate as to have you over even without the music!'

'Very well, we'll do that,' Saswati smiled.

'Such a ready yes can only mean no. But I shan't give up hope.'

. . . The joy she had not been able to digest because she couldn't talk about it kept her awake a long time. How nice it would have been if Majumdar had been part of their family. He could have been—couldn't he still? What do you mean couldn't?—The thought struck her so violently that she almost sat up in bed—that was just what Prabir Majumdar wanted, wanted desperately, that was what all this was for . . . all of this! First it was a joke, nebulous, but now . . . Over these past few days it had become clear, obvious; and this evening it had been announced in large letters like on a poster—it had been obvious in Majumdar's expression, his behaviour, the way he avoided Swati, and what he had told her on the stairs. Strange—how could she not have realized it all this while.

Saswati felt a desire to wake her husband up immediately to tell him. She felt other desires too. The thought of Swati's getting married generated a different sort of excitement in her. The first days of her acquaintance with Harit returned to her physically, and then the first few months after the wedding. Had it lasted only a few months? . . . Saswati turned towards her husband—but Harit was facing away from her again—so all she could see was the sleeveless vest covering half his back, his slumbering back. She moved closer, running her hand through the fine hair at the back of his neck . . . never mind, she wouldn't wake him, he wouldn't wake up even if she tried, such a sound sleeper . . . and really! He worked so hard all day!

∽

The last thing that Saswati had wondered about before falling asleep was whether Prabir himself would approach them with a proposal or whether they should do something about it. In the morning she tried to bring it up once or twice with Harit—she thought he might not consider the subject completely unsuitable for discussion—but the office-bound Harit spent this time in such a rush that Saswati didn't get the opportunity, or perhaps she didn't want to cast her pearls hastily, deciding it was best to wait for a more conducive atmosphere. She examined the whole thing over and over—but there didn't really seem much to examine, she must be right, definitely!—in fact she even felt that living proof would be available soon. But even Saswati had not imagined how soon.

Almost an hour after Harit had left—Saswati was in bed, leafing through a bunch of film magazines supplied by Biju—the servant announced the arrival of a stranger—'He's looking for you.'

'Who . . .?' Saswati named one of her husband's closest friends.

'No,' replied the ancient retainer, imported from the in-laws, 'I've never seen him before.'

Immediately a loud voice was heard from the drawing room—just a single curtained-door away: 'I'm Prabir Majumdar, I had something to tell you.'

Oh! Saswati rose, ran. And as soon as he saw her, Majumdar began, still standing, 'I'm sure I'm intruding at this hour, it's probably rude too; certainly I should have come when—the first time, at least—when both of you were home; but there's something I have to tell you—it's for your ears only; so I've deliberately come at an hour when Mr Nandy wouldn't be home.'

Saswati felt her heart lurch suddenly, her face reddened, her legs seemed unable to support her. Had she misunderstood? Was he actually . . .? But well before a word, a single word, could appear on her lips, Majumdar continued, 'Since it's about your sister you should be the first . . .'

Saswati breathed again, relaxed, was about to smile but suppressed it, saying gravely, 'Please take a seat.'

About twenty minutes later—for not much needed to be said—when the stranger rose, there was no obstacle to Saswati's finally lavishing on her lips the smile she had been saving within herself, but Prabir Majumdar's face, which Saswati had never seen except with a smile, was now tightly serious. He'd fired the first arrow from his bow, it had struck the target; but this was only the first—and the nearest—target. He would have to fire the next one further, and that wouldn't be simple. He'd better not lose the war in the delight of winning the battle. So he was now grim, prepared.

'If you permit,' Majumdar bowed his head, 'I can escort you to your father's residence this evening.'

'Certainly.' Responding impulsively, Saswati recollected the very next moment that this man was not yet her sister's husband, would going with him . . .? So she made up an excuse immediately, 'But we're supposed to be somewhere else this evening.'

'In that case . . .?'

Saswati pretended to think. 'All right, I'll make the time and go myself.'

'Today?'

'Today—or tomorrow.'

'Should I come tomorrow then?'

'Here?'

'Wherever you want me to. My fate is in your hands now.'

Saswati glowed with pleasure. 'All right then, come.'

'Tomorrow?'

'Tomorrow.'

'Same time?'

About to nod, Saswati stopped. 'In the evening.'

'At that hour . . .'

'I'll try to ensure my husband is present as well.' Every sign of a married woman's dignity was visible in the way Saswati stood up. 'Since we're the only ones near at hand, perhaps my father will seek his opinion too.'

Glancing at Saswati for an instant, Majumdar said, 'I am grateful to you.'

Saswati went over to Tollygunge that very afternoon. And was pleased to see her husband at home when she returned. Normally, either Harit was not home at this hour, or his friends were over; but—and Saswati interpreted this as a good omen—this evening he was not only alone but also at home, a combination she did not remember from the recent past. He was scribbling something in English on sheets of foolscap paper, several pamphlets scattered on his desk, Saswati went up to him, saying, 'Oh, you're home!'

Harit did not respond to this redundant observation.

'No guests today?'

'No.'

'Then you could have come over to bring me home.'

'After all these days you should at least be able to travel to and from your father's house by yourself.'

'It's not as though I can't, but since you were free today. . .'

Detecting an unfamiliar note in his wife's voice, Harit looked up at her. 'What do you mean free? Can't you see?' He waved his arms towards the pamphlets and the sheets of paper.

The room was a small one, the desk nestled next to the head of the bed. Sitting down on the edge of the bed, as close to Harit as possible, Saswati glanced at what Harit had written. 'Is what you're doing very important?'

'Very.'

'Will you make some time to listen to me?'

This time Harit detected an even more unfamiliar note. Raising his eyes again, he looked at her for a while before asking, 'What's the matter?'

'Listen . . . Listen to me . . . Forget about what you're writing for now . . . This is important too . . . Extremely. . .'

'What is it?'

'Majumdar wants to marry Swati,' said Saswati after catching her breath.

'Who?'

'Prabir Majumdar . . . You know . . . Biju's . . .'

'Oh!' Harit made a small sound, a small, contemptuous smile appearing on his lips.

Saswati waited for Harit to say something more, but his eyes descended to the foolscap sheets again. As though in pain, Saswati cried, 'Is there nothing more you have to say?'

'What should I say?'

'Why, doesn't Swati mean anything to you? Doesn't her future matter to you?'

Capping his pen, Harit asked, 'Well, then . . . When's the wedding?"

'What! Just like that . . . Men, honestly!'

'But you said . . .'

'What did I say? Can't you pay attention to me for once?'

Harit gathered up the pamphlets, arranged his foolscap sheets—even those few moments felt intolerable to Saswati— put them all to one side, leaned back in his chair and said, 'All right, tell me.'

'I want to know your opinion.'

'It would be very natural for any man to want to marry Swati,' said Harit after some thought. 'But it would be preferable for the man to be unmarried or a widower.'

'Uff!' Saswati yelped. 'Don't you think of *anything* except the war and Stalin?'

Having read some documents smuggled in freshly from Moscow, Harit's anxiety for Stalin was a little lower that evening, so, forgiving the utterance of the name of the worthy by the unworthy, he said, 'And Swati too—yes, she's what people refer to as marriageable now, she certainly is, beyond doubt.'

Saswati didn't realize this was just a variation on what Harit had said earlier, so she assented eagerly, 'Exactly! This—*this* is the right time for Swati to get married. Baba's getting older—

he'll be retiring soon—what does it matter to me, I don't belong there—but Baba didn't even consider it!'

'Hmm?' Harit made a sound expressing sympathy with both his wife and his sister-in-law at the same time.

'. . . "Are you mad," he said.' Saswati choked with grief.

'Indeed!' Harit's forehead creased. 'Poor Majumdar!'

'Not Majumdar . . . It's my father . . . He's not in his senses . . . He thinks there's no better girl in the country than his Swati. But that isn't really the way it is—would she really get a better prospect!'

'Why don't you let your father worry about that—and didn't you just say you don't belong there any more?'

'Of course!' Saswati sighed. 'I get ticked off here, and I'm nobody there! Women have worthless lives!'

Harit glanced at his wife once more. 'If you're going to get agitated at trivial . . .'

'Trivial! I tried so hard to explain, to make him understand—Baba didn't even answer properly—you call that trivial!'

'Why you?' For the first time during the conversation, Harit seemed surprised.

'Why me . . . what?' Saswati didn't understand the question.

'Why are *you* the one who has to explain, to make him understand?'

'Who else is interested—who else do we even have to do all this?'

'But when Majumdar has got the answer, then why . . .?'

'No! He doesn't even know as yet. He came and spoke to me this afternoon—I didn't tell you earlier because I was going to tell you the whole story at one go . . . and where's the time anyway . . . of course I had already . . . I'd thought of it last night, in fact . . .'

'Why did he come to you?' Harit interrupted his wife's account.

'He'd have spoken to Ma if she'd been alive, but since she isn't . . .'

'When did you become a mother figure for Swati?' Harit laughed softly, as though he'd just been told something amusing. 'When the girl's mother is dead you have to talk to the father—that's what I did—after talking to you, of course. If your father hadn't agreed, you would have had to fight it out with him. Swati'll do the same! . . . And I for one think she can fight for herself quite well. Where do *you* come into the picture?'

Saswati's torrent of words froze suddenly. She was quiet for a while, eyeing a light brown patch on the desk, then said, her eyes still lowered, 'Majumdar has not told Swati yet.'

'He's hired the lawyer before arresting the accused!' Harit burst out laughing, relaxing his thighs and stretching his legs out under the desk. 'How strange!'

'What's so strange about it . . .' But Saswati's protest didn't carry any conviction; she gave a forced laugh. 'Not everyone is as fearless as you! He's on the reserved side . . .'

'Aaaaah!' Harit opened his mouth wide in the English style, making the sound in English, the word disappearing into an exhalation of breath. He continued in English—he was a little fatigued having spoken in pure Bengali for such a long time—'What will we hear next?'

This time Saswati was silent even longer; even more meekly she said, 'Just as well he didn't.'

Harit took his time too before responding. Rolling his pen on the desk with his fingertips, he asked, 'Does that mean the bride isn't willing?'

Saswati didn't reply; the expression that appeared on her downcast face suggested a recent bereavement, and, noting that expression, Harit arched his eyebrows, creased his forehead, and said with a small clap of his hands, 'Hea-a-vens! Then why did you put me through all this?'

Raising her face, Saswati said, 'But should the whole thing just be dismissed out of hand? What certainty do we have that Swati isn't making a mistake?'

'We don't, just as there's no certainty of the opposite either! Mistake or not, a marriage involves two people, and if one of the two isn't willing, then who's marrying whom?' Harit spoke quickly, his eyes darting around, as though he could just as well not have spoken, or as though he was thinking of something else—and, at the same time, for that very reason, deliberately twisted a simple idea, as though it was very entertaining.

Looking at the empty, white expanse of wall in front of her, Saswati protested, 'Does Swati even understand it all? She's still a child . . .'

'Child? How much older were you when you got married?'

'I took the right decision!'

'Swati too . . .' Harit didn't finish, didn't think it necessary either; suddenly he rose from his chair, and then sat down again immediately, drawing the pamphlets and the sheets of paper towards himself.

'I knew you'd say that.' Saswati stood up.

Although his eyes were on the last thing he'd written on the foolscap sheet, Harit replied at once, 'Of course! If you don't know, who . . .' Suddenly he raised his face and smiled, saying in an altered tone, 'When you had decided to marry me, if your father had wanted someone else instead—say—that singer with the moustache, Abhro or was it Shubhro, with him . . .'

'What nonsense . . .!' Saswati turned away, as though she wouldn't remain in the room any more, but turned back instantly to argue, 'But Swati's not in the same state of mind that I was in.'

Harit straightened his back, leaned back in his chair, virtually slumped in it. He looked a little too cheerful—by his standards—as though he was quite relaxed, as though he was ready for a tête-à-tête with his wife even at the cost of his mission of saving the world, or as though—after a long time—this conjugal intimacy itself had made him cheerful. 'But you wouldn't have married any Tom, Dick or Harry simply because you hadn't met me. And besides . . .' He didn't let his wife say anything, savouring the colour of rage on her face, saying, 'How much do we know anyway of what's really on Swati's mind?'

That 'we' offered a little consolation to Saswati; Harit had acknowledged that in this matter at least they were 'we'! She came closer to him again, sitting down slowly on the bed. Her voice couldn't be heard clearly when she said, 'How does it matter to you—it's all a big joke for you—I'm the one caught in the middle!'

Harit seemed to grow even more cheerful, with bright eyes he said, 'You're talking as though someone wants to marry *you*—and you want to, as well—but your father's coming in the way.'

'I'm your wife.' Saswati suddenly spoke loudly. She breathed heavily.

'Is there any doubt about that?' Harit avoided his wife's eye, but maintained the levity in his voice. 'But really—I don't know why you're so worried.'

Swati waited till her breathing became normal again. Then she said in an everyday, domesticated voice, 'Majumdar will come again tomorrow . . . what do I say to him . . .'

'Why say anything at all?' Harit suggested quickly. 'Send him to your father . . . he might even run into Swati there.'

It took Saswati a while to understand the entire significance of this. She gulped, ran her tongue over her lower lip, then said softly, 'You can do whatever you like with me, but don't you feel any pity for anyone else?'

Harit was taken aback; he had not expected to hear this from his wife. But—for that very reason—he paid no attention to it, as though he hadn't even heard, smiling teasingly, his lips curled, he said, 'Maybe you gave him a little too much hope? You probably didn't even consider that his wish and your initiative wouldn't be enough.'

Saswati was close to tears, she wanted to undo everything. And because, at any time, in any situation, married women have no greater friends than their husbands, she appealed again to her husband, 'Can you be at home tomorrow evening?'

'I'll have to be!'—Harit's voice acquired a practical note— 'I have visitors tomorrow evening.'

'I was thinking . . . when Majumdar comes, if you could also . . . it's your house, after all . . . and besides, he has to be told . . .'

'Do you really need me? He won't like what he's told, but at least if you're the one who tells him . . . and . . . you'll be able to soften the blow too. But where will you entertain him?'

Saswati frowned, not understanding.

'If he turns up early, that's fine, or else once the others have arrived . . .'

'What'll we do then?'

'We can't have outsiders present at our conversation,' Harit informed her gravely.

'Does that mean . . .' Saswati looked at him with bewildered eyes, 'there'll be nowhere to meet him?'

Harit dispelled his wife's anxiety easily, 'You can sit in the dining room.'

In the dining room! That fan-less cubicle! The balcony of Metro Cinema, Chang-Aan restaurant, Kaufman's Coffee—all of them flashed before Saswati's eyes. Harit had been with them too that evening, and—no matter how little it had been, or how brief—he too had enjoyed himself, hadn't he?

His eyes on his wife's wan face, Harit applied the ointment now. 'It won't be comfortable, but you do need some privacy. If I'd known beforehand . . .'

'I was wrong to have done all this without asking you,' Saswati had to acknowledge.

'There's something you could do,' Harit continued his ministrations, 'send word through Biju . . . some other time . . . or some other day . . .'

'And why does he even need to come. Biju can give him

the news.' Saswati's lips clamped shut, as though not another word would escape them.

'Bijon the bearer of bad news!' Harit laughed uproariously at his accomplishment of wiping out the last vestiges of colour from his wife's face.

◦◦

Bearer of bad news? Was it so simple?

Bijon created a furore. Why? What's wrong with Majumdar? Is he ugly? Or poor? Or immoral? Too old? Uneducated? A businessman? Didn't you get your daughter married to another old businessman who hadn't passed his exams either? In what respect is Prabir Majumdar worse than the rough-and-tough bald Bardhan from Burma? Is he a good-for-nothing? He knows important people in Calcutta, keeps track of things, he's a connoisseur of music, he's interested in the fine arts. A gentleman! And how rich he is! Do you know he owns land in Ballygunge? Do you know he's buying another car? Do you know how large his insurance premium is? How much do you even know about him—is he a skinflint like your son-in-law Harit, or selfish like Calcutta babus. What a large heart he has. See how he's brought his niece to stay with him, and how many poor relatives he's rescued by giving them jobs! And remember where he's risen from—he had nothing to begin with—so poor—and look where he is today! Is this a mean achievement? So dedicated to his work—he'll be another Sir Biren! Your daughter's very lucky that such a man has chosen her. And you just dismiss him with a snap of your fingers? You don't even want to consider it? Why, what do you have to be so vain about? Fine, so you won't get her married to him, but may I know the reason? I know why—because I know him, because he's my friend, because I'm the one who introduced you to him, that is his fault, isn't it? Rajen Mitra cannot survive unless he does the very opposite of what I want. If the same proposal had come through someone else, anyone else, you would have happily got your daughter married to him! Do you suppose I don't know you!

Mornings and evenings—when Rajen-babu was at home— Bijon continued this diatribe at the top of his voice, charging out into the road even while regurgitating it, coming back the very next instant like a football rebounding off a goalpost, raised his voice again to a fever pitch, threatening to choke himself to death. His voice—his ranting—was clearly audible next door in the congested neighbourhood; women lined the windows nearby, men came out on the street, and the two people at home who were the object of all this remained holed up in silence in their respective rooms, praying for temporary deafness. Repetition made his eloquence flower even more; more information was added, the logic was strengthened even further: using delightful descriptions, amazing adjectives and heart-rending hints, Bijon almost displayed talent at times.

At one point he said, 'If this was going to be your decision, didn't the two of you know it beforehand? If you were not going to agree to this marriage, why did you go so far!'

'Do you even *know* what you're saying?' said Swati, emerging from her room.

A wild grin ran across Bijon's face at finally having provoked Swati into joining battle with him. 'I know exactly what I'm saying. Didn't you know beforehand when you accepted his invitation—when you flirted with him—when you spent an hour with him at home alone in the afternoon?'

'Don't you shout.'

'Why shouldn't I—am I afraid of you or your father? Let everyone know of your scandalous behaviour . . .'

'. . . Biju!' Standing near the door, Rajen-babu shouted, as much as it was possible for him to shout.

Bijon's bluster was not diminished. He kept bursting out, 'Yes . . . Let everyone know! Do people know—does even Baba know what you . . . On the sly with someone else . . . That petty professor of yours . . . All those letters, such loving exchanges— don't imagine I won't reveal your exploits—will you be able to snare anyone after this? Either you shall marry Majumdar . . . Or no one shall marry you . . . Listen . . . Listen carefully . . . No one else . . . eventually it *shall* be him . . . yes, I'll keep my word!' He thumped his chest, leapt into the air, and shot out like a red-hot cannonball.

Swati was trembling, Rajen-babu put his hand on her back and brought her to his room. For a while both were quiet, then, when it became clear that Bijon wouldn't be back for the time being, a stifled 'Oh!' emerged from Rajen-babu's throat.

The sound faded gradually, without raising an echo.

Sinking into the depths of silence again, Rajen-babu suddenly found some ground beneath his feet. Raising his head to take a deep breath, he said, 'I have an idea . . .'

Swati raised her head too to listen.

'He's going to keep tormenting you like this . . .' Rajen-babu left out Bijon's name . . . 'I'm not home all day, and even if I am . . .' his voice choked.

Swati felt a sharp pang for her father.

'You could . . .' Rajen-babu paused . . . 'Maybe your Bordi's place . . . She'll be so happy . . . I can take a day or two off to . . . Or else to Saraswati in Delhi . . . do you want to go?'

'No, Baba, there's no need to go anywhere.'

'You might enjoy it . . . Feel better too . . .'

'No,' said Swati again.

'But . . .' This time Rajen-babu resorted to vague generalization, 'If they . . . How unpleasant . . . Something terrible here . . .' He seemed to have temporarily lost the ability to form an entire sentence.

'Do you expect me to leave home to run away from

Dada?' Swati curled her lips, almost smiling, and continued in response to her father's silence, 'What can Dada do to me?'

After this neither said anything, neither rose from where they sat. Although she was the one who had offered her father courage, yet she didn't want to go away from him, and Rajen-babu suddenly realized with a jolt that this was the beginning, and that this beginning signalled the end—the end, meaning, Swati's new beginning. It was evening then, darkness had descended on the room; the calendar flapped on the wall flapped in the wind as though impatient for the next few months to arrive.

Light footsteps were heard outside. 'Saswati, probably...' said Rajen-babu, getting up to switch on the light in the room.

Entering, Saswati looked in turn at her father and her sister. Swati rose, saying, 'I'll just have my bath and come back, Chhordi.'

Saswati hadn't visited them for a few days. 'Saswati,' said her father, glancing at her grim expression.

Although the chair Swati had vacated was close by, Saswati walked up to the bed and sat on it, sideways, facing her father. 'What's the matter?' she asked.

Rajen-babu didn't reply.

Her eyes on her father's pale, lined face, Saswati couldn't help repeating her question.

'Biju's tormenting her...!'

'Biju? Forget about Biju!' Why torment, what kind of torment... Saswati seemed to understand all this without asking.

Rajen-babu sighed from deep within his heart.

After a pause Saswati said, 'But you mustn't be blind because Biju's demented, Baba.'

Rajen-babu suddenly shut his eyes, as though he had seen something fearful.

'Saswati... Let it be... Not now...'

'No, Baba, I'm not going to argue with you. There's just the one thing I need to say. After that it's up to you.'

Rajen-babu waited like a patient waits for the doctor's needle.

'Here's the thing.' Saswati stirred. 'Forget about Biju, don't bring Swati into this either; just consider that you're the father of a girl—who has no mother—the entire responsibility is yours.'

Silently, Rajen-babu accepted the fact that Saswati was reminding him of his responsibility.

'Now, if there's a proposal for your daughter's marriage, surely you're going to think about it at least. Are you sure that where this . . . this matter is concerned, you've given it as much thought as you should?'

Rajen-babu did not say anything this time either, and, encouraged, Saswati continued, 'Or did you simply, without considering anything seriously, or because you want to keep your daughter with you for some more time . . .'

'Is that what you think?' Rajen-babu interrupted suddenly.

'Nothing wrong if you do . . . Considering what Biju is like . . . And among us she's the one you most . . .'

'Really?'

'If that is so . . . No problems, Majumdar will wait . . . Six months, a year, even two years . . .'

'Did he come running to you?'

'I'm not saying anything on his behalf . . . He doesn't mean anything to me . . . All I can see is that he can fulfil, if not all, many of the hopes that parents nurture for their daughter and . . . And Swati might also change her mind altogether, mightn't she?'

'Who's taking the responsibility for getting her to change her mind? You? Or he himself?'

Even more seriously, Saswati said, 'No, he won't visit your house any more, he won't bother you, until and unless you send for him.'

Rajen-babu accepted this promise in silence.

'I felt it necessary to let you know—not for Majumdar's

benefit, but for ours. Simply because Swati's heart isn't responding right now, or because you don't like such people, don't just dismiss it out of hand; think it over. I don't have anything more to say.'

Saswati rose, and, instantly contradicting her last statement, continued, 'If she'd been alive, Ma wouldn't have disapproved of him. It was she who had chosen the grooms for three of your daughters.'

'Since then it's been you, of course,' said Rajen-babu.

'Is my choice very poor?' Saswati flashed a smile, and Rajen-babu twinkled at once. 'And what sweet have you got this evening?'

'I have to go, Baba.'

'So soon?'

'Yes, I have to go to Bhowanipore . . .'

After a pause Rajen-babu said, 'So you get around on your own these days?'

'I like it. And who will escort me around?'

'Is Harit there already?'

'He isn't even back from office yet—or maybe he is by now—he'll go when he's ready to. All right, don't forget what I said.' Saswati left with a clicking of high heels. Rajen-babu suddenly felt he didn't know this lady.

'Where's Chhordi?' said Swati, returning after her bath.

'She was in a hurry . . . They're invited to the in-laws—and her father- and mother-in-law love her very much . . .' Rajen-babu said more than he needed to.

Left! Swati didn't say it in as many words, but Rajen-babu saw it written all over her face. And for the moment he seemed to run out of things to say to her.

Swati went into the drawing room with a book. The drawing room made you think differently; it was the place where you invited the world in; even when empty, even when you were alone, you felt involved with people at large, with things at large, your own situation, the elements unique to your own life didn't seem as overwhelming any more. Swati went into the room with this hope; the hope of lightening the burden she was carrying all by herself, the hope for at least a glimpse of the world outside through the window. But her expectations were more than met, much more, because within a few minutes of her settling down—instead of offering a glimpse through the window, the outside world entered in person through the open door.

'Have you heard the news? Have you heard?' Harit's hair was flying, eyes shining, and a different ruddy hue stirred restlessly under the sunburnt skin on his face.

'What? What's happened?' Swati stood up, terrified, wondering what might have happened.

'Hitler has invaded Russia! Hitler has invaded Russia!' Harit punched the air both times. 'Haven't you heard yet?'

Swati sat down again, disappointed, relieved.

Pacing about the room, Harit sounded the war bugle. 'Decimated! They'll be decimated now! They'll be sliced up by the sickle, shattered by the hammer! All this while it was just the rehearsal—the show begins now! What do you know, Swati, what do you think—you can't imagine what will happen—we'll have to fight, everyone will have to fight—everyone everywhere in the world—prepare, prepare, all of you.'

After a silence, Swati said, 'Are you coming straight from office?'

'You could say that . . .' Suddenly slumping into a chair, Harit said in an altered tone, 'Of course the news means nothing to you—not yet—but it will one day, it'll compel you to understand.'

'Chhordi left just a few minutes ago,' said Swati.

'Really?'

'She's gone to your Bhowanipore house.'

'That's fine. But I didn't come here for your Chhordi, I came here to give *you* the news.'

'Me?' Swati chuckled. 'What made you consider me suitable for this honour?'

Harit's expression relaxed, a small smile appeared on his lips. 'I have to say you've become quite suitable of late. Poor Prabir Chandra Majumdar.' Despite the world-shaking event, the playground for humour still seemed wide open in Harit's brain. 'Poor fellow! He hasn't give up hope yet—he was nagging Saswati about something yesterday! Poor man!' Harit couldn't seem to have enough of stabbing the rejected suitor with this particular description.

Swati was surprised by this information. What was the substance of all the nagging? She didn't ask, but she hoped Harit would divulge it on his own.

The hope wasn't fulfilled. Harit said, 'That's fine, that's excellent! May you attain more glory, may you break a few more hearts—or else what's the point! According to the French only that woman is worth marrying for whom at least seven . . .' Harit didn't finish, he probably recalled his global message again, the muscles on his face hardened, with a jerk he straightened his body, which was tired with all the wandering around he had done.

'What, you're leaving?'

'Yes, to Makaranda's now . . .'

'Some tea . . .'

'No . . .' Harit turned around to see Rajen-babu, and tried to look amiable in deference to his father-in-law.

'Saswati has already . . .' began Rajen-babu.

'I heard,' Harit didn't waste time. 'Oh yes . . . Ma has some ritual today . . . They believe in all these things!' Harit's smile expressed pity for both his mother and his wife's father.

'Are you also . . .'

'Not sure. I'm going somewhere else . . . Maybe after that . . . No,' he answered his father-in-law's unstated request in advance . . . 'No tea now. I was leaving . . . All right, I'm off now.' Harit turned around swiftly, disappearing quickly outside the door.

Rajen-babu sat down near his daughter. With a smile he said, 'Harit *had* come for your sister, when he discovered she wasn't here he didn't wait.'

'No, Baba,' Swati also smiled in response to her father. 'Harit-da came to inform me that Hitler has invaded Russia.'

'Really?'

'Yes, that's why...'

'So the war's spreading.'

Swati stopped on hearing her father say this. 'Is it really going to get very bad? Harit-da made quite a fuss.'

'What use is it for us to worry. We have even bigger things to worry about.'

Her father's last statement depressed Swati again.

Rajen-babu didn't say anything for a minute or so. Then, slowly, he started speaking: 'Swati, listen to me. In the absence of your mother, *I* have to talk to you—and you're an intelligent girl, you know very well what's right for you.'

A blue vein became faintly visible on Swati's fair cheek.

'And you must have realized by now,' Rajen-babu's voice seemed to acquire a lighter tone, 'that for people—for women, in particular—marriage is a very important event, the factor behind much of life's happiness.'

Rajen-babu looked at his daughter. And though every nerve in her body was under stress, she didn't reveal any of this to her father, answering while averting his eyes, 'Unhappiness, too.'

Rajen-babu was a little surprised at his literature-loving daughter. But then, he thought, if she knows that too, so much the better. The daughter seemed to provide the next cue to the father in this difficult dialogue. 'Yes, unhappiness too. And hence all the trouble we go to, all the anxiety we experience. Nobody wants to be unhappy, it's happiness they all strive for.'

Swati was silent. Then:

'But can you ever tell in advance?'

'That's why we have a word named fate.' As soon as he said

this Rajen-babu realized this wasn't the right response, so he continued, 'Of course you can't. Choices that don't seem attractive often turn out to provide happy experiences. That Prabir—maybe his wife will be very happy.'

Swati's head tilted back a little on her neck. Composing herself, she said, 'Why maybe—certainly!' Then she asked suddenly, 'What did Chhordi tell you?'

'You know what Saswati wants,' Rajen-babu answered bluntly. 'I want to know what *you* want, so . . .'

'Don't you know?' Swati couldn't control herself any more, hiding her face with her hands.

Rajen-babu's eyes alighted on Swati's thick, curly, jet-black hair; taking his time, he said, 'I didn't ask you earlier, I just assumed what I want is also what you want. But if your decision is based only on my disapproval . . .'

'Is that what you think of me?' Swati raised her face and looked at him with blazing eyes.

'Isn't it natural for you to try to avoid,' Rajen-babu spoke softly, 'what I don't like? But think about it without worrying about my viewpoint, and then if you feel even the slightest . . .'

'Baba!'

Rajen-babu heard an anguished cry. Glancing at his daughter calmly, he said, 'All I want to tell you is that you mustn't think of my approval or disapproval. What *you* want is what will happen.'

'That settles it then.' Colour, emotion, life . . . All of these returned to Swati's face.

'So that you can be sure of what you want . . .'

'Do you need to explain to people what they want?'

'Sometimes you do,' Rajen-babu smiled. 'Does the little boy know he's hungry?'

'I'm not little any more, Baba.' Swati stood up, tall, delicate, lovely.

But was she really as grown-up as she looked? The

protection she had from the harshness of life was still intact, she enjoyed everyone's plentiful indulgence, much of life was still make-believe for her, her days and nights were delineated in the black-and-white of love and hate. What did she know of the apprehensions, uncertainties, compulsions, responsibilities of adult life? She had read about a hundred different complications of life, but when her own condition threatened to become even slightly complex, was she able to take care of it all by herself? Didn't she immediately fall back on her usual, and first, source of support? . . . Had this too been shattered today? Had even her father abandoned her to this terrible world? . . . She may have displayed a great deal of courage at the time, but all night long she lay curled up on her bed with fear, her throat running dry. Somewhere she sensed a similarity between what her brother and Harit had said, and did her father also think that she was the one to have . . .? Was it her fault then? If only she had made the effort, been careful from the beginning, could she have averted this threat? The risk may have been avoided, but still, did it amount to this: that this was what she had actually wanted? But if someone made incorrect assumptions about her, what could she do about it? Would she have to prove that she had no contribution to this mistake? And even if she did, would she still be accused all her life? How troublesome—would this nuisance dog her all her life!

Swati didn't sleep well that night. The next day she got out of bed rather late, and soon afterwards, well before his usual hour, her father went off to work. Swati felt he was avoiding her.

She didn't do her hair, or have a bath, or open a book. She merely ran her eyes over the spines of the stacked titles, without pausing at any of them, none of the books spoke to her that day, for the first time she got no response from any of them. Perhaps the answer lay elsewhere? Not in the printed word, then, but handwritten? She pulled them out of the drawer—letters, one of them in a blue envelope, the rest in white. She looked them over, touched them fleetingly; then began to read them, one by one, starting with the one in the blue envelope. But these were like books too! To the last 'y' of the last letter she applied all her desires, all her will; scoured the lines for some meaning between them. Twisting and turning the words over and over, she tried her utmost to extract some significance, to wring out a single drop of assurance. But nothing! Just words in a row, well-composed words, beautiful words—but what would she do with this beauty, books held words much more beautiful. He was travelling in the hills, he was happy, pausing occasionally to hone his writing skills with letters. The vacation was almost over, but what of that? He wouldn't return until the last possible moment.

As she put away the letters, Swati felt as though she had been walking for ages without getting anywhere, on a road without end, just as in a dream. And just as a dream ends with a jolt, so too did she suddenly wake up to clarity, identifying the dream as just that, while the road to reality stretched ahead.

Taking a sheet of paper, she uncapped her pen. The first time she had addressed Satyen very formally, relaxing the formality only a notch since then. That day, she used no form of address at all.

'When are you coming? The vacation's almost over, and you *have* to return. I don't want another letter. Letters are no good. I want you to be the reply.'

Adding her name, she looked at the letter.

Two minutes later, Swati submitted to the trusted darkness of the postbox her life, her future, her fate.

2

It was a joyous, gorgeous, luminous day. Cloud-smoke in summer's smoky mouth, the clouds smoky-black in colour, a skyful of black, sky-shattering rain, then incessant drizzles cooled the earth, the clouds hid themselves, blue splintered the sky, real blue, a soft but dazzling dark blue, the blue that appears in Bengal's skies—although it was famous for its blue—no more than nine or ten days a year. The sun outside must have been hot, but indoors there was just a soft light, a yellow–green–indigo glow, as though the wet green of the trees had poured this light on itself. The breeze was moist too, spreading a chill, it was chilly even without a breeze, even the electric fan, although it was afternoon, could be given a break. Swati, at least, paid no attention to the stilled fan; dressed in a sari the colour of grass, the parting in her bowed head a thread of light, all the joys of this luminous day reflected on her face, she read her letter standing up, and behind her, gazing at her bent neck, stood someone taller than she was, in a floppily wrapped dhoti and a shirt, sandals on his feet, holding two books and an exercise book. His posture suggested he was waiting for Swati to say something in particular, something on which much depended for him. He waited as long as he thought it should take to read a letter, then said, 'What has Ma written?'

'All well,' Swati replied without lifting her eyes.

'About me?'

'Bordi has put you under my wing,' Swati turned towards him, looked at him, smiled.

'Am I going to stay here or at the hostel?'

'Very keen on the hostel, I can see! Sir will dress up in style and skip classes every day! No such luck—just see how strict I am!'

'Ma had said I would stay here, but Baba said—no, it won't be convenient for them.'

'What else did your father say?'

'Baba had wanted to bring me too—when everyone came here during Durga Puja. But Ma said no. Exams, she said. I was very angry with her.'

'Very angry?' Swati arched her eyebrows.

'Naturally! The exams were six months away . . . And anyway do you think I studied during that time. I needn't have missed the trip.'

'That's all right, now you've come to stay instead of just visiting.'

'Do you think this was easy either? Ma went on and on—why not a college here—he's still a child, alone in Calcutta—etcetera, etcetera, the things Ma can come up with! Tell me, is a college back home even worth its name? Is a sixteen-year-old boy still a child?'

'What's most surprising is that Bordi actually let you go, considering how much she loves her children!'

'All mothers love their children; what's new about that?'

'Lovely! Less than a month in Calcutta and already a big talker.'

'So you think I'm a child too.'

'No such luck—how tall you've become already! I couldn't recognize you at first—*this* is Dalim? *Our* Dalim? When did he grow up so much?'

'You've grown up a lot too, Chhotomashi.'

Swati didn't reply, taking a few steps to sit in a chair. The chairs, which used to be in the middle of the room, as they should be, had been pushed to one side, close to one another, because half the drawing room was now Dalim's; a narrow cot, a small desk—Saswati's old desk, which used to occupy a corner in Rajen-babu's room—a new chair that didn't match with it at all—his uncle's gift—books on the desk, a round alarm clock, a calendar on the wall, but most of it covered by the shining new square mirror, purchased by the owner himself, which hung from the same nail. The room was definitely crowded, but now—on this day of light, on this joyous, gorgeous, luminous day it looked quite airy, open, lean, although on the ground floor, but because of the extra windows, and because Swati had drawn the curtains to cash in on the privacy offered by the afternoon, and in honour of the extraordinary light and breeze of this day, the affluence of the sky's blue-gold had made its way into the room.

Dalim neither sat down, nor moved, remaining where he was and saying, 'Am I rather too tall, Chhotomashi?'

'It's good to be tall.'

'Good, perhaps, but is it good to be too tall? I'm thin too—what do you think I should do? Should I exercise? But is it true that if you stop exercising once you've started you become fat?'

'Won't remain thin, won't get fat—what do we do with you!'

'But isn't there anything between thin and fat?' Dalim looked at his aunt, paused, and then continued, 'You told me to backbrush my hair, is this all right?'

'Let me see.'

The lanky Dalim bowed his head. Like his father's, his hair was also wiry and curly, he had brushed it back, obliterating the memory of the parting he had had in his hair as a child.

'Too much oil, don't put so much,' said Swati. 'Did you choose that blue shirt yourself?'

'Don't you like it?' Dalim raised his face.

'It's a nice colour—for curtains. And are you totally opposed to the normal way of wearing the dhoti?'

Dalim bowed his head again. He glanced at the detestable—that was how it felt now—way in which his dhoti had puffed up, at the detestable blue shirt; then, frowning, his head still bowed, he raised his eyes and said, looking at the wall behind Swati, 'No matter what I try, I'll still be me.'

'Do you want to be someone else?' Swati smiled quietly, recalling her own pain and agony when she was thirteen or fourteen.

'Wanting isn't enough, is it?' His eyes still on the same wall, Dalim continued, 'Do you suppose I can be Satyen-babu just because I want to?'

Laughing loudly, Swati said, 'Of all the people in the world, he's the one you picked?'

'But Satyen-babu is so handsome.'

'Handsome?' Another gust of laughter from Swati. 'Nobody on earth has used that word about him before you.'

'I know, people just think handsome means fair skin and nice features. But we say, no, grace is what matters.'

'Who are these "we"?'

Dalim chuckled, displaying his irregularly spaced teeth. Shifting his gaze to look directly at Swati, he said, 'Wouldn't you say Satyen-babu is handsome, Chhotomashi?'

His chhotomashi bantered in response, 'No one has ever seen anyone so handsome, isn't that so?'

'I don't care what others say,' said Dalim gravely. 'I use my own eyes.'

'Is that so!' All the brightness of the day broke out in song as Swati laughed. 'Why do you run away at the sight of him then.'

'What do I have to talk to him about.'

After a pause Swati said, 'It's probably not very comfortable for you in this room.'

'Not comfortable? Why?'

'It's the drawing room, after all. In case we have a visitor . . .'

'Oh, do you think I'm the kind to have my nose buried in my books all the time! And what guests are you talking about . . . only Satyen-babu now and then . . .' Dalim stopped abruptly, then continued immediately, 'Does it get uncomfortable for any of you?'

'Very,' said Swati. 'Baba simply can't sleep at night worrying whether you're feeling scared alone in this room.'

'What!' Dalim curled his lips, with the faint shadow of a budding moustache on them, in a way that made him look rather sweet. 'Why should I feel scared?'

'That's what I tell him. But Baba insists on waking up in the middle of the night to make sure—you never know, what if a ghost came for you or a demon ate you up!'

'It isn't right for him to have to...'

'Baba would prefer it if you stayed in his room. "There's so much room here," he says, "and I'm not even home all day..."'

'Dadu's very...'

'Yes, Baba's very. What would you prefer?'

Casting his eyes on his desk, his cot, his mirror, his minuscule, well-organized kingdom, Dalim said, 'I ... I'll stay here ... all right, Chhotomashi?' He even managed to improvise some logic in favour of his preference, 'It's convenient for all of you too—in case there's a guest I can inform you immediately.'

'Extremely convenient!' Swati smiled, then looked sternly at him. 'Is this how you plan to spend the day, or do you have a college to go to?'

Throwing a glance at the alarm clock on his desk, Dalim answered, 'I have some more time. Your classes start very early—but then, you have the whole day to yourselves.'

'I don't like it.'

'Me neither,' said Dalim immediately. 'Have to wake up at the crack of dawn. What does Satyen-babu teach your class, Chhotomashi?'

'What you don't read at all—that's what he teaches us.'

Dalim smiled with his eyes. 'You think I don't read any poetry at all? Haven't you seen *Sanchayita* on my desk? ... He must teach very well, mustn't he? If only I'd known, I'd have joined the college where he teaches. But Baba had told me about Presidency—he went there too; besides, I'm reading science, as he wanted—but I'm not enjoying it at all, Chhotomashi.'

'Run now, off with you, no more of this,' his chhotomashi chided him. 'Aren't you getting late for college!'

Dalim took a few reluctant steps towards the door, carrying his books. Stopping again, he said, 'Who knows whether we'll even have classes today.'

'Why?'

'Rabindranath...'

'No! Don't even think of such a thing.'

'But everyone was saying yesterday and in this morning's papers too . . . all right, I'm going.' Dalim had to shove himself out of the door.

Swati stayed where she was. She felt comfort, physical comfort, the comfort of the shimmering afternoon, the comfort of smooth digestion following a little chat after lunch. She was feeling drowsy—in fact, sleep was on its way—when, hearing a light sound in the room, she asked without opening her eyes, 'Did you forget something, Dalim?'

Not getting an answer, Swati opened her eyes, and then sprang to her feet.

'. . . What? What is it?'

Pale face, dishevelled hair, pinched lips and unshaven cheeks—in all this time Swati had never seen Satyen Roy looking like this. And when he spoke, his voice sounded strange too: 'Haven't you heard yet?'

'Heard what?'

Satyen Roy lifted his eyes towards Swati, then lowered them again, saying, 'Rabindranath . . .' He couldn't continue.

Swati bowed her head too at once, clasping her hands together at her breast. Her posture was similar to the one in which she had read Shweta's letter, standing; and in the lines of her shoulder, her neck—where earlier a joyful grace had almost spoken out aloud—now the same lines drew a picture of sorrow, a silent submission, the deeper grace of sadness.

They stood face-to-face. But not face-to-face either, for both had their heads bowed, both were silent. A little later Satyen raised his eyes; Swati did not see this, but she raised hers too immediately: in an unquestioning serenity they looked into each other's eyes.

'Let's go,' said Satyen Roy.

'Go? Where?'

'Don't you want to go? To see him?'

'Of course.' But go without telling Baba? Swati wondered.

'Let's go then.'

'But you—where were you?"

'I was there—I wouldn't have come—but I came for you. You've never seen him—you didn't—but still, for the last time at least . . .'

With a look at Satyen Roy's wan, stubbled face, Swati said, 'But you haven't eaten or . . .'

'No time for all that now,' Satyen's shoulders signalled something, a slight impatience. 'We're getting late. Let's go.'

'Do have something to eat. Haven't you eaten anything since morning?'

'No,' Satyen said, perhaps a trifle too loudly. He seemed a little disappointed—seemed hurt—at Swati's insistence on such trivial things as food at a time such as this. It was true he hadn't eaten anything since his first cup of tea in the morning: but he had no sensation of hunger, nor of fatigue; he had no sensation at all, other than that of grief; an expansive, rare, incomparable grief; familiar through imagination, ancient through possibility, and yet strange in reality, as unknown as the unexpected, as intolerable as the incredible . . . Arriving there in the morning, as soon as he had realized today was the last day, he had decided to stay till the end . . . The hours passed somehow after that, the crowds swelled, the large rooms and verandas at the poet's Jorasanko residence filled with people, more of them in the courtyard . . . A perspiring man in a vest passed on the news over the telephone; besides him everyone was silent, not one among all those people spoke, even after spotting familiar faces no one said anything, newcomers understood at a glance, without having to ask. Waiting, waiting mutely, just waiting—for what? Then, after a long time, he had sat down for a bit, he suddenly heard a sound—from the next room—like a single long-suppressed heart-rending gasp, and immediately people glanced at the watches on their wrists, at the clock on the wall, something past twelve, a whisper rose. A little later, when they allowed a single visit into the room—he had entered too. The head had seemed even bigger than earlier, enormous, but the body seemed to have shrunk a little, although the wrist was as broad as always, as powerful, the fingers as formidable. For the last time he had set eyes on that long-familiar face; on that head, that brow, that greatness; touched the ice-cold feet just once . . . And as soon as Satyen recalled that moment, as soon as he saw in his mind's eye the exhausted slump of that gigantic head, a red-hot shiver rose in his chest, he turned his face away quickly. Collecting himself in a moment, he said, as though offering a faint smile, 'All right, give me a glass of water.'

'Nothing else?' Swati quickly fetched him a glass of water from Dalim's pitcher.

Draining his glass, Satyen said, 'Quickly now. Let's go.'

'But . . . I was thinking . . .' Swati said.

'About what your father will say?' Satyen guessed right—half right . . . 'He'll be back any moment. All offices have been closed.'

Swati's face brightened. 'Then . . . can't we wait a little bit?'

'You'd rather tell him before you went?' Satyen finally understood, and was jolted. Couldn't the rules be broken even on a day such as this? Couldn't the daily compulsions be forgotten even for once? Did the same things have to be considered as on other days? But he had not; winding his way out through the crowd, he had run off to take a bus all the way from Jorasanko to Tollygunge, meaning to rush back to Jorasanko from Tollygunge immediately. But why had he?

The question died as soon as it had risen in Satyen's mind; he was in no state of mind to quiz himself, nor did he have the time. 'Your father won't mind, I know.'

'So do I.'

'Well, then?'

Swati didn't reply.

'Then you'd better stay. But I can't any more.'

'No, I'm going too,' said Swati at once.

She rushed inside, wrote a two-line note for her father and handed it to the maid, changed her clothes and shoes, took her handbag, and, stepping out on the road with Satyen, the first thing she noticed was that the day was still just as joyous and gorgeous and luminous.

The bus filled before they reached Kalighat. Still people kept getting in; college students, schoolboys, shopkeepers, the unemployed, young men who chatted with one another all day. The bus was so crowded she felt suffocated. But the seats reserved for women, one of which Swati occupied, were safe— and she was seated by the window, staring out fixedly. The roads were full of typical late afternoon crowds, schoolboys in groups, but without their boisterousness; several older people wandered around aimlessly; groups of people gathered at any shop where the radio played; and there were small crowds at every street corner, hoping to board any bus or tram that came by. Cinema posters were covered in black; the doors shut. Women stood in verandas, at windows, their hair open, children in their arms, taking in as much of the road as they could. Everyone's eyes, everyone's mind, were trained on the road.

The day became cloudy, it started raining by the time they reached Chowringhee. But when the bus came to a halt at Esplanade, the sun was shining again, brightly; and in that soft-moist light, Swati saw an extraordinary swirl in the crowd, extraordinary even for Esplanade. The office-goer in a suit, the lawyer in his black coat, middle-aged clerks with umbrellas in hand, thin young clerical workers, Englishmen, Chinese, Madrasis, priests, Parsis—they were all rushing to and fro between Chowringhee, Dharmatalla, Curzon Park, Corporation Street, but without any specific destination, seemingly a little bewildered; many of them seemed to have forgotten the axiom that you go back home when the office is closed. No matter how fragmented they looked, Calcutta's crowds were never aimless; everyone usually knew where they were going and why; but today they had all forgotten their destination, the certainty of a destination—and that was why these crowds were unusual, extraordinary.

Some people just stood stiffly, staring straight ahead, some just walked around, some seemed to make up their minds and walk a few steps, only to stop suddenly, some read the papers, each with two or three more peering over their shoulder. The special edition had just hit the streets, disappearing in a sea of hands.

Sitting behind Swati, Satyen reached out through the window to buy a newspaper, handing it to her after a single glance. Swati gave it just one glance, putting it on her lap. The girl of about fifteen sitting next to her took it without asking for permission, her eyes moved from the top to the bottom, and from those eyes tears fell on the newspaper with words printed on it in black, smudging the still-wet ink fresh from the presses.

The bus all but emptied out at Jorasanko. Everyone ran towards Dwarakanath Lane, but, about to cross the road, Satyen paused. When he had left there had been a barrage of people—what had happened to them? Where was everyone?— 'Have they taken him away already?' the words escaped his lips.

'Yes, they have—if you want to see him go to College Street . . .' answered someone as he passed.

Swati had never been to Chitpore before; she watched with amazement the jostling trams and buses on a street that was more of a lane; even more of a lane further down, dark, twisting; tall buildings, cheek by jowl, shutting out the sky; strange crowds on the pavements and in makeshift roadside kiosks selling peculiar things. She almost forgot why she was there; remembering only when Satyen said, 'They've taken him away already. Let's go to College Street. You *can* walk quickly, can't you?'

They walked swiftly, silently along the nominal pavement, avoiding brushing against other pedestrians. After a few minutes they turned left, entering Muktaram Babu Street. All these Calcutta neighbourhoods—Swati felt—were like a different land, a different world; the light, the air, even the smell was different.

She looked around her, but couldn't see anything clearly because of the pace at which Satyen-babu was walking.

The long, dark, serpentine Muktaram Babu Street ended at Cornwallis Street; and the crossing of College Street and Harrison Road appeared soon afterwards.

Satyen stopped on the covered pavement in front of the College Street market, climbing the steps of a shoe-shop. Many more people stood there, mostly college students. They were heard saying, any moment now.

'Did the walk tire you out?' Satyen asked.

'N . . . no!'

'Do you wish you hadn't come?'

'No.'

The conversation ended there, both of them were silent again. Some people stood on the dangerous bare roof of a shop on the opposite side of the road, their cameras aimed; women and children thronged the first-floor balcony next door; there wasn't a single window nearby without three or four faces peering out of it, and no one moved on the road, everyone waiting. Satyen felt the weight of that waiting, that mute waiting, on himself again.

'Here they come . . . here they are . . .' a buzz rose through the crowd.

Swati had expected a long, intense, overwhelmed, silent, slow procession of bowed heads; but only a handful of people bore him away on their shoulders, rather quickly—from north to south—a few people straggling behind them . . . Like a flash of lightning they disappeared from Swati's vision— the long white mane and the enormous, pale, tranquil, contemplative brow glinted in the sunlight. That was all Swati saw, nothing more.

Satyen saw Swati standing rigidly upright, hands balled up in fists, her lips clamped together; saw the trembling in her throat, the quivering of her lips, the deep colour in her cheeks.

He saw her liquid black bright eyes become brighter, become shining mirrors, then the mirrors shattered, became liquid again, brimmed over, the head was bowed.

And at this sight, Satyen had a catch in his throat all over again, his eyes misted over, and he embarrassed himself. This death demanded no tears, this grief, this immense, invaluable grief, this final jewel of eighty years of uncompromising labour—was it to be squandered in tears?

'Let's go now,' Satyen said.

Swati did not try to conceal that she had been crying, she wiped her eyes on the end of her sari, coughed, and then said hoarsely, 'Let's.'

But the trams and buses were choked. From every direction, on every road, people rushed towards Nimtala, for the last rites. They waited helplessly, their feet aching as they stood there.

'Should we try walking?' Swati said. 'A little further ahead we might . . .'

'Walking a little won't help. Only if we can go all the way to Esplanade . . .'

'Is that very far?' Swati asked, unsure about the geography of this part of town.

'Not all that far,' Satyen said encouragingly. 'Down Chittaranjan Avenue—shall we walk then?'

'Why not.'

As soon as they had traversed Colootola Street to reach Chittaranjan Avenue, the skies became dark, opening up suddenly. They took shelter under a portico. Dense was the rain cascading to the ground, and, drenched in that rain, there passed a group of calm, silent, grave Chinese men, each with his head bowed, each with flowers in his hand, each barefoot.

Swati looked at them as long as they remained visible. 'How beautiful they are,' she said.

Satyen nodded in assent.

'Where are they going?'

'Must be Nimtala.'

Swati had heard of Nimtala, so she understood. 'Aren't you going?'

'I would have . . . but . . .'

'Can't I go too?'

'You can, but I can't take you.'

'Why not?'

'You can't imagine how crowded it will be.'

Swati didn't like this. Even on a day such as this, she reflected, Satyen-babu remained far too cautious, conventional, mindful of dos and don'ts. Meanwhile the rain didn't let up.

Another group appeared, Englishmen, priests, bearded old men, dressed in long white smocks, flowers in their hands, tranquillity on their faces, prayer in their eyes. Soaked to the skin, they passed by.

The rain lessened, the rain stopped, they resumed walking under a light drizzle, raindrops on their hands, lips, heads. The sun came out; the yellow sunlight, slanted in the late afternoon, glinted on the wet, black surface of the road, glittered in the soft-moist air.

'Tell me if you're feeling tired, I think we can get on a bus here.'

'I'm enjoying the walk,' said Swati. As soon as she spoke she felt remorse, felt guilty; on this day, at such a time, was it right to 'enjoy' anything? Even if you did, did you have to *say* so? Swati glanced apprehensively at Satyen Roy out of the corner of her eye, but the grief-stricken professor appeared not to have noticed the discordant note of enjoyment, on the contrary, he said, pleased, 'You are? That's fine then.'

They walked on in silence, but not the way they had on Muktaram Babu Street after being thwarted at Jorasanko; back then their pace was swift, the lane narrow, the mind anxious; and now before their eyes lay the generous neatness of Chittaranjan Avenue—an enormous, broad, large-hearted expanse, uncrowded,

without trams, the cars floating by lightly, silently; huge, tall
buildings lined the road on either side, but even larger, even
higher was the sky, and the road was so spread out that the
buildings appeared weightless—the houses on the two sides of
the road seemed to belong to two separate neighbourhoods;
and over the entire road a curtain with the subtle, transparent
tinge of the rainswept yellow-green late afternoon rippled,
swayed, glowed. They walked slowly, there was no hurry now; the
climactic moment had passed under the portico of the College
Street shoe shop; the nerves weren't drawn tight like bowstrings
any more, they had gone limp now, now there was time to
gaze—at the afternoon, at the light, at the bright, beautiful sky.
Swati felt an undefined joy in her heart; a little later her guilt
vanished too, but she herself remained unaware of this change of
season within, didn't think about it, didn't consider it specifically,
gradually sinking into her sensation of happiness.

And Satyen—passionate about poetry, he had worshipped the
poet all his life—he too experienced an elusive joy; just as
the blue pennant was hoisted at that moment over the dispassionate
gateway of the sky over post-Rabindranath Bengal and grief-
stricken Calcutta, so too was the deep dank grave of historic grief
in his mind covered by the green of the present, the immediate,
the living moment—so effortlessly that even he did not realize
it. In silence, each of them accepted this happiness they were dimly
conscious of—their own, as well as that of the other person—they
had not spoken earlier because there was nothing to say, now
they didn't because there was no need to.

At Esplanade the screaming wheels, the orbit of the crowds,
the jostling and shoving began again. They crossed the road
after several stops and starts. At Chowringhee Satyen said, 'Would
you like a cup of tea?'

'You haven't had a bite all day,' Swati remembered suddenly.
'If you feel you're late . . .'

'How late can I be?'

'You mean—you're already fearfully late?'

At this Swati remembered that she had not thought about going home even once, about the need to get back home, about her father. Was he worried? How long had she been out? What time was it? She tried to catch a glimpse of the Whiteaway-Laidlow clock, but from where they were standing . . . never mind. 'Which of these?' she said.

Each of the small restaurants, all in a row, were packed. Satyen took Swati into a large English restaurant set amidst them, the window facing the road covered in frosted glass panes, the stairs encased in rubber. From the upheaval of the glare-crowds-bustle outside they were suddenly transported into a silken silent, roomy, solemn darkness. A new aroma wafted into Swati's nose, a sort of foreign aroma, dry, light, warming . . . unfamiliar, but nice . . . nice.

They were threading their way past several empty tables towards one in the corner when a solitary occupant of one of the tables suddenly called out to them.

Satyen stopped, raising his hand in greeting. But without returning the greeting noticeably, the gentleman said, 'Coming from Nimtala?'

'No, we didn't go all that . . . Swati, you know who this is, don't you . . .'

Swati did. Dark, discontent, unkempt, Dhruba Datta was sprawled on a chair, a cigarette between his fingers, a light brown drink in a glass set before him, just like—the memory suddenly flashed in Swati's mind—she had seen on the table shared by the two middle-aged foreigners at Chang-Aan. Noting that Satyen's greeting was wasted, she did not attempt to emulate him, only trying to indicate through a humble expression that she had already had the fortune of being acquainted with this genius.

But this wasn't necessary either, Dhruba Datta did not even notice her presence. Looking at Satyen, he asked, 'What was it like—all the breast-beating and the excitement?'

Satyen couldn't find an instant response, and Dhruba Datta continued immediately, 'I feel sorry for Rabindranath. He tried so hard to die in Europe, said as much so many times, wrote about it too, but eventually . . . "Allow me to die in the land of my birth"!' Dhruba Datta smiled a tiny, bitter smile, and in the dim darkness of that large, empty restaurant, his voice sounded far too loud and harsh. Satyen may have been about to say something, but he realized in an instant that Dhruba Datta didn't want to hear anything, only wanted to spew out what was on his mind—taking a drag on his cigarette, but leaving his drink untouched, the poet spoke through curled lips: 'I came out, wandered around the streets for some time, but I couldn't take it any more and came in here. What an opportunity this is! Those who have read no Rabindranath except *Katha O Kahini,* or even if they have, have not understood any of it, or even if they've understood, have not accepted it, all those cunning idiots who chant the word Gurudeb with their oily lips, yet whose very existence is an act of enmity against Rabindranath, and all those faddists, who will not know, all their lives, will not want to know, what Rabindranath means, why and how—what an opportunity it is today for all these people that our nation is full of. It's bigger than ten IFA Shield Finals, bigger than a hundred Kanan Devi-Saigal concerts! Roaring business for newspapers, peak season for meeting-mongers, publicity sprees for commercially minded bosses! What excitement, what antics, what revelry! People to whom it makes no difference whatsoever whether Rabindranath is alive or dead are the ones who are wildly celebrating this festival of grief. Hah!'

Speaking slowly and deliberately, choosing his words with care, the successor delivered the funeral oration of the predecessor in a loud, stern, harsh voice, stopping at the appropriate point after the last syllable, leaned forward and stretched out his hand, ingested a little of his drink, and then leaned back in his chair to communicate that he had nothing more to say on the subject.

Satyen had been listening in silence, his expression becoming graver as he listened, then sadder, even a little pained. A little later he said, 'Well, then . . .' raising his hand in farewell.

'Why don't you . . .' Dhruba Datta suddenly looked at Swati, as though he had only just seen her, 'join me.' Swati felt uncomfortable, more than she had when she met him at Satyen-babu's house, she turned away at once, but still sensed a pair of sharp, glittering eyes on her face—and her victory was in moving ahead a few steps to ensure Satyen-babu didn't actually join Dhruba Datta at his table.

Saying, 'We'll just . . . Over there . . .' Satyen followed her. They sat at a corner table quite some distance away; pouring the tea immaculately, sipping it noiselessly, and unwrapping a sandwich with her left hand, Swati said—in a tone somewhat too angry for her—'He may be a poet, he may be famous, but a nice man he's not!'

Satyen had been thinking of Dhruba Datta all this while; smiling a little, he said, 'A nice man? Someone who can't speak his mind, can't protest against injustice, who is more embarrassed than courageous, and therefore is exploited by everyone according to their needs—that's who a good man is, right?' As he spoke, Satyen considered the fact that he did have something to say in response to Dhruba Datta, he should have said it, too, but he hadn't been able to say anything at all—and this happened to him all the time, for which he suffered in his head.

'No, why do you say that?' Swati protested. 'A nice man is someone who doesn't hurt others even if he's suffering himself.' She thought of her father immediately—or perhaps she said this keeping her father in mind.

Satyen glanced at Swati, kept looking for a while. The colour of a warm emotion had risen in her face, her hair a little awry after all the walking she had done, the candour of confidence shining in her eyes. This was the first time in all these days that she had spoken so freely; even the other day there used to be a tentative nervousness in the presence of the professor—Satyen had observed the change since his return from Shillong—the deference owed to a teacher had been wiped out—although they routinely met once a week in college for an honours class. Satyen had tried not to notice it—at least, not to acknowledge it—but at this moment, it became obvious, concrete, well defined, in Swati's spontaneous, lively protest; he averted his eyes, lowered them towards his cup of tea. What about me—have I maintained the teacher's sense of proportion and protocol? Am I not a collaborator in this closing of the gap, this exposure of the heart, am I not the one responsible, am I not the one who started it all? What am I doing, where am I heading? Why had I rushed off from Jorasanko to Tollygunge, unbathed and fasting, on this grieving afternoon? Rabindranath's death! Is it not an event that should for the moment make me forget everything else, all effort, need, eagerness? But still, when he had breathed his last, when I came out after paying my respects for the last time, my first thought was of . . . her; I felt I had to ensure that she shared this sublime experience, that it was my duty, my responsibility . . . but why? But why? . . . Satyen bowed his head under an odd sort of shame, of protest, of self-chastisement, to conceal which he sipped his tea several times.

The entirety of this thought didn't take Satyen more than a few seconds; which was why Swati, unable to sense any change in her companion, continued to talk freely. 'Is there nothing positive in this country as far as he's concerned?'

Satyen suddenly realized Dhruba Datta had spoken the unadulterated truth, that his grief was far more sacred, his respect for Rabindranath far more unselfish; and the reason that he—Satyen—was feeling unhappy as he listened was his temporary sentimentality, for today he had also been infected by the mass hysteria. Raising his eyes, he said, 'Does one have to be positive even if there isn't any reason to be?'

'But,' Swati argued, 'does he understand his own flaws as well as he does the nation's?'

'Of course he does!' Satyen smiled gently. 'His four successive books of poetry are proof of that. He tries tirelessly to overcome his flaws, to surpass himself every time. And you do understand,' he almost added a teacher's note, 'how difficult it is to identify one's shortcomings, and how painful.'

'I don't know about his writing, but does he understand the flaws in his own character?'

'What do you mean by flaws in his own character? And what do you know about him anyway?' Satyen was almost severe this time.

Swati suddenly asked, 'What's that he's drinking?'

'He uses those . . . substances . . . probably,' Satyen answered gravely.

Swati paused. So what she had surmised, but hadn't wanted to, was true. Dhruba Datta the poet was drinking what is known in plain language as alcohol. Like all middle-class Bengali girls, Swati too had learnt from childhood to consider that substance with dread. And although she had recently got a different picture from a foreign novel, it still seemed to belong to a different world, sounding right only in English—hearing the word spoken in Bengali made her shudder. She had heard plenty, read Saratchandra Chatterjee, seen it in films too, but this was for all intents and purpose the first time she had actually seen a flesh-and-blood person drinking. And who was that person? A poet. And when? Just when the heartbeat of poetry had been stilled a few hours earlier, and the entire nation had lost itself.

'A wonderful time for all this!' She spoke what was on her mind.

'But we're having tea too,' Satyen said softly, 'what's wrong with that?'

Swati didn't like this support for Dhruba Datta from Satyen. Was he also one of them? Did he also 'use' 'those substances' from time to time? Poetry was good, poetry was very good, but did the rumours spread by fools actually have some basis in truth; were those who wrote poetry, those who spent all their time with poetry, all a little . . . a little . . .?

'Besides,' Satyen continued, 'if you want to say something about someone you should do it to their face; what we're doing now is backbiting—literally.' He looked across several empty tables at Dhruba Datta's *panjabi*-covered back.

Swati followed Satyen's gaze. From where she sat, a part of his face was visible too, and coiling-up cigarette smoke, and from the little she could see Swati realized that his entire attention was now concentrated solely on the glass before him. Her gaze seemed to ricochet from the impact, as though dealt a body blow, and settled on Satyen's distracted face, on it she saw simplicity, honesty, tranquillity; saw a promise she could trust, an assurance of certainty; her eyes clouded over with remorse at what she had thought a minute ago about people with a poetic bent of mind, and, knowing it wasn't real, the clouds dispelled.

As though he had sensed the intimacy of Swati's gaze at him, Satyen turned to look at her, and as soon as his eyes met hers she chuckled—a sudden, irrelevant, even a little unwarranted, chuckle.

'What is it?' he asked, frowning.

'Nothing. Everything you said is correct, but there's something I *shall* say—it isn't nice the way he looks at you,' she said, glancing again at Dhruba Datta's back.

At that precise moment Dhruba Datta rose, his tall frame a little hunched, walked out swiftly without looking to left or right, disjointed, restless, aimless. Satyen looked at his retreating back, then said, 'You're completely wrong there. His talent is in his eyes . . . But no more of this. Let's talk of something else.'

But Swati was still thinking of Dhruba Datta's offensive gaze.

It was Satyen who changed the subject—'Did you see Dalim?'

'Dalim? Where?'

'When we were waiting at College Street. He was in an overcrowded bus. Didn't see us. Quite a nice boy.'

This last statement sounded unnecessary—that is, it didn't sound strong enough to Swati. 'Quite? Why quite?' she asked.

Satyen answered after some time, 'No particular reason, just . . .'

Dhruba Datta's departure had relaxed Swati fully now, leaning back comfortably in her chair, she said, 'That "quite" is one of the methods used to write people off.'

'And it isn't nice to hear someone else say "quite" either, is it?' Satyen smiled.

'Meaning?'

Without answering, Satyen said, 'And your Bordi . . . how is she!'

'You ask after Bordi quite often—tell me why!'

'I think of her quite often.'

'But how many times have you met her, after all.'

'That's probably why.'

'Do you think of people less when you see them often?' Swati asked logically.

'We remember what isn't. What is, always is.'

'Then isn't is better,' said Swati.

'Why? Is it better to think of someone?'

Swati thought for a bit. In her head she sniffed the soft new soil of the small mound of silted memories of her young life. 'Of course it is. Much better.'

'And this?'

'What?'

'What is. What's happening.'

'I don't know!' Reddening a little, Swati smiled.

'This is our problem.' Satyen leaned back in his chair. 'We're always wiser after the event. What *is*, what's happening, means nothing to us; we perceive our moments of happiness not at the time, but later—much later; which is why we always feel that, ever since then, nothing has matched what happened, nothing can. Of course,' he added with a smile, 'this is not *my* observation, nor is it new, but what's old suddenly seems fresh when we perceive it with our own life.'

Having finished, Satyen straightened his back, picked up his cup, drained the tea in it and wiped his lips with his handkerchief. The impact of breaking his day-long fast, of the warmth of the tea, of the warmth in Swati's eyes, made Satyen feel alive, he was enjoying the moment, watching, talking, listening. And listening to him, Swati wondered, is this one of those moments of happiness, then? Will I realize it now, or later? But Swati tried to capture it at once, tried to catch the thief in the act, as it were—and immediately chided herself for even imagining that a moment of such grief for the entire nation could be a happy one for herself. But Satyen-babu's expression held no sign of grief either.

The plates had been removed, the bill had been paid, there was no excuse for not leaving, but still Satyen dallied. Finally he noticed that the crowds were swelling, the lights were brighter, and the few people he had seen on entering had left. His eyes returned to Swati after the survey; very simply, lightly, as though it was related to the earlier discussion, he said, 'You seemed a little troubled earlier.'

'Troubled? When? About what?'

'That last letter of yours I got in Shillong . . .'

This was the first time that Satyen had referred to that letter. That he hadn't all this time had left Swati quietly grateful. Embarrassed from the moment she had posted the letter, she had felt even more so four days later when Satyen returned and visited her almost immediately. But when neither his conversation nor his behaviour indicated that he had received the letter, she breathed a sigh of relief. In fact—although deep in the recesses of her mind she knew perfectly well that her letter had not been misdirected, that it had not failed, for otherwise he would have spent the last few days of his vacation in Shillong instead of returning immediately—she even pretended to herself that the letter hadn't reached, thank goodness, good riddance! And although, right now, she felt herself blushing hotly and lowering her face to her breast, her lids to her eyes, to conceal it, the same self-delusion gave her the strength to defend herself, allowing her to ask directly, 'Which letter?'

'The one you wrote me—to come back.'

'You got that letter?'

'Did you imagine I didn't?' Satyen, so artless, added force to her self-deception.

'Who knows!' Swati recovered her composure, her eyes wistful, and breathed a sigh in secret, in perfect secret. She'd been very scared, almost unable to breathe . . . A small smile appeared on her face, which she tried to conceal by lowering her face again.

Meanwhile Satyen was thinking about the letter, seeing the blue notepaper before his eyes, sensing its opaque scent in his breath, no introduction, a few, just a few words, and below them the name, the beautiful name, the loveliest name in the world. On the way back, every word in that letter had resonated in his mind to the rhythm of the train, flowing into an exquisite current of joy that flowed in the crevices between half-sleep and half-wakefulness on the moving train; and at the back of his mind, that current, that undiscovered, secret joy, that subtle, unfamiliar tremor—although it was impossible to tell from his appearance, and his days were passing the same way as before, too—had not yet ceased. And now, at this moment, it seemed to rise to the surface, it wanted to manifest itself as words on his lips, but in the period that it took for the words to be transferred to language, Swati spoke up, 'Shall we go now?'

'Yes, let's go.'

It was nearly dark, and overcast once more, a slight drizzle, packed trams. Swati found a place on the seats reserved for women, and though Satyen stood directly behind her, knowing that conversation was impossible—or perhaps deliberately—neither of them even tried. Swati reflected how, barely a couple of months earlier, she had been but a child, been a silly girl, but now she had found herself, found that self whom she most wanted to be like. And, looking alternately at the melancholy evening outside and at Swati's mass of hair, come loose from its restraining clip, Satyen realized she hadn't answered his question about the letter.

Swati was astonished when she saw her father back home. Had Rabindranath's death so overwhelmed him? He looked forlorn, his lips were dry, his eyes were sunken. 'Did you get my note, Baba?' she asked, going up to him quickly.

Rajen-babu nodded.

'I'm rather late, aren't I?'

When her father didn't say anything, didn't ask anything this time either, Swati suspected something. 'Baba, you . . . You look . . . What's happened, Baba?'

'There's a telegram.'

'Telegram? Show it to me . . .' As she spoke, Swati's eyes fell on the pale envelope lying near her father. She read it in a moment, then looked at him. He didn't say anything.

'What's a stroke, Baba?' she asked.

'It's an illness . . .' Rajen-babu didn't elucidate.

'A serious illness.'

'Yes . . .' He didn't look at his daughter.

'Where's Dalim . . .' Swati looked around.

'He isn't back yet.'

'He must leave today, mustn't he? But is there still time for the train?'

'They've changed the time, it leaves at nine now. If he isn't back by eight . . .'

'He will be . . . Any moment now . . . Today of course everyone . . . But he'll definitely be back by eight.'

'. . . Then I'll go,' Rajen-babu finished what he was saying.

'You? Why you?... No, of course you must, Bordi will be relieved... is it very bad?'

Rajen-babu didn't reply.

'Bad... Very bad... How bad can it be...' Swati paced up and down restlessly, speaking. 'People do fall seriously ill, don't they... They do, they get better too... Don't worry so much, if the doctors there aren't good enough let him come here... Yes, that would be better, so many good doctors here in Calcutta... They can cure anything...' Swati stopped suddenly, like a stabbing knife came the reminder that if Calcutta doctors could indeed cure any illness then her mother... And Rabindranath... But she couldn't be quiet either, this silence without anyone speaking was unbearable, so she spoke again, 'What time did the telegram arrive?'

'Around... two.'

'When did you get back?'

'Just before that.'

Two o'clock! Four or five hours! He's been waiting here alone, worrying all by himself! And I...

'Have you sent word to Chhordi?'

'I sent Hari... She wasn't home. Today of course...'

'Send him again.'

'Never mind, what's the use of bothering her now. She'll be tired anyway!' Rajen-babu looked at the old, yellowing wall-clock.

'Dada?'

Rajen-babu indicated helplessness with his hands.

'If Dada were home at least... The telegram came at two, you said?... Have you had your tea?'

'They gave me some.'

It wasn't clear from this whether he'd had his tea or not; but saying anything more about this—or asking for another cup of tea for him—seemed meaningless, saying anything seemed meaningless. Swati read the telegram again, turned it round and round in her hand, then ran out to the drawing room on hearing footsteps, expecting to see Dalim or her brother . . . But no . . . There was no one there.

Rajen-babu rose, packed Dalim's things into a hold-all with Hari's help, and wrapped a sheet, a pillow and a few clothes of his own into a bundle.

Looking on, Swati said, 'Are you going, Baba?'

'Let's see.'

'Yes, Baba, go . . . Don't worry about me . . . I can manage.'

'You could stay with Saswati . . .'

'But why? Hari's here, so's Ram-er ma—what can go wrong? And you'll be back soon besides . . . and Jamaibabu will get well too . . .' The sight of the packed hold-all and bundle made Swati feel an emptiness, a suffocating desolation seemed to spread all over the house.

After getting everything ready, Rajen-babu waited again quietly, and Swati ran out of things to say, she felt like a wrung-out wet towel, and inside the room the aged yellowed clock kept ticking.

Dalim returned before eight after all. His clothes caked in mud, a humble victorious smile on his face. He hadn't given up, he had gone all the way to the crematorium, entered, almost died in the crush of people, and all the way back had been planning how he would describe everything to Swati and how astonished she would be. 'Chhotomashi . . .' He was calling her already as he entered, and stopped abruptly near the door. His aunt lay on the bed, and his grandfather looked odd, and there was packed luggage on the floor . . . Why?

. . . Dalim didn't take more than a few minutes to get ready. He had a so-called bath—didn't even manage to scrape all the mud off—and just about sat down briefly at the table to eat. It wasn't as though he was supremely anxious, but his self-esteem shot up considerably at being given the responsibility of going home immediately because of his father's illness, his swiftness peaked as a result, and he looked grave, very grave. 'Should I take some fruit from Sealdah?' he asked intelligently.

In response, Rajen-babu said, 'The taxi's here. Let's go,' and made to go with him.

'But you . . . Why do you . . .?'

'Let me see you off . . .'

'Oh no, you don't need to . . . Do you suppose I . . . Of course not!' Dalim practically pushed his grandfather away, bending to touch his feet the very next moment, springing into the taxi with a look at his aunt.

Finally Swati said, 'You didn't go, Baba?'

'So I see. Maybe . . . Tomorrow . . .' Finally Rajen-babu looked directly at his daughter.

3

Swati awoke in darkness. But she realized immediately it wasn't night any more. She heard crows cawing, Hari hammering away at the coal pieces, water warbling in the bathroom. From that last sound she knew her father was up. She got out of bed too.

She almost stumbled on her way out. Just outside the door, in the slice of corridor between two rooms, the maid was sprawled on the floor, asleep—was this how she slept every night, so helpless, destitute?

Swati practically stepped over her, meeting her father in the veranda at the back—he was on his way out of the bathroom after a morning wash. In the ashen gloom Swati saw her father's face was ashen. In the pale darkness Rajen-babu saw Swati's face was pale. Neither of them spoke.

Swati entered the bathroom. When she came out, she had to step over the maid again to enter her room; she changed out of her creased, dirty, dreary violet sari into a freshly ironed mill sari—white, far too white, like limestone, white and dismal.

After she had changed, Swati went to the veranda at the back. This was her father's sitting room, as well as their dining room. It held a long, narrow, rexin-topped dining table—like something used by doctors to examine patients, as though there would be an operation soon. Her father sat in a chair at one end, facing the yard; Swati also faced the yard as she took the chair at the head of the table. Neither of them spoke.

Darkness withdrew, dawn advanced. After the ashen half-light came the pale ashen dawn; the dirty smoky light blended into the spiral of smoke from the kitchen; the kitchen wall was blackened, the yard was filthy and full of coal dust; it was a dirty, bleak, chilly dawn. Swati wrapped her sari around herself— winter in the air already! When had summer ended? When did the monsoon run away?

Having woken up, the maid was passing, her head uncovered; she came to a halt at the sight of Rajen-babu, made a cowl for her head with the end of her sari, peeped at Swati from beneath it and went back. Her expression was forlorn—Swati observed in an instant—crestfallen, contracted, creased.

Darkness withdrew, daylight emerged. A thin sun lit up the filthy roof of the kitchen, a weak, square, dirty patch of yellow sunlight illuminated the yard. Hari brought tea from the kitchen, with bread-and-butter. He looked forlorn too, drawn, unhappy, melancholy. Swati had seen Hari every day since her childhood; for the first time she saw his face etched in sadness.

They had their tea in silence. The maid, her head covered, came in silence to deposit the newspaper and glasses on the table, left in silence.

Rajen-babu unfolded the newspaper, reading it through his glasses with extra attention. Swati sat in silence.

The weak square patch of yellow sunlight disappeared; thin, long beams of white sunlight advanced. Swati rose in silence, returned to her room in silence. Rajen-babu read the newspaper in silence.

No—there was nothing to say, nothing to do. What she had been constantly reminded of over the past few days, what she had not forgotten even for a moment in her sleep last night, was something about which there was nothing to say, nothing to hear—even nothing new to think. Yet, there was nothing else to talk about either, nothing else to think about. You had to think about the same things that you had already thought about a thousand times.

This was Swati's first real encounter with death. Her mother had died too: how had she felt then? Her constant exposure to her mother's illness had made her get used to it, ever since her earliest memory she had known that a mother was not an unshakeable idea. And she had been a child, too; it hurt, it hurt very much, but there was comfort too; the more it hurt the more she cried, and the more she cried the easier it was to forget. Then there was the news of Maya Sanyal's death when college reopened. That day—she realized now when she thought about it—her greatest sensation had been that of victory—someone else had died, she had not had to; and for that reason when she had come out on the road, things had seemed much more wonderful—everything; it was wonderful merely to be alive. And Rabindranath the other day—but that was not a death at all. The Rabindranaths of the world don't die; they go away from time to beyond time, out of their body into people's minds, they're immortal. But what of others, people, everyone? They're dead when they die, lost the moment they exit their bodies, nothing remained.

And this was the death everyone had to die.

Swati recollected reading the English poem 'We Are Seven'. The girl kept saying, seven are we, nay, we are seven! Although two of the seven were dead. A child, she did not understand what death meant. Swati had found it funny. An eight-year-old girl who didn't understand death! As far back as her memory went, Swati couldn't remember a single day when she was like the girl in the poem. Very very early on in childhood—possibly at the age of four or five—she had been informed that everyone had to die, including her—she would have to die too. Here she was, playing, laughing, eating, sleeping, doing as she pleased; but all the time, an archer had an arrow aimed at her back, the bowstring drawn back, standing with his feet apart—the archer could fire the arrow any time, no one knew why he hadn't yet; but fire it he would eventually, no one knew when, and when he did that was it. Whenever she was alone in her room, she'd be scared to look behind her, her back seemed to tingle. But it wasn't just her, everyone was targeted by the same archer, the same arrow, didn't they know? Didn't they think about it? Weren't they afraid? Swati had looked at grown-ups' faces to gauge their thoughts about this—but none of them seemed afraid, they were just fine!—then would she also not be afraid once she had grown up—when would she?—how grown-up do you have to be before you can be as secure? The little Swati had lived in hope, but today's Swati could no longer remember when that propitious moment had come and gone, when the tingling in her back had stopped, when she had succeeded in forgetting that archer. All she remembered was that she hadn't recollected the archer in many, many years—not since that faint memory of her childhood—not even when her mother had died—she had lived many, many years, one after the other, as though there were no such thing as death.

'Telegram!'

Her heart had quaked at the sound, although this was just what she had been waiting for since the afternoon, along with her sister and brother. She was just a little late getting up from her chair, her father got to his feet before she could; Swati saw the shadow of a demon at the door, and, a little later, on the road a cycle-lamp like a one-eyed monster. For a moment her father's face seemed to crumple into an entirely different form, then he spoke in a whisper, 'I'd better go to her.'

'I'm coming too,' said Swati.

'No.'

'Baba!'

'No.'

His luggage had been packed already from the previous day, Saswati packed a few more things quickly—it barely took five minutes, and there was just about enough time to get the train. Rajen-babu dropped his daughters at Saswati's house . . . Since he *was* having to go eventually, if only he had gone the previous day—but what purpose would that have served either!

Seeing them, seeing their expressions, Harit said, 'Bad news?'

Saswati didn't respond.

'Your father's left?' Harit looked at Swati.

Swati nodded slowly.

Harit frowned. 'Is it very bad?'

'It's all over,' said Saswati.

Harit was silent for a minute or so, then remarked gravely, 'Hmm . . . all that overeating . . . if he had even cut down towards the end . . . there's no other treatment . . . and once you've had a stroke it's very difficult!' He uttered the word "difficult" loosely, as though there was still hope of recovery.

Saswati sighed.

Swati was unhappy with both Saswati's sigh and Harit's response. She was unhappy staying with them—why couldn't she have stayed at home, but her father simply wouldn't allow that. How horrible the days had been till her father's return. She hadn't even been able to pay a short visit home, because there was no question of Saswati going there during those few days, and although her brother had been over a few times, he had refused to take her home—and yet, it was necessary to conceal from Saswati that although her father wasn't home—no one was, for all intents and purposes—her heart still lay there.

Swati was living away from home for the first time in her life. You couldn't follow your daily routine when you were living somewhere else, but these were small inconveniences, and she was not in a state of mind to fret over such things. But because it was her sister's home, her sister's and nobody else's, every difference seemed exaggerated. Saswati was the one she had been closest to; after Mahashweta and Saraswati had got married, even more so after their mother's death, she couldn't manage for a moment without Saswati. And now where that same Saswati was concerned, meeting her from time to time was wonderful, realizing that she got a little tired at the prospect of spending an entire day alone with her, Swati felt a stab of conscience. Many of Saswati's habits were different, her conversation was different, much of it didn't match with hers. Swati assumed that Saswati was still the way she used to be, that she herself had changed; so she blamed herself, and to cover up for that blame she tried to lavish extra love on her sister. Lying by her side in the afternoon she tried to be intimate using the memory of their childhood, but she couldn't hit the right note, and Saswati spared her too by falling asleep in a short while. She tried again after dinner—but if Saswati spent too much time with her, then Harit—she could clearly make out—didn't approve; and if Harit had a long conversation with her, Saswati looked grumpy. At any other time Swati would have found this amusing; but now she only felt unhappy, all she felt was that there was no room for her here, why was she even here.

But worst of all was Saswati's and Harit's indifference to death. Harit's response was the preferable one; he had made it clear that the death of his wife's sister's husband meant nothing to him, but to preserve his wife's honour he was willing to spend a few days quietly. But Saswati maintained an almost constant pall of gloom, talking of her brother-in-law and sister every now and then, sighing heavily at regular intervals, sobbing frequently. This was what Swati couldn't bear.

Why? Was Saswati deceitful, or was Swati's grief deeper? No, Saswati's sorrow was genuine, and hers wasn't deeper either. How *could* hers be deeper, she hadn't spent any more time with her brother-in-law than Saswati had. Maybe she had liked him a lot, very much; but had she lost anything because he was lost to them? Nothing at all. That a Pramathesh Chowdhury was no longer in this world made as much difference to Saswati as to her—not a bit. Saswati's grief was for Shweta, and that was right, natural; but Swati didn't think of her eldest sister much, not even of Dalim, but thought only of her brother-in-law over and over again. Over and over again she imagined him lying flat, cold, stiff—a corpse! What did he look like now? Was there even a trace of a smile on that ever-smiling face? Or was it twisted in pain? Or was it just . . . empty? Nothing, just emptiness.

Swati thought—no, not of Pramathesh—but of death. So this was what it was like? Was the invisible archer always prepared with the infallible arrow, after all? Just like in her childhood? The same way then, the same way now, the same way always. We forget, we keep forgetting, but he doesn't forget. He's always there. He's there. Aiming at my back, at me, at the totality of everything that is mine and everything that is me. All my wishes, thoughts, efforts, above them all, he; all my conspiracies, quarrels, celebrations, above them all, he; all my hopes and love, above them all too, he. How could I have forgotten!

Swati was surprised at having forgotten about death all this while, she was even more surprised at seeing others still forgetful about it, and at Harit's and Saswati's behaviour. Harit's relationship with death was one of formality, and Saswati's, of pity; each of them was busy living their own lives after paying the debts that their relationships entailed; not once did they remember that death is an even bigger creditor; they didn't remember that they had been sold to death as soon as they had been born. They had never seen that unavoidable, confident, dreadful archer, they did not see him now either.

Swati sensed a huge gulf between herself and Saswati and Harit. Not just with the two of them, but with everyone. Those who were alive, those who made up the world, seemed to Swati not to be part of her world any more. She had come to know a great deal that no one else knew; that was why she was now cut off from everyone else, she was alone in the world. Everyone else was headed in one direction, dancing, leaping, running, circling, quickly, slowly; like sacrificial lambs being herded in flocks, none of them knew where they were headed, she alone knew. She alone knew that all living people were dying people, those who were alive were dying by the day, only death had no death. She alone knew there was no truth other than death, we only evade death as long as we can, by whatever means we can, and that evasion is known as life. And this life—in it only unhappiness is true, only unhappiness is certain and unshakeable; we avoid it, we cheat it, as long as we can, by whatever means we can, and that cheating is known as happiness, hope, desires. That too only she knew, she alone.

Just like the tanpura that is strummed sonorously before the song begins, a similar drowsy, sombre, continuous tune played within Swati all the time, a melody of sadness, an all-encompassing sadness; a pensive, slow, relentless current of sadness flowed continuously; not stopping, not shrinking; not growing, giving up; unchanging. Her father returned, she returned home—still the same. Day after day passed—still the same.

Satyen-babu came home the day she returned. He too seemed a little distant, not someone she could think of as her own, but she also felt that if anyone could understand her current state of mind, it was he. He was about to say something smilingly when he set eyes on her, but his smile disappeared at the second glance, standing up, he asked, 'What's the matter?'

Swati couldn't reply immediately.

'Did you go somewhere? . . . I came twice . . . The house was locked . . . Where did you go? . . . What? What's happened?'

Swati waited a little longer, arranged the words in her mind, then spoke slowly, 'Boro-jamaibabu—Bordi's husband—he . . . He's died.'

Satyen-babu gave her just a single glance—a fleeting, swift, slightly apprehensive glance. Then he sat down abruptly, remained sitting silently with his head bowed; he didn't say anything, didn't ask any questions, didn't demand details; he only sat in silence for some time, for a long time; and Swati too stood in silence, she recalled, just the other day, he had come with the news of Rabindranath's death. That day there had been something to do at once, lots to do, and lots to talk about afterwards; today there was nothing, today there was only silence. All over the city, all over the country, there was still an uproar over Rabindranath, it was still the top headline in the papers; so many journals, so many speeches, pictures, songs, statements, committees, organizations—this would go on for some time more—and in the midst of all this an even more momentous piece of news arrived to just a handful of people, this group was singled out from everyone else, becoming even more tightly knit. Death was nothing, people were dying every day, a single 'How sad' as you passed by was where it ended; but the few who grieved, there was no grief like theirs, there was no grief but one's own—that was the only grief; everything else was news, events, talking points. Suddenly Swati recalled what Dhruba Datta had said in the restaurant—she had hated it then, she had been furious, but—how right—he had been right. Could grief spread that way across a city, could grief raise such a hue and cry? How was that possible—grief was what isolated people, you couldn't grieve together with others, with a lot of people. We don't just fear unhappiness, we evade it too; so, as long as possible, we behave as though there's no such thing, as though it's nothing.

Did the news that had made Satyen-babu sit d affect him in any way? F:
                                                                   ..u sit down so heavily
                                   ..y. rixing her eyes on his face, Swati looked

for an answer to this question. But the way he sat, his head bowed with his forehead resting on his hand, only his chin was visible. His posture looked as though it really had been a blow. But why should it be a blow to him, and why am I assuming it is—he does not, for all intents and purposes, even know them. This is his politeness—a superior politeness to Harit-da's—charming courtesy, but I can be polite too, I should be the one to talk now so that he can feel comfortable.

'You said you'd been here,' Swati sat down and started conversing.

Satyen-babu moved his hand from his forehead, but still didn't speak.

'I haven't even been to college these past few days,' Swati continued the conversation, 'I was staying with Chhordi. Baba went to Bordi's house, you see.'

Satyen-babu looked up, but still he didn't speak.

'It was so sudden—we couldn't inform you earlier.' As soon as she said this Swati felt silly—did he have to be informed of everything? As though it was important for him to know? So she continued quickly, 'What have you been doing all these days?'

Finally he looked at her, finally he spoke. 'I . . . Never mind what I was doing. I'm going now.' His eyes met Swati's briefly, then he left.

Swati could not disbelieve the intense stillness in those eyes. She was a little surprised, she wondered briefly. Has he then grasped what lies in my heart? Has he too seen that terrible archer? What I alone know, what no one else in the world knows, does he know it too?

The maid entered with a bucket and a rag to swab the floor. Looking at her, it was Satyen whom Swati saw, saw his stilled, intense eyes. In her mind played the thought: 'I am grieving, this is his grief; I love Bordi, that's why he loves Bordi even though he practically doesn't know her.' The thought had peeped into her mind earlier too—she hadn't acknowledged it—

didn't acknowledge it now either. But unknown to herself, she kept thinking of Satyen. He had been visiting more frequently these past one and a half months; in recent months, more than half of the words that Swati had uttered had been to Satyen. Her father had become very quiet these days, and a little worried, anxious; his glasses perched on his nose, he wrote letters to Shweta, to Pramathesh's younger brother; Swati had never seen her father write so many letters personally. All this while she had been her father's secretary; but she didn't even know what was in these letters, her father didn't even give her the letters that came from her other two sisters. One day she had asked, 'What are you writing, Baba, to Bordi?'

'I've asked her to come.'

'Bordi's coming!' She didn't say it with joy, with exuberance; it was more of a question, a hesitant question. How would she manage to even look at Bordi, how would she manage to talk to her?

'Yes, that would be best.' Her father said this in a way that suggested there were counter-arguments too. Swati realized that it was no longer easy for Bordi to come and live here—it hadn't been easy earlier either, but the obstacles then and the obstacles now were diametrically opposite, so she said, 'Won't she come if you ask her?'

'Let's see.' He continued writing, raising his eyes towards her a little later. Swati seemed to see something in his squinting, aged eyes behind the glasses; she didn't look any more, she didn't wait any more.

Her father's face disappeared, she thought of Satyen again. His eyes were clear by nature, he emanated a certain dignified elegance, he spoke slowly, but never vaguely. And he said the kind of things that didn't always need a reply, even listening in silence made it seem like a conversation. It wasn't just about books any more, it included many more things now; in the past one and a half months they had spoken more than they had in the previous three years. Swati tried to recollect what they had said; but how strange—she couldn't remember any of it. What? What does Satyen say to me, she thought.

Swati startled herself, was startled to realize that she was thinking of Satyen-babu as Satyen. She reddened all by herself in her room, seemingly averting her own gaze; and in that instant there spread across the room a cool, bright autumn morning, a morning that had been dead to her until now... Satyen. Moving her lips without making a sound, she pronounced the name. When had he become Satyen?

There was a sound in the room, she looked up to discover it was Saswati. They exchanged glances in silence, then Swati said, 'How early you've come.'

'Yes, I came as soon as I woke up, and I woke up quite early.' As she spoke Saswati remembered how, having woken up well before she did on other days, she had enjoyed the early morning, enjoyed taking the tram by herself to get here. But she spoke about something else, 'I didn't sleep well at night either, such strange dreams.'

Perhaps because of the somewhat sleepless night, Saswati's cheeks appeared a little more flushed, her eyes a little more glittering. But Swati did not mention what she saw.

Saswati continued, 'It was a morning just like this one when Bordi came last time.' Pausing, she added unnecessarily, 'Wasn't it, Swati?'

Swati had just had the same thought, but she didn't give her assent, didn't speak.

'What fun it was! Jamaibabu in such a good mood, and having Bordi always made it wonderful. And now B- '' Tears welled up in Saswati's ~~~ Bordi...'

has ever ~~~ eyes. And she thought, nothing ~~~ ever seemed more wonderful, she had never been happier in her life—though she hadn't realized it then; on the contrary, she had felt upset almost every day at Harit's unwillingness to participate in their family celebrations, and at his open contempt for this kind of entertainment. Her mind went further back, stopping at her wedding; the radiant morning after the first night spent awake, Pramathesh's exuberant laughter as he sat cross-legged on the bed, and Shweta forcing him—Harit had become 'he' to her just that day—to eat. He looked funny, how different everything was. Saswati sighed—not for her eldest sister, but for herself this time. 'Do you remember,' she controlled herself as she was about to say something else, 'all of us going to the theatre together?'

Didn't she just? She remembered everything. Shweta came; and immediately started plying everyone with her handmade sweets; then that *alusheddho* in the kitchen—the smoky flavour—no other *alusheddho* in the world would ever have that flavour. But she had run all this through her mind a thousand times already.

'How he used to laugh!' said Saswati.

Yes, he did. And when leaving, had smiled in a different way as he got into the taxi . . . 'We're going now . . . don't know when we'll be back . . .' But she had run all this through her mind too, a thousand times already.

To prevent herself from having to do it again, Swati said, 'Have you had your morning tea?'

'Yes . . . Harit wasn't up yet . . . I made a cup for myself . . .' Saswati's changed tone virtually told Swati that she had rather enjoyed an independent cup of tea before her husband had awakened. Pausing, Saswati asked, 'Is it time?'

'Already?' Swati shuddered.

'What time is the train?'

'Something past eight . . .'

'Then there's still some time,' Saswati glanced at the tiny gold watch on her wrist—her wedding gift from her brother-in-law. 'Has Baba gone to the station?'

'I'm not sure . . . Probably . . .'

This 'probably' about her father's whereabouts sounded

out of place to Saswati. 'Let me check.' She returned immediately. 'Yes, he has.'

Now it was Swati's turn to feel something was out of place. Her father's going out without informing her, without meeting her before leaving, was new to her.

'What about Biju?' Saswati asked.

'Not up yet, I think.'

Saswati felt Swati was thinking of something else, unconnected to Shweta's arrival today. She went to Bijon's room herself. The door was shut. She knocked, called out his name. There was no response. Returning, she said, 'Does Biju sleep in so late?'

'It's not all that late,' Swati said. 'Just seems that way because we were up early.'

'I'm asking for a specific reason. Biju should be up too.'

Swati was silent.

'Why don't we try to wake him up?'

'I heard you try.'

'But . . . What if he's asleep even when they arrive?' Saswati's expression betrayed anxiety.

'How awful! What *will* Bordi think? I think we should wake him up somehow,' Saswati was worried.

'Go ahead and try.'

'You sound like you don't care.'

Swati was silent.

'Are you still angry with Biju?'

'Was I ever angry with him?' Swati smiled thinly.

Saswati smiled. 'With me too.'

This was the first time there was any reference between the sisters to the Majumdar episode since it had ended. 'How can I be angry with you?' said Swati.

Saswati looked at Swati, then around the room. This was where she used to live, used to sleep—along with Swati. A little vaguely, she said, 'I did what I thought best then. Forget about it.'

Both of them were silent after that.

'I saw Satyen-babu at the tram-stop,' Saswati changed the subject.

'Satyen-babu who?'

'Satyen-babu . . . Satyen Roy . . . what on earth is wrong with you today?'

Swati had indeed not realized that this everyday reference was to the very person she had been thinking of in the recesses of her mind during the sparse conversation with Saswati. But this was correct, to others he was merely Satyen-babu, merely some Satyen Roy. Copying her sister's casual tone, she said, 'Must be on his way to college.'

'Haven't the holidays started yet?''

'They will soon.'

'I looked at him, but he didn't notice me—or else I'd have talked with him.' Saswati continued a little later, 'He's quite nice.'

Swati had noticed that Saswati had begun to view Satyen a little differently these days. Her attitude seemed to have clearly changed. Whenever she saw him here she came up to talk to him, perhaps a little more than she needed to—at least, that was what Swati felt. Her brother must have told her something—that was what she had assumed, as she hadn't considered that the sight of her and Satyen together was reason enough to pay more attention to Satyen these days. She tried to gauge from Saswati's expression how much of what Bijon had told her she had believed, and then looked at her shoulder to say, 'Lovely blouse!'

But Saswati returned to the original topic. 'I've been thinking of inviting him to tea; but . . .' she now shifted the blame from her husband to his friends . . . 'Satyen-babu will not exactly get along with Harit's friends.'

'You needn't invite anyone else.'

'That's true, but you know what Harit is like, he can't enjoy himself unless some of his own friends are also there; and besides, it's not much fun without a few people, and . . . and will Satyen-babu enjoy himself if you aren't there?'

'All right, if you invite me I'll come too.' Swati laughed.

'No, I won't invite you.' Saswati smiled mockingly.

This wasn't far from what was on her mind. On at least four or five occasions that she had been here in the recent past—although at different times of the day—she had found Swati with the professor; when she came Swati seemed a little fidgety—wandering around the house—but not comfortable enough for the three of them to chat together either. Saswati had drawn her own conclusions, but because the Majumdar affair had left a bitter taste in her mouth, she had not told anyone, neither her father nor her husband. She had been nurturing it in her mind, quite enjoying it; she kept recollecting her—hers and Harit's—budding relationship; what a special time in one's life it was! She wished she could talk to Satyen in private, squeeze the truth out of his heart—but her husband wasn't like that, he didn't like this kind of behaviour with people, liked spending money even less. Majumdar wasn't a bad sort, if only they could still have met socially—but how was that possible after what had happened—really, Majumdar had ruined everything by wanting to marry Swati.

Saswati forgot for the time being that she was the one who had added the most fuel to Majumdar's fire; nor did it occur to her that she was thinking of him only as an instrument of her own desire, that she expected the impossible from him—that he would cheerfully offer someone else the woman he had not got for himself. A number of incoherent, improper, mutually contradictory thoughts passed through Saswati's mind in the space of just a few seconds.

Even after trying for three years she had not been able to blend into her husband's entourage, she had given up trying now. Her father was getting older, and Swati was a different kind of person, after all, and there were a lot of problems because she wasn't married yet—problems for Saswati. The only place where she enjoyed herself now was her in-laws' house; it was quite lively at times with her sisters- and brothers-in-law all together, but their ways were a little orthodox, the women's interaction with the outside world was still limited to buying clothes at neighbourhood shops and not missing a single Bengali film. She liked it there, but she was also happy that Harit had come away; a world of socializing after her heart, whose taste Majumdar had offered her during that far-too-brief period, was yet to come her way again. Seeing Satyen, seeing Swati with Satyen, gave birth to fresh hopes.

Swati took advantage of Saswati's silence to ask, 'Want to try waking Dada up once more?'

This time her effort was successful, shutting the lid on the box of her mind, Saswati rose at once. 'Yes, let me try.' She left with the expression of one who had taken on a gigantic task, which no one else could accomplish. She returned with a red face a few minutes later. 'No use! Called him so many times, tried to drag him out of bed—not a peep out of him. I thought I heard him groan a couple of times, so I waited a bit, but silence again! Honestly!' Saswati looked grave the way grown-ups do when confronted by the disobedience of children.

Swati had heard the din, and had guessed the outcome, so she didn't say anything.

'How can anyone sleep so much. It's impossible that he hasn't woken up—he's just staying in bed deliberately, not answering, in case he's asked to do something. You're quite right, Swati, Biju's not human.'

'When did I say that?'

Saswati ignored Swati's protest, continuing, 'Such an awful thing to have happened—and he's not the least bit perturbed.'

Swati was in fact quite relieved at Biju's quiet acceptance of what had happened—he was such a crybaby. So she said, 'What can you do... That's what men...'

'Rubbish! As if anyone can really hide their feelings! Biju isn't human, he has no soul; don't you see what a self-centred existence he has—besides his meals and his bed, what does he have to do with the family!' Saswati grew furious with her brother as she spoke, she suddenly recollected that it was Biju who had planted the misguided notion of marrying Swati in Majumdar's head. 'Doesn't he know Bordi's coming?'

'He does,' Swati answered succinctly.

'If he does how can he pretend to be asleep—and I called him so many times, too. He can at least be polite.'

'He really may be asleep,' Swati said.

'Nothing of the sort! He just won't go to any trouble, that's all.' Saswati paused for breath. 'Are things under control here?'

'What are you talking about?'

'So many people on their way, we have to make arrangements, don't we! Let's take a look.' Saswati got up again in a businesslike way, took a tour of the small house, including the kitchen. In the kitchen Hari had boiled the milk, laid out the cups and saucers for tea, and was now busy preparing breakfast; in the veranda the maid was slicing pineapple, the pieces falling on a white plate, a basket on her left was piled high with oranges, apples and other fruit. Unable to find anything that needed to be done, Saswati went back towards the room, asking as she walked, 'How does it feel to think about it, Swati?'

'About what?'

'That Bordi . . . she won't eat and dress the way we do any more.'

'It's a horrible system.'

'Lots of people don't follow it any more. But Bordi probably . . . I can't imagine. That white sari . . .' Saswati paused, sighed. 'How beautiful she is, and how young still!'

Listening to this expression of reasonable, natural sympathy, Swati suddenly felt a sharp pang of grief for her brother-in-law. Saswati was almost blaming him for having died. This was the end for Bordi—but that was just something people said, a figure of speech. It was actually the end for the other person—

the one who had died had lost everything. Swati felt a blurred notion that the sympathy we felt for the grieving was because we had forgotten the one who'd died, because we always forget death. Despite all its efforts death had not succeeded in getting people to remember it.

They went into their father's room. His large bed and Saswati's small one from long ago had been made, the larger one covered with a bedspread and the smaller, with a sheet; everything was ready. Their father never forgot anything, did everything well in time, got it done in time, never left anything unfinished for anyone else to complete.

It would have been better right now if he had, for the closer the hand of the clock approached eight, the more the conversation between them dwindled, and both felt a sort of restlessness within themselves. Spending a few minutes in one room, a few more in another, they finally went into the drawing room. The chairs were still pushed against the wall, just as before, Dalim's cot on the other side was still covered with a sheet, the books were arranged neatly on the desk. Swati hadn't forgotten to wind his alarm clock every day either.

The sisters sat at a distance from each other. As soon as she sat down, Saswati said, 'Open the door, Swati.'

Swati rose to open the front door, then resumed her seat.

A little later Saswati said, 'The curtains . . . Can you draw them? Never mind, I'll do it . . .'

Saswati rose herself, drew the curtains shut, then sat on a different chair. 'Warm . . . isn't it?' she said a little later.

Swati got up, switched on the fan, and moved to a different chair.

A little later Saswati said, 'The fan's too strong . . . A little slower . . .' She herself rose to reduce the speed of the fan and went back to her original chair. At once her gaze fell on Dalim's alarm clock. 'Eight-twenty!' Saswati seemed to jump.

'Twenty!' Swati's voice trembled too, as though she had never heard of it being eight-twenty before.

For a while both of them tried not to look at the clock with its round face, and both their gazes kept returning to the black-and-white round face.

'Exactly what time is the train?' Saswati said.

'I'm not sure.'

'Isn't there a timetable at home?'

Swati shook her head.

'The newspaper?'

'Let me see.' Swati found the newspaper on the dining table, gave it to her sister and sat down again.

Quickly, busily, Saswati started turning the pages over, as though it was a matter of life and death. 'Where is it? . . . Which page? . . . Which newspaper is this? . . . Here we are. What's the name of the train?'

'No idea.'

'No idea?' Saswati practically snarled. 'Dhaka Mail . . . no, how can it be Dhaka Mail . . . they're coming from Mymensingh . . . don't you know the name of the train from Mymensingh?'

Swati didn't answer.

'Useless!' Saswati flung the paper to the floor. Swati bent to pick up a page, spreading it on her knees and training her eyes on it.

Saswati bent too and picked up another page, but instead of holding it before her eyes she kept rolling and unrolling it, and after doing this several times her hands paused, she said, a trifle calmly, 'I think it's time now.'

'Really?' Swati trembled, looked, rose. Saswati rose too at once. Saswati observed that Swati's face was pale, her lips dry. Swati observed that Saswati's face was pale, her lips dry. Then, without any words, both of them sat down again, Swati in the chair Saswati had been sitting on, and Saswati, about to sit down in the one vacated by Swati, changed her mind and sat down next to her sister.

They gave up all attempts to converse now. Seated side by side, they stared ahead, at the door, at the street through the gap in the curtains. Both of them ashen, wan, pale, both trembling within. Side by side, close to each other, their hands almost touching, but without looking at each other, and without the slightest movement, they remained sitting in a way that would suggest to anyone who happened to see them from the street that two young women had struck a pleasant pose for a photograph.

. . . But when the maroon taxi flashed in the window, they rose calmly, walked slowly—although neither of them looked at each other—crossed the distance to the curtains in a few steps and pushed them aside to emerge outside, stopped on the top step, side by side, without looking at each other.

The first to leap out of the taxi were the sisters Ata and Tata—how they'd grown!—then Chhoton—how tightly he had drawn the belt around his shorts!—then the tall, grave, newly responsible Dalim in a cap—why the cap? Of course, he had had to shave his head, and he'd put on some weight too from what he'd had to eat at the rituals! The last time he hadn't come with them, and this time he had brought everyone along—and they'd all fitted into one taxi this time.

Their father got out of the taxi, the baby in his arms—not much of a baby any more, such a lovely smile, displaying small white teeth—so very sweet! Swati forgot everything else, she went down the stairs to the street, took the baby from her father into her own arms, pressed her to her breast, kissed her on her cheeks. And as soon as she set eyes on this new person, the baby wailed in a thin, small but surprisingly powerful voice.

'That's your Mashi, mustn't cry, Chhotomashi . . .'

Swati turned when she heard the voice. White: the sari

white, the parting in the hair white; but Bordi nevertheless. That moment, when Swati set eyes on her, seemed to blur.

'Let me have her,' said Shweta, glancing at her with happy, sorrowful, smiling, liquid, tearful eyes before kissing her on the cheek. Swati trembled, lowered her eyes, a few teardrops ran down her cheek, one after the other.

Climbing the steps with her baby, Shweta said, 'Well, Saswati? Where's Biju?'

'Biju . . .' Saswati tried to make up a story, but it wasn't necessary. Just as Shweta was entering the house, Biju raced in, freshly awake, hair tousled, his dhoti wrapped around him somehow, dressed in the top half of a striped Western-style sleeping suit, unbuttoned at the top, displaying the hair on his chest. He halted on seeing his eldest sister, and instantly his face took on a terrible, evil, contorted expression, suddenly rearing up like a horse he put his arms around his sister, the baby still in her arms, and burst into tears, 'Oh . . . Oh . . . Oh . . . Bordi! Oh . . . Oh . . . Jamaibabu! Jamaibabu-u-u-u!'

The baby was almost knocked out of Shweta's arms at this onslaught, she clung to her somehow, extricating herself with considerable effort, and Biju, seemingly robbed off his support, slumped to the floor at her feet. He didn't try to get up, didn't cover his face, which twisted in unbelievable ways under the onslaught of his tears, and in a hoarse, loud, dreadful voice, words emerged from his mouth in gulps: 'Who else . . . Like him . . . Who was it who . . . Gave me the money . . . With whose money . . . Today I . . . Jamaibabu . . . Oh . . . Oh . . .' Drawing up his knees, his arms splayed behind him, his fingers scrabbling at the floor, displaying the black hair on his chest through the gap in his unbuttoned striped sleeping shirt, Bijon went on sobbing grotesquely.

The taxi had not left yet, the gigantic Sikh driver with his moustache and beard was still waiting, Rajen-babu was out on the street too, Hari had stopped in the process of getting the luggage out, Swati and Dalim had halted on the steps, one or two people were gathered on the street. The door was wide open, the curtains drawn apart, everyone could see, everyone could hear; Bijon's heartfelt, spontaneous, heartbreaking lamentation found its way into the houses nearby too.

Saswati stood in the room, turned to stone; Ata, Tata and Chhoton stared in round-eyed astonishment; Shweta tried to calm her baby with one hand and her brother with the other. And outside, Dalim kept glancing at Swati repeatedly, but Swati didn't raise her face, didn't move, and, unable to think of what to do, he too stood on the steps, his back to the street, and Hari threaded his way between them to bring the last of the luggage into the house. Rajen-babu paid the taxi fare, checked inside the taxi one last time, and as the gigantic Sikh departed along with the vehicle, the lane seemed to breathe again. Rajen-babu didn't go in, didn't climb the steps, looked at Biju without seeing him, heard him without listening to him. He wasn't thinking of Biju at all, or of anything else. He was recalling his first thought of the morning after waking up, and over and over again during the day. He was thinking of the day Shweta had been born. That was the first time. The labour room in their impoverished Beleghata home, the first view from the door; a tiny red figure in the midwife's arms; and on the bed, loose hair, an ivory-white face with its eyes shut, an ivory-white arm outside the quilt. That glimpse of ivory had made him think of the name. Shweta. For ivory-white.

4

The Durga Puja vacations came around again, there was a rush to leave the city for the holidays. Train tickets seemed to be cheaper than usual this year; out on the street you kept coming across taxis loaded with luggage.

Harit's family were in Deoghar en masse; Saswati's father-in-law had a house there. Harit and Saswati were supposed to have joined them as soon as his holidays began, but on the last day of work Harit came home to announce he couldn't go.

'What's the matter?' said Saswati.

'I have to stay in Calcutta.'

'Why?'

'Our organization is now going to focus on resistance, but merely changing the charter isn't enough, everything has to be rebuilt from scratch. We've been talking about it for a long time, but no actual work has been done yet. But now we can't wait any more. We have to during these holidays . . . Thandani is coming from Bombay just for this. And Makaranda is off to Billibakam.'

'Then why can't you go?'

'That's why. Makaranda has been working very hard these past few months, the doctor's ordered rest. He *has* to go.'

'But you work thrice as hard as Makaranda Mukherjee.'

'Don't argue.' Harit spun around the room as he talked: first he took off his coat, hung it on the hanger and slotted it into the bracket, then took off his shoes near the clothes-rack, hung up his tie in its rightful place, then came up to the desk to check for letters. Saswati had been sitting in his chair, her arms on its armrests. 'Do you need the chair?' she asked.

'No, don't get up. I . . .' Harit walked towards the bathroom . . . 'As you see, I can't go. But you can.' He turned back from the bathroom door to say the last few words. But Saswati no longer subjected her eyes to the labour of following him across different parts of the room in order to listen to him.

Over tea Harit brought it up again. 'If I'd known earlier I'd have sent you off with them. But Thandani's telegram only just came.'

'I can go to Deoghar by myself,' said Saraswati.

'Of course.' Harit was pleased. 'It's a day train, I'll see you off here, they'll meet you at the station. No need to change trains—how difficult can it be? When would you like to go? Tomorrow?'

'I'm not going.'

'Not going! Why?'

'I'm not.'

Harit consumed three or four of the snacks that had come with his tea in quick succession. Why hadn't these displays of injured outrage been eradicated from the country yet! Harit hated all this; not only did he hate them, he felt quite helpless when confronted by them. He didn't know what he should do, what he should say, he seemed to turn into an idiot, and this made him seethe so much within himself that it eventually made things very ugly. Muffling the rising voice of anger, he said in a placatory tone, 'Why not? You'd enjoy it, and recover physically too.'

'Recover physically from what? Am I ill?'

'No—but this monotonous life, and this cage-like flat . . . At least a holiday now and then . . .'

'I don't find it monotonous.'

Harit gestured with his hand like an Englishman to indicate he had no time for such meaningless exchanges. 'As you please,' he said in English, adding in Bengali, 'All I wanted to say was that you don't have to be stuck here because of me. You're independent, you should do as you please.'

'What if I were to tell you I don't want to go because you're not going?'

Harit had lowered his head to sip his tea, he straightened it with a jerk to look at his wife. With a sardonic smile he said, 'Then I'd say you *are* ill, and you *should* go to cure yourself of it.'

Now Saswati smiled mockingly too. 'Would you be happier if I went?'

'Oh.' Harit made his viewpoint clear with just that one powerful sound.

Putting on his socks and shoes again, Harit marched out triumphantly. He didn't have to go anywhere that evening; didn't have anything much to do at home either; after a long time he had an evening to himself; and, to tell the truth, he had planned to go out with Saswati in the evening to buy a few things—he had meant to take her to New Market, which Saswati enjoyed. With the Deoghar trip being cancelled at the last minute, he had been feeling unhappy because Saswati would be unhappy; but Saswati wouldn't be entirely disappointed, he would arrange for her to go, in fact, he had even planned to steal a couple of days to take her to Deoghar himself. But nothing was turning out as he had planned—the very opposite, in fact. Was it his fault? Saswati's fault? Harit went to New Market alone, bought himself two vests and half a dozen handkerchiefs from Calico Mills, and two coloured brassieres and a hair-net for Saswati—you didn't get these things in Ballygunge—and thought it over in between. No, it wasn't anyone's fault, this was the way these things happened. It had happened this way many times before; it would happen this way many times again, many more times. What takes place is bound to be the precise opposite of what you imagine, what you're prepared for. It was all laid out sequentially: the sullenness, the oppressive atmosphere; then at night, one night, the act of forgetting all of it, the act of getting it all back. But how long, how many minutes did *that* last? Then the exhausted sleep, and after the sleep, the day. And if something else were to happen again the very next day, the smallest of things, then the same things would be played out all over again, the opposite of your plans, the opposite of your wishes, the sullen face, the sullen heart, the unhealthy damp atmosphere, and then again the night. The fatigue of conjugal life!

It happened that night too. And then Saswati asked in a very small voice, 'Would you be happy if I went?'

'What's all this!'

'Would you be happy if I stayed? Would you miss me if I went?'

Harit shifted on the bed. What kind of questions were these—would it do much harm to possess an iota of intelligence?

'Tell me.'

'I don't answer silly questions.' Harit answered in a way that suggested the answer was self-evident, and needn't be given, therefore.

But Saswati wasn't satisfied. 'No, tell me. Would you be unhappy if I went away?'

Harit saw Saswati's eyes dimly in the darkness. He shut his eyes, thinking, must she make me lie? And will she be happy just to hear a lie? He sidestepped the question, saying, 'When it comes to duty, I don't consider unhappiness relevant.'

'What is your duty?'

'To stay in Calcutta during these holidays.'

'And my duty is to go to Deoghar?'

'No, this is what your duty is,' said Harit, moving closer to his wife and putting his head on her pillow. Saswati could not neglect her duty. She sighed almost a minute later, a long sigh of happiness. And Harit also let out a small, secret sigh at not having had to lie blatantly. To seal his triumph he stayed where he was.

Saswati buzzed softly, 'You know, it's just as well we couldn't go.'

'Why?'

'Just the other day Bordi . . . and here we'd have gone off for a holiday . . . I was feeling uncomfortable.' As she tasted the warmth of existence, the last remnants of it, Saswati felt a heartbreaking sadness for her sister, and her happiness of the moment felt like a crime. Adding a dash of unhappiness made the happiness more delicious—she felt completely at one with her husband, which she had never felt before. 'Really, a woman is nothing without her husband,' she said in a muffled, indistinct voice.

The same litany. Was this a ghost of the Hindu faith? But Harit did not give the command to his troops of logic, polemic and objections, sleep had invaded his eyes, and besides he was feeling indolent too, indolent and happy.

Saswati spoke with a small sigh, 'You've heard about Jamaibabu's brother?'

He seemed to have heard something, Harit stumbled on the staircase to sleep. 'Yes, it's always been like this,' said Harit, descending to the plains of wakefulness. 'The Hindu widow has always been cheated, from ancient times!' He didn't pass up on the joy of poking at old ghosts.

'As for those brothers of his, I've heard that Jamaibabu . . . They're stepbrothers, much younger, practically brought up by Bordi.'

'There you are!' Harit moved back to his own pillow to talk. 'This is what joint families mean for us! Help everyone else, but let your wife and children fend for themselves. And still we don't learn. I'm sure Pramathesh-babu hasn't left much for his family?'

'So I heard,' Saswati admitted in a high-pitched voice, as though it was her fault.

Harit rolled around a bit, then turned over on his stomach and thrust his hands under his pillow. This was his most comfortable position to go to sleep in. Turning his head to look at Saswati, he said, 'Such a spendthrift!'

Harit's tone was sympathetic, but Saswati was hurt. She had benefited from her brother-in-law's prodigality too, and was this giving of pleasure, this feeling of pleasure, such a bad thing? She tried to tell her husband what she had heard from her father; in a very low, embarrassed tone, used by one honourable man to talk about the secret vice of another, she said, 'It wasn't just that. He gave away money too.'

'Gave away!'

'He used to help people. Many families in poverty, poor students . . . Whoever asked him for money. . .'

'That's even worse!' Harit stifled a smile. 'What can one person do to solve the problem of poverty? Nothing at all, and in the bargain he becomes poor too. The only way out is a system where no one will be poor. Of course, no one will be rich either.' Finishing, Harit decided that it might be wise to divert half his monthly savings into another insurance policy. In case of untimely death an insurance policy was far more beneficial.

Saswati didn't speak any more; she turned over on her side. Harit shut his eyes too, mentally listing the things he had to do for their resistance movement. But a little later he heard the clinking again. 'Are you asleep?' asked Saswati.

'No,' answered Harit, his eyes still shut.

Shifting, Saswati said, 'Jamaibabu gave Biju two thousand rupees too.'

'To Bijon?' Harit opened his eyes. 'Why?'

'Biju asked him. No one knew all this time; Biju confessed the other day.'

Harit lost his inclination to sleep, feeling pangs of regret. Was it that simple! He too could have extracted a fat donation for the party; if he hadn't mentioned the party directly but referred to it in a roundabout manner, he would surely have got the money; what a golden opportunity he had lost. Two thousand for that Bijon at one go! And it hadn't occurred to him even once. All he had done was to rant at Pramathesh thinking he was a Fascist. Really—you needed to be as cool-headed as Thandani to make things work!

Sitting up in bed, Harit said, 'What's Bijon doing with the money?'

'He claims he's put it into his business.'

'What kind of business?' Harit couldn't abandon the discussion.

'I'm not sure. Something to do with the war . . .'

'The war? That's good.'

'Good? But Baba's very worried . . .'

'Why?'

'Apparently this kind of business is nothing but daylight robbery!'

Harit smiled generously. Saswati could see a row of white teeth in the darkness. 'It isn't?' she asked.

'Even if the fathers feel that way do you suppose the sons will sit back and do nothing? And it's everyone's duty now to help with the war effort. Russia must be protected, by hook or by crook.'

Saswati found it difficult to imagine Biju doing something to beat back Hitler. Giving up, she said, 'How long are you going to stay awake? Go to sleep.'

'Yes,' said Harit, resuming his position on the bed. 'Biju is quite efficient, I notice.'

'There's a reason for that. Prabir Majumdar is behind him.'

'Who? Oh . . . that Majumdar. Then it wouldn't have been a bad thing for him and Swati to have got married. Why didn't they?'

Saswati was astonished. A little later she said, 'A marriage needs two people; how can it take place if one of them is unwilling?'

Harit remembered saying something similar himself to Saswati once. 'That's true,' he said quickly. 'And Swati's very romantic. Likes poetry. Dangerous.'

'Why?'

Harit didn't answer. After fidgeting a bit he settled down, asking in a sleep-laced voice, 'Not a peep out of Majumdar any more?'

'None.'

'And what about Swati?'

'What about her.' Saswati curled up in preparation for sleep. 'Want to go over tomorrow?'

'Hmm?'

'Tomorrow, go over . . .'

'Hmm.'

'You'll go?'

'Yes. Be quiet now . . . I'm very . . .' Harit fell asleep without completing what he was saying.

Saswati remained awake by herself, her eyes shut. It was a long time since she had had such a long conversation with her husband in bed at night. Perhaps because of this, and because of a sense of new, intimate harmony with her husband, she wasn't sleepy at all. She thought about the persons they had been discussing all this time, their faces swam up in succession before her ceyes: Shweta, Pramathesh, Rajen-babu, Biju, Majumdar, Swati. And then, although they hadn't discussed him, Saswati was reminded of Satyen Roy too, before falling asleep she thought a little of Satyen Roy too.

The last thing that she had said at night, had wanted to say, was what she repeated the next morning, 'Shall we go over today?'

'Now?' said Harit, reading a letter that had just been delivered. 'I have to go to Shyambazar now.' He returned the letter to the envelope. 'Why don't *you* go?'

'I shall go in any case. I've been going every day.'

'So shall I,' Harit smiled vaguely. 'Tomorrow—definitely.'

'You haven't been at all since the day Bordi came. Now that the holidays have started, you could, sometimes.'

'I will.'

'I think Bordi's going to stay on here,' said Saswati and looked at Harit, but she couldn't see his face, because Harit was looking for something in his drawer, his face lowered. Still bent over, he said, 'What's the hurry then?'

Realizing that Harit hadn't understood, Saswati waited. When he had straightened after taking some papers out of the drawer, she repeated, 'Baba's probably going to ask Bordi to stay here permanently.'

'Permanently?'

'So it seems. And it's a good idea, don't you think?'

Harit tried to convey with a smile that he had no difference of opinion with his wife on this matter. Even though she realized Harit didn't want to listen, that he was thinking of other things, Saswati couldn't help saying what she wanted to. 'Of course it's a good idea! A thousand times better than living on the charity of your husband's brothers. But Baba will never get his rest. He should have been resting after his retirement, and look what's happened!'

'Is he retiring soon?'

'I told you the other day, didn't I . . .'

'Oh yes. Any day now, isn't it?'

'You could say so. He's on long leave now, immediately after that . . .'

'In that case . . .' The crease disappeared from Harit's brow almost as soon as it appeared, for he saw the bright side of things instantly. 'There's the pension after all . . . getting half your pay without having to work is no small thing, our jobs don't have anything like that—heaven knows what will happen when we're old!—and your sister will get something at least, won't she?'

'But the responsibility is all Baba's, an enormous responsibility. That's why I tell him, "Don't worry, we're there." '

Wondering whom the 'we' referred to, and what the 'there' meant, Harit answered warily, 'It's pointless worrying too much about all this when there's nothing to be done.'

'Not at all,' Saswati answered at once. 'It matters a lot that we're close by, that we're part of everything—good or bad. And think of it from Bordi's point of view. She was married at fourteen; that house, everything there, everything was hers— and now to have to leave all that behind at a moment's notice, can that be easy?'

Harit had been reassured at his wife's explanation of 'there', he said amiably, 'That's true. And that's why I feel awkward going over. You know very well I'm no good at all this consolation business.'

'Consolation!' Saswati had been grave throughout the conversation, now she became graver still. 'Is there really any consolation for this, and console whom in any case? Bordi can console you if need be. She's extraordinary.'

Harit had been perched on the edge of his chair, he stood up suddenly. Enough of domestic life—the world was calling. 'All right, I'm off,' he said quickly.

'So am I,' said Saswati.

The room bustled with activity. Standing in opposite corners, their backs to each other, they changed their clothes. Standing behind Saswati, Harit combed his hair in the long mirror on the almirah. Saswati transferred some small change out of Harit's moneybag into her own yellow handbag.

At the tram-stop Saswati asked, 'When will you be back?'

'Not sure. I have to go to several places.'

'I'll be back by twelve.'

'All right.'

The tram was empty, they found seats next to each other. Harit began to think about what he had been thwarted in last night—about how well he could organize things before Thandani arrived; and Saswati thought about . . . her eldest sister. She too had been worried like Harit—but Harit had not seen Biju's violent display of grief. Amidst a roomful of astonished people it was Shweta who had taken him by the hand into the room, calmed him down by talking to him—as though this concerned him and not her. Just like she used to be—no, not exactly—quiet, she had become quiet inside—but otherwise, just like she used to be. It felt good just to be near her—just like before—but who knew how she felt. I used to think Bordi was a very happy woman, fulfilled and happy, and that happiness spilled over sometimes, though very carefully. But now? Can someone who isn't happy themselves make others happy? Or does it have nothing to do with being happy oneself? Or is happiness . . . who knows! Here we are.

Bidding Harit goodbye with her eyes, Saswati got off, watched Harit's tram take a right turn. Harit was submerged in his thoughts about the resistance movement, but when an old man with a bundle took the seat next to him a little later, he recalled Saswati! He was travelling with Saswati in just such a tram, he thought—or in a train compartment—a long journey, not too many stations, quite often there would be no one else in the compartment, then they were forced to be together. But Saswati remained unaware of these thoughts of Harit's; she crossed the road in peace and waited for a tram to Tollygunge.

∾

She saw Satyen as soon as she entered. Satyen stood up with a shy smile.

'Oh please don't get up. When did you come?'

'A moment ago.'

'Where's everyone?' Saswati looked around. 'Have they been told you're here?'

'I don't know.'

Saswati found the answer funny. 'All right I . . .' she said with a smile and was about to leave the room. Her way of turning on her heels, Satyen saw, was similar to Swati's. Quickly he said, blurted out, 'Won't you sit down too?'

'Sit? All right . . .' There was a slight hesitation in Saswati's voice, but also pleasure. 'Please, do sit down.'

After this exchange of courtesies, Satyen asked decorously, 'How is Harit-babu?'

'Yes. You must come over to our place sometime,' Saswati said on an impulse.

'Of course,' answered Satyen at once. 'When?'

Saswati hadn't expected such enthusiasm, she felt in a bit of a spot. Harit had his Thandani, and she didn't want to get into trouble again by inviting anyone without informing him. 'When are you available?' she asked after a few moments.

'Available? I'm available every day. Do you imagine I am swamped by engagements?'

'Nor am I. I think one a day is sufficient.'

Suddenly, Satyen reddened slightly. Noticing this from the corner of her eye, Saswati said, 'Of course, that one engagement must be the one after your heart.'

'Some days I don't even have a single one.'

'Give me one of those available days.'

Looking at Saswati's smiling face made Satyen feel a little silly, and he enjoyed the feeling too. But in order to hide both feelings, he said seriously, 'There's no engagement at all. I'm going away.'

'Where . . .?' Saswati seemed startled.

'To Ranchi first . . .'

'Ah, for a holiday. I thought . . . When are you going?'

To maintain the gravity of what he had just said, he would now have to give a date in the very near future, but the only response that Satyen could summon up was a vague 'Very soon!' This time he really felt unhappy. Six days had already gone by since the holidays had begun. He had targeted Chhota Nagpur this time; Ranchi, Topchanchi, Hazaribagh, a bus to Giridih— he would climb to the top of Pareshnath Hill, spend the night at the transit bungalow on the peak, and finally a few days' rest at Maheshmanda—someone he knew had a house there—he had planned it all out beautifully. He'd heard so much about that part of the world, and he had loved the couple of afternoon hours he had passed in that hilly terrain on his way back from Delhi. Everyone had left Calcutta on packed trains; and these Durga Puja days would be nothing but noise—did anyone in their senses stay in Calcutta at this time? They didn't? Everyone in this family has, as they always did. 'Aren't you going anywhere?' Satyen found something to say.

'Us? No, it isn't easy for us.'

It's easy enough for me, Satyen thought, I have no impediment. But why am I not going? Six days have gone by. This horrible crowded Calcutta of Durga Puja—versus the dimpled green earth. Why do I keep postponing my departure every day? Why?

'Chhordi! When did you come?'

'Just now. We couldn't go to Deoghar after all.'

'Couldn't? I thought as much . . .'

'I didn't particularly want to this time anyway,' Saswati acknowledged freely in Harit's absence. 'Harit is the one who needs the rest, but he won't budge.'

'The progressive movement?'

'Resistance, not progressive.'

'Resistance,' Swati burst out laughing, and Saswati joined her fearlessly.

During this conversation between the sisters Satyen looked in turn at Swati and Saswati, but when neither of them glanced at him, he looked away with a detached expression. At least, he tried to look detached. Swati seemed very happy today, very pleased to see Saswati; he couldn't fathom the reason for so much happiness. There was no happiness in his heart, unhappiness was stuck in its side like a thorn. The sound of the combined laughter of the sisters seemed to prick him like a thorn too. Why was he . . . Where was he? Why was he here this morning? Didn't he have anything else to do? How time went by! He had bought the Yeats anthology the other day, hadn't even leafed through it, nor the book of Maugham's short stories—that one was for reading on the way, though. Satyen saw himself by the window of a moving train, a book of short stories in hand, and a book of poems on the veranda of a bungalow en route early in the morning . . . Ah! . . . He'd go . . . Definitely . . . Tomorrow . . . Yes, tomorrow . . .

'Let's go inside,' Swati told Saswati.

'But . . .' Saswati addressed Satyen.

Swati said, 'He'll wait a bit,' then added—looking at Satyen for the first time—'Please wait a bit.'

'I . . .' Satyen seemed on the verge of saying something, but before he could say anything more the sisters went inside.

Swati returned a little later to sit in the chair opposite Satyen's. Their eyes met, and they lowered them immediately. When their eyes met again, Swati said indistinctly, looking at him steadily, 'What?'

Satyen gazed at her slightly reddened face, her moist shining eyes, and the slight curve in her moist lips. He saw this sight often, and yet there was so much to see still.

'So early today?'

Satyen didn't speak this time either. A moment ago she had been talking to Saswati, he thought, and now—how different the two Swatis were. Which one was better? Each was better than the other.

'The two of you seem to have hit it off.'

'The two of us?' He understood the implication as soon as he said it. 'Yes, but as soon as she saw you your sister forgot all about me.'

'I thought I heard Chhordi's voice, but wondered whom she was talking to.' Swati uttered this unadulterated lie without batting an eyelid. She had spotted Satyen through the window while he was still on the street—her brother was   there too, he was smiling, and talking excessively with her. Nothing specific . . . Just dragging the conversation on. He was so . . .!

'Of course . . . your sister's voice,' Satyen smiled. 'And once you'd seen her, of course . . .'

'So I noticed,' Swati answered without smiling.

Dalim entered from the street. 'Chhotomashi . . .' he paused on seeing Satyen.

'Got it?'

Dalim lowered his voice. 'Couldn't get the imported one . . . This is local.'

'Let me see.'

The lanky Dalim positioned himself sideways, so that he didn't exactly turn his back to Satyen-babu, but so that he couldn't see him, either. By now fresh hair had sprouted on his head, like a skullcap. The tenderness he had brought all over again with him from Mymensingh had been washed away in Calcutta. His expression was even more solemn than earlier, but a thin, curling growth of a first beard at places on his cheek gave away his age accurately. Looking at his profile, Satyen remembered being the same age once upon a time, although he didn't have an aunt like Dalim's.

Swati accepted the bundle from Dalim, unwrapping and examining it.

'Is it all right?' Dalim asked anxiously, quietly.

'Yes.'

'The colour will match, won't it?'

'I think so.'

He didn't get the chance to recount how many shops he had had to scour to match the shade, how he had had to go to Dharmatalla because he hadn't found what he was looking for in all of Bhowanipore; accepting just that small reward for his exertions, and with a swift glance at Satyen-babu, reddening a little himself, departed quickly.

Looking at the white and brown wool unravelling on Swati's lap, Satyen said, 'Do you . . . knit?'

'I don't really . . . But Dalim's been clamouring for a jumper.' Swati scanned the brown wool closely. Her head still lowered, she continued, 'Just as well, thanks to Dalim I'm learning how to knit from Bordi.'

'So he prefers his aunt's work to his mother's?'

'He does have one she knitted for him, but he's shot up suddenly, you see. I'm thinking of taking that one apart and . . . Tell me,' Swati raised her face, holding the two balls of wool in each of her hands, 'which colour do you prefer?'

'I don't quite . . .' Satyen looked at her with all his deep, primal indifference about things like knitting, but when he did, he realized clearly that the business of knitting was by no means insignificant to human existence.

'Dalim may not share my preference.'

'Of course he will. His ideal is . . . Satyen-babu.'

Swati uttered the name softly, a little indistinctly, and, hearing Swati say his name, Satyen could hardly believe that the Satyen-babu in question was nobody but him. 'I didn't know that,' he said a little later.

'Why, all his effort is to . . . Didn't you see how he's worn his dhoti and *panjabi*? Doesn't suit him at all.'

'If he were to follow his ideal he would never get to wear woollen clothes.'

'Why? Don't you ever wear any?' Swati asked with pretended artlessness.

'Me!' Despite identifying the pretence, or perhaps because of it, Satyen's self-esteem was hurt.

'Why don't you start? Shall I ask Bordi to knit you one? She knits them so beautifully . . .' Swati swept the hair away from her brow.

Satyen's heart lurched. He had seen that gesture of hers so many times, and every time he had . . .! But as much as he liked it, he disliked it too; he seemed to die of shame at Swati's lack of restraint, her rampant boldness. More than ever before, even more strongly, even more sharply, the running train came to his mind, the long night, the book of poetry in a new green morning. When would he go? Tomorrow . . . Why tomorrow? Today . . . He'd go today.

Leaning forward to look at Satyen's bowed head, Swati continued, 'Will you? I'll ask Bordi right away.'

'No,' said Satyen, raising his head.

Still Swati pretended not to understand the change in Satyen's reaction. 'All right, let her knit it first,' she said casually, 'if you don't like it then we can . . .'

'Listen,' Satyen interrupted Swati gravely. 'There's a reason

I came early. I came because there won't be time later. I'm going away today.'

Swati was silent for a while, then she said, 'I see!'

'I'm taking the Ranchi Express,' Satyen informed her unnecessarily. 'First to Ranchi . . . then . . .'

'I hope to learn all that from your long letters.'

'I know you don't like my letters,' said Satyen.

'Who says I don't. Such lovely descriptions!'

'Really, I don't know how to write letters.'

Swati bowed her head and proceeded to wrap the balls of wool in paper.

Satyen gazed at the plump balls, strangely captivated. But soon the wrapping was completed, the white and brown colours could no longer be seen. He waited a little, to hear 'Are you really going?', but Swati stood up holding Dalim's purchases.

Immediately Satyen stood up too.

'You're leaving?' asked Swati.

'Yes . . . er . . . may I meet Bordi?'

'Just a minute.'

And the very next moment Satyen found himself sitting alone in the room. He tried to picture the train journey tonight—tea at Muri at dawn—Ranchi in a few hours after that—he tried to picture it with great enthusiasm. And as soon as he sensed a hint of Shweta this side of the curtain—before she had even entered the room—he stood up quickly, saying, 'I'm going out of town today, I wanted to see you before I left.'

'Today?' Saswati asked from the background.

Satyen remembered he had said something else to her a short while ago. Quickly he said, 'Yes, I decided to go today. The holidays are going waste . . .' Realizing what he had said was not very complimentary to the people present, he quickly added, 'When I'm back . . . if I still have your permission . . . I'll visit you.'

Saswati was relieved that the question of inviting Satyen home during this uncertain busy period for Harit no longer arose, but she said, 'I can see how anxious you are for my permission. You've decided to leave Calcutta immediately so that you don't really have to visit us.'

'Stay for a while,' said Shweta.

'I can't stay long.'

'Just for a bit.'

After everyone had sat down Shweta said, 'Are you going home?'

With a slight smile, Satyen Roy gave his favourite answer: 'I have no such thing as home.'

Shweta smiled too. 'Home isn't a place of its own. It's wherever your people are.'

'People meaning family?'

'Don't you care for your family?' There was sympathy in Shweta's eyes, disguised as amusement.

'I don't even know anyone in my family,' Satyen's answer held a touch of bravado.

'Don't they know anything about you either?'

Satyen glanced at the blue curtain for the third time in as many minutes. After a moment's delay, he answered listlessly, 'There's nothing to know.'

'Which of your relatives live in Calcutta?'

'In Calcutta?' Satyen paused. 'There was an uncle, my brother's brother, he . . . he's no longer alive.'

'His wife? Their children?'

'They're still there.'

'How many of them?'

Satyen was surprised at this detailed inquiry from Shweta.

'One girl—two boys,' he answered reluctantly.

'Is the girl the youngest?'

'No, the daughter is the eldest—she's married.'

'Do they live here?'

'No, they live in . . .' Where was it that Bulu lived? Was it Bajitpur? Pabna? Never mind. 'They live in Pabna,' Satyen concluded the discussion.

'Don't you visit your aunt sometimes?'

'Yes . . . No . . . Not exactly . . . Just . . .' Satyen's voice crumbled towards the end. He had just realized he really couldn't remember when he had last visited his aunt.

'She must visit you sometimes.'

'No, she's . . . she lives very far away, you see . . . in Baranagar!' And it was from that distant Baranagar that her ten-year-old son had tracked him down to Tollygunge one day, in watery ink on a scrap of paper she had asked for a loan of ten rupees. He had given the money at once, and told the boy, 'Tell your mother I'll visit her soon.' A long time had passed since then.

'Just the one uncle?' asked Shweta.

'Yes.' Satyen had planned to stop there, but someone within him brushed aside his plan and made him speak, 'Mama was a very nice man . . . And rather young when he . . .'

Satyen almost bit his tongue when he heard himself speak. Why was he saying all this, and to whom? He himself . . . And just the other day! He recollected Pramathesh-babu's round jovial face, and his uncle alongside—his uncle used to love him, even in a household where it was hard to make ends meet, he had had a place in his home as well as his heart for Satyen— then looked at Shweta apprehensively to gauge the outcome of his carelessness.

But Shweta asked, 'What kind of work did he do?'

'Mama? He was a schoolteacher. That's why Mamima is now . . .' Satyen paused again. She did have a hard life now! Living in a slum in Baranagar . . .!

'How old is the eldest son?'

Satyen saw from Shweta's expression that she had understood what he hadn't said. 'Not very young,' he seemed to reassure himself. 'He even has a job.' But not much of a job . . . a factory labourer! At an age when he should be in college! How would they survive? 'Still—' this 'still' was like an excuse for his behaviour—'I feel bad about them. They didn't even have a chance to complete their education!' Satyen made the last statement so regretfully that his face looked different for a moment. Saswati— she had been listening to the conversation in silence—was a little . . . surprised, in that one statement she seemed to penetrate his crisply creased courtesy to see the real person within, in that single moment she got to know him much better. And she realized, too, why she felt happy just to be near Shweta. Shweta never talked about herself, only about the other person—as though she were a part of everyone's life—and this was her nature, as in good times, so in bad, and for that very reason she didn't ever seem unhappy—not even now. Saswati looked again at Satyen's slightly embarrassed expression, by chance Satyen glanced at her too— and looked away apprehensively. He realized too that he now appeared different to these people, in a way he didn't want to be seen, he wanted to hide; his embarrassment spread across his face. His habit, his efforts were of no use; he ended up saying things he didn't want to say, had never wanted to say, never did say anywhere. Never anywhere? But had anyone anywhere ever asked him?

The blue curtain shifted, and the person to enter was . . . Ata. She walked in gingerly holding a brass tray with the tea things on it; her face lowered, she carefully negotiated her way to the circular centre-table and put the tray down, then disappeared at high speed behind the curtain. And almost immediately, Tata charged in at the speed of light, diving into her mother's lap.

'What's the matter?' asked Shweta, placing her hand on her daughter's curls.

'Mm . . . Maa . . .'

'What?'

'Ma . . .!' Ata rubbed her face on her mother's lap twice.

Cupping her daughter's face in her hands and bringing her own face very close, Shweta said, 'What? Tell me in secret. Mmm? . . . Oh, I see. Yes, Didi wasn't right to do that. I shall scold her.'

Saswati said, 'Why did Ata have to bring in the tea-tray?'

'Exactly, as if Tata couldn't have! She'd have done it far better than her sister. There's something I want you to do now . . . Get some of those nice mints on a plate. And tell Chhotomashi to come here.'

'Chhotomashi is angry.'

'Angry! Why?'

'With Didi. Ma, you have to pour the tea first and then the water, don't you—everyone knows that—but Didi . . .'

'Really, Didi can't do a thing. Tell Chhotomashi she needn't be angry any more . . . Ma's calling her.'

Pleased, Tata left, tossing her curls, hurling a sideways look at Satyen on the way.

'How you spoil them, Bordi,' said Saswati.

'Do you remember, Saswati,' Shweta said a little later, 'this is exactly how Swati used to behave with you.'

'Only with me? She used to harass Mejdi and Shejdi too.'

'Tata is very keen,' Shweta looked at Satyen, 'to make friends with you, but she's very shy. Ata too—did you see how she ran away after putting the tray down?'

Satyen had been engrossed in all that had been going on; it took him some time to realize that Shweta's last statement was addressed to him. 'One of my many shortcomings is that I can't make friends with children at all,' he said softly, lowering his eyes to Shweta's fair-skinned feet. He intended no humour, he really did feel he didn't know, didn't understand, didn't have too many accomplishments.

'The tea's probably . . .' Saswati looked at the teapot. 'Ah, Swati. Come and pour the tea.'

'When you're here why do you need me?'

Saswati smiled. 'Tata was right. You really are angry.'

'See, even Swati hasn't managed to give up her childhood habits yet, never mind Tata,' said Shweta.

'All right, I'll pour,' Saswati said. 'How many spoons of sugar?'

'Swati knows everything,' said Shweta. 'Let her pour.'

'I asked her to,' Saswati moved away.

But Swati remained at a distance.

'Come, Swati,' said Shweta.

Swati rose, poured the tea without a word, her head bowed, and, watching the milk turn the brown of the tea gradually to gold, tried to hide the changing colour on her face too.

Satyen must have been watching the colour of the tea too, but when Swati pushed the table lightly towards him after pouring just one cup, he raised his eyes to say, 'Anyone else . . . Everyone else . . . You, Mrs Nandy?'

'I don't much like the sound of that Mrs Nandy.'

'In that case . . . Saswati-debi?'

'Directly to "debi"?'

'Why all these formalities? You can call her Chhordi,' Shweta solved the problem simply.

'That's another of my defects,' Satyen looked at a spot between Shweta and Saswati, 'I'm no good with all those names. Besides, I'm the older one.'

'How much older can you be?'

'To answer that I have to ask a forbidden question.'

'I'm twenty-four,' said Saswati. 'You?'

'Twenty-six. Can twenty-four be compared with twenty-six?'

'A woman of twenty-four can't even be compared to a man of thirty-two.'

'So Harit-babu is thirty-two?'

Shweta giggled at this, Saswati laughed in embarrassment, Swati couldn't help smiling either. 'Drink your tea. It's getting cold,' said Shweta.

'Just me alone? Tell her, Bordi . . .' Satyen indicated Saswati with his eyes.

'Didn't you just say you're no good with all those names!' Saswati laughed.

'No good doesn't mean . . .' Shweta looked away from Satyen's red face. 'Have some tea, Saswati . . . You, Swati . . .?'

'No,' Swati finally spoke.

'We're not great fans of tea, but . . . all right, might as well have a cup of Swati's brew . . .' Saswati brought her chair closer. 'Bordi, ask Satyen-babu to have something.'

'No, nothing else. I like my tea just by itself.'

'All right, no need to if you don't want to,' said Shweta.

'I simply cannot have my tea just by itself, though.' Saswati reached for a biscuit. Satyen was suddenly enticed by the appearance of the biscuit in her hand, he took one too. Then—although he was very dismissive of sweets—he even had a shondesh as he was talking, and after the tea—although he wasn't in favour of overwriting the flavour of tea with something else—he accepted a mint from Tata, who was all knotted up with shyness, not just that, he placed his hand on her head, took his face close to hers—though very stiff himself—and even managed a 'How nice!' for her. And instantly he realized that he was enjoying the flavour of the very family-life that he claimed to despise. Immediately afterwards, he thought, there's no more excuse to stay on. He would have to go now.

'It's time I went.' He hadn't wanted to, hadn't wanted to say it so soon, but someone seemed to push the words out of his throat. And since he *had* said them, he had to get up.

'So you're leaving today?'

That's right, so he was. Where was it he was going? Oh yes, to Ranchi. 'I'm leaving today,' Satyen's voice sounded a little harsh.

'When are you back?'

'When the holidays end.' The same person, who had been

exuberant a moment before, suddenly became stern, grave and taciturn.

'The holidays are rather long, aren't they? Saswati tried to extend the conversation. 'Maybe after a few days . . .'

'I cannot,' Satyen summoned a thin smile to his lips.

'Well, if you *have* decided to go . . .' said Shweta.

To leave no option open, Satyen glanced at Shweta and Saswati individually, saying, 'I'll meet you as soon as I'm back. I'm going now.' After the last three words—finally, after all this time—he turned towards Swati, as though he had just remembered there was someone else in the room. He had bid his final farewell from the door, Saswati standing opposite him, Shweta a little further back holding Tata's hand, and, even further back, half concealed behind Shweta, Swati. When he looked at her, Swati stirred a little, returned his look. And on the street Satyen felt Swati hadn't stopped looking at him yet, she was still looking, her glance was following him, was with him, was skewering his body with every turn of the screw. He felt something like pain, physical pain, it brought tears to his eyes. He walked swiftly, reached the tram-stop swiftly, boarded the tram to buy a ticket for Ranchi from the railway counter at the Hazra Road crossing.

∽

'Loton!' Swati called, going inside.

Loton was close by, she came crawling on hearing her name.

'Come on—bath time! Will you let your Mashi give you a bath?'

Loton staggered to her feet, clutching her aunt's sari for support. Raising her face, she emitted a sticky cry, lisping 'Matee! Ba-a-a-at!' supplementing her words by raining blows on her own head with her arms, but with so much force that she sat down on the floor under the impact.

'With Mashi, yes?' Swati laughed.

Still sitting on the floor, Loton stretched her arms out. 'Matee! Lap?'

'Nothing doing!' Swati retreated a few steps. 'Get up and walk. Come on!'

Loton increased her volume in a nasal tone, 'La-a-a-a-ap!'

'All right, lap . . . but who's giving you your bath?'

'M-m-a-a-a . . .'

'Ma! Ba-a-a-ye-bye, I'm not talking to you.' Swati pouted and rolled her eyes.

'Matee-e-e!' In stretching the ending, Loton grimaced till her lips also stretched from ear to ear, bubbles appeared in her mouth, her eyes turned round.

'No! I'm not talking to you!' Swati arched her eyebrows, turning away.

'All right, enough of this circus,' Shweta laughed. 'And anyway it's the same act every day.'

With a stern look and in an admonishing tone, Swati said, 'Now make up your mind—who's giving you your bath?'

Looking at her, Loton went off into peals of laughter.

'Ma?'

Loton shook her head with gusto, the way people say 'no'.

'Mashi, then?'

Loton shook her head with even more gusto.

'Silly girl! Hasn't learnt a thing yet!' Swati demonstrated how to nod in agreement, and, picking this up at once, Loton started nodding like a wind-up doll, refusing to stop.

'All right, all right, that's enough. Come along now. Bath time.' Swati wrapped the end of her sari around her waist in preparation.

'Bordi! Is Swati really going to give her a bath?' Saswati stirred anxiously.

'Look at that girl! Pretending she doesn't know anyone else now,' Shweta said.

'And look at Swati. Pretending she really can give her a bath,' Saswati smiled.

'But she does sometimes.'

'Is she able to? Is Swati able to?' Saswati was visiting at this hour of the day after a long time, so the whole thing was new to her.

'Come and see if I can!' said Swati, going off to the veranda inside the house with Loton perched on her shoulder.

Saswati had never handled a baby herself—she hadn't had to, yet—which was why she was uncertain despite her sister's calmness. 'I don't know, Bordi, Swati won't drop her or hurt her or something, will she?'

'Of course she won't.'

'Let's go and take a look.'

Saswati went to the veranda, Shweta following her after a few minutes. By then Swati's pair of assistants were jumping up and down with excitement. Ata had pulled Loton's frock off her, Tata had fetched the soap, towel and can of oil from the bathroom at a run, and, hearing the noise, Chhoton had turned up, his hands in the pockets of his shorts, to see all the fun.

Brushing against Swati as he walked past indifferently, Bijon said, 'I believe he's going away today, Swati?'

Swati pretended not to hear.

'Is he really going?' Bijon persisted, moving a little further away, and not looking directly at Swati,

'What are you talking about!' Swati half-raised her eyes at Bijon.

'I hear Satyen's going away?'

'Where on earth will he go?' Swati was about to say what was on her mind, but restrained herself to say, 'You're home far too long these days, Dada.'

'Poor fellow,' said Shweta. 'Gets ticked off when he isn't home, but no one's happy when he is.'

'See, Bordi! I'm not even allowed to stay at home peacefully on a holiday . . .'

'Didn't you say you're so busy you have to work Sundays too?'

'It's all up to me whether I take a holiday or not,' said Biju immediately without smiling. 'I don't work for anyone, after all.'

'That doesn't mean you have to walk around the house in that vest full of holes. Look at you!'

Twisting his arm to scratch himself on the back through one of the holes, he said, 'I have to tell Satyen something. Did he go home?'

'Biju thinks he's such a clown,' Saswati said in a low voice to Swati.

Swati said nothing; sitting cross-legged on the floor, she made Loton lie down in her lap, wrapping her arms around her, and Loton flailed her legs and hands as usual to provide entertainment.

'What fun!' Tata clapped.

'What sort of fun is this!' said Chhoton.

'Of course it's fun! Lots of fun!'

'Not at all!'

'Then go away!'

But Chhoton didn't budge, he kept watching the non-fun. He didn't think very highly of the small human being known as his sister; nasty, dirty, still wet the bed—ugh!—with brains to match, she had put the entire top in her mouth the other day— cut her tongue, what a scene—and their mother had scolded him instead! But she was so stupid, didn't even know you're not supposed to eat tops . . . but no scolding for her!

As soon as Swati tried to rub the oil into Loton's body she jerked as though she was going to turn a somersault.

'Should I hold her hand, Chhotomashi?' Ata asked quickly.

'And her legs,' added Tata.

'No, really, Bordi,' Saswati threatened her sister, 'who knows what awaits your daughter today.'

Swati concentrated on her task. First slowly, carefully, then confidently, unhesitatingly, her oil-soaked hand began to move over Loton's sweet, small, warm body in different directions—first just the one hand; then, when Loton had stopped her fidgeting to lie back in bliss, purring to please the audience, with both hands; she tried to rub, stroke, knead just the way she had seen Shweta do it; putting drops of massage oil into the folds of her neck, into the spaces between her fingers, didn't forget her tiny earlobes; in silence, her head bowed, in silence, solemnly, unknown to herself she began to prepare for her own future. She knew that the future was at hand. She trembled, just like the station does well before the train actually arrives, because of the rumbling of distant wheels borne along the ground. And that was why, just like the bustle on the platform when the bell was rung to announce the train, her entire being became busy, busy hands, busy gestures, busy movements; she felt so alive that she wouldn't be able to live without expending some of this energy. She was tense, her fingertips throbbed, she had forgotten what tiredness was, she had forgotten what peace was too . . . He was going away? Going away today? No, he won't, he won't. I know he won't.

Suddenly Loton cried out sharply.

'Oh dear,' said Saswati. 'It's got into her eyes.'

'No no, nothing's the matter. How Loton likes an oil massage,' Swati copied Shweta's tone perfectly, 'she doesn't cry at all . . . Have any of you ever seen anyone like her . . . No one can do it so well . . .'

'As if!' Chhoton was heard. 'I can do it so much better!'

'That's true. Loton has learnt from her brother how to bathe so beautifully!'

Chhoton was silent at this, as befits a responsible elder brother.

'Give him a proper bath one day, will you, Swati?' said Shweta. 'He never lets me, maybe with you . . .'

'Never!' said Chhoton.

'So Chhoton doesn't like bathing?' said Saswati.

'Just like his uncle here,' Shweta smiled. 'The things we had to do sometimes to get Biju to have his bath!'

'What's that you're saying about me?' Biju appeared at the door. He was dressed in a creased silk *panjabi* to conceal the vest—he looked most villainous in it—a cigarette glowed in his hands. Saswati said, looking at Shweta, 'Don't you have anything to say to him, he's smoking in your presence!'

'Bordi doesn't mind all that.' Biju puffed on his cigarette solemnly, then came a couple of steps closer to peer at Loton.

'Ugh!' Bijon said, wrinkling his nose. 'Mustard oil!'

'Will you take a look, Bordi, is it all right?' said Swati, running her hand once more over the small, undressed, soft, smooth body. Gazing at her, Saswati thought how nice it would be to have one of her own ... But Harit simply wasn't willing.

'Mustard oil turns the complexion dark,' said Bijon. 'Babies need olive oil.'

'Really? What else do they need?'

Bijon smiled pleasantly. 'I'll get you everything, Bordi, don't you worry.'

'Thank goodness. You can finally breathe, Bordi,' said Swati, standing up with the glazed Loton in her arms.

'You'll see,' Bijon twinkled, the half-smoked cigarette dangling from his lips.

Swati took the steps down to the courtyard, where Loton's bathwater had been warmed in the sun in her tub for quite some time. Loton sat down in the tub, the water coming up to her neck, splashing happily, and, displaying astounding manipulation of her vocal cords, practised her consonants at the top of her voice; and, watching her, happy in her happiness, the anxiety that had welled up within Swati a short while ago disappeared, she knew for certain in her heart that Satyen wouldn't go, he couldn't go.

Ata poured water from a mug on Loton's head, Tata didn't relent till she had soaped her sister a little, and the two of them completed half of their own baths too as Loton splashed around, so did Swati in trying to rescue Loton from their clutches. Loton laughed, Ata and Tata laughed, Swati laughed with them, the white clouds of autumn floated above, and a placid sky looked on.

'No more now. Take her out!' Shweta called out from the veranda.

But it was no easy task. Loton kept saying, 'N-n-no . . . Ba-a-a-ath!' She held on to the handles of the tub with her hands—such tiny fists, but so strong!—she defeated her aunt not once but twice, got her face completely wet, and Swati thought all this so much fun that she didn't try any more.

'Is it like this every day, Bordi?' Saswati wanted to know.

'A little extra for her aunt. She has to show off all she knows, after all.'

Saswati fidgeted. The girl wouldn't get a fever, would she, playing around in the water for such a long time? She wouldn't tumble into the water while holding the handles, would she? 'Get her out, Swati,' she shouted. Then she stood up herself. She half-wanted to join them in the courtyard, to take Loton in her own arms for a bit; she seemed to have finally found a pretext for it. 'I'll fetch her, Bordi,' she said, heading towards the steps, but Swati brought Loton in at the same time, setting her down on the floor, screaming and wet, and knelt on the floor to wipe her dry with a towel.

'Let me, Swati,' said Shweta softly.

'I can.' Swati tilted her perspiring face to wipe it on her shoulder. 'So naughty, Bordi, your . . .' Seeing Shweta's expression, she stopped. Her eyes had changed . . . What was it? Swati looked quickly at Saswati, at Bijon, both were staring straight ahead . . . What was it? Letting go of Loton, Swati stood up, and instantly, even before she turned, something leapt up in her heart to tell her what it was; that's why she wasn't in the least bit surprised to see Satyen standing in the middle of the courtyard with a red, sunburnt face.

Bijon climbed down the steps to the courtyard quickly to welcome him. 'Please come in.'

Finally—when he saw the bathtub, saw everyone—Satyen realized it hadn't been proper at all to have walked into the house directly through the back door. 'I . . . I . . .' He stopped after getting as far as that.

'Do come in,' Bijon said in an even more magnanimous voice.

'The other door was shut . . . No one answered . . . So I thought . . . Let me try . . .' What had he thought? When he had already spent all that time here in the morning, why had he come back in the middle of the day, at this inconvenient hour? Once more, just to see her once more.

'That doesn't matter. Please—do come in.'

'No, no . . . Not now . . .' Satyen's heart wanted to run away immediately, but his body refused to move—that is to say, it moved mechanically, he followed Bijon up the steps with light footsteps.

'Shall we sit here? No . . . Let's go into the other room . . .' Bijon dripped with politeness.

'Oh, you can sit here,' Shweta stood up after dressing Loton.

'No, how can we sit here . . . Please . . . come with me. Actually,' Bijon paused, 'whatever you prefer.'

Prefer! Satyen didn't even seem to understand what that might mean, he sat down listlessly in the same Venesta chair that Bijon had pushed forward initially.

Bijon sat down too, starting an informal conversation, 'Where did you go?'

'Now? I'd gone to get my ticket. Here . . .' There was no need to, no one did such a thing normally, but still he fished out the green railway ticket from his pocket. Needlessly, it was like throwing away money, but still he had bought the costlier second-class ticket, so that he did not change his mind, so that at least the extra money spent dragged him to Ranchi. He waved the ticket—as though he wanted to display it to everyone—then looked around. He spotted the two older sisters by the door, standing next to each other, saw Swati too—saw her dimly—standing against the wall at a distance. Stiffly, indistinctly, Swati stood with her face half-turned: as soon as she had seen Satyen she seemed to have seen her own appearance in the mirror too—her hair all over the place, her sari sopping wet with massage oil and water; should she change? No. Should she go away? No. Should she stay? No. She stayed, however, wondering every moment, why am I still here, and as she wondered she remained rooted to the same spot, not moving, not speaking, not looking.

'Are you travelling somewhere?' Bijon the innocent asked.

'I'm going to Ranchi today,' Satyen answered grimly. 'Have you been to Ranchi, Bijon-babu?'

'I'll be back in a minute.' Shweta took Loton inside, and a little later Saswati came in too, stuffing the end of her sari into her mouth and laughing silently but uncontrollably.

'What's the matter, Saswati? What is it?'

Saswati couldn't talk, shaking with laughter she buried her face in her sister's shoulder.

As she powdered Loton, Shweta said, 'Look at her! What are you laughing at?'

'Bijon-babu . . .' Saswati's voice rang out like a slap punctuating her laughter.

'What's wrong with that! At last we have someone to address him respectfully.'

'And Biju too. Did you just hear him talk—and to think he's hardly ever spoken to Satyen in his life.'

'But then all these days there wasn't . . .' Without finishing, Shweta started scanning Loton's neatly folded clothes.

'I know!' Saswati said in a different tone, not laughing any more. 'Why on earth is Satyen even going . . .'

'Why not? Let him go.'

'Let him? But meanwhile . . . isn't that Baba?'

Shweta slipped a thin white silk vest on Loton.

'Where was Baba all this time?'

'Apparently you didn't like the sari you got . . .'

'Oh my God! When did I say I didn't like it? All I said was . . .'

'It's the same thing. He won't give up till it's perfect.'

'And so he went off to change it? Honestly!'

Rajen-babu entered, looking tired. Spotting the box in his hand, Saswati exclaimed, 'This is too much, Baba.'

'Tell me if you like the too much.' Rajen-babu handed the box to his daughter.

Lifting the lid for a quick peep, Saswati gave her opinion: 'It's lovely.'

'You didn't even see it.'

Saswati controlled her impulse to open the box and examine it thoroughly. She remembered Shweta didn't dress in such saris, wouldn't any more. She felt a little ashamed.

'I can tell at a glance. But why did you have to . . . It would have been better to have changed that fancy dhoti.'

'Why?' asked Shweta.

'He doesn't like such stuff. Calls it son-in-law attire.'

'That's right then,' said Shweta, 'he *is* the son-in-law.'

'And how often does he dress in a dhoti anyway! Why bother . . .'

'The less frequently he does, the better the dhoti should be,' Shweta replied at once.

'Hmmph!' Using that noise to smother something she left unsaid, Saswati turned to her father, 'Did you meet Satyen, Baba?'

'Yes, I met him.'

'Is it all right for all of us to have come away?'

'About Satyen? But I saw him leave just now.'

'Already? He only just came.'

Rajen-babu didn't respond.

'He came in the morning too.'

Rajen-babu didn't respond this time either. Saswati couldn't find anything more to say, Shweta started combing Loton's hair with a small red comb, and the maid came in a little later with a bowl of milk for Loton.

'Swati!' Saswati called out loudly, suddenly. Receiving no response, she called out again. Then, looking around, she asked slightly anxiously, 'Where's Swati?'

'Didimoni's gone for her bath,' the maid was heard whispering.

There was silence again. None of the three looked at anyone else; and after a minute of this, Rajen-babu left for the other room, his feet dragging. Saswati didn't speak after that, nor did Shweta; Loton gulped down her milk, lying back in her mother's lap, she dropped off to sleep, picture-perfect, as soon as she had emptied the bowl.

∿

Saswati went back home, everyone had lunch, the neighbourhood fell silent for the afternoon. Even more silent was Swati's room in Rajen-babu's house; Saswati's old bed had been laid out in it once again, Ata and Tata slept on it at night—and Loton was asleep on it now. Her puffy, pale pink but also bluish eyelids, covering her sleeping eyes, looked enormous now. But the other two people in the room were not looking at this beautiful sight; Shweta sat with her back to her daughter, resting her chin on her drawn-up knee, while Rajen-babu sat on the cane chair in which Swati read her novels, looking with concentration at a particular spot on the floor. They seemed to have been in this pose for some time, silent, as though perturbed. A little later Shweta said softly, 'So, Baba?'

Rajen-babu raised his eyes from the floor.

Shweta said, 'Everything seems fine; only—he has no family . . .'

'Why not? He has us!' said Rajen-babu, getting off his chair. On his way out, he stopped at Swati's small clothes-rack; three pairs of shoes were laid out, two of them were ancient, but she simply couldn't bring herself to throw them out. He moved towards the desk; the old cane bookshelf was bent under the weight of books; on the bottom rack her school textbooks were covered with a film of dust—the atlas had a blue cover—the desk held her current books, storybooks, notebooks. He opened a notebook; there was an analysis of Portia's character, he read a little of it, the words appeared blurred without his glasses, but still he gazed at them, and from the wall opposite, Shishirkana, now a portrait trapped behind a sheet of glass covered in dust, gazed at him with blurry eyes. Rajen-babu didn't get to know.

Shutting the notebook, he put it back in place and went into the next room. Ata, Tata and Chhoton were playing ludo, as soon she saw him Tata said beseechingly, 'Will you play with us, Dadu?'

'Will you?' said Ata. 'Then we'll start over again. We asked Chhotomashi so many times—it's no fun without four players.'

'Dadu and I on the same team!' Chhoton settled down, cross-legged.

'After you've finished this round,' said Rajen-babu, going out to the veranda. Half the courtyard was in the shade now, clothes were drying on the clothesline, somewhere a crow cawed, and Swati sat silently on the steps. Rajen-babu didn't call out to her, didn't go near her, just looked at her from the back. Swati turned round a little later.

'Have you seen my box of paan?' Rajen-babu said quickly.

'It was right there . . . Let me look . . .' Swati rose quickly too.

'Never mind, I'm sure I'll find it.'

'I'll fetch it . . .'

'Swati . . .'

Swati paused. Rajen-babu looked at his daughter, but

Swati didn't stop, didn't look at him, avoided her father's eyes and left. For the first time, for the first time in her life, she felt embarrassed in her father's presence.

She went to Shweta. Who was asleep. It needed a second look for Swati to realize she was wrong. Shweta lay there, her hand on her forehead, and beneath the hand covering her eyes, from the corners of those eyes two clear streams of tears were flowing, curving past her nose down to her lips, the lips were parted slightly, a blue vein in her ivory-white neck throbbed ever so slightly. Swati stopped, she was astonished, she couldn't take her eyes off her sister. Even Shweta cried? And she had thought—relieved by the notion—that Shweta was excellent at hiding her unhappiness. Hide! What option did you have in this world but to hide your unhappiness, where was the time, the space, to be unhappy? But what if you did have the time? On such quiet afternoons, and when everyone else was asleep, those endless dark nights—what did she know of them, what did she know of Shweta's nights and her days? And what, for that matter, did she know of unhappiness—or had known, before today—whatever did she know of unhappiness?

The moment this occurred to her, the moment she remembered that Satyen was indeed going away today, tears welled up in her breast. But where could she cry, where could she hide, someone or the other was bound to see, what would she say then? Shweta was her safe refuge— at least, used to be—but what if she too drove Swati away with her own tears!

Swati was about to leave, but Shweta's eyes opened. Looking at her, Shweta said in a dewy voice, 'Come to me, Swati.'

Swati stopped.

'Come here.' Clearing her throat, Shweta called her again. Her eyes acknowledged that she had been crying, but the tears stopped instantly too, only their memory lingering in her voice.

Swati approached her, sat down near her head.

'Want to stretch out? Come.' Shweta made room, and wiped her face with the back of her hand.

Swati lay down next to her, nestling against her; without a word, they remained that way side by side.

'Heeeeao,' Loton cried out in her sleep.

Shweta's left arm moved. 'Oh God, sopping wet . . .' She sat up to change the sheets, stroking her daughter back to sleep. 'This girl is such a bedwetter! That's why I can't stand her!'

At this Swati felt her sister had returned to her. Relaxed once more, she said with a smile, 'All you do is badmouth her, Bordi. Such a good girl—see how long she's been napping.'

'What does she have to do besides eat and sleep anyway!'

'Come on!' Swati's voice acquired a cadence. 'She's learning new words every day, isn't she? And how lovely she is!'

'Really?' Shweta glanced at her daughter from the corner of her eye.

'I'm sure she'll be the loveliest among all of you,' Swati lifted her father's words shamelessly.

'Not to my eyes! Such an ugly forehead!' Shweta touched the ugly forehead with three fingers.

Gazing at Loton's puffy eyes and reddish face, Swati said, 'I love her so very much, Bordi.'

'But how much longer? Soon there'll be a mouthful of teeth, a stream of words—and a stream of slaps!'

Swati laughed loudly. 'She won't be nice any more?'

'Not like she is now.'

Swati thought about it. Babies were beautiful, very beautiful, but they were for others—grown-ups—to get pleasure from, what difference did it make to them? They didn't know they were beautiful, they didn't even know they existed, and the day they did that would be the end of beautiful. No, Loton was beautiful, but it wasn't beautiful to be Loton. Poor thing—she spent sixteen out of the twenty-four hours in sleep; how many years more would it take her to get to where I am today, where a person knows she exists, knows what she wants, what she really wants, and can hear in her breast the pulsating truth that she will get what she wants, that what she really wants will take place, has to take place, there's no alternative to its taking place.

Listening to what pulsated within her, Swati said, 'But I think it's better to be a grown-up.'

'Of course it is,' Shweta agreed. 'Self-sufficient—freedom.'

'You don't seem too happy about it?'

'Not much to be happy about either,' Shweta lay down again next to Swati. 'Nothing can be as good as the first three years.'

About to respond, Swati stopped. Something else—something strange—occurred to her: this experience of the 'first three years' would end for Shweta with Loton, and had ended for her father with her. She seemed to see her father's face in Shweta's, the face that she had seen a little while earlier, that different, unable-to-talk face, and then her father seemed to turn into her mother; not her sick mother, not her suffering mother, but her radiant mother with lips reddened from paan; and before her very eyes, the colours were wiped away to be replaced by white. Suddenly she said, 'Why have you given up paan, Bordi?'

Shweta didn't answer.

'Why? Surely it's allowed.'

'Of course it is.'

'Then why not?' Swati spoke emotionally, as though this business of giving up paan was the most important thing. 'Why not? You loved it, I remember . . .'

'So did he,' Shweta said in a small voice.

For the first time Swati heard her sister refer to this person, the person who was no longer present, whose absence everyone had accepted already. Everyone . . . But not one person, and how did that one person feel about everyone else? Swati looked away; the tears lurking at the bottom of her heart seemed to have found a pretext to well up again. Sounds of merriment came from the next room—they were playing ludo. People had discovered so many different ways to pass time, yet time was the problem, yet there were times when time would not pass. He was going away! Swati felt a sledgehammer blow on her heart—was he going away? What do I do now?

∽

What do I do, Satyen was wondering too at that moment, what do I do. Night was still a long way off, there was plenty of time before he had to leave for the station. At least six hours. And he would have to spend those six hours just this way, lying back in his easy chair, not awake, not asleep, not alive; for the one thing that he had always been terrified of, the one thing that he had avoided at any cost, had now materialized, for the next six hours—until he could take the bus to Howrah Station—he had nothing, nothing to do either.

Satyen looked around. A clean, cool room; the lords of literature all in rows on the two bookshelves stacked with books; on the desk, near at hand, a few fresh ones. He remembered he had thought of this room as heaven after moving from the mess in Bhowanipore; remembered thinking at some point that he would be able to spend his entire life just reading. Life! How long was life? He had got what he wanted; he hadn't wanted much, but what he had wanted he had got—a job that offered low pay but lots of holidays, a secluded home, the living environment of Calcutta, freedom, and the mentality that didn't make him think about himself all the time. But all those other thoughts— the brisk walk of the brain after digesting a book—where were they? Literature, why have you failed me today? The pretty, small frame within which he had confined his life . . . Within which, whatever else may happen, he had never had to worry about how to spend his time . . . was it not enough for him any more? Had his life suddenly expanded! Did he have wants that had not yet been fulfilled? But wanting didn't exist in isolation, to want was to get, he couldn't die of thirst with want, could he! To want was to get—it wasn't a question of less or more; for everyone wanted what mattered to them the most— if you wanted it, you got it, and if that wasn't the case, then you had no choice but to not want anything!

An image swam up before his eyes. Of that day when he had been standing in the veranda and had seen a girl walk across the field. It had been the monsoon season then, he had just moved into this house; the sun was up in the late afternoon after the rain. In one glance he had taken in the red sky, the spread-out field, and—when the girl came nearer, and he recognized her—the ribbon of yellow sunlight on her black hair. How self-controlled he had been then, detached, in love with beauty because it was beautiful. And now? A different image this time. The middle of the day, a busy household, amidst all this, suddenly . . . Standing in the courtyard . . . He himself. What had everyone thought? What had they thought when he had fished the ticket out of his pocket? He hadn't managed to say a single word to her, hadn't even managed to get a look at her properly. Useless . . . all useless. If all you wanted when you saw someone often was to see them again and again, then . . . then it was best not to see them at all. And then, at that very moment, his coming away suddenly—running into her father just as he was leaving—what was it he had said, he hadn't replied, lest he ask him to stay a little longer, and lest he agree, too. Foolishness . . . it was all foolishness! The essence of beauty was that it was fleeting; the condition it set was that we must not claim it. You can't live in the Taj Mahal, a touchstone idol was only fit for a temple, those who live in Puri round the year don't even spare a glance for the sea. That's why flesh-and-blood people couldn't be beautiful, if they seemed beautiful, if you liked them, if for some reason you liked a real person, and if you wanted them . . . To want something . . . Beauty had nothing to do with that male dance of desire! And that's why you should be careful of loving real people: you can love poetry, you can love wisdom, you can love the sky—but be very careful about loving a real person. Take him, a civilized human being, a well-educated man—he had behaved as foolishly as a seventeen-year-old just a short while ago, and now—although he lacked for nothing, had no reason to be unhappy—was gasping for breath under deep water while sitting in his chair.

A metaphor came to Satyen's mind. Standing on the bank, he was watching the beautiful river scenery, he was captivated, increasingly captivated; and the more he was, the closer he edged to the water, to see it even better, and suddenly he slipped and fell in. The water was dangerous, deceitful, treacherous, slippery; pushing here, pulling there, buffeting elsewhere; the more yielding it was, the more obdurate it was—and even if you could feel the ground beneath your feet, it was perilous. But you knew, Satyen told himself, you knew this is what water is like, didn't you? Then he answered himself, how would I know, I've never fallen in before. But didn't you know you could slip in if you went so close? Satyen didn't answer this time.

He raised his arm in desperation. His fingers curled, as though they were going to make a grab for the three books laid out on the desk, but the very next moment his arm sagged into his lap like a limp rag. Pointless! From whom would he hide himself with those books? From whom would he conceal the fact that all his heart lay there, in that house, which was two minutes away, but could also be at the other end of the world right now. He wouldn't have to hide, wouldn't have to think, just a few hours more, then it would be night, the train, another land. What did that other land hold? Peace? Deliverance? Shelter? No . . . It held just what this room of his did right now . . . Emptiness, just emptiness. Still, this trip was at least an attempt; an attempt not to accept the impossible condition that if just that one person was missing, everything was missing, and maybe the attempt would strengthen his resistance, he would find beneath the silt in his own heart the much older rock. But he would return, wouldn't he? And then again...? No, after his return he would move from this house, move from this neighbourhood, stop taking classes for girls at the college. Everything would be fine if only he didn't have to meet her. He would traverse the desolate landscape of emptiness to return to the comfort of routine, to the protection of habit, to his former identity, to his independent will. Yes, that was the right course of action.

Having written his own release order and signed it, he left unburdened. A little too unburdened: as though the doctor had said there was nothing to worry about, he would be cured, but a leg would have to be amputated. Immediately he reflected: I won't see her again after this, so just this once . . . As soon as he did, he sat up in his chair, seemed to come to life again, returned to the real world. Go over again? Once more, after that late morning visit! In his mind's eye Satyen saw those three grey steps, the green door, the blue curtain opposite it, and Swati parting the curtain to enter the room. What would he say? There was nothing to say, or there was so much to say that it would never end. Even after so many things had been said over so many days, everything remained unsaid. Let it. Why go over—Satyen slumped in his chair again—if he went it would only be to come back.

The house, the steps, the door vaporized; only Swati remained, the blue curtain behind her, only Swati in the emptied-out universe, just like you felt, when lying back on the grass, that there was nothing else but that white cloud in the sky. She didn't move, didn't shift, stood still. Swati's eyes, the moist glow in them—Satyen saw that too—as though she were waiting, for someone to say something, for something to happen. Swati was waiting for him—for something he hadn't said, for something he had forgotten to say; and as soon as it was remembered, as soon as it was said, everything would be solved, everything would be all right.

All this while there was emptiness, now disquiet took its place. This didn't concern him alone, someone else had a share too, an equal share. And yet all this time he'd been thinking only about himself, how he would get his tranquil life back, that was all he had been thinking of, had been preparing himself to accept the resultant unhappiness. His life! Did he have control over his life any more? Could he defy his desire only because he desired to, what if the desire was not his alone, but someone else's too? Could he cause himself pain?

Responsibility, the weight of responsibility forced Satyen's head down on his shoulders, shut his eyes. He tried not to think, not to think of anything, to lose himself in a hazy, sleepy cloud. But the eyes gazed at him, twinkling eyes with a moist glow, awake in the darkness behind his closed eyes, looking into his eyes, into his heart, piercing him, piercing. To be released from those eyes Satyen opened his own, and, staring at the floor, clearly realized that he—they—had only one option, and that option was marriage.

Marriage! It sounded very strange to him. Why, he asked himself, hasn't the idea peeped into your mind even once all this time? Perhaps—but did that make it real? But it would become real some day. That didn't mean now! But this is good, this is best . . . This is natural. Natural? Or routine? But then the biggest routine of them all was the act of living.

Satyen took his mind on a journey through the early years of his youth. His was a world bereft of women in every sense. Did he feel something was missing? Maybe, but he felt no impatience. He had seen unlimited initiative among his fellow-students for the company of women. He had seen particularly bold people among them. With what motivation had he succeeded in passing those years, refusing to spend himself meaninglessly despite the taunts of the courageous? Not because he was superior—God knew he wasn't—not because he was more intelligent, and definitely not because he was insensitive; the reason was probably the fact that, having read poetry since childhood, he had conjured up a certain idea about this in his mind's eye, and he had made a secret, very secret, vow to his imagination. He had sometimes felt that he might see that figure from his imagination in real life too, but that had nothing to do with marriage, at least, there was no compulsion. Get married? So what if he didn't—and if he had to, he would sometime or the other. Earlier, he had lightly tapped the whole business away from this side of his mind to the other, but he couldn't now, suddenly it stuck in his side like a thorn.

Suddenly? Nothing was sudden, we make everything happen out of choice. The truth, tell the truth, did you raise your eyes from your textbook one morning three years ago while taking a class in a college and immediately see your imagination converted to reality? Or did you over those three years prune and reshape your imagination to match it to reality. Come now, confess, did this descend on you from the heavens, or was it you who had built it day by day, then breathed life into the straw-and-earth-and-colour of the figure! Me alone! Both of us, both of us; . how could it have happened without the two together? And not two any more either, a single life now; you're one now.

Satyen felt a shiver run down his spine. They were one! Never to be separated again! And that could only mean . . . Marriage? Celebrations, stupid priest, alcoholic smell of new furniture! Broadcast to the world what had grown between them, been nurtured between them, the beauty of it all! But what was the alternative? Was there another way that would let you gaze to your heart's content, say every last thing, stay without having to come away?

The question seemed to float for a while on the surface of the mind, then sank slowly when no answer was forthcoming, and immediately everything returned in an enormous muddy torrent—all of it, his ticket for Ranchi; saying goodbye twice over; all his resolve of a few minutes ago. Which of the two? He would have to decide—today, now. If he went, it wouldn't merely be a short trip out of Calcutta, it would mean a permanent trip out of this entire existence, the existence which . . . could have been, could still be. And if he didn't go today, then he wouldn't be able to delay things either. Which?

Satyen rose from his chair. He felt weightless, as though he were floating over the floor. He went into his bedroom, combed his hair before the mirror, his face looked unfamiliar. He just couldn't think about all this any more—he'd go out, somewhere, anywhere, there were still a few hours to go, he didn't have to do anything definite for the next few hours. He took some money; suddenly recollected Shillong, the day he'd received the last letter, and immediately taken the train back. That very day he had realized a day like today would come, had to come. He had understood it all, known it all, so did Swati, so did everyone in her family—all this while it had just been pretence, increasing his self-importance. Whatever he did, whatever he thought, would he really be able to leave Calcutta now? He wouldn't? Of course he would! Satyen arrived at the street at high speed; walked swiftly along the left-hand side towards the lane to the right—towards the single-storeyed white building— didn't even give it a glance; went directly to the tram-stop, straight into the tram and to Esplanade.

He paused outside Metro Cinema, as though this was what he had come for. Not able to get tickets, he went to another cinema hall, entered. The film had begun. There was a bluish darkness. The presence of so many people with the same objective, and the moving pictures flickering on the screen under the harsh light made him feel a little lighter. He tried to immerse himself. Two friends were in love with the same woman; she married one of them, the other went off to become a sailor.

Time went by. The sailor returned, they met again, and as soon as he did the woman fell in love with him. But the sailor wasn't willing to betray his friend; meanwhile the husband guessed what was going on and found consolation with a dancing girl, that in turn offended the wife. The to-ing and fro-ing continued; time dragged. Satyen began to feel the chair wasn't all that comfortable, people were coughing too much, it was high time the film ended. War broke out—the universal solution—the husband became an air-force pilot, the sailor a submarine commander, and the woman gloated with photographs of both the brave men—time for 'God Save the King'. But Satyen left before that, emerging blinking in the yellowed sunlight. It was still daylight! Now what . . .? All right, how about a cup of tea. Reaching Chowringhee, he entered the first restaurant he saw.

As soon as he sat down, someone spoke from the next table. 'What a surprise! Satyen!'

Satyen turned to see Kiran Bakshi looking at him, a fork embedded in his mutton cutlet. But this was not the Kiran he knew, the one he had spent four years in college with, the eternally unshaven Kiran Bakshi in handloom; now he was in a silk *panjabi* with gold buttons, well-groomed hair; radiating, all told, the conspicuous glitter of all things brand new. 'Why don't you join me!' Kiran waved his other hand in the air and, no sooner had Satyen taken the chair opposite him than he said, 'It's been ages. What are you up to?'

'It's you who have been up to something,' Satyen cast an eye at Kiran's cheek—he hadn't merely shaved, he seemed to have scraped the skin off, and powdered it too—'but what?'

'Oh, don't ask, you know, *that* happened.' Two large creases appeared on Kiran's shining cheeks as he smiled.

'When?'

'First of August.' Kiran announced the date sonorously, as though the date of his wedding was extremely special to

Satyen—to everyone, in fact. 'I couldn't let you know . . . It was all very sudden . . . And besides I didn't even know where . . .'

'That's all right. Eat your cutlet.'

'Yes, of course. How about you . . . What would you like?'

'Some tea.'

'And what else? Nothing else? Have something. Anything you want. It's my treat.'

Satyen smiled.

'Please . . . do have something!' Kiran bubbled with camaraderie. 'If you'd rather not have a cutlet try something else. Sandwiches? A piece of cake? Of course—it's cake you like—don't you remember Cornfooly Cabin?'

Satyen wondered, are we really as intimate as Kiran suggests? And meanwhile, Kiran called out, 'Waiter!'

The waiter put a slice of cake before Satyen, a fat crescent studded with raisins. 'Won-n-n-derful,' said Kiran, pleased. 'It's no fun eating alone.'

'But you were, weren't you?'

'You weren't here then.' Finally at peace, Kiran returned to his mutton cutlet—and to the earlier topic. Chewing, he said, 'That's true, I couldn't inform many of our friends. And you don't even meet them these days—everyone's so busy—life as a student was such fun, wasn't it?' He laughed in a self-satisfied way.

'How's your legal practice going?' asked Satyen.

'That's another story. I was trying my luck at the Alipur courts—didn't make enough even for the tram fare. So I've switched to income tax, things look hopeful—my father-in-law's an ITO, you see.'

'ITO?'

'Income-tax officer. That's a huge advantage, don't you see! And income-tax practice means quick money too. Damn—this knife is blunt!'

'Why bother with all that. Use your fingers.' Satyen broke off a piece of cake with his hand and popped it into his mouth.

WHEN THE TIME IS RIGHT 429

'You're right! You can't do justice to this with a fork and knife!' Kiran pushed the cutlery aside to get going with his hands, but said just a little later, 'Oh dear!'

'What's the matter?'

Kiran said sadly, his mouth full, 'I spilt some sauce on the sleeve.'

Satyen observed that Kiran actually looked as if he was in mourning. With a glance at his sleeve, he said, 'But you can hardly see it.'

'You can't?' Kiran swallowed the piece of mutton in his mouth without chewing it properly. Raising his arm, he examined the sleeve carefully, his diamond ring flashing. A little later, he said, 'It's not showing now, but as soon as it dries . . . Should I rinse it off?'

'No,' said Satyen. 'It'll only spread, and ruin the crease too.'

'You're right. Then might as well let it stay this way, don't you think?' Expressing his regret again after one more glance at the tiny stain, he lowered his arm and settled back in his chair. Listlessly, he said, 'How about you . . . You're still teaching . . . Where are you coming from?'

'I went to watch a film.'

'Which one?'

Satyen realized he didn't know the name, hadn't even noticed the posters. He named the cinema hall.

'Ah, *Ends Meeting*. What's it like?'

'Not bad.'

'I heard good things . . . Janet Green's in it . . . I won't get to watch it.'

'Why not?'

'Oh, don't ask. Anita is obsessed with Bengali films . . . Anita is my wife's name. Isn't it a nice name?'

'Amita is a very nice name.'

'Not Amita, A . . . *nita*.' Kiran laughed loudly. 'Everyone makes this mistake. It's a new kind of name, isn't it?'

'Yes,' said Satyen. He wished parents would put more thought into their children's names, so that the names meant something, at least. Bengal was being overrun by Anilendus and Anitas.

'Those Bengali films, you know, I can't stand them, but what can one do, I *have* to go—already been to two this week. Then again, if nobody goes, how will the local film industry grow.'

'That's true,' said Satyen.

'No, really, marriage robs you of your freedom. Take this holiday today—shouldn't a man be resting—but no, I have to do the rounds of my in-laws' relatives. Now I have to go to Creek Row, and then to Farepukur; someone's ill here, someone's had a baby there—how are they and all that.' Kiran looked at his plate as though he was extremely annoyed, then ate the last piece of his cutlet.

'Fortifying yourself before that?' Satyen said.

'Hah . . . Yes . . . You could say that!' Kiran laughed loudly in enjoyment.

'But why are you alone?'

Kiran's smile turned to grimness instantly. In a low voice he said, 'Exactly! We were about to leave when my mother suddenly decided she had to go somewhere with her daughter-in-law. Boy!' He called out angrily. 'Finger-bowl!'

'Is that why you got upset and didn't have your tea at home?'

Kiran rinsed his fingers clean in the bowl of warm water. Wiping his hands with his handkerchief, he said, 'Mothers have no sense, and as for wives—they will keep everyone but you happy. I mean, the illness is nothing serious, mother and baby are fine too—is there any point in my going by myself? But if I don't . . .' Kiran shook his head, finished his now-cold tea in a single gulp and ended, 'You're better off, far better off.'

'Are you done?' Satyen asked a little later.

'Yes—let's go. You hardly ate your cake . . . The bill's mine, all right?' Kiran paid, drew back his sleeve to glance at his gold watch. The expression in his eyes changed slightly, a small sound of regret emerged.

'No one will spot it,' said Satyen, 'unless you show them.'

'Yes!' Kiran stood upright, shifted a little. 'And it'll go with a wash.'

'Yes, it will certainly go with a wash,' Satyen got to the street first. 'So it's Creek Row for you now.'

'Don't ask!' A smile creased Kiran's cheeks again. Crossing Chowringhee, he said, 'But I didn't ask anything about you. Still at that mess . . .?'

A lorry passed with a deafening roar; answering became unnecessary.

'It was very nice meeting you after so long,' Kiran continued the conversation. 'Do come over some time . . . Sardar Sankar Road, you remember, don't you! Come tomorrow, Anita will be very happy. Come for tea, all right?'

Reaching the pavement, Satyen said, 'That would be wonderful, but I'm leaving for Ranchi tonight.'

'Leaving for Ranchi? Oh well, why not—you're a free man— whereas people like us . . . Ah, here's No. 3! After you're back then—you won't forget? All right . . .' Kiran climbed into the bus quickly, waving goodbye once more from the window.

The bus left, Satyen stayed rooted to the spot. The sun had declined. Unobstructed on the western side, Chowringhee glittered like a sheet of gold, the sunlight bouncing off some of the shop windows was blinding. He stood watching the stream of cars, the buses stopping and then leaving one by one. The sunlight darkened, the diagonal shadow of the lamp post crossed the road and, becoming indistinct, ascended the shop-steps. Satyen turned towards the tram-stop, stood facing the west. The colour green was spread across the Calcutta Maidan, golden; with the grass, trees, streets, benches, the children at play, the statues, all included in its fold, golden; orange-red; the fort became visible for an instant in the distance, like a dimly seen hillock;

towards the Eden Gardens the green turned to blue. Satyen stood watching the trams stopping and then leaving one by one. The nannies finished their gossip and rose, the British children began making their way back home, a blood-red sunray fell on a black stone statue in the distance. A cawing sound rose above his head, the bird flew to the tree in front of him. Satyen got into a tram.

～

'Aren't you coming, Chhotomashi?'

'Yes, let's go.'

'Why don't you come!'

'Let's go,' said Swati.

'You keep saying let's go,' said Tata. 'It's getting so late.'

'Uff!' said Shweta. 'Why are you bothering Chhotomashi?'

'But Chhotomashi said yesterday...' Ata pouted.

Swati arranged her sari, touched a comb to her hair, left with the two of them in tow.

'Children's park, Chhotomashi.'

'Let's go to that field today,' said Swati.

'No, Chhotomashi...'

'There's a jasmine tree. We'll gather flowers.'

'Jasmine! So many jasmine trees we had in Mymensingh. Who needs jasmine!'

'Then who needs anything?' Ata dismissed Tata's protests. 'I love gathering flowers. Let's go.'

With a fleeting glance at Swati, Tata said, 'I'll get more flowers than Didi, see if I don't. Walk faster, Chhotomashi.'

Swati arrived at the field, flanked by her nieces. It was a field no more, having almost become a neighbourhood in itself. There was an unpaved red road, electric cables, small, freshly painted houses; some more were under construction, others were complete but still unoccupied, a few had people living in them even before being completed, and as for that house of Anukul-uncle's—tenants had moved in—the walls, painted white, had already started to blacken. No, it wasn't a field any more, but there were still open spaces here and there, and to the extreme west some parts of the original field were intact. What had this place been like three years ago? But Swati no longer felt it was the same place: that enormous field, those dense trees— you could see them from the car back then—it wasn't as though all of those things had disappeared, some remained, somewhere else, always would. She felt like a stranger in her own neighbourhood, crossed the unpaved road quickly, didn't glance at the houses; went directly to the field in the west with its uneven dead grass.

'Where's the jasmine tree, Chhotomashi?'

'Here it is.'

'Oh my God, is that it! Didi, remember that jasmine tree by the tank! That was hu-u-u-ge!'

'Not at all,' said Ata at once. 'It wasn't very big at all!'

'Not very big! Look, Didi . . .'

'Flowers! There they are, see?' said Swati.

'Where?'

'Go look.'

'Chhotomashi, aren't you coming with us too?'

'I'll wait here. Let me see who can gather more.'

Swati looked around . . . sometimes at Ata and Tata, sometimes in other directions. It wasn't a beautiful place, just the opposite, in fact, but it still made for a picture. One side was dark with trees, on another side you could see the high roofs on Russa Road, and in that corner the colours of the sunset were still entangled in the shaggy tops of a few trees taller than buildings. A day, one more day, died slowly before Swati's eyes. The place changed its appearance suddenly; no light; nobody; a void. As always in October, after the glittering heat of the day the chilly foggy evening appeared, looking forlorn. 'Ata! Tata!' called Swati.

'Co-o-o-ming!'

Going up to them, Swati said, 'Home now.'

'Just a little longer, Chhotomashi,' they said and moved away.

Swati called them again after a while. Ata came first, saying, 'There weren't a lot of flowers, Chhotomashi, I only got a few. And so dusty and filthy!'

Tata ran up too, saying, 'See, I've got more. Haven't I?'

'Mu-u-u-ch more!' But there was no adolescent enthusiasm in Swati's voice.

'Where shall I put them, Chhotomashi, the flowers?'

'Give them to me,' said Ata. 'I'll tie them up at the end of my sari.'

'No. You keep mine, Chhotomashi.'

Making a fist around the flowers, Swati said, 'Let's go.'

'But this isn't the way home,' Ata said.

'Let's take a small walk first.'

'Good idea! You know, Chhotomashi, the flowers here are kind of thin. Oh, if only you could see the flowers we used to get back there, Chhotomashi!'

Taking Swati's hand, Tata said quickly, 'Do you love flowers a lot, Chhotomashi? Which one's your favourite?'

'I know!' Ata spoke up from the other side.

'Shut up, Didi! Which one, Chhotomashi?'

'Which one? . . . Which one? . . .' Swati stopped suddenly. Not just stopped talking, but also stopped walking. A sound was heard in the distance, a rumble.

'What is it?' asked Ata.

'Can you hear that?'

'That's only a train!' After a bit Ata continued, 'So what?'

'We can hear trains every day,' said Tata.

'You can even see them ever so often,' said Ata. 'What fun that Tollygunge Bridge is! Trams below, trains above! Shall we climb up to the tracks one day, Chhotomashi?'

Swati didn't speak, didn't move. She couldn't possibly move—or so she felt—till the sound died away. She clenched her fist tighter, thinking, the flowers are going to be spoilt. Unravelling itself gradually, the coiled thread of sound eventually disappeared. Swati realized that tears had sprung to her eyes—she allowed them to flow, it was dark by then.

'Let's go, Chhotomashi!'

Swati resumed walking, swiftly this time, but as soon as they were near the house—*that* house—her footsteps slowed down. The door was shut, the room, dark. Lights glowed upstairs, but downstairs it was shut, dark.

'Ow!' exclaimed Tata. 'Didi trod on me.'

'Do you *have* to walk at my heels?'

'Look at her, Chhotomashi,' Tata began in a quarrelsome tone, but stopped on seeing the expression on Swati's face. She resumed a little later on a different note. 'Tell me something, Chhotomashi.'

Swati looked at her.

'Isn't this where your Satyen-babu lives?' she whispered.

Swati nodded.

'Is he home now?'

'Why?' Ata laughed. 'Do you want to pay him a visit?'

For once Tata let her elder sister's response go without repartee. Craning her neck upwards, she whispered, 'He's probably home.'

'How silly,' Ata laughed. 'Some other people live upstairs. And what are you whispering for? As if it's some huge secret!' She laughed again.

'Shut up, Didi.' Tata raised her voice palpably.

'Let's go,' Ata urged her sister. 'No need to gape in the middle of the road.'

The sisters quarrelled all the way back home. The sound of their voices reached Swati's ears, but she grasped not a word. Suddenly she remembered: the flowers? In her hand. Shut, dark. What time was the train? Her hand perspired. Should I shift the flowers to my left hand?

Ata's and Tata's voices stopped suddenly. One of them tugged at Swati's sari.

'What?'

'Chhotomashi!' Tata whispered even more softly than before.

Swati realized they had arrived at their own house. And Satyen stood on the steps. Three knocks sounded on the front door.

'Are they deaf?' said Ata softly. 'I'd better go round the back...'

'Me too.' Tata ran after Ata. Satyen turned. Swati climbed the three steps.

'I'm here again,' said Satyen.

Swati said nothing.

'That is to say—I had to come.'

Still Swati said nothing. Satyen continued after a pause. 'I had to come. Couldn't keep myself from coming. Well . . . It's probably time I . . . All right then . . .'

'No,' said Swati. A few flowers escaped her clenched fist to fall near her feet. 'No,' she repeated. 'Don't go.' Someone opened the front door from within.

5

The short winter day ended quickly, evening fell. Standing at the door between the two rooms, Tarulata said, 'Time to get ready, Satu.'

Satyen smiled. Every time his aunt—the wife of his mother's dead brother—had addressed him as Satu today, the same small smile had appeared on his lips; a mocking smile, but it held something else too. It was amusing, really, to consider the fact there was no one today but this solitary aunt to address him by that nickname, to speak to him with the familiar *tui* for 'you'.

'What do you mean, ready?' Satyen said.

'Aren't you going to dress?' Kiran Bakshi looked at him sternly.

'Dress for what? And I *am* dressed.'

'This dress?' Kiran looked Satyen up and down, then said, 'Haven't you put shades on the lights yet?'

'What for?'

'That's my question too—what for! But those ARP boys in our neighbourhood keep threatening us. No, you know,' Kiran looked up once more, 'the light *can* be seen outside. I'd better shut the windows.'

'Oh, let it go.'

Kiran got up to shut the windows. Returning to his seat, he said, 'Apparently the Japanese have entered Burma already, seems Rangoon was bombed too last night?'

Kiran had ended with a question mark, so Satyen had to say, 'Must be.'

'I don't like it,' Kiran said succinctly. 'Burma's fallen.'

What if it has, Satyen thought. What did it matter, what was worth protecting in Burma? The only valuable thing there was Swati's sister Mahashweta and her family, but they were in Calcutta already—her husband Hemanga-babu too, they'd been very worried for him for a few days—but he'd arrived too, thank goodness. Why worry about Burma any more?

Akhil came in from the other room and placed a new silk *panjabi* on the chair next to Satyen's. 'What?' said Satyen, glancing at it.

'Ma asked you to put this on,' smiled Akhil. His teeth were crooked, his face angular, but—Satyen mused—his eyes are very lively, I hadn't noticed earlier. This same Akhil had come to him one day to borrow ten rupees—and how different he looked today. Looking at him for a few minutes, he said, 'That's quite a hairstyle, Akhil.'

Touching his hair lightly, Akhil tilted his head sideways

in embarrassment. 'Have you clipped your nails, Satyen?' asked Kiran.

About to examine his fingernails, Satyen noticed the yellow thread on his right wrist. Apparently it was mandatory.

A little later Nikhil said, 'I'm wondering what you'll look like in a silk wedding dhoti.'

'What do you mean silk wedding dhoti?'

'Don't you know about the groom's wedding attire?'

'You mean all those practices are still followed?'

Kiran kept smiling, as though wreaking fitting revenge on Satyen. Speaking slowly, he said, 'Imagine: people all around you, strangers, women—all eyes on you—and you in their midst. Two people will hold up a large sheet and wrap it around you, and you will change your dhoti in that position while maintaining as much of your dignity as you can. The dhoti is usually a little short, doesn't quite cover your legs entirely, and what they give you for the rest of you—of course, you're quite slim, you'll pretty much be able to cover your body.'

'Impossible!' exclaimed Satyen.

'You can say what you like; but you can't get married in cotton.'

'Can't?' Satyen looked around with terrified eyes. He grabbed the silk *panjabi*, saying, 'Right! I'll just put this on, that'll do.'

'You're not allowed anything like a *panjabi* or shirt,' said Kiran relentlessly.

'Are you mad! Lucky I had this, and Mamima also was clever enough to . . .' Satyen changed in a flash, put his handkerchief in his pocket and said, 'So unnecessary—going to all this trouble! I kept telling them we should just call the registrar and be done with it, they refused to listen.'

'Why should they?' Kiran smiled. 'What if you then say one fine day, "All right! You're on your own now. I'm done!" What then?'

It took Satyen some time to understand. But when he did, he answered, 'That's exactly why! If there's no way to leave, then what value does not leaving have?'

'There's always a way,' Kiran said lightly, 'or what are we lawyers here for?'

Satyen didn't reply. He remembered saying the same thing to Swati; not once, not even twice, but several times. Swati had at first pretended not to have heard, and then frowned, saying, 'What . . .!' and had finally said, her eyes blazing, 'Don't talk of this ever again.'

'Why?'

'Isn't it obvious? Are you ever going to leave me?'

'No. And that's why I don't want compulsion without choice.'

'Maybe you don't, but I do.'

'You want compulsion? You don't want a choice?'

'No. I don't want the choice of leaving you.'

'Why?' Satyen had asked even after this. 'Don't you have enough faith in yourself?'

'If I didn't I would have been afraid of a formal ceremony the way you are!' Swati had thrown him a single glance after saying this, the glance of a queen. Satyen had felt inferior for a moment.

Nikhil came inside, dressed in a warm brown shirt, holding a folded copy of the one-paisa evening newspaper. Satyen liked the sight of that shirt, it was familiar, he had seen his uncle wear it often, and the boy looked like his father too . . . Nikhil had turned out well.

'Any important news?' asked Kiran.

'Nothing at all. Just the morning news all over again.' Nikhil tossed the newspaper on the desk.

Kiran picked it up and glanced at it. 'Fifteen thousand people in three days . . .'

'Probably more,' said Nikhil. 'You can't get on the trains any more, the Biharis are running away on foot . . .'

'You can't blame them. Even the gentry...' Kiran didn't finish, thinking of his father-in-law. He had already rented a house in Rampurhat—away from Calcutta—he was planning to send all the women there—apparently Anita would have to go too. Unfair obstinacy!

'Yes, no one's talking of anything else,' Nikhil smiled. 'I just heard someone say...'

'Really, I wonder what will happen!' Kiran turned to Satyen. 'What do you think?"

'What can happen!' Satyen smiled amiably. 'Nikhil, were you over there just now?'

'Yes. They're coming to fetch you.'

Satyen felt like laughing. I suppose I won't be able to go on my own unless they fetch me. Ridiculous customs! Swati's sisters had been shooing him away for quite some time now— no need to meet, only at the wedding now! And then yesterday the second sister—or was it the third—Saraswati was the third sister, wasn't she?—told him very seriously, Satyen, you mustn't come tomorrow, is that clear? And that was why the day had been blurred since morning; it was the first day in the past two months that he hadn't met Swati even once between morning and evening.

Tarulata entered with a traditional cane tray, putting it on the floor and laying out a low wooden stool adorned with patterns in white specially painted for the occasion. 'Come, Satu,' she called.

'Now what?' Satyen frowned.

'Come along. Have to sit here.'

'All this nonsense.'

'Won't work today,' Kiran said. 'You'll have to do whatever they tell you to do.'

That *is* what I'm doing, thought Satyen, the I in me is all but gone. There had already been one round of it in the morning— his aunt had simply refused to relent—a priest arrived, a man with a tail of hair on his tonsured head, packets made with banana leaves, a porridge of rice and banana—uff!—two hours of incomprehensible muttering—they actually asked him his great-grandmother's name!—as if anyone had ever been told their great-grandmother's name!—what a farce! But on the other side of this farce lay reality; all these lies would shed their layers and eventually arrive at the truth. Would he have known that truth if he had gone off to Ranchi two months ago on that foggy evening? All the sounds in the world had stopped then, when Swati had talked to him on the veranda steps, so had he; it had felt as though they had said everything in their hearts, everything in their lives; it had felt as though even after a lifetime of talking they wouldn't be done, but they were, they didn't talk any more, unless they began over again they wouldn't talk any more. This was that beginning.

'What are you waiting for?' Kiran chivvied him. 'Get up.'

Satyen rose, sat on the low wooden platform with motifs painted on it. A lamp burnt on the tray, blades of grass and grains of rice and similar things were arrayed on it. His aunt squatted before him, said something soundlessly with her hand on his head, then put a drop of sandalwood paste on his forehead with the little finger of her left hand.

'Me too . . .' Kiran came forward and stooped.

'No . . .' Satyen tried to block Kiran with both his hands.

'Forget it!' Kiran used his bulbous fingers to decorate Satyen's forehead with palpable drops of the paste. 'This is the only day of your life you're going to get married!' Stepping back, he said, 'Very nice.'

Tarulata put the grass blades and rice grains on his head, raised the tray to touch his forehead, the lamp still burning on it, then suddenly took his right hand and nipped his little finger. Satyen rose hurriedly.

'You've forgotten something,' said Kiran, referring to the ritual touching of the feet with the hands.

'Never mind,' said Tarulata, putting away the tray and the low platform.

'Such a sticky mess,' Satyen made to wipe the sandalwood paste marks off his forehead.

'No, don't. Leave them be—they can hardly be seen. Here you are reacting this way, and how my aunts had chastised me.' Kiran smiled at Tarulata.

'Our boy objects to everything—' Tarulata arranged the chairs in the room neatly—'tidy up the bed, will you, Nikhil.'

'Are you sure no one can see?' Satyen asked worriedly.

'What if they do. This is nothing compared to the sight when they put the groom's *topor* on your head. What a clown they make of you then!' Kiran laughed in delight.

Surveying the room by walking around it, Tarulata said, 'Nikhil, can you check where Mahesh has disappeared. He only went to get the paan.'

'I'll check,' Akhil ran out.

'Why isn't anyone else here yet?' Kiran looked in the direction of the road. Not getting a reply, he said, 'Aren't any of your other friends coming?'

'Do you suppose he's invited anyone? He has an uncle in Calcutta—his father's first cousin, no less—I begged and pleaded with Satu to inform him—he didn't bother! How much can I do on my own!' Tugging twice at the already impeccably laid out bedspread, she went out.

How much can I do alone! Satyen had had to hear this several times already! But she could do quite a lot—she had tidied up that desk alone several times during the day—not that there was really anything to tidy up! Satyen looked round the room, everything looked neat and clean, perfectly arranged—why, there wasn't even a single book leaning against another on the shelves. He suddenly felt as though he were somewhere else—and it wasn't untrue either, it wasn't his own room any more. He had had to bring his aunt over two days earlier;

and immediately, a different world dawned in this room of his. People, visits, people. And when empty, shockingly empty. He had been to Swati's empty home this afternoon—no one was there—he was actually a little surprised not to find her at home. He had spent some time stretched out on Dalim's bed.

'Really? You haven't asked anyone? Not even your colleagues from college? Your writer friends? . . . No one? . . . Wonderful!'

Satyen only smiled vaguely in response to Kiran's noises.

'This isn't right. If I'd known I would have asked a few of them myself—definitely Bhabesh Chanda and Phani Bhattacharya.'

'I can see you're feeling a bit lonely,' said Satyen.

'Not because of that. That you've asked me alone and no one else is a matter of pride for me, after all.' Kiran gave Satyen a different kind of look.

Satyen looked away in embarrassment. They'd met at the restaurant purely by accident. Just as well, for he had at least managed to ask one person to come. And Kiran was quite nice, he thought—yes, rather nice, actually much nicer than the people I used to spend my time with back then. As a student he hadn't thought highly of Kiran, had even joined others in making fun of him, recalling all of this Satyen felt remorseful now.

'They're coming, Satu-da!' Akhil came running. 'Hu-u-u-ge car!' He raced out again.

There was a little silence. Satyen saw that Nikhil stood by the door looking suitably solemn, his aunt behind Nikhil, even as Kiran sat up straight. How strangely the day had passed! An entire day through which he did nothing, agonized over nothing, after all these days of turmoil he had no sensation today, he was able to think of Swati without a tremor in his heart. Emotion had deserted him since this morning, expectation had died, only his existence floated along the surface of the currents of time. All this time it had been just their world, exclusively for the two of them; now it belonged to others, to everyone, to no one—now it was time for announcements, axioms, arrangements. All lies!

'Well?' A hand was placed on his shoulder, gently.

Raising his face, Satyen saw the pleasant-faced Arun. A little dark in complexion—the correct complexion for men—his unkempt black hair greying at the temples, and the thick black frame of his glasses over that smoky colour suited him rather well. Satyen had liked him at first sight—only at sight, and then more after talking to him—a little shy, he talked a little vaguely, it sounded sweet when he switched from the formal *aapni* to the informal *tumi*.

Looking for a moment into Arun's eyes, dilated behind his glasses, Satyen said, 'Kiran, this . . . this is Arun-babu, and . . .'

Kiran smiled. 'That's enough for me. Please, take a seat,' he said, being polite on Satyen's behalf.

Arun took the chair next to Satyen's. 'How's our girl?' asked Tarulata, coming closer.

'You know how it is!' Raising his fingers to the corners of his eyes, Arun traced them down his face.

'She's crying?'

'That's all I've seen her do ever since I came.'

'Even though she's chosen her own husband?'

'That's what I tried to tell her! But it's no good—she's crying herself to distraction.' For a moment Arun's voice sounded different, his smiling expression disappeared too.

Putting his feet up on the cot, Hemanga said in his high-pitched voice, 'I hope you're listening, Satyen, you have to make up for all those tears!'

'It's because she knows he will that she's crying so much!' Kiran answered immediately, representing the groom's side.

Satyen had smiled faintly at Hemanga's banter; he did the same in response to Kiran's repartee. It was neither a willing smile nor a reluctant one, it was one of compulsion; it had become second nature for now. He had no choice, no powers, he was mired in this; events unfolded around him, but he was neither responsible for them, nor able to prevent them, he could only watch and listen, and not prevent himself from smiling in this manner from time to time. He wasn't listening closely now; his aunt's movements looked like a scene in which he had no role to play; she was laying out plates laden with sweets before each of the guests, Mahesh brought in several glasses of water on a tray—how well groomed he looked today—while Akhil arrived with a bowl of paan for everyone.

His aunt paused in front of Kiran. 'Have some.'

'I already have.'

'You must have one more before you leave. Dalim, some more . . .'

'Shall I spill the beans, Dalim?' Arun glanced at him sideways.

Standing at a distance, Dalim reddened.

'He has refused to address you as Meshomashai, he wants to call you Satyen-da . . . Dalim has been quarrelling with his mother every single day over this.'

Satyen shuddered at 'Meshomashai', and, importing a degree of animation to his red face, Dalim said, 'Meshomashai is so awful . . . it's meant for old people.'

'Right you are, Dalim!' exclaimed Hemanga. 'Even we weren't born as uncles, you know!' He touched the small bald patch—not all that small—on his head.

At this, Satyen suddenly felt very fond of Hemanga. Yes—he was very nice too, grave in appearance, a man of few words, but witty when he did speak. And Dalim—the poor fellow was beetroot red—how sweet he looked!

Glancing at Tarulata, Hemanga said solemnly, 'Uncle to eleven children overnight.'

Satyen winced, as though pricked by a pin, and Tarulata answered equally gravely, 'He's lucky to be part of a family with all of you in it—of course, you're getting a jewel too—another of these, Dalim?'

Dalim looked at Nikhil with assent written on his face. 'Paan,' said Nikhil, indicating his cheek.

'Right, paan it is!' Dalim said, in a manner that suggested substituting a sweet with a paan was a new and amazing idea; he popped one into his mouth.

Mahesh took the plates and glasses away, Akhil patted his hair into place with his left hand, Dalim's lower lip acquired a faint tinge of red. Tarulata appeared before Satyen with a garland on a plate. 'Here, Satu!'

'What?'

'Put it on.'

'A garland?' Satyen retreated, arms upraised. 'No, never, I simply cannot.'

'What do you mean cannot? You can't have a wedding without a garland. Come on now . . .' Satyen fidgeted fruitlessly, Kiran Bakshi forced the garland on him, a thick, white, fragrant garland.

'That looks nice,' Arun said. 'You must take one too.'

'Me? All right!' Kiran smiled, picked up a small garland, and, about to wrap it round his wrist, coiled it instead and put it carefully in his pocket, beneath the handkerchief. He'd give it to Anita at night.

Satyen had taken the opportunity to remove the garland, Kiran jumped down his throat in protest. 'What kind of childishness is this! Keep it on!' Abashed by this strong reprimand, Satyen looked suitably chastised and put it back on. The plate held more garlands; Akhil took one, Nikhil took one for himself and gave one to Dalim too. Suddenly the room filled with the scent of the flowers, and everyone remained silent to breathe in this fragrance deeply.

Then, popping a clove into his mouth, Hemanga said, 'Well, then . . .'

'Yes, enough talk. Let's go, Satyen.' Arun rose, clutching the end of his dhoti.

Dalim came up to them quickly. 'Should I get a taxi?'

Looking around briefly, Hemanga said, 'Do we need one?'

What do we need the car for either? Satyen reflected. It was easy enough to walk across. But even if the wedding had been at Rajen-babu's house they would probably have had to take a car.

'Can you believe it.' Kiran adjusted the shawl on his shoulder and stood up. 'He hasn't asked any of his friends—kept it from every single one of them. Imagine getting married with just a single friend in tow!'

'Satyen cannot think beyond a single person these days,' Arun said softly, and Kiran laughed uproariously at this. Releasing a thin stream of chuckles at the end, he said, 'Very well . . . We'll get our revenge later.'

Arun picked up Satyen's shawl from the shoulder and put it on his shoulder. Satyen looked back, reddened a bit. Hemanga's high-pitched voice was heard, 'With your permission then.'

Tarulata looked at Satyen without talking. Satyen took a few steps, then stopped suddenly, saying, 'Aren't you coming, Mamima?' Seeing the smile on the corner of her lips, he said, 'Oh, you're not supposed to?'

'Silly custom!' Arun exclaimed. 'You must come!'

The smile spread wider on Tarulata's lips. 'I'll just welcome the bride and bring her home,' she said.

Behind Satyen, Kiran asked surreptitiously, 'Are you planning to stay on here?'

'Let's see.'

'Plenty of flats available in our part of town. I can find one for you.'

New, thought Satyen, all this is new. Everyone was thinking of him, everyone wanted the best for him, everyone wanted to be useful to him. There she was, his aunt, the loveliness of sorrow on her face, she had worked so hard all by herself since she came, and Nikhil had been so busy too—he really had been wrong to have ignored them all these days—he would visit them regularly from now on—for sure!

'Then may we go now?' Hemanga spoke to Tarulata as though he were seeking permission.

Satyen's gaze shifted. They were standing in a small circle—he had never seen so many people in this room. His eyes touched on each one's face—everyone was pleased, happy, even his aunt's face radiated nothing but happiness now—what was everyone so happy about? Nothing, everyone was nice, so everyone was happy. He spotted Mahesh as he left—he stood in a corner, Satyen remembered scolding him once for being late getting him his tea, he felt a brief stab of remorse.

Everyone went outside. Tarulata stood near the door, shielded her mouth with her hands and ululated. Long out of practice, she couldn't do it the first time, but the next time, it came out loud and clear, two young women appeared in the upstairs balcony, a plump housewife behind them, after a quick look the elder of the two went into the room to get dressed—they were going to the wedding too.

The black car had almost blended into the darkness in the narrow lane; now a light went on within, the chauffeur reached out to open the door.

'What a big car,' said Satyen from the steps.

'Bijon has a friend—Majumdar,' behind him, Arun responded. 'It's his car. Brand new.'

Satyen didn't know Majumdar, hadn't even heard of him before; but as soon as he was told he realized this Mr Majumdar was very nice too—maybe he had offered his car even at the cost of personal inconvenience. He was a little surprised—so much decency in the world and he had no idea!

'Take the taxi, Dalim,' said Hemanga.

'I'll come with you,' said Nikhil.

The rest fitted themselves into Majumdar's car. The light went out. Akhil and Kiran sat on either side of Satyen, Arun next to Kiran, and between Akhil and Satyen lay the *topor*. The shiny foil on that awful thing with tassels flashed at him.

This too? . . . The car set off, and at that precise moment, Satyen forgot everything else and had just one thought: then it was real? All of it real?

Tarulata's figure in the lit-up doorway disappeared, behind them lay Satyen's book-wormed ground-floor room, the upstairs balcony emptied out. The car negotiated the lane slowly; Arun—his eyes held a trace of the brightness of Delhi's Connaught Circus—said when they reached Russa Road, 'How dark it is here!'

Hemanga—who was seated next to the chauffeur—turned back to say, 'The blackout has spoilt everything. Imagine a wedding without lights!'

'But what a lovely house! How did you ever get hold of it?'

'I don't think it's difficult getting a house in Calcutta right now.'

'That's true,' Kiran exclaimed. 'Everyone's running away! Especially the servants.'

In the taxi behind them Nikhil tapped Dalim on his shoulder. 'Want one?'

'Cigarette?' Dalim's eyes widened. 'You smoke?'

'When I can get one,' Nikhil smiled. 'Try one? . . .'

'Oh no,' Dalim moved away, feeling his mother's eyes on him.

'State Express! 555!' Nikhil caressed the cigarette with a finger.

'Really? They won't be back in Calcutta till the war ends?' Arun laughed loudly. 'How convenient, a perfect venue for the wedding, and a wonderful house for you as soon as you arrived from Rangoon.'

'You're coming from Rangoon?' Kiran straightened his back. 'When did you arrive? What's the news from Burma?'

'How will he know,' answered Arun. 'He boarded his ship the very next day after Pearl Harbor!'

'Oh!' Kiran said, partly admiring, partly disappointed. He leaned back again in the comfort of the cushioned seat.

In the dark, Nikhil's face looked reddish in the glow of the matchstick; Dalim watched, fear, respect and envy in his eyes. Emitting smoke through pursed lips, Nikhil said, 'Bijon-babu is very generous. A cigarette whenever you meet him!'

Arun said, 'Luckily the rest of them had come away earlier! You would have been in trouble if you'd had to bring all of them with you.'

'Not all that much.' For a moment Hemanga remembered his house of fourteen years in Rangoon, a house full of furniture, curios, his local servant Chonchu, who had been with him since childhood. 'I hadn't even imagined this trip would mean a permanent move.'

'Just as well! But for something like this, you'd never have left Burma. Mahashweta is very pleased.'

'But not Saraswati.'

Arun knew what he was hinting at. 'Let the goddesses say what they will, I won't let go of the opportunity.'

'You'll go to war?'

'Or else I'll have to spend the rest of my life as Second Surgeon at Irwin Hospital.'

Satyen was a little surprised that a man as fine as Arun-babu wanted to leave his wife behind and go off. Surely he must be joking—he wouldn't really go. He was about to say something, but the car took a turn; they had arrived.

They stopped in front of a house built at an angle to the road, at the point where Southern Avenue branched out at an acute angle from Russa Road. Satyen had noticed the house when he had passed this way, it looked beautiful in the late afternoon light; but—he looked out through the thick windows of the car while Nikhil threw the glowing, only slightly smoked State Express out the window before getting out of the taxi; what a waste! If he'd known they'd be here so soon he wouldn't have lit up—but now the house looked completely different, the roof was covered with a canopy, you could make out the crowd even from the car, multicoloured saris leaning over the balcony railings upstairs, unknown people on the stairs—it was a different world. Another, unfamiliar, strange world, belonging to others, belonging to everyone else . . . Unreal, this wasn't true, it would vanish in an instant, and then he would be back to his own world—his own newly discovered world, though he no longer remembered when it wasn't his.

Satyen got out of the car. Inside the house, music rang out loudly, conch shells rang out sharply.

Mahashweta opened her eyes, sat up. She'd gone to bed only after two in the morning, and then had been up again at dawn for the first ceremony of the wedding; all day she had been feeling faint, and from the afternoon onwards her head . . . how effectively she'd managed to ruin her health! Even amidst all the commotion she had forced herself to lie down with the lights out, so that she didn't get a headache which would spoil everything, a nap now would . . . yes, of course. She would be fine, wouldn't miss out on anything, wouldn't have to give up a single drop of the wedding excitement. How long, how long it had been since she had experienced a life such as this! Getting off the bed, she switched on the light; it flashed in the two mirrors of the almirah and the dressing table which were placed opposite each other, the fresh varnish on the oily frame of the double-bed glistened. Mahashweta enjoyed the sensations, enjoyed the sharp tang of the varnish, the smell of new, a new life—not just for those who would spend the night in this room, but hers too, yes, hers too.

Mahashweta shut the door. Undraping the upper half of her sari, she put cream on her face and neck, then slowly dabbed some pink powder on herself.

There was a knock on the door.

'Who's there?'

'Me. Saraswati.'

Trailing the end of her sari on the floor, Mahashweta opened the door, concealing herself behind it. As soon as Saraswati entered she shut the door again.

'How long it's taking you to dress!'

'Nearly done.' With lean fingers, Mahashweta repaired whatever little damage had been done to her hair by the nap, stroked her hair-bun twice. 'You still have plenty of hair,' said Saraswati.

Which means, thought Mahashweta, that's all that's left, nothing else is. And not much by way of hair either—long, but as thin as wire, and absolutely straight. She glanced for an instant at the thick curly mop on her sister, smiled drily and said, 'Hair! It's one long agony—I go mad putting it up and then letting it loose!'

Saraswati smiled from the corners of her lips.

'No—really!' Shedding the expensive silk sari she was dressed in, Mahashweta stood for a minute in her imported sleeveless chemise and milk-white satin petticoat. Looking at her eyes, Saraswati said, 'Were you asleep?'

'No,' Mahashweta denied it. She inserted her pale, reedy arms into a jet-black blouse, loosened the waist of the petticoat to tuck in the trailing ends of the blouse, then said as she tightened it again at the waist, 'I was resting a bit. The groom's arrived, hasn't he?'

'Yes, let's go. How's the headache?'

'I didn't get one after all,' said Mahashweta happily. From the bed she picked up the sari that she had bought a few days ago after doing the rounds of dozens of shops.

Scanning the end of the cream-coloured silk sari from Benares, made with real silver, Saraswati said, 'You must get yourself treated properly once all this is done. There's a very good new medicine for anaemia.'

'What's the use!' Mahashweta put on her sari with great

care. 'Having so many children takes a heavy toll on women!' She finished dressing, draping the glittering end of the sari over her shoulder.

'That's rubbish!' Saraswati quoted Dr Arun's current viewpoint.

'Not that you've demonstrated much there, my dear.' Mahashweta fixed a choker with pearls the size of turtle eggs on her throat. 'All quiet after two.'

'As if you have a lot more? Just four!' Saraswati offered a congratulatory smile.

'Five, Saraswati,' Mahashweta answered drily, and attached pearl danglers to her ears.

Saraswati's expression changed. It was true she always forgot that Mahashweta's first child, a daughter, had died at the age of eight months. To say something quickly, she said, 'Bordi has five too,' and instantly realized this was a mistake as well.

And yet, Mahashweta mused, how lovely Shweta still looked. People looked old in the white widow's garb, but when she and I stand next to each other, it's I who looks like the elder sister. Why did it have to be like this for me? It wasn't this way for Shweta, it wasn't this way for many people. Why don't I have enough blood, enough flesh on me—I never shall either. Tugging at the part of her sari covering her sagging breasts, she said, 'It's so painful to carry each of these children inside you, give birth to them, bring them up! They suck everything out of you!' She said all this looking into the mirror, in a low voice, as though addressing her own pale, far too pale, face. Then she uncorked a bottle of perfume, dabbed it on her shoulders, breasts, neck.

'Smells lovely—give me some,' Saraswati tried to change the subject.

Handing the bottle to her, Mahashweta said, 'Saswati has managed well. Isn't it four years since she got married? How has she done it?'

Saraswati relaxed. With a covert smile she said, 'It's time for her to have one now. She's getting fat.'

Mahashweta looked enviously at Saraswati's mostly slender, ever-so-slightly thick figure, at her firm, slightly full breasts, at the thin fold on her stomach. But then Saraswati had held the winning hand from the beginning; Arun had been in *her* future. Suddenly she said, 'I heard Arun's going off to the front? Really?'

'I don't know.'

'You don't know?' Mahashweta came away from the mirror. 'Tell him not to.'

'Why don't you try talking to him,' Saraswati said grimly.

Mahashweta smiled at her sister, but spoke sadly. 'Men. All they're concerned with is their own work and career.'

'That's fine. Am I holding him back—*can* you ever hold anyone back, for that matter!'

This last statement pleased Mahashweta somewhere at the back of her mind. But with an innocent expression she said, 'You're wrong there. Arun didn't accept a government post only because you wouldn't like living in a small town, right?'

'That was then! . . . And now!' Saraswati glanced into the long mirror set in the almirah door, and behind her Mahashweta observed in the mirror her younger sister's coral necklace, the glittering earrings under the cowl over her head, her brocade blouse, her sari of French silk. Then she looked at her own reflection once more, and now Saraswati looked at Mahashweta in the mirror. Suddenly they exchanged looks, there was a quick knock on the door.

Saraswati opened the door. Saswati entered, worried and sombre, slightly out of breath. 'Ni-i-i-i-ce! A lovely chat behind closed doors!'

'What are we needed for?' Mahashweta smiled.

'Get moving! We haven't even begun to dress Swati, and Satyen is sitting in a room full of unknown people looking utterly miserable!'

'Let him.'

'What were you doing?' asked Saraswati.

'Me? You think I have a moment to spare! I must have gone up and down the stairs at least ten times in the past thirty minutes alone.' The satisfaction in Saswati's voice was palpable. 'I'm just going to catch my breath.' Looking around, she said, 'Swati's furniture is lovely. Hemanga-da knows his business!'

'Oh yes . . . He knows his timber, his iron, his cement . . . very well,' said Mahashweta.

'What's going to happen to all your things in Rangoon?' asked Saswati.

'What do you suppose? The Japanese will chop them up for firewood.'

'How can you say that? Doesn't it hurt?'

'Not at all.' Why should it hurt? They had managed to flee Burma: what more could they ask for? Furniture, utensils, radios, gramophones, cars—you could get all those things again; but would she ever get back those years of her life? Wasted—the best time of her life had been wasted in Burma, in exile; without joy, without company, without a life; it had passed only in the satisfaction from the expansion of her husband's business enterprise, only in giving birth to and bringing up children. How could she feel any pain for the house in which her health and youth had been squandered over fourteen years!

'The dressing table's lovely.' Saswati looked at it once more.

'So you don't like your own any more?' said Saraswati.

'No, it's not that.' Saswati sounded casual. 'Let me go find out what's going on.'

Looking at Saswati's retreating back, Saraswati said, 'She's getting worked up needlessly. With Bordi around nothing will remain incomplete!'

'Let's go see Satyen,' said Mahashweta, moving towards the door.

Saraswati and Mahashweta left the room. The passage was crowded, a fresh set of people came up the staircase. The sisters stepped aside, after the group had gone past Saraswati asked, 'Who were they?'

'If I knew them so would you,' answered Mahashweta, climbing downstairs.

'You've been here a month, I came just the other day.'

'Must be neighbours. Yes, I think I've seen that fat woman before.'

'Baba, really! Just look at the number of people he's asked.'

'Biju's worse. Swati's getting married—no one must be left out. It was he who remembered Nepal-pishemoshai from Santragachhi.'

'That decrepit old fool is still alive!' Saraswati smiled.

On the lowest step, a young woman with hexagonal glasses stopped on seeing them. 'Are you Swati's sisters?'

They accepted this identity with smiles.

'Are you Mahashweta?'

Arching her eyebrows a little, Saraswati said, 'This is Mahashweta.'

'Then you must be Saraswati,' the woman offered a dazzling smile. 'I've heard so much about all of you from Bijon-da. I'm Urmila, Prabir Majumdar is my uncle. We've just arrived.'

Saraswati sprouted a skilful smile. 'All right, why don't you go upstairs. Swati's friends are all over there.'

'Very smart girl,' said Mahashweta.

'Very.' Saraswati went towards the front room, two people passed them, carrying a basket piled high with earthen cups. 'This Majumdar seems to be a very special friend of Biju's.'

'And her lips—she's made them blood-red!'

'It's still rare in Calcutta; almost all women use lipstick these days in Delhi.'

Six or seven little girls ran towards the staircase, giggling.

'Are you all right with that?'

'As if it makes a difference. Even Geeti has started!'

'. . . Hong Kong!' A robust voice was heard as soon as they neared the door to the front room.

'Indefatigable—our Harit Nandy,' said Saraswati. 'All roads lead to the bomb.'

The sisters came to a halt near the door.

'After evacuating Hong Kong the English are now . . .' said Harit.

'Evacuate! Fled, you mean! For fear of the devil!' This came from a powerfully built man, dressed in an off-white flannel *panjabi*–churidar ensemble, his parted hair seemingly plastered to his scalp with glue.

Several people laughed. Entering, Saraswati said, 'So Nandy's finally found the time to come?' Many of the people looked up when she spoke.

So did Satyen. It wasn't an uninviting spectacle—he had concluded as soon as he had entered—the pile of shoes at the door, the yellow carpet on the white sheet, and a small red one at one end, with a deep red silk bolster on it, and two even redder, almost black, bouquets of roses. He was about to sit with the rest, but no—Arun and the rest piloted him to that kingdom of red, disappearing after depositing him on the double-layered carpet. He almost choked on the heady fragrances, there were plump bunches of roses, stalks of rajanigandha—so many of them!—but anyway, he breathed a sigh of relief at being able to take off his garland. Nikhil and Akhil sat stiffly and silently, Kiran was silent too—and everything was new—he only caught a quick glimpse of Saswati—more guests were coming; lemonade, tea, plates piled with paan and cigarettes—smoke curling above dark heads, conversation, laughter, noise and movement outside— little girls peeping in at all three doors—thank goodness Harit had just arrived. They were discussing the war, he listened for a bit—they were right, if there was an attack people would be in trouble—if only he could lean back against a wall his back would feel better—ah, there they were!

Satyen set his eyes on Mahashweta first. Extraordinarily thin, oddly fair, virtually yellow—a blue vein standing out clearly on her cheek—her skin and sari had almost merged, and a silvery fabric glittered as it cascaded on to her black blouse. Then at Saraswati: she stood erect, smiling eyes, smiling mouth, the head set beautifully on her shoulders, dressed in a blue sari—peacock blue—and a blouse the colour of hyacinth. Then he looked at both of them together.

'Is everything all right? Do you need anything?' asked Saraswati.

Realizing the questions were meant for him, Satyen said, 'Can't these bouquets be removed?'

'Don't you like flowers?' asked Mahashweta.

'Flowers are very nice, but a bouquet on either side . . .'

'Leave them be, they're a lovely sight.'

'All right, I'll take them away,' said someone in a deep, hoarse voice behind him.

Satyen turned around. 'Bijon-babu! . . . Have you caught a cold?'

'Hah!' Bijon smiled, coughed twice, then bent towards the flower vases.

'Biju!' Mahashweta exclaimed, 'Leave them be!'

'Then may I shift a bit?' Satyen appealed to her.

'Oh, please don't,' said the powerfully built man in the off-white outfit. 'You're a lucky man—we want to gaze upon you!'

'Here you are—make yourself comfortable,' Biju arranged the bolster for Satyen to lean back on it.

'No, not that, please.' Satyen moved away in terror.

'Biju's looking terrible,' said Mahashweta in a low voice. 'He's been working very hard!'

'And his tears. That's the trouble with him, he keeps crying!'

'And he insisted on fasting too!'

'Really, this Biju . . .' Saraswati tried to smile, but what came out was a small sigh, and Mahashweta sighed too along with her.

'Mejdi, Shejdi, this is Prabir Majumdar.' The man in the off-white outfit stood up on the yellow carpet.

'This is Satyen-babu's friend,' Bijon indicated Kiran, 'these are Akhil and Nikhil-babu . . . And these . . .'

'We're all family!' Someone spoke up from the back, and the rest—most of them distant relatives—declared their assent with low murmurs.

'Was that your car?' Satyen said.

'Honoured,' said Majumdar, sitting down again, crossing his plump legs.

'What do you do with such a big car?'

'Nothing. I use a small car.'

'How many cars do you own?' asked Kiran.

Majumdar didn't answer, only smiled, displaying large teeth.

Patting his knee, Harit said, 'Laugh while you can, do you know what the Japanese have in store for us?'

'Has Hong Kong really fallen?' asked a sturdy man of advanced years, with a formidable white moustache, dressed in a warm coat.

'I heard it just a few minutes ago on Radio Saigon. They've almost reached Tavoy too! No escape!' Announcing this catastrophic news in a rather pleased voice, Harit looked round at everyone, becoming even more pleased at spotting fear on some faces.

'Will they really bomb Calcutta?' someone asked from a distance in a rheumy voice.

'Do you suppose Bengalis will wake up before that? But the point is . . .'

Nikhil cocked his ears to listen to the rest, but Saraswati said at once, 'Not now. There'll be plenty of time for all this.'

Harit turned to look at her immediately, snorted with laughter.

'Ma . . .' a small sound rose behind Mahashweta.

Mahashweta seemed to be surprised afresh when she caught sight of Iru. Who could tell she was just twelve—how much older she looked this evening in that scarlet crepe sari. There's Geeti—just two months younger, but the gap looks more like two years; and the fourteen-year-old Ata looks about the same age as Iru. Mahashweta glanced at all three once more; suddenly narrowing her eyes, she said, 'Have you girls used lipstick?'

Saraswati turned as well.

'The bell's tolling for us,' Harit informed Majumdar softly. 'The day the *Prince of Wales* and the *Repulse* were sunk, it was obvious that . . .'

Saraswati turned her eyes from Mahashweta towards Majumdar and shook her head violently. And in the process of taking another look at the three scarlet–green–orange girls he didn't hear a word of what Harit said.

Iru looked at Ata, Ata at Geeti, all three smiled with blossomed lips. 'Now, Ma?' Iru said, pointing at the notebook in her hand.

'All right.'

'You tell him, Ma.'

'They want to tell you something, Satyen,' said Mahashweta.

'Thailand, Malay and the Philippines in a week . . .' Now Nikhil made up his mind and edged closer to Harit.

Satyen saw three girls coming towards him, all three about the same height, not children, not adults, weightless, three colourful feathers floating in the breeze, scarlet, orange-red, green.

'Please write something in my notebook,' said Iru.

'Now?' Leafing through the yellow–white–pink pages of the notebook with the violet covers, Satyen said, 'But there's nothing in here.'

'There's one,' said Geeti. Bubbles of laughter rose in the other two. 'Near the beginning . . .'

Craning his neck over Satyen's shoulder, Akhil saw written on the white page at which the notebook was open, 'Swati Mitra', and then, below that in smaller letters, 'Swati Roy'.

As soon as Satyen looked at it all three spilled over with giggles. What fun it had been getting Chhotomashi to write this.

Satyen looked at the name—the names—for a while. 'Please write on the same page,' said Iru, handing him a slim, lustrous, black pen. 'No—on the same page.'

Satyen wrote his name.

'Put the date.'

Pen in hand, Satyen looked at the picture, a multicoloured picture of three waiting girls.

Harit had stopped talking to observe the proceedings benevolently, he prompted quickly, 'Fifteenth of December . . .'

'No, in our style,' Kiran intervened. 'Twenty-ninth of Aghran.'

'No need to tell him' Majumdar raised his hand. 'He's memorized both.'

'Got them by heart, you mean.' Kiran laughed all by himself.

Taking the notebook back, Iru said, 'Let's go.' Laughter flashed in three pairs of eyes: what fun—they'd show everyone now! Iru collided with her father as she ran off—no, Swati first.

'They're saying Tokyo by Christmas . . .' Harit lowered his voice again.

Majumdar spotted a bald head by the door.

The man said something to the sister in the black velvet blouse. Was he the husband? . . . Must be, or else wouldn't his expression have changed even slightly when talking to her? The sister in the black blouse said something to the sister in the red necklace: both turned, left.

Harit regained his independence. Turning to Satyen, he said, 'Well timed, this wedding. Just as the shelling is about to begin!'

Making some quick calculations, Kiran said, 'If we'd finished it off even by early November, none of this . . .'

'The delay was on my account,' said Hemanga, advancing to the yellow carpet.

'Indeed—you had them quite rattled here!' Harit spoke as though 'their' worries were quite meaningless.

Not spotting Bijon anywhere, Majumdar started the conversation himself. 'So you've just come from Burma?'

'Give us some news of Burma.' Kiran jiggled his knee, and Nikhil looked at Hemanga for an answer.

Hemanga smiled thinly. 'You're Mr Majumdar? We must have a chat soon.'

Majumdar bowed his head, as though gratified, then raised his face to smile broadly. Through a mutual glance, they established kinship, competition too. Hemanga realized that though he looked naive the man was a professional, and Majumdar realized that the son-in-law with the high-pitched voice hadn't exactly come away bankrupt, he had plenty of cash and it would come in useful too, here, now.

'News of Burma?' Harit took the opportunity to pick up the thread, and Nikhil shifted his gaze towards him from Hemanga. 'Our news will be the same, too, in a couple of days, unless we . . .'

'But has Rangoon been bombed?' The rheumy voice asked a question again.

Harit curled his lips in contempt. This bombing was the only thing they were worried about—as though escaping the bombing was all that mattered. Illiterate, the whole lot of them! Putting on a detached expression, he said, 'It could be, easily. What prevents Calcutta from being bombed too?'

Suddenly shuddering as though with the cold, Kiran chortled, rubbing his hands. 'That's true. Calcutta could easily be bombed. Suppose tonight—suppose this very night . . .' He looked at Satyen.

Satyen smiled faintly. Bombing? The Japanese would bomb Calcutta? But then the Japanese were not really all that bad, were they? And even if they did, even if they did tonight—so what? The bombing wouldn't hurt anyone, no one would die, not a house would be destroyed—and even if they were, or were set on fire, he wouldn't . . . He wouldn't be hurt, and those whom he loved wouldn't be hurt either; everything would be fine.

Hearing Kiran chortling, Harit hurled a thunderbolt at him with his eyes, then turned back to Majumdar to begin an organized lecture. 'Here's where it stands. Assume Japan is bound to overrun India. Assume the English will retreat further for now. Now if we . . .'

'Let's go!' Arun appeared by the door. 'Come along, let's go.' He couldn't speak very loudly, he had to repeat himself several times to spread the message. Impossible—Harit shrugged with one shoulder—it was impossible to hold a discussion at a wedding!

A glance at the pleasant-looking man in glasses told Majumdar he was another of the sons-in-law—red necklace's husband? Must be, the eldest was a widow, wasn't she? Bijon's stories had made all of them familiar, but he didn't actually know any of them, except Mrs Nandy—and, of course, her eccentric husband. Might as well not have come, he suddenly thought.

A slow stir began around the room.

'Come along, come along everybody. Come, Nikhil, Akhil. Kiran-babu, you must stay for the wedding ceremony.'

'What time will it start?'

'After ten—please do stay, don't leave. Harit-babu, you're among the invitees too, please come along now.'

Harit was polite enough to create a smile-like slit on his face, displaying his teeth briefly. Never mind, he would finish over dinner, Majumdar had better not slip out of his grasp. To ensure he didn't, Harit said suavely, 'Shall we go, Mr Majumdar?'

'Oh, so you're the one!' Arun approached Bijon's large-car-owning friend. 'You've been extremely helpful. Now if you'd take the trouble to . . .' Arun moved on to the others.

'Please . . . Do come along . . . Straight up the stairs . . . Oh yes, keep your shoes on.'

∾

'Nice house you've got for yourselves,' said Saraswati as they climbed the stairs.

'Nice?' Mahashweta said in a stifled voice. She hadn't yet identified the house as nice in itself; this was Calcutta, she was in Calcutta, she would stay here, she wouldn't have to cross the sea any more, this realization alone had taken up her days. How fortunate the Japanese had declared war.

'How long since you were here last?' she asked, taking a turn in the stairs.

'About three years. You?'

'Five years,' Mahashweta replied immediately. 'The last time I came was when Baba had the house built, and this is the first time since then.'

'Yes, you couldn't come for Saswati's wedding,' Saraswati remembered.

'You and I are meeting after seven years. The last time was when we lived in the Jatin Das Road house . . .' Mahashweta paused on the first floor, caught her breath. 'And I'm meeting Didi after ten years.'

'Ten years!' Saswati tried to smile, but it turned into a sigh. 'I know, Bordi . . .' she didn't finish; 'I know . . .!' Mahashweta said to herself too. They evaded each other's eyes.

Shaking the curtain at the door, three slim giggling girls emerged from the large room in the centre of the house, one scarlet, one green, the third orange-red. 'Take a look, Ma . . .' said Iru, flashing her black eyes.

'Whose handwriting is better, Ma?' Geeti asked.

'Definitely Chhotomashi's,' said Iru.

'Never! Satyen-da's,' said Ata.

Without waiting for the verdict, they disappeared in a wave of colour.

What a quaint accent Iru has, observed Saraswati mentally, is that how they talk in Burma? Why does Geeti have that funny dancing gait like foreign women, Mahashweta wondered. The sisters appeared at the door to the large room.

'Well, Mahashweta, Saraswati, where were you all this time. You must make sure everything's all right.'

It was a great-aunt of theirs, the second wife of their great-uncle Bhupesh, plump and shiny, a mountain of paan in her mouth, not more than eleven or twelve years older than them.

'It's a good life for Kunda-didima with her ancient husband,' said Saraswati quietly. She entered.

Mahashweta didn't hear what she was saying, she was busy staring. There was no furniture in the room, it would have been overcrowded had there been. It was full of people. All women; young women and married women of different ages. They were all chatting, in scattered groups of two or three, since there was nowhere to sit, there was a continuous swirl of movement; a small group stood in a circle in the middle. Throwing glances at some, smiles at others, Mahashweta and Saraswati joined the group.

Finally, Mahashweta got a chance to look around. Everyone was a relative; members of the families of both her parents; those she had known when she was young, those she had known since they were young: her entire childhood seemed to have materialized in this room, the memories emerging from her mind to appear before her eyes. She hadn't expected to see them ever again in her life, she had forgotten many of them, but the moment she set eyes on them she realized she hadn't, you never forget anyone, you expect to meet every single person you knew at some time or the other. As she swept her eyes over the people present, Mahashweta's eyes met Shobha's!

Shobha—she had spotted Mahashweta already—smiled and

looked away, and Mahashweta scanned her cousin, the same age as her, carefully, tried to recall her face as she had known it. No, Shobha really had aged—she had a hard life, they weren't very well off. A 'poor girl' appeared in her mind and disappeared instantly, a different sort of sigh emerged. I . . . do I look the same?

'Have you seen Mahashweta's choker?' The woman next to Shobha whispered in her ear.

Not seen it? Was there a choice? The collarbones were so high, they had to be covered with large pearls . . . But envy retreated instantly after baring its fangs, happiness triumphed. Shobha was happy, from the moment she had set foot here, the previous morning, and her happiness kept growing—she would be here tonight too, and the night hadn't even begun yet. Two days, her uncle had rescued her for two full days from her existence of deprivation and life on the brink: she had been eating without cooking, having a good time instead of slaving all day, laughing, dressing up, talking to people whenever she wanted to, and so many people to talk to—everyone! She had so many relatives in Calcutta—she couldn't even imagine this being the case any more. They didn't even meet one another normally, didn't even think of one another ever; but here they were—and she felt so strong a bond with each of them, everyone did; a contagious happiness was spreading from one person to another—really, there was nothing happier than a wedding! Everyone would disperse to their own homes after this, everyone would rejoin their own families, the same distances would spring up, the same weakening of the bonds; again that dawn-to-midnight . . . But not now, not just yet.

Shobha lowered her eyes. She noticed two white feet on the beautiful silk mat on the lovely white floor, turning red slowly under Saswati's brush, a long cascade of hair flowing over the curved back—behind her, squatting on her haunches, Usha was running a comb through it. Swati looked like a figure from a painting, her chin resting on a raised knee, her hands clasped around her leg just below the knee, her eyes downcast, silent. But why did she have to lower her eyes, she had chosen on her own, she wasn't getting married blindly like the rest of us. Never even seen the man before, didn't know anything about him, overnight the emperor of your life, a completely unknown person—Shobha was suddenly surprised at this age-old custom. But then life did go by quite happily that way too, and in any case, did this other way of doing it always lead to happiness?

'What kind of hairstyle, Saraswati?'

'You're asking me! You're the expert, Usha-boudi.'

'Tell me about a couple of Delhi styles.' Pleased, Usha picked up a ribbon. 'All right, Mahashweta, you tell me. I believe there are many different hairstyles in Burma.'

'Not Burma, Japan,' Saswati said without raising her eyes from Swati's feet.

'What's all this I hear?' Kunda said, her cheeks puffed with the paan in them. 'Are we getting a Japanese king? Will prices fall?'

'Forget about doing your hair,' Usha bunched up the hair behind the shoulder, 'soon you won't need to any more.' She tied the ribbon tightly around the hair.

'Why not?' asked a young woman laughingly.

'All bobcuts!' Usha rolled her eyes, as though the future was clearly visible in that direction. Her eyes met Mahashweta's.

'What's wrong with that, bobcuts are better than these cake-buns!' Having said this, Leela, standing next to Mahashweta, was vastly amused at her own wit and kept laughing. Those who heard her pondered for a minute over the state of their own hair.

Twice, Usha stroked the thick tail of hair tied up with the ribbon. Looking at Saraswati, she said, 'What lovely hair you sisters have really, makes me envious.'

'Let's hear you say something, Swati.' Kunda targeted her

with smiling eyes. 'You've gone and done it, there's no need to be embarrassed now.'

'Swati won't waste her words now,' Usha said, coiling up her hair from the waist upwards. 'She's hoarding them all.'

'But you must have used up some of them already,' Kunda said, dragging her words. 'Let's hear a few samples. What did you say to conquer such a learned man! Is it true, Swati, that he's read all the books in the world?'

'He's going to begin the best book in the world now.' Usha began patting the coils into a bun.

Shobha smiled, tried to catch the expression on Swati's face. But all she saw was a portion of her cheek; an eyelid trembled, Swati unclasped her hands, seemingly startled all of a sudden. Every time there was a sound, she was startled, and every time she was startled, she was surprised by that fact. This time too Swati was surprised when she saw her own arms—bangles of so many different kinds—and next to those shining animated bangles the *shankha*, that symbol of marriage, with the yellow thread tied around it, so beautiful, so serene in its whiteness. It was difficult to slip a *shankha* on, it had to be done very gingerly so that it didn't snap, but in her case the tiny *shankha* seemed to arrive on its own around her wrist, faced no obstruction at all at her knuckles. A good omen, everyone said.

'Done, Chhordi?' Swati said softly.

'Almost.' Saswati took her hands away, leaned back and tilted her head to survey her handiwork, then used her fingers to get a fine tip on the brush. 'Raise your foot slightly, Swati.'

Resting her heel on the floor, Swati raised her toes. The brush tickled her between the toes. Swati twitched involuntarily, the brush jerked.

'Don't move . . . Yes, this is perfect. Keep it that way.' With great concentration, Saswati ran her brush through the channels between the toes, and Swati gazed at the yellowish hue on the sole of her foot. As was the custom, she had been doused in turmeric paste earlier in the evening, then made to dress in this coarse red-bordered sari—they had sent the sari—they—he—he's sent it for me. Swati glanced at the striking red border just above her feet. The sari would apparently be given away to someone. This one? Couldn't they give away another one?

'And where are all the princesses?'

Saswati raised her face, Swati too; they exchanged glances, both realized they had had the same thought. The words, the manner of speaking, even the voice, were a lot like their father's—the way he used to speak years ago—they kept making the same mistake. As soon as she thought of her father grief twisted in her breast again, and Mahashweta and Saraswati both remembered how, when they were children, the three sisters used to quarrel for the right to sleep in the same bed at night with this aunt, their father's sister.

'No princesses here any more,' Kunda smiled, 'all queens.'

'Put your foot down flat now,' said Saswati in a low voice. Swati did; Saswati put a drop of red on each nail and stood up.

'Very nice,' approved Leela.

Rajen-babu's sister looked around, the sindoor bright in her grey hair. Smiling sweetly with her sunken cheeks, she said, 'All five together again. How long Raju has wished for this.'

'So have we,' Usha said casually, proceeding to put pins into the enormous dense black hair-bun.

'That's true! And our girls! No one can beat them in looks or accomplishments!' Smiles rippled through dimples in the sunken cheeks of their childless aunt.

She'll never learn to be sensible, Mahashweta reflected; should you talk this way in a room full of women? To change the subject she asked what she already knew, 'Were you here for Saswati's wedding, Pishima?'

'How could I!' She put her hand on her cheek to display astonishment. 'I was very ill! Your Pishe was sure I'd die.

Hmmph! As if I'd die that easily—kowlera, tyfote I've seen them all, none of them could get me!'

A wave of laughter went round the room; Swati felt Shweta had the same manner of speaking—and the fog of happiness wrapped itself even more tightly around Shobha, the faces blurred, no one's features were clearly visible, all the faces were dressed in nothing but a smile—the same smile. Everyone here was related to Swati, but they weren't all related to one another; many of them didn't even know one another very well, many of them would never even see one another again; but still, all this was for now, no one was distant, they were all close to one another, the wedding had turned them all into one large family, and she was in the midst of it all.

Unwrapping the golden-red silk sari from Benares that Swati would be married in, Saraswati said, 'At least we're all meeting one another thanks to Swati. It's been so long!'

So long, not so long, it had never happened, thought Mahashweta. I've never seen all these people together, why, I'm actually seeing some of the wives, the sons-in-law, the children for the very first time. She swept her eyes around the room once more, then, glancing at her aunt's creased face, thought, all of us are alive at the same time, I too, along with everyone else. The thought surprised her, pleased her.

'Yes, everyone,' Mahashweta said. 'No one left out.'

No one?—a mute cry rose within Swati—Jamaibabu! Doesn't anyone remember, doesn't anyone even remember he existed once? In a single stroke Saswati's wedding came back to her, the next morning, cross-legged on the bed, laughing uproariously, the infinite goodness in those easily surprised round eyes. All wiped out? So soon? A quiet pain found release, rose in her throat after a long time. Now she was no longer the woman she didn't know earlier, with the *shankha*, the reddened feet, dressed in the sari 'he' had sent, the focus of everyone's joy, happiness; now she was Swati all over again, eleven, fifteen, with curly hair, clinging, crying herself to sleep without dinner, waking up in fear on rainy nights, lighting up winter mornings in her red-bordered sari, now she was snuggling up to her mother again, now she was her father's girl again. Swati buried her eyes in her knees.

Saraswati came up to her, the golden-red sari in her hand. 'Get up, Swati. Time to put the sari on.'

'Swati,' Saswati called more gently. Footsteps were heard on the stairs, many of them, more, many people were climbing the stairs together.

Raising her face, Swati wiped her eyes with her palm. Swivelling her head, now with an enormous bun atop it, from side to side, she looked around with reddened eyes, she saw laughter, saris, a profusion of colours, clashes between necklaces and earrings, an enormous peacock spread its plumage under the dazzling electric light, happiness surrounded her, everyone's happiness. Her eyes moved from face to face, searching.

'Looking for something, Swati?' Saswati said.

'Where's Bordi? Swati asked in a very small voice.

'Bordi? You want Bordi? I'll fetch her . . .' Saswati went towards the door, the sound of footsteps diminished as they went past the first floor towards the roof, she should check on Satyen.

'Ah, Bordi. I was looking for you. Swati's asking for you.' Saswati didn't pause, going off towards the stairs.

'There she is,' said Saraswati. 'Come, Bordi, Swati won't put her sari on without you.'

'Go on upstairs, all of you' said Shweta as she came in. 'Take them upstairs, will you, Leela-mashi? Pishima, ask everyone to go, please.'

'Men first,' said Kunda.

'Ancient history,' said Rajen-babu's sister, waving her hand. 'Women are equal now. Come along. Come along, all of you.'

A stir of movement from the distant wall reached the group in the middle. Silk and gold flashed, emeralds and rubies glittered. And amidst this extraordinary roomwide dance of jaunty gold and voluble jewellery and silk and satin brocade, she saw Shweta, even more extraordinary, white, in her widow's garb, as extraordinarily white as the *shankha* on her hand next to her bangles, and just as serene, beautiful.

'Well, Swati?' Swati lowered her eyes, Shweta sat down by her side. 'Have something to eat, all right?' she said in a low voice.

'No.'

'Let me get you a little fruit juice—you must be thirsty.'

'Not now. Stay with me for a bit, Bordi.'

'Swati . . .' Saraswati hurried her.

'All right, she'll be ready in a bit.' Shweta put an arm around her, she could feel Swati trembling. The crowd in the room started shrinking, shrank, the sari, blouse, veil and jewellery lay on the mat; up on the roof, people sat down to eat.

Halfway down the stairs Saswati saw Harit coming upstairs with Prabir Majumdar. Saswati stopped, Majumdar stopped too when he saw her. Just like before he brought his palms together in greeting, bowing his head deeply; just like before a smile suffused his face. 'How are you, Mrs Nandy?'

'Very well, and you?' said Saswati, nodding.

'It is my fortune,' Majumdar glanced at Saswati, 'to have met you here.'

Saswati smiled, not sure how to respond. Since the day Majumdar had been informed of the rejection—she was the one who had had to break the news—and had left, Saswati had not met him, she hadn't expected to either. She hadn't expected Majumdar to be present at Swati's wedding. Never mind being present, he seemed quite enthusiastic; he had sent a gramophone as a gift, sent his car for use all day long, and looked as happy as before. What kind of a man was he?

Unfeeling? Or generous? Or had all of that just been a passing fancy—nothing more?

'Your gramophone's lovely.' Saswati felt this could be said, this should be said.

'But it's not mine!' Majumdar smiled.

'Let's go,' Harit urged him. He wasn't enjoying this conversation, wasn't even listening to it, but Majumdar seemed gratified. 'Let's go,' he said again.

'It was very nice meeting you,' Majumdar took his leave.

'Likewise,' Saswati smiled again, gesturing with her head.

Saswati went downstairs, Majumdar went upstairs, Harit looked back, and as though she was hoping as much, Saswati raised her eyes. Harit suddenly found his wife looking very beautiful.

No, Majumdar was a gentleman; no other description suited him, he was what you call a genuine gentleman. How pleasing Majumdar's . . . extraordinary courtesy—yes, certainly extraordinary—was. How easily he accepted what was not to be, how quickly he was delighted at others' happiness. Saswati's happiness increased too, she thought of this as an extra gain for herself, none of my sisters know anything about it, none of them is as much a part of Swati's wedding as I am. I made a mistake then, she thought, but Swati did not, no one but Satyen would have suited her—really!—they were made for each other, they had met, were getting married; they would be happy, so happy, there wouldn't be the slightest blemish. Saswati's heart filled with joy, she seemed unable to hold it in, seemed to float on a current of air to the front room.

The yellow carpet lay on the sheet stretched out from wall to wall; bowls of paan and ashtrays lay scattered, Satyen was alone in the room, away from the red carpet. 'Wonderful!' said Saswati, approaching him quickly.

A magenta sari glowed before Satyen's eyes, a yellow-and-green blouse, a filigree necklace in read and green. First he saw the lips move, then heard the voice: 'They've left you all alone here! Wonderful!'

'Arun-babu was here. He'll be back. And it was quite nice by myself.'

Looking at Satyen's soft eyes, listening to his soft voice, Saswati's heart spilled over, not exactly in happiness now, but in something surpassing happiness, this was a new feeling, she had never felt it for anyone else: what can I do for this man, she thought. Surprised, Saswati wondered, had Satyen become more important than Swati? Surprised, she wondered: is this what it means to become fond of someone?

'By yourself? Then I shouldn't have come?'

'No, this is even better,' Satyen said quickly.

Saswati smiled. Looking around she said, 'Weren't there some flowers here?'

'I put them away. And if you'll permit me, I'd like to stand.'

'Of course!'

Satyen rose, the two bouquets of red roses flashed behind him.

'You must be feeling tired,' said Saswati. 'Have you had a cup of tea?'

'Probably.'

'What do you mean probably?'

Satyen walked a few steps on the carpet. 'I mean, when everyone was being given tea they gave me a cup too, but I can't quite remember whether I had it or not.'

With every word, Saswati came to love him a little more. 'Want another cup now? Though it's not a good idea to have too much tea on an empty stomach.'

'Empty? But I ate.'

'Ni–i–i–ce! Our girl has fasted all day.'

'She has? But I told her not to.'

Saswati wanted to laugh. Suppressing the urge, she said, 'So did we, but she refused. Anyway a day's fasting does no harm. Then you . . . Let me get you a cup of tea, all right? I'll be back in a moment.'

'I was thinking . . .'

'Yes?'

'Could I sit somewhere else?'

'What's the matter here?'

'If there was a chair or something . . .'

'I see!' Saswati smiled with her eyes. 'All right, come with me.' She took Satyen into a smaller room through an inside door, where a three-piece sofa-set had been placed without any space between the pieces.

Satyen sat down, resting his back. 'Comfortable now?' asked Saswati.

'Very. A little too comfortable.'

'Do you like the blue?'

'This sofa? Very nice.'

'Good. So you don't dislike it? That's good enough.'

'Why?' asked Satyen, not understanding.

'Because it's yours, you see . . .'

'Mine? Why?' Satyen continued after a pause. 'What am I going to do with all this? Where will I even put all this?'

'Now you have someone to worry about all that too.' Saswati left, leaving behind the radiance of her laughter, came back a little later with a steaming cup of tea, put the tea on a small table with a yellow glass top by Satyen's side.

'Please, sit down for a few minutes now,' said Satyen.

'No, I won't. Have your tea.'

'Ahh!' said Satyen, sipping the tea. He realized he had been craving a cup of tea.

'Is it all right? Not too much sugar?'

'No. It's perfect.'

Still standing, Saswati watched Satyen for a while, then said, 'Can I tell you something.'

'Tell me.'

'You must address me as Chhordi.'

'I will.'

'And I'm going to use *tumi* from tomorrow.'

'Of course,' said Satyen, looking at her.

'You can too if you like.'

'I will. From tomorrow?'

'Yes, from tomorrow.'

They laughed together, softly. Arun entered anxiously, saying, 'So this is where you've hidden Satyen, Saswati! And here I was, wondering where he'd disappeared.'

'I know how worried you were. You'd left him all alone!'

'Just went to make sure everything was all right upstairs. Ready, Satyen? Not much time to go.'

'I'm going too. Take care of him, Arun-da—he mustn't get lost.' Saswati looked back at Satyen as she left.

❧

She went directly to the terrace. It was a huge space, covered with a canopy, surrounded on all sides by dark blue screens like a tennis court because of the blackout and the cold, another screen ran alongside the single room on the roof, dividing the terrace into two unequal portions. The smaller part was where the wedding would take place, and the larger was for the feasting—which was under way. People had sat down at long narrow trestle tables facing one another in double-rows; men sat at five of the tables, women at three; it was a pleasing sight. Saswati walked through a narrow channel between two rows of backs, stopping at a brown shirt. 'Is the food all right, Nikhil?'

About to put a piece of fish-fry into his mouth, Nikhil looked back, reddened considerably on seeing Saswati. 'Need anything?' Saswati continued.

'No, nothing.' What could he possibly need? Between the salad and the sweet there were eighteen different kinds of dishes—yes, eighteen, he had counted—along with scented water and even a paan with a clove on a separate dish—and, probably for those who weren't paan-eaters, mouth-fresheners like cardamom and aniseed. The image of a wedding feast etched in his memory, which he had seen many times as a child, had nothing in common with this. Those used to mean sitting down at congested tables, the lower half of your shirt getting wet, waiting for the daal while the fries went cold, the sweets ladled out into the curry, everything running into each other, and when you've already eaten your fill of whatever's been served, the glamorous import of the mutton and the pulao—but here, there was none of the perspiration, stench and labour of serving at the tables; and—best of all, unusual, and new to Nikhil— no screaming and shouting, very quiet, only the buzz of conversation among the guests could be heard. And it was possible to be choosy about what to eat, in comfort; although there were eighteen different things to be eaten, everything could be tried without wasting anything because the servings weren't too big. As he finished his bhetki, Nikhil tuned in to the conversations around him.

'. . . The issue is, what shall we do now.'

'We?' A middle-aged man of refined appearance in a long black coat closed at the neck lifted his eyes towards Harit. 'What can we do. Slaves once, slaves always.'

A few people laughed. Harit's face reddened, he snorted his small laugh. Another person, a shawl draped over his shoulder, said, 'Not necessarily. This could be an opportunity for us.'

'It's certainly an opportunity.' Harit fired a question like an arrow. 'But for what?'

~

As he ploughed through the daal with the stuffed kachuri, Majumdar lifted his eyes and saw Saswati pass. He looked at her for a while, but their eyes didn't meet. Saswati moved ahead, two people carrying jugs of water went off in two different directions, in the distance the Rangoon son-in-law smiled at someone, and over on the other side, where the women were sitting, there was a momentary flash of silver draped over a black satin shoulder. I shouldn't have come, Majumdar thought again, really, why did I? He remembered that last day with Saswati—he had meant to say several things, but didn't have to say much—didn't have to! Bijon had come to him looking like a plucked bird, raving and ranting; but he didn't hear almost any of it; just the one thing kept ringing in his ears—no luck. Was he upset? Did his heart break? Nothing like that. He had felt nothing like the descriptions in novels suggest. No pain at all, nothing else, just the humiliating sting of the scorpion, the damning cries of defeat. He couldn't, he had failed; he, Prabir Chandra Majumdar, the eldest son of a shrimp of a clerk, brought up in deprivation, the lord and master of a hundred and fifty people today, owner of a large car and a small car, for the first time he had attempted something without succeeding. Or hadn't he tried hard enough, hadn't he wanted hard enough—the way he had said sixteen years ago, pumping his fist, 'I *must* have money.'

'. . . Nobody understands the situation. What do you think?' Harit Nandy's confidential tone attracted Majumdar's attention.

'Me? . . . I don't quite . . .'

'It's very simple. Do you want the Fascists to win?'

Majumdar looked at Harit for a while. Dripping obsequiousness from the creases in his cheek, he asked softly, 'Will you tell me what the word "Fascist" means?'

Harit laughed, waving his hands.

'Please do explain it to me, Mr Nandy,' Majumdar pleaded solemnly, even more obsequiously. 'I haven't been to college, I don't understand these things.'

'I've been telling these young men for a long time,' the

rheumy voice was heard behind them, talking loudly, 'never mind the degrees, just learn Japanese.'

Harit looked back quickly to put a face to the voice, and Majumdar took the opportunity to attack the *shorshe chingri bhaape* . . . He'd failed, he'd tried but failed; hope died, but the craving didn't. When Bijon came the other day, looking guilty, to inform him of his sister's wedding—to invite him—he was the one who had to express happiness, eagerness—he was the one who had to put Bijon at ease—and the pretence turned into reality. He sent a four-hundred-rupee gramophone as a gift, sent a favour in the form of the larger of his cars for use all day; and arrived himself on time with his niece, an embodiment of courtesy. Why? To make them feel grateful? To show his magnanimity? Rubbish! Maintaining a relationship, through any means, on any terms, was that what he wanted? Wasn't that what he wanted? Was he so desperate?

'. . . But will the pension be maintained?' A thin question emerged behind Majumdar through a pair of formidable grey moustaches; and opposite him, about to put a piece of cauliflower from the fish curry into his mouth, Kiran Bakshi said, 'Is it really time to send the family out of Calcutta?'

Kiran Bakshi's question was directed at Harit, but Harit merely raised his head and contracted the muscles in his cheek; he had tried to smile, but it came out as a grimace.

Standing behind Kiran, a curly-haired teenager poured water into his empty glass. Nikhil looked back to find Dalim had changed his clothes; instead of the floppy *panjabi* he now had on a striped grey silk shirt, sleeves rolled up, a gold watch on his wrist—what was the watch for?

When their eyes met Nikhil asked, 'What time is it, Dalim-babu?'

About to glance at his watch, Dalim caught on to the joke and reddened, he moved on along the channel between the tables.

'. . . Those who are about to retire have little to worry about. They can get extensions whenever they want.'

'Really?'

'Of course, the ARP supply. . . Excuse me, some water please. Oh, this fish is heavenly!'

Hemanga ran up. 'Some more for you . . . A little more . . .?'

'Will the Japanese fly in from their bases to bomb us, or will they bring an aircraft carrier into the Bay of Bengal?'

Harit didn't even deign to raise his eyes at Kiran Bakshi's nuanced military query; seemingly overburdened by the weight of the stupidity all around him, he picked out the nuts and almonds from his pulao to eat, then quickly tasted the mutton—not bad at all, quite delicious. He ate some of it, then began in a very low voice, 'Fascists are those who . . .'

'Are you taking an extension?'

'No, not me . . .' The food being masticated in his mouth suppressed the rest. 'But Rajen probably . . .'

'Rajen-babu? I thought he couldn't wait to retire.'

'It's all fathe!' A very old man spoke for the first time, Rajen-babu's sister's husband himself, whose being alive was publicized amply in the red streak in his wife's hair. 'With his eldhesth dhaughther being widhowedh . . .'

Dalim moved away quickly, Saswati beckoned to him when she saw him; and, listening to Harit's unrelenting whining—rather, not listening to it—Majumdar suddenly raised his eyes and immediately noticed her gesticulating.

'Why dhoes Rajen's fathe holdh this for him?' The lack of teeth softened the hard consonants; then, trying to speak forcibly, he acquired a pronounced lisp. 'Becauth he'th honetht!'

'That's true!' Rebati Sinha, Rajen-babu's neighbour, agreed at once. 'Rajen-babu is a real gentleman. In our neighbourhood . . .'

'Give me some water. They've covered the whole place, it's so . . .'

'Thank goodness it's winter!' Dalim said gravely. 'If it had been warm I don't know how in this blackout . . .'

'Will the blackout last that long?' Saswati was worried. 'What a situation, really! But why are you serving water? Isn't there anyone else?'

'There is, and that includes me,' Dalim smiled engagingly. Then, suddenly putting the jug down, he took off his watch and put it in his pocket.

'Why did you take it off?'

'Comes in the way,' Dalim smiled faintly.

'It was looking nice. Jamaibabu's watch, isn't it?' Saswati said lightly, going off towards the women's tables.

Dalim paused, then put the watch back on casually.

'. . . Swati is the apple of her father's eye! Now that she's getting married . . .' Without completing what she was saying, Kunda looked down at her plate, biting into the aubergine fritters.

'You get used to everything, everything works out fine.' Smiling, Leela proceeded to the fish-head with cabbage.

'This lobster is amazingly delicious!' Appreciation spilled over from Shobha, her mouth full of food.

'Show me what isn't!' exclaimed Rajen-babu's sister. 'With Pratap as cook you can't do better!'

'Is he very famous?' asked a much younger woman from a distance.

'Oh my God!' The aunt showed her amazement with her hand on her cheek. 'Haven't you heard of Pratap? His father was the best cook in Bikrampur, there wasn't another one like him in . . .'

Standing behind her, Mahashweta pinched her shoulder.

'Very nice!' The sound came from the gap in the grey moustache which had just begun to glisten from the olive chutney. 'You have to say Rajen has made excellent arrangements.'

'Yes, superb!'

'Fabulous cooking!'

'His youngest daughter's wedding, after all, so he's spent a lot of money. And his sons-in-law are all so worthy too . . .'

'This one's low on salary though,' remarked the balding middle-aged man in gold-rimmed glasses, the five sisters' uncle Prabhat, Leela's husband, in a low voice.

'Never mind,' Rebati-babu delivered his judgement, withdrawing the fingers soaked in tomato chutney from his mouth. 'The boy's excellent! I've known him quite some time—he lives in my house—doesn't even look you in the eye!'

'He was looking where he needed to,' the rheumy voice said loudly.

Arranging the long white central bone of the fish she'd eaten by the side of the plate, Chitra said, 'So this was what Swati was angling for.'

'I knew all along,' Anupama smiled.

'Since when?' Chitra sounded disbelieving.

'There were certainly no signs during the honours class. Satyen-babu would never look at Swati, Swati would never look up from her book.'

The older, oversized, overdressed, unmarried-and-out-of-place Iva Ganguly said in a baritone like a man's, 'Whatever you may so, for a professor and a student to . . .'

'Shh! That's Swati's sister over there!'

'No daal for you?' Rajen-babu's sister frowned at a complete stranger.

'I've overeaten already,' the lady answered shyly.

'Do try it.' It was evident from the questioner's smile that daal of this quality had never been made in the history of the world, nor would again.

'But you're not eating either, only talking,' said a satiated old lady in a red-bordered silk sari, Harit's mother.

'I will now,' said Rajen-babu's sister, concentrating on her pulao.

'Ve-e-e-ry nice!' Chomping on the mutton with her

gold-capped tooth, her mouth open, a woman in an unsuitably gaudy sari seemed to suddenly remember the occasion for the feast. 'A very good match. Getting a groom for your daughter these days . . .'

'Quite true!' Rajen-babu's sister stopped eating to look at her gravely. 'It's the same everywhere, most people are barely able to get one or two out the door. And all five of ours . . .' An engaging smile suffused her entire face, sweeping her eyes over everyone she continued, 'All five simply flew away . . . The first one that saw them liked them . . . And the sons-in-law too, wonderful boys . . .'

'All right, enough!' Several people heard Mahashweta's whisper, but not the one it was directed at.

'But then our girls don't go looking for husbands themselves.' Rebati-babu's wife whispered to the lady sitting by her side.

The recipient merely gestured with her hand, without speaking. A grain of rice was dislodged from the stone set in her ring.

'Swati will probably give up studies.'

'She has to,' replied Iva Ganguly in the authoritative tone of her uncle the vice principal.

'It was nice to have Swati in class,' Anupama's voice held a trace of sadness. Remember that class on "The Ancient Mariner"?'

'And that day we were all in the tram together, and Satyen Roy got in?'

Anupama and Chitra sighed in unison. Those days seemed so far in the past already.

'Does Supriti write?'

'Not at all. Friends mean nothing after you're married.'

'It's hard to say what makes some people attractive.' Iva Ganguly lowered her mannish voice considerably, but still sounded loud after the soft voices of the other two. 'A brilliant young man like Satyen Roy should have been more . . . more . . .'

Without finishing, Iva Ganguly started picking at her yet-to-be-touched food with her eyes. From a little distance a pair of sharp eyes looked at her through hexagonal glasses, and Chitra and Anupama looked at her in surprise at hearing her finally say something complimentary about Satyen Roy.

'. . . ambitious,' concluded Iva, picking up an olive. 'My uncle keeps saying, "I simply don't understand why Satyen is rotting here; he can get much better jobs." That's his problem—no ambition.'

'Please don't mind,' the painted face with the hexagonal glasses leaned forward as much as possible in that crowded space. 'Please don't mind—I don't know any of you—all of you are Swati's friends, aren't you? So am I—and I *shall* say this, Swati's an extraordinary girl, and Satyen-babu is extraordinarily. . . lucky.'

Even Iva Ganguly was taken aback at this candid statement, and Chitra seemed to find in it the inspiration she needed to express a sincere opinion she held. 'Satyen-babu isn't much to look at though.'

'I don't know whether he's much to look at, but he's very attractive!' A new classmate of theirs, a dark, slender girl, with no jewellery to accompany her formal sari, spoke up clearly.

'Do any of you . . . Anything more . . .' Saswati came near them.

'A little water, Chhordi,' said Urmila. Although she addressed Bijon as Biju-da she hadn't yet addressed Saswati as Chhordi, but she did now so that the rest of them could realize how intimate she was with this family.

'Water? Just a minute . . .' As she looked around Saswati's eyes met Dalim's, she summoned him with a glance.

The dutiful Dalim approached them obediently. He had replenished many an empty glass of water by now, but had carefully avoided this one table. Even looking at its occupants from a distance made his eyelids droop. Why was it this way? Why were girls so beautiful, and why couldn't you just go near them?

Stiff, solemn, trying his utmost not to blush, Dalim, lanky, bent to pour water into Urmila's glass. A fragrance leapt up at him—strange, unknown, new, unusual, amazing.

'May I have some water, please,' Dalim had seen the girl who made the request in a clear voice earlier too. She was some sort of cousin of his aunt's husband's—and a little while earlier on the staircase—he hadn't seen her properly, hadn't been able to, only a glow of beauty, a flash of colour had passed before his eyes. Dalim tiptoed a few chairs away, raised the jug with his fair arm in the rolled-up sleeve and the gold watch, and at that precise moment, completely without provocation, the beautiful girl raised her face, her round earrings swayed, the light fell on the slight down above her upper lip. The jug suddenly felt very heavy in Dalim's hand, and behaved in so unruly a manner that despite his holding on to it with all his strength, water spilled from it, the glass overflowed, wetting the thin sheet of paper covering the table and dripping on the glittering sari, the water splashed on the satin shoes, then sprayed all over. The some-sort-of-cousin of Mahashweta's husband's bent for a moment and then, with equal promptness, looked daggers at Dalim, the faint golden down over her comely lips became even more visible. A current of laughter ran through everyone nearby; Harit's brother's wife—who had sat at the same table as the young women in order to avoid the company of her mother-in-law—of course, she was young herself, but there was a lifetime of difference between married and unmarried women—tried to suppress her laughter with unnecessary sips of water, and, at one corner of the table, three blossoming angels laughed like the music of a waterfall, one scarlet, one green, one orange.

His mouth full of shondesh, his brown shirt unbuttoned at the neck because the food had made him feel warm, Nikhil turned back at the sound of laughter. All three of them had leaned back while laughing, Nikhil saw them a little more clearly now, and he saw Dalim very clearly, well groomed, handsome, dressed in a tantalizing grey striped shirt, displaying his wavy hair with his head bowed, still standing with the jug of water in his hand. Dalim looked as though he was smiling too, Nikhil felt a sudden stab of envy, the delicious dessert suddenly stuck in his throat.

∾

'So the Japanese really will bomb Calcutta?' asked Kiran Bakshi. He didn't know himself whom the question was for, the 'so' was meaningless too; because he hadn't got any answer to two earlier far more subtle and serious questions: 'What's the minimum distance from Calcutta for safety?' and 'Unless there's a direct hit there shouldn't be any problem, should there?'; while eating he had been lost in his own thoughts, his father-in-law's obduracy, his imminent, uncertain, Anita-less situation, this unimaginable calamity threatening immortal Calcutta, and, following that very thread, while biting into the crisp papad just placed on his plate, that original question had escaped his mouth in a rather serious vein.

'No, they won't bomb Calcutta,' the refined gentleman in the long coat and long sideburns answered suavely. 'They will simply swallow the plump juicy city—like this,' he said, holding his rashogolla in two fingers a few inches from his upturned mouth and dropping it in whole on to his tongue.

Fifth Column! Fifth Column, all of them! No, not all—some of us are still here! We'll fight, we'll resist, we'll win—we're going to exterminate them like bugs! Harit's face grew feral with these thoughts, his fingers moved swiftly on his plate, he picked something up at random from the plate—he had finished long ago, hadn't touched half the things—without even looking, he bit into a sliver of ginger from the chutney. Oh God—it was hot!

'No papad for me!' The sharpness of his tongue, mingled with the rage in his heart, made it sound angry, like a belligerent rebuke.

Hearing Harit draw in his breath, Majumdar said in his smoothest of voices, 'Anything spicy in there, Mr Nandy?'

Harit tried to smile good-naturedly in response.

'Have some sweets—this one looks delicious!' Majumdar gathered up the rashomalai, in its own bowl, to put it on his emptied-out plate, breaking off a piece of papad to use it as a spoon. 'See how useful this is—use it as a spoon, use it as food. But you don't like papad, do you?' Even as he was about to look at Harit with an expansive smile, his eyes shifted, his thick lips became softer, banter was replaced by intensity in his eyes, which met Saswati's as she passed by.

'I hope you're staying,' Saswati tilted her head as she spoke, hurrying along. Downstairs by now Swati must be all dressed up—but she stopped suddenly on spotting her father. In the distance, in the corner, where the pitchers of water and plates and glasses were piled, stood her father, next to Hemanga. Saswati felt as though she was seeing him after a long time, he seemed to look different. His face had shrunk, the man himself seemed to have shrunk. Creases on his face, squinting eyes, loose folds of skin at the neck, the grey shawl wrapped around him like melancholy—from a distance, and her father was looking the other way, Saswati saw it all very clearly. She turned—though she did want to go downstairs; through the bright corridor between the tables, brushing past the shining hair of the young men and the multicoloured clothes and jewellery on the women, avoiding the baskets of papad being taken around, Saswati proceeded towards the dimly lit corner in the distance. It wasn't as though she had remembered something important to tell him—nothing specific, she just felt she wanted to go to him.

'The problem with our country is that we have no political education here.' Having overcome the impact of the ginger, Harit was his usual grave self.

Majumdar was sipping water, but he didn't speak immediately after putting his glass down. Squeezing some lime juice on his palms, he rinsed them in the water remaining in the glass, used his left hand to pull out his imported cotton handkerchief and wiped his hands on it carefully; crumpling it up and returning it to his left pocket and pulling out a large patterned silk handkerchief from his right pocket to wipe his lips, he said slowly, 'The problem with silk handkerchiefs is that you can't wipe your hands with them properly. That's why I never forget to take two to wedding invitations.' Glancing at Harit out of one eye, he continued, 'But you're absolutely right! For instance, I didn't even know that the Japanese slaughter cows on the streets and eat them. I learnt a lot from you today.'

Harit's nostrils flared slightly, Majumdar's silk handkerchief gave them a gift of a lavender fragrance, Harit snorted. No, he wouldn't lose his temper, losing his temper would achieve nothing; even the enemy had to be utilized, that was what counted. For now, if he could stick to this man there would be no need to walk after dinner. Harit glanced at him amiably, as though he hadn't understood the mockery, or as though he was joining in too; casually, he asked, 'Where are you off to now?'

'I'll . . .' Majumdar stopped. Go home? Right away? But where else could he go? There was no happiness anywhere—happiness! This commodity named happiness was only a consolation prize for those who hadn't got anything else. What would he do with happiness?

'If it's on your way, could you drop me home?' Harit came out in the open.

Majumdar turned round to look at him. 'Aren't you staying?' His voice held a note of surprise.

'I was thinking—the thing is, this business of weddings is very boring.'

'Which? The ceremony or what comes afterwards? Please don't mind my asking, you're experienced, after all.'

Kiran Bakshi considered the response abhorrent, but the man with the sideburns as well as two others laughed, but Harit stopped as he was about to smile, as though he had only just remembered that this man had been actively trying to woo Swati, and suddenly, even the sure-tongued Harit felt a little subdued, and Saswati, happy, stood by her father watching the glowing scene. Although it would end soon, the place throbbed with life now; more vociferous than before; the voices louder than before; many of the guests were done with their dinner, they distributed their conversation generously among nearby people and waved at those in the distance; some reclined in their chairs, savouring their paan, some braced themselves against the surface of the table to get to their feet; many rinsed their hands in their glasses! Sweets were still being served at the tables for women and for the older men, Bhupesh-babu ate fourteen rashogollas, everyone laughed.

'Lovely dinner, Baba. Everyone enjoyed it so-o-o-o-o-o much,' Saswati looked glowingly at her father.

'How can you not stay?' Majumdar said in a low voice to Harit. 'What will people think? And Mrs Nandy . . .'

'Let's go, Baba,' said Saswati. 'Once the stairs get crowded . . .'

'. . . You simply have to stay!' Majumdar urged Harit.

'Are you staying?'

Should I? Mrs Nandy asked me to, didn't she? Oh but everyone says that. And do I have to just because she did? No, enough—no more! Why am I even asking Nandy to? Who am I to? How does it matter to me? And there are far better pastimes on a winter night in Calcutta than watching this play with fearful dolls that passes for a Hindu marriage! What would it be like to take this trigger-happy madman to one of those places? Majumdar found the idea extremely funny, but suppressing his laughter, he answered Harit. 'Me? Am I anywhere near as important here as you?' He concluded with a smile and a display of his large teeth.

Harit admired the man mentally. Even he wouldn't have been able to talk this way, smile this way.

About to leave with his daughter, Rajen-babu paused at the table for the elderly, Shobha made up her mind to loosen her petticoat as soon as she went downstairs, Nikhil wondered where Dalim was, Iva said Christmas is ruined this year, where will all of you be, Leela mused that her husband would want to leave immediately but without watching the ceremony, Kunda stuffed four paans into her mouth at one go, Harit thought so the circus starts now what are we waiting for, Saswati tugged at her father's clothes, her sister-in-law hoped her son Babla hadn't woken up back home, Urmila put a few more cardamom slices into her mouth, and Mahashweta wondered whether her curls were natural or machine-made. 'We're off to Jamatara as soon as the holidays start, after that who knows . . .' Iva said as she rose, Harit rose, Prabhat-babu and Rebati-babu's wife both rose, everyone rose together with a whooshing sound, some of the young men lit their cigarettes as they rose, Nikhil ran off to exploit the State Express in his pocket in the seclusion of the ground floor, chairs were scraped back and people started moving about, the uncle who had lost his teeth coughed, family members looked for one another, thank goodness there was still time to take a tram, Hemanga moved from the dimly lit area to the part where the wedding would take place, Urmila spoke to her uncle and the girl with the down above her lip told Mahashweta, Mahashweta moved towards the stairs, and three of them scarlet–orange–green flashed past her, flew down the stairs, laughed and scattered midway, overtook their aunt and grandfather and thudded on to the first floor.

On the first floor Saswati said, 'Have you seen all the gifts Swati's got, Baba?'

'Not all,' Rajen-babu answered after what seemed to be some thought.

'Want to see? Come along. Come with me.' Saswati took her father into the room that Mahashweta was resting in when Satyen had arrived. Sitting at the brand new dressing table, Dalim was absorbed in combing his hair, he leapt to his feet on hearing them.

'What are you doing here, Dalim?'

'I . . . I was er . . . Just passing . . . The room was empty . . . So . . . All these things . . . Is it wise to leave it empty?'

'Not at all.' Saswati answered, her mouth round, her eyes wide.

'And almost everyone was upstairs,' Dalim offered more justification in all seriousness, 'so I . . .'

'You *have* to be useful all the time, Dalim?'

Dalim blushed all the way to his neck. Seeing him redden Saswati was reminded of the incident of the jug, which she had forgotten almost instantly.

'There's something you *can* do. Go find out if your new Mesho is all right downstairs.'

'No, Shejomashi, not Mesho please?'

'All right, your Satyen-da then . . .'

'Certainly!' Dalim sprang to attention like a soldier. 'Is there something I should tell him?'

'Just have a chat. He's probably all by himself.'

'All right.' Dalim sounded subdued. Why didn't Saswati ask him to carry the almirah downstairs instead? What on earth would he say to Satyen? How would he begin the conversation? Or would Satyen do it? A worried Dalim went towards the door, pausing on hearing footsteps on the staircase leading to the second floor. 'They're all coming downstairs, Shejomashi,' he said happily, turning back, 'I'd better . . . What do you think?'

Saswati didn't reply, she didn't appear to have heard. With a glance at her back, the sari cascading across it, Dalim left.

'. . . This tissue sari is from Leela-mashi, real silver, Baba.' Positioned near the clothes-rack stacked with saris, Saswati touched each sari as she described it. '. . . And this French chiffon is from Tapan-da—sky-blue—the colour of the night-sky actually—this maroon silk from Paresh-kaka, it's from Murshidabad, and this one—the silk from Dhaka—this one's from Shobha-di . . .' Saswati's voice dipped here, a little embarrassed, implying that it was a very generous gift from Shobha considering her finances.

'Very nice sari.' Rajen-babu glanced at his daughter.

'Yes, very!' Saswati's voice seemed a little too enthusiastic. 'About twelve rupees or so I'd say. And look at that one—she's got two of those—and you know, Baba, this new style here, five of them!'

'All right, I . . .' as soon as Rajen-babu stirred Saswati held on to his shoulder. 'Take a look here, Baba . . .' She guided him towards the dressing table. 'These vases are unusual, aren't they, Baba? And this little box with gala inlay, how sweet . . . And this minaret . . . And see . . .' Saswati opened the drawer, 'This pen . . . The new Parker for ladies . . . From Swati's friends . . . And have you seen . . . So-o-o-o many cases for her sindoor . . . I like the ivory one the most . . . What'll she do with so many! And this silver-framed mirror . . .' Saswati shut one drawer and opened another, then another . . . Touched an object here, picked another one up there, and kept talking enthusiastically and continuously, 'Toilet set . . . Trinket-box . . . Kashmir handicraft . . .'

'Anyone in here?' A deep matronly voice sounded near the door.

Rajen-babu moved away from his daughter at once.

'Let's see the gifts . . .' said Rebati-babu's wife as she entered, drawing the end of her sari over her head and looking a little stiff despite her bulk when she caught sight of Rajen-babu.

'Come in, please . . .'

Saswati went up to her with a smile, Rajen-babu flattened himself against the wall. Rebati-babu's wife entered, followed by two others; the footsteps died on the staircase. As he went out Rajen-babu heard a voice, 'First show us what she's got from her sisters . . .'

Rajen-babu didn't look at the room Swati was in, he didn't look anywhere; he went directly to the balcony in front, over whose railing the young girls had been leaning to watch the arrival of the groom. He stopped at once. Biju lay sprawled on the cot on his stomach, his arms splayed out, his shoulders heaved, his torso shook, an ugly sound like the hissing of a cat burst out of him from time to time, and near his head Shweta was bent over, gently running her hand over him and talking to him. 'What's the matter?' said Rajen-babu, going up to them.

'I tell you,' Shweta seemed to be whispering, 'this Biju . . .'

Rajen-babu's expression became stern, his brow creased in annoyance. 'Biju . . . Get up now . . . There's a good boy . . . It's almost time . . .'

'What's the use—oh—of crying—oh—this is how—oh—the world turns!'

Rajen-babu turned round. Walking quickly to the other end of the balcony, he said, 'Is it very bad, Beli?'

A young widow, almost wasted away herself, said hesitantly, 'When he gets an attack it's better in the open, so this balcony . . .'

'Of course, of course . . . Anything else we can . . . Some medicine . . . Make him more comfortable . . .'

'No—oh—nothing—oh—nothing works—oh—I—I was telling—oh—Bijon . . .'

'Don't talk any more, Dada,' said the widow, kneeling on the floor and fanning him.

But, gasping with asthma, Nepal-babu wouldn't stop. 'I was saying—oh—on such a day—oh—should—oh—should you cry—later—oh . . .'

Rajen-babu was watching him so closely he didn't listen. Nepal-babu squatted on a blanket laid out on the floor, a spittoon next to him, a shawl of impossible vintage around his waist, two arms as thin as rope dangling over the knees placed like a cone; like a blade of grass or two on subsided ground there were a few strands of beard in the hollows of his cheek, and the opaque eyes seemed to be desperate to reach the forehead above them. The flesh and blood had all been consumed, but still he was alive, and within that frame his throat—with thick veins within compartments created by walls of skin, and with an Adam's apple like a lump—had a life of its own like an amazing breathing-machine.

'There's no—oh—need to cry—oh—should be happy—oh—so happy—when I—oh—when—that—oh . . .' Nepal-babu either wasn't able to talk any more, or forgot what he wanted to say.

Rajen-babu didn't linger. He recalled that Nepal-babu too had arranged his daughter's wedding once upon a time—his only daughter, his only child—the girl died within two years of her marriage, the grandparents brought their granddaughter over to live with them, arranged for her wedding too, she came back a widow, and now this emaciated widower eked out a living somehow in Santragachhi with his granddaughter on a monthly pension of thirty-six rupees. And when he died what would Beli . . . But all thoughts had to stop somewhere.

'. . . The priest's gone upstairs, they're going to fetch Satyen, quick now, Biju . . .'

Biju emitted steam like a boiler at this information.

Rajen-babu's upper lip clamped down on his lower one, his brow furrowed so much that his eyes contracted. Looking at his son for a bit, he said, 'Get up, Biju!'

Biju's body jerked, then calmed down after he clutched the edge of the cot in his fist.

'Get up,' Shweta said gently, briefly.

'What is it? What's the matter?' Mahashweta and Saraswati came and stopped near Biju's feet.

'Nothing,' said Shweta. 'And over there?'

'Almost ready. Why isn't Biju getting up?'

'He will. Just resting a little—he's been working very hard.'

The younger sisters had believed their elder sister, but they realized the truth when Biju sat up. His eyes were so swollen he could barely be recognized. The younger sisters exchanged glances, Saraswati curled her lips and even as she was about to do the same Mahashweta's expression changed suddenly, and this change was reflected on Saraswati's face. They looked away from each other.

'Bijon—oh—go and do—oh—what you—oh—such a happy—oh—such—oh—such—khh!' There was a sound like an old but sturdy object exploding, Nepal-babu emitted some of the endless supply of phlegm in his lungs, his head slumped to one side, the widow Beli held the spittoon before him.

Saraswati threw a sidelong glance in that direction, then went to her father, saying, 'Baba, come and see Swati. I think she's looking very nice.' She said it humbly, having contributed considerably to the process.

'Get up this instant!' Rajen-babu suddenly shouted at Biju, his voice sounded unfamiliar.

Curled up, Biju looked at his father, his lips moved, he probably tried to say something, but both nostrils were blocked and he had lost his voice. Breathing hard through his mouth, he got up and went away quickly, without looking at anyone.

'Baba, Swati . . .'

But this time too he seemed not to hear Saraswati. 'Let them make a bed for him here,' he said anxiously, 'tell them to raise the pillow . . . Bringing Nepal-babu . . . Such a sick man . . . Why on earth . . ?' It wasn't quite clear what the last part referred to, or whom he was instructing.

A feeble hand shook like a rag to indicate refusal, and Beli said softly, 'This is fine, why unnecessarily . . .'

'No . . . How can we do that . . . He has to be helped to

sit up . . . And a little peace and quiet . . .' Rajen-babu looked around helplessly.

'I'll look after it,' said Saraswati capably.

She fetched some people to help, they made a thick comfortable bed on the cot, placed half a dozen pillows, Rajen-babu helped Beli lift the patient on the bed and made him sit comfortably, plumping up the pillows behind his shoulder and head quite unnecessarily, he said, 'All right? Better now? Feeling better now?'

'Oh, please don't bother . . . I . . . I'll do it,' said Beli, troubled.

'No need to do anything now,' Rajen-babu told the maid who had arrived, 'stay here, in case he needs anything . . .'

'Don't worry, Rajen-dadu . . . There's no need . . . As it is . . .' The tentative Beli could go no further, half-turning her back to the two glittering sisters, she sat so close to her grandfather that she was barely visible any more. Nepal-babu didn't try to talk any more, he didn't even seem to understand what was going on; his round, opaque eyes rolled up and became still, his mouth stayed open like the hole in the leather of a pair of torn shoes, he just drew air into the black cavity of his mouth like a set of bellows, air, just air, breaths. Maybe resting back against five pillows on the soft bed had made him comfortable, or maybe he was immersed for the moment in that insensate detachment which is the final solution to all the agonies of sickness.

As they stood there, Mahashweta and Saraswati watched this scene; Saraswati tried to signal to her father with her eyes, but she couldn't even meet his eye. Returning, she whispered, 'Baba overdoes everything.'

'The old man won't die here, will he?' Mahashweta asked anxiously.

'Of course not! No one dies of asthma.'

At this Mahashweta began to worry about what Nepal-babu

would die of in that case. But instead of expressing this, she said, 'Biju shouldn't have made him come.'

'Biju's got no sense!' Saraswati stopped at the door of the room where Swati was being dressed. Nepal-babu stretched out one leg, the other remained drawn up, Beli gently stretched that one out too, covered both with the shawl, and Rajen-babu remained on the spot. The concern in his expression made him look very worried. He had forgotten something important, something he should do, do immediately, but he couldn't for the life of him remember what it was. He glanced at Beli, at Nepal-babu; suddenly he wondered who they were. Looking around, he couldn't see anyone else. Where were all of them? Rajen-babu crossed the balcony, walking along the corridor between the rooms facing one another, he suddenly heard someone call, 'Baba!'

Nothing special, he had heard that word in a girl's voice a million times in his life, but suddenly he felt as though he couldn't breathe. A little later he realized Saswati was standing before the curtained door.

'Baba!' Saswati smiled. 'You no longer seem to know us.'

Rajen-babu didn't speak, didn't even try to smile.

'Come in here . . .' Saswati was about to go downstairs for another quick chat with Satyen before the wedding ceremony began, she had stopped on seeing her father, she returned with him. The crowds were gone now, most of the room was empty, but the group in the centre was larger now, and more silent than before, more absorbed. Everyone seemed to be looking at one person with deep attention, no one spoke much.

'Come, Baba!' Saswati entered the room and called him again. 'Come and see how beautiful Swati looks!'

Some of them turned at the sound of her voice. Saraswati came forward, Usha covered her head with her sari, Rajen-babu's sister's expression became a little forlorn. The women standing in a circle divided into two halves to make way for him, Saswati and Saraswati brought their father to the middle, face-to-face with her. Swati. Swati stood on a pretty white silk sheet on the pretty white floor. Her feet were covered by the golden border of her sari, only the tips of the toes were visible. The hair on her head was covered by the golden border too, only the thin parting in her hair was visible. Swati. The sari, golden lit-up stars flared into red, fell again to gold, like a bridge over black hair, nestling against ears which were like young sea-shells that had just become heavier under the weight of emerald earrings, dazzling against the background of the lotus-red blouse, skirting the ruby-and-emerald necklace, barely touching the comparatively less fair outer side of the arm—temporarily robbed of its free will—as it cascaded downwards. Swati. Her forehead, where a lock of her hair always dangled disobediently, was now as silken as the full moon under the tightly done-up hair, decorated like the blemishes on the moon with drops of sandalwood paste. And the hands that usually rose all the time to sweep those recalcitrant locks away now hung uselessly at her side, a finger on the left hand was bent, probably unused to the ring on it, the pink nails touched the golden border of the sari unknowingly. Swati. Her face—that active theatre of joy and sorrow—seemed to have got a respite finally; the lights were on, the sets were in place, but the actors were missing, it was empty, quiet, her slightly swollen pinkish lids were lowered on her eyes, her full moist lips were closed, besides the almost invisible quivering of the nostrils like a flute, there were no words on her face.

The room was silent for a minute after Rajen-babu's arrival, then the buzz rose afresh, 'Beautiful . . . How beautiful she looks . . . A beauty indeed.'

'The sari looks very nice on her, doesn't it, Baba?' Saswati asked in a low voice.

But Rajen-babu wasn't looking at the sari. Dazzling in golden-red sari, lotus-red blouse, emerald earrings and ruby-and-emerald necklace, the bangles and bracelets glittering next to the white of the *shankha*—he noticed none of it; he didn't even seem to see the person everyone was crowding around, in whom every pair of eyes was absorbed, but it *was* she whom he was looking at. He was looking at Swati, the tiny turbulent restless Swati in a frock, who kicked up fearful rows with her elder sister, who cried herself to sleep after a scolding from her mother, who went to sleep in her father's arms, her curly head resting on his shoulder, without having her dinner. Suddenly a fog descended over Rajen-babu's eyes; the enormous room, the lights, the people all disappeared; he had just calmed Swati down and put her to bed beside her mother, and sitting on the bed, her knees drawn up, her mother gazed upon her with her large eyes on her thin face. Forgetting the daughter, Rajen-babu looked at the mother; she would raise her face, say something any moment now. But the exhausted eyes on the slender face did not move, they only gazed at her daughter in silence.

'You know . . .'

Rajen-babu started. Who spoke?

Saraswati said into his ear, 'We didn't make her put on all the jewellery, Baba. It would have been too much.'

Rajen-babu exhaled. Everything came into focus again, reality reappeared, he saw before him the dazzling, beautiful, distant Swati. When did she grow up? When did she grow up so? Rajen-babu was astonished.

'Swati, turn this way.' From a short distance, Usha's sharp eyes had led her to suspect that a small lock of hair next to the parting had already broken ranks, so she said again, 'Let me see—don't lower your head now.'

But Swati bowed her head even more. Baba, she said to herself. She hadn't seen him all day. For ever so long now he hadn't looked at her—hadn't been able to look at her. She hadn't been to him either, hadn't stood by his side, hadn't said anything. Again she said to herself, Baba. She saw the faded colour of his shawl, the sleeve, an arm, as she gazed the arm was lowered, then she saw the folds in his dhoti, its border, the sandals. Swati couldn't look at her father's face, the embarrassment, glory, responsibility of being born a daughter made her lower her eyes even more.

∾

The guests were leaving, the excitement stretched all the way to the street. Instead of unnecessarily prolonged farewells, most of them hurried off to get trams; divided into small as well as large groups, to the sound of pointed as well as heavy shoes, with words in deep as well as high voices, they created a sudden flurry of activity on Calcutta's blacked-out, fearful, silent, winter streets; on the other side, about ten cars stopped at a distance, reversed their way up to the gate one by one, honking continuously; some of the guests sought out taxis or rickshaws, some said let's walk, and as they passed by some pedestrians stopped to avoid the crowds, glaring at the house and thinking with bomb-besieged minds, yet another wedding!

Near the gate a couple of people were busy supervising the reversing cars, and on either side of the exit from the balcony Iru and Geeti stood holding silver salvers piled with paan—in case anyone wanted one more on their way out—and Hemanga stood on the top step, bidding goodbye to everyone. Depending on age, relationship and degree of intimacy, he exchanged a few words with almost everyone, saying 'goodnight' only to those whom he did not know at all. Many of them didn't even notice his farewell; talking amongst themselves or wondering whether they'd get a tram; but still, every time Hemanga spotted someone he didn't know, he tilted his head the same way and said 'goodnight' the same way.

When the crowd had thinned considerably, Rebati-babu emerged with his waddling wife and grown-up unmarried daughters. Although Hemanga had only seem him once fleetingly,

he recognized him at once—he remembered faces perfectly.
Rubbing his hands together, he said, 'So soon . . .?'

'Yes, we'd better . . .' Rebati-babu answered even before
Hemanga had finished. 'I'd have liked to have stayed . . . They
even more . . .' He tilted his head towards his wife, who seemed
indignant at this flippancy and turned away her hard face—
'but I'm not feeling very . . . If I catch a cold . . .'

'Then shall I get you a car . . .' said Hemanga quickly.

'Not necessary.' Rebati-babu raised his hand. 'It's a very
short way, too short to . . . All right then, we had a wonderful
time.' The entire family descended the steps.

The next people he met were Majumdar and his niece.
Hemanga's expression turned into a smile at first, then into
disappointment. 'You're leaving too?'

You too. Why, am I supposed to be someone special? 'I
am,' he said briefly.

'We were really hoping you . . .' glancing at Urmila,
Hemanga corrected himself quickly, 'both of you would stay.'

'It's not much of a thing to hope for.' Majumdar didn't
smile, the way he spoke made it sound almost rude. Then,
probably realizing as much, he smiled broadly, saying, 'Not today.
We'll meet again, I'm sure. This is where you . . . This is your
house now, isn't it?'

Urmila took the opportunity to express her wish once
more. 'Can't we stay a little, Mama?'

Majumdar's expression changed instantly, he looked at his
niece sternly. She knew the meaning of this look, if you listen
to me you'll get all you want, and if you don't like that I can
send you back immediately to your mother in Nathurampur.
Urmila shrank back in silence.

Smiling again, Majumdar told Hemanga, 'If you don't
mind, I'll take the Pontiac. The driver's taken the Austin
back, you see.' He spoke as though the driver had done
this of his own accord, that his employer had nothing to
do with it.

Hemanga smiled to himself in sympathy. He was a young man—with a new car. 'Of course! You must take your own car back—there's no question of . . . And everything is done here anyway. Really, you did us such a big favour.' Hemanga realized Majumdar wanted to hear this once more, which is why he ended the way he did.

Majumdar enjoyed hearing this, but at the same time he felt a stab of rage. Favour! Was he a professional do-gooder? He recalled Harit Nandy coming downstairs with him—how the man could rave!—as soon as they reached the first floor the sister in the red necklace emerged from somewhere to ask him, 'Where are you off to, Nandy? Forget it, come this way!' She seemed to turn the horse into a lamb in a moment and dragged him away, and while doing that managed to incline her head and smile at Urmila. Majumdar had breathed a sigh of relief at finally having escaped Harit's clutches, but just a few minutes later he felt humiliated when he recalled it; the more he realized there was no question of an insult here, the angrier he felt, he wanted to say something harsh, something that would really hurt, but he couldn't work out what he could say without crossing the bounds of decency, and by the time he looked again Hemanga had shifted his attention to another group of people who were leaving, it was a large group, a dark-complexioned, handsome middle-aged man was talking to the two girls in scarlet and orange saris holding salvers of paan, if he'd been younger he'd have looked like Nandy.

'Fine girls! Fine young women!' said Harit's enthusiastic father, smiling with abnormally white false teeth.

Hearing themselves described as young women, Iru and Geeti smiled broadly, then, moving away and catching each other's eyes, burst out in unnecessary laughter, and the last wave of that laughter hit Nikhil, dressed in the old brown flannel shirt, as he returned after finishing his second cigarette out on the street.

'A paan for you?' Hemanga turned back towards Majumdar. Iru appeared quickly and held out her salver. Majumdar set his eyes for a moment on the blossoming girl in the scarlet sari, smiled a little and took a paan.

'My daughter,' said Hemanga, possibly a little anxiously.

Majumdar didn't notice his anxiety, his anger subsided. The appearance of the slender lovely elfin young girl near him seemed to touch a soft spot somewhere in his heart, a line of grace suddenly appeared at the corner of his lips when he said, 'I realized as much. How else could she be so beautiful?'

Hemanga Bardhan ran his hand over his bald patch and smiled deferentially at this, as though the credit for his daughter's beauty was all his own; and immediately afterwards he moved towards Saswati's in-laws, who were heading for the stairs.

Trying to step back Majumdar heard his niece's soft voice, 'Let's go too, Mama . . .'

Half-turning towards her Majumdar said, 'Very well, why don't you stay?'

The painted face with the hexagonal glasses brightened at once. Urmila wasn't surprised, she was used to these sudden changes of fancy in her uncle. She wasn't stupid, she had realized her uncle liked to make those under him dance at his bidding, was fond of tasting his authority over them in various ways. Urmila was about to provide something for his taste buds immediately by saying things that would please him, but she didn't get the opportunity.

'I'll send Subir with the car about an hour later.' Majumdar didn't give his niece another glance, seeing Hemanga standing before him he inclined his head and said, 'Goodnight,' then ran down the steps two at a time, overtook the Nandy family to reach the street almost at a run, seemed to be reunited with a friend when he climbed into the black Pontiac which had blended into the darkness.

Where to? Where to now? Where else but . . . home—that

same home, that very home, where there were comforts that could drown him but no happiness. But happiness or not, at least there was sleep; and then the day again, work again. But sleep so soon? The moment you hit the bed, now *that* was sleep. He needed exhaustion, more exhaustion. Majumdar changed gears . . . Where to? Don Juan's revelries? Geetali? Or maybe tonight . . .? Or should he go home and summon his office manager, the old man would get out of his warm bed and run quaking to meet him. No, he wouldn't go anywhere, there was nothing to be had anywhere. Only flattery. Even his father spoke to him cringingly—it was loathsome. How appalling life was without money, but how appalling with it too. If only his mother hadn't died . . . There was a screeching sound.

Majumdar braked, an expletive on his lips. In front of the car—a cow? Can you imagine, no wonder people called them cows. Majumdar blew his horn long and loud . . . But even at the sound of that all-new electric horn that made people jump out of their skins, the cow was not perturbed at all, didn't realize even remotely that the enormous and expensive Pontiac had stopped just because of her, very unhurriedly shifted a step or two, barely moving, as though laboriously making just about enough room for the car to pass, craned her neck from the same spot to graze on the dry grass on the verge running down the middle of Southern Avenue, and Majumdar brushed past her tail to take a bad-tempered turn into Lansdowne Road. This was another nuisance of these blackouts—there was no joy any more to driving either.

∾

By then the crowd in the large carpeted ground-floor room at the venue of the wedding had dwindled to about fifteen men, close relatives, or those who had been unable to refuse their wives, or those who were eager or curious themselves. They had moved closer to the groom now; most of them knew one another, they had just completed an excellent dinner; except for the slightly older men who were feeling drowsy already, the rest were enthusiastic about conversing.

No one discussed the war any more—even Kiran Bakshi had forgotten the bomb for now, Harit wasn't there either to remind them. They discussed the evening, a few remarks also being addressed to the protagonist present on the scene.

'. . . I've known her since she was a child,' the round-faced Prabhat-babu in the thin gold-rimmed glasses said, 'wonderful girl, absolutely brilliant. Rajen-babu had been worried about a suitable groom for her . . .' Not that he had ever heard Rajen-babu profess any concern in this matter, but there was no harm making the claim . . . 'But then the girl made sure to give her father no cause for concern. Very nice!' Concluding, he looked at Satyen with admiration, but also with amusement.

'This sort of wedding is the norm these days,' said Tapan, the smart mint-fresh barrister lately back from the UK.

'Norm? What do you mean norm? How many such weddings do you get in all?' Even after fourteen rashogollas the sixty-plus Bhupesh-babu joined the argument intrepidly.

'If it isn't, it should be,' announced Tapan firmly, for, far from having children readying for marriage, he himself was yet to be married; using a comparison of their respective beauty, accomplishments and fathers' wealth, he was wooing two young women simultaneously, unable to choose between them yet.

'Why should it?' Paresh-babu, an engineer, took Bhupesh-babu's side.

'This practice of the groom's family approving of the bride is barbaric.'

'What? Barbaric!' Prabhat-babu threw his head back and laughed. 'So you're branding everyone in this land a barbarian.'

'Never mind our land, it's the same system everywhere in the world,' Paresh-babu spoke in the low tone of someone whose logic cannot be refuted. 'It's the parents who arrange these things everywhere, after which it's all for form's sake.'

'Really?' Tapan glanced mockingly at him.

'Of course I'm talking about good families. For them the system is rigid even in an England or a Europe.' Supreme confidence oozed from Paresh-babu, for after having spent his youth virtually trouble-free in the industrial areas of England, Scotland and Germany, he had been forced to get married in Glasgow, to a woman of his own choice, not that she was from a 'good family', but he had been considerably harassed trying to extricate himself; and now even his uneducated Bengali wife of twenty years was sometimes startled at his orthodox views. Noting the mockery in the callow young barrister's eyes he said, 'I lived in those countries for ten years, I know.'

'That was a long time ago!' Tapan expressed contempt through the shape of his lips. 'Everything has changed now.'

'Changed? Didn't Edward VIII have to abdicate just the other day?'

'Oh, that! That's different. But . . .'

'Is this even worth talking about?' Prabhat-babu interrupted loudly. 'It was our parents who arranged all our marriages . . . Has it turned out so terrible for us . . . We *have* managed to go through life haven't we . . . Heh heh!' Running his hand over his socks-encased foot he swayed his torso, beaming silently all over his round face and then even blushing a little suddenly.

But the other two didn't even hear him. Ignoring—almost forgetting—everyone else, Paresh-babu and Tapan conversed amongst themselves; a competition had been sparked off between them over which of them knew Europe better. Paresh-babu's argument was that he had lived there longer, had travelled a great deal too, therefore there was at least no one here who could possibly overrule him; and Tapan wanted to say that since he had been there recently, he was much better informed.

Prabhat-babu listened to the argument for a while, but was unable to make much sense of it, as soon as he turned around his eyes met Kiran Bakshi's, who had been craning his neck to listen.

For quite some time now Kiran Bakshi had been on the verge of participating. He had listened closely, it made him uncomfortable, he positively hated the conversation. What strange things they were saying about marriage, as though humans had ever had any control over it. It was a . . . a . . . Kiran couldn't quite say what, couldn't find a word for it, but felt it deeply within himself. Take Anita . . . How long have we been married after all, even the other day I knew nothing about her, but now it seems it was always this way, so many lifetimes . . . That kind of thing. There was such a hunt for a bride, Ma surveyed so many different girls, so did I now and then . . . But now can I even imagine anyone but Anita? Satyen too the same way—and in Satyen's presence these people . . . How peculiar they are! All these thoughts ran through Kiran's mind, and, craning his neck to look at them alternately, he looked for an opening to speak; after catching Prabhat-babu's eye he didn't hesitate any more.

'I agree completely with you,' began Kiran, stressing on the 'I'.

Prabhat-babu was surprised, perturbed too. He couldn't imagine what he might have said that had made none other than the groom's friend agree with him.

'What you said about marriage,' Kiran reminded him. 'You're right. The marriage is what matters, not the circumstances leading to it.'

'Exactly,' agreed Prabhat-babu, forgetting that the speaker was only echoing his own statement.

'What these people are saying makes no sense,' Kiran indicated them with his eyes. 'Actually . . .' Having discovered the word he seemed to clutch at it . . . 'Actually marriage is a . . . a . . .'

Kiran paused to look for an appropriate word, but Prabhat-babu said at once, 'Right! Right you are!' He nodded, and then, turning to the groom, said deferentially, 'You're a college professor, aren't you?'

Satyen suddenly realized he was being addressed. But . . . What? What had he said? Seeing him hesitate, Kiran answered on his behalf, mentioned the name of his college.

'Excellent,' Prabhat-babu said, looking at Satyen. 'You must go to England, though. As you can see, no matter how much of a scholar you are, without a British stamp you're a nobody.'

Satyen smiled amiably in response.

'Our Harit now, a fine boy—and doing very well at work too I hear.'

Unable to understand the connection between the successive statements made by this cheerful, kind, bespectacled fine man, Satyen smiled again, this time a little stupidly.

'Excellent!' Prabhat-babu didn't specify what or whom he was praising, looked around with happily approving eyes and said, 'But where's Harit?'

At the time Saraswati was telling Arun on the first-floor landing, 'Take Nandy with you.'

On hearing his name, Harit glanced at them with detachment. He had accepted his current predicament bravely; he leaned against the wall in a pose that tried to express his generous contempt for the idiotic world of women and ceremonies. But still, he was stuck, unable to budge, because either Saraswati or Mahashweta, and sometimes both, kept drawing him into conversation—meaningless exchanges!—but . . . All right . . . Since they insisted, might as well listen. He had even told Saraswati in English, you haven't grown a day older, she had laughed, so had he with her.

'Don't delay things any more,' Saraswati urged her husband.

Running his hand through his unkempt hair, Arun went up to Harit. 'Let's go, Mr Nandy.'

'Where?'

Listening to someone else meanwhile, Saraswati turned her head to give him a quick look. 'Go fetch the groom, Nandy.'

'Fetch the groom? He's been here a long time already.'

At this Saraswati, Mahashweta and her pretty sister-in-law with the slight down above the upper lip, who was passing by, all broke into peals of laughter. Harit reddened; he simply couldn't understand what they were laughing at.

'Come along, never mind them.' Arun touched Harit's shoulder lightly; rescuing him from the clutches of flighty women he took Harit downstairs.

Paresh-babu and Tapan were still arguing. The engineer resorted to his seniority in age to say, 'You don't know anything my friend!' The barrister answered by the law, 'It's better to know a few things correctly than many things wrongly.' Paresh-babu didn't offer a retort, Tapan fell silent too; both of them realized simultaneously that no one else in the room was speaking; so they stopped speaking too. As it often happens when people are waiting for something, everyone suddenly fell silent at the same time.

Arun and Harit entered, all eyes turned towards them. By now Arun had summoned an almost medical gravity to his expression, and as Harit trailed him with a munificent smile, he suddenly recollected his own wedding night.

Arun came up to Satyen, said, 'Shall we go?'

Picking up the garland lying next to Satyen with both his hands, Kiran said, 'Here you are.'

This time Satyen did not attempt revolt, he took the garland.

'Forget the shawl,' said Kiran, removing it himself from Satyen's shoulders and handing it to Nikhil, who was nearby, to put away. 'Put this on now.'

Satyen slipped the garland on, almost everyone present rose too, only a few of the drowsy old men stayed put. But when he tried to walk, the groom hopped like a frog instead.

Arun's medical gravity didn't last; chuckling, he asked, 'What's the matter?'

'Pins and needles.'

'Pins and needles?' Harit suppressed his laughter. 'Can't blame them, given how long you've had to sit without moving.'

'Take my hand then,' Kiran offered.

'No, it's fine,' said Satyen, hopping again on one foot.

'Give it a good shake,' whispered Kiran.

'No need!' Instead of hopping, Satyen now placed the edge of his foot on the floor with each step, limping, the garland flopping around his neck in rhythm with every stride. He tried to maintain his dignity as much as he could through all of this, but the mixture of pain and the attempt to conceal it made him look like a naughty boy being marched off to the teacher to be punished, while trying to convince his classmates that he didn't care at all.

This expression on his face suddenly endeared Satyen to Harit. Once outside the room, he asked, 'Better?'

'Better,' said Satyen, about to put on his shoes, but he couldn't slip one on around his still-swollen left foot. Supporting himself against the wall, he tried to manoeuvre, but it was no good.

'What's all this!' Kiran exclaimed. 'Do you plan to get married with shoes on?'

'Never mind then.' Satyen proceeded barefoot, seemingly disappointed, unhappy. Harit and Arun flanked him, Kiran walked directly behind, behind Kiran, Nikhil, and then the long winding queue of people from the bride's side.

Kiran tapped his shoulder at the foot of the stairs. When he looked back, Kiran said in a low voice, 'Well? How do you feel?'

'I feel nothing!' Satyen answered openly, instantly, at a volume everyone could hear.

'Hah!' Kiran dismissed this, but Satyen had told the truth. He really did feel nothing, no frisson, not even a frisson of novelty. It was as though all this was familiar, as though he knew beforehand that at this particular time these particular things would happen. That on this specific date at this specific time he would set foot on this red step, then this one. Emotion had vanished this morning, but a faint awareness of its absence had still been present; now it wasn't even faint. Everything was clear now—natural, in other words. He felt normal, calm, absolutely level-headed. There was neither a tremor, nor an aftershock, in his heart! Neither hope nor fear, neither suspicion nor joy. Just like his college days, when he wouldn't be able to sleep on the eve of the exam out of anxiety, but as soon as he sat at his desk to take the exam, as soon as the huge exam hall fell silent at the rustling of the question papers being distributed, instantly his mind would be freed of curiosity, of anxiety, becoming calm. In the same way now too everything was clear, simple, so simple that it was normal. He was surprised himself, even tried to feel something, but felt nothing, besides the comfort of the pins and needles going away completely. Satyen climbed the stairs easily, crossing the first floor and going on up to the second; at the last step he suddenly walked ahead of Arun and Harit to proceed on his own; spontaneously, confidently, freely, he stood at the door to the lit-up terrace.

The larger portion of the terrace, where dinner had been served, was quiet now. The chairs had already been put away, only rows of tables remained. And where there were barely a couple of people earlier, that smaller portion was now packed, humming with activity, laughing, colourful, but also solemn.

All this while, Ata had been gazing entranced at Swati in her bridal finery, suddenly turning round and unable to find her friends, she ran to the terrace. Where were they? But instead of looking for Iru and Geeti, Ata found a vantage point, she had to watch the wedding from the beginning, after all. Now if only they'd come quickly.

It didn't take long, someone clapped her on the back soon afterwards. 'Here she is! Didn't I say she'd be on the terrace!'

Looking at them with shining happy eyes, Ata asked, 'Where were you?'

'Us?' Geeti's look suggested deep mystery. Turning to Iru, she asked, 'How many did you have?'

'Twenty-six.'

'Show-off!'

'At least eleven or twelve,' said Iru.

'I had eighteen, exactly,' said Geeti.

'Paan?' Ata pouted, looked daggers. 'So *that's* what both of you were doing all this while. Paan in secret?'

'In secret? Who says?' Iru sent a message with her eyes too. 'Openly. In front of everyone. We were giving people paan, and while we did, we too . . .'

'Didn't you get any for me?' Ata set off a wave of indignation.

Without replying, Iru grabbed Ata's right hand with her left, then, prising open her fist, placed in it a small paan with a clove, warmed by her own hand.

'I had a lot too,' said Ata. 'So many, I didn't even count. Anyway, since you got this for me, I'll have this one too.' Popping it in her mouth, she laughed with her eyes at Iru, saying, 'Your lips really have turned red.'

'Mine?' asked Geeti quickly.

'As if yours need to be red,' said Ata, 'you've already turned it into a postbox.'

Geeti's painted cheeks turned redder still, as though to prove this statement of Ata's wrong. 'As if Iru hasn't used lipstick,' she said, nudging Iru with her shoulder.

'Move aside, O goddesses,' said the thin priest in a surprisingly deep baritone as he arranged things on a copper salver.

Like a wave the scarlet–green–orange saris rolled away. Iru and Geeti thought 'O goddesses' was hilarious, trying to suppress

their laughter they let it out in gasps. 'What's so funny?'
Realizing the reason, Ata arched her eyebrows.

'What's that the priest has on?' Geeti whispered in her ear.

'Don't you know?' Ata smiled. 'It's called the *namaboli*.
Got the different names of God written on it.'

'Oh, so *that's* a *namaboli*.' Geeti looked solemn, but giggled
immediately. 'Seen that tail of hair?'

'Stale tail,' said Iru.

Even Ata found this funny, controlling herself she mixed
admonition into her laughter, saying, 'What nonsense . . .! He
isn't some common priest, you know, he teaches in a school.'

'What rubbish! As if a priest can be a schoolmaster!'
said Geeti.

'But I know he is. All right, check with Mama . . .'

'Shh!' said Iru, tapping Ata on the shoulder. 'There's Mama.
It's starting now.'

They nestled closer to one another.

Wrapped in silk fabric, Bijon walked up to the priest
unnaturally quickly and was about to plop down on one of
the mats when the priest stopped him with upraised hand.
'That is your seat. Facing north.'

Bijon sat on the correct mat, woven with grass, facing north.
He shuddered as soon as he sat down. 'Sit still,' said the priest.

Bijon was still. Several pairs of eyes observed him—by
then many more people had arrived, most of them women.
'Who's he?' Iva Ganguly asked Chitra.

'I think he'll give the bride away.'

'Really? Isn't he too young to give the bride away?'

Standing close by, Urmila overheard them. Looking at them
out of the corner of her eye, she said, 'He's Swati's elder brother.'

Iva remembered the hexagonal glasses, they had had no
choice but to notice when they were eating. Now she looked at
the face closely, it looked familiar. Urmila turned towards
them at the same moment, smiled, came closer. 'Are you one of
the family?' Iva asked.

'No, I'm not part of the family. I said I'm a friend, didn't I? But . . .' Urmila said many things more without pausing. And within five minutes a friendship sprung up between her and Iva Ganguly, the kind that's possible only between two women in a railway compartment or at a wedding, not anywhere else or between any other people.

After getting to know the most important things about each other, Urmila said, 'Bijon-da looks so helpless! I'm referring to Swati's brother.'

'But he's not doing anything, he only seems to be sitting there.'

'No, can't you see him moving his lips?'

'Yes!' Iva laughed. 'Only the priest mutters all those words, the others merely move their lips.'

Urmila laughed too. 'Complicated, too! Can't they get it over with quickly?'

'It's nice to look at though,' Anupama remarked gently.

'Yes, very nice for others.' People nearby looked back on hearing her masculine voice. 'But so painful for the bride and the groom.'

'Is it really?' Chitra interjected suddenly. A wave of laughter swayed the four young women standing side by side, all the way to Urmila.

Chitra felt someone tug at her sari. 'Didi . . .' whispered a girl of about ten.

Turning back, Chitra's smiling face turned glum instantly on seeing her mother. 'Are we going now, Ma?'

'Yes, let's. It's late—and there's the blackout too. You're coming with us too, aren't you?' said Chitra's mother, looking at Anupama.

'So soon!' Anupama's voice sounded like a plea.

'Please stay a bit,' said Iva. 'I'll leave too in a while, we can all go together. You're not too far away—they can send someone with us.'

But, already burdened with husband and family, Chitra's mother wasn't willing to stay any longer. Suddenly Urmila said, craning her neck to look at her, 'May I say something, if you don't mind! My car will be here after some time to pick me up, I can drop all of you home.' What if it was the smaller car though? Then it would need two trips—not all that much of trouble! Reassured, Urmila looked at Chitra's mother again. 'Will that help?'

Chitra's mother couldn't reject the proposal from this bright unknown young woman out of hand. In her heart she wanted to stay too, but how often do such wishes come true anyway. Taking advantage of her hesitation, Chitra said, 'Let's stay, Ma.'

'All right . . . You're not sleepy, Tunti?'

'Not at all! I'm not in the least bit sleepy.' The ten-year-old opened her eyes wide to prove her point visibly. Then she stirred, saying with trepidation, 'There's the groom, Ma!'

The little girl's observation seemed to spread across the gathering, everyone stirred. Along with the groom, well behind him, many more people arrived, all men, and behind them arrived a gaggle of children between five and ten. A few bold ones among them approached and sat very close by, and noticing that no one objected, the rest also arranged themselves near the wedding area.

Satyen sat down on the low platform with patterns in white, facing east; another platform next to him was empty, a little smaller, the pattern different too. Satyen looked all around after he sat; the first thing he saw was the group of children sitting all bunched up together! There he was . . . What was his name now, Saraswati's son . . . Yes, Dipu; and Mahashweta's three sons, almost of equal height . . . And Chhoton in front of everyone . . . Just look at him, the dandy in a dhoti, sitting cross-legged. There was Tata with her group . . . All of them in glittering saris tonight, all with lips reddened by paan . . . And so what if they were children, the differences between the boys' group and the girls' group were palpable. Satyen moved his gaze, suddenly saw Akhil nearby; he had summoned up a solemnity suitable to the occasion on his lean face, standing with his arms folded across his chest.

'Sit down, Akhil,' said Satyen softly.

Akhil hadn't even dreamt that Satu-da would actually talk to him during the wedding ceremony; instantly his solemnity fell away, and a crooked row of teeth was bared in a smile.

Overhearing Satyen, Arun put his hand on Akhil's shoulder. 'Why don't you sit down here,' he said, making him sit practically in physical contact with Satyen. Akhil was finally comfortable—he'd been standing a long time, but was it right to sit so close to Satu-da? He moved away a little, but not towards the children—ugh! With those shrimps!

'Wonderful! You left the most important thing behind!' said Hemanga, bending over him from behind and depositing the *topor* in his lap. Satyen frowned at it; moving the ugly glittering object gingerly with two fingers, he said pathetically, 'Do I *have* to?'

'Repose it on your head,' instructed the priest.

'Now?'

Looking at the groom for a moment, the priest said, 'All right, later.'

'One more thing. I'm not taking off these clothes,' said Satyen, meeting the priest's lustreless eyes under his bushy salt-and-pepper eyebrows.

He had expected the priest to be astonished, but there was no sign of it on the tonsured priest's lean, clean-shaven face. In a slightly tired voice he said, 'You may don the upper covering at the appropriate juncture.'

Satyen was pleased; but he didn't seem quite as pleased at such a ready solution, he didn't feel it was a victory.

The wedding ceremony began. Holding out a copper plate before Bijon, the priest said, 'Gather a handful of rice with your right hand.'

Bijon picked up a fistful from the fine rice piled on the plate.

'Now repose the left hand above the right.'

Bijon complied.

Positioning Bijon's left hand correctly, the priest said, 'Now touch the groom's right knee with your right hand,' using an arcane Bengali word for knee.

Bijon could not remember which part of the body the word referred to, he looked at the priest's face.

The priest personally brought a finger on Bijon's right hand in contact with the groom's right knee. Bijon had to lean considerably towards Satyen, his upper covering parted to reveal a slice of skin. The priest recited the Sanskrit words slowly, with gaps, and in an indistinct, sibilant, hoarse voice Bijon went on muttering something similar. Satyen felt a tickling sensation on his knee where Bijon's finger was touching it, a smile appeared on his lips.

Noticing this, Usha said, 'The groom's quite lively. He's smiling.'

Without taking her eyes off the scene, Shobha said, 'Yes, very. And why shouldn't he be!' She wondered how a wedding felt if you already knew the man you were marrying quite well, but in a moment she moved away from the thought and became absorbed watching.

Removing his finger from the groom's knee, Biju straightened up, the priest turned his head to say something to Hemanga, Hemanga signalled to Arun, Arun hurried off. The children sitting close by turned their heads to see. Shobha looked at two of the girls for a moment, in a moment her eyes shifted—because of the happiness she was allowed to feel after such a long time, even her own children appeared irrelevant on this last night of happiness.

Someone said in a grandmotherly voice from the back, 'What's the groom waiting for? When will he put on the wedding dress?'

'Have they gone to fetch the bride?' A much younger voice was heard.

'The bride's coming. The bride's coming?' Beginning at the parapet towards the road, the buzz among the girls spread to the room on the terrace at the other end. The first floor was silent; the room where the bride was being dressed up wasn't crowded any more, the handful of people still there were silent too.

Arun, dishevelled, materialized suddenly, saying, 'Come, Swati.'

The words fell on the floor like a spark. Swati's aunt and Kunda exchanged glances, then Kunda said, 'Come, Swati. It's time.'

Swati didn't move. She kept standing as she was, head bowed, her arms inanimate, just as Rajen-babu had seen her, but her clothing had changed. Her face was now half-veiled in a transparent pink veil, a light tiara—made of the same pith as Satyen's *topor*—adorned her hair, and over the emerald-ruby gold-and-red a thick, white, fragrant garland reached down from her neck almost to her knee.

'Let her walk upstairs,' said Leela softly.

'Walk!' Her aunt had been gazing at Swati through calm, slightly melancholy eyes all this time, but now she was galvanized into activity. 'The bride will walk? The idea!' With a flash of her eyes she extracted support from Kunda, then, vaporizing Leela with a single sidelong glance, she called out slightly hoarsely, 'Who's coming to carry Swati upstairs?'

Dalim came forward, rolling up his striped sleeves.

'Who else?'

'Me,' said Arun from the back.

'Come, Swati, sit down on this.' Her aunt's tone changed suddenly, becoming soft, moist, as she pointed to the low platform on which Swati would sit to be carried upstairs.

Swati stirred, she stepped on the platform painted in yellow, white and red; she sat down cross-legged, almost half of the garland coiled into her lap, white on red. Her sisters surrounded her; between Mahashweta and Saraswati, Shweta looked as white as the garland round Swati's neck.

Saswati kneeled behind Swati. Putting her hand on her sister's back, she said ever so softly, 'Swati.' She was close to tears suddenly, unable to breathe, so she called softly.

Swati trembled. She raised her face, covered with the scarf, turned her face, everything was blurred, through blurry eyes she saw Shweta.

'Silly girl!' A smile, the trace of a smile, floated across Shweta's lips. 'Arun . . .'

Saswati rose, her sisters stepped back, Arun and Dalim bent and lifted the platform from either side, Swati sitting on it. As soon as they had raised her a little, Swati swayed, quickly put her arms around their necks to balance herself.

Straightening, Arun said, 'Can you manage, Dalim?'

'Of course,' said Dalim, puffing his chest.

'No, two aren't enough. Wait,' said Shweta, going quickly to the door and calling out with her hand on the curtain, 'Paresh-kaka, we need your help to carry Swati upstairs.'

'Carry? All right!' Tossing his cigarette away, Paresh-babu tugged at the curtain. He had only meant to part them, but the lightly set curtain dropped to the floor, bringing the brass rod down too. Shweta put it aside.

'Come along, Mr Barrister!' The short but well-built Paresh-babu took a step.

'Me too? All right.' Tapan, a bit of a fop, came forward slowly. Unable to forget the acrimony of their argument, he said with a touch of contempt, 'Why don't you let go, Paresh-da?'

'What? You think Paresh-da's getting old? I can still take on half a dozen like you . . .'

The four strong men took hold of the platform on four

sides. Lifted into mid-air, Swati began her journey towards life. The sound of conch shells rose louder than the ululation, the women trailed behind, in the balcony the napping Nepal-babu started, Beli abandoned him for a few minutes to take a look, Rajen-babu's grey shawl was seen fleetingly in the corridor.

'Careful now,' said Paresh-babu as they reached the staircase.

'All right,' said Dalim.

Swati ascended the stairs, Arun and Dalim on either side, Paresh-babu behind her, Tapan in front, facing her. Tapan had the lightest load, but the hardest job, for he had to climb the stairs backwards. When turning at the landing between floors, he tripped on his dhoti.

The platform tilted to the front, there was enormous pressure on Arun's and Dalim's necks, Paresh-babu saw Swati's back bending like a swimmer's. Quickly grabbing her with one hand, he said, 'Never mind Tapan, let go.'

'Why don't you take my place instead,' said Tapan.

Paresh-babu and Tapan exchanged positions, but even after that they had to stop at the door to the terrace. Tilting the platform, tilting themselves, as soon as the four of them reached the terrace with Swati, her face veiled, her head bowed, golden-red, new, the women's buzzing increased, 'There she is . . . The bride's here . . . Swati . . . so lovely . . .'

A flock of pigeons rose into the air, dispersed in different directions with a beating of wings. Just as before an important scene in a play is about to begin, everyone stops looking around, abandons personal thoughts, settles down in their seats with their programmes folded out of the way and looks at the stage, in the same way, after a quick succession of shimmering waves of movement, everyone settled down for a better look. Some shifted sideways, some moved forward, carrying Satyen's now-useless shawl, the slightly perturbed Nikhil shifted his weight from one foot to the other. Anupama put her hand on Chitra's shoulders, Kiran Bakshi's perfectly folded shawl was now draped over his left shoulder instead of his right, Nikhil said to himself I won't look anywhere else now, some of the children rose from their cross-legged positions to kneel for a better look, Chhoton shook himself to shake off sleep. Satyen saw many more people had arrived—a smiling Saswati stood opposite him—the place looked different now that it was so full of people.

The platform was lowered; from the one painted in yellow, white and red, Swati now sat on the one meant for her, to Satyen's left. 'Will the bride circle the groom on foot?' inquired the priest.

'No, she will be carried,' said Hemanga, unfolding a crisp, off-white, ironed scarf with a scratching sound, putting it around Satyen's shoulder, and telling him, 'Drape this around yourself.'

Saswati immediately bent and placed the *topor* on the groom's head. His eyes downcast with embarrassment, Satyen waited for the sound of laughter, but no—no one laughed, not one of the people present laughed at the site of Satyen Roy putting on a *topor* during his wedding. Satyen Roy was somewhat surprised.

'Let the groom stand,' said the priest.

The *topor* on his head, the garland round his neck, Satyen draped the scarf around himself as he stood up. He didn't feel uncomfortable, there seemed to be a chill in the air. Bijon-babu was bare-bodied too, didn't he feel cold?

Dalim, Arun and Paresh-babu lifted Swati, seated on the wedding platform, into mid-air again—it was easier with three than with four. Tapan wasn't exactly dejected at being excluded, on the contrary, he happily stepped back to watch the scene.

To raise Swati in the air and make her circle Satyen seven times made the veins bulge in Dalim's fair-complexioned arm, Arun's upper lip disappeared inside his mouth with the effort, Paresh-babu's expression stiffened too. Swati felt progressively and palpably heavier to the three pairs of arms, and as though to encourage the three of them Hemanga counted at the top of his voice, 'One . . . Two . . . Four . . .'

'No, no, this was the third,' Chitra exclaimed.

'No, he's right,' said Anupama.

'You can hardly see Swati's face.'

'How will you see it? They fix the tiara with a thread so that the veil doesn't shift.'

'The groom's face is veiled too. They're even holding a sheet before him. Rubbish!' Iva glanced at Urmila.

'Don't you know!' Urmila smiled slyly. 'No looking till the first meeting of eyes.'

'Oh, so you're not supposed to see each other's face till that first meeting of eyes?' Iva laughed so loudly in her masculine voice that a lot of people near her looked at her, startled.

'. . . Five.'

The platform stopped. Hemanga shouted in his high voice, 'Five . . . Five . . . Twice more.'

'Dalim, are you all right?' asked Paresh-babu.

'Yes!' Dalim panted.

'Come on.'

The platform moved again. Arun's upper lip parted, running his tongue over his lower lip, he said very softly, 'Easy, Swati.' But Swati either did not hear, or did not understand, she continued to wrap her arm tightly around Arun's neck.

With one more round, Iva Ganguly noticed Dalim, lanky, his adolescent face under his curly hair now red for a different reason. Tapping Urmila on the shoulder, she asked, 'Do you know the people taking Swati around?'

'The one in the glasses is her sister's husband.' Urmila had seen Arun for the first time today, she had guessed his relationship with the family as soon as she saw him, but she spoke as though she had known him for a long time.

'And the other one? That fair boy?' Iva didn't even acknowledge the existence of the short old third man.

Urmila hadn't seen the fair boy earlier either, but she had heard Saswati address him as Dalim during dinner, and she had heard from Bijon, a regular visitor to their house, about his sister's son with that name. Once a piece of information, any information, had penetrated Urmila's ears—no matter how it was conveyed—she never forgot it; so she answered easily, 'Oh, that's Dalim. Swati's eldest sister's daughter. What a mess back then with the water, poor fellow!' Urmila smiled.

Iva remembered the incident too, but didn't find it funny. 'How painful for the people doing that job,' she said.

'Not all that much,' said Anupama.

'Of course it is. Brides are all grown up these days . . . Can they be . . .'

'But Swati looks very young.'

'All girls look young at their wedding.' Chitra added something of her own to what she had heard her mother say. 'But that doesn't mean Iva will too.'

'Thank goodness!' Iva laughed, rather too loudly. Once again some people turned to look at her.

Tilting her neck to look at Chitra, Urmila regurgitated something she'd read in a newspaper, 'Now that girls are becoming independent they're getting taller too. Earlier . . .'

'Seven!' Hemanga's high voice sounded out sharply.

The girls advanced in a wave, many of the children stood up, Kiran Bakshi craned his neck over Hemanga's shoulder, Hemanga moved out of the way in deference to the groom's friend, Saswati appeared by his side, Harit, present because he didn't have an option, looked at Swati with curious eyes.

The platform stopped opposite the groom. 'Not so high,' said Hemanga.

The platform dropped a few inches.

'A little higher. Their eyes have to be level.'

The platform rose. Paresh-babu looked at Hemanga through slanted eyes. 'Check . . . Level now?'

'Almost . . . A little closer . . . Yes . . . Perfect,' said Hemanga, examining the scene closely.

The platform became still, the sheet held all this while before the groom's face fell away; standing on either side of her, Mahashweta and Saraswati removed her veil. But Swati couldn't raise her eyes.

'Look at him, Swati,' said Saraswati.

'Look at her, Satyen,' said Kiran on the other side.

But Satyen had been gazing at her already. This was Swati? Long black lashes on lowered eyes. This was Swati.

Eyes met eyes, conch shells were blown. Nobody knew why, but everyone present, men and women, children and the old, all felt especially happy at that moment. The platform was lowered to the floor, after placing Swati opposite the groom, Dalim, Arun and Paresh-babu were finally free. Arun rubbed his neck immediately, Dalim rubbed his hands, Paresh-babu only took a single deep breath, his well-exercised chest expanding. 'Now for the exchange of garlands,' said Hemanga. 'Stand up, Swati.'

After her seven rounds, Swati felt a physical comfort at being able to stand. But that sense of comfort was wiped out in an instant; she wasn't able to sense anything other than Satyen standing near her, opposite her! She didn't know her legs were trembling after her day-long fast; didn't register her awkwardness at being draped in the sari and jewellery; forgot the unbearable pain of having to leave her father; she only sensed Satyen—didn't see him, only sensed him.

Garlands in hand, they stood face to face. The head with the *topor* on it was lowered, the garland of white flowers around Swati's neck flowed down Satyen's neck to his chest. The veiled head was lowered, on Swati's breast flowed the smaller, slightly soiled garland around Satyen's neck. There was no need for, no meaning to, all this; a million rituals would go waste if there were no truth in the heart; but for the moment a breeze of happiness, of joy, of well-being, blew soft, spread in every direction, stretched from Shobha's overwhelmed gaze to Harit's lips, curled in amusement. Harit didn't find that amusement abhorrent.

'Sit down now, Swati,' said Saswati softly.

Satyen also bent to sit, but before that a plump dark woman of advanced years came up to him, saying, 'Come downstairs for a minute.'

'Downstairs. Why?'

'Because. Come now.' The dark woman winked, smiled.

Satyen looked around with surprised eyes, but no one told him anything, no one explained anything to him. 'I'll come too, Kunda-didima,' said Saswati, moving forward.

'Do I have to come too?' asked Satyen helplessly.

'Come,' said Saraswati. 'Don't be scared.'

'No one else?' Satyen turned his face slightly towards Swati.

Light laughter blew across the room at this question, then Mahashweta said with slitted eyes, 'Of course not, we won't leave you alone. We're coming along as bodyguards. Let's go.'

The three sisters and Kunda escorted Satyen to the first floor as though they had arrested the commander-in-chief of the enemy. They arrived at the room where Mahashweta had been resting, where the married couple would spend the night. Rajen-babu's sister was waiting.

As soon as Satyen entered she proceeded to chase him with a stick. Satyen was a trifle alarmed, but the grey-haired woman did not hit him with the stick, only used it to measure him from head to toe. Then he was made to stand facing the wall, to walk a few steps, the dark woman tapped him on the head thrice as she muttered something. Then Satyen gave up being surprised.

The grey-haired woman came up to him with some things arranged on a copper salver. 'What's this in my hand?'

Satyen answered innocently, 'A plate.'

'Swati is your fate.'

Satyen's ears felt hot, he felt pinpricks on his face. And enjoying his predicament with silent laughter were not just the grey-haired and the dark women, but also the sisters—even Saswati, although she sympathized with him, for she too hated this old-fashioned humour.

'All right, now tell me what this is.' Kunda touched the knife on the plate.

'That?' Satyen paused. Knife? Which meant—'wife'! Therefore—'That's a blade.' Satyen pierced Kunda with his eyes triumphantly.

'Lovely!' Saswati clapped. 'Match that!'

But after only a short pause Kunda retorted gloriously, 'Your marriage to Swati was in heaven made!'

'Superb!' The sisters laughed in appreciation, Satyen smiled too. It was quite a good response at short notice.

'May I go now?' Satyen, now animated, looked at the woman with grey hair.

'Aren't we in a hurry! All right, come here.'

The women took him to a corner of the room, where a lamp burned on a cane tray. It was similar to the one his aunt had used earlier at home, but more decorated, and laden with many more objects, some of which Satyen was made to touch, and then the dark woman immersed a paan-leaf in the small bowl of water and splashed him with it. Assuming that the tray would now be raised to touch his forehead, Satyen leaned forward in anticipation, but for some mysterious reason this step was omitted; the women rose, the entire group returned to the terrace, including the woman with grey hair.

Poking Chhoton on his back, Tata said, 'You're asleep, Chhoton!'

'Of course not!' Chhoton straightened his head, which had slumped forward, with a jerk.

'Go to bed downstairs!' Having played elder sister, Tata

turned to Bijoli. She was Shobha's eldest daughter, they had become friends over the past two days.

Glancing at the freshly returned groom, Bijoli said, 'At weddings, it's the women who win.'

'Why win?'

'So many saris and so much jewellery as gifts! What fun, isn't it!'

'Fun, my foot! Don't they have to go away from their parents! Oh my God!'

'But Swati-mashi's mother is dead,' remembered Bijoli.

'So what, what about her father! It's the same thing.' Tata remembered her own father fleetingly, but continued without a pause, 'It's the men who have the real fun. How pampered they are by their wives' families! But when it comes to how the women are treated by their husbands' families . . .'

'But men don't live with their in-laws,' interjected another girl from the other side. 'How long do you suppose the pampering lasts?'

Bulan, Mahashweta's second son, overheard this. Rubbish, he thought, as if men would ever want to live with their parents! These girls! Nothing but marriage on their minds! Let them get married if they want—what else are girls good for—but why must the men. 'Tell me, Dada,' he couldn't keep his thoughts bottled up, 'why do men get married?'

'What a stupid question!' Amal, one and a half years older, smiled at his brother's ignorance.

'Why is it stupid . . .'

'Don't you know!' Ottu, two years younger, interrupted Bulan. 'People have babies because they get married!'

'Ottu!' Tata scolded him from her position behind him. These boys, so cheeky, really.

Ottu fell silent after throwing a harsh look at Tata, and Bulan thought, babies? But it's the women who have the babies. Then . . . And must those wailing babies be born! Ottu knew nothing! Bulan pondered a little more, but simply couldn't work it out; he turned his attention again to this new person who had agreed to get married despite being a man.

By then the process of giving the bride away had started. The bride and groom sat face-to-face, and the priest, having placed the sacred pitcher between them, was arranging strands of stiff thread over it. Suddenly seeing Arun by his side, Kiran said, 'No priest from the groom's side?'

'The groom needs one too?' Arun smiled faintly.

'Ha!' Kiran laughed too. 'And Satyen being what he is . . .' Without finishing, he lowered his eyes.

'Establish the groom's right hand at this spot,' enunciated the priest.

Satyen put his hand, palm downwards, on the pitcher.

'Heavenward.'

Satyen looked at the priest, the priest took his hand and placed it palm upwards. So that was what he was referring to! Satyen was pleased by the image, and a few moments later Swati's right hand descended on his own, spread out facing the sky; a hand pointing heavenward, gentle, extreme gentleness in it, almost without touching. The priest bound their hands together with a stiff thread, then sat opposite Bijon and opened his manuscript.

Bijon had been sitting in the same pose all this while, his head bowed, chin almost scraping his chest; he looked up with fearful eyes on hearing the incantation again. Fixing his gaze on the priest's face he moved his lips inaudibly; while Satyen actually tried to listen closely and repeat clearly, as though here too his educational status needed to be preserved.

'*Enang kanyang salankarang . . .*' said the priest.

'*Enang kanyang shankaralang . . .*' Bijon muttered.

'*Shavastrachhadanang . . .*'

'*Shastrachhedanang . . .*'

'*Prajapatidevatakang . . .*'

'*Prajapatidevatatang . . .*'

'*Tuvyamahang sampradade . . .*'

'*Tumbabhayang sampradade.*'

'What was that he handed to the groom?' Anupama asked.

'No idea!' Chitra turned to Iva. 'Look at that girl.'

'Which . . .'

'Violet sari. Isn't her necklace interesting?'

'Hardly. That's a radio-necklace.'

'*Avih kanya maya dattaa rakshanang poshanang kuru.*' The priest's baritone rang in Iva's ears. Smiling, she said, '*Rakshanang poshanang kuru*! Why, can't women look after themselves!' She glanced at Urmila, but even to such an apt remark her new friend only signified assent with a nod of the lashes, she didn't say anything.

She didn't, because Urmila was particularly busy. Busy looking at Bijon. Bijon's expression was extremely grave, but also that of someone who had been beaten up, someone who was afraid. None of this matched her Bijon-da, whom she knew, knew very well, whom she had identified mentally as the first victim of her artificial laughter. Urmila looked for a flash of that silly, nice, handsome, funny, and, all-told, desirable face—but found nothing. Not for a moment did his expression change; not for a moment did he raise his face to look around and notice her. Even after a prolonged stare, followed by frequent glances, Urmila could not manage to meet her Bijon-da's eyes even once.

For the moment Bijon had forgotten everything and everyone else as well, not Urmila alone. That the responsibility of giving Swati away had fallen upon him had overwhelmed him since morning. He wouldn't allow any deviation from the ritual; the poor fellow had fasted all day. Towards evening his father's sister had said, 'Why can't Swati have some fruit and sweets, no harm in that surely?'The moment he heard Bijon had protested desperately. What harm could it have done? No one knew. But just because we don't know, can anyone say for sure there's nothing to it. If there isn't, why does the rule exist in the first place? And as he proceeded with the ceremony for his sister's wedding, this astonishing feeling of who-can-tell didn't leave him, kept growing, in fact. Swati and Satyen didn't seem to be real people; they seemed to have retreated to a distance, become characters in a story; as he watched the battered face of the Sanskrit teacher of Dinabandhu School with a salary of sixty rupees, he thought he was seeing a saint, and that, on this saint's instructions, he dipped his hand in the water, that he held his right hand with his left, that he upturned his left hand on his right, and that he then touched the hard, empty floor with his forehead—all of this appeared very strange to Bijon, strange, mysterious, almost supernatural.

The priest straightened his back, reorganized his upper garment. Then, arranging several other pots of water properly, he opened the manuscript and looked at the groom: '*Om yaa akrintanyavayan . . .*'

'How odd!' Harit said suddenly. 'It's all for the groom? Nothing for the bride?'

'Of course not,' Tapan quipped. 'The bride's only role is to be willing.'

'That's actually to their advantage!' Arun cast an eye on the barrister. 'Get the husbands to make impossible promises and do nothing themselves.'

Savouring Arun's observation, Kiran Bakshi said, 'And what the groom recites—it's all flattery!'

The priest stopped suddenly. Adopting the gaze that he did when his class grew very unruly, he directed the same reluctant, fish-like glassy stare at the bride's family, asking, 'Will the groom speak for the bride?'

'All right,' said Hemanga at once.

'But why? Let her speak for herself,' said Arun.

The priest looked at Satyen. 'Of course,' said Satyen. 'The bride will speak for herself.' There was a soft roll of male laughter.

After the laughter had died down, the priest looked at the bride and said, even more softly, '*Om pra mey patiyanah panthah kalpatang, shiva arishtha patilokong gameyam.*'

The priest's baritone and the rhythm of his Sanskrit chant seemed to create reverberations within Swati's breast suddenly; she couldn't repeat the words.

'Say the words, Swati,' Bijon said in a very low voice.

Swati turned towards her brother, as though she had only now sensed his existence close by, so close; only now did she see his face clearly. But she couldn't see at all the Bijon she knew, the one who had been with her since birth, the one with whom she had battled since birth, that stubborn bad-tempered quarrelsome wet-blanket crybaby lazy lying Bijon. This seemed to be someone else altogether—she had never seen him before.

'*Om pra mey patiyanah panthah . . .*' the priest repeated.

Dropping the aspirated endings, Swati repeated slowly, '*Om pra mey patiyanah panthah kalpatang, shiva arishtha patilokong gameyam.*' Accompanying the male baritone, her girlish voice, further weakened by fasting, sounded unfamiliar to Satyen, unfamiliar, unusual, gracious, infinite in its grace.

Shutting the manuscript, the priest untied their hands. Thank goodness, it's done. Satyen stretched his back, then took the horrible object off his head, holding it lightly with two fingers.

'What!' Mahashweta exclaimed. 'Why did you take that off?'

'No need any more!' Satyen answered suavely, confidently.

'There's more,' said Saraswati in brief. 'Children, give way.'

Chhoton widened his eyes, the children used the opportunity to raise a din as they shifted, Bijon left his seat to stand by Hemanga's side, the priest used the cleared space to light the fire for the rest of the ceremonies, Swati rose from her seat, Saswati changed its position, Swati sat again by Satyen's side. Feeling a light touch on his shoulder, Satyen turned back. 'What?'

'Nothing,' said Saraswati, holding up a corner of the off-white scarf draped around his body, Mahashweta handed her a corner of Swati's pink scarf, and, knotting them together with nimble fingers, Saraswati repeated, 'Nothing.'

'It has to stay this way?' Satyen's eyes widened, even after all that had happened it seemed unbelievable.

'Yes, and this way too,' said Saraswati, planting the *topor* back on his head. Satyen bowed his head, the tassels on the *topor* tickled his ears.

'Isn't the fire ceremony meant to take place later?' asked Shobha.

'What difference does it make?' answered Leela.

'But isn't it meant to be next morning?'

'It varies—in our family they finish it all on the wedding night!'

'Good thing, too. It's not easy doing it again the next day—I still remember how my eyes smarted from all that smoke.' Leela smiled.

The bluish smoke rose before Satyen's eyes. He remembered Raghuvansh: Sita's eyes reddened by the smoke rising from the ceremonial fire. Swati's too...? He was about to look, but at that moment the priest handed him an object like the seashell-shaped spoon used to feed babies with, saying, 'Cast this into the flames.'

At first Satyen had thought the entire thing had to be thrown into the fire, but then he discovered it contained a little ghee. He flung the ghee into the fire, had to do it six times in all. Each time the flames grew redder, the blue smoke fainter. And then came the incantations again.

So it continued. Trying to pronounce the words correctly, Satyen wondered: how much longer? When would it end? The place seemed quieter than before, the priest's professional baritone sounded even deeper. Satyen looked around every now and then: red necklace, silvery sari, Saswati's smile now replaced by solemnity—was he going to address her as Chhordi from tomorrow? He spotted Shweta, Loton in her arms, spotted Rajen-babu's grey shawl indistinctly. And look! Chhoton had fallen asleep.

Dalim took Chhoton away quickly. The night advanced, Nikhil moved from his position behind Kiran to stand near Bijon, it grew colder, Nikhil unfolded Satyen's shawl and draped it around Bijon, wrapping it around himself Bijon glanced at Nikhil without a word, for some time no one said anything, the hum of muted conversations stopped, only the flames forcing everyone to stay awake crackled with Sanskrit words, the rhythm of the classical language floated like a memory over all the other silences, ebbing as soon as it flowed, just like promises. Mahashweta and Saraswati recalled that night, when they had dressed up the same way to sit in the same pose in two different parts of a terrace; the sisters exchanged glances, Saraswati looked at Arun, Mahashweta at Hemanga, then Mahashweta at Arun. We'll do this too one day, thought Anupama and Chitra—when? Opposite whom shall we be sitting? Who would it be—as soon as they had this thought they blushed, and their eyes met precisely at that moment. Urmila suddenly remembered her mother, her childhood, Nathurampur, the match arranged for her when she was fourteen—the would-be groom had sneaked in to steal a look at her—the wedding had almost taken place, but her father suddenly . . . If her father hadn't died, if she had actually married Indu Nag—she still remembered the name—who had stolen in for a look when she was fourteen . . . how would things have turned out, Urmila wondered about all that for a while, and Iva Ganguly's eyes, wandering in search of someone, or something, suddenly stopped at Dalim's fair face under a mop of curly hair. So very young still!

Shoving Dalim aside, Kunda appeared, holding an earthen

pot. Dipping her finger into the white liquid in it, she bent to draw seven circles on the floor in a diagonal line in front of the bride and groom.

'What's she doing?' asked Iru.

'The seven steps,' answered Ata.

'Seven steps? What's that?'

'You'll see.' Ata offered more information solemnly. '*This* is the real wedding.'

The bride and groom rose, Satyen felt a tug on his back as he moved. The knot. How long would it have to stay?

'Get off those seats now.' Rajen-babu's sister came up to them.

Tethered together, they stepped off gingerly. 'In front, Swati,' said the aunt.

The tug as Swati moved forward almost dislodged the scarf from Satyen's shoulders, standing behind him, Saraswati put it back in place. Swati came round to the front, Satyen stood behind her, circling her with his arms from the back Satyen cupped his hands, and Swati cupped hers over his. Mahashweta and Saraswati quickly took up positions on either side, Saswati was at hand with the plate of *khoi*. The aunt murmured instructions to them.

'First the right foot, then the left . . . On each of the circles, one at a time . . . You have to guide Swati's hands to scatter a handful of *khoi* each time and . . . It's pointing north-west, isn't it?' She turned to check with Kunda, who still held the pot.

She chuckled instead of answering. She knew this whole business through and through, how could she get it wrong?

First the right foot, then the left, they stepped into the first circle on the north-east side.

'Perfect!' Saswati filled Swati's cupped hands with the *khoi*, Satyen aimed with his eyes and nudged her hands upwards. The *khoi* scattered from Swati's hands, most of it falling outside, only a few grains ending in the flames.

'*Om sakha saptapadi bhava, sakhyante gameyang,*' the priest's voice rose once more. '*Sakhyante ma jyoshah, sakhyante ma jyoshthah.*'

Hemanga had nodded off, he stumbled while going up the wooden stairs of his office in Rangoon. The wedding: Calcutta. It was all to the good—Mahashweta's long-standing wish had finally been fulfilled, now if only her health . . . The way her mother after that endless illness . . . These aren't good thoughts to have. Running his hands over his face Hemanga stood upright, saw Arun in front of him. Arun smiled, but not for Hemanga, he smiled in memory of that day when Shishirkana had scolded him for bringing an expensive box of chocolates. How fortunate that she had, how else would he have realized his heart had been surrendered, then when he was on his way back home for the holidays, somehow he realized while lying in his bunk on the train that Mahashweta was very nice but Saswati . . . What *were* these thoughts! And why had they come back to him after so many years.

'*Om samanjantu vishwe devah, samapo hridayani nau. Sammatarishwa sang dhata, samu deshtri dadhatu nau.*'

The ghee went into the flames, the *khoi* went into the flames, the women scattered the *khoi*; Kunda repainted the already faded white circles. Shobha thought: it's over, almost over. The holiday is over, the period of escape is over, back to . . . Suddenly she thought: what about him! Oh yes, he's left. When did he go? Didn't even tell me. But then why bother . . . And so reticent . . . So crowded here, besides . . . And working so hard all day . . . And I've been here the past two days . . . Or was he angry? Normally you couldn't get a peep out of him, but where I'm concerned he can certainly get angry!

'*Om mama brate te hridayang dadhatu, mama chittamanu chittang te astu.*'

Swati in front, Satyen behind, their hands cupped together—beautiful, how well they were matched. Tears sprang to Rajen-babu's sister's eyes. Her husband wasn't watching. He was sleeping downstairs. He hadn't woken up, had he? As soon as he did he needed a glass of water, paan, the paan mashed—having lost his teeth the old man was very demanding! And this same man, how handsome he had been when . . . She felt a gust of laughter coming.

'*Om annaprasena manina praanasutrena prishwina.*' Approaching the end, the priest's enthusiasm seemed to increase, his voice rose. '*Badhnami satyagranthina, manashcha hridayancha te.*'

What did all this mean, wondered Usha, but they sounded beautiful. He had apparently read Sanskrit in college. But what purpose did all that serve . . . Worked in the Railways all his life . . . And what a job it was too . . . Tours all the time, round the year. He was supposed to be back on Friday—but who could tell—he could have come a day or two earlier for the wedding. But no—he wasn't that kind of a man. Work was worship.

'*Jadetadhridayang tava, tadastu hridayang mama. Jadidang hridayang mama, tadastu hridayang tava!*'

Hriday! The heart! The word suddenly penetrated Iru's, Geeti's, Ata's ears, the scarlet–orange–green saris trembled. The heart! It was still an object of amusement for them, a joke, laughter tickled them when they caught sight of it in print—but now they trembled not in amusement, nor in curiosity, the word thrilled them for a moment. A spark from the woman in them who had not yet awoken, but would any day now, electrified them for a moment, and Nikhil suddenly felt, so what if he only hammered nails at a factory, so what if his was a life of hardship, he wasn't afraid, he wasn't unhappy, he could do anything, he had everything, and Kiran Bakshi understood—understood clearly—what he had not realized conclusively earlier, that it was impossible for him to live without Anita, impossible. No, he wouldn't let her go; let his father-in-law be upset, let her quarrel with her parents; even if all of Calcutta fled out of fear of the bomb Anita would not, he wouldn't either—or else they'd both go together. Was that garland still in his pocket? Yes, here it was.

They stepped into the last of the seven circles, the *khoi* fell into the flames again, more *khoi*, more incantations, conch shells, breaking the barriers of that strange silence, conversation laughter movement again, Prabhat-babu wondered if Leela wanted to stay longer; removing his hand from Bijon's shoulder Hemanga said now you'd better, and Dalim told Nikhil do you want to, and Harit moved his eyes away from Saswati and stepped away from the crowd. Oh, so much time wasted, he could have written the manifesto by now. Everything came back to him: Japan's conspiracy, Russia's danger, idiotic Bengalis, the enormous responsibility of their resistance movement. To think I'd forgotten all of this all this time. No wonder he called it the opium of the masses! No, must go home this very moment, on foot, go to sleep at once, and from tomorrow morning . . . Obstinately, Harit went downstairs before everyone else, but stopped as soon as he reached the first floor. Would Saswati . . .? No, she would stay, she was for all intents and purposes living at her father's home these days . . . Bengali girls had this thing about going back home. And now Swati's father's home had become her home too. Harit went down to the ground floor a little slowly, as he did he remembered the house on Jatin Das Road; meanwhile a group of women surrounded Swati and Satyen, tethered together; the soirée on Swati's birthday, his first time there; meanwhile the bride and groom walked gingerly; Swati had really given that singer a piece of her mind; everyone walked behind them; the rascal. And Saswati that day; and Saswati put her hand on Swati's back, Bijon shivered in the cold, the distant half of the terrace emptied out, and Mahashweta, just behind Swati, as soon as she set foot on the first step she feared she'd get a headache any moment.

∾

But as soon as she entered the room where the bride and groom would spend the night, she forgot her headache. Was this the room she had spent the evening in? The light seemed far brighter now, the room larger, it seemed lively, as though it had finally come to life; as though this room in this rented house that they had found suddenly, unknown to them all this while, had been made just for this, and after being made had been waiting for just this moment. Amidst the different colours of the saris arranged on the clothes-rack, Mahashweta met the eyes of the lights; with their eyes they said, 'You here? You here?' The mirror brimming with light beamed the answer towards the oily varnish, 'Here they are! Here they are! They've come!' Every single thing in the room said this with a smile, the four white walls too. Mahashweta's eyes turned away from the surroundings, turned towards Swati and Satyen, they sat down on the sheets laid out on the floor, picked their positions wrongly—'The other side, Swati.' Swati moved to Satyen's left, once upon a time I had also the same way . . . How had it felt? . . . No one could tell . . . She didn't remember any of it, but the smell was familiar . . . Of what? Of nothing in particular, of rooms where couples spend their wedding nights, of new, the lovely subtle fragrance of new. Mahashweta drank in the fragrance—suddenly the headache? No.

No, Mahashweta didn't get a headache, or didn't realize it even if she did, she was fine till the end, didn't lose a bit of her enthusiasm; she saw everything, all the games with the rice, with the water, Saswati's extra-busy appearance—as though nothing could have been done without her; she listened to everything, her aunt saying the same thing over and over again in her hoarse voice, Saraswati's comments, Kunda's jokes—she laughed again and again, with and without provocation. Then Prabhat-babu suddenly turned up from nowhere, saying, all right then we're; Leela stirred, Usha said then I should also, some more people stirred, he came and said let's go—what do you need the muffler for?—no need to come downstairs, let's go, we're going then, all right, coming, leaving, the crowd dwindled, Geeti's head lolled on Ata's shoulder, conversations dwindled, Mahashweta's vision suddenly grew blurred, the sound of laughter petered out, leaving only a trace of it in the air, the trace trembled, disappeared, then suddenly everything was silent.

Suppressing a small yawn Saraswati said, 'Let them go now, Kunda-didima. Let them sleep.'

'Are you sleepy, Satyen?' she hurled a glance at him.

'Remember your wedding, Mahashweta?' Rajen-babu's sister recalled. 'It started only at two in the morning, it was the monsoon, before the night could end . . .'

'. . . It was dawn!' completed Kunda. 'That was fun.'

'And it started raining during the ceremony. And at that moment Shishirkana . . .'

Our mother? Mahashweta looked at Saraswati, both sisters recollected their mother. They remembered how ill she had become during their weddings, how despite the late night and pouring rain the doctor had to be called to give her an injection . . . They had got to know the next day. They had been a little upset.

Realizing as much, their aunt changed the subject. 'And how Swati cried the next day because she had missed the ceremonies.'

'There was another reason for Swati to cry at Mejdi's and Shejdi's wedding,' Saswati smiled, exchanged glances with Mahashweta and Saraswati. They recalled the five-year-old Swati's 'I'm going to marry Arun-da' tantrums, a secret amusement flowed between their eyes, but the amusement also pricked Mahashweta somewhere slightly.

'Shall I spill the beans?' Saswati threatened Swati.

Arun coughed.

Shweta came in, went up to Swati. 'Swati, I have to go now . . .'

'Do you have to, Didi?' Mahashweta looked at her. 'Stay for a bit.'

'No, I'd better go.' Turning towards Swati, towards Satyen, as though their permission was what mattered, Shweta said, 'I'll be back first thing in the morning, all right?'

'What were you doing all this while?' asked Saraswati.

'Just getting the children . . . They were lying there like soldiers on a battlefield! Geeti, go to sleep now . . . You're dropping off in any case.'

'Iru . . .?' Mahashweta suddenly remembered her daughter.

'Your daughter's sleeping in her silk,' Shweta smiled.

Sleeping? Geeti heard the word. Who? Me? No, I'm awake . . . Here, see! But her eyes shut again almost immediately, she felt the swaying of a train, train, We've reached Tundla, Ma.

'Do you *have* to go tomorrow, Shobha?' Shweta tilted her head to look at Shobha.

Shobha was sitting behind Mahashweta, plucking at the turtle-egg-like pearls around her neck, moving her hand away in a flash she said shyly, 'Yes, Shweta-di, I have to.'

'Your mother-in-law . . . Never mind, I'll tell you tomorrow.' Shweta went up to Swati, bent to put her hand on her covered head, met Satyen's eyes for a moment. Straightening, she said, 'Don't keep them up too long, Pishima. They'd better not fall ill or something.'

'Does Swati think so too?' The indefatigable Kunda now tackled Swati.

'All right then . . .' Taking leave of Swati and Satyen once more with her eyes, Shweta went outside. And ran into Dalim immediately. He now had a brown sweater on over his striped shirt.

'The rickshaw's here, Ma,' he said.

'All right.' Shweta was about to leave, Dalim continued quickly, 'I . . . I'm not going home, Ma.'

'Of course, you can stay here. But don't stay up too late.'

Biju came out of the opposite room. He had wrapped himself entirely in his shawl, even his arms.

'Not asleep yet, Biju?' said Shweta.

'Why should I be asleep,' croaked Biju. 'Are you going now?'

'Yes . . .'

'Have you got a taxi?'

'The taxis refused, Mama,' Dalim said. 'I got a rickshaw.'

'These taxi drivers think they're lords. Keep Loton well covered, Bordi, she'd better not catch a cold.'

'Yes sir!' Shweta patted Bijon on the cheek. 'Whose shawl is that, Biju?'

'This one? Satyen's.'

'So Satyen's shawl is warmer.'

Bijon didn't seem to have heard. Looking at the door to the other room, he said, 'How much longer in there?'

'Nearly done.'

'It's very late. I'd better tell Pishima now to . . .' Bijon moved towards the door to the room, Dalim went with him, they entered together, Shweta walked along the corridor between the rows of rooms, arrived at the balcony in front, where the girls had lined up to watch the arrival of the groom in the evening. One side was covered with blinds now to keep the cold out; Nepal-babu still lay on the bed made up on the cot, his eyes half-closed, not moving, mouth open, lips twisted, at first glance . . . No, the hollow chest could be seen rising and falling beneath the shawl . . . Let him sleep, poor man . . . Beli was sleeping too on the floor under a blanket . . . Had she eaten? Yes . . . Shweta moved away, an easy chair was drawn up to the wall at the other end of the balcony, a grey shawl, eyes trained outside, her father.

'Baba,' Shweta called him softly.

Rajen-babu turned.

'The rickshaw's here, Baba.'

'Let's go.'

Rajen-babu rose, his eye fell on his daughter's shoulder, only a long cloth blouse. 'Don't you have anything warm . . .'

'I do. Let's go . . .'

'Is Hemanga back?' Rajen-babu asked as they walked.

'Not yet. Lots of people to be dropped home.'

'Isn't he taking a bit too long?'

'Not at all. He didn't leave all that long ago . . . Are you worrying again?'

'No. But . . . It's late, and the blackout . . .'

'No need to worry. Just a minute, Baba.'

Shweta carried the sleeping Loton out of the largest room on the first floor, where Swati had dressed for the wedding. She had wrapped her daughter in a pink woollen muffler, draped a white scarf around her own back.

Shweta stopped again after a few steps. 'Want to peep in before we go, Baba?'

Rajen-babu paused at the door. Through the gap between Biju and Dalim, standing in front of him, he glanced fleetingly at Swati; through the gap between Dalim and Arun, at Satyen. Ata nudged Geeti, saying, get up now; Saraswati said, all right then, Satyen; they climbed down the brightly lit staircase, and crossed the brightly lit ground floor; no one anywhere, all was silent. Saswati said, well, Swati; Shobha thought, sleep. Calcutta: dark, black, both eyes of the rickshaw glittering, ting-ting, silent, silent everywhere, ting-ting, the sky overhead blacker still, stars in the sky bright, stars, so many of them! Mahashweta said, Saswati you; Kunda said, Satyen, this lamp must burn all night; ting-ting, the rickshaw in the dark; no one anywhere; dim under the shade; fireflies, large houses, darkness. Water for the night, and here, and if you need to; black, the trees black, the unused tramlines black; a solitary cat on an empty pavement; which room, said Arun; coming out, Bijon said, Hemanga-da's still; here's Hemanga-babu, let's go, Dalim; Shweta said, Baba, it's cold; Rajen-babu said, but Loton's very; the rickshaw rang ting-ting;

darkness, and in the dark the rail embankment appeared to be a hill; Tollygunge Bridge; Rajen-babu's sister pushed the cane tray with the lamp against the wall; Shobha thought, it's over after this; where to, Babu; Shobha yawned, it's over; Saswati said, Pishima; Kunda came away; the rickshaw turned; the neighbourhood was asleep; glittering fireflies, glittering saris; Mahashweta and Saraswati rose to their feet, their bangles clinking; the rickshaw stopped its ting-ting. All right then, all right then, Rajen-babu getting off first, Loton in his arms, and then Shweta getting off, taking her daughter from her father; Mahashweta and Saraswati came out; Shobha, it's over; Rajen-babu climbed up the three steps, empty; Saswati and Kunda switching off lights on the way, dark; dark, closed, keys from his pocket; Rajen-babu's sister coming out, shutting the door behind her; Rajen-babu stooping before the door, silent; the entire house silent; the earth silent; Shweta looked up at the sky, stars, silent; Swati didn't stir, Satyen didn't stir, both silent; the shadowy light from the lamp on the tray; hidden, shy, words that couldn't be said, unforgettable; the door opened, dark; neither of them spoke, neither of them forgot; two of them in the dark room, two of them in the dark, side by side; shrunk, taut; didn't speak, didn't forget; Shweta stopped; Rajen-babu, with his hand on the wall; taut; two lives, creatures, throbbing hearts, throbbing bodies; no eyes, eyes, open, open windows, black; black outside; stars in the black sky; distant, other side, other world; all that had happened, not happened, would keep happening, eternal; a skyful of stilled stars looked on.

Scan QR code to access the
Penguin Random House India website